The
box set
OUT OF LINE
Series

Lauren,   —

Thanks for being
so awesome! The
sun is finally
shining because of
    you!! :)

Jen McLaughlin

Jen McLaughlin

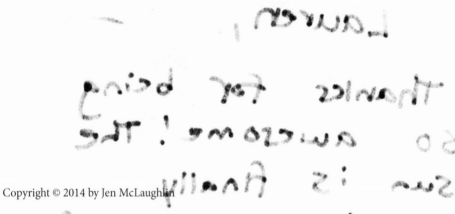

Manufactured in the United States of America

Interior Design and Formatting by: E.M. Tippetts Book Designs

OUT OF LINE

a novel

Jen McLaughlin

Edited by: Hollie Westring at hollietheeditor.com

Cover Designed by: Sarah Hansen at © OkayCreations.net

Interior Design and Formatting by: E.M. Tippetts Book Designs

This book goes out to Caisey Quinn, my wonderful critique partner.

Without you threatening my life if I didn't finish this book…it wouldn't be here.

Desperate to break free…

I've spent my entire life under my father's thumb, but now I'm finally free to make my own choices. When my roommate dragged me to my first college party, I met Finn Coram and my life turned inside out. He knows how to break the rules and is everything I never knew I wanted. A Marine by day and surfer by night, he pushes me away even as our attraction brings us closer. Now I am finally free to do whatever I want. I know what I want. I choose Finn.

Trying to play by the rules…

I always follow orders. My job, my life, depends on it. I thought this job would be easy, all the rules were made crystal clear, but when I met Carrie Wallington, everything got muddy. She's a rule I know I shouldn't break, but damn if I don't inch closer to the breaking point each time I see her. I'm ready to step out of line. And even worse? I'm living a lie. They say the truth will set you free, but in my case…

The truth will cost me everything.

Trying to resist…

Her lips parted to let out a little moan, and I swooped in, entwining my tongue with hers. She gasped, almost as if she'd never been kissed before, and then melted against me. She wrapped her arms around me, urging me even closer, and my hands fell to her hips. Unable to help myself, I pressed my cock against the soft curve of the side of her ass, reveling in the feel of her softness pressed against my hardness.

Fuck, I wanted her.

Tearing my mouth free, I took a ragged breath and held her still. She kept trying to wiggle in my lap. If she kept that up, this would be more than a cover kiss. It would be a cover fuck. I tightened my fists on her and opened my eyes. She did the same, looking back at me with smoldering blue eyes.

Well, that answered my question from earlier.

Her swollen red lips begged to be kissed some more, but I tamped down the urge. I had to remember the game. Stay on course. "Shit. I shouldn't have done that. Pretend it never happened."

She blinked at me, the heat fading from her eyes and being replaced by confusion. "Why?"

OUT OF LINE

CHAPTER ONE

Carrie

I leaned against the wall and surveyed the crowded room. All around me, people were in pursuit of the three majors of college: getting drunk, getting laid, and then getting even drunker. They were shouting in each other's ears to be heard over the deafening music, sucking on each other's body parts, or throwing up in a corner. The overachievers would do all three by the time the night ended.

It was freshman year at its finest—and I was the only freshman not fitting in.

But at least no one had been *paid* to hang out with me at this party. When I was twelve, my father had thrown me a huge birthday party. The turnout had been particularly surprising to me, considering the people who came were the same girls who told me what a loser I was while in school. Of course, as soon as my parents left the room to get cake, the girls had backed me in a corner and pulled at my hair and dress. They had told me that I was such a loser my father had to pay their parents to make them come. Susie had gotten an iPod. Mary received a phone. Chrissie—a pony.

I had gotten a cold, hard dose of reality.

A tall guy bumped into me, hauling me out of memory lane. His beer tipped and spilled all over my open-toed sandals. The cool liquid was almost a welcome change from the stifling hotness.

"Oh, shit. I'm sorry." He dropped to his knees and started patting at my feet with the closest object he could get his hands on. It looked like a shirt. "I wasn't watching where I was going."

I laughed and shook my head, dropping a hand on his shoulder. He felt a tiny bit sweaty, but who could blame him? It was freaking hot. "Don't worry about it. Seriously."

"No, it's not." He lifted his head and his eyes went wide. "Oh, fuck. Do I know you?"

My smile slipped a little bit, but I forced it back into place. He wouldn't recognize me. I had been out of the public eye for well over a year, and I'd made sure to change my appearance quite a bit. I also had much longer hair, and my body finally grew into itself. My braces were gone, and I outgrew those god-awful bangs, too. I liked to think I didn't look anything like the gawky girl I'd once been.

Please, God.

"No, I don't think so. But don't worry about my feet. It's not a big deal. I was just leaving anyway."

He stood up. "Are you sure?"

"Positive." I smiled at him, hoping my sincerity showed. "Thank you, though."

He gave me one more smile and headed back toward the bar. I watched him go before I worked my way across the room. I needed to get out and breathe some fresh air. Somehow I even managed to make it through the crush without spilling my Coke. As I pushed through the door, the ocean breeze washed over me, immediately calming my pounding heart.

One thing I hadn't managed to change about myself in my big transformation: I still didn't do well in crowds. I never should have listened to my new roommate, Marie. I had only been at the University of California in San Diego for two days and had already been invited to four parties. I'd turned down all but this one. It wasn't because I was a prude or anything. I just didn't like the craziness that parties entailed.

After all, I had ultimately picked this campus because the occupational therapy program was excellent—not because of the parties. It also had the added bonus of being on the beach *and*

2

as far away from my parents as I could possibly manage without leaving the country. They were great, and I loved them, but man, they liked to smother me. The "hold me down kicking and screaming as I tried to break free" type of smothering.

That was the last thing I needed at this point in my life. I needed to try to be on my own. To try to make my own place in the world. And for once I was really, truly on my own…outside of a raging party that I didn't belong in, hiding in dark shadows that hid only God knew what.

But still. Awesome.

I kicked off my sandals and trudged down the sandy hill to the dark beach, sinking my toes into the chilly sand. Probably not the best combination with the beer bath I had just taken, but whatever. My mom and dad had never let me walk barefoot in the sand. It was too unclean, and syringes might be buried deep down—plus other unmentionable items Mom blushed just thinking about. She couldn't even say the word *condom* for cripes sake.

I was convinced I must have been conceived via subliminal messaging or something. My parents were far too proper to do the down and nasty. Too proper to walk barefoot on a dark, scary beach. And I was supposed to be the same. Grinning, I dug in even deeper, loving the way the sand felt between my toes.

I scanned the shadows and found a bench a few feet away. When I sat down, I swung both of my bare feet in the air and let out a deep sigh. There was probably a homeless guy sleeping a few feet away from me in the darkness, but I didn't give a hoot. I was alone, in front of the ocean, listening to the waves crash on the sand.

For the first time since coming here, I felt at peace. Maybe I could fit in. There had to be some people here who were like me—a little bit dorky and a lot awkward. The door opened behind me, and the sound of heels clacking on the pavement interrupted my thoughts. "Carrie? Are you out here?"

"Yeah. Over here," I called out.

"Are you trying to get mugged?"

"No. Just trying to find a homeless guy to fall in love with," I replied, keeping my voice light. "So far, no one wants me."

"Whatever," Marie said, snorting. After a few moments, she stood in front of me, heels in hand and hands on hips. Marie frowned at me from behind a veil of perfectly arranged blonde hair, which blew in the ocean breeze. "You totally bailed on me."

I flinched. Yeah. I kind of had. "Sorry. In my defense, I did tell you parties aren't my thing."

"That's something girls say when they don't want to seem like sluts." Marie waved a hand and shoved her hair out of her face. Within seconds, it was back. "I didn't think you actually *meant* it meant it."

"Well, I did." I swung my legs some more, trying to distract myself from the righteous anger being thrown my way. "You can go back in. I just needed some air."

"Will you be back?"

"Maybe." I blew out a breath. "No."

Marie's light blue eyes pierced into me. "Are you going to be like this all year long? I like you and all, but you're kinda lame."

"I'll try not to be," I said as honestly as I possibly could. Because I *would* try to be sociable and outgoing and not so lame. I would probably fail. "But it will be a while till I'm there."

Marie rolled her eyes and fluffed her hair with her hand. "Well, hurry up. I'm not going to be lame with you as you struggle to adulthood."

"You don't *have* to do anything. Go back to the party." I shooed her away, a smile on my face. "I kind of want to be alone with my homeless boyfriend."

Marie eyed me, the hesitation clear in her eyes and the way she held her weight on one foot, the other slightly lifted. "Are you sure?"

"More positive than a proton."

"Oh my God. Never say that again."

I laughed. "Fine. Now go have fun."

"Okay." Marie hugged me tight, and her hair tickled my nose. "But next time, you stay whether or not you want to. Enough lameness."

I watched her go. We were complete opposites, but maybe it would make us great roommates. Marie might be the person to pull me out of my self-imposed shell, and I could make sure

Marie studied as hard as she partied. It had the makings of a win-win situation. Maybe. Of course, it could be a complete and utter disaster too.

But I was trying to be optimistic, thank you very much.

I leaned back against the park bench, letting out another sigh. I would sit here for another minute before I headed back to my room. Once I got there, I'd curl up with a good romance book with my current book boyfriend and pretend the real world didn't exist for a little while. It would be the perfect Saturday night…for a sixty-year-old woman.

Lame, lame, lame.

After a couple of seconds of pure relaxation, I stiffened. Someone moved in the shadows. I almost missed it, but out of the corner of my eye I caught movement. Who was out here with me? If Dad were here, he'd be saying it was a druggie desperate for his next hit. He'd sic his private security team on whoever dared to walk near him. I used to go back to the spot and give whoever had been held back by my father's team some money. One of Dad's security officers would go with me.

But I wasn't my father, and I refused to jump to the worst conclusions. I stood up and crept toward the shadows, my heart in my throat and my legs feeling less than steady. My mind screamed at me to turn around and run home, but I ignored it.

"H-Hello?" I called out, but it sounded more like a croak than a word. I licked my lips and swallowed hard, taking another step toward the ocean. "Is anyone there?"

Nothing but the waves crashing. I hesitated. Someone was there. I knew it. "I know you're out there. You might as well come out. If you don't, I'll…I'll call the cops."

I held my breath, waiting to see if the hidden person would call my bluff and come out. After a few seconds, a shadowed form stepped forward. As the shadow grew closer, I realized it was a man. A guy who stood at least six feet tall and had muscles that I thought only existed in the romance books I read.

He had to be a couple years older than me, maybe a senior, and he had on a pair of cargo shorts and nothing else. Hot damn, he obviously worked out. A lot. He had short, curly brown hair, and he looked harmless enough. But those muscles…

Okay, when I goaded the guy out of hiding, I hadn't been expecting a freaking bodybuilder to walk out of the shadows. I backed up a step, biting down on my lower lip. "Who are you, and why are you hiding in the shadows?"

He had a black tattoo of some sort on his flexed bicep. Wait. Scratch that. He had tattoos pretty much from his elbows up and all across his shoulders and pecs. Hot. *Really* hot. This was the type of guy Dad kept me away from. He had bad boy written all over him. In numerous ways.

He rubbed the back of his neck and stepped closer, towering over me. "Who are you, and why are *you* hiding in shadows?"

I blinked and forced my eyes away from his ink. "I wasn't. I was sitting on the bench."

"Maybe I was too, before you came out." He grinned at me. "Maybe you stole my seat."

"Did I?"

"Maybe."

I shook my head and tried not to smile, but it was hard. For some reason, I liked this guy. "You like that word, don't you?" I held my hand up when he opened his mouth to answer. "Let me guess. Maybe?"

He laughed, loud and clear. I liked the sound of it. "Perhaps."

"Oh my God, he says something else." I held a hand to my forehead. "I might be imagining things."

"Hm. You *do* look a little flushed."

Probably because an off-the-radar hot guy was talking to me. Maybe even flirting? Crap. I had no idea. The last time a normal boy had flirted with me, Dad had his security team drag him out of the mall by both arms. I had no doubt this guy would get the same treatment if he ever crossed paths with Dad. "I do?"

He stepped closer and bent down, his eyes at level with mine. They were blue. Really, really blue, with little specks of darker blue around the pupil. People were always telling me that I had the prettiest blue eyes in the world. They were wrong. This guy did.

"Yep. Definitely flushed."

I cleared my throat and tucked my hair behind my ear. Until I remembered it was in a ponytail. Then I ended up kind of rubbing against my ear, trying to make it look like I'd *meant* to do that. And probably failing miserably. "I'm fine."

"I didn't say you weren't." He backed off and smoothed his brown hair, but it bounced right back into perfect disarray. He headed for the bench I had been sitting on and lowered himself onto it. "So, tell me. Why are you outside instead of partying inside?"

I followed him, scooted my shoes between us to maintain a safe distance apart, and then sat down on the edge of the bench. "Uh...I needed some fresh air. And this party is a little bit too crazy for my tastes. The frat boys are a little crazy too."

He nodded. "So, you new here?"

"Yeah. I'm a freshman." After smoothing the stupid skirt Marie had conned me into wearing, I looked at him. "Do you go here?"

"Yeah, I'm a senior." He cocked his head toward the house. "And I'm in that frat."

"Oh." I looked down at my lap. So I'd insulted his friends. Great. Just great. "I'm sure it's a lot of fun."

He grinned. "Even though they're crazy?"

"Uh, sure." I smiled back at him, but inwardly flinched. It was too late to tell him that the guys were perfectly normal. I was broken—not them. But I would look even more like an idiot than I already did if I told him I'd left because of my own lameness. "Maybe I'll give it another chance."

He chuckled. "Not tonight, though, right?"

"Nope. Not tonight." I played with the hem of my skirt. "I'm all partied out. I drank too much."

He looked at my cup. "You better watch yourself. A lot of guys will take advantage of a girl who drank too much."

"But not you?"

His eyes darkened, but he looked away. "Not me."

It was a pity. I'd never been taken advantage of by anyone, but if I was going to be used, I'd prefer he be the one doing it. I kind of snort-giggled at the thought, earning a weird look from him. Oh well. He wasn't exactly the first person to shoot me that look. "Then I guess I'm in good company."

He shrugged. "You should go home and sleep it off."

"It's only eleven," I argued. I conveniently ignored the fact that I'd been planning on going home mere moments before. That had been before *him*. "Why would I go to bed already?"

He looked at me, running his gaze up and down my body. "You look like the type of girl who's used to playing by the rules. Good girls go to bed early."

I was, but I was also freaking sick of being that girl. All my life, Dad had neatly moved me around on his chessboard, a pawn to his own plans. I was done being a pawn. I wanted to be the queen of my own life from now on.

Leaning in, I caught his gaze. He stiffened, a light shining in his eyes I didn't fully comprehend. "Maybe I'm the type of girl who's sick of living by the rules and who's ready to have some fun."

CHAPTER TWO

Finn

When she leaned in close to me like that, I gripped my thighs. I felt ridiculously out of place right now. I was in a pair of board shorts, pretending to be a carefree surfer dude so that my overprotective, needs-therapy boss could "rest easily" while his perfectly capable daughter attended college. I didn't even have my *gun* on me. And to top it off? Carrie was a cute little thing who was looking at me as if she wanted nothing more than to crawl all over me.

I needed to get close to her, but not *that* close. Even if I wanted to.

Her soft red hair reminded me of Scarlett Johansson as Black Widow. I had always had a thing for her—what kind of hot-blooded American man hadn't at one point or another? I especially liked her when she carried a kick-ass gun and wore black spandex and boots. It wasn't a far stretch of my imagination to picture Carrie in Scarlett's getup. Her short skirt left little to the imagination, and I wanted her. Bad.

I'd never had such an instant attraction to someone before. The type that demanded I find a way to get her in my arms, naked and writhing, before the end of the month, but I couldn't have her. I forced myself to picture Senator Wallington's face instead of Carrie's. That should help. "I think you look like a good girl who wants to try her hand at being a bad girl."

"Maybe." She shrugged. "But maybe not. You don't know anything about me."

Ah, but I did. I had her file memorized. And I'd been watching her from the shadows all night long. I also knew enough about her to know she hadn't been drinking tonight. Knew enough to know the real reason she wasn't inside was because she hated crowds. She hadn't been to any real parties until now. And I knew her father was controlling enough to send an undercover agent to watch his nineteen-year-old daughter fumble her way through freshman year.

One thing I knew about repressed girls who went away to college: They went all *Girls Gone Wild* on crack as soon as they got even the slightest taste of freedom.

The girl was looking for trouble with a capital T. Even I could see that.

She licked her plump, red lips and met my eyes. "So, you going to your room or staying out here with me?"

Oh yeah. Trouble indeed. I shifted in my seat. The girl had no idea what kind of attention she was welcoming. She might only be a couple of years younger than me, but even so, she had *off limits* stamped across her forehead. I forced a lighthearted laugh. Something I suspected a California boy would do. Hell, something *I'd* once done. "I don't really live here. I was fucking with you."

"Oh." Her brow furrowed. "Which dorm do you live in?"

"None." I grinned at her, even though my cheeks hurt from smiling so damned much. "I don't even go here. I'm just a surfer who lives nearby. Can't afford the fancy education."

That much had once been true, at least. When I'd been eighteen, I couldn't afford the tuition. That's why I had enlisted in the Marines. My plan had been to use the GI Bill to earn my degree, but I hadn't gotten to that point in my life yet. As it was, I had shadowed my father's footsteps and joined the Marine reserves fresh outta high school. I had been ooh-rah'ing it for five years now and had attained the rank of sergeant. On top of that, I held the title of "assistant private security officer" with the senator's security team.

I could afford to go to college now, but I was too busy. And now I was here in California. I'd been picked for this assignment since, as the youngest employee at twenty-three, I was the most likely candidate to blend into a college campus.

And if I managed to keep Carrie out of trouble, I would return to work minus the "assistant" in my title—and a spike in my pay. But first I had to get close enough to her to be able to be in her company, but not so close that she wanted me even *closer*.

"Oh, I totally get that," she said, nodding as if she had a clue about what it was like to be poor. She didn't.

Her daddy could afford to buy this whole campus without blinking. Hell, he'd already made a *sizable contribution* to get the dean to allow an undercover agent to linger around campus and follow a student. "Yeah?"

"Yeah." She plucked at her skirt again, her shoulders hunched. "I mean, not personally, but I know how bad the economy is right now. I'm not some bimbo college student. I watch the news."

Sure she did. Maybe TMZ was her version of "news," but it sure as hell wasn't mine. "I'm sure you do, Ginger."

She gave me a look. I could tell she wasn't sure if I was insulting her. Maybe she had more brains in her pretty head than I gave her credit for. "My name's not Ginger."

I gave her a cocky grin. "I think it has a nice ring to it, though. Don't you?"

"No," she said flatly. "So if you aren't going to college, what do you do?"

"I'm a Marine," I said. "And the rest of the time I surf."

I tugged at my Hollister cargo shorts. Apparently that's what all the California kids wore nowadays. I must've grown up since I left, because I preferred wearing a suit with a Glock or a pair of cammies…with a badass M-16.

"Nice. I'd like to learn how to surf sometime. It looks so freeing."

I cocked a brow. What an odd choice of words. "Freeing?"

"Yeah." She stole a quick look at me, her cheeks pink. "Like…it's just you and the ocean, and no one can tell you what to do or how to act. No one can yell at you for riding a wave, or just sitting out there, watching the world pass by. I don't even really know how that feels, and I doubt I ever will."

With a father like hers? Doubtful.

I'd resented being asked to come here to babysit some spoiled little brat, but seeing her look so despondent tugged at the little bit of heartstrings I had. "I'll teach you, if you want."

Fuck. Why had I opened my stupid mouth and blurted out that shit?

"Really?" She perked up, her shoulders straight and her sapphire blue eyes shining. She looked way too pretty right now. Way too much like a pretty woman, and not enough like an *assignment*. "Do you mean it?"

Hell no. "Sure. Why not?"

I could think of at least a hundred reasons why not. The last thing I needed was to spend time with her out in the ocean. She'd probably wear a tiny bikini underneath her wetsuit. And she'd cling to me in fear, her slender body pressed to mine as she learned how to ride the waves...

Maybe she would chicken out and say no.

"Can we start now?" she asked, practically shouting in my ear. She hopped off the bench and did a little dance thing that was way too fucking cute. Her whole body trembled with excitement. I could *feel* it rolling off her. "I'm game if you are."

I choked on a laugh. So much for her chickening out. Some small part of me admired her enthusiasm. A lot of girls wavered and couldn't make up their minds. I was getting the sinking suspicion she wasn't that kind of girl. "I think we should do it when we can actually see what we're doing."

"Tomorrow morning?"

I scratched my head and scrunched my nose. "Uh, you'll need a board, a bathing suit, and a wetsuit first."

"I have a bathing suit already." She cocked her head. "Wait. Does a bikini work, or does it have to be a one-piece?"

It was on the tip of my tongue to say she needed a one-piece. At least it would cover more of her skin, but she might find out I lied, and then she would start to question everything I told her. I couldn't afford that right now. "Bikinis are fine. Preferred, even."

She nibbled on her lower lip. "Would you go shopping with me tomorrow? Help me pick out the right gear? Then maybe we could head out to the waves."

Shopping? Hell no. I didn't want to go shopping. For girls, shopping was a marathon sport. I'd probably be dragged through ten stores before she could find the perfect color surfboard. And a matching wetsuit. And probably a fucking hair bow, too. "I'd *love* to."

I forced a smile and tried to look on the bright side of things. I needed to spend time with her, and this would accomplish that. After the heinous shopping experience, I would be rewarded with surfing. It wouldn't be so bad, would it?

"Thank you." Her cheeks flushed and she gave me a shy smile. "Where should we meet?"

"At your dorm around eight?" I met her eyes. "Or is that too early for you, Ginger?"

She stiffened, the fetching pink color leaving her cheeks. That was probably a good thing, since she looked far too cute wearing a blush. There was that steely determination again. When she looked at me, her eyes flashing with challenge, she looked like her father. "I'll be there. I don't sleep in till twelve."

"All right." I inclined my head. "Then off to bed you go."

She laughed. "You can't send me to bed. Who do you think you are? My father?"

Hell no. But I worked for her father, so that had to count for something. "Hey, if you want to surf, you need to be well rested. If you're hung over and tired, I'm not taking you."

"I won't be hung over."

I eyed her cup, even though I knew damn well it didn't have alcohol in it. "Tell that to the judge."

"Fine. I'm going to bed." She clamped her mouth and grabbed her shoes. "I'll see you in the morning."

"I'll walk you," I offered, standing up. It would make me feel better to know she was safely ensconced behind locked doors before I went back to my apartment. It *was* my job, after all.

She flushed and ducked her head. "If you want to. But you can't come in."

She was probably thinking I wanted to walk her home to try to steal a kiss or cop a feel. Well, she could think that all she wanted. It wasn't happening. In fact, it had been strictly forbidden. I had even gotten a lecture from the senator about what was allowed and what wasn't—complete with a signed contract. As if I was a child who needed to be shown on a fucking doll where I could and couldn't touch.

I shoved my hands in my pockets, feeling ridiculous. "I wasn't planning on it."

"Then why walk with me?" she asked, her head cocked.

"So I'll know where to meet you tomorrow." I shrugged. "Ya know, for our shopping."

"Oh. Right." She started walking, and I fell into step beside her while scanning the shadows for any threats. "I knew that."

I laughed lightly. "Sure you did."

"I can't think of any other reason you'd want to walk me."

I shook my head, then realized, like an idiot, I'd never asked her what her name was. If I accidentally blurted it out before she told me who she was, the gig would be up before I even got started. "What's your name, anyway?"

"Carrie. Yours?"

She left off her last name just as her father instructed her to do. I could report back that she was following instructions like a good little girl. Although…walking with strange men she met on the beach after dark wasn't exactly playing by the rules. But since it was with me, I would let the infraction slide this time.

"I'm Finn. Finn Coram."

She gave me another smile. She looked so pretty, smiling at me in the moonlight. It would be a hell of a long year keeping the horny college boys off her. "Nice to meet you, Finn."

"Back atcha, *Carrie*," I said, forcing a grin. I hated acting like a foolish boy. Hated pretending to be something I wasn't. "But I still prefer Ginger."

She hesitated, licking her lips. "Can I ask you something?"

"Sure. Go for it."

"Why are you teaching me how to surf? What made you offer?" She stole a quick glance at me. "Why are you being so nice to me?"

Already, she was questioning my motives. My respect for her grew. This wasn't a bimbo socialite. She knew to use caution, even if she wasn't using enough of it. I shrugged. "Why not?"

"In my world, there's always a reason." She lifted a shoulder and stopped at a pathway leading to a big dorm. "So you've got to have one."

"Yeah, well, I don't." I leaned against the building next to hers and crossed my ankles. "This your building?"

She didn't answer my question, but narrowed her eyes on me. "I'll meet you out here at eight."

"All right."

She stared at me. I arched my brow in return, waiting to see what the hell she was waiting for. If it was a good night kiss, she would be waiting a hell of a long time. She tapped her foot. "You can go now," she said.

"I'll wait until you're safely inside."

Her foot stopped tapping and she glowered at me. Oh, yeah. She definitely took after her father. "And *I'll* wait till you leave."

We stared each other down, neither one of use seeming to want to be the one who looked away first. After a bit more of our little Mexican standoff, I chuckled. "I can do this all night, Ginger."

"So can I." She tilted her head and studied her nails. "You know, you're starting to remind me of my father's private security firm."

"Your father has private security? Or he works in it?"

She flushed. "Yeah, he has security."

"Why?"

"None of your business. Is there something you want to tell me?"

"Of course not." I laughed but shifted on my feet. She was way too close to the truth already. I would need to back down to remain undercover. "Do I *look* like private security?"

She ran her gaze over me. "Not really, but that doesn't mean anything. You're being awfully…protective."

"Ya know, I'm a Marine. It's kind of our thing to guard people."

She pursed her lips. "Fair enough, but still. Go *home* before I call security on your butt."

"There you go, bossing me around again." I picked up a piece of her hair without intending to do so. It was so soft and pretty. "Fine, but I'll see you right here in the morning."

"Okay." She nodded and bit her lower lip. "Bye."

I dropped her hair and headed back toward the beach, where I could then hop on my motorcycle and ride back to my empty apartment. As I turned the corner, I stopped and peeked out. She headed toward her building, her head low and her steps unhurried. I pulled out my iPhone and jotted off a quick text to update the senator.

I'm here and have seen her. All is well.

As I slid the phone into my pocket without awaiting a reply, I watched her go with a smile on my face. The senator had obviously underestimated his daughter's street smarts. Sure, she'd made a few blunders, but she'd also made some smart choices. She hadn't given me her full name, and she'd lied to me to hide her true location in case I was some creepy stalker.

Her father would be proud.

CHAPTER THREE

Carrie

With only ten minutes to spare, I hurriedly applied the last touches to my lip gloss, checked out my hair, and turned off the bathroom light. If I had primped right, I looked effortlessly, naturally beautiful. That's what the website said I would look like, anyway. I had never really bothered to primp for a boy, so I'd had to rely on my best friend for help.

Google.

Was it pathetic that I had no one else to ask? Sure. But at least Google never let me down. It had also given me *the talk*, the same one my mother avoided until right before I left for school. And when I'd finally been given *the talk*, it had been with so many euphemisms even I had become confused while trying to figure out what drumsticks had to do with warm apple pie.

I smoothed my tank top over my stomach. I had paired it with some yoga pants, and I wore my red bikini underneath the simple outfit just in case Finn wanted to go out in the water afterward. Tiptoeing past a snoring Marie, I managed to make it out of the dorm without waking her up.

I probably worried for nothing. I doubted a stampede of elephants would have woken Marie up. The girl had been snoring loud enough to wake the dead. Her arms were flung out to her sides, and a huge puddle of drool gathered under her cheek. She'd probably have a hell of a hangover when she woke up, so I had set my bottle of Motrin next to her bed on my way out.

I glanced at my phone and walked faster. A quick call home would be a good idea. That way I wouldn't have to deal with my parents while out with Finn. I quickly dialed home and leaned against the wall. They picked up on the first ring, as if they'd been hovering by the phone waiting for me to call all morning.

"Hello?" Mom said.

A line clicked as Dad picked up the phone in his office. "Carrie?"

I smiled. "Hi, guys."

"How's college going?" Mom asked, her voice trembling.

"Have you met anyone nice yet?" Dad asked.

"Yeah." I pictured Finn and smiled. "A couple of people."

"What are their names?" Dad asked. I could picture him sitting at his desk, pencil in hand, waiting to look into anyone who dared say hello to me. "I'll do a background check."

"Dad. No."

"But—"

"*No.*"

Mom sighed. "Let her be, dear."

"Fine." I heard something slam down. "But if you get involved with someone, I'll expect to get his name from you."

"She's not going to do that yet." Mom paused. "Right? We had our little talk. Do we need to have another one?"

I flinched. "God, no." I cleared my throat. "I mean, uh, no, thank you. I'm good. And I'm not seeing anyone yet. I've only been here two days."

Dad laughed. "That's my girl."

I peeked at the time. I had less than one minute to get downstairs. "I'm about to go out with a friend of mine, though. Shopping."

"Oh, how delightful." Mom, of course, perked up at the word *shopping.* "Where are you going? What are you shopping for?"

"Do you need more money?" Dad threw in. "I can transfer more to your account."

"No, I'm fine. And I'm shopping for..." I pictured the dead silence that would come if I said what I was really shopping for. It would be amusing for two-point-two seconds...until all hell broke loose. "I'm just shopping for fun. Hanging out and stuff."

"But what for?" Mom asked.

Geez. Enough with the details already. "I think swimsuits and beach gear."

"Oh, how fun."

Dad yawned. "This is my cue to say goodbye. I've got meetings all day long."

"Yeah, I have to go." I gripped the phone tight. "I love you guys."

"We love you, too," Mom said.

Dad mumbled something that might have been *I love you*, but he never said it, so it was doubtful. "Bye."

"Bye, dear."

I hung up and headed outside. I needed to get down to the meeting point before Finn did, or he would see me come out of the correct building. He didn't need to know where I lived. Didn't need to know anything about me…yet. If he proved trustworthy, then I would tell him more. Little by little. But for now, I was just a girl who liked sitting on benches at night.

A girl who wanted to surf.

It was probably the one place private security couldn't follow me. It's not like a bunch of men in suits would blend in out there in the great big sea. As I crossed the lawn, I glanced around. No one lurked in the bushes. No one suspicious followed me. I didn't believe my father gave in to my request to go to college minus a bodyguard, but I hadn't *seen* any yet.

Was it possible he had trusted me enough to be on my own? Doubtful. When I had gone abroad last year, it had been with not one, not two, but *three* security guards. He was ridiculous when it came to my safety. He'd probably installed a GPS tracking system under my skin when I was a kid. I wouldn't put it past him.

I rounded the corner and saw Finn standing there, facing the other way and looking as sexy as I remembered. I had thought he was gorgeous last night. Holy freaking bananas. In the morning light, his sun-kissed skin glinted and highlighted his hard muscles. Muscles covered in tats that begged to be stroked…by my hands. With his brown hair in as much disarray as it had been last night, he quite easily emanated the surfer look he wore so well.

Oh, so well.

As I approached, he smiled at me. "You're two minutes late, but you look pretty enough that I'll let it slide."

My heart sped up at his backhanded compliment, but I refused to show it. I shrugged and said, "A girl's gotta primp. Get used to it, Marine."

"Especially girls like you?"

I stiffened. That sounded an awful lot like an insult. And even worse, it sounded as if he knew something about me that I didn't want him to know. Did he know who I was? "What the hell is that supposed to mean?"

"Nothing." He straightened, looking less like a laid-back surfer and more like a man. A man I didn't know at all. Maybe this had been a bad idea. "You just look like the type of girl who likes to spend hours getting ready before she walks outside to get the mail. I mean, you're gorgeous. Just look at you."

"And you look like the type of guy who makes presumptuous assumptions about other people, while keeping your own nose firmly pointed in the air." I marched past him. "Forget it. I'll learn how to surf with someone else."

He grasped my elbow as I passed, his touch burning me and yet somehow sending a shiver through my veins. "I'm sorry," he said, his voice soft. "I shouldn't make assumptions. You're right."

"Damn right I am." I tossed my hair over my shoulder and glared at him. Turns out, this close, his eyes were even bluer. Really, really blue. "Now let me go."

He dropped his hand immediately and dragged it through his curls. "Can we start over? I get cranky before my coffee and say stupid things to beautiful women I'm supposed to be flirting with."

My lips twitched. Truth was, so did I. Well, the first part, anyway. I usually didn't bother to hit on pretty girls since I didn't swing that way. "Okay. Coffee, then shopping?"

"Deal." He motioned me forward as he walked beside me.

"Where will we shop?" I asked.

"At a store? I hear that's where most people do it."

I laughed lightly and stopped at the coffee booth. "You're weird."

"Aren't we all in our own way?"

"Yeah, I guess so." I nudged him with my elbow. God, he was solid. "But you're weirder than most."

He let me order my mocha latte before he stepped forward to order a plain black coffee. As I reached into my pocket to grab some cash for my portion of the order, he handed the barista his card. "I got you."

A warm flush spread through my body. No one ever paid for me. The few people I had hung out with in school had always been relying on me for purchases, but no one here knew how much money I had. No one knew my father was on the short list for presidential candidates. The anonymity was a refreshing change of pace. "Thank you. I'll get the next one."

He shrugged. "If I let you have a next time. You might kill me with boredom during the shopping trip."

"Haha. So funny." I grinned, then decided to get some payback for the trick he'd played on me last night. "Do you think I can find a Swarovski-encrusted surfboard? I'm willing to go in every single store in San Diego if needed."

"Oh, hell no." He shot me an incredulous look and turned a little bit green. "Please tell me you're kidding."

I blinked innocently and managed to keep a straight face. "Is that a no?"

He grabbed our coffees and handed me the bigger one. Once I took it, he shoved his sunglasses up his nose. "No. It's fucking fabulous." He shot a quick look at me. "Oops. Sorry."

"For what? Cursing?" I laughed at the absurdity of it. Who the heck apologized for cursing? "Sometimes I say *fuck* too. I'm not a little kid, you know."

He took a sip of his coffee. How did he do that? I would have burnt my tongue. "It feels like you are at times. Like you could be my little sister or something."

Sister? Ouch. Guess I knew where I stood with him. "How old *are* you?"

"Twenty-three." He looked at me. "What about you? Are you jailbait?"

"*No.*" I looked down at my cup. How much should I tell him about myself? I wanted to make friends. To be normal for once, but I couldn't be stupid. "I'm nineteen. I took a year off and went abroad before starting college."

He took another sip of coffee. "That's a good idea. It's how I would have done it, if I'd gone the college route."

I hesitated. I didn't want to overstep my boundaries and had no idea what a friend should or should not say to that. Or if we even were *friends* yet. "You still could if you wanted to. Do you want to?"

"Maybe someday, when I have time." He laughed. "Right now? I'm good in my career field."

"Well, you never know. You might decide to go officer someday."

He shot me a weird look. "Maybe."

"There's that word again."

"It's a good word, especially when life is filled with maybes." He stopped in front of a surf shop on the beach. "This would be a good place to start. I can't promise Swarovski, but there might be something pink."

"I don't do pink. It doesn't match my hair."

"Heaven forbid," he said, holding the door open for me. "We can't have that."

"Darn right we can't." I ducked into the store and took a cautious look around. Surfboards of every imaginable color lined the left wall, while wetsuits filled up the other half. In the back, a bunch of boogie boards hung on the wood wall. Maybe boogie boarding would be a safer choice. It wasn't too late to change my mind…

No. Not happening.

A blonde girl wearing a bikini underneath a transparent top stood behind the counter texting. She looked up when the bell on the door chimed, quickly assessing me before moving on to Finn—and staying there. She straightened and smoothed her hair. "Hello. Welcome to Surf's Up. What can I do for you?"

Finn smiled at her a little bit too widely, and his eyes dipped far too low to be staring at her face. Jerk. "My friend here needs a good beginner's board."

The girl looked at me again, but quickly turned back to Finn. "The blue one in the back is good for her. Perfect size."

"You think?" Finn walked over to the board in question and cocked his head. I followed Finn, but practically got shoved aside by the worker. I struggled to right myself before I went legs over head in the rack of wetsuits, but Finn caught my elbow without even looking my way. "You should watch where you're going, Ginger."

"I told you." I tried to pull free of his grip, but he didn't budge. "Stop calling me that."

Finn looked at me. "Why? It's cute."

"Says who?"

"Me." He dropped his hold on me and turned back to the employee, who'd been watching him as if he was her next meal. "So this will work for her?"

The employee moved closer to Finn, brushing up against him. And Finn, the perv, didn't move away. Of course not. He was a guy. The girl ran her fingers over the board, caressing it as if it was a person instead of an inanimate object. "Yes. The lines are smooth, and the finish flawless."

"What do you think, Ginger?"

I rolled my eyes at the nickname, but didn't bother to correct him again. No matter what I said, he would use it. "Sold. I'll take it."

Finn turned to me with wide eyes. "Really? That quick?"

"I don't care what it looks like. If you say it's good, it's good."

He tugged on his ear and looked at me as if I had sprouted two heads overnight or something. "All right. Next up? A suit."

I turned to the employee, using the no-nonsense tone Dad used when he wanted shit to get done. "I'd like a blue and white one, to match the board."

"Measurements?" The girl eyed me. "I'm guessing 32A?"

Total, petty lie. I was *not* a 32A, and it was obvious. "No, I'm—"

"34C," Finn replied, grinning. "Am I right?"

I blinked at him, taken off guard by that statement. Was it normal for a guy to know that crap? "Dude. What the heck is wrong with you? And *why* do you know that?"

"I'm kind of an expert in the frontal area." Finn grinned, and his eyes sparkled. "It's my thing."

"Obviously," I drawled, smiling.

He shrugged. I gave the rest of my measurements to the worker, and within ten minutes we were finished shopping. I carried my wetsuit and coffee, and he carried my board for me. I headed toward the ocean, so eager to hit the water I could barely stand still, and then sat down on a bench. He eyed me, but didn't sit. "That was a hell of a lot faster than I expected. I didn't even bring my board with me."

I took a sip of my coffee and watched the waves crashing on the sand. A surfer effortlessly rode one in, and a bunch more of them bobbed out in the water. They made it look so easy. So simple. I knew it was anything but. What the heck was I thinking? I couldn't do this, could I? If my father knew...

I straightened my back. The hell with that. I was going for it. The fact that my father didn't approve only made me want it more. Childish? Sure. Who cared? I was allowed a little bit of rebellion now and then. "Do you want to go to your place and get it?"

"I could, I guess." He looked over his shoulder toward the road. "Do you want to wait here for me?"

"Can't I come?"

He hesitated, shifting on his feet. "I only have a motorcycle. I'm not sure you want to ride that."

A motorcycle? Hell to the yes. Dad called bikes *donor cycles*. Told me if I ever even thought about setting foot within ten feet of one, he'd ground me for life. I wasn't ground-able anymore, was I? God, this freedom I now had was exhilarating. A girl could get used to this kind of life. "Oh, I'd love that."

"Seriously?" he asked, looking a little pale. "I'm not sure that's a good idea."

I propped my hand on my hip and stood. "Why not?"

"I only have one helmet."

"So what? I'll be fine. I trust you."

He looked up at the sky. "*You* might," he mumbled under his breath. Then he perked up. "What will we do with your board?"

"I'll have the store hold it for me."

He sighed. "I guess I'm out of arguments."

"I guess so," I said cheerily, my heart accelerating at the mere thought of climbing on a bike with Finn. "Cheer up. You're acting like my dad again."

He stiffened. "Stop saying that."

"Then stop acting like him," I said, smiling to show I was teasing him. "You better be here when I come back out, or I'll skin you alive."

I grabbed my stuff and headed toward the store. After a quick conversation with the employee, I came back out and found Finn standing there, his hands in his pockets and his shoulders hunched. I held my hand out and waited for him to take it with bated breath. I don't know why I did that. We weren't dating. We weren't even friends yet. I couldn't resist. He stared at my hand for a second, muttered something under his breath, and closed his fingers around mine. A shot of electricity skittered up my arm, making me jump slightly.

24

What the heck had that been?

His eyes darkened and something weird twisted in my belly in response. Something I was only loosely familiar with. Desire. I was a virgin, but I'd read about sex enough times to recognize the sensation. And I would bet my favorite pair of Converses that he was feeling it, too.

"Ready?" he asked, his voice deeper than usual.

"*So* ready," I said, peeking up at him through my lashes. "I've always wanted to ride one, but my dad wouldn't let me."

He perked up. "Maybe we shouldn't. You know, if your dad would be mad."

"Oh, please. I'm nineteen." I tugged him toward a Harley I could only assume was his. "I'll ride what I want to ride."

He groaned under his breath. "I bet you will." When we reached the bike, he grabbed the helmet off the handle and slid it over my head. I tried to pull back, not wanting to wear the ugly thing in front of him, but he didn't let me. "My bike. My rules. You wear the helmet."

"What about you?"

"I'll be fine." He gently slid the helmet the rest of the way down over my head, making sure to keep my hair out of my eyes as he did so. My heart did a weird little flip flop at the way he watched me, his eyes hot and his lips soft. His touch, gentle as it might seem, held a strength behind it.

"How do I look?"

"Perfect," he said lightly. Then he climbed onto the bike and looked over his shoulder at me. That look he gave me was the look that so many books described. Like he was inviting me to fall into his arms and stay there forever. God, I wanted to. His muscles flexed, teasing me with his perfection. "Climb on and hold on as tight as you can."

I swallowed hard and slid on the back of the bike.

CHAPTER FOUR

Finn

One thing I knew with picture perfect clarity? The senator was going to fucking kill me for taking his precious little girl out on a bike. Skin me alive and castrate me. Hang me up as a warning to all the other low-level security officers he employed. I would deserve every second of the pending torture, because not only did I want to take her on the back of my bike—but I also wanted to *take* her.

In several positions.

The second Carrie backed me into a corner and insisted she ride my bike with me, I'd known I was fucked…but not in the good way. Just the idea of her wrapping her pretty little arms around me and squeezing those perfect 34C's against my back made my cock hard. The reality of her pressed against me might be the death of me.

Everything I'd thought I knew about her so far had been wrong. I'd been so sure she would turn out to be this spoiled brat who thrived on shopping, drinking, and defying Daddy. Okay, the last part might be true, but she was also more. A lot more. I wanted to get to know her better. Preferably while naked in my bed.

No. My job was to serve. Protect. Keep my cover. And most of all? Not touch her. The bad thing was, I couldn't seem to stop *thinking* about it. For some reason, the little socialite who wasn't really a socialite was getting under my skin, and I had to find a way to get her out before it was too late.

If only my Glock protected against that shit.

Carrie slid onto the bike and wrapped her whole body against me. I bit back a groan and tried to ignore the way my cock was screaming for attention. Her legs wrapped around me, pressing against me. It would be so easy to turn around. To rip the helmet off her head and kiss her until she realized that the best way to get back at Daddy was through me.

But that wasn't my job.

And that wasn't me.

I didn't play the part of bad boy. Never had.

I revved the engine to life, taking my frustration out on the throttle, and she squealed and hung on even tighter. I couldn't tell if she was more excited or terrified. Probably an exhilarating mixture of both. The girl was getting a chance to live, and she obviously loved life.

Grinning, I shouted over my shoulder, "Hold on tight, Ginger."

Her nails dug into my waist and she scooted even closer, if that was possible. My grin faded away to a grunt, and I pulled away from the curb a little too hard. She didn't panic and cry out. Instead, she whooped. Actually whooped, for fuck's sake.

If she were anyone but the senator's daughter, I would be bringing her back to my place so I could show her how to *really* live. How to feel more alive than ever—and I could show her every damn night if she wanted me to. I twisted the throttle and turned the corner on the PCH, letting the bike climb up in speed slowly. Instead of clinging to me for dear life, she loosened her hold on me and laughed.

By the time we completed the short ride to my apartment, I was ready to explode with want. As I booted the kickstand into place, she hopped off of my bike and ripped the helmet off her head. Her wild red hair was a complete and utter mess, but she looked beautiful.

She did a little dance and handed me my helmet. Her blue eyes were sparkling. Vibrant. Full of life. I couldn't help but wonder what they would look like if I kissed her. Would she look up at me like that, with sapphires shining in her eyes? Or would they smolder and simmer, slowly heating me and making me need more?

"That was freaking awesome," she said, spinning in a circle. "I want to do it again and again and again."

My cock twitched, giving a whole new meaning to those words. "Anytime you want it, you let me know. I'll be at your beck and call."

"Really?" She gave me an odd look, as if she was wondering if I meant something else.

And, fuck me, I did. "Really."

"Why are you being so nice to me? It doesn't make any sense." She tucked her hair behind her ears and flushed. "I can't help but think there's a motive behind all this that you're not telling me. Are you…did someone…send you here?"

My heart twisted at the look she was giving me. All puppy-dog eyes, begging me for the truth. I wished I could give it to her. Wished I hadn't signed a contract stating I would keep my cover, no matter what.

Wished I wasn't a liar.

I hadn't expected it to be this hard. I hadn't expected her.

The girl was too smart for her own good. She was onto me. The only way to blow her off course was to confuse her. I couldn't blow my cover. Couldn't be exposed. No matter what. I grabbed her hand and yanked her sideways onto my lap. I liked the way she felt there. "You want motive? I'll give you motive."

She looked up at me, her mouth in a perfect *O*. Her hands fell to my shoulders, and she clung to me. "What are you—"

I slammed my mouth down on hers, telling myself the whole time that I was only kissing her because I had to keep my cover. That this wasn't *real*. Didn't mean anything. But the second her soft lips gave in to mine, I knew I was full of shit. I might be doing this to keep my cover, but I was also doing it because I wanted to see what she tasted like. To hear her little sounds of pleasure.

Her lips parted to let out a little moan, and I swooped in, entwining my tongue with hers. She gasped, almost as if she'd never been kissed before, and then melted against me. She wrapped her arms around me, urging me even closer, and my hands fell to her hips. Unable to help myself, I pressed my cock against the soft curve of the side of her ass, reveling in the feel of her softness pressed against my hardness.

Fuck, I wanted her.

Tearing my mouth free, I took a ragged breath and held her still. She kept trying to wiggle in my lap. If she kept that up, this would be more than a cover kiss. It would be a cover fuck. I tightened my fists on her and opened my eyes. She did the same, looking back at me with smoldering blue eyes.

Well, that answered my question from earlier.

Her swollen red lips begged to be kissed some more, but I tamped down the urge. I had to remember the game. Stay on course. "Shit. I shouldn't have done that. Pretend it never happened."

She blinked at me, the heat fading from her eyes and being replaced by confusion. "Why?"

"Speaking of favorite words…" I mumbled under my breath. I rubbed the back of my neck and sighed. "Was that motive enough for you?"

"Y-Yeah, I guess so." She licked her lips, her gaze on my mouth. "I didn't know…didn't realize you were thinking about kissing me. I wasn't expecting…that."

She sounded so innocent right now. Had she ever been with a man? I couldn't imagine a girl that looked like her still being a virgin…but then again, with her father, it was definitely a possibility. "Well, I'm a guy. We're always thinking about—" I broke off, swallowing the word *sex*. "Kissing. Surely you've been kissed before."

"Of course," she quickly said, her cheeks red. "Tons of times."

Tons? Why didn't I like the sound of that? "Oh really?"

"Really. You're hardly the first guy to show an interest. I'm not some meek little virgin girl."

She had to go and tell me that, didn't she? "Good to know."

I set her on her feet and stood, my heart pounding in my ears. That kiss had been a huge mistake. An even bigger mistake than accepting this assignment in the first place.

She pressed her fingers to her lips and looked at me. "So that's why you're being nice to me? Because you want to kiss me?"

"Occasionally." I forced a nonchalant shrug. She had to think I wanted her, but I couldn't actually *have* her. What a fine line I walked. One step too far to the left and I would be a goner. "I'm a guy. I'm always in the mood to kiss someone."

"Anyone will do?"

"Pretty much."

"Oh. I see." She cocked her head. "So that's your motive."

I dragged a hand through my hair and started for my door. "Sometimes there isn't a reason or a motive. Sometimes it just happens."

"Not in my life."

"Well, maybe you need a new life."

"Maybe." She bit her lower lip. "It's not that easy to just trust someone, especially when you don't even know them."

I swallowed the guilt choking me back. I knew she was suspicious, and she had every reason to be wary of me. I was a fraud. A phony. A fake. And most of all? An asshole for kissing her under false pretenses. "Why are you so damn suspicious of everyone and everything?"

She didn't follow me, but put her hands on her perfect hips. "I don't know."

"Why are you glowering at me like I drowned your kitten in front of you?"

"Because I thought we were friends."

"We are."

She lifted her chin up. "Friends don't kiss friends then say *shit*. You obviously don't like me very much, so I'm going to make this easy for you. I'm leaving—and you're staying."

"No, you're not." I rubbed my eyes. Unbelievable. Instead of fixing this screw up, I'd managed to make it worse. "I'm your ride."

She pulled out her phone and put it to her ear. "Yes. I'd like a cab, please. It's an apartment building. Brick with patios and balconies. I'll be outside." She rattled off my address, an address I didn't even know she'd be able to figure out, and then slid the phone back in her purse. "Problem solved. Now go away."

She sat down on the curb, her back to me, and promptly ignored me. I hesitated. Should I do what she wanted and go inside to come up with a plan? Or should I try to fix this now? The urge to bang my head against the wall was almost as strong as the urge to pull her into my arms was. She looked so alone sitting there and staring out in the road. I approached her slowly, uncertain how to tackle this.

"Look, I'm sorry." I sat beside her, my leg touching hers. She shot me a dirty look, but didn't move away. "I didn't mean to kiss you. Not because I don't want to, but because I just want to be friends."

"Then why did you kiss me?"

"Because I couldn't stop myself," I admitted. It was one of the most honest things I had said to her all day. "But I should have."

She finally looked at me again. "Why can't you kiss me? What's so wrong with it? I mean, if you want to, why is it bad?"

Good question. "It just is. In my career, I could be gone at any second if they call up my unit. I can't have relationships."

"That's bull." Her hands tightened on her knees. "If you don't want to be with me, just say it. Don't give me half-assed reasons why you can't."

"I don't want to be with you," I said, my voice coming out harsher than I intended. I reached out and closed my hand over hers, trying to soften the blow. "Not in that way, but I do want to be friends."

"I'll think about it." The cab pulled up and she stood. Her hand on the door, she glanced at me over her shoulder. "But if you want to be friends, keep your lips off mine from now on."

"Deal. Still want to surf?"

She hesitated. "Not today. I have a headache. See ya some other time."

And with that, she closed the door in my face and left me standing on the curb. My phone buzzed, and I pulled it out. Her father, of course. The man had impeccable timing.

Things going well?

I tightened my grip on the phone and typed fast. *I got it covered.*

Good. Don't forget the rules.

The ones I'd already broken? As if I could.

CHAPTER FIVE

Carrie

Later that night, after Finn kissed me and dissed me, so to speak, I came out of the bathroom in a pair of frog jammies and found Marie sitting on my bed, a short dress in her hands. Since Marie was already wearing a way-too-short black dress, I could only assume the tiny blue dress in Marie's hands was for someone else. That someone else better not be *me*.

I raised a brow and eyed the contraption. "What's up?"

"What's up is you're going to lose the froggies and slip into this." Marie tossed the dress at me and I reflexively caught it. "And we're going to go party. And for once in your life, you're staying."

I held the dress to my chest. "I told you, I don't like parties."

"That's because you never drink at them, I'd bet." Marie stood up and gave me a little push toward the bathroom. "But tonight, you are. I'll get you something good, and we'll party the night away. Monday classes start, so we'll have a boring week. But tonight?" She shoved me into the bathroom. "We dance!"

As the door closed in my face, I flinched. Marie might be pushy—literally—but she had a point. The week ahead of us would be long. Would it be so wrong to let loose and have some fun tonight? Look at all the other stuff I had already done since getting here.

Buying a surfboard? Check. Riding a motorcycle? Check. Kissing a hot surfer boy? Double freaking check. As long as I wasn't crazy and didn't get caught on camera naked or something, there wouldn't be any backlash. Surely Dad drank in college, right? Oh, but that was different. *He* was a man, and *I* was his baby girl.

Rolling my eyes, I sent a mental eff you out in the universe. I made quick work of shedding my froggie pajamas and slid in to the short dress. Spinning in front of the mirror, I cringed. The thing barely covered my butt. Wait. Maybe it didn't even cover it at all.

"I'm coming in," Marie called. As she opened the door and barged through, she paused. "Wow. You look amazing. All you need is makeup and we'll be ready to go."

"I don't really—"

"Wear makeup? I know." Marie pulled out an eyeshadow brush. "But tonight you're different, remember?"

Different. That sounded nice. I closed my eyes and let Marie work her magic. But when I closed my eyes, I remembered that amazing kiss Finn had given me. And then I remembered our fight afterward. He was always acting so…contradictory. It didn't make any sense. Marie started applying the eyeshadow, and I belatedly said, "Not too dark."

"I know, I know." Marie set to work, and I tried to relax. This was supposed to be fun. "Your dad called. I told him you were studying at the library."

I swallowed. "Why did you do that?"

"He calls every hour. He needs to back off. He a cop or something?"

I laughed. "No. Just overprotective."

"Ah." I felt Marie's shrug, even though my eyes were shut. "My dad was like that before he died."

"I'm sorry," I said. Dad was annoying, sure, but I couldn't picture life without him. "How long ago?"

"Two years." Marie closed the mascara, and seemed to close the topic. "Open your eyes now."

I refused to look at myself yet. I was scared I would look more hooker than sexy. "Done?"

"Not yet."

I fidgeted. "Are you *sure* it's not too short?"

"Positive." Marie applied a layer of lip gloss, grabbed a piece of toilet paper, and said, "Blot." I pressed my lips down on the toilet paper. "There. Now you're ready to go."

I peeked in the mirror. Smoky gray eyes and black eyeliner stared back at me, making my eyes seem brighter than usual. And the red lip gloss actually looked…good. "Wow."

"Right?" Marie put the rest of the makeup away, fluffed her blonde hair, and grinned. "We'll be the prettiest girls there. Now let's go."

We linked arms and walked out of the dorm. As we passed, boys gaped at us, making me smile. Okay, maybe Marie was right. Maybe I needed this. After Finn kissed me and practically wiped his mouth to remove my taste from his lips, my self-esteem had been lagging. It might be fun to go out and drink. Flirt a little bit too much.

And then Finn could kiss my un-kissable ass.

Marie dropped my arm when we reached the crowded frat house. Girls in dresses even shorter than mine filled the room, as well as guys in plaid shorts and solid-colored shirts. From a distance, they all looked the same. Marie tugged me toward the "bar" area, which was really just a bunch of wine coolers and beer cans on a folding table. "Which one do you want?"

I eyed the choices skeptically, then reached for a pink drink with a picture of the beach on the label. "This one, I guess."

"Good choice." Marie opened it for me and grabbed a beer from the table. After opening her own drink, she nodded to the room. "Next assignment is for you to find a cute guy and start talking to him. Think of this like a class. A class at how to party properly."

I rolled my eyes. "But—"

I turned around and Marie was gone, already chatting up a guy I vaguely recognized. Great. Just freaking great. Now what? Everywhere I looked, people were already engrossed in conversations. I wasn't the type of girl who just barged in and invaded other people's conversations. Giving up on finding someone who wasn't already busy, I scanned the room, looking for somewhere to sit. As I searched, I tilted my drink to my lips. It tasted sweet and a little bit like pink lemonade.

Whoever came up with this type of alcohol was *brilliant*.

Spying an empty spot by the door, I carefully made my way across the room in my heels and sat down on the step leading outside. I hadn't left, but it gave me room to breathe. It was a win-win. No sooner had I sat down than a man was next to me, a beer in his hand and a sloppy grin on his face.

"Hey, there," he said, his voice slurred. "Haven't seen you around here before."

How many drinks had he had? I got nervous around drunk people. They were too unpredictable. Dad had thrown a dinner party once and a man had gotten drunk and punched another guy for looking at his wife too long. He'd been perfectly fine, and even polite, before the drinking.

Though my urge to run was strong, I forced myself to take a sip of my drink. I'd been running away enough. It was time to stand still. "Yeah, I'm new here."

"Freshman?"

"Yep." I took another sip. The drink was delicious. "You?"

He scooted closer to me, pressing his body against mine. I could smell the alcohol on his breath, overwhelming and sickening. "I'm a junior."

I stiffened. Though Finn had done the same thing earlier, his body pressed to mine hadn't made me want to gag. It hadn't made me feel like a thousand worms squiggled under my skin. I scooted away from him. "Nice."

He reached out and played with my hair, leaning so close that his beer breath washed over me. "I like this color. Is it real?"

"Uh, yeah." I pulled my hair free and slid into the corner of the banister. "What's your major?"

"You are," he said, following me.

That had to be the corniest line I had ever heard or read. And I'd read a heck of a lot of books. I couldn't help it. I laughed. "Okay, that was funny."

"It's only the beginning."

Without warning, his lips closed over mine. Instead of the electric whir I had felt when Finn kissed me, the itchy need to get closer to him...I couldn't breathe. I tore free of this man's smothering mouth, but he moved on to my neck without a second's hesitation.

"Get off me." Shoving at his shoulders, I stood up and took a calming breath. After setting my half empty bottle on the step, I said, "I have a boyfriend."

"Oh. Why didn't you tell me before you kissed me?" Beer Breath asked. He stumbled to his feet and adjusted his junk.

So freaking attractive.

"I didn't—"

"Get lost," a hard voice that I recognized said from the shadows. "You'll go back to your stupid little party and find another drunk girl to hit on."

"Says who?" Beer Breath asked, a cocky grin on his face.

"Says me," Finn said, stepping out of the shadows. He flexed his fists and stepped closer to me. "Go ahead. Give me a reason to punch your fucking face in, and I'll gladly oblige."

Beer Breath paled and shuffled backward. "Dude. She kissed me."

"No, I didn't."

"We wouldn't expect you to know the difference, now would we?" Finn asked, his voice mocking. He was practically begging for a fight. And all because of what? Because some dude kissed me? Why did he even care? "You have five seconds to be gone."

Beer Breath turned red. "You know what? Run off with your little boyfriend and don't ever come back to this frat again."

Beer Breath stormed off, leaving Finn and me alone on the porch. I pivoted and gave him what I hoped was an annoyed look. "You do realize I can handle a grabby-hands boy by myself, right? I dealt with you, after all."

He stepped closer, towering over me. "Ginger, you have no idea how to deal with me."

I stiffened. "I know that if I kissed you now, you wouldn't push me away."

"Of course I wouldn't. Look at you." His gaze dipped over my body, and when he met my eyes again his own were blazing and hot. "Any man would kiss you back."

"You'd push me away after."

He lifted a shoulder but said nothing.

He was so darn condescending and cocky. "Why are you at another frat party that I just *happen* to be at? Who are you? Why are you following me?"

Finn leaned against a palm tree and looked far too casual, but he reminded me of one of those lions on the Discovery Channel. He looked perfectly calm on the surface, but in a second he could be all deadly and lethal. "I'm here because I was taking a walk down the beach, and I saw you and that loser kissing. Then I saw you push him away. I wanted to make sure you were okay, but now I'm wishing I had bashed his head into the fucking wall before I let him go."

My heart rose to my throat. "Why?"

"Because you should be kissing *me*," he practically whispered. "Not some college boy who doesn't know what he's doing."

He closed the distance between us. And as soon as his hands were on my hips, his mouth was on mine. The familiar sensations he'd awoken in me came to life, and I clung to him. His tongue entwined with mine, and he grabbed my waist, yanking me against him.

I lifted up on tiptoe, trying to get closer, and moaned softly. He needed to do that again. And more. This is how a kiss was supposed to feel. This is what it was supposed to do to me. I might be inexperienced, but even I knew what a good kiss felt like.

And. This. Was. It.

CHAPTER SIX

Finn

As soon as my lips touched hers, I knew I was making one of the biggest fucking mistakes of my life. I shouldn't have done that. I *really* shouldn't have done that. Seeing her in that bastard's arms had triggered something deep within me. Something had made me go crazy and come down on her like a barbarian or some shit like that. I'd needed to show her who she should really be kissing. That same primal urge had apparently taken away the common sense God had given me. This was strictly off limits. Forbidden.

Yet I couldn't stop.

When she whimpered into my mouth and pressed even closer to me, pressing her soft stomach against my hard cock, I wanted so badly to forget all the reasons why I couldn't kiss her. Forget all the reasons I couldn't bring her back to my place and spend all night making her scream my name.

But then my phone buzzed.

And all the reasons I *shouldn't* be kissing her came flooding back. I jerked free and stumbled back, a hand over my mouth. As if that would help remove the memory of how wonderful she tasted. "Fuck."

She stiffened, her sapphire eyes going narrow. "No. Fuck *you*." Flinging her hair over her shoulder, she headed for the dorms.

I ignored my phone and stumbled after her. "Wait. I'm sorry."

"Sorry about what?" She spun around, arms akimbo and eyes blazing. "Sorry you kissed me again? Sorry you keep kissing me and then regretting it? Sorry you keep following me around?" She shoved my shoulders hard, but I didn't move. Not much could move me anymore. "What's your deal, anyway?"

I clenched my jaw. "The truth is, I don't want to want you. I'm a Marine. I could be out of this place in days for all I know. And I barely know you, and yet I can't stay away. That's what I'm doing here. That's why I keep coming back."

Even if it is my job to follow you around.

"Why aren't you supposed to want me?" Her eyes went wide and she pointed a finger at me. "Oh my God, you have a girlfriend. Don't you?"

My heart stuttered to a stop before speeding up painfully. For a second, I thought she knew who I really was. For a second, I thought my cover had been blown. And I had been relieved. Maybe I needed to stop this game. Quit.

"No. I don't." I held my hands out to my sides, palms up. "I'm not a cheater."

"Just a player."

No, just a liar. "Pretty much. And I'm already committed to my work."

She pressed her lips together. "The Marines."

I wanted to correct her. Tell her it was my other job that was causing problems, but then she'd want more info. Info I couldn't give her. "Right."

She smoothed her hair. "So what are we supposed to do? Stop seeing each other?"

I couldn't do that even if my job *wasn't* to see her. I wanted to be with her, plain and simple; no matter how wrong it might be. "No. I can't do that."

"Then what do you want from me?" She tilted her head back and looked up at me, her lips soft and her eyes even softer. I wanted to kiss her again, but I held back. "You aren't making any sense."

"I want to...I want to teach you to surf, and ride on my bike, and be with you, but I can't *be with* you."

I cupped her cheek and kissed her forehead. Her lids drifted shut, and she swayed closer. It took all my control to not capture her lips. To not take what she so freely offered, but she didn't realize who she offered her lips to. If she knew she would hate me.

More than I hated myself right now.

She held on to my biceps and gave me a small smile. "Friends?"

"Friends."

She nodded and dropped her hold on me. I let her go, but it was hard. Way too fucking hard. "Then you can't be mad if you see me kissing other guys. You can't not want me, but not want me to be with someone else. That's not fair."

The hell it wasn't.

"I can't promise that." I gritted my teeth. "I don't make promises I can't keep, and I don't think I can keep that one."

"Then at least promise you won't lie to me anymore." She canted her head. "Can you promise me that?"

I swallowed hard. "I can't promise that either," I managed to say. "But I can promise to do my best not to hurt you and to be a good friend."

She gave me one last look and turned on her heel, leaving me behind. I followed her, even though I had been clearly dismissed. Yep. She was just like her father. "Would you rather I lie and say I'll never tell you a lie? Who can promise that?"

"Honest people. That's who."

I laughed hard. "So you've never lied to me?"

She hesitated. I could see her recalling our time together, going over every conversation in detail. After licking her lips, she finally admitted, "No. I guess I can't say that."

"See?" Of course, I already knew all about the lies she'd told me. Every single one. "No one can promise that. People lie all the time, especially when it comes to little things."

My phone buzzed again, but I ignored it. Hers buzzed too and she pulled it out. After quickly typing on her phone, she gave me her attention again. "Fine. You win." Her phone buzzed again and she rolled her eyes. "What is he even doing up?"

"Who?" I asked, even though I knew who it was. I hadn't answered his text soon enough, so he'd texted his daughter. The dude needed some form of medication and some *serious* help.

"My dad." She stole a quick peek at me as she texted. "He's kind of crazy protective."

"No kidding."

She snorted. "I wish I was kidding. It's, like, after midnight there."

"Where are you from?"

She froze, her fingers hovering over her iPhone screen. "Washington, D.C."

"Nice." I rocked back on my heels, slipping back into my role. It was time to play the part of interested friend again. Asking questions I already knew the answer to. "What does he do?"

"Oh, nothing too interesting." She put her phone away and gave me a calculating stare. "Something to do with billing."

Or *making* bills. "Oh, that sounds fun."

"Not really," she said, smiling. "It's pretty boring. What do your parents do?"

"My mom died of cancer when I was sixteen." I ignored the pang of pain I still felt at the loss. There was no use living in the past, and it would never go away. "My dad is in security."

She placed a hand on my shoulder. "I'm so sorry for you loss. I can't even imagine…"

I knew she was close with her mother. Much closer than she was to her father, who seemed determined to run her life for her, no matter how old she might be. "Thanks."

"Can friends hug?"

"Hell yeah they can."

She flung her arms around my neck, holding me close. For a second, my arms lingered at her hips, but then I let myself pull her close. I may have buried my face in her neck, but that was pure speculation I would deny even under torture if asked later.

She stepped back and grinned up at me. "So…surfing tomorrow?"

"Sure." I headed toward her dorm room, but she didn't follow me. I stopped walking. "Hello?'

She grinned. "Hi."

"Why aren't you coming with me?"

"I have to go back to the party." She pointed over her shoulder. "Marie's waiting for me. I promised her I wouldn't leave early again."

I stiffened. I didn't like the thought of her hanging out with more guys like the one who'd just kissed her. "You're going back to that place? To that guy?"

"Yeah, I can handle him."

She started for the party, but I grabbed her elbow. "Don't go. Those places are asking for trouble. What if something bad happens?"

She raised her brows. "What if it doesn't?"

"At least let me go with you."

"Nope." She wiggled free and started walking again. "I want to be on my own. I'm ready to go back into the masses. If I'm going to be in college, I have to get used to this type of thing, right?"

"You don't have to party to be in college," I said tightly. "You can, ya know, study."

"I plan on doing that." She stopped on the steps of the party. The loud music came out the windows, and I could see a couple getting pretty hot and heavy almost directly behind her. Would that be her soon? "But tonight I'm being someone besides myself. And I'm going to go have some fun, even if it kills me."

It might not kill her, but she might be the death of me.

She wiggled her fingers in my direction and disappeared inside the building. I stood there awkwardly, my hands in my pockets, and shifted on my feet so I could see her. She grabbed another wine cooler and made her way over to a young man sitting in the corner. He had blond hair and screamed of money.

He was probably born with a silver spoon in his mouth, just like Carrie. He wore high-quality clothing and his Rolex glinted in the dim lighting. The boy looked up at her as if she were a goddess and moved over so she could sit beside him. They conversed quietly, and then the boy laughed at something Carrie said.

While I watched from outside, like someone who didn't belong.

Because I didn't, in more ways than one.

CHAPTER SEVEN

Carrie

The next morning, I struggled to get to the surface, my lungs bursting with the need to breathe. The need for air. I kicked wildly but seemed to be getting nowhere fast. I knew time was running out. Knew I needed to breathe sooner rather than later. If I died in this ocean, Dad would kill me.

Finn had given me a ten-minute lecture about the dangers of surfing. Telling me to never leave his side, never take a wave that wasn't the right size for me, never take chances, and above all—never disobey him out in the ocean. Out there, he was my boss and I would "fucking listen." Well, I had followed all those rules. I had fucking listened.

But I was *still* drowning.

Just as I was certain I would never see the light of day again, a strong hand closed around my wrist and tugged me to the surface. As I gulped in a deep breath, the air stinging my oxygen-deprived lungs, I opened my eyes and saw Finn looking down at me with a tight jaw. Little droplets of water spiked on his long lashes, and his hair was soaking wet.

"Got you," he said, his voice rough.

"Thanks," I sputtered, struggling to catch my breath. I shivered, and he frowned down at me even more. "It's c-cold under there."

"Yeah. I noticed," he said. A muscle ticked in his jaw again. What was his deal? "You almost drowned. You know that, right?"

"I was fine." And I was also a big fat liar. I hadn't been fine. Far from it. And truth be told? I'd been terrified. But that was all the more reason for me to keep going. To try again until I got better. I refused to back down. "Ready to go again?"

"Hell no. You're done for today, no matter what you say," he said, paddling toward the shore and towing me behind him like an errant child. "If I have to save your life one more time today, you'll owe me your first born son."

I could fight his hold and insist on continuing, but the truth was I was worn out. I could feel my exhaustion all the way to my bones. We'd been in the water for three hours. I was tired, achy, and freezing. California water might look inviting, but it was freaking frigid. "F-Fine. We'll do it again next weekend."

He shot me an incredulous look. "You want to go back out?"

"Of course," I said through numb lips. "I want to learn."

"You're something else," he muttered, shaking his head.

"W-What's that supposed to mean?"

He lifted a shoulder. "I would've thought one time would be enough for you."

"I don't give up easily." As soon as my feet hit sand, I pulled free of his grip. His assumptions about me were getting awfully annoying. "I get my steely determination from my father and my need to succeed from my mother. So don't *assume* I'll quit so easily."

"Relax. I didn't mean to insult you."

"You did."

I waited for him to apologize. To say he was wrong about me. Good thing I didn't hold my breath, because I'd have died waiting. Instead, he shot me an amused look and slung his board under his arm. When he reached for mine, I shook my head and mimicked his hold with my own.

"Refusing help now?" he asked, his eyes lighting up with amusement.

I had to know how to do this myself. He wouldn't always be with me. "I don't need you doting all over me, thank you very much."

"Doting?" he spluttered, his face turning red. "I'm not *doting* on you. Christ."

"I'm perfectly capable of carrying my own board."

"Unbelievable," he muttered under his breath. He shook his head and walked toward our towels. "Take off the wetsuit."

I looked down at the only thing keeping me warm right now. "Why? That doesn't make any sense."

"Can you *not* argue for one time in your life?"

"Excuse me for speaking my mind, master." I stiffened. "I'd say it'll never happen again, but it would be a lie."

He laughed. "Just trust me, okay? You'll warm up quicker without the suit." He held out my towel. "And put this on once you're out of it."

Why did I have to wear a towel? Maybe he couldn't stand the sight of me. "Right here?"

He cocked a brow. "Yeah. What's wrong? You naked under there?"

"No, of course not." I looked around. A bunch of surfers were stripping out of their suits without a shred of modesty a few feet over, chatting about the waves that would be coming from the storm tonight. Apparently undressing in public was normal. "I just didn't realize…"

I drifted off, feeling stupid. It's not like my bikini I wore underneath was something I never showed anyone. It was meant to be worn out in public, for Pete's sake. I might be undressing in public in front of a bunch of men, but it was a bikini. No big deal.

After taking a deep breath to calm my stupidly racing heart, I peeled the wetsuit off my body. For a brief second, I thought my bikini top had gone off with the suit, but a quick glance showed it was still in place—but slightly skewed. As I adjusted the top, I lifted my head and found Finn watching me with dark eyes. As our gazes collided, he turned away.

I had caught him watching me, and the look in his eyes had sent a fist of something crashing through me. Desire? Need? Both.

God, he didn't make any sense. He watched me as if he couldn't get his mind off me, and yet he kept insisting he couldn't have me. Heaven forbid another man looked my way though. He'd be all over the guy in two seconds flat, just like a jealous boyfriend. All the cons without the pros.

I tugged the wetsuit past my hips, but stopped when I realized the wetsuit wasn't the only thing I was removing. "Oops. My bikini bottom almost came off."

"Please make sure it doesn't," he said over his shoulder. "Unless you want to put on a show for a bunch of older men."

Were they all older? I scanned the men surrounding us. A guy was about my age leaned against a tree, his eyes on me. "They're not all old.

The guy watching me over there is my age. Actually, he's kind of cute…"

Finn spun around so fast he should have gotten whiplash. Within seconds, he was in front of me, his hands on my hips and his back pressed to my front. "Who? Where?"

Yep. Jealous boyfriend, only without the perks. No way I was letting him go all alpha male on the poor guy for daring to look at me. "I think he might have left."

I pretended to look around his wide shoulders, leaning against his back for support. When my breasts brushed against his damp skin, my already hard nipples pebbled into even harder beads, seeming to beg for his touch. Could he tell? Did he know? When he tensed up and drew in a deep breath, I got my answer. "Fuck, Carrie. What are you doing?"

"Just looking around for that guy," I breathed, finding boldness in his obvious reaction to me. "Why? Is something wrong?"

"You aren't ready for what you're starting, Ginger."

Yeah, I was. *He* was the one who wasn't ready. Not me.

I didn't know what struck me, what made me think that I could seduce him. I didn't know what the hell I was doing. He'd probably been with countless women, while I was nothing but a nineteen-year-old virgin who read too many romance books. One who didn't know what to do with a man like Finn.

But I tried anyway. I trailed my fingers over his shoulders, then leaned in and pressed a kiss to the back of his shoulder. Reaching around him, I let my hands slide down his hard pecs, toward his abs. He tensed and hissed through his teeth. I bit down on his shoulder and tried to get up the nerve to go even lower.

He shuddered and leaned back into me, his hands reaching around to grab my butt. His fingers fanned out over the top of my thighs, so close to touching me where I needed him most, yet not close enough. "Carrie…" he said, his voice strained. "You need to…I need to…back away. Now. Or you'll be mine in more ways than you can handle. Right here. Right now. In front of everyone."

After a second of hesitation, I backed off, the intensity in his voice almost too much for me to handle. I didn't doubt that he meant it. That he would kiss me in front of everyone. But surely not…not what he said. He acted as if he was about to bend me over the bench and have his way with me.

"You wouldn't." I pressed my hands to my cheeks, which suddenly felt way too hot.

"I would." He spun to face me, his face red. "What game are you playing?"

My gaze fell to his erection, which strained against his swim trunks. He wanted me, just like I wanted him. I swallowed past the Sahara Desert that was now my throat and forced my eyes northward. "I'm not playing any games. I just wanted—"

"I know what you wanted." He flexed his jaw and stepped back from me. His gaze dipped below my face for a second, but then he turned around again. My stomach coiled, as if he'd touched me instead of simply looking my way. "Put the towel on."

I scowled at his back. If he wanted to ignore the desire between us, I would let him, but I didn't have to make it *easy* on him. After drying my hair, I flung the towel across the bench before I sat down and reclined against the seat. Covering a yawn with my hand, I dropped my head back against the wood.

"You got something against a towel?" he asked.

"Yeah. I want to feel the sun."

"Feel it through a towel," he said.

"Nah. I'm good." I bit my lower lip to keep it from lifting into a smile. I kind of liked the fact that he couldn't bear seeing me. At least, now that I knew *why*. "That was fun but exhausting."

I heard him move closer, but didn't open my eyes. "Maybe you're tired because of the partying and not the surfing," he said.

"I doubt it." I cracked one eye open to look at him. He was watching me, but he wasn't staring at my face. "Though, I did meet a nice guy."

His fists went even tighter. "Oh yeah?"

"Yeah. His name's Cory." I shrugged. "He gave me his number. We're in a bunch of classes together, and we even have the same major."

He was exactly the kind of man Dad would pick for me. The kind of guy he would want to call his son-in-law. If they ever met, Dad would probably start drawing up wedding invitations within minutes of meeting Cory. I, however, preferred my men with tattoos and attitude and perpetually disheveled hair.

Men like Finn.

"How perfect," he said, his voice tight. "I'm sure Daddy would approve of him."

My eyes flew open. His thoughts mirrored my own way too well. "Excuse me?"

"I-I mean, he sounds like the kind of guy a father would like." He sat down beside me, hanging his hands in between his knees. "From what little I know of fathers, anyway."

I relaxed again. For a second, I thought he knew something more about me than he should have. "Did any of your girlfriends' fathers like you?"

He shrugged. "I haven't really had any. I've been married to my work for the past five years. Not much free time."

"Oh." I looked at him out of the corner of my eye. "I can't imagine you being single. I figured a guy like you would have numerous women in his life."

"Now who's making assumptions?" he asked, giving me a pointed look.

"I'm sorry," I quickly said. I hated when he did it to me, and I'd gone and done it to him. "I didn't mean to be rude."

"Apology accepted, but it just so happens you might be right."

My jaw dropped open. He didn't make any sense. "You said you've been single."

"I've been single." He grinned at me. "Not celibate. Two different things."

I rolled my eyes, disappointed by his honesty. I'd been hoping… what, exactly? That he'd spent his whole life waiting for the right girl to come along? As if.

He shifted on the bench and stole a glance at me. "Are you going to see this guy again?"

"I'm sure I will. We do have classes together."

He sighed. "I meant outside of school."

"I don't know." I looked up, watching the clouds move lazily across the blue sky. One of the clouds looked like the Washington Monument, and it made me miss home and my mom. Heck, even my dad.

"What's his last name?"

I eyed him. "Why?"

"Just curious if I knew him."

"Oh. Pinkerton." I watched the monument cloud until in merged with another, making it unrecognizable. "I'll probably see him again. He seems nice."

"Nice," he muttered. "That's a word for a puppy, not a man. Nice won't make you scream out in bed."

I choked on a laugh, but something inside of me responded differently. Finn would probably be able to make me scream his name. Too bad he didn't want to. "I can't believe you said that."

He lifted a shoulder. "If the shoe fits…"

"Well, I like puppies and nice guys like Cory," I added. Even though I was lying. I much preferred Finn.

"You're a dog person?" he asked.

"Some dogs." I smiled and pictured Mom's dog running through the yard with a pink bow around its neck. "I like the little terrier my mom has. She's cute."

"Do you miss home?"

"Yeah." I nodded and swallowed hard. "I mean, it's been less than a week, but I definitely miss certain things. Although it's nice being on my own. Making friends. Surfing. Riding a motorcycle." I hesitated. I wanted to tell him more about myself. Wanted to trust him. "I couldn't do that stuff at home. There were too many eyes on me all the time."

"Too many eyes," he said softly. "That doesn't sound fun."

"It kind of sucked," I admitted. "My dad is kind of…important in his company. He's in politics, and with politics…people are always watching."

He cleared his throat. "You didn't mention that before."

"I didn't trust you before." I met his eyes and bit down on my lip. "I do now. I'm hoping it's not a mistake."

"It's not," he said, but his eyes looked shaded with something I couldn't name. "I won't tell anyone."

"Yeah, I'm trying to keep a low profile. I look a lot different than I used to, and I was lucky enough to be out of the media for the last year. Hopefully it stays that way."

"So, you're like a Kennedy?"

I laughed. I wasn't nearly so high up on the political food chain, nor did I want to be. "Hardly so glamorous."

He elbowed me in the ribs. "I like the idea of being friends with a Kennedy. It sounds impressive, don't ya think?"

"No," I managed to say with a straight face, but then I ruined it by laughing. "I'm not as cool as them."

"I think you're just fine the way you are," he said. "How did you manage to come here without security?"

My breath caught in my throat, but I refused to read into that too much. "Dad wanted to send private security with me, but I refused. He probably sent some out here anyway, knowing him."

He tugged on his hair. "Do you think he'd do that?"

"I *know* he'd do that." I played with the string on the side of my bikini bottoms, not wanting to look at him when I told him this part. "They're probably watching us right now."

He gave an uneasy laugh. "If so, they'll probably kick my ass for taking you surfing."

"If they're smart, they'll never show their faces."

He snorted. "Should they be scared of you?"

"Scared of how I'll react? Yes." I stood up and held out my hands. "I want to be normal. Have normal fun and kiss normal boys. Study late at night and party occasionally. Is that so *wrong*?"

"Whoa." He stood up and grabbed my hands. "I didn't say it was."

"I know. Sorry." The righteous anger seemed to disappear, leaving me as deflated as a leaky balloon. "I get all worked up when I think of those sickos out there, following me around. Watching everything I do. I mean, get a life. Who in their right mind takes a job watching someone else 24/7? It's like being a glorified stalker if you ask me."

He gave an uneasy laugh. "Come on. Let's get some coffee and forget all about the men possibly watching us."

"All right." I took a deep breath and dropped one of his hands. "This time, it's on me."

He stiffened. "I'd rather—"

"And so would I. We're not dating. We're friends, and friends split bills."

He hesitated. "They do," he admitted. "I have to ask. Why is it you never had friends?"

"Uh…" I nibbled on my lower lip. "Well, not many of them passed by Dad's scrutiny. If their parents had even a whiff of scandal attached to their names, we were done hanging out. The few who did pass were major bitches."

"Ah." His fingers flexed on mine. "What about boyfriends?"

"Please," I scoffed. "Do you really think they passed Daddy's test?"

He flinched. "That bad, huh?"

"Worse. I stopped trying after tenth grade."

"What about in Europe?"

"Not a chance." I tightened my grip on his hand. "I had security with me the whole time. I met a cute Italian boy while I was there, but that was it."

His thumb stroked the back of my hand. "*Ciao, bella.*"

"You speak Italian?"

"Nope. That's all I know," he admitted, laughing. Dropping my hand, he stopped at the coffee stand and propelled me forward with a hand splayed across my lower back. "Ladies first."

My cheeks went all hot, and my body all tingly. From a simple touch. "Uh, a nonfat iced mocha, please."

"I'll have a black coffee," he said, smiling at the barista.

The barista almost dropped the cup in her hand, then dipped her head low. I rolled my eyes, but realized I probably looked that stupid around him half of the time. I shook my head. "Don't you ever branch out? Try something new?"

He eyed me from under his shades. "I like my coffee black."

"Did you ever get a mocha or a latte?"

"Nope." He shuddered. "I don't drink girly coffee."

"It's not girly. Besides, if you've never had it, then you can't know that you don't like it." I headed for the end of the counter. His hand stayed on my back, as if he didn't want to let me go. And I didn't want him to let me go. I pulled a twenty out of my bikini top and handed it to the cashier. It had actually stayed dry.

"Because I know." He cleared his throat. "Did you seriously just take money out of your bra to pay?"

"It's not a bra. It's a bikini." I shot him a grin over my shoulder. "But yeah. Strippers do it, why not surfers?"

He grabbed my coffee and handed it to me. "Did you know two out of six dollar bills have been shoved down a stripper's G-string at one point in time?"

"No." I shuddered. "Thanks for that."

I dropped all the ones I'd gotten back into the tip jar and walked toward our bench. Our surfboards still sat there. God, I loved California. In D.C., they would have been gone within seconds. I could get used to this place. Used to the way of life. Especially the cute surfer boys who came with it.

"So, you ready for school to start tomorrow?" he asked, blowing on his coffee as he sat down beside me.

"Yeah, I guess so." I held out my drink and pressed my straw to his lips. "Take a sip."

He clamped his mouth shut and shook his head. "No."

"For me?"

His eyes flashed. "You don't play fair."

"I'm the daughter of a politician. What did you expect?"

"Touché." He leaned in, closed his lips around the straw, and took a sip. When he pulled back, he swallowed. "It's not too bad, I guess, but I'll stick with my black coffee."

"Hm." I lifted the cup to my own lips and sipped. I couldn't help but think that my lips were where his had just been. I wished he would kiss me again. Wished he would stop being all honorable and stuff. As I pulled back, I flicked my tongue over the tip of the straw. "Tastes good to me."

He leaned in, his gaze on my mouth. I held my breath, waiting to see what he would do. Waiting to see if he'd stop fighting and start kissing, but he froze a few breaths away from me. "It's okay." He leaned back against the bench and took a long swig of his coffee. "So, what else are you doing today, Ginger?"

Hello, change of topic. "I have this thing," I mumbled.

He sat forward. "What thing?"

"Does it matter?"

His gaze pinned me down. Made it hard to concentrate. "Yes. Friends tell each other their plans."

"What are yours?"

"I'm going to lay around in my boxers and watch TV all night. Maybe drink a few beers." He pointed at me with his coffee. "Your turn."

I was too busy picturing him in his boxers to fight him. "I'm going to the soup kitchen to help serve Sunday dinner."

He paused with his cup halfway to his lips. "Seriously?"

"Seriously." I took a long sip of coffee, uncomfortable with his scrutiny. "It's important to give back to the community."

He set his coffee down and cupped my chin with his thumb and finger. "You're one amazing woman. You know that, right, Ginger?"

The nickname that had once annoyed me sent shivers through my veins now. "Not really. I'm just a college girl."

"Most college students are too busy partying to care about feeding the poor."

"I've gotta share what I can." I shrugged. "It's only right. Karma and all that."

He pressed his lips together, seeming to be stopping himself from saying something. "I'm going with you. I want to help."

"You don't have to," I protested, even though my whole body quickened at the thought of spending more time with him. "I'll be fine on my own."

"I know you will." He brushed his thumb over my lip. "But I *want* to go with you."

"All right," I said breathlessly. "Wanna pick me up on the bike at six?"

He laughed. "I created a beast with that thing, didn't I?"

"Yep." I stood up, tossed out my empty coffee and grabbed my surfboard. "I'll be waiting. Don't be late."

CHAPTER EIGHT

Carrie

It was almost time to meet up with Finn, so I hurried down the stairs, my heart beating a little bit faster than usual. After I warned him not to be late, there was no way I could be late myself. He'd never let that slide. As I passed the last dorm in my hallway, a girl came out and grabbed my wrist. "Hey, you the one who put all those designer clothes in the communal room?"

"Uh, no." Well, crap. I didn't think anyone had seen me earlier. I tucked my hair behind my ear and smiled. "I have no idea what you're talking about."

The girl adjusted her top. The top I had put in a box for others to take a few hours ago. "Darn. I could've sworn they said it was the redhead in 123."

Well, there went my career as a super spy. I had tried to be sneaky about it, but I couldn't help but share some of the clothes my mom constantly sent me with the other people in my dorm. I mean, why not? I'd seen and heard how some of the students didn't have much money for clothes…and I had too many. That's all. "Nope. Wrong room."

"Oh, well, sorry. I just wanted to say thanks. I've always wanted a Gucci top."

I smiled and waved over my shoulder as I started down the hallway. "Well, if I figure out who it is, I'll pass the message along."

"Thanks."

I made a mental note to put more Gucci out next time Mom sent a care package. Most of the stuff went to the local homeless shelters, but it didn't hurt to anonymously help my fellow classmates, did it? As I pushed through the doors to the outside, I smiled at the sight of Finn waiting for me. He leaned against a tree, looking completely at ease in his board shorts and red T-shirt. His ink stood out even more against the contrast of the red. When I approached him, he cocked a brow.

"*I'm* on time."

"So am I. Look at us, being all grown up and stuff." I patted his arm. Hot damn, his arm was hard. And huge. "You ready?"

"Yeah."

He fell into step beside me, like he always did. I wished I was bold enough to grab his hand again, but he'd clearly told me he didn't want anything to do with me, romance-wise. So I kept my grabby hands to myself. "Have you ever helped out at a shelter before?"

"No." He stole a quick look at me. "That's probably pretty crappy of me, huh?"

I shook my head. "Nah."

"Why do you do it?"

"Why not?" I stopped at his motorcycle. As I watched, he climbed on and handed me his helmet. Maybe I should have went out and bought my own earlier. Then he would stop insisting I use his. Would that look too forward? Be too pushy? I had no idea. "Shouldn't you be wearing this instead of me?"

"No." He looked over his shoulder at me. "Now put it on."

I took the helmet. I could argue, but I knew when it came to my safety, he wouldn't budge. He was a lot like Dad in that respect. Once again, the niggling doubt that said he'd been sent here by my father to befriend me came to mind. I shoved it down as best I could. Finn hadn't given me any reason to suspect him. Just because the past hadn't worked out so well for me didn't mean history was repeating itself.

After shoving the helmet over my head, I climbed on behind him and held on tight. The whole ride to the soup kitchen, I went over all the different ways he'd proved he wasn't Dad's lackey. He'd kissed me—which Dad would never allow. Taken me surfing—which Dad would hate. Driven me around on his bike—which Dad would flip his shit over. And he was…Finn.

There was no way Dad would send a guy who looked like Finn to protect me unless he was blind, dumb, and stupid. Or incredibly naïve.

We turned into the parking lot, and he shut off the bike. I removed the helmet and handed it to him, but he was too busy scanning our surroundings as if the Big Bad Wolf lurked in the shadows or something. I nudged him with the helmet and he took it without taking his eyes off the people around us. "I don't like this setting."

I followed his gaze, but saw nothing out of place. A man in tattered clothing sat on the ground outside the door, but he looked harmless. Hungry, but harmless. A woman leaned against the wall a few feet past him, watching us. Her face was filthy, but her eyes seemed kind. "Don't be a hypocrite. These people just need food."

Finn looked at me again. His face softened and he cupped my cheek. I liked it when he did that, but I had to remember it meant nothing to him. Not like it did to me. "Your kindness might be the death of you."

I climbed off his bike, letting his hand fall to his lap. He quickly followed me, staying close by my side. I stopped walking, giving him a stern look. "I don't need protecting."

"I'm not." He threw an arm over my shoulders. "I'm just being friendly."

I rolled my eyes. "Yeah. Sure." As I approached the woman I'd seen earlier, I reached into my pocket, took out a gift card to McDonald's, and pressed it into the woman's hand. "Here. For this week."

The woman took the card and smiled at me, her eyes lighting up. "Thank you."

I nodded, uncomfortable with the gratitude. This should be something more people did, and it shouldn't bring about such appreciation. I wished I could help everyone. I went to the man on the other side of the door and did the same. He thanked me and fell back asleep.

As we entered the building, Finn shook his head. "Does your father know you do this?"

"No." I tucked my hair behind my ear. "I use the money he sends me every month. He always sends twice what I need. Sometimes more."

Finn fell silent, but he looked at me weird. As if I was an enigma he couldn't figure out, which was silly. It was a simple matter. I had money, they didn't. Easily fixed. It wasn't exactly rocket science.

We walked up to the woman who looked to be in charge. "Hi. I'm Carrie, and this is Finn. We're here to help."

The woman eyed me. Her weathered face cracked into a disapproving frown. I'd been judged and found wanting within seconds. "You okay with getting your hands dirty? A pretty little thing like you?"

Finn stiffened. "Excuse me? I'll have you know—"

"It's okay." I placed a hand on his arm. There he went again, going into knight-in-shining-armor mode. It was cute and all, but I could take care of myself. "I'll be fine. Where do you want us?"

"The kitchens. You're on dish duty."

I nodded and headed for the kitchen. Finn started to follow me, but the woman stopped him by stepping in his path. She barely reached the bottom of Finn's shoulders, but he stopped instantly. "Not you. You're out front. Watch for trouble and break it up if it starts."

He hesitated. "I'm with her."

"I'll be fine back there." I shooed him away. "Go be a protective Marine for someone else tonight."

"All right." He gave me a hard look. "Don't leave this building without me. Not even for air."

I saluted him. "Yes, sir."

He grinned. "Good girl."

I shook my head and headed into the kitchen. The whole way there, I could feel his eyes on me, but once I got inside the kitchen, I was too busy to focus on Finn. The rest of my night was spent scrubbing filthy dishes. By the time I was finished, I was coated in a sheen of sweat and feeling pretty darn gross.

I came out of the kitchen and scanned the room for Finn. He was at the door, his arms crossed. He looked more like a bouncer at a popular nightclub than a volunteer. I shook my head and smiled. He looked as out of place here as I did at the fancy balls Mom always dragged me to.

The woman in charge came up to me. "Thank you for the help."

"Thanks for letting us contribute." I swiped my wrist across my sticky forehead and then reached into my pocket. "Do you mind if I leave these with you? If any families come in, or anyone you know who needs the extra help, just give them one."

The woman took the gift cards, but her forehead wrinkled. "Are these all from you?"

"They're from Senator Wallington. He likes supporting the less fortunate."

The woman's eyes lit up. "Wow. A politician who actually cares?"

"He tries." If Dad ever found out about me spending the funds he sent me on someone else, I could at least point out that it helped his campaign. That would end the lecture pretty fast. I squeezed the woman's shoulder and winked. "Remember him if he's ever up for president."

"I will," the woman said, wonder in her voice. She headed straight for a family eating in the corner and gave them two cards. When the family looked my way, I smiled and headed for the door. Time for me to leave.

Finn stood there, watching me. When I reached his side, he looked at the family who had just received the gift cards. "More Robin Hood acts?"

"Yeah. And?"

"Nothing." He shook his head. "Let's go home and eat something ourselves. I'm starving."

My stomach chose that particular moment to sound like a hungry beast. I pressed a hand to it and smiled at him. "Deal."

"Islands?"

"What?"

"Don't tell me you've never been to Islands…"

"I've never even heard of it. What is it?"

"Only the best burgers this side of the Mississippi." He handed me his helmet. "I solemnly swear that you'll never be able to eat McDonald's again once you've tasted their burgers."

I laughed. God, he made everything so much fun. "Oh yeah?" I put the helmet on and watched him climb on the bike. "We'll see about that."

"Want to make a bet?"

If I was betting with Finn, then I was in way over my head. "Sure. What's the bet?"

"If I win and you love the burgers…you have to spend the whole day with me next weekend, watching movies."

Please. I'd purposely lose just to spend the day with him. I better make an equally enticing deal for if I hated the burgers. "Deal. And if I win and I still prefer McDonald's, you teach me how to ride the bike."

He shook his head. "Hell no."

"Then no deal." I leaned in and ran my finger down the side of his cheek and lingered at his jaw. His eyes lit up at my touch, smoldering and hot. I wanted to run my hands through his light brown curls, but I resisted the urge. Barely. "I bet you would've won."

He captured my hand in his, holding my palm against his skin.

"Damn right I would, Ginger. The bet is on. Now climb on and hold on tight."

I got on the motorcycle behind him, my heart still racing from earlier when he'd held my hand close. The look in his eyes did weird things to me. "Don't I always?"

"Yeah. My favorite part of the ride is feeling you plastered against me."

My breath caught in my throat. "What?"

He revved the bike, not bothering to answer. I clung to him as he sped down the road, obviously in a hurry to leave the shady part of town far behind us, but even over the whirring of the engine…

I heard him laugh.

CHAPTER NINE

Finn

Almost a week later, I leaned against the tree and watched Carrie through the window, firmly in stalker mode, as requested by her father. She sat in the library with Cory. The senator had done a background check on him, and he'd gotten the Daddy stamp of approval. He was probably picturing all the perfect little grandbabies he could get out of the perfect little couple already. What a picture they would make on the campaign poster.

I hated the fucking kid for being so perfectly suited for Carrie. Plus, he sat too close to Carrie all the time, and Carrie smiled at him too much.

I sighed and leaned my head back against the tree, closing my eyes. All I wanted was a cold beer and a good game to watch. I was fucking beat. I was getting pretty damn tired of following Carrie around. Not because I didn't like her, but because I liked her *too* much. It's not like she needed me supervising her all the time. It was Friday night, and she was studying instead of partying. Besides the few parties she'd gone to, she'd been remarkably tame. Well-censored with a good head on her shoulders.

She didn't need me. Didn't need Big Brother watching.

I had been even more convinced of this fact after I helped Carrie at the soup kitchen last week. That had been a side of her I probably would have been better off ignoring. Just like the sight of her in a bikini. I could have done without that too. Both made me like her even more. Both made me want things I shouldn't be wanting. Things like her in my arms, smiling up at me like I owned the fucking world. I liked when she looked at me like that. No one else did.

She leaned over and pointed at some nerdy-looking guy's page, her hand gesturing wildly while she explained something to him. The guy looked like he'd never had a friend in his entire life, but Carrie had drawn him under her spell. Cory watched with a disgusted look on his face, but Carrie was oblivious to that. She was too busy smiling at the tiny nerd to notice.

That was Carrie. Loving and accepting of everyone—even a liar like me.

I glanced down when my phone lit up in my hand. It was Carrie. I looked up, checking to see if she was still in the library. She was. So…she was texting me while studying with that Cory kid?

I looked down at her text. *Surfing tomorrow?*

I smiled. *It's supposed to rain.* I tapped the phone against my chin. *Movie marathon at my place? You owe me my winnings.*

She picked up her phone and smiled. *Deal, but that's not fair. It's a bet you knew you would win. Pick me up at ten?*

Hell yeah I did. I never make bets I'll lose. See you then.

Before putting my own phone away, I jotted off a quick text to let her father know that she was in the company of Golden Boy, and then I slid the phone into my pocket. As she came out of the library with Cory, she laughed and swatted his arm. The nerd was with them. She hugged him goodbye and promised to call him next week to hang out. Looked like I needed to do another background check.

Once the gleeful nerd walked away, Cory sighed and pulled Carrie to a stop. They stood at the end of the path, where the boy's dorm went to the left, and Carrie's to the right. If I had to watch her kiss another guy, I wouldn't be responsible for my reactions. I couldn't have her, but I didn't want anyone else to have her.

Yes, I knew how horrible that sounded. I didn't care.

Cory crinkled his nose. "What's with the new guy?"

"I don't know. He seems nice. Why?" Carrie asked, seeming confused.

"Word has it he's an orphan with no one who loves him."

Carrie flinched as if she'd been hit. "Aw, the poor guy. I can't even imagine what he's been through."

"But—"

"No buts. He's nice and I like him." She stared Cory down. "I think I'm going to head up now. Thanks for the study session."

"Want to come to the party over there with me?" Cory asked, pointing behind him. "It's supposed to be fun."

"No, thank you. I have plans already."

She did?

"All right." Cory hugged Carrie close. "Good night."

"Night."

Carrie headed to her dorm room alone, and I breathed a sigh of relief. I didn't want to watch her drink herself stupid tonight. I wanted to drink *myself* stupid, in my quiet, empty apartment. Cory mumbled something under his breath as he passed me, and then headed toward the party raging a few buildings down.

My phone buzzed, and I took it out of my pocket as I headed toward my bike. *Want to start our movie fest tonight? I'm in the mood for a sleepover…*

My eyes went wide. *You want to have a sleepover? At my place?*

Barely a second passed before she replied. *Why not?*

I could think of at least ten reasons "why not" off the top of my head. Every single nerve in my brain shouted no. Screamed it was a bad idea. Even so, I typed: *Sure. Be there in five.*

I waited the required time and walked up to her dorm door. Or, the one she *showed* me was her dorm door. She stood there, wearing the same outfit she'd had on earlier but holding a bag on her shoulder. "Hey."

I caught my breath at the sight of her, her eyes shining as she smiled at me. I swore she got more beautiful, more irresistible, each time I saw her. I took her bag from her and slung it over my own shoulder. "Hey, yourself. How was your night?"

"Good. Marie is at a party, so my dorm was quiet for once. I studied with Cory until a few minutes ago since we have our first exam on Monday, but he went to the party. Now I'm with you."

Thank motherfucking God for that. "So, I'm not your only friend anymore?"

"I guess not." She lifted a shoulder. "I don't even know if Marie is my friend. I think we just kind of deal with each other. We get along and all, but we're really different."

I'd say so. I had seen Marie come out of at least three different guys' rooms during the week, but hadn't seen her crack open a book even once. "Yeah. Not all roommates are instant friends like in movies."

"I guess not." She stopped at my bike. "I like her, but she's not my friend. Not like you are."

I swallowed hard. "Not like Cory, either?"

"Cory is nice. I like him."

"There's that word again. Nice." I flexed my fingers on her bag. "Future boyfriend material?"

She stole a peek at me and her cheeks went all pink. "I have no idea. I'm not really into planning out that portion of my life. If I find someone I like, it'll happen. Until then, I'll focus on my studies, and keep my lips to myself."

I tried to ban the memory of her mouth on mine from my memory. Tried to forget how much she'd seemed like she liked me as she moaned into my mouth. I failed. Miserably. "That's a very mature way to think of it."

"If you say so. I just call it common sense."

I sat down on the bike and handed her the helmet I bought for her. She looked at me with wide eyes, as if no one had ever bought her a fucking present before. "Did you buy this for me?"

"I did." I shrugged and slammed my own helmet over my head, more to hide from her scrutiny than anything. I liked having her on my bike, so I bought her a helmet. Nothing more to it than that. "If you're going to be riding with me, it makes sense for you to have one."

"I'll pay you back." She pushed the helmet down on her head. "How much was it?"

"I don't want your money." I booted up the kickstand. "Now hold on tight."

"But—"

"Just close your eyes and relax."

I revved up the engine, bringing the bike to life. I waited for her to argue, like usual, but she didn't. And when she wrapped her body around mine, laying her head on my shoulder, *I* closed *my* eyes. For a second, I pretended she wasn't my boss's daughter or my assignment. Pretended I wasn't lying to her, and that she wouldn't hate me when she found out the truth. For a brief second, I let myself enjoy the way she felt pressed up against me, her body all soft and willing.

I inhaled deeply, memorizing her scent. She smelled amazing, even when fresh out of the ocean. It haunted me daily. *She* taunted me daily, without even trying. I wanted her.

Too bad I couldn't have her.

I opened my eyes and pulled out onto the road. I took my time on the ride there, taking as many back roads as possible for the short ride. This was the only period I got to feel her arms around me without feeling guilty as hell about it. The only occasion I was permitted to touch and be touched. If I had my way, we'd drive around all night long.

But I didn't.

When I pulled up at my place, I killed the engine and sat there for a second, not moving. Interestingly enough, neither did she. As if by some unspoken agreement, we held each other. It wasn't until a truck drove by that either one of us moved. She dropped her arms from around my waist and removed her helmet.

I took mine off too and our gazes clashed.

She was so beautifully off limits that it hurt. Her hair was sticking up, she had no makeup on, but she looked abso-fucking-lutely perfect. She licked her lips and didn't drop my gaze. "Thank you for the helmet," she said softly. So softly I almost didn't hear her. "And the ride."

"Don't mention it," I said, my voice gruff.

I slid off of the bike and offered her my hand. I should stop doing that. As a matter of fact, I should take her home right now, before I proved myself unworthy of trust—hers and her father's. But sending her away now would only hurt her feelings, and the last thing I wanted to do was that. She would hate me once she found out who I really was.

I didn't want to hurry the inevitable along.

She slid her fingers inside of mine, her fingers so small and dainty, and I held on tight. Right or wrong, I didn't want to let go. I wanted to hold her close, cherish her, and continue to show her how fun life could be when you spend your time with the right person. I wanted to show her *everything*.

"Why are you so quiet?" she asked, darting a quick look at me. "Is something wrong?"

Shit. How long had I been quiet? "No, nothing's wrong." I led her up the walk toward my small studio apartment. "I'm just tired."

"Oh. Do you want to cancel?"

Yes. "No." I unlocked the door. "It's nothing a little bit of coffee won't help."

"No beer tonight?" She nudged my arm.

"Not for the nineteen-year-old. Your father would kill me if he found out I was giving alcohol to a minor."

"You don't know him and he doesn't know you." She rolled her eyes. "I think you're safe."

My heart squeezed tight. "Not if he has security watching you like you said." I hated this game. I hated lying. I hated not telling her *I* was the security watching her. "I'm not going to jail for supplying a minor with booze."

She huffed. "What's the good of having a friend who is older than twenty-one if he won't get me drunk?"

"I'll tell you what I'm good at," I said, stopping and slinging her over my shoulder. "I'm good for surfing, riding a bike, and carrying your cute little ass around."

She giggled and tried to squirm free, but I tightened my grip on her thighs. I liked her in this position. I had a great view. "Put me down!"

"Nope." I juggled her weight and my key, finally managing to open the door to my apartment without dropping her on her perfect little ass. "I'm keeping you forever. Tell your bodyguards that, nice and loud."

She snorted. "If they're watching, they'll come running."

"Then this is a good way to find out if they're here. Play the part of damsel in distress properly." I slapped her ass and stood on the threshold. "Call out for help, or I'll smack you harder."

"Help!" she cried, her voice convincingly strained. "Someone, help me!"

"Nice." I slammed the door behind us and set her on her feet, even though I didn't want to. She rushed to the window and peeked out. "You should get into acting."

"No one's coming. I can't believe it," she said excitedly. "He actually trusted me enough to send me here alone."

Guilt slammed into me, hard and fast and merciless. "See? You were worried about nothing."

"Words cannot describe how happy I am right now that you offered to be my guinea pig." She turned and flung herself at me, hugging me tight. "So I'll show you instead."

My arms closed around her, and I held her close to my chest. I could

Jen McLaughlin

feel her heart beating fast against mine, as if she'd just caught a huge wave and rode it through to the end. "Hey, now, it wasn't exactly rocket science."

"Still." She rested her cheek on the spot right above my heart. I forgot how short she was until times like this. She didn't even reach my shoulders. "Now I know I can really relax. No one's watching me. You have no idea how wonderful that sensation is. At home, I'd wake up and find security officers watching me sleep. As if a man was going to break in and ravish me in my sleep or something. I had no freedom. None. But now I do, and it's fabulous."

"Your dad had people watch you *sleep*?"

She averted her face. "Yes."

I swallowed hard. I hadn't known that part. That went beyond loving parent and into loony-toon territory. "I'm sorry. That's insane."

"Yeah, that's my dad for you." She lifted her head and smiled up at me, her eyes sparkling. "But I'm finally free."

She was so easily tricked. So gullible. And I was an ass for taking advantage of that innocence. My throat threatened to close up on me and kill me, right then and there in my own apartment. At this moment, I felt that it would have been a well-deserved death. "Right."

She pulled back a little bit, her hands resting on my shoulders, and looked up at me with those big blue eyes. If she kept looking at me as if I owned the sun, I would die trying. After holding my gaze for what seemed like an eternity, she rose up on her tiptoes and didn't stop until her mouth was a scant inch or so from my ear.

"So...since no one's watching..."

I tightened my grip on her. If she suggested we have wild, crazy sex on the balcony...I wouldn't say no. I was too weak right now. "Yeah?"

"How about that drink?"

I swallowed a laugh. I didn't know if I was relieved or disappointed she didn't want crazy balcony sex. "No way."

"We've quite clearly established there is no one watching. That was your excuse."

I dropped my hold on her and removed her hands from my shoulders. "You're just using me for my age, aren't you? Admit it."

"That and your bike." She cocked her head and put her hands on her hips. "Plus, you surf. That's nice too."

"I'm hurt." I held my hand over my heart. "Really."

69

"You're not bad on the eyes either, when you're not being annoying. Unfortunately for you, that's almost never." She headed for my kitchen, tossing me a teasing grin over her shoulder. "Now show me where you keep the good stuff."

I entwined my hands behind my neck and followed her. Since when did I have to be the voice of reason when it came to drinking? I wasn't old enough for this shit. Wasn't old enough or responsible enough to slip into the role of responsible adult for her. And I didn't want to. "You know you can't drink."

"Says who?" She opened the fridge, grabbed two beers, and set them on the counter. "Everyone else on campus is drinking right now. You know it. I know it."

I dropped my hands and scowled at her. She had a point about everyone else drinking in college, but I still didn't want to be the man who got the senator's precious little girl drunk. That wasn't on my job description. Then again, keeping her from having a drink or two wasn't on it either. At least she was in a safe environment with me.

I crossed my arms. "That's not playing fair and you know it."

"Neither is acting like you're my protector. We're *friends*." She struggled with the beer, trying to open it. Her face turned red as she twisted as hard as she could, and she bit down on her lip. "How the hell do you open this thing?"

I sighed and took it from her. With a simple twist, the beer was open. I held it out to her, but caught her gaze. "I still don't like doing this."

"I know."

She rose to her tiptoes and kissed my cheek. She had to stop doing that shit to me. It wasn't good for either one of us. Her soft lips teased me, and it took a hell of a lot more control than I thought I had to not turn my head and catch her lips with mine. It would be so easy to do.

"Do you now?"

She nodded, her lips brushing against my cheek. "But you need to get over yourself, open a beer, and come watch a movie with me."

With that, she dropped back to her feet and sashayed out of the kitchen, her hips swinging and her red hair looking way too enticing. Hell, *she* looked too damn touchable. My fingers twitched, and my whole body screamed at me to chase after her and claim those soft lips. To make her mine in every way.

Yeah. Get over it.

Easier said than done.

CHAPTER TEN

Carrie

I walked into the living room, my heart racing at light speed due to the fact I'd just kissed Finn. It was on the cheek, but still. It was a kiss. I tipped back another sip, cringing at the taste. Apparently, I didn't like beer, but I was beyond caring. I wanted to relax and enjoy my new freedom, and who better to do it with than Finn, the one guy I trusted? The one guy who made me feel like I could trust him, and let go of all my doubts and fears. Let go of my suspicions even.

He made me want to have fun. Be free.

Be someone else entirely.

Someone he could want like I wanted him.

My phone buzzed, and I glanced at it. It was Dad. I ignored the call, then shot off a quick text telling him I couldn't answer because I was in the library. I felt a little bit guilty at the lie…but really. He needed to back off.

When Finn came into the living room, his beer pressed to his lips and his head tipped back, I couldn't tear my eyes away. His Adam's apple bobbed as he swallowed, and he pinned me down with his penetrating stare. He flopped down next to me on the couch and rested his feet on the coffee table.

"What now?" he asked, not looking at me. "Why are you staring me like that?"

"I'm not staring at you. I was just watching you."

I averted my eyes, taking the chance to shove my phone back in my pocket, and inwardly cursed my heating cheeks. I used the time I needed to regain my composure after getting caught staring at him to survey his home. Everything looked way too fashionable, from the bamboo rug to the grey couch. And he had curtains. What kind of surfer dude cared about curtains?

A neatly made, and *huge*, bed sat in the corner of the room. It had a light blue bedspread and the pillowcases matched. Opposite of the bed was the kitchen, and his black surfboard leaned up against the wall next to his bed. His perfectly ironed military uniform hung in the open closet, along with a ton of t-shirts and board shorts. On top of the closet rung, a shelf held a bunch of socks and boxers. It looked so neat and orderly. So unlike Finn.

It looked like he even folded his *socks*. Who did that?

"Did you decorate this place?" I turned back to him. He sat next to me, doing something on his phone. His brow was furrowed and his fingers flew over the screen. "It doesn't feel like…you."

He threw a quick glance across his apartment and shoved his phone into his pocket. "No. It came furnished."

"Ah. That explains it."

"Explains what, exactly?" He looked over at me, his lips pursed.

"It just doesn't seem like the way you'd decorate your house. It's too… girly."

He grinned. "Worried I'm hiding a wife somewhere in here?"

"Maybe." I stood up and crossed the room, stopping in front of his closet. I ran my hand over the crisp cotton sleeve of his shirt, my heart twisting at the thought of him wearing it in battle. "I forget sometimes that you're in the Marines. Why don't you live on base? Do you like it? Will you get sent overseas?"

"Slow down, Ginger. I can't keep up." He stood up and approached me, stopping at an appropriate distance for friends. I couldn't help wishing that for once he'd stop pushing me away and instead pull me closer. "I don't live on base because I don't want to. I hate base housing and hate the barracks even more. Yes, I like it." He picked up a piece of my hair, toying with it. "And yes, I have gone on deployment before, but I haven't fought yet."

When he rolled the piece of hair between his fingers, tugging gently, I shivered. As if he sensed it, his grip on my curl tightened, then he dropped it.

I turned to him. "That doesn't answer my question. Will you get sent over there any time soon?"

I held my breath. God, please no. Just the idea of Finn in harm's way was enough to make me want to hurl. What if he got injured or…no. I couldn't finish that thought. Ever. He wouldn't go over, and he would stay safe. The most dangerous things he would ever do would be surfing and riding his bike.

"I suppose it's likely. I've heard word of my unit possibly getting sent out sometime in the summer." He leaned against the wall and crossed his ankles. He took another swig of his beer, so I did the same. The thought of him going to war was enough to drive me to drink *anything*. "So I guess anything is possible."

I swallowed hard. "I hope you don't go."

"It's part of the job."

"Still."

Our gazes latched, and for once he didn't back off or turn away. "Don't worry about me. If I do leave, you probably won't even remember my name after a while."

I set my empty beer bottle down and smacked his arm as hard as I could. "Not remember you? What the hell is the matter with you? Of *course* I'll remember you." I shoved his shoulders, wanting to hurt him for insinuating I was so flaky I would forget all about him the second he left, but he simply raised a brow at me. "Of *course* I'll care."

He finished his beer and set his down too. "No, you won't. You'll move on with your life and be fine. You'll probably marry Cory and have little Ginger babies."

I smacked him again. Really hard. "You're such a jerk."

"Stop hitting me." He caught my wrist and narrowed his eyes at me. "And I never claimed not to be one, did I?"

I tried to jerk free, but he didn't let go of my wrist. "Good. Because you're a big, fat, stupid jerk."

His jaw ticked. "What are we? Kindergartners? Resorting to name-calling? Should I call you a poopy-face now?" He released my wrist and slid his hand into my hair. "Tug on your hair and pretend I don't like you?"

I curled my free hand into his shirt and pulled him closer. "Go ahead."

"No." But he did bury his hands even deeper into my hair, making my scalp tingle ever so slightly. And then he pulled. Gently. My stomach clenched with need.

I licked my lips. "Why not?"

"Because I'd rather do this."

He lowered his head, tenderly brushing his lips against mine. He kept the kiss so soft I barely felt it, yet it rocked me straight to my core. That something so little could feel so powerful should have scared me, but it didn't. It made me want him even more because it felt so right. I wanted his real kiss. The one where he held nothing back and gave me the passion I so desired from him.

"Carrie," he sighed against my lips, his fingers tightening on my hair. "You're killing me."

That gave me the courage to try for more. To get something more than a chaste peck on the lips from him. He'd taught me what desire was, and I wanted to learn more—with *him*.

"Then let me help."

Rising up on tiptoes, I tried to catch his mouth again. Tried to get him to break his impervious self-control. But he pulled back without giving me a chance. His hands shook as he disengaged himself from my clinging hands, and he looked down at me with heated eyes.

"You can't help me with this," he rasped. "I'll go get you another beer. Stay here."

Without another word, he grabbed our empty bottles and headed off into the kitchen. I wrapped my arms around myself, shivering slightly. I'd thought I had seen desire in his eyes before I tried to kiss him again. I could have sworn he wanted it as much as I did. Obviously, I'd been wrong. I kept throwing myself at him, and he didn't even want me.

I needed to stop being so freaking pathetic around him. And I really needed to stop melting into a tiny puddle on the floor every time he flexed his hot muscles at me and smiled. He only wanted to be friends, and if that's all I could get, then so be it. I would have to take it.

He came back into the room, a full beer in each hand and his mouth pressed tight. "Look, I'm—"

I held up my hand, knowing exactly where he was going. "I know. You don't need to say another thing. Seriously."

"You're upset," he said flatly.

"I'm not. We're friends, nothing more."

He hesitated. "It's not that I don't want to be more. Believe me. I just can't."

"I know. You've told me." I took the beer from him and took a long, hard drink. "Stop worrying so much. It was fun. It doesn't mean we're anything more than friends, right?"

His knuckles went white on his beer. "Right."

"Good. Glad we're on the same page." I sat down and reclined on the couch. Hopefully I didn't look like I wanted to scream and tear my hair out right now. Because I did. "So, what are we watching?"

He stood there for a second, looking at me. Then he crossed the room and sat down on the opposite side of the couch. Much farther than he had last time. The message was clear. He didn't want any more accidental kissing to happen.

Fine. Neither did I.

He flipped through the titles and then hovered over a movie. "*The Hangover*?"

"What's it about?"

He stared at me as if I had sprouted horns or something equally appalling. "You've never heard of it?"

"My father didn't like me going to the movies. He didn't like movies in general. Said they were nothing but goop for the mind. I snuck into one once, but got dragged out halfway through." Why did all of my stories end with "and I got dragged out?" Geez. Maybe I should see a therapist or something. Or become one so I could talk to myself about my messed-up childhood. I read the blurb on the TV. "And judging from the description and rating, he definitely wouldn't have wanted me to watch *this*."

He shook his head and selected the title. "Oh, Ginger, you don't know what you've been missing."

"Why don't you show me?" I asked, issuing a challenge I knew he wouldn't accept. "All of it."

His mouth clamped down tight. "Don't tempt me."

"Maybe I like tempting you."

"No, you really don't. Now knock it off, or I'll show you what I do with annoying women who don't know when to stop."

Was it wrong I wanted to find out exactly what that was?

And was it just me, or was it hot in here? I took another drink, set my beer down, and pulled my oversized sweatshirt off. Avoiding his eyes, I flung it across the room to my bag. Even though I wore a tight black camisole tank underneath, I felt indecently exposed. What if he thought I was trying to seduce him or something?

Was I trying to seduce him…or something?

As I smoothed my hair with my hand, I stole a quick glance his way. He watched me with hooded eyes. Eyes that saw things I didn't think I wanted him to see. Standing up, I walked to my bag and dug out my pink shorts I'd brought to sleep in. Shorts that seemed way too short now, but that's what I always wore to bed. Shorts and a tank top.

Why should I let it bother me now? After all, we were just *friends*.

Lifting my chin, I squeezed past his outstretched legs, brushing against his thigh as I passed. He stiffened and clung to his armrest, his knuckles white. "What are you doing?"

"Changing into comfy clothes." I grabbed the waistband of my pants, preparing to strip down behind him. "Don't turn around. I'm doing it behind you."

He cleared his throat. "Let me guess. Your 'comfy clothes' are the tiny shorts you're holding and the tank top you're wearing?"

"Mmhm."

He dropped his head back against the chair. "Fucking fabulous."

"If you say so." I stepped out of my pants, feeling out of place in his apartment. It was the first time I stood in nothing but my underwear in front of a guy, and he wasn't even looking. Didn't even want to look. "Do you have a problem with my pajamas?"

"No. Not at all." He adjusted himself on the chair and paused the movie at the starting sequence. "But I'm gonna need another drink before we start. Let me know when you're dressed."

I slid my shorts up my legs slowly, enjoying the freeing sensation I felt at being half naked with him in the same room. "You're good to go."

He stood up and turned around hesitantly. Almost as if he was afraid I'd lied about being dressed. His gaze ran over me, sending liquid heat flying through my veins. Why was it that he set me on fire just by looking at me, and Cory didn't even make me the slightest bit warm?

Without a word, he emptied his beer. My full one sat on the table untouched. He gave me a dark look and walked past me toward the kitchen, his stance rigid. "Stay here. I'll be right back."

I settled down into the corner of the couch, stretching my legs out in front of me, and picked up my own drink. When he came back out, two beers in hand, he set them down and headed for the bed. "I still have a whole beer," I said.

"Then I'll drink them both."

"Okay..."

Reaching out, he ripped the blue quilt off and came back to the couch. He spread it out over my legs and settled down next to me. After removing his shirt, he tucked himself in before he hit play. So he was cold...but he took off his shirt. That was a contradiction if I'd ever seen one. "There. All settled."

"Are you cold?"

"Yeah. Sure. Freezing," he mumbled, taking another swig of his beer.

A thin sheen of sweat appeared on his forehead almost instantly after getting under the blanket. "You don't look cold," I said, unable to stop myself from commenting on his strange behavior.

He sighed. "For once, stop questioning everything I do."

He lifted his beer to his lips, his brooding stare never leaving the screen. Though I would have rather spent the night watching *him* watch the movie, I forced myself to pay attention to the antics on screen. And within seconds, I was laughing hysterically.

When I looked over at him about halfway through the movie, he was watching me with a smile. I froze mid-laugh, my heartbeat increasing when our gazes clashed. Maybe it was the way he was looking at me that sent a surge of heat through my veins. He watched me as if...

As if he'd rather be watching *me* than the movie.

CHAPTER ELEVEN

Finn

The next morning, the first thing I noticed was the sun shining through the slats of the living room blinds. The second thing I became aware of was the warm body pressed against mine. My hand rested on the curve of her hip, and my hard cock was touching her soft ass. There was no question as to whose ass I spooned.

Carrie.

We must have fallen asleep during the last movie we'd been watching. What had it been? Something about a haunted house. Carrie had gotten scared, so I'd thrown my arm over her and cuddled her. Apparently, I had proceeded to cuddle her all fucking night long. She stirred in my arms, wiggling her ass. I gritted my teeth and pushed closer, unable to resist. She let out a soft moan and rubbed against me in her sleep. Fuck. If she kept that up, I'd forget all about the rules and stipulations.

Hell, I might just forget them now and blame it on my foggy head. I dropped a kiss to the spot where her shoulder and neck met, then nibbled lightly. She tasted good. So good that I decided to move an inch to the left and taste her there too. Even better.

She let out a soft moan and rubbed against my cock, making me moan. Fuck me. I shouldn't have started this, but now I couldn't stop. I bit down on her shoulder again and palmed her ass. I squeezed hard, acquainting myself with how perfectly she fit in my hand. She should be mine, no matter what her father would say.

She was mine, even if she couldn't be.

Her head rolled toward me, and I held my breath. Had I woken her up? I studied her face for any signs of her being out of dreamland, but she didn't move. She just crinkled her nose and let out a sigh. I gently removed my hand from her ass and ran it down her cheek, memorizing how peaceful she looked when she slept. It was the only time I'd get to see it, so I didn't want to miss a fucking detail.

When my hand slid down her throat, she arched her back and moaned something that sounded a hell of a lot like my name. I froze, my heart racing, and looked up at her again. Still asleep…but she kept squirming. As if…

As if she wanted more, even in her sleep. I let my hand slide over the curve of her breasts, lightly tracing over her perky nipple. Seeing that she was turned on by what I did sent pure need slamming into my gut. I rolled her nipple between my thumb and forefinger, tugging just enough to pleasure her.

While I played with her perfect breast, she drew in a ragged breath and moaned my name. This time I *heard* it. She was fucking dreaming about me as I touched her. That was too much for me to let go of. I knew I should stop. Knew I should get my hands off her, but she needed me as much as I needed her.

Slowly, I slid my hand down her stomach. When I reached her waistband, I pressed my lips to hers, unable to resist a kiss. I kept it light. Almost nonexistent. But even so, she moaned and stirred in my arms. Damn it all to hell…she was waking up. I didn't know whether to be happy or pissed about that.

I pulled back and moved my hand to her flat stomach before she knew what I'd done. She may expect more out of me than I could give, and I couldn't have that. Her eyes fluttered open, her lids heavy with sleep. "Finn?"

"Sh." I pressed a finger to her mouth, wishing she hadn't woken up yet. Now I had to stop kissing her, even though I didn't want to. "It's all a dream."

She licked her lips, and her tongue ran along my finger, hot and moist. The sight of her pink tongue on my skin was almost enough for me to stop giving a damn. I wanted to press my mouth to hers again. Take her. Keep her.

"No, it's not," she argued.

"You always fight me."

Her lips quirked. "You always say stupid things."

I laughed and forced myself to stand up. To let go. "Get ready. We have a tide to catch. Get dressed out here. I'll get ready in the bathroom."

I headed across the room, grabbing my bathing suit along the way. Thanks to my morning make out session, I now sported a hard-on that I wouldn't be able to hide from her. I'd need a few minutes to myself before I was fit for polite company.

An hour and a half later, I watched Carrie ride the wave I'd sent her out on. She stood on the surfboard, her arms stretched out precariously, grinning with pride as she rode the tiny wave I told her to take. I was probably wearing an even stupider, bigger grin than she was. Miraculously enough, she was starting to get the hang of surfing, and it had only taken a tiny bit of practice.

She was a natural.

Too bad I wasn't a natural at this spy business. Every second spent in her company blurred the lines between friendship and assignment more and more. And every time we were together, it got harder and harder to remember all the reasons I *shouldn't* when all the reasons I *should* were staring me back in the face. Like right now. She was everything I would have hoped for in a girlfriend, and then some.

Kind. Giving. Adventurous. Never afraid to try something new.

And I wasn't allowed to have her.

She tumbled into the water, and I hastily dove for her wrist. She could come up on her own, obviously, but I wouldn't be doing my job if I didn't do anything while she struggled to get to the surface. Eh, who was I trying to kid? I didn't find her because I had to, I found her because I had to make sure she was okay. For *me*—not the senator.

Hauling her up to the surface, I said, "Got you."

She spluttered and swiped her red, drenched hair out of her face. "Did you see that? I had it!"

"You did." I couldn't help it. I grinned with pride again. She was an excellent student, and I was having fun playing the part of teacher. "Soon you won't need my help to catch a wave."

"I wanna go again," she said, struggling to get back up on her board.

Though I wanted to refuse, to drag her to the shore where she could rest up a bit, I couldn't find the heart to make her leave. I could feel the excitement bouncing off her, and I couldn't make her stop now. In fact, I reached out and hauled her onto the board by the back of her wetsuit, then helped her paddle back out to the open water.

Once we reached the optimum surf point, I stopped dragging her, and instead dragged a hand through my damp hair. I hadn't been surfing today. Just supervising. And yet, I didn't give a damn. Normally, I'd be itching to catch a wave myself, but watching her have fun seemed to be enough for me.

She squeezed her hair tight and lifted her face to the sky, letting out a contented sigh. "I never thought I'd have so much fun doing something like this."

"Me either," I said before thinking it through. Then again, I *hadn't* expected to have fun watching her surf. But I did. "I mean, surfing isn't for everyone. I'm glad you like it so much."

"I really do," she said, staring off toward the shore.

I scanned the beach, watching all the tiny people walk around. One in particular caught my eye. She wore a green shirt I'd swear I saw Carrie wear last week. "Uh, Carrie?"

"Yeah?"

"Did you leave a shirt out there?"

She blinked at me. "No…why?"

"I see a girl wearing your shirt. I recognize it. It's the one you wore to the soup kitchen last week. I made fun of the color and you said—"

"That green was the luckiest color in the world." She put her hand above her forehead and squinted. "Yeah. That's mine."

"Why is she wearing it?"

Carrie dropped her hand and fidgeted with nothing at all. "Every once in a while, I put a box of clothes in the dorm. Anonymously."

"Why?"

"Because I have too many."

I shook my head. "Every time I think I know everything there is to know about your giving nature, I discover something new."

Her cheeks went red. "It's nothing." She squinted at the shore. "Oh look. Cory's out there."

I stiffened. She and Cory had been spending more and more time together during the week, and that was all well and fucking dandy. But the weekend was supposed to be my time. It wasn't written down and signed in blood or anything, but it had become our thing, and I didn't feel like fucking sharing. "Why's he here?"

"What time is it?" she asked.

I looked at my watch. "Ten-thirty."

"Shit. I was supposed to meet up with him at ten. I totally forgot. It's so easy to lose track of the time out here, isn't it?"

"Yeah, it is." I cleared my throat. "I didn't know you had any other plans today."

"It came up last night. Cory needs tutoring in anatomy, and I offered to help him today." She dipped her fingers into the water. "I told him we'd meet up after surfing, but I guess when I didn't show up, he came looking for me."

"Smart guy like that shouldn't need help in anatomy," I mumbled. "Then again, guys like him always do."

She shot me a look that suggested she wondered if she'd misheard. "Are you upset? I know we normally hang out after surfing, but we have a big test Monday, and I wanted—"

"I'm not upset," I said, shaking my head at her as if I was amused by the mere idea. But I *was* upset. This was my day, not Golden Boy's. "Now get ready, Ginger. Here comes a good one."

She waved erratically, and Cory waved back. Looking over her shoulder, she started paddling in front of the wave. "See ya at the shore."

"I'll be right behind you."

And I would. There was an even bigger wave coming behind hers, and I could ride it out and meet her at the beach. First real wave I would ride all day. As she took off with the baby wave I sent her on, I watched her safely ride it to shore. Once she made it without wiping out, I readied myself for my own ride. As I rode it, slicing in and out with expert precision, I tried not to watch Carrie as she made her way over to Cory on the beach. Once I hit the sand, I purposely took my time walking over to them, watching from a safe distance. She started taking off her wetsuit, and Cory practically convulsed right then and there on the beach.

What a fucking newbie.

He wouldn't know what to do with Carrie if he got her. Carrie deserved someone more experienced. Someone who would know how to make her scream out in pleasure and wouldn't completely miss her clit while going down on her. Someone like…me.

I walked up behind Carrie and started stripping. "Hey," I said, nodding at Cory. "What's up?"

Cory ripped his eyes from Carrie's sleek body for all of two seconds to nod in my direction. "Hello. Nice surf out there, huh?"

"Not too bad." I threw my wetsuit on the sand and shook my hair in Cory's direction, spraying both Cory and Carrie. Carrie laughed, but Cory gave me a death glare and brushed his hands over his dampened Oxford shirt. "Oops. Sorry."

"No worries," Cory said, smiling, but his attention was *still* on Carrie's body. Didn't she see the way Cory ogled her? Did she know how much the boy wanted more from her than mere studying?

Or, my inner voice whispered, *maybe she knew it and liked it.*

"You should go surfing with us sometime," Carrie said, her voice muffled from under her short blue sundress she was pulling over her head. "It's so much fun."

I snorted. "I don't think Cory is the surfing type."

"I *beg* your pardon." Cory looked down his nose at me, and I stiffened. "I don't expect someone like you to know what I do or do not like, thank you, so kindly refrain from voicing your opinions."

Oh, hell no. No one looked at me like I was gum stuck to the bottom of their shoe and walked away without getting well acquainted with my knuckles. Not since kindergarten. I tightened my fists and advanced on the little fucker. "Oh yeah? Want to know what I do know?"

"No." Carrie pressed a hand to my chest and I stopped. Just like that. The girl held way too much power over me. "I don't think Cory meant that as an insult. Did you, Cory?"

"Of course not." Cory smiled again, just as falsely as the last time. I still wanted to punch him, just as strongly as the last time. "No harm meant, man."

"My name's Finn. Not man."

I looked down at Carrie's hand, which still rested on my chest. My heart sped up at the sight of it, and my vivid imagination ran wild. I pictured her with her hand on my chest, but it wasn't innocent. No, it was while I drove her insane with need. My body buried deep inside hers as she cried out my name over and over again.

That was more like it.

I should kiss her right now, in front of this little jerk. Stake my claim.

"Sorry." Cory held up his hands and backed away from me. *The boy has a brain after all.* "Finn."

"Okay, I'm ready to go." Carrie gave me one last warning look, then bent to grab her board and suit. "You ready to head back to the dorms?"

I clenched my jaw, knowing a dismissal when I saw one.

"Sure. Here. Let me carry that for you. See ya later, Finn," Cory said.

He reached out and tentatively took her board from her, holding it out as far from his perfect pink shirt and plaid shorts as he could get. So she let Cory carry her board, but wouldn't let me? What the fuck did that mean?

"Later," I said, my voice rock hard.

Carrie looked at me over her shoulder, hesitating. "I'll call you later, okay?"

I wouldn't be home. I'd probably be out getting blasted to try to forget how stupid she was making me act lately.

Carrie waited for a reply, but when it became obvious I wouldn't be giving one, she walked off with Cory. As I watched, Cory threw his arm over Carrie's bare shoulders, hauling her close. Her musical laughter came back to me, making me grit my teeth. I'd never wanted to punch someone as much as I wanted to punch Cory right now—and he hadn't even done anything *wrong*.

In fact, he was the perfect match for someone like Carrie.

While I was not.

A few beers later, I leaned back on the bar and took a long pull of my beer. I'd spent the last three hours watching football and was slightly buzzed. For the first time in a long while, I felt free to relax. Free to chill. I knew Carrie was safe. She was with Golden Boy, and he wouldn't harm her.

Hell, he couldn't even get enough balls to kiss her.

Someone tapped my shoulder, and I turned around. A brunette with huge—and obviously fake—breasts sat beside me. She was gorgeous and totally my type. "Hey there."

I tipped my beer at her. "How's it going?"

"Good." She sidled closer, running her fingers over the tattoo on my bicep. "Better now that I've met you."

I should be turned on right now. I *should* be wanting to bring her back to my place so I could fuck her brains out until I forgot all about Carrie. Until I forgot all about everything. But I felt…nothing. "Is that so?"

"It is." She pressed her thigh against mine and caught my gaze. She had blue eyes, but compared to Carrie's, they were dull and boring. "Wanna buy me a drink?"

I took another sip, trying to decide how best to answer. I'd like to pretend I was attracted to her. Maybe even force myself to pretend she was Carrie, and fuck her in the dark. But it felt as if I was betraying Carrie somehow, even though we weren't and never could be a couple.

"Maybe another night." I pulled out my wallet and tossed some cash on the bar. "I was just leaving."

"Your loss," she called out, her tone seductive.

I shook my head and walked out onto the crowded sidewalk. I had enough to drink that I should have been able to finally shake the hold Carrie had over me. But no. She still had her claws knuckle deep in me, whether or not she knew it. For the first time in my life, I didn't know what to do with a woman. Didn't know how best to solve this issue I had where she was concerned.

A laugh came back to me, and I stiffened. Lifting my head, I scanned the crowd. I slowed my steps when I spotted her. She was, of course, with Golden Boy. Cory stopped walking and hugged her close. From my vantage point, she looked stiff. Cory leaned down and kissed her, and she didn't move out of his arms. Didn't squirm or squiggle or try to break free.

Instead, she kissed Cory back.

I clenched my fists and ducked behind a nearby building, waiting to see if she needed any help. When would she push Cory away? Tell him to fuck off? Apparently never. When she pulled back and smiled up at Cory, her hand over his heart like she'd done earlier with me, my own heart twisted and turned.

Fuck that. And fuck this job. I quit.

I turned on my heel and headed home, red coloring my peripheral vision as I shoved my way through the crowd. I knew I had no right to be angry with her. None at all. I'd been the one to insist we be friends, and only friends. I'd been the one who constantly pushed her away, refusing to admit I wanted her, no matter how hard it had been.

Hell, I had practically given her to Cory on a silver platter. If I was in Cory's place, I'd be doing the exact same thing, only I'd be doing it in private, where I wouldn't have to stop. Fucking newbie.

I unlocked my front door and went straight to my fridge. After pushing aside the wine coolers I kept stocked for Carrie, I grabbed a cold beer and cracked it open. Crossing the room, I kicked off my sandals and ripped off my shirt before reclining on the couch. My gaze fell to the spot where Carrie always sat on our Saturday night hangout. The spot she was supposed to be in right now.

It looked ridiculously empty without her there.

"Pathetic," I mumbled under my breath. "You're fucking pathetic, Coram."

I pulled out my phone and dialed quickly. It would be late back home, but I'd bet Dad was still up watching Conan. After two rings, he picked up. "Hello?"

"Hey, Dad." The TV quieted, but not before I heard Conan. I'd been right. Homesickness washed over me, and I swallowed another swig of beer. "Watching TV?"

"Yeah. Nothing's changed out here," Dad said. "How's it going out in California, son? Enjoying the sun, sand, and surf?"

"You know it," I said, smiling at the enthusiasm in Dad's voice. We'd lived in California when I had been a boy, before Mom had died. Before everything had gone and changed. "I missed this place."

"I know," Dad said, his voice gruff. "And I miss you."

"Speaking of which," I cleared my throat. "How likely do you think it would be for the senator to let me off duty earlier than planned? On a scale of one to ten?"

"Zero." Dad sighed. "Why? What happened? Sick of babysitting the brat already?"

"It's not that. She's not a brat at all."

"Then what's the issue?" Something crinkled and Dad munched

down on something crunchy. Sour cream and onion chips, no doubt. "You're back in your home state surfing and getting paid to do it. What's the problem?"

I hesitated. I didn't want to tell Dad how deeply watching Carrie was affecting me. The jealousy. The guilt. The feelings I didn't want to name. "It doesn't really seem like I'm needed here, but I don't know how my suggestion of terminating this assignment would go over with the senator."

"Senator Wallington feels differently," Dad said. "Every day, he checks your updates. Every day, he tells me what a fine boy I've raised. He's even suggested when I retire, I'll be getting double my allotted retirement fund thanks to my son's 'go get 'em' attitude and willingness to please."

I dropped my forehead to my palm. There was no getting out of this now. I couldn't do that to my dad. "That's…great, Dad. Really great."

And it was. Dad could definitely use the added money. Getting double his retirement would let him set up home pretty much wherever he wanted. Live comfortably. Not worry about money or bills or food. And when it came down to it, being in California wasn't half as bad as I had thought it would be. If I could get my emotions under control, and get it through my thick head that Carrie would never be mine, it might actually be enjoyable.

"Is something wrong, son? If you're miserable, I'd rather be fired than get double my retirement fund," Dad said, his tone dead serious. "I'll be fine without it."

No, he wouldn't. Not when I could suck it up and be a man. "I'm fine, Dad." I rubbed my forehead. "I was just being stupid. Homesick, I guess."

"I miss you too, son."

I swallowed hard. "Thanks for the talk. I'm gonna go now."

"All right. Good night, son."

"Night, Dad."

I hung up and closed my eyes. Enough of this shit. Enough wanting and wishing and hoping. I needed to focus on the cold hard truth of the matter. If I fucked this up, Dad wouldn't get his nice, cushy retirement pay off. If I fucked this up, I wouldn't be the only one to suffer. It was time to suck it up and stop mooning all over Carrie Wallington, for Dad's sake.

She was an assignment…nothing more.

CHAPTER TWELVE

Carrie

A few nights later, I hugged Cory good-bye, making sure to keep it friendly and not too personal. He went in for a kiss again, but I ducked my head just in the nick of time. After he caught me off guard last Saturday, he'd been trying to kiss me over and over all week long. Of course, I might be partially to blame for that. I hadn't ended our first kiss right away, and had probably given him the wrong impression.

But I hadn't kept the kiss going because I'd liked it so much I couldn't break it off. Not because it set me on fire in ways even twenty thousand romance novels could possibly describe. No, I hadn't ended the kiss because it hadn't done anything at *all*. Zilch. Nada. Zero. Zip.

No matter how many ways I said it, I may as well have been kissing a poster of a fat, balding man for all the excitement the kiss had given me. But when Finn kissed me…

Now, that was another story all together.

"Good night, Cory," I said, patting his shoulder.

Yep. I actually patted his shoulder.

"Night." He gave me a long, almost pleading, look. "See you tomorrow afternoon for another weekend study session?"

"I'm hanging out with Finn," I said, my tone apologetic. "Sorry."

Cory nodded but looked unhappy. Guilt struck me, but I didn't know the right way to let him know I wanted to be friends and only friends.

Maybe I could repeat the speech Finn had given me. It had worked well enough for him. "No problem. See you Monday."

"Bye."

I headed up the stairs to my dorm, expecting to find the room empty. It was Friday night, after all, and Marie surely had plans. But when I opened the door, I found Marie on the couch, hot and heavy with some guy I didn't even recognize.

Marie opened her eyes mid-kiss and pointed at the door. What was I supposed to do? Sit in the hallway? Marie narrowed her eyes and pointed at the door more emphatically. I slowly backed out and closed the door behind me.

Leaning against the hallway wall, I closed my eyes. Okay. Now what? I could call Cory and hang out with him some more, but I was already struggling to find a way to break it to him gently that I wasn't interested in a relationship with him. That left two other options. Walking around without a destination or even an idea on how long it would be until I could return to my room…or Finn.

Easy decision. I missed Finn anyway.

I headed back outside and called a taxi. I knew I should call him first. Make sure he didn't mind if I stopped by. But what if he told me no? If I just kind of showed up, it would be hard to send me away. At least I hoped so.

Of course, by the time the cab arrived, I was losing my confidence in this decision. And after I paid the cab and started up his walkway, I was ready to run back toward the car, even though it was halfway down the road. His bike was outside, so I was fairly certain he was home, but what if he had company? The kind of company he didn't mind kissing?

I hovered outside of his door, pressing my ear against the cool steel door, listening for the telltale noises of sex. All I heard was him talking. Something about watching "Golden Boy." No one responded, so I could only assume that he was on the phone. That was a good sign.

I swiped my hands over my thighs. Taking a deep breath, I raised my trembling fist and knocked. His voice paused, and then I heard footsteps approach. He opened the door, and my breath *whooshed* out of my lungs. He didn't have a shirt on, like usual, but instead of his normal shorts, he wore a pair of camouflage pants. His dog tags, which I'd never seen him wear, hung off his neck, and his hair was shorter on the sides than it had been the last time I'd seen him. A little shorter on the top, too, but there were still some curls.

He looked like a Marine. The type of Marine that went to war. The thought chilled my blood. War had always seemed so far removed from my own life that I never really thought about it besides the occasional story I saw on TV. I'd never known a soldier or a Marine or anyone who would be in harm's way to keep me safe.

Not until Finn.

"Of course, sir." He clenched his phone tighter and held a finger in front of his mouth in an obvious attempt at keeping me quiet. Was he on the phone with his superior? "Yes, sir." A pause. "I will update you on that status when I return from duty." He hung up and shoved the phone in his pocket. "Hey."

"Hi," I said, biting my lower lip. "I haven't seen you in a while. Or heard from you. Are you…is something wrong?"

…and now I sounded like a desperate girlfriend seeking attention.

"I've been busy." He gestured down his body. "Getting ready."

I nodded. "You look ready to go to war."

"Not quite." He raised a brow at me. "I'm missing a few key components. Namely, a weapon."

"Well, duh." I flicked a glance over him again, my legs going all weak. He was always hot, but wearing his uniform, he was catastrophic to my health. "Why are you wearing that? And why did you cut your hair?"

"Because I had to for drill." He tugged on his dog tags. He still hadn't moved out of the opening of the door or invited me in. In fact, he hadn't even smiled or looked happy to see me. "Are we doing surprise visits now? I hadn't realized we were there yet."

I stepped back and glanced over my shoulder. A couple came up the walkway, a young child at their side. They were talking about not having enough money for food again. I made a mental note to drop off a gift card to a local grocery store at their door. "What's drill?'"

"It's something I have to do the first weekend of every month," he said, his jaw tight.

"O-Oh." I cleared my throat. "Are you leaving now?"

He hesitated. "No, I have to report to duty first thing in the morning. Why?"

"So, I guess we're not surfing tomorrow, huh?"

"No, we're not."

I shifted on my feet, not sure what to say next. He was acting cold and uncaring, and I didn't know how to talk to a Finn who acted this way. I'd obviously made a mistake coming here. "You weren't going to tell me?"

"No, I wasn't." He sighed and leaned against the doorjamb. "I didn't realize I had to."

I crossed my arms. "Well, I'm new to this whole 'friend' thing, but it's kind of common courtesy to let someone know when normal routines will be broken, right?"

I forced a laugh, but it hurt to know he hadn't even been planning on letting me know our usual plans were off. Then again, hadn't I done exactly the same thing to him? Yeah. I had. Just last week. Well, *crap*. I'd been a horrible friend and hadn't even known it.

"Yeah." He cocked a brow, his thoughts clearly along the same lines as mine. I could *see* it in his eyes. "Yeah, it is."

"I'm sorry, okay?" I played with the hem of my shirt. "I'm not the best at this stuff. I didn't realize…"

He studied his nails. "What exactly are you apologizing for?"

"For not hanging out last Saturday after surfing. You're obviously mad, and it wasn't right for me to not let you know about it."

"Nope." He looked up at me with something that could only be described as disinterest. "I'm not mad about that. I got over it quickly enough."

I curled my hands into fists. My nails dug into my skin from the force I used, but I didn't even care. "Then *what* are you mad at?"

"Why do you think I'm mad at all?"

"For one?" I craned my neck to look past him. "You haven't invited me in. Do you already have company?"

"Nope."

"If you're not mad, then why aren't you—?"

"The better question is," he crossed his ankles and checked the time, "why are you here unannounced at nine o'clock on a Friday night?"

"I…I wanted to see you."

"Why?" he bit off, as if he couldn't spare more than a single word on me.

"You know what? Never mind." I brushed past him, muttering, "Good luck this weekend."

94

"Thanks, Ginger," he said, his voice taunting me. "Don't get lost in the ocean without me. I won't be there to save your pretty little ass."

I froze mid-step, my whole body trembling with frustration and anger and hurt. "You know what?" I turned on him, swinging my fist toward his hard, bare bicep. "Fuck you!"

He easily caught my wrist, preventing the blow. His jaw ticked, and his eyes spit fire at me. "What's the matter? Do you not like being blown off? Well, neither do I."

"I *knew* it. I knew you were mad at me." I tried to yank free, but he didn't loosen his grip. "Let *go* of me."

"Or what?" he asked, clearly daring me to do my worst. "What could a little brat like you possibly do to me that would make me let go?"

I knew one thing he didn't want from me. One thing sure to make him release me. I grabbed his dog tags and yanked hard, bringing him down to my level. He didn't even fight me, probably because he'd been expecting me to hit him or shove him or something else painful. Instead, I melded my mouth to his, kissing him with everything I had.

All of my frustration, anger and yes, *need*, came pouring out of me.

He dropped my wrist and gripped my hips, neither pushing me away nor pulling me closer. Spinning me around, he trapped me between the brick wall and his hard chest. When he tilted his head and deepened the kiss, clearly taking control, I clung to the cool metal of his dog tags. With my free hand, I ran my fingers over his abs. I'd wanted to do that since the first time I saw him.

His muscles clenched, and he rubbed his erection against me, teasing me. Taunting me. God, this was how a kiss was supposed to feel. This is how I *wanted* to feel. And I wanted to find this bliss in Finn's arms. No one else's.

I lowered my hand, brushing against the top of his waistband, and then lower until I reached his penis. He arched into my hand, groaning into my mouth. When I closed my hand over him, marveling at the size and feel of him, he jerked and jumped back from me as if I'd punched him instead of touched him. As if I hurt him, instead of bringing him pleasure.

"Damn it, Carrie," he swore, dragging his hands down his face. When he turned to me with blazing eyes, I flinched. "You just go around kissing anyone you want, don't you? Don't care who or where or when? Or how many of us there are?"

I tensed. "What the hell is that supposed to mean?"

"I saw you," he said. No, *snarled*. "I saw you kissing Cory just a couple of days ago, and now you're here, kissing me?"

My heart ached at the accusation in his tone. And the hurt in his eyes… "I didn't kiss him. He kissed me."

"You looked pretty damned happy about it to me." He grabbed the bannister and looked out at the road, his shoulders tense. "As a matter of fact, you looked like the perfect couple, so I really don't know why you're here with me."

I took a step toward him. If he was mad about Cory kissing me, did that mean he was jealous? And if he was, what did his jealousy mean? "I didn't kiss him back."

He spun on me. "Bullshit. I *saw* you. And you liked it."

"No." I held my hands out, desperate to make him understand why I had kissed Cory. To make him see I only wanted him, not Cory. "I kissed him because I was curious. I wanted to know why he doesn't—"

"I don't care why you did it. Just leave me alone." He started for his door, but I stepped in his path, resting my hand on his chest. His whole body tensed, but his heart raced beneath my palm. "Carrie, move out of the way. I'm done here."

I tilted my head back and met his eyes. "No."

"Go bug Cory. He'll welcome it. I don't." He removed my hand from his chest. "I don't play games, and I don't share."

Finally, the anger came back. Thank God, because I needed its strength right now. "Funny, but you told me you didn't want to be with me. Told me you weren't interested. So how is it *sharing* when you never wanted me in the first place?"

"When you came here and kissed me, it became sharing." He still hadn't dropped my hand, but his grip wasn't harsh or even strong. "I'm not willing to be some man you kiss when the mood strikes, before you go running back to Cory."

"That's not fair."

He squared his jaw. "Tell me, were you with him tonight before you came to me?"

I trembled. "I was, but not like you're insinuating."

"There's no insinuation."

"Sure there isn't." I glared at him. "And I'm Mother Teresa."

"Nice to meet you." He dropped my hand. "Now get the hell off my porch."

He was halfway inside the door before I got up enough nerve to ask, "Do you want something different now? Do you want to be with me?"

He froze, his hand on the doorknob. When he looked back at me, his eyes were open and vulnerable. He looked at me as if he did want more. As if he wanted me. But then he opened his mouth and ruined everything. "What I want doesn't matter. It's not happening. Ever. Go chase after Cory instead of me. He'll let you catch him."

"I don't want him," I whispered. "I want you."

He shut the door in my face, and I was alone. I swallowed back tears and started down the steps. Well, that was it. It was over.

All because I'd gone and kissed him.

CHAPTER THIRTEEN

Finn

After drill on Sunday night, I unlocked my door and kicked it open. My eyes strayed to the spot Carrie had stood when I told her to go chase someone else. Even though I tried not to remember what had happened right in this spot on Friday night, it was useless. She'd been on my mind all weekend at training. Haunting me. Annoying me. Making me wish I'd done things differently from the start.

Now that I was back from training, nothing had changed.

She was still on my mind. Still bugging me, even though she wasn't by my side. What was wrong with me? Since when did I let one little spoiled brat of a girl get under my skin so deeply? I squeezed my eyes shut and leaned against the wall, the silence of my empty apartment surrounding me. But the silence soon gave way to her whispered words—the ones that wouldn't leave me the hell alone.

I don't want him. I want you.

And what had I said to her? I'd told her to spend her time with Cory instead of me. It was better this way. The right thing to do. She would move on to someone more suitable, and I would be safe from ruining everything for Dad's retirement. It's not like I needed to hang out with her to watch over her. That had been my first mistake—trying to become her friend. The second had been kissing her. And the third?

Wanting more from her than grade school kisses.

I banged my head back against the wall. "Idiot."

Pulling my phone out of my pocket, I powered it on. It had been off since Friday night, and I was sure I'd have a waiting text or a thousand from the senator. No sooner did the Apple icon disappear from the screen than my phone buzzed.

Everything okay over there? Have you seen her tonight?

I rolled my eyes. *Just walked in. Haven't gone out yet.*

Do so and report back.

Yes, sir.

Apparently my time to sit around moping had come to an end. Duty called, and I couldn't ignore it. After making quick work of changing out of my uniform, I opened the door and headed out to search for Carrie. It's not like I could text her and ask what she was doing. I'd kind of ended that aspect of our friendship the minute I rejected her and acted like an ass.

I'd have to go over to the dorms and see if I could find her. It was five thirty, so chances were she'd be out and about. Maybe at the library. Probably with Cory. Making golden fucking plans for a golden fucking future.

The whole ride over to the school grounds, I was tense and strung out. I wasn't ready to see her with Cory. To see what I'd orchestrated. I pulled the bike up to the curb and took off my helmet. After scouring the library, I came up empty. Everywhere else on campus turned out empty too, but then it occurred to me what day it was.

Sunday. She was probably helping out at the soup kitchen. Alone.

Son of a bitch.

I jumped back on my bike and took the quickest route to the local shelter. By the time I arrived, the sun was down and I had every intention of hiding in the shadows of the parking lot. Once she got in a cab, I could tell her dad she was fine. But as I pulled up on my bike, she walked out the door. She was pale and her hair was frizzy. Huge bags were under her eyes, making her look exhausted. A family came out of the soup kitchen at the same time as her, and Carrie handed them three gift cards.

The family hugged her and she hugged them back. Carrie watched them walk away with a smile on her face. Once she was alone, she stepped under the streetlight and I saw a thin sheen of sweat covering her skin. She'd worked too hard tonight. Then again, she always did, especially when it came to helping others.

As she reached into her pocket to grab her phone, I swore I saw a shadowy shape move behind her, but it could have been a trick of the light. I tried to sink back into the shadows before it was too late and she spotted me, but she turned my way. At first, she didn't see me, but I knew the exact second she spotted me. Her nostrils flared and she gave me her back. Clearly, she planned on pretending she hadn't seen me.

When she pulled out her phone and started texting or calling someone, I hesitated before I walked up to her. "Hi."

"Are we surprising each other now? I didn't realize we were there," she murmured, still not looking up at me.

Okay. I deserved that. Maybe we weren't supposed to be friends anymore, but I could at least apologize for my bad behavior. "I'm sorry I lost it the other night."

"It's fine."

She still didn't look at me. I shifted on my feet and scanned the dark alley behind her. I couldn't get rid of this uneasy gut feeling that something was back there. "No, it's not."

Finally, she lifted her head. "You're right. It's not, but if nothing else, I now know exactly how you feel about me. So thanks for that."

"No, you really don't." I ran a hand through my hair. "I don't even know how I feel most of the time."

"Well, good for you."

Yeah. She was pretty pissed at me. Well, I'd been pissed at her too. "Thanks, Ginger."

She stiffened. "Don't call me that."

"Or what? You'll kiss me into submission again?"

The glare she gave me should have turned me into nothing more than a pile of ashes. Instead, it made my whole body quicken with excitement. I liked when she played hard to get, damn it. "Go away."

"And leave you standing here all alone in the worst section of the city?" I snorted. "Yeah. Not happening. Where's your cab?"

"Late." She walked past me, her shoulder bumping into my arm. It was probably supposed to be a shoulder bump, but she was too damned short to pull it off effectively. "If you won't take the hint, then I'll leave you."

I fell into step beside of her, my hands in my pockets. This wasn't a good section of the city, and she was playing stupid games. I thought I heard a footstep behind us and spun, ready to protect Carrie, but nothing was there. When I turned around, Carrie had an eyebrow raised and an amused expression on her face.

"Chasing shadows?"

"In this section of town, it's probably not a shadow." I searched the darkness, certain someone or something was out there. "Let's go. Now."

"Not with you."

There it was again. A footstep. A shuffle. I grabbed her elbow. "This is an even stupider move than kissing me. You looking to get robbed or worse?"

She broke free and stumbled backward. "I'm looking to get rid of *you*."

"Well, newsflash. Storming off in the worst section in San Diego isn't the way to do it." I reached for her, but she skirted out of my reach again. "Get on my bike, and I'll drop you off."

"Not happening." She tried to step around me, but I blocked her again. She stomped her foot. Actually stomped her foot. "Get out of the way!"

"No. We need to leave. *Now*."

Something fell in the alley behind us, clattering against the pavement. Carrie seemed oblivious to the threat, but I wasn't. My entire body knew a fight was coming, and I wanted Carrie far, far from it. A shadow moved behind her as my worst nightmare came to life. A man wearing a black ski mask and a pair of black gloves appeared seemingly out of thin air, holding a knife to her throat.

"No quick movements," he rasped, his eyes on me.

I held up my hands and surveyed the rest of the shadows. Nothing else moved. It looked like the mugger was working alone. "Easy now. We're not fighting back."

Carrie's eyes went wide, and her face ghostly white. "Finn?"

"Just do as he says," I said, keeping my voice calm and soothing, while inside I was ready to rip off this asshole's face piece by piece. The man pressed the knife against Carrie's white skin and I saw red. Lots and lots of fucking red. My heart pounded in my head, and my whole body braced for a fight. "Let go of her right now."

The man laughed. Fucking laughed. "Give me all of your money and jewelry, and I'll think about it. Now."

"*Finn*," Carrie said, her voice soft. I could tell she was seconds from panicking, and if she panicked, there was no telling what this man would do.

"Look at me." When she followed my command, I saw the fear deep in the depths of her blue eyes. It was like pure acid in my stomach. I didn't want to see her look at me like that ever again. I didn't drop Carrie's gaze, making sure I looked calm and collected for her. "Do what he says, babe. It'll be okay."

She fumbled with the bracelet on her wrist, her fingers slipping on the clasp. Once she finally managed to get it off, she handed it to the man holding her. He snatched it up and shoved it in his pocket. Judging from the way he shook as he held Carrie, the money he earned from the sale of the bauble would go straight into his veins. Or up his nose.

His unsteady hand made the knife slice Carrie's throat. It was just a tiny scratch at best, but it made me ready to make him bleed a hell of a lot more. "Let go of her."

"Once I'm done, you'll get her back," the man sneered. He pressed the knife even deeper into Carrie's neck and a tiny trickle of blood rolled down her throat. "Money. *Now*."

I wanted to throttle the piece of shit. *Now*. But I knew I had to set the scene right. I needed to get the threat away from Carrie before I made my move. Then it was game fucking on. The asshat wouldn't know what hit him.

"Here you go," I said.

I took a wad of cash out of my pocket and held it out, waving it around just out of reach. The fucker reached for it, but couldn't quite touch. He extended his arm, letting the knife fall away from Carrie's throat. Bingo. Just what I'd wanted.

Moving so fast the man never saw it coming, I captured his wrist and spun it behind his back. The knife clattered to the ground and Carrie leapt back from it, her eyes wider than ever before. Yanking the guy's arm up behind his shoulders, I kept a firm pressure on him. I wrapped my forearm around the guy's neck in a chokehold, squeezing tight enough to knock the guy out but not kill him.

No matter how tempting it might be.

"Come near her again, and next time you won't wake the fuck up," I snarled in his ear, fury making it hard to keep my grip loose. The thief tried to break free, but went limp in my arms. I let him drop to the ground and took the bracelet out of the guy's hand, then shoved the cash back in my pocket too. "Let's go *now*."

Carrie nodded quickly, taking my hand when I offered it. Neither one of us spoke as we climbed on the bike, helmets on and tension high. She clung to me, so I could feel her entire body shaking. Trembling. She might be in shock. I didn't know if the shock was from my quick reaction to the robber, or the robber himself.

Either way, it wasn't good.

I choked the throttle, speeding down the PCH to my apartment. When we got there, I hopped off the bike and yanked off my helmet. After helping her to her feet, I gently removed hers. She looked at me, not touching me but not moving away either.

"Why did you bring me here?" she asked.

I looked around. Though I hadn't thought it through, I'd brought her back to my place. Leaving her alone was out of the question right now. "I don't want you to be alone tonight."

"Oh." She took a shaky breath, her face still far too pale for my liking. "I'll be fine. You don't have to—"

"I want to," I said simply, making sure my tone left no room for arguments. Though I wanted to rail at her, *scream* at her, I swallowed back my anger. Now was neither the time nor the place to release my frustrations at her actions.

She didn't say anything. Just swallowed hard and nodded.

I brushed her hair out of her face tenderly and her eyes drifted shut. "Are you okay, Ginger?"

"Where did you learn how to do that?" she asked, her voice tiny and soft. "It was…crazy."

"The Marines," I said, swallowing past the huge lump in my throat threatening to choke me. So, she was *scared* of me now. Fucking fabulous. "You know I would never hurt you, right?"

She bit her lip and latched gazes with me. I couldn't read the emotions in her eyes. Fear maybe? "Of course."

"I'm sorry you had to see that." I hugged her tight, resting my head on hers and breathing in her scent. "But I'm not sorry I did it. He could have…you could have…"

She gripped my sides, fisting my shirt, and my stomach clenched. "I know."

Seeing that man holding a knife to her throat had done weird things to my insides. I'd be a fool to deny she meant something to me. Something real and huge and unstoppable. Like a force of nature, only stronger. How much longer could I push her away? How many times could I deny the feelings that were so clearly there before I gave up trying?

She shuddered and buried her face in my shirt. "Just take me up to your place, please."

Not trusting myself to speak right now, I swung her in my arms, carrying her up to my apartment. For once, she didn't fight me. She just lay there, letting me cradle her in my arms. Once we were inside, I sat down on the couch with her still in my arms.

I couldn't hold it in anymore. "That's was the stupidest, most stubborn, idiotic—"

"I know."

"—thing I've ever seen you do."

"I *know*."

"And you will never, ever go there without me again. Understood?"

She swallowed and nodded. "Yes."

Her easy acquiescence did nothing to soothe my temper. I needed a fight. Needed to make her see how stupid she'd been in storming off like that. "If I hadn't been there—"

"But you were," she said quietly.

"But *if* I wasn't." I tightened my arms around her, picturing all the horrible things that could have happened to her. All the gruesome things men liked to do to defenseless women like her. "Do you have any idea what it would do to me if you were hurt? I can't even imagine—"

She lifted her head and kissed me, shutting me up quite effectively. For once, I didn't want to fight her off. Didn't want to give a damn about my duties or expectations. Didn't give a damn what kind of contract I'd signed that said I wasn't allowed to touch her. For once, I...

Didn't want to stop.

CHAPTER FOURTEEN

Carrie

I held on to Finn as tight as I could, kissing him for as long as he would let me. At any minute, he would push me away and curse, but I didn't care right now. After the scare in the street, and his even more impressive saving of my stupid butt, I couldn't stop thinking about how it had felt with that knife to my throat. I hadn't been as scared for myself as I had been for Finn when he went for that guy. I'd been terrified he would get hurt trying to save me.

Frightened he would get stabbed or worse…die.

All because I had to go and be a stubborn idiot who refused to leave with him. I *knew* better than to walk off into the dark city streets. Knew not to storm off in a huff when danger lurked nearby. My actions had put myself, and consequently, Finn, in danger. If he had been injured trying to save me, I never would have forgiven myself.

I strained to get closer, but his hold on me didn't allow me to move. He broke off the kiss and dropped his forehead on mine, taking a shaky breath. "I don't want to stop, babe. I swear it. But you could be in shock…"

"I'm not," I said quickly, grabbing his hand and holding it to my cheek. "I'm fine. I want you so bad it hurts."

His jaw flexed, but I could see his answering need in his eyes. "I shouldn't."

"You should."

"Carrie..." He closed his fingers on my hips, lifting me up and lowering me on his lap so I straddled him.

"Oh my God." His erection pressed against my core, making me moan. I entwined my hands behind his neck, the cool metal of his dog tags digging in to my skin. He hadn't even taken them off before seeking me out. "You really should, Finn."

He made a long sound, half groan and half agreement. "I can't fight this anymore. I don't even want to."

And with that, he buried his hands in my hair and tugged me down, his mouth seeking mine. For that brief second, the time that our mouths hovered close to each other, I knew I hadn't made a mistake in falling for him. I had fallen hard, and there was no going back.

His lips touched mine and all thought fled. All I knew was Finn was kissing me, and things finally felt right. And this time when he kissed me, he held nothing back. I knew it from the way his lips moved over mine. His mouth devoured mine hungrily, and he arched up against me, letting his erection rub where I needed him most. I dug my fingernails into his shoulders, holding him closer.

Begging him not to leave with my actions instead of my words. If he pulled away now, I didn't think I would recover. If he stopped now, I just might break. But he didn't. Instead, he stood up and cupped my butt, holding me in place as he headed toward the bedroom. Slowly, he lowered me to his bed, never breaking off the kiss.

My head spun as his lips worked mine, making everything but him disappear from my mind. The way he kissed me. How amazing his hands felt on my body. The feel of the soft bed underneath my back, contrasting with his hard body on top of mine. Pressing me down and making me want more.

Tentatively, I ran my fingers down his back, sliding them up his shirt when I reached the hem. His hot skin burned my fingers, and the way he moaned into my mouth set me afire. I traced my nails down his spine, growing bolder the lower I went. When I reached the waistband of his shorts, I scraped my nails against his lower back.

He hissed and tore his mouth from mine. "Are you sure you want this?"

Unable to talk, I nodded and reached for him again. He stretched and ripped his shirt off over his head, and then melded his mouth back to mine. His free hand, with the other firmly on my hip, roamed all over. My sides. My stomach. My neck. When he traced the curve of my breast, I gasped into his mouth and arched my back.

He needed to do that again.

Apparently I said that out loud. He chuckled. "I will."

"Please," I whimpered.

Slowly, he crept my shirt over my stomach, stopping at the bottom of my bra. I caught my breath, afraid to move. Afraid if I made a sound, he would grow a conscience again and stop doing those magical things to me. He met my eyes, his own hot and unwavering. "Have you kissed Cory again?"

"W-What?" I asked, caught off guard.

"Since you kissed me, have you kissed him?" he asked, his jaw ticking.

I shook my head. "No. Of course not. Just the once."

"Good." He lifted my shirt a little bit more, his fingers brushing my bare skin, never dropping my gaze. "You're mine now. Don't forget it."

I swallowed hard at the possessiveness in his tone. I should argue or say I didn't belong to any man. Assert my independence. But right now? Right here? I was his. One hundred percent his, and perfectly happy to be there. "I won't. Now kiss me again."

He took off my shirt the rest of the way and closed his mouth over mine. As he worked his magic with his tongue, his fingers toyed with the strap of my bra, tugging gently. Before I could even blink, he had the strap undone and was lowering the tiny scrap of fabric off my breasts. For a second, I worried he might not like what he saw. Worried I would disappoint him somehow.

But he reared back and looked down at me…and I was lost. He was seeing what no man had ever seen before. I didn't want to hide from him. Didn't want to deny him a single thing. Not tonight. I let my hands fall to my sides. He swallowed so hard I could see it, and then traced a finger over my bare stomach, creeping closer and closer to my left breast.

"You're the most beautiful woman I've ever seen," he uttered, almost as if he didn't realize he said it out loud.

Before I could respond, or even decide if I *should* respond, he lowered his head to my breast, flicking his tongue over my sensitive nipple. "*Finn,*" I cried out. I gripped his head, urging him closer. Needing him closer.

His slid his hands under my back, arching my back for me. I bent one leg, spreading my thighs to let him in. Knowing instinctively that he needed to be there to ease the ache building inside me, begging for release. He moved into the crook of my thighs, but didn't press his erection against me. Instead, he scraped his teeth against my nipple and sucked harder.

"I-I need you." I licked my lips and added, "Please."

His hands trembled as he let go of me and undid my pants. I lifted my hips, letting him undress me, and didn't so much as flinch as he lowered them down my legs. When he reached for my panties, I grabbed his hand and swallowed the nervous bubble of laughter threatening to escape me.

I might be a virgin, but I knew what came next. And before I was completely naked, things needed to get taken care of. "Do you have protection?"

He pushed off the bed and opened the nightstand next to it, pulling out a purple foil package. He tossed it onto the bed and made quick work of removing his shorts. When he ripped off his boxers, I didn't drop my gaze from his body. If he saw my shyness and my uncertainty, he might back down. As it was, he surely thought I was more experienced than I was.

I knew if *he* knew I was a virgin, this wouldn't be happening.

As he stepped out of the last piece of clothing he wore, I feasted my eyes on him. Tattoos covered his upper arms and shoulders. That I already knew. But his lower half was devoid of any ink. In a way, I was glad. The perfection of his body was an artwork all by itself, and I couldn't help but think any more ink would detract from the muscle and flawlessness I saw right now.

When my gaze dropped to his penis, I practically choked on the deep breath I took. No matter how many romance books I read, I hadn't been expecting *that* much length. Holy crap. No romance book could ever have prepared me for this. He was magnificent.

He approached me, his steps sure. When he lowered his body over mine, I stopped trying to do calculations on the likelihood of him fitting all the way inside of me without tearing something vital. I wasn't a fool. Women had been doing this since the beginning of time, and I was no different than any of them.

Though Finn might just be bigger than all the other men.

He sucked my other nipple into his mouth, ripping open the condom as he did so. After a few quick movements, his hands were back on my skin, burning paths everywhere he touched. My blood heated, and my stomach clenched tight, building a pressure that I was powerless to stop. Powerless to control.

When he kissed a path down my stomach, taking little bites as he went, I went mad with desire. Tossing my head back and forth on the pillow, I moaned and cried out and dug my nails into his skin. He flicked his tongue over my clitoris before taking that into his mouth too.

Oh, holy mother of freaking God. That felt way too good to ever stop. I would make him stay down there forever. He could take breaks for water and food, but that was it. I dug my heels into the mattress, letting out a whimper that didn't even remotely sound like me.

He groaned and adjusted his hold on me. I, in turn, tightened my legs on his head, refusing to let him move until he gave me what I needed. Until I found the release I knew his mouth could give me. "Don't stop," I demanded, panting for air.

He ran his hands up my calves, then down my thighs. When he reached my hips, he lifted me higher. Something in the changed position must have made for optimal pleasure, because my whole body tingled and went weak. I clung to his hands, needing to hold on to something secure before I let go of all control.

And when I did, letting the pleasure wash over me, all of the pressure that had been building inside of me burst into a million pieces. As my whole body went limp with gratification, he dropped my hips and settled in between my legs. He rubbed against me, exactly where his mouth had just been, and another wave of intense pleasure crashed over me.

Capturing my face in between both of his hands, he kissed me gently. As his mouth played over mine, I could taste the familiar flavor of Finn I'd come to know and also myself on his tongue, making for an intoxicating combination that made me even more eager for him to come inside me. More desperate for him to fill me completely.

"Carrie," he gritted out, his hold on my hips tight. "I can't go slow or be gentle."

I opened my mouth to warn him about the technicality of me still being a virgin, but it was too late. He thrust inside of me with one quick movement, and the pain of him ripping through me blended with the satisfaction at having him buried deep inside of me, where I'd wanted him for weeks.

CHAPTER FIFTEEN

Finn

Having Carrie in my arms was more than I could bear. Better than I'd imagined. Nothing could describe the way she made me feel, so I wouldn't even bother to try. I fused my mouth with hers before surging into her, unable to believe how fucking amazing she made me feel. How she could bring me to my knees with a simple touch. Make me want to stay there too, I'd bet. I'd had sex with a good amount of women during the years, but I'd never done this.

Never made love before.

But then I crashed through the resistance I'd suspected might be there. I reared back, looking down at her with concern. "Are you okay?" Then, realizing I should act surprised, I added, "Wait. You're a virgin?"

"Y-Yes." I started to pull out of her. She closed her legs around my waist, blinking back tears even as she tried to keep me inside of her. But I was *hurting* her. "No. Don't stop. I want…I need…"

She rolled her hips up tentatively, more than likely experimenting with the sensation of having me inside her. I gritted my teeth and forced myself to remain still, letting her test out the waters, so to speak. "You should have told me."

"I was afraid you'd stop," she said, running her fingers lightly over my back. "Please don't stop. Don't let go."

"I've got you," I promised, nibbling on her ear. I knew I should stop.

Should end this right here and now, but she kept moving underneath of me, and letting out tiny breathy moans that drove me fucking wild. I couldn't stop. Not ever. "And I won't."

She thrust her hips up again, and a sheen of sweat formed on my forehead. Her tight pussy gripped me more closely than I could ever have imagined, and my cock screamed at me to move inside of her. To finish what I started.

She dug her heels into my ass, urging me closer. "It doesn't hurt anymore. Move inside me."

I pulled almost all the way out of her, then slowly drove back in. I groaned at the pleasure she gave me, unable to bite it back. Her body fit mine like a glove. It was as if she was made for me and me alone. My arms trembled from the strength I exerted to hold myself back. To not hurt her. I kept my weight on them, not wanting to crush her. "That okay?"

She nodded and lifted her head. "Kiss me and move faster."

The control I'd had over my motions snapped, and I crashed my mouth down on hers. I moved inside of her, hesitantly at first, but growing more and more sure as I went. She moaned and squirmed beneath me, begging for more. Once I was certain I wasn't hurting her, I lifted her hips in my hands and drove deeper. She cried out and scratched her nails down my back, probably drawing blood and waking up the neighbors.

I didn't even give a flying fuck.

I needed her too badly. It had all started with an immediate attraction, but now it was more. So much more. As I grew closer and closer to the precipice, I tried to focus on her. The way her eyes were slit, barely letting me see the bright blue sapphire. The way she let out tiny puffs of air through her swollen lips. But most of all, the way she moaned my name as I brought her higher and higher, refusing to stop until I made her come again.

When she finally tensed and bowed against me, frozen in time, I let myself go. I thrust one more time inside of her, going as deep as I could possibly go, and cried out, "*Carrie.*"

As the strongest orgasm I'd ever had rushed through my veins, I collapsed on top of her, keeping my weight on my elbows. She tightened her legs around me, seeming to not want to let me go, and hugged me close, her own breathing as ragged as mine. If she didn't want to let me go, that was fine by me. I could happily lie here as long as she wanted me to.

I buried my face in her neck, closed my eyes, and waited for the regrets and the guilt to come. Waited for cold, hard reality to come crashing over me once I remembered all the reasons I shouldn't have done this. And even more terrifying? Knowing she would hate me for taking her virginity while lying to her. When she knew what I really was—*who* I really was—she would never forgive me for taking her under false pretenses. And I would never forgive myself either.

I needed to find a way to fix this.

I lifted myself on my elbows and looked down at her, sweeping her sweaty hair off her face. I knew I should be feeling that suffocating guilt right about now, but it wasn't coming. She smiled, her eyes warm and soft and on me. "Wow."

"Yeah." I grinned at the wonder in her voice, despite myself. "You okay, Ginger?"

She nodded and arched a brow. "Are *you* okay?"

I laughed. "I think so." I slowly withdrew from her, watching her for any signs of pain. She flinched when I pulled out of her completely, but besides that she seemed fine. "You really should have told me, though."

She didn't even pretend to misunderstand me. She was a smart girl, my Carrie. "Would it have made a difference?"

I thought about it, but I already knew the answer. I wouldn't have stopped. I'd been lost in her the second she walked out on that beach more than a month ago, demanding for whoever was hiding in the shadows to show themselves. I'd been lost this whole time, but I'd been fighting it. I was done fighting her. From now on, I would fight *for* her.

For us.

"No, it wouldn't have. I couldn't have stopped any more than you could have," I admitted. "But now I need to take care of you."

I brushed my lips over hers before sliding off the bed. As I walked to the trash can to remove the condom, I took a deep breath. This *obviously* changed everything between us. I couldn't ignore my need to be with her any more than I could ignore the pressing need to admit my real identity to her before it was too late.

She would be angry with me at first, but if I came clean on my own— without her finding out when I wasn't there—then maybe she would understand. Maybe she could find it in her heart to forgive me and allow us to continue on as we had been, only without any lies between us. Yeah, and maybe some pigs would fly by wearing Wonder Woman costumes too.

Actually…that might be more likely.

I turned around and crossed the room to my bed. She let out a squeal when I picked her up and carried her into the bathroom. "I can walk, you know."

"You can, but I want to carry you." I kissed the tip of her nose before I set her down in front of the shower. "And you like making me happy, so you'll let me."

She huffed. "So, that's how you're gonna play this, huh?"

"Uh-huh." I turned on the shower, grinning the whole time. I couldn't remember the last time I'd felt so happy. Probably never. "Is it working?"

She splayed her hands over my shoulders, sliding them in front of my body. She rested them over my heart, pressing her cheek against my bare back. "Yes." I stopped moving, not wanting to break her hold. Not wanting her to let go. But then she did, and she slid her hand under the water. "Perfect. You coming in, too?"

I cocked a brow. "You have to ask?"

She laughed. "Guess not." She stepped into the shower and smiled at me. "This is weird. I've never showered with someone else."

"Well, it's another first for you then." I joined her and pulled her into my arms. Her naked body pressed against mine, making my cock harden again, but I wouldn't touch her. Not tonight. She needed rest. "I want to be all your firsts from now on."

She laid her head against my chest, directly over my heart. Did she know she owned it yet? "Sounds like a plan."

I grabbed her hair and got it damp, watching the water cascade down her bare back, only to roll down her ass. After clearing my throat, and mentally slapping myself in the face for being a perv, I reached for the shampoo. As I washed her hair, her eyes drifted shut and she let out a happy sigh.

I rinsed out the suds, watching her face as I did so. She looked so peaceful and innocent. "Sorry, I only have men's shampoo."

"That's okay." Her lids drifted up. "I'll smell like you."

I made a mental note to buy her some girly shampoo in the morning.

And a toothbrush. If I had my way, she'd be spending a lot more time here with me from now on. "Next time, you'll have something better."

Her eyes drifted shut again and she yawned. I made quick work of washing her body, pausing at the blood smeared between her legs. I'd done that. Taken her innocence. The fact that she'd chosen me, trusted *me*, was enough to make me want to scream. Soon, she would hate me. Soon, she would regret this.

I rinsed her off, and then quickly washed my own body. She leaned against the tile wall, her eyes devouring me. "Can I do you?"

I bit back a groan. "I don't think that's a good idea. I already want you again, but you can't handle that. Your body needs rest."

She licked her lips. "Are you so sure of that?"

"Yes." Fuck my fucking conscience. "Positive as a proton."

Her eyes went wide, then she let out a nervous laugh. "You heard that?"

"I did," I admitted, shooting her a sheepish grin.

"Oh God." She dropped her forehead onto her palm. "How embarrassing."

"You mean adorable?"

"Nope," she quipped.

I turned off the water and grabbed two towels. As we dried off, my eyes never left her. She was so gorgeous. Her pale skin contrasted fantastically with the smattering of red curls between her legs. She had a few freckles across her body, but for the most part, she was all ivory skin and temptation. I dropped my towel and cupped her face, tilting her it up to mine.

I ran my fingers over the line of freckles that ran across her cheeks and over her nose. "I love these little freckles. You know that?"

"I hate them."

"They're perfect, just like you."

I kissed her, making sure I kept it light. I swung her in my arms and carried her to the bed. After I gently set her in the middle of it, I reached down to the foot of the bed and lifted the covers over her bare body. She lay on her side, her hands folded under her cheek, watching me. I pulled my phone out of my pocket and quickly let her father know she was safe and sound.

I just neglected to mention she was safe and sound *in my bed.*

When I crawled under the blanket with her, she smiled and ran her fingers through my damp hair. Something that had nothing to do with lust rolled over me, like a tidal wave. She nibbled on her lower lip and tugged the blanket higher. The pink tinge in her cheeks hinted at her vulnerability.

"Stay the night with me?" I asked.

She gave me a small smile. "Do I really have a choice? You already tucked me in."

"Not really." I pulled her into my arms. "I was simply pretending to be a democracy."

She snorted, but burrowed closer. "Fine, but are you going to wake up and then curse and apologize in the morning?"

"Nope." My arms tightened around her. "I'm done fighting."

She smiled up at me, her eyes shining. "Really?"

"Really."

She smoothed a piece of my hair off my forehead. "So, uh, are we still just friends? Or…?"

I laughed and hauled her against my body. "Some friends might do that, but not me. We're more than friends now, Ginger."

"Do we have a name?" she asked, her voice soft.

Yeah. Mine was *liar*. Hers would be *mad*.

The guilt I'd been expecting had arrived right on schedule.

But for one simple night, I didn't want to think about anything. Didn't want to think about repercussions, or what her dad would say when he found out I hadn't followed the rules. Even worse? What *my* dad would say. Would my actions ruin Dad's chances at getting the big retirement pension?

No, I couldn't let it. I'd find a way to fix this, but it started with telling Carrie the truth.

"I'm not sure yet, but I know this changed everything," I said, kissing the top of her head. "Every fucking thing."

Her fingers closed around my shoulders, holding on tight. She yawned loudly. "You don't exactly sound happy about that."

"I'm happy." I swallowed all of my fears and doubts, trying to drown them out with a bright smile. "I have you. What more could I need?"

"How was drill?"

"Boring and utterly exhausting." I hesitated, then added, "And I missed you."

118

"I missed you, too." She smiled and snuggled into the crook of my elbow. "Can you wake me up at seven for class?"

"Yep."

I reached out and switched off the light. I lay there, holding her close, and tried to come up with the best way to tell her what I was. Tried to come up with a gentle way of breaking the news. Bad thing was? There wasn't one. No matter how I said it, she would hate me.

Her breathing evened out almost immediately, but the weight of my lies pressed me down into the mattress until I couldn't breathe anymore. How was I supposed to sleep when I could think of nothing but what I'd done?

And what I had to do. I had to tell her.

"You awake?" I whispered.

She mumbled something and scooted closer to me, letting off a soft snore. I wanted to wake her up and spill my guts, but I forced myself to lie still.

Tomorrow. Tomorrow I would tell her the truth.

CHAPTER SIXTEEN

Carrie

This afternoon class was never going to end. I sat back in my seat and eyed the clock. Only three more minutes until my class was over, and then I could see Finn. He'd promised to meet me at the dorm afterward, and I couldn't wait to see him again. Couldn't wait to kiss him and hold him and hug him. And, well, more.

I fanned my cheeks with my notebook as I recalled exactly what we'd done last night, and how amazing it had made me feel. How amazing *I'd* made *him* feel. I wanted more. Lots more. I'd known sex brought pleasure. Known I would enjoy it. But with Finn, it far surpassed pleasurable. As a matter of fact, what he did to me just might tip the Richter scale.

Cory elbowed me and tipped his head toward the professor. The professor, meanwhile, was looking at *me*. No. Scratch that. The whole class was watching me. I sat up straight in my seat and smoothed my hair. Why were they all staring at me?

Professor Hanabee turned red and shoved his hands in his pockets. "Would you be answering my question anytime soon, Carrie?"

"Uh," I said, looking to Cory for some help. He didn't even look at me. Just stared at the front of the classroom. "What was the question again?"

The professor rolled his eyes. "Cory?"

Cory gave the answer easily.

I looked down at my notebook. All I'd done was draw squiggles and a few random words like *bilateral* and *hemorrhage*. I thought I saw Finn's name in there too, but I could be wrong.

Professor Hanabee gave me one last, piercing look, then turned back to the class. "There will be a quiz tomorrow. You may go now."

While everyone else got up, I kept my head lowered. My cheeks were on fire, but I knew that I had no one to blame but myself. I'd always been at the head of my class. Straight A's. Eye on the end game. What the heck did I think I was doing, neglecting my academic obligations to daydream about a guy? I slammed my book shut and stood. After collecting the rest of my stuff, I started down the steps.

"A moment, please?" Professor Hanabee called out.

"Yes?" I climbed the rest of the way down and stood in front of his desk.

He wore one of those god-awful professor jackets with the patches on the elbow, and his glasses kept sliding down his nose. He jammed them back up with a short, stubby finger. "Did I mention I'm friends with your father? He calls for updates every so often. I'd hate to give him a bad answer."

I swallowed hard to stop the scathing reply trying to escape. Of *course* Dad would have friends on staff. He had spies *everywhere*. "Yes, sir."

I headed for the door, mentally figuring out how much time I would need to cram a day's worth of missed lesson into my head. Would there still be time for my fun evening with Finn? Could I do both? Cory waited at the door for me, his sandy blond hair perfectly in place like usual. The complete opposite of Finn's messy curls. He leaned against the wall, phone in his hand.

When I came to his side, he lifted his head. "Hey."

"Hey." I scanned the crowd for Finn. "Sorry about today."

He followed my gaze. "Looking for someone?"

"Yeah," I answered distractedly. "Finn."

"Marie said you didn't come back to the room last night." Cory shoved his phone in his pocket and gave me a look. A look that said he had his suspicions where I had been, and what I'd been doing. "Where were you?"

I stiffened. "I don't see how that's any of your business."

"I thought that we had something going between us, so, yeah, it kind of is."

Cory yanked on the collar of his polo. His pink-and-yellow striped polo, buttoned all the way up to his neck. Did he ever let loose? Wear a T-shirt that didn't come from a brand name store, or stop thinking so much about what everyone would think about him if he did?

"We're just friends. I like you a lot, and you're a great guy. Excellent, really. Any girl would be lucky to have you." I sighed. God, I sucked at this stuff. "But I'm kind of with someone else right now."

He stiffened. "The surfer?"

"Yeah." I swallowed back my arguments that Finn was more than a surfer. More than what Cory decided to label him as. He was smart, funny, handsome, brave…

Cory chuckled and his shoulders relaxed. "Good."

I blinked at him. "Good?"

"Yeah." He stared at his impeccable nails. "It won't last, and when it falls apart, you'll come back to me."

"That's a really shitty thing to say," I snapped, heading toward the doors. "He's a great guy."

Cory's mouth pressed tight. "He can be great all he wants, but it still won't work. You aren't the same type of people."

"You're wrong." I stopped walking. "You don't know him like I do."

"No, I'm not wrong," he said, his face red. I opened my mouth to slam his opinions to the dirt, but he didn't give me a chance. "You've got plans in your life that don't include a surfer boy who has no immediate goals in *his* life besides when he should catch his next wave."

"He has a great job. He's a Marine." I took a breath. "How dare you pretend that's not a career."

Cory rubbed his temples. "He's got nothing to offer you, really. Can't help you study. Has no knowledge of what you'll be doing with your life. Won't get along with your father. He's a rebellious stage in your life. Nothing more."

"I don't *need* him to help me study. I'm fine on my own."

"Sure you are," Cory agreed, nodding. "But that's not the biggest problem. The biggest problem is that you two have nothing in common. The things you like about him now? The stuff you think you admire most because he's so different?" Cory leaned in, latching gazes with me. "That's the stuff that will make you hate him later."

Could he be right? Would I eventually hate Finn's laid-back lifestyle? His quest for fun? The way he laughed as he surfed, his eyes lit up and his laugh blending with the sounds of the waves crashing on the shore? "You're wrong."

"No, I'm not. I learned it in psychology." He nodded his head toward the dorms. "Speaking of the devil…"

Finn came up to my side and cleared his throat. He wore a light yellow shirt with a surfboard on it and plaid shorts. His shades were firmly in place, and his short curls were a little messy. Not messy enough, though, due to his haircut. "I was starting to think you forgot about me."

"No. No, of course not. I'm just a little bit late because I got in trouble."

"You?" Finn raised a brow. "How could *you* have gotten in trouble?"

"We'll talk about it later." I knew I should get ready for the quiz tomorrow, but I didn't want to give up time with Finn. I could make time for both. "Come on."

Finn took my hand and nodded at Cory. "Later, Cody."

"My name's Cory," Cory said, his voice hard. "But you already know that, don't you?"

"I have no idea what you're talking about," Finn said, his tone completely innocent.

Even I believed him…almost.

Cory grabbed my arm as we passed, and Finn stiffened next to me at the touch. "Are you going to study?" Cory asked.

"Yeah. Later."

Cory flexed his jaw and let go of me. "Fine. See you later."

"What was that all about?" Finn steered me toward his bike.

"Nothing. We have a quiz coming up. I'll study later tonight."

He stopped walking and looked over his shoulder at Cory. "Are you sure? Your grades come first. Maybe you should go with Golden Boy."

Golden Boy. Why did that name ring a bell? I shook my head, shaking away the niggling sensation that I'd heard those words before. "No, I'll be fine. You promised me cheeseburgers and milkshakes, and I intend to collect."

He wrapped his arms around me and tugged me close. "First, you need to pay up."

He lowered his mouth to mine, giving me a passionate kiss that quite literally knocked the breath out of me. I curled my hands into his shirt, trying to urge him closer, and he moaned before breaking off the kiss. Before I could so much as blink, he slid the helmet over my head and reached for his.

"I've got a surprise for you."

I bit down on my lower lip. "Oh? What is it?"

He sat down on the bike and looked straight ahead before slamming on his own helmet. "You'll just have to wait and see."

CHAPTER SEVENTEEN

Finn

I pulled the bike up to the curb and closed my eyes, relishing the way her arms felt around me. Loving the fact that I could show how much I liked it when she clung to me, now that we were together. Now that she knew how I felt about her. I tore my helmet off, and then picked her up, setting her on my lap.

She shrieked at the sudden movement and flung her arms around my neck. Her sweet ass pressed down on me, making my cock hard, but I wasn't looking for that right now. I just needed to hold her because I fucking could. "Hey, babe."

I gently removed her helmet and set it aside. The way she looked at me...

I loved it.

I could get used to seeing that same light shining in her eyes for the rest of my goddamned life. And that's what I wanted. Not a short period of her life. I wanted forever. Even though I knew, subjectively, that we were doomed from the start. I'd started this relationship with lies, and it would end the second the full truth came out.

And even if I hadn't lied to her, she was too young to even contemplate forever. A baby, practically. When I'd been nineteen, the furthest thing from my mind had been love or settling down with someone. To her, this was nothing more than the obligatory college fling.

"Why are you looking at me like that?" she asked breathlessly.

I snapped myself out of whatever unicorn land I'd been stuck in. "Like what?"

"Like I bit you or something."

I snorted. "You can bite me anytime you want, babe."

She slapped my arm, but I barely even felt it. She was like a mosquito bite on my arm. "Keep it up, and I just might. And I bite really hard."

"I hope that's a promise."

She rolled her eyes. "So is this the surprise? I already knew you had an apartment."

I chuckled and nuzzled her neck. "That's not the surprise."

"Then what is?"

She arched her neck to allow me better access. Nice. I nibbled some more. "You'll have to go in and find out."

She hopped off my lap and practically ran up to the door. *Note to self: she likes surprises.* I followed her more slowly, grinning at her exuberance. When she turned to me impatiently, her hand out, I set the key in her hand. She burst inside the door—and then stopped.

She scanned the room, looking for any signs of something different. Turning to me, she cocked a brow. "Uh, where's the surprise?"

"Right here."

She eyed me, her eyes dancing. "Is it you?"

"I wrapped something with a bow."

Her gaze dropped to my cock, and her voice came out breathy. "Seriously?"

I burst into laughter. "Nope."

"Darn, that would've been fun."

I made a mental note to remember the idea. "It's better than that." I reached into her bag and retrieved the item I needed. I brandished her anatomy book with more flair than I knew I had in me. All for the greater good, of course. "We're spending the night...*studying*!"

"Studying. Really," she said dryly. "I can hardly contain my excitement."

"I see that," I said, laughing. "But that's not all."

She perked up. "Oh? What else?"

"Every time you get an answer right, I get to kiss you anywhere I want." I let my gaze dip down low. "And I've got a few ideas where I'd like to start."

Her cheeks flushed and she licked her lips. "And if I get it wrong?"

"Then you don't get kisses and you go home with Cory to study."

"I thought you hated him."

I gently shoved her down on the couch and laid my body on top of hers. "I do." I nibbled on her ear, biting a little bit harder than necessary. "So you better get the answers right."

She dug her nails into my shoulders. "Fine, but I need time to study."

"Time granted." I gave her a long, searching kiss, my tongue circling hers. When she kissed me back without hesitation, her body melding into mine more completely than her mouth, I almost forgot her need to study. Almost forgot part of my job was to make sure she didn't get distracted from her duties.

I was distracting her, and I had to stop.

With a groan, I pulled back and ended the kiss. "No more of that until our studying session starts." Hopping to my feet, I handed her the textbook and headed for the kitchen. "I'll be out on the patio, cooking you dinner."

She blinked up at me. "You cook?"

"Hell yeah, I cook. Better than that, I *grill*. I have one on the back porch." I gave her a cocky grin. "I'm more than a pretty face, Ginger."

"I already knew that," she said gently, meeting my eyes. "In fact, I knew it as soon as you opened your mouth and told me about yourself."

I froze. I had been mostly joking, but I'd dealt with the assumptions I was nothing more than a pretty boy with no goals all my life. Hell, right now I was playing the part of that exact type of person. She saw the real me? Knew I had goals and aspirations?

I cleared my throat and forced myself to stop standing there like an idiot. "Uh, good. Now off I go. Study hard, woman. I don't want you hanging out with Cory."

She laughed and cracked open the book while I set about getting ready to grill some burgers outside. But first, I pulled the vanilla ice cream out of the freezer and grabbed some milk. I scooped half the container into the blender, added milk, then threw in some Oreos for good measure. I had promised her a milkshake before realizing she had to study, and she'd damn well get it.

I switched the blender on, and she looked up at me. When she saw what I was making, her eyes went wide. After I switched off the blender, she said, "You make milkshakes too?"

"Yep." I pulled two red cups out of the cabinet. "And they're the best you'll ever have."

"Really?"

I emptied the contents of the blender into the glasses and stuck two straws into the cups. "See for yourself."

I crossed the room and gave her the glass with more in it. She took it from my hand, her fingers brushing mine as she did so. She wrapped her perfect lips around the straw and closed her eyes. And I was jealous of a fucking straw. "Holy crap, you're right."

"I know I am." I grinned. "Now get back to studying, or I'm taking it back."

She hugged it to her chest. "Never."

Her phone rang and she dug it out. "Hello?" Silence. "Yeah, of course I can help you. How about tomorrow after class?" More silence. "Sure. I'll see you then, Keith."

Keith. Who the hell was Keith?

She hung up and smiled at me. I arched a brow. "Should I be worried about this Keith guy?"

"Nope." She pushed her hair out of her eyes. "Remember the guy Cory was mean to?"

Nerd boy. "Yeah."

"He asked me to help him plan the booth the school is running at the Relay for a Cure taking place next week." She set down her phone. "I told him to contact me if he needed help. His parents died of cancer…and so did your mom. So I wanted to help."

I swallowed hard, moved by her compassion. "That's nice of you."

"It's nothing at all," she murmured distractedly, taking a sip of her milkshake. "I wish I could do more."

Her attention was on her book, so I left her alone. She was always so busy wishing she could do more that she didn't see she was doing enough. Her heart was big enough to encompass everyone around her, including me. I headed back into the kitchen, sipping my own milkshake. As I sliced the tomatoes and onions, I kept stealing glances at her. She sat on my couch, completely silent with her head bowed over the book, and

I couldn't get my mind off how much I liked this little bit of domesticity. I could get used to cooking while she studied.

And I could *definitely* get used to helping her study.

Hopefully when I told her the truth later tonight…it wouldn't be a thing of the past. I just wanted to let her study before the fighting began. Or so I kept telling myself.

Though studying hadn't been in my plans for the night, I hadn't missed the way she'd hesitated when Cory asked her if she wanted to study. I knew she was torn between doing what she *wanted* to do, and what she *should* do. Hell, I knew that particular dilemma all too well. So I made the decision for her. She could have both. She didn't need Cory to study.

She had me.

I might not be going to college to become a doctor, but I could certainly hold up a flashcard and help her cram words into her head. When I finished cooking dinner, I headed back inside. She was still on the couch, but she'd sprawled out across it and was balancing the book on her chest. I set the platter of burgers down on the kitchen counter, cracked open a beer, and took a long draw, my eyes on her the whole time. She'd finished her milkshake. Maybe I'd make her another one later. Anything to make her happy.

Her mouth moved silently as she read, but otherwise she was still. Yep. I definitely could get used to this. "Dinner's ready."

She jumped slightly and looked at me. "What?"

"Dinner." I motioned to the plate behind me. "It's ready."

"Oh." She set the book down and rubbed her temples. "I didn't realize I'd been reading that long."

"Yep, you were."

I stood in front of her and tugged her to her feet. She wrapped her arms around me once she was standing, then kissed the spot directly over my heart. I hugged her close, my heart speeding up at the soft kiss. I wished…

Wished these things would never change. Wished she wouldn't have to hate me. Wished I didn't have to tell her the truth tonight. The cowardly part of me wanted to hold back. Wait. But I knew it was the right thing to do, even if I didn't want to.

She rose up on tiptoes and kissed me. "Ready?"

Hell no. "Yeah, come on."

I grabbed her hand and led her into the kitchen. As we built our burgers, mine with mustard and ketchup, hers just ketchup, I kept stealing glances at her. She was tapping her foot as she created her meal, her lips moving silently. I had no idea if she was singing or citing medical terms, but either way…fucking adorable.

I grinned. "You singing a song over there?"

"Hm?" Her foot stopped mid-tap. "Maybe."

I scooped her up in my arms. "Don't stop. I love it."

Her cheeks tinged pink. "Really?"

"Really."

She pushed out of my arms and tucked her hair behind her ear. "Well, then, you better get used to it. I'm kind of a dork."

"I find you adorable."

She snorted. "That was a pretty adorable thing to say."

"We have to stick together."

She flopped down on the couch. "I have to eat this, then give me ten more minutes to study." She picked her burger up. "Then we play."

"Deal."

We ate in companionable silence. Once she was finished, I cleared our plates and busied myself with the dishes while she studied. I leaned against the counter and dried my hands. "How's it going over there?"

She glanced up at me. "I feel like I ate a house, but I think I'm ready."

I crossed the room and took the book out of her hands. I glanced down at the page and scrunched my eyebrows together. "Exciting stuff, huh?"

"It's anatomy." She stretched her arms over her head, baring a tiny strip of stomach. That was all I needed to want her. Hell, I didn't even need that. "None of it is exciting."

"I beg to differ," I said. I dropped to my knees in front of the couch and pushed her shirt back up. She sucked in a deep breath and held it, her bright blue eyes on me. "I find anatomy, yours in particular, quite exciting."

She arched a ginger brow at me. "Oh really?"

"Mmhm." I ran my fingers over the bare strip of skin and kissed it. "Really."

She threaded her hands through my hair, holding me there. I closed

132

my eyes and practically purred like a cat. This. Right here. I could live like this quite happily for the rest of my life. I nibbled on the patch of skin right under her belly button, tightening my grip on her hips when she started squirming.

"Don't stop doing that," she whispered, her eyes drifting shut. "Like, ever."

I didn't want to. "Are you sore?"

"No." Her cheeks turned red, and she opened her eyes to peek at me. "My lower extremities are fine."

"Look at you, showing off your medical vocabulary." I kissed her stomach, this time a little bit lower and grabbed her waistband. "Say something else the book taught you, and I'll kiss you again."

She spouted off some medical jargon I couldn't really understand, but it sounded legit. As long as I got to kiss her some more, I'd be happy. I undid her pants and pulled them off her legs. She had a dark purple satin thong on that just might be my favorite color in the whole world right now. I ran my fingers over the soft satin, dipping down to brush across her clit.

Her left leg fell to the floor, granting me better access. I took full advantage of this, slipping in between her legs and nibbling on her upper thigh. "Say something else or I'll stop."

"The way you make me feel…" she moaned. "Will soon cause a series of muscle contractions in the genital region…that will be accompanied by a sudden release of endorphins."

I blinked up at her, amusement threatening to overtake my desire. "Did you give me the medical definition of an orgasm?"

"Yes," she said through her teeth. "Now kiss me again."

I laughed and flicked my tongue over her clit, through her panties. "More."

"Argh." She yanked on my hair with just enough force to make my scalp sting. I liked that too. "When the endorphins rush to my head, I'll experience a sudden sensation of…"

I tugged down her panties, listening to her medical talk, but not really paying attention. At this point, I was a little bit too distracted by the fact that I wanted to make those endorphins she'd mentioned rush to her head. Repeatedly. When her thong fell to the floor along with her pants, I nibbled my way up her thigh. The closer I got to her clit, the faster she babbled. And the faster I forgot all about studying, and could only focus on her.

She whimpered and tried to urge me closer. I let her take control of me. Let her put me where she wanted me…but only because I wanted to be there. When I flicked my tongue against her clit, her legs jerked and she moaned. I liked the sounds coming out of her mouth. I needed more.

I rolled my tongue in a lazy circle, keeping my touch light. She dug her nails into my scalp and lifted her hips, begging for more. Her soft scent teased me. She smelled like lilies and something else. Something fruity and intoxicating and *her*. I gripped her hip with a trembling hand, holding her in place, and slipped my other hand in between her thighs. She said she wasn't sore, but I wasn't about to thrust inside of her without making certain of that fact.

I swirled my tongue a little harder this time, then gently slid a finger inside her. She was tight. Too tight. My cock ached to be buried inside her slick folds, but I ignored it. Her muscles clenched down on my finger, hard, and I increased the pressure of my mouth a fraction more.

"Don't stop, don't stop," she panted, over and over again, her nails digging into any piece of skin or scalp she could reach. She'd apparently given up on medical lingo. "*Finn.*"

As soon as she said my name, I pulled out and put another finger in, my tight hold on control slipping fast. I needed her too badly. Power like this wasn't good. Wasn't right. Yet, she held it over me without even trying. And worse yet? I didn't think I stood a chance at breaking free because I didn't even want to.

Her muscles clamped down on me, and she froze, her entire body rigid and held taught. Then she breathed my name again and collapsed to the couch, her breathing erratic. I stood up and crossed the room, going to the nightstand to grab protection. As I approached her, I undid my shorts. Her cheeks were flushed and her hair was messy. She looked fucking hot right now, right after I made her come.

She sat up and licked her lips. "Can I…can I do that to you?"

"Fuck yeah, you can." I kicked my shorts off and let them fall to the floor. All of the contents of my pockets spilled on the floor, but I didn't give a damn. All that mattered was *her*, and making her happy.

She reached out and trailed her fingers over my abs, her touch feather light. I closed my fists, nearly crushing the condom in the process. This might be the most torturous thing I'd ever put myself through, but it just might be the most pleasurable too. She pulled me closer, and I stumbled forward, letting her put me where she wanted me.

When I stood between her bare knees, she looked up at me through her lashes, almost as if she tested my reaction before she even started. I slit my eyes, making it look as if I wasn't watching her, but I'd be dead before I missed the sight of her mouth on my cock. She leaned in and flicked her tongue against the tip of me, and every muscle in my body jerked in response.

"Hm," she said, shifting her weight on the edge of the couch. She cupped my balls gently, running her fingertips over the sensitive skin. I hissed and tightened my jaw. She was going to kill me with her almost-there caresses. "Do you like that?" she asked, her tone throaty and whispery and oozing of sex.

"Yes," I managed to say through my swollen throat. "Do it again."

She grinned and rolled her tongue over the head of my cock, this time doing a complete circle. I'd tried to keep my hands to myself, but she broke my restraint. I dropped the condom on the floor and buried my hand in her red curls. I urged her closer, gently, in case she changed her mind.

She didn't.

Without warning, her mouth closed around me and she sucked me in, keeping the suction constant and the pressure *just right*. I looked down at her, watching her fuck me with her sweet red mouth, and couldn't look away. Each time she drew back, she took more of me in. And she didn't stop playing with my balls, increasing the pleasure by tenfold. My fingers flexed on her head, and I forced myself to stand still. To not thrust into her warm mouth...but it was the hardest thing in the world to do.

To just stand there, while I wanted to bend her over and fuck her senseless.

When she sucked me in more, making me grow horribly close to an orgasm, I placed my hands on her shoulders and pulled out of her mouth. My entire body tensed when she increased the suction, trying to keep me in, but I refused to come in her mouth. I needed to take her gently and sweetly. I needed to make love to her the way I would have if I'd known it was her first time last night.

"No more," I rasped.

"But—"

"*No.* If you keep doing that, I'll come." I ran my finger over her hard nipple, squeezing gently. "But when I come, I'll be buried deep inside of you. I won't accept anything else."

I ripped open the condom and slipped it on before bending down and carrying her to the bed. After laying her down gently, I lowered my body over hers and kissed her. She wrapped her arms around my neck and tentatively slid her tongue between my lips. It was the first time she kissed me like that, taken the initiative during sex, and the devastating effect it had on me was not missed.

My arms tightened around her, and I wished I could hold her close forever. Keep her safe forever. Make sure no one ever hurt her again. But *I'd* be the one hurting her. *I'd* be the one ruining the very thing I so cherished…her trust.

She curled her legs around my waist and lifted her hips. "Now," she demanded.

After taking a calming breath, I slowly inched inside of her, making sure to be gentle. To go slow. My body shook with the effort it took to hold back, but it was worth it. She deserved this and more. When I pulled out and moved inside of her even slower, she broke free of our kiss and looked up at me.

"What's wrong?"

I gritted my teeth when she dug her heels into my ass. "Nothing, babe."

"Then move." She arched her hips up while slamming her heels into my ass, and I surged inside of her another few inches.

Still, I held myself back, even though the sweat pouring down my forehead was stinging my eyes. "I…don't want to…hurt you."

"You won't." She cupped my cheeks and smiled up at me, her eyes shining with tears and something else. "I trust you."

I swallowed hard, the guilt threatening to overwhelm me. To choke me. I needed to tell her the truth. Now. "I have to tell you something. I'm—"

She curled her hands behind my neck and jerked me down, kissing me passionately. When she arched her hips up, taking me completely inside of her, I groaned and pressed even farther in. She increased the pressure of her lips, her teeth digging into my lower lip, and moved again.

"Carrie, I—"

"Tell me *later*," she demanded against my mouth. "I need you. Harder."

And that? That was my undoing.

I pulled out of her and thrust inside, sure and fast. She moaned and scratched her nails down my back, so I repeated the gesture. As I moved inside of her, something inside of me gave way, and I knew I would never go back to the way I'd been before her.

Her legs clamped around me even tighter, and her breathy cries grew quicker. She was close. So close. I reached down between us, never breaking the kiss, and pressed my thumb against her clit. She moaned into my mouth and pumped her hips up once, twice, then came—her body tensing all around me. I slid out of her and drove back inside, my own orgasm taking control of my body within seconds of her release.

I collapsed on top of her and buried my face in her neck. Taking a deep breath, I tried to remember the last time I'd felt this way after sex, but I came up empty. I had never felt so damned happy and satisfied after sex until…until Carrie.

I couldn't lose her. Not now. Not ever.

CHAPTER EIGHTEEN

Carrie

Now *that* was what I called a study session. I closed my eyes and took a nice, long breath. No matter how many times I read the why and how of sex, nothing compared to the reality of it. The reality of Finn touching my bare skin, moving inside of me and taking me higher and higher…

Yeah. Nothing.

I shivered and within seconds he had a blanket over me. He was always so considerate and compassionate. I shivered, he got a blanket. I yawned, he got me to go to sleep. I needed to study, he kidnapped me and forced me to do so. He was supportive, hot, and honest.

Cory didn't have a clue what he was talking about.

Finn was everything I wanted in a partner and more. I wouldn't grow to hate him for his "faults." Heck, I had yet to *see* any faults at all. Surely he had some, everyone did, but he hid them well. He stood up and headed for the trash can as I watched. The back view was almost as enticing as the front.

Almost.

He turned on his heel and scratched the back of his head. He always did that when he was nervous. I knew that about him. Why would he be nervous?

"You want another milkshake now?" he asked, his voice uncharacteristically hesitant. "We can sip on them while we finish studying."

"I already got my reward." I sat up, bringing the blanket with me. "What possible reason do I have to study now?"

He raised a cocky brow, and just like that, the Finn I knew was back. "Your grades? Your father? Your whole life?"

"Eh." I shrugged. "I like your methods of persuasion far better than those."

He grinned and crossed the room, then bent down to give me a lingering kiss before pulling away. His hand remained on my neck, his touch gentle. "Then far be it for me to leave you hanging. I'll go clean up, but we need to talk. Deal?"

"Talk? That sounds serious."

"Nah. It's just something I have to tell you." He gave me a lingering kiss, but seemed as if he didn't want to let go. As if something was wrong. "I'll be right back."

He gave me one last look before he headed into the bathroom, closing the door behind him. I let out a little sigh and slid out of the bed. As much as I'd like to remain here all night, he was right. I had studying to do, and I wasn't about to do that naked. I got dressed in my clothing, but couldn't find my shirt anywhere. When I spotted his red shirt lying on the floor, I grinned and slipped it over my head.

It smelled like him. Delicious.

As I hugged the shirt close to me, I caught sight of his phone lying on the floor under the table. I reached down and pulled it out, intending to set it down on the table so he wouldn't be looking for it later, but right when I picked it up, the screen lit up. I tried not to look. I really, really did. It's not like I wanted to be that girl who snooped through my boyfriend's phone for hints of other women in his life. And yet…

My gaze flitted to the closed bathroom door before it returned to the phone in my hand, and what I saw there made my heart stop and my stomach twist in tight, painful knots. As if the floor dropped out from underneath me, letting me crash to my death five hundred feet below. At first it was the all capital letters in the text message that drew my attention. Dad texted in all caps, as did most older people. But then I looked at the number, and my entire body went all weak and shaky with disbelief. Confirmation came swift and hard, like a kick in the stomach. I'd know that phone number anywhere.

I read the text again.

Have you seen her today? Is she studying with Cory?

For a second, I hoped I picked up the wrong phone. That I held my own phone in my hand, and not his. That would be so much better than the alternative. So much better than knowing that the first person I trusted enough to let get close to me, the first man I could possibly see myself falling in love with, was nothing more than a spy sent by Dad.

Oh my God. I was such a fool. I'd fallen for it all, without even questioning why a guy like Finn would want me. Without a second thought or a backward glance. Now I was staring the truth in the face. Dad was texting Finn, and Finn was hanging out with me because he *had* to, not because he *wanted* to. He'd been sent here to babysit me, and I'd been dumb enough to believe he might actually be interested in me.

That he actually cared.

I blinked back tears when the bathroom door opened, and Finn came out wearing a pair of boxers. "About that talk, how about if we—?"

He scanned the room until he found me, and then he broke off midsentence. He looked first at the phone in my hand, then at my face. He paled and stopped walking midstride. He opened his mouth, closed it, then tried for a casual tone of voice. "You okay, babe?"

Okay? No, I was not okay. I was horrible. Terrible. Ready to cry and scream and kill Dad for doing this to me. For sending Finn to watch me. For sending a man I could so easily fall in love with, then ripping him away from me without a second thought.

And I was even madder at myself for falling for it.

"Was it all a lie?" I asked, my voice miraculously even, even if it came out soft. I slowly lifted my head. "Tell me the truth for once. Was it all a *lie?*"

He flinched and seemed to break out of a trance. He crossed the room and held his hands out in front of him. "No. Please, let me explain."

"*No.*"

I stumbled to my feet and backed away from him. I couldn't bear his touch after all of this. After he…oh, God. No. I couldn't even think about it right now. I tossed his phone onto the couch, not wanting to hold it another second. In some sick way, I almost blamed the phone for all of this. If I hadn't picked it up, I wouldn't be feeling like the world had stopped spinning.

"Carrie, I didn't pretend to like you. It's not history repeating itself."

"Oh my God, you know all about that too?" I covered my face with my hands. Somehow, him knowing all about my embarrassing past made it worse. So much worse. "Did you get a file on me? All my dirty little secrets?"

He flinched. "Yes."

"Unbelievable." I swallowed hard, my head spinning so fast I couldn't even keep up. "I can't believe it was all a lie. Do you have any idea how much I liked you?"

"Please. Let me explain."

My heart twisted so hard it hurt. "Explain what, exactly? How you lied to me to get close to me? How you pretended to care about me? Or maybe how you slept with me because my dad told you to?"

"*No.*" His voice broke. "It's not what it looks like."

"So you're not watching me for my father and reporting back to him?"

He flinched. "I am. But—"

"There are no *buts* in this situation. None at all." I let out a harsh laugh. "God, I'm such an idiot."

"It wasn't all a lie. Not the way I feel about you."

"Don't even go there." I stared at the bed, the sheets still rumpled from our recent bout of sex. Swallowing hard, I covered my face with my hands. My stomach lurched, and I swallowed back the bile threatening to rise. "I can't believe I…we…"

"Carrie, don't think like that. What we did there has nothing to do with your father," he said, his voice raspy. His hand rested on my shoulder. "I wasn't even supposed to—"

I shrugged off his hand and dug my nails into my palms. The pain was a welcome distraction from the stronger, more mind-numbing pain he was causing me. "Don't touch me! I trusted you. Actually *trusted* you."

His shoulders drooped and he held out his hands. "I know. I'm sorry. You have no idea how sorry I am."

"I don't want to hear a single apology." I pushed my hair out of my eyes and shook my head in disbelief. "What you felt or pretended you felt means nothing to me anymore. Just tell me everything from the beginning. How do you know my father?"

"I work for him." He clenched his hands at his sides. A muscle in his jaw ticked, but otherwise he looked completely unaffected. "I was sent here to watch over you because I'm the youngest in the security squad."

"Wait…what?" He couldn't possibly work for Dad. I'd have remembered seeing *him* around the house. "I've never seen you there before. I know all the guys."

"I started working for him while you were abroad. When you came back, the senator hid me. His plan was already in motion," he said, his shoulders straight and his head held high. "I didn't want to do it, but he promised me a higher position and a raise if I stuck it out for a year."

Stuck it out for a year. As if it would be so horrible spending time with me. At least he had found a pleasing way to pass the time for himself. Seduce the senator's daughter and laugh about it after. I swallowed past the tears threatening to escape. "Wow. So you get paid for banging his daughter behind his back. That must be poetic justice, huh?"

"No." He reached for me, but before he could touch skin, I stepped back and gave him a dirty look. His hands fell back to his sides. "It wasn't like that. It's not like that. If he knew what I did, I'd be fired, and so would my father. He works for your dad too."

"Your father?" I eyed him, trying to figure out who his father could possibly be. There was only one man with a son who could be Finn's age, and he was the one I liked the best, of course. "Oh my God. Not Larry?"

Finn flinched. "Yes."

"But his son isn't called Finn. He's Griffin…oh…" I sank onto the couch, my legs trembling. "Oh my God."

"I didn't lie about my name. Finn is my nickname, and I kept my mother's name because she was worried her side of the family would die out. There were lots of Hannigans, but no more Corams." He tugged on his hair and shook his head. "I didn't want to lie to you. I didn't like doing this. I'm sorry."

It hurt enough knowing he'd been lying this whole time. To know that he hadn't really liked me or even cared about me. Hearing him apologize for the farce was too much. "Stop *saying* that."

"But I am sorry."

I ignored him. I had to keep focusing on finding out the why and how, or I would break. I needed cold, hard facts. "How often did you have to report back to him? Did he…?" I paused, scared to ask this next question. Scared of what the answer might be. "Did he tell you to pretend to want to be with me? To act like you were interested in me?"

"*No.*" He dropped to his knees in front of me, his gaze latched with mine. "I swear to you that nothing between us was a lie on that front. Not the friendship. Not the sex. Not a single conversation. I fell for you, and I fell hard. There was no fighting or pretending. None of it was a ploy to get close to you."

"You're telling me that you came up to me on the beach simply because you *had* to know me?" I leveled a look on him and when he flushed I had my answer. "Exactly. Contrary to what I've shown you so far, I'm not gullible."

"I know you're not, but I'm telling you the truth." He looked toward the bed, then back at me. "I care about you, Carrie. More than I care about my job or myself. More than I should ever have let myself care for you."

"Stop saying that," I demanded, covering my ears. I couldn't believe him. Not ever again. "You're a liar and I don't trust you, so just *stop*."

"I know." He nodded and stumbled back from me, his mouth held taught. "I'm sorry."

If he said he was sorry one more time, I'd scream. Literally scream. I pulled my phone out and started typing Dad's number. This was over right now. "I'm calling him."

"I know." He paled even more. "Go ahead. Tell him how much I fucked up."

I paused with my finger over the screen. He'd said something about his father earlier. If I called Dad, would Larry get fired? "So what happens if I call my dad and tell him I know what he did? Will he send you home?" I hovered with my finger over the send button.

His shoulders drooped and he fell back against the wall. "Yeah. I'm sure I'll be fired, and you'll never have to see me again."

Still, I hesitated. "Why did it have to be a lie? Why you too?"

He took a shaky breath. "Carrie, please." He dragged his hands down his face. "I swear to you I didn't mean to hurt you. I tried so hard not to fall for you. To push you away. But I couldn't."

I swallowed hard. "Are you really twenty-three?"

"Yes."

"Are you really a Marine?"

He dropped his head into his hands and sighed. "Yes." He lifted his head. "I told you, the only lies between us were the fact that I didn't tell you why I was here." His jaw flexed and he pushed to his feet. "The rest is real. I am still your friend and your—"

I laughed harshly. "You're not my friend. You were never my friend. It was all an assignment."

He flinched. "At first, maybe, but not now. Not for a long time."

My heart squeezed so tightly I couldn't breathe. Oh, how I wanted to believe him. How much my heart begged for him to be telling me the truth. But that's exactly why I couldn't. I'd fallen for his lies once. I wouldn't do it again. "Just stop. Stop the act. I'm not standing here so you can lie to me. All I want is information."

He just stared at me. "What else do you want to know?"

Everything. Nothing. What I really wanted was for us to go back in time to a few minutes ago. Back to when I'd been blissfully unaware of the fact that Finn had been spending time with me because he had to.

"How often do you report to him?"

"Every day," he said. "I watch you and report back to him every day. I'm supposed to keep doing so throughout the next year."

I clung to the table next to me, giving him my back. He'd been following me. Studying my motions like some sick stalker or something. All in the name of Dad's twisted need to control me. To control my life. The thought left a sick taste in my mouth. "Why did you let me get this close when you knew it would come to this?"

"I couldn't stop myself." His footsteps crept closer. "I fell for you hard, Ginger."

I whirled and shoved him backward as hard as I could. So hard my palms hurt, but it still wasn't hard enough. I would never be able to hurt him as much as he hurt me. "Don't you dare call me that now. Not ever again. You don't have that right anymore."

"Fine." He didn't back down at all, his eyes flashing. "Go ahead and call it in. Tell your father I failed. Tell him to fire me."

"So he can send another man out here in your place?"

He shrugged, the motions carefree, but the look in his eyes did nothing to hide the tension swirling inside him. "The next one will probably be better at keeping his hands to himself."

I curled my fists. "Unlike you?"

"Unlike me." He met my eyes again, challenging me. "Go ahead. You know you want the satisfaction of seeing me canned. I can see it in your eyes. You hate me. Get your revenge."

I didn't hate him. This would be *so* much easier if I did.

I swallowed past the words dying to come out. The ones that begged him to not really be a spy or a traitor. The ones that would kill my pride with one great, sweeping blow. I should do exactly what he said—call Dad. But if I did that, Dad would simply send another spy in. At least with Finn, I knew what to expect.

Was that reason enough to keep him around? I couldn't imagine having to see him every day after this. To be reminded of how much an idiot I had been, time and time again. "What will happen to your dad?"

Finn's façade crumbled. Guilt took its place, and he yanked on his hair. "He'll lose his big pension, but that's my responsibility to bear, not yours. Do it."

I liked his dad, but that wasn't why I hesitated. That wasn't why I wasn't pulling the trigger, so to speak. No, something besides empathy drove me. Something uglier and more self-serving. "You want me to do it. You want to be sent away, don't you?"

He held his hands out to his sides. "I don't know what you're insinuating."

"Ah, but I think you do." I pointed the phone at him, laughing lightly. "Is the guilt too much for you? Can't stand seeing the effects of your lies? Ready to run?"

"Yes, it's too much," he cried. "I hurt you and I'm *sorry*. I know you hate me, and I know why, but just fucking end it already, or I will."

I shook my head. "No, you're going to stay. You're going to watch me forget all about you. Watch me move on. You're going to do your duty, and you're going to report back to him like the good little spy you are."

He gave a harsh laugh. "Why the hell would I do that?'

"To save your father." I tilted up my chin. "And because you owe me. You made me want to be with you, then you turned out to be nothing but a fraud."

His face crumpled and he sank down on the couch. He looked as if he gave up. Stopped caring or hoping. "Fine. I'll do it."

"Good."

"I really am sorry," he rasped, his head low. I couldn't see his face, but the sincerity in his voice almost broke me. "I hope you know that."

I tensed, my whole body aching to go to him. To comfort him, of all things. I was really messed up in the head from all this crap. "The only thing I know now is what my father's spy looks like, and I want to *keep* knowing. You'll do your duty, but you'll stay the hell away from me. I don't want to see you, smell you, or even hear you. Just report back to my dad while leaving me the hell out of it."

He lifted his head, and the vulnerability I'd caught a glimpse of was gone. "I can't follow you around, watching you flirt with other men. Not anymore."

"You should have thought of that before we did what we did." I collected my books and lifted my phone to my ear. "Yes, I'd like a cab, please." I told the operator my location and hung up. "Text him and tell him I studied and went to bed early."

Finn picked up his phone and quickly typed. Then he threw it down on the couch. "You have no idea what you're starting here. You should report me immediately."

"I should, but I won't." I looked out the window, waiting for the cab.

"Why not?"

I forced a shrug. "Because I want to know what to expect. Because I'm more like my father than I realized. I like being in control too."

"With me, you've never been in control."

"Yeah, I know that now." I blinked back tears, refusing to show him how much I hurt. Refusing to show him my weakness—him. "But from now on, I will be."

I hurriedly gathered the rest of my things, including my shirt I couldn't find earlier, and he stayed quiet. Thank God. I couldn't pretend like I wasn't dying inside any longer. Couldn't pretend he hadn't broken my heart, when he had. If he knew how hard I had fallen, he would never leave me alone. Never let me move on. And I *needed* to move on.

The cab beeped from outside, and I turned to face him. He watched me with a weird mixture of apprehension and longing. "I don't want to see you watching me. Just do your job, and stay out of my way."

When I headed for the door, he stood up. "I'm sorry, Gi—" He broke off. "Carrie. I really am."

I paused with my hand on the knob, squeezing it so tightly my knuckles hurt. "So am I."

I opened the door and walked out of his apartment for the last time. I had no intention of ever stepping foot inside it again. I didn't want to see him again either. Didn't need the reminder that he had stolen my heart and then stomped it into the dirt.

If only he had buried it too.

CHAPTER NINETEEN

Finn

A few days later, and a hell of a lot of thinking and heartache later, I grabbed my phone, jotted off a quick text to Senator Asshole letting him know his daughter was still alive, and then grabbed my surfboard. It had been too long since I'd been out in the ocean alone. Too long, especially since it was pretty much the only place that no one bugged me or talked to me or told me to fuck off.

The past few times I'd come had been with Carrie, but those days were obviously over. Shit, we *were* over, and I was miserable because of it. I missed her. Missed having her in my arms. Missed the man I was with her. She made me better. Different. Whole.

But not anymore. I was destined to walk around half-filled for the rest of my miserable life. With a sigh, I juggled my board and closed the door, making sure to lock it, then headed for my bike. After sliding my surfboard into the special slot I'd had added on to the side earlier this week, I revved the engine and pulled away from the curb. The wind blew through my hair since I hadn't grabbed my helmet, and I took a deep breath.

I hadn't expected to miss her so damn much once she left me. It had been a relationship born out of lies and pretenses, but now I couldn't stop thinking about her. And she probably hadn't even thought of me once since the other day, besides to curse me out.

In all three languages she spoke.

She'd told me she could speak three languages. I also knew she let out a tiny little snore every once in a while when she slept. She gave almost all of her allowance to the poor and rarely spent any money. She liked her milkshakes creamy, not watery. I hadn't read any of that in her file. There was so much I knew about her that her damn file didn't know. We had surpassed the working relationship I'd meant to maintain a long time ago. But to her, that's all I'd ever be.

The guy who was sent to spy on her by her daddy.

Ever since she told me to leave her alone, she'd spent almost every passing second with Cory. They ate together. Walked together. Studied together. They seemed to be attached at the hip, and it was driving me insane with jealousy each time I saw them. Ripping my chest open until a tiny little monster grew bigger than fucking Godzilla. A part of me was sure she was hanging with that loser just to hurt me.

But she didn't believe me about how much I cared for her—refused to believe me. So she wouldn't be trying to hurt me if she thought I was just talking to her for the job, which only made it worse. It meant that every time she laughed at something Cory said and hugged the jerk closer, it was *real*. It wasn't some scheme to torture me.

She actually liked the little fucker.

I parked my bike and slid off the seat. After taking off my shirt, I put on my wetsuit, my eyes on the blue water. It looked particularly impetuous today. Good. I was in the mood to get tossed around. Hard. I headed for the beach, excitement taking over for the first time since Carrie had broken it off with me. I would get out there, ride a few waves, and forget all about—

"Why are *you* here?" Carrie asked from somewhere behind me.

I paused midstride, my heart leaping at the sound of her voice. God, I had missed hearing that sass in her tone. That spark of something that no one else could possibly bring out in me. I forced a neutral expression to my face and turned to face her.

She wore her wetsuit, but had it down around her waist, and her unruly hair was pulled back in a ponytail. She had big bags under her eyes, as if she'd been sleeping poorly. I forced my attention to return to the ocean, and said, "I'm going to church."

"Haha." Out of my peripheral vision, I saw her eye my surfboard, her blue eyes cold and her lips pressed tightly together. Her small spattering of freckles danced across her nose, and her curly red hair already whipped across her forehead. She looked perfect. "Very funny, but don't quit your day job of stalking college girls."

"It wasn't supposed to be funny or a joke. This *is* my version of church." I felt stupid for letting her know how I really felt about surfing, but there was no going back now. I'd already opened my big fat mouth. I shrugged and tried my best to look like I didn't give a damn what she thought about me. "When I'm out there, it's just me, God, and the ocean. No one else can interfere with me except Mother Nature herself."

She nibbled on her lower lip. "That's awfully profound for a surfer boy."

"I'm more than just a surfer boy, but you already knew that, didn't you?"

She crossed her arms. "I'm going surfing today, so you can't go."

"Excuse me?" I laughed at her audacity. "I hate to break it to you, but you don't own the ocean, Princess."

She stiffened. "No, but you work for my family and I don't want you out there with me, so you have to listen to me. I'm your boss."

Okay, that stung a little bit. It would be a lie to say it hadn't. "The hell you are. I work for your father."

Her face turned red. "Just go away. I don't want to be out there with you."

"Then surf farther south. Or north, for all I care." I gestured toward the ocean with my board. "This is my beach, and I'm not leaving it. Not even for you."

"I thought no one owned the beach," she called out, taunting me. Even her stance was aggressive, her feet spread wide and her eyes flashing with anger. She wanted a fight, and she wanted it bad.

I wouldn't rise to the bait. Wouldn't fight. But I sure as hell wouldn't back down either. "They don't, but this is the beach my mother took me to every weekend as I grew up. It's where we had our last night together, before she was gone forever. And it's the beach I rode my first wave on, with her by my side. I'm sure as hell not leaving it because you hate me."

I brushed past her, fully intending to leave her standing on that beach alone, but her soft word stopped me. "Wait."

"What now?" I asked, my entire body tense.

"I'm sorry. You're right." I turned to face her, and she swept her hair out of her face with a frustrated sigh. "I'm being a bitch. Just because I can't stand the sight of you doesn't mean I get to tell you to leave."

"Such a heartfelt apology."

She lifted a shoulder. "It's the best I can do, considering."

"May I go now, *boss lady*?" I cocked my head toward the ocean. "I'd like to enjoy the type of solitude only the ocean can give me before it's too late."

"You never mentioned wanting solitude out there before."

"That's because I was with you," I reminded her.

She cocked her head. "Why did you take me, if you didn't like going out there with other people?"

"Because with you? I didn't mind."

I headed for the ocean once more, leaving her standing there. She wouldn't believe me anyway, so there was no point in waiting to see if she replied. She'd just accuse me of running a play on her, or trying to win her over so I could babysit her better. I wasn't in the mood to get my heart trampled again.

Just my body.

I almost made it to the water before I got interrupted again. I bit back a curse when a blonde in a skimpy bikini stopped me. "Hey. Remember me?"

I scanned her face. Nope. I didn't. "Uh…?"

"I work at Surf's Up," she said, punching my arm lightly. "I helped you pick out your girlfriend's surfboard."

"She's not my girlfriend," I said, my eyes automatically scanning the beach for Carrie. She stood a few yards away, her own gaze on me…and the blonde at my side. "We're not even friends anymore, really."

Her nostrils flared. Could she hear us? She looked ready to kill someone. I wasn't sure if her target was the girl or me—maybe both.

"Oh, well, I like the sound of that." She trailed her fingers over my tattoo, giving me a flirtatious smile. "I like your ink. What's it mean?"

I hated when girls asked that. It wasn't any of their damn business what my ink meant. "Thanks, and nothing. It's just ink."

"Oh. Hot."

That was…deep. About as deep as a puddle. I cleared my throat and looked at Carrie again. Her fists were clenched at her sides. Was she jealous? Nah. Not possible. "You surf?"

The blonde laughed and punched me again. Why did girls think that was sexy? I only liked one girl hitting me, but she didn't even want to touch me right now. Or ever. "No, I just help out at the store, and I date a lot of surfers. *Only* surfers."

Before I could reply, Carrie walked up to some shirtless guy. She smiled at him and handed him sunscreen. The jerk smiled back at her and Carrie turned her back to the guy. When the jerk squirted sunscreen on his hands and massaged it over Carrie's shoulders, I clenched my teeth. Carrie laughed at something the guy said, slapping his arm lightly. The jerk didn't seem to mind either.

"You've got to be kidding me," I murmured. "I'm going to kill her."

Blondie shot me the dirtiest look ever. "Just friends, huh?" Then she was gone.

I stood there, trying to figure out what the hell had just happened.

Carrie. That's what happened.

She thanked the helpful guy, then headed for the water, pulling up her wetsuit. I caught up to her within seconds. "What was that all about?"

"What?" She blinked at me innocently, but the smirk was harder to hide. "I needed sunscreen."

"Under your wetsuit?"

"Sure. You can never be too careful." She shrugged. "Did you have fun with Bambi over there?"

And just like that, I relaxed. "You're jealous."

She snorted and snorted again. As if such a preposterous statement required a double snort. "I am *not*."

"Oh. So, if I go out there and flirt with her, you won't give a damn?"

"Good luck with that. She probably hates you now." Carrie splashed into the water, sending droplets my way. "As a matter of fact, I might have to watch you get rejected. It'll be funny and good for your ego."

I stared at her. "Is that a challenge?"

"No." She eyed me. "Knowing you, she'd be in your bed by nighttime. You'd like that, wouldn't you?"

I tensed. She made me sound like a manwhore, and I wasn't. I wasn't a virgin, but I didn't sleep around either. "Because I've given you reason to believe I'm a manwhore?"

"Stop asking me rhetorical questions."

I gripped my board tighter than I should have, but I couldn't help it. I wanted to scream. "That wasn't rhetorical. I'd *love* to know why you think I'd bring her home with me mere days after we broke up."

"You brought me home."

I rolled my eyes and fought against the huge wave trying to knock me down. "Oh, well, then I must be a whore. If I'll bring you home, anyone will do."

She whirled on me. "Yeah, pretty much."

"Wave."

"*What?*"

A wave knocked into her, throwing her in my arms. I caught her, stumbling back a bit before I caught my own balance again. As soon as I gained my footing, she quickly shoved out of my arms. "Wave," I repeated.

"I noticed." She shoved her damp hair out of her face. "Thanks for the warning."

I couldn't tell if she was being sarcastic, so I nodded. "Might want to face outward from now on."

"Gee, thanks for the pro tip." Another wave crashed into us, and she stumbled back. I started to reach for her elbow, but she shot me a supersonic death glare. "I'm fine. Stop protecting me."

"It's my job. Don't want my help? Go over there." I pointed to a crowded spot in the ocean. "They won't give a damn if you wipe out."

She lifted her chin. "I'm staying here."

"Thought you didn't want to be near me."

Did her chin go even higher? Yep. It did. "I don't, but I refuse to run away just because you're here."

"Lucky me," I drawled.

Another big wave came, and she stumbled backward again. I swallowed the sense of premonition creeping up. The ocean was perfect for me today, but for a novice like Carrie, it could be a deathtrap. If she got taken under by a monster wave, I might not be able to reach her in time.

She glanced at me out of the corner of her eye. "Why do you look like someone might take away your favorite toy?"

I shook my head. "I was quiet. That's all." Another wave came, and

154

I made a big show of getting knocked back. "Wow, the waves are pretty rough. Maybe we shouldn't surf today."

She eyed all the other surfers, who were smiling and laughing and catching waves. They weren't exactly helping my cause. "They all look fine to me."

"They're idiots for being out here in this. I don't know what I was thinking." I grabbed her elbow. "Let's go back to the shore."

She jerked free. "No."

"Carrie—"

"*No.*" She kept going farther into the ocean. I could tell by the way she stomped through the water that I wouldn't win this one. "Now go away. You've got an appointment with Jesus, and he doesn't like to be kept waiting."

I squared my jaw. "It's too dangerous for a newbie like you."

"For your charge, you mean?" She glanced back at me over her shoulder. "Oh well. You'll be earning your keep today, *guard.*"

Fine. She wanted to be like that? She could be like that. I followed her, muttering under my breath, "After you, *boss.*"

Looked as if my day of planned solitude was off. I wouldn't get the brief time of no one bossing me around or bugging me. Instead, I'd have to save her life time and time again. If she went and tried to drown on me, I'd rescue her and then throttle her little ass for being so damn reckless.

CHAPTER TWENTY

Carrie

Once I got out into the ocean, I straddled my board, determined not to let Mr. Worrywart take the fun out of my morning. It had been a long, painful week and I needed to let go. Needed to relax. But then he came. I knew there was an easy fix to this annoyance. Knew I could swim away from him, and our entire interaction would be over. But if I did that, he might start flirting with Bimbo Bambi again. And for some reason I didn't want to name right now, thank you very much, I didn't want him talking to her.

Or looking at her.

Or thinking about her.

No big deal, right? Right.

He paddled closer to me and gave me a long, hard look. "So, where's Lover Boy today?"

Lover Boy? As if. "Don't you call him Golden Boy?"

"Yeah, I did, but I changed my mind lately. Where is he?"

"He's not the surfing type," I said simply.

The truth was, I hadn't invited him. Why would I? This wasn't his thing. It was mine. Besides, I had been spending way too much freaking time in his company lately. He was a perfect gentleman. He didn't do a single thing wrong. Never lost his temper or fought with me. Never called me annoying nicknames. He treated me like a princess.

Turns out, I didn't like being treated like a princess.

I liked annoying surfer boys who lied to me.

"No kidding," he said dryly. "I never would've guessed that."

"Talk to Jesus, not me."

"I can't. I only talk to him when I'm alone."

I saw a wave coming in the distance, but quickly realized it would be too big. I knew not to ride the huge ones. Knew I was a novice at best. He worried for nothing. Small correction—he worried about me because he was *paid* to do so.

"You get this one."

He hesitated. "You going to be okay alone?"

"Yes, yes." I rolled my hand in a sweeping gesture. "Just *go*."

He gave me one last look before paddling forward. Despite my annoyance with him, I couldn't help but watch in admiration. He sliced through the wave as if he was born on a surfboard, and he made it look damned sexy. Effortless too. I could sit here all morning, watching him surf.

Talking to him. Fighting with him. Kissing him…

God, what was wrong with me? Why was I still thinking about him like this after what I'd found out? After knowing he'd been paid to get close to me? To fool me into liking him. I was sick. I would never have believed myself possible of such weakness before Finn.

By the time he made his way back, I was thoroughly disgusted with myself. He grinned at me and shook his head like the dog he was. Droplets landed on my nose, and I swiped them off. "That was a great one."

I clucked my tongue and kept staring straight ahead. Not looking at him. "I saw."

"You okay?" he asked after a moment's hesitation.

"I'm freaking wonderful."

I checked over my shoulder, but it didn't look like any waves of an appropriate size would be coming anytime soon. Maybe he'd been right, and I should've left, but then I'd have to admit defeat to him…and I wasn't willing to do that. Not ever again, if I could help it.

He looked out at the ocean too, his brow furrowed. "We could just head in. You can try tomorrow."

"Not happening. I'm riding at least one wave before I go home."

"You don't have to prove anything to me," he said, his voice low. "We both know you're good at surfing, but that's exactly why you can't take one of these. You know you're not ready."

"Don't tell me what I can and can't do," I said, my grip on my board tight. "I'll take whatever wave I want, whenever I want it, and you can't do a darn thing to stop me."

"The hell I can't," he snapped, throwing his left leg over the side of his board. "Watch me."

"Stop right there," I warned, holding my hand out. If he touched me, I would be done for. I couldn't ever feel his touch again, because if I did, I might just forget all about the lies. I might not care anymore. "I'm warning you."

"Or what? You'll yell at me some more?"

He hopped off his board and started swimming to me. Oh God. I had to get away. Needed to escape. He'd triggered the fight-or-flight response in my system, and I chose flight. I glanced behind me just in time to see a wave forming. It was bigger than usual, but nothing too insane.

He must've seen the look in my eyes, because his own went wide. "Don't do it, Carrie. You can't—"

"The hell I can't," I echoed back at him, paddling forward.

"Carrie, no!" he yelled. He leapt on his board, clearly trying to catch the wave with me.

I had no idea if he succeeded, because I was trying to keep my balance since the "not so big wave" turned out to be *humongous*. I was an idiot for trying to ride it. Within seconds, I wiped out, the salt water stinging my eyes and filling my mouth. I hadn't held my breath. Hadn't been ready. I'd been too busy worrying about him and what he was doing.

I went under hard, and my tethered surfboard hit me in the back of the head. Stars swam before my eyes, but I tried to wait out the torrential wave like Finn had taught me. I got thrown around like a limp rag doll in a washing machine. Oh, God, I was going to die out here in the cold Pacific Ocean, all because I'd been too much of a fool to know when to call it quits. Too darn full of pride for my own good.

What would happen to Finn when he realized I wasn't coming back up? How could it be that we would never see each other again? There was so much more to talk about. Things to figure out and fights to have. I wasn't ready to die yet.

A hand closed around my wrist, yanking me up to the surface. Before I could so much as blink in surprise, my face cleared the water. Finn took a deep gulping breath, then disappeared below the ocean.

"Finn!" I screamed, paddling around in a frantic circle. "*Finn!*"

Nothing. He was gone.

I took a deep breath and sank under water, but I only just got my head under when someone from behind me yanked me back up. I let out a broken sob and broke free. "No! He's missing!"

I dove back under the water, but my captor caught my arm again. I swung a fist at him, refusing to be held back when Finn needed help. Refusing to let him die because he'd saved me.

"Jesus, Ginger," Finn said, shaking me. "I'm right here." He shook me again. "Carrie, I'm here."

I stopped fighting and took a deep, ragged breath. He was here. Alive. I burst into tears and threw my arms around his neck. He hugged me tight and kissed my temple, then my cheek. I held my breath, waiting to see if he'd take it further. If he'd kiss me. He seemed to hesitate, his lips hovering near mine. So close I could move just a tiny bit, and we would be touching.

But I held my breath for nothing, because he didn't move that inch, and neither did I. "Sh. It's okay. You're okay. I got you."

I choked on a sob and hit his shoulder. "I wasn't worried about *me*, you idiot."

"Well, you should have been." The calming tone he'd been using disappeared and was replaced by the hard, cold tone he'd never used on me before. "Fuck, Carrie. You could've died. All because of what?"

"Because of you!" I hit him again, but he didn't even flinch. "Because you won't leave me alone! I had to get away."

He flinched. "Well, from now on, I will. Believe me, I will," he rasped, his voice breaking on the last word.

He started for the sand. Part of me wanted to continue this fight out here in the ocean, but the other part of me wanted to get him safely to the shore. I had almost *lost* him. Really lost him. When he'd sunk under the water, I had gone insane with worry. And the way I felt at the mere idea of losing him told me something I should have known already.

I wasn't over him. I might never be completely over him.

As soon as my feet cleared the hectic rush of the water, he let go of me and dragged his hands down his face. "Jesus."

"What did you mean out there?" I asked, unable to stop myself. "About leaving me alone?"

He turned to me, his face drawn and ragged looking. "I didn't know you hated me so much you'd rather die than surf next to me."

I swallowed hard. That wasn't it at all. I didn't hate him. That was the problem. "I can't surf with you or be your friend. I don't even want to see you. It hurts too much."

He paled. "It hurts me too. You have no idea how damn much it hurts because you think this was all a game to me. It wasn't. And seeing you every day? It *kills* me."

I pressed a hand to my heart, the pain he'd sent slicing through it with his words was almost knee buckling. Okay. So maybe he really had cared about me, at one point. But it didn't change the fact that he'd lied to me. Or the fact that he'd been spying on me for money. For my father. I cared about him too, but nothing could change any of those things… no matter how much I wished it could.

Because I really did.

"Then it's settled." My throat was so swollen with pending tears that I could barely speak, let alone breathe. "It's better if we avoid places we used to hang out. You watch me from a distance as you have been this week, and we don't come out here anymore. Don't see each other."

He cleared his throat. "You won't see me again. Goodbye."

Wait. I couldn't do this. Couldn't let him walk away from me. There had to be a way to at least be friends. Or to try. "Finn, I—"

"Don't. Just don't." He shrugged. Actually shrugged, as if he didn't care at all. "It doesn't even matter, does it? We didn't ever stand a chance."

My throat ached from the tears I held back. The tears I wasn't sure I could hold back anymore all because I'd gone and fallen for my bodyguard. "Not with all the lies."

"Right." He laughed. "It was all a mistake. One huge fucking mistake, but it's easy to fix. As easy as walking away." He gave me one last long, hard look, then said, "Goodbye, Carrie."

"Finn…" I held my hand out, but he'd already turned his back on me.

He walked away, his back stiff and his head held high. The tone in his voice was so…so final. As if he meant what he said, unlike me. And I had a feeling he would be better at sticking to his word than I was too.

I wouldn't see him again.

CHAPTER TWENTY-ONE

Finn

Three agonizing weeks later, I sat on a bench, an open technology textbook perched on my knee and a hat pulled low over my head. All part of my incognito spy outfit. That way if she saw me, I wouldn't be instantly recognizable. It had worked so far. We hadn't spoken since that day in the water, and she hadn't looked at me even once.

I'd seen to it.

It was five o'clock, and the soft ocean breeze calmed my otherwise fraught nerves. Soon she would come out. I'd been following her around. Watched her help out at the cancer race. Watched her go to the soup kitchen, even though I stood outside of it now. Watched her give away clothes and food and money—but not once had she done anything fun for herself. She just studied and helped and volunteered.

No fun. No games. Hardly ever any smiles.

If I didn't know better, I'd think she missed me. But she didn't.

Carrie came out of the building five minutes earlier than usual, her hair frizzy and her face lowered. Even with her hair sticking up every which way to Sunday, she was the picture of perfection. A breath of fresh air on a hot, smoggy day. I tensed as she walked right past me, but she didn't even glance my way.

She pressed a hand to her stomach, her steps quickening. Was that a groan I heard? No, I must've been imagining things. I stood up, tucking the book into my bag as I shadowed her steps. She walked faster than usual, but had some odd kind of shuffle to her step. Like a supersonic zombie. What was wrong with her?

When she slapped a hand over her mouth and ran for the cover of the bushes that lined either side of the walkway, I got my answer. She was sick. I sprinted after her, my stomach twisting in response to the retching sounds that came from her. Any time someone vomited, I always felt sympathy nausea. Sometimes, that sympathy turned into my own bout of puking my guts up.

So, as a rule, I avoided people who were throwing up, but this was *Carrie*.

I dropped to my knees at her side, grabbing her hair and holding it back from her face so she wouldn't get it dirty. She didn't even bother to look my way or tell me to fuck off. She just kept puking. A cold sweat broke out on my forehead, but I tightened my grip on her hair and made sure to breathe through my mouth—not my nose.

Shallow, slow breaths.

"Sh. It's okay." With my free hand, I rubbed her back in wide, sweeping circles. "I've got you."

She shuddered, one last gag making its way out of her body before she let her head hang. Not knowing what else to do, I kept rubbing her back and holding her hair. After what seemed like an eternity of sitting by the putrid vomit, she lifted her head. Her blue eyes were hard, but they held a touch of vulnerability to them.

"Go away, Finn," she mumbled. Swiping a hand across her mouth, she struggled to stand up. "I'm fine."

I quickly rose and lifted her to her feet. When she stumbled sideways, almost right into her puke, I gripped her hips. "Shit. Stay still."

"I'm trying," she muttered, clinging to my shoulders. "The world won't stop spinning."

"Can you walk?"

She lifted her chin. "Of course I can."

"Okay."

I let go of her, even though every instinct screamed at me to hold on tighter and never let go. She took one step and almost fell flat on her face. I caught her effortlessly, swinging her up in my arms.

Her head flopped down on my chest, and she looked anything but ready to be released. "God, it hurts."

"I'll take care of you."

"I can take care of myself," she mumbled, her eyes drifting shut.

My heart seized at the look on her face as she drifted off. She was pale and listless. Her small hand rested on my chest, right above my heart. She liked putting it there, as if she knew she owned it and was re-staking her claim. "I know you can, but I want to help you. Now rest."

I dropped a quick kiss to her clammy forehead and headed for my bike. I almost reached it before I realized I couldn't ride home with an unconscious Carrie on my lap. I hesitated, not sure what to do. Should I get a cab and take her back to my place? Or should I carry her up to her room and take care of her there?

I spotted Marie walking to the dorm, three girls on either side of her. They were laughing loudly, talking about a study session involving alcohol in Marie's room. Carrie stirred at their laughter, her brow furrowing. I held her closer, kissing her temple.

"Take me home," she muttered restlessly. She burrowed closer to me, let out a ragged sigh, and fell asleep.

Well, that settled it. Home. *My* home.

Walking right past my bike, I managed to call a taxi without waking Carrie. Once it arrived, I settled into the back of the cab with her curled up on my lap. I smoothed her hair off her face, studying her delicate features. Her small nose was red at the tip, and she had bags under her eyes that hinted she hadn't been sleeping well lately. I hadn't been either.

I missed Carrie too much.

Somehow I doubted I was the cause of her insomnia, though. More likely, it had been because she'd been hitting the books harder than usual. Midterms were coming up, so she had been preparing for those. I had seen her in the library with Lover Boy almost every day this week. Whenever she studied, Cory did too.

Fucking annoying pansy.

The cab stopped in front of my place, and I shuffled Carrie in my arms so I could reach my wallet. The cabbie eyed Carrie. "Is she dead? If so, it'll cost extra."

I rolled my eyes. "Glad to know humanity is still at its peak."

"Hey, I'm just sayin'."

"So am I." I tossed the cash at the man. "She's not dead. She's sick."

"Then get her out of my cab before she ruins it."

I glanced pointedly at the cigarette burns covering the seat and the crack in the glass of the window. "I think it's too late for that."

"Whatever." The man dismissed me with a casual flick of his wrist. "Just go."

I was getting damned sick of people telling me to "just go," but now wasn't the time to address that. I had a sick Carrie on my hands—one who might explode at any given time. I opened the door, hugging her closer to my chest as I bent to get out. She jerked awake, her eyes wide. She looked...ah, fuck.

She looked green.

I picked up the pace. "Are you going to make it inside?"

She nodded frantically and squeezed her eyes shut. I practically ran to my door, unlocked it, and deposited her in front of the toilet. She waved her hand at me, clearly wanting me to leave, but I hovered in the doorway. Though my stomach demanded I do as she wished, I couldn't *leave* her.

When the first tortured groan escaped her, I stopped trying to fight the inevitable. I kneeled beside her, grabbing her hair to keep it out of the path of destruction. Her body tensed, but she didn't have a chance to tell me to go away before the vomiting started again. My own stomach twisted in reply, but I gnashed my teeth. By the time she was finished, I knew I would be throwing up today too.

I stood, my legs shaking, and wet a washcloth with warm water. She rested her cheek on her forearm, which was flung over the side of the toilet. When I came back to her side, she opened her eyes and blinked at me, a tear rolling down her face. "This sucks," she whispered.

I dabbed the washcloth over her forehead and across her mouth. "I know."

"Why are you doing this?" She closed her eyes and took a deep breath. "It's not in your job description, is it?"

"Knock it the hell off." I flexed my jaw, tossing the washcloth in the corner of the bathroom. I picked her up. "I'm taking care of you, and you're not going to stop me."

She rested her head on my shoulder, her hand once again over my heart—which traitorously sped up. "I don't know why you could possibly want to."

"It should be obvious. If it's not, I'm not sure what to say." I lowered her to the bed and lifted the blankets until she was covered. "I'm going to go grab you some medicine. I'll be right back."

I headed for the bathroom and closed the door behind me. After turning on the shower, which I hoped would be loud enough to drown out the sound of what I was about to do, I fell to my knees in front of the porcelain god. I flushed the toilet, and within seconds my own stomach emptied itself.

By the time I was finished, I felt as shaky and weak as she'd looked. I flushed again, then hopped in the shower to make it look as if I'd showered instead of ralphed. I allowed myself a minute to quickly scrub down, brush my teeth, and throw a towel around my waist. Opening up the cabinet, I pulled out the Pepto-Bismol I'd bought a few weeks ago after I'd had some bad tuna.

I took a dose for myself behind the closed door, and then came out of the bathroom with hers. She was curled up on her side, her eyes open but sleepy. I sat down beside her and held out the medicine. "Here. Take this."

"Thank you." She sat up slowly, her gaze drifting over me. "Can you please lose the towel?"

I tensed. "Why?"

"Because I don't want to see you half naked." She licked her lips, her stare somewhere around the level of my abs. "Not anymore."

Liar. "Sure."

I stood up, dropping the towel to the floor. Her indrawn breath almost made me crack a smile, but I forced myself to remain dead serious. Hell, I even stretched my arms over my head, letting her look her fill for however long she'd like.

"Finn."

I looked over at her, butt-assed naked. "Yeah?"

"You're *naked.*"

"I know." I looked down at myself. "You said to lose the towel. You also said you didn't want to see me half naked anymore, so here you go."

She set down her empty cup on the nightstand with a trembling hand, but her lips quirked as if a smile was trying to escape, but she didn't want to let it. I hadn't realized how much I missed her smile lighting up my life until now. "When I said 'lose the towel,' I meant put on some clothes. And by not wanting to see you half naked, I meant clothed."

"Oh." I shrugged. "I guess I could get dressed."

I crossed the room wearing my birthday suit, then opened my top drawer. She let out a strangled groan, but I heard her lay back down. Did she face the other way so she wouldn't have to see me anymore? Or was she watching? I dared a glance over my shoulder and quickly turned back around.

Oh, she was watching, all right.

I slowly stepped into a pair of boxers and pulled out a pair of khaki shorts. After I slid those on, I turned to face her. My stomach was a little bit steadier now. "Better?"

She cleared her throat. "Shirt?"

"Nah. I never wear one at home. You know that." I sat down beside her, reaching out to feel her forehead. It was blazing hot. "Shit, you have a fever."

She blinked at me. "Yeah, I've had one all day. Woke up with one."

"And you went to school *why*?"

She laid back down, cuddling into my bed as if she belonged there. And she did. She really fucking did. "I can't afford to miss classes right now."

"You can't afford to neglect your health either."

She rolled her eyes. Even sick and wasted, she had enough energy to give me sass and attitude. I loved it. Hell, I loved *her*, but that wasn't exactly a surprise to me. Not after all the moping I'd been doing ever since I lost her.

"My mom is all the way across the country and I'm single. Who am I supposed to get to take care of me?" she asked.

She didn't have to be single if she would give me another chance, but I didn't point that out. "Me."

"I can't call you for help anymore." She stared up at me. "We're not even really friends."

My heart wrenched, but I refused to show her how much it hurt for me to follow her rules. I pushed off the bed, heading into the kitchen. "I'll go make you some chicken broth."

"I'm not hungry." She rolled over and curled her knees into the fetal position. "Not even in the slightest."

I didn't stop walking. "You need something in your stomach, or it'll just hurt more when you puke."

"You don't have to do this," she called out, her voice shaking. "I'll be fine on my own."

"Yeah, I do. And no, you won't."

Because if I didn't take care of her…

Who would?

CHAPTER TWENTY-TWO

Carrie

I leaned back in the couch, holding the bowl in the crook of my lap. As I sipped down the chicken broth, I felt immensely better before it even hit my stomach. But even if it hadn't made me feel better, it was quite easily the most delicious soup I'd ever had. It didn't even have anything in it. Finn sat beside me on the couch, eating his own plain broth. He still hadn't put on a shirt, and I still hadn't stopped thinking about touching him again, even though I felt like I was on death's door.

I wouldn't follow through with my thoughts, but it didn't stop me from *wanting*.

He had a way of touching me that made me forget all about the outside world. All about how much he'd betrayed me, and how much I was supposed to hate him. I shouldn't be here, eating his soup and using his bed. I shouldn't be near him at all.

I still cared about him too much.

He looked at me out of the corner of his eye. "You okay?"

"Yeah." I set down my bowl. "That was really good. Thanks."

He finished his own bowl then set it next to mine. "It was my mom's recipe. My dad gave it to me when I was old enough to cook it myself. It always made me feel better when I was sick, so it seemed appropriate."

"Thank you," I said softly, oddly moved that he'd made me the same soup his mother made him. I wanted to hug him. To take away the brief shadows of grief I saw before he looked away.

He tugged at his brown hair. "Don't mention it. How about we get you back in bed now?"

I swallowed hard. Even the thought of crawling back into his bed sent shivers down my spine. The things we had done there... "I should go back to my dorm."

"Why bother? You won't get any sleep there with Marie. She has company." He pinned me down with his stare, his bright blue eyes on me. "I promise I won't touch you. You'll be perfectly safe here."

He didn't need to touch me to make me want him. That was the scary part. "Still."

"No." He stood, his jaw ticking. "I tried this the nice way, but I'll put it simply: You're not leaving. End of story."

Okay, that took away any lingering desire to kiss him. Then again, his arrogance usually did. "You don't own me. You're not my dad, and—"

"No, but I work for him, as you've reminded me every chance you get." He picked up his phone and waved it in front of my eyes. "And I'm not afraid to call him and get him down here. I'll tell him you're refusing medical treatment from the hospital."

I drew in a deep breath. "You wouldn't."

He raised a brow and started typing. I stood up and tried to snatch it out of his hands. My stomach protested the fast movement with a loud gurgle. "Stop it. Don't you *dare* call him."

"Then get in the fucking bed." He narrowed his eyes at me. "I can tell you're making yourself even sicker by arguing with me. Just lay down."

"I'm fine." My stomach twisted again, and I clutched it tight. Oh God, I was going to...

"Yeah. Sure you are," he drawled. He picked me up, and I closed my eyes as the room spun. I should point out I could walk on my own, but I didn't want to open my mouth right now. "Bathroom or bed?"

"Bathroom," I gasped, the vomit trying to escape even with the single word. "And leave me alone this time. I don't want you to see—" I broke off and covered my mouth.

He made it to the toilet in record time. "Not leaving."

I opened my mouth to argue, but the torrential vomiting pouring out of my system swallowed up the words. By the time I was finished, I felt more like the stuff floating in the toilet than a person. I hadn't even realized Finn held my hair until he released it, heading for the washcloths again.

Why was he being so…nice? So darn courteous and thoughtful and perfect? He needed to open his mouth and say something annoying really quickly before I fell for him all over again. He returned with a wet washcloth. He looked sweaty and a little pale himself. What was wrong with him?

"Here," he murmured, wiping my face down as he did last time.

I closed my eyes, tears threatening to escape me at his tender touch. "Why are you being so nice to me? And why are you shaking?"

"Because I care, even if it hurts." He tossed the washcloth aside and rose to his feet. "Do you want to shower?"

"Yes." I opened my eyes. He was leaning against the sink clutching his stomach. As soon as he saw I watched him, he straightened and headed for the faucet. "Are you okay?"

"I'm fine," he said dismissively. "Just worry about yourself."

I frowned. "Are you sick too?"

"No." The shower turned on, and he stuck his hand under the stream of water. Seemingly satisfied with the temperature, he went back to the sink and pulled out a light blue toothbrush. He opened the case and set it down on the sink. "Here. Use this."

I stood up and he grabbed my elbow. As if he was ready to catch me if I fell. But that was his job, wasn't it? I couldn't read anything more into it than that. "I don't have any clothes to change into."

He hesitated. "I don't want to leave you here alone to go get some."

"I'll be fine alone."

"I'm not leaving you."

I sighed, but inwardly I smiled. He seemed so worried about me, and it was hard not to be affected by his concern. No matter how stupid that made me. "I'll wear these again." I looked down at the dirty, wrinkled clothes. The ones that probably smelled worse than I did. "It's not a big deal."

"No, you won't." He let go of me. "I'll go get a T-shirt and a pair of boxers for you to wear. They'll be big, but it's better than what you've got on."

Wear his clothes? Somehow that didn't seem like a grand idea. His scent was already ingrained in my memory. Did I really need to wear it too? "But—"

"No buts." He headed for the door. "Just get in the shower. I'll push the clothes in through the door once you're in."

The door shut in my face, making me flinch. I took off my clothes and stepped into the water. Closing my eyes, I took a long breath. This is exactly what I'd needed—a fresh shower. A clean start. Hopefully the puking portion of my illness would be over now, and I could actually sleep.

I turned to search for the shampoo, but stopped mid-reach. Next to his manly shampoo he had apologized for last time I'd been here rested a fruity, girly shampoo and conditioner. When had he put that in there? Back when we were "dating"? Or was it for another girl? Even as I thought it, my heart screamed no. I didn't think he was seeing anyone else. He'd never given me a reason to believe he was. For all intents and purposes, the only woman he ever talked to was me. Just me.

But only because he has to, my inner voice so rudely reminded me.

I poured the shampoo into my palm, then scrubbed my scalp a bit harder than strictly necessary. Maybe that would make my smarter, annoying inner voice shut up. But instead, it simply reminded me of the last time I'd been in this shower. I hadn't been alone, and Finn had washed my hair far gentler than I was doing to myself. He'd been tender and loving and kind.

And then the next day, I'd found out who he was.

By the time I was out of the shower, I felt better physically, but much worse *emotionally*. After I dried off, I padded over barefoot to the toilet, where he'd apparently left a folded up T-shirt and a pair of boxers for me. I recognized the T-shirt. It was the red one I'd been wearing the day I found out who Finn really was.

I had washed it and set it on his porch step weeks ago.

Of course, that was after I'd slept with it on for a week. I hadn't wanted to give it back. It had smelled like him, even after a washing. He hadn't said anything to me about me bringing it back, but he hadn't had a chance to say anything at all until today. I hadn't even seen him in three weeks. Part of me had wondered if he'd quit and gone home.

That same annoying part of me was thrilled at being proved wrong.

I pulled the shirt over my head, inhaling deeply. Had he known giving me this shirt would affect me so deeply? Or had he just blindly reached in and grabbed the first thing he saw? Probably the latter. I picked up the toothbrush, did a quick cleaning, then steeled myself to face him again.

I opened the door and peeked out. He sat on the couch, texting someone. His girlfriend? My dad? The freaking Pope? Who knew. "Hey."

He clicked his screen off and stood up. He still didn't wear a shirt. Probably just to taunt me with the muscles I would never touch again. "You look like you feel better."

"I do." I crossed the room and climbed into the bed, tucking myself in. "Thank you."

He stood up and came to my side. Gently, he pressed his hand to my cheek. "You feel cooler too," he murmured, his blue eyes examining me.

Looking for signs of…what?

"Good."

"Yeah. Good," he said.

We fell awkwardly silent, neither one of us so much as moving. Daring to be the first to break the hold we had over one another. His phone buzzed, making me jump. He dropped his gaze and checked the message. I swallowed back the jealousy threatening to take hold. "Who are you talking to?"

"Hm?" He typed a quick reply. "No one."

"Is it her shampoo in there?"

That got his attention. He looked up at me, his brow furrowed. "Whose?"

"You tell me." I touched my damp hair. "There's girl shampoo in there. Are you seeing someone?"

"What? No." He shook his head, as if he couldn't believe I'd asked him that. "I got that for you, back when we were…well, you know."

"You did?"

"Yeah." He flushed and rubbed the back of his neck. "That's where the toothbrush came from too. After that first night, I went shopping while you were at school. I thought that maybe you were going to be spending a lot of time here, so I wanted you to have what you needed. But then…well, you found out who I was, and that was that."

"That was that," I repeated, thoroughly and utterly confused. Nothing about this man added up. He acted as if he really cared about me and wanted to be with me, but he worked for my *father*. And he was a liar. And manipulative. And bossy. And annoying.

And irresistible.

There were a million things I wanted to say, and at least a million reasons why I shouldn't say them. So I said nothing at all. When I remained silent, he shifted uneasily on the bed. "I'll sleep on the couch tonight. You can have the bed."

"Don't be ridiculous."

He arched a brow. "How am I being ridiculous?"

"You can sleep in the bed too." I flushed, searching for the right words to make it look like I offered because of practicality. I couldn't let him know how much I ached to sleep in his arms again. Or how horribly I'd been sleeping ever since we had broken up. Or how I missed him so much it *hurt*. "It's not like we've never, well, you know. Worse things have been done in this bed than sleeping together."

"Worse?"

"Crap." *Mental facepalm.* "Not that it was bad or anything—what we did. I mean, you know it wasn't."

His lips twitched. "Do I?"

I covered my face. "I'm done trying to talk."

He laughed and pulled my hands down. "Relax, you're fine."

"No. I'm not fine." I looked at him and his laughter faded away. "I'm not fine at all."

He swallowed hard. "Carrie…"

"Don't say it. Don't say anything." I rolled over on my side. "Just turn out the light. I'm tired."

After what felt like an hour, he finally turned off the light. I released the breath I'd been holding, willing my racing heart to calm down. As he lowered himself on the bed, keeping above the covers, he also let out a deep whoosh of air.

He remained blessedly silent. I didn't know if he went right to sleep, because as soon as I felt him next to me, I zonked out. When I woke up in the morning, he was gone. My clothes were washed and folded nicely at the bottom of the bed.

A note rested on top of it. I opened it with trepidation. What would he say? What could he say?

I'm sorry.

--Finn

That's it. Just three little words. And yet, they were more than enough.

CHAPTER TWENTY-THREE

Finn

Two days later, I leaned against the outside of Carrie's dorm, my eyes on the building she was currently in. I knew exactly who it belonged to, and I also knew how much I hated that she was inside of it. With the man she should have fallen for all along.

Fucking Lover Boy himself, in the flesh.

Ever since the night she'd spent at my apartment, I'd resumed following Carrie around sight unseen. Just like she wanted. Yesterday, she'd kept darting glances all around, watching for me. Almost as if she wanted to catch me out of place. I'd made sure to stay out of sight, and she had eventually stopped looking.

I didn't blame her in the least. If our roles were reversed, I would've felt the same way. I wouldn't want to ever see her again, but that didn't make it any easier on me. Losing her had only made it all the more evident that I loved her. And all the more evident that I was an idiot too. The two kind of went hand in hand, didn't they?

Love didn't come without a little bit of stupidity. Okay. A hell of a lot of it.

The door opened, and Cory came out, his arm thrown around Carrie's shoulders. I tensed. She didn't shrug free like she normally did. If anything, she snuggled in closer. I clamped my jaw tight and proceeded to try and come up with at least twenty different ways I could shove

Cory's arm up his own ass. I'd only reached option three when Cory kissed Carrie's cheek, then went back inside.

Cheek? Fucking pansy...

I'd never like that guy as much as I did right now.

Carrie hugged her books tight to her chest and searched the empty courtyard. I should slink back into the shadows. Hide. But I didn't want to. Maybe I was in the mood for a fight. Maybe I just wanted to hear her voice as she told me to go away. Either way, I was completely pathetic.

I straightened, waiting to see if she would see me. Equally worried she might not. Her gaze skimmed over me, then slammed back. I stood my ground, waiting to see what she did. How she would react to my blatant disobedience to her request.

Mumbling to herself, she crossed the yard. "Hey. Thank you for taking care of me the other day."

She said it so fast that I had a hard time keeping up with the torrent of words coming out of her mouth. I cocked a brow. "You're welcome. Sorry I'm still here. I wasn't expecting you to come out of his room so soon." I shrugged and focused on the door behind her. "I figured you might be...ah, *busy* for a little while. Ya know."

Her cheeks turned pink. "We weren't...I didn't..." She pressed her lips together. "We were studying, not doing *that*."

Relief rushed through me, heady and unstoppable. Relief I didn't have a right to feel. "I figured as much when he kissed you on the cheek. Anyone who has earned the right to kiss you wouldn't go for your cheek."

She opened her mouth, then slammed it shut. "Good night, Finn. You can go now."

I cocked my head. "I'll leave once you're inside."

"I'm not going inside." She fluttered her hand. "Well, I am, but I'm coming back out. I'm going to a party."

I stood up straight at that. "What kind of party? And do you really think that's best after the way you felt a couple nights ago?"

"A frat party, and I'm fine."

She moved past me, going inside. I should go back into the shadows, but I didn't like the idea of her going to a party tonight. After the type of night she had the other day, she needed rest and tea. Not dancing and beer.

I paced for what had to have been twenty minutes, my impatience growing with each step I took. She had no place partying tonight. None at all. The door opened behind me and I spun. "You're not going to that party. If you think I'll sit there watching—"

I stopped talking, and my jaw dropped. Holy. Fucking. Shit.

I'd seen her in a bikini. I'd seen her surfing. I'd even seen her naked, but I had never seen her like *this*. She wore a tiny, poor excuse for a dress, a pair of *fuck me* heels that were meant to be over my shoulders, not on the ground—and wore more makeup than I'd ever seen on her before. Her red lips begged to be kissed, and the rest of her…well, it matched the shoes.

"*No.*" My jaw ticked. "Go upstairs and put on some real clothes."

She laughed. "Yeah, not happening."

"You're right. It's not." When she tried to pass me, I stepped in her way. "I said get dressed."

She shook her head. "No."

"Do it."

"Or what?" She put her hands on her hips. Actually put her hands on her hips and stared me down. "What can someone like *you* do to hurt me?"

I'd said almost those same exact words to her not long ago. Turns out, someone like her could hurt me too easily by refusing to be with me. By not loving me back. "I'll kiss you, like you did to teach me a lesson, if you don't change right now."

"Please." She huffed. "I'm not the one who can't handle a simple kiss."

Challenge. Accepted.

I hauled her close, making sure to press my body fully against hers. Closing my hands around her ass, I rubbed against her as I fused my mouth to hers, not wasting even a second in ravishing her. Her hands pushed at my shoulders, but then she stopped pushing and started pulling me closer. When her tongue dueled with mine, I barely managed to hold back my shout of satisfaction.

She might keep saying she didn't want to be around me, but her body obviously did. Thank fucking God. She whimpered into my mouth and lifted her leg, wrapping her calf around mine. I would like nothing more than to keep this going. To take her home with me and show her exactly how much she hated me while I made love to her repeatedly. But I knew as soon as the kiss ended, so would we.

Again.

I pulled back and rested my forehead on hers, wishing that things could be different. "I miss you," I whispered. "So damn much. Please give me another chance."

Her fingers tightened on me, and for a second I thought she might pull me closer. For a second, my heart leapt. She pushed me away. "I'm sorry, but I *can't*."

My heart leapt right into a gnarled mess at her words, but I forced myself to let her go. "Fine, but either you change out of that poor excuse for a dress, or I stay by your side all night instead of letting you do your thing undisturbed. Your choice."

"Why do you give a damn what I do? Just tell Dad I'm in bed. He won't know."

I shook my head. "I care because I care about you, Captain Obvious."

"Stop *saying* that."

"No." I advanced on her. "I care about you, and you telling me to stop isn't going to work. Get changed, or hang out with me."

"I'm this close," she held her fingers close together and shoved them in my face, "to calling my Dad and telling him I know exactly who you are."

I cocked a brow. "Go ahead."

Bluff. Called.

She stomped her foot. "What would your dad do without his pension?"

"If he was here, he'd be stopping you from leaving in that too." I dragged a hand through my hair. "This isn't you, Carrie. If you have to dress like this to get a guy's attention, he's not the right guy for you."

She held her hands out to her sides. "What would you know about what kind of guy I need?"

My jaw ticked. "I know it's not whoever you're wearing this outfit for."

"Oh?" She paced in front of me. "Let me guess. You're the type of guy I need?"

"No," I said honestly. "You deserve much better than me."

That made her stop pacing, and she looked at me in surprise. "Excuse me?"

"You heard me." I caught her jaw and tilted her face up to mine. "I'd like to say I deserve you, but the truth is I don't and never will. You deserve a prince, and you're not going to catch him wearing that."

"Finn…" She swayed toward me, her eyes soft. "I wish—"

"Is there a problem here?" Cory asked, his voice tight. He glared at my hand, which was still on Carrie's jaw. The little fucker was probably mad I dared to touch her. "Carrie? Are you all right?"

"I'm fine," Carrie quickly replied. "We were just finishing up here."

I dropped my hold on Carrie. "There's not a problem, Cody. Carrie was about to go change."

"Change?" Cory looked her up and down, and I swore the idiot's tongue hit the dirt. "She looks great to me."

"Of course she does," I muttered.

Carrie shot me an angry look. "Thank you, *Cory*."

"This is touching and all," I said as I crossed my arms and rocked back on my heels. "but what's your choice?"

"I *choose* to ignore you and leave with Cory," she said, tipping her perfect little nose up in the air. "Now, if you'll excuse us?"

Cory threw an arm over Carrie's shoulder and shot me a triumphant grin. "See ya later."

I fell into step beside them. "No need for goodbyes. I'm coming along."

"No, you're not." Carrie stopped walking and shot me down with her sapphire eyes. "Finn. *Please*. Just go away. You're going to ruin everything."

She gave me the look she probably gave her father. The look that made her get away with everything in the world, and then some. The one that begged me to back off, before her cover was blown. If I kept insisting on accompanying her, questions would be asked. She would no longer be just another girl who went to college. She'd be the senator's daughter—complete with bodyguard.

"You heard her." Cory pulled Carrie closer to his side, eyeing me cautiously. "Go away. You don't even *go* to this school, do you?"

As if she needed protection from me. I was trying to help her, not hurt her.

Wasn't I?

Or was my jealousy the thing leading me to protest her outfit? Was it really any worse than what every other college girl would be wearing to the party? Maybe I needed to take a step back and stop playing the part of the overprotective boyfriend. I wasn't hers, and she wasn't mine. It was none of my business what she did or didn't wear anymore.

"Fine." I flexed my fingers. "You know where I'll be."

Carrie bit down on her lower lip and glanced away from me. "Thank you."

I inclined my head, shot a death glare in Cory's direction, and faded back into the shadows where I belonged.

CHAPTER TWENTY-FOUR

Carrie

Seeing Finn earlier had messed me up. Especially when he asked me to give him another chance. God, I wanted to, but I was too scared. Too scared to put myself out there again. Once a liar, always a liar. If he lied to me about his identity, what else would he lie to me about? What else had he *already* lied about?

I grabbed my fourth drink of the night, tipping it back and drinking deeply. It tasted like crap, but I didn't care. Not tonight. Seeing him had thrown me off-kilter. I'd been so sure I could get over him. Sure that eventually I wouldn't miss him or need him or want him. Then he'd had to go and kiss me. That had ruined everything. My body had responded immediately to him, as if it remembered the things he could do with his hands and tongue.

And it wanted more. *I* wanted more.

Marie came over to me, grinning. "Well, if it isn't the prodigal roommate. Out drinking like the rest of us college kids."

"Yeah." I forced a smile for my roommate. We weren't friends, but I didn't hate her. "Crazy, huh?"

"A welcome crazy." Marie nudged me with her shoulder. "I was starting to think I bunked with Mother Mary or something."

I rolled my eyes. "Believe me, that's not the case."

"Coulda fooled me." Marie took a long sip of her beer. "Although, I saw you on the beach the other week. Surfing. Who was that fine hottie you had with you? And more importantly, who is *he* to *you*?"

I tensed. "Him? No one. Nothing."

"Can you tell me where to find him? I'd like to be his something."

If Marie thought I would give her Finn's info, she was barking up the wrong tree. No one would be getting near him with my help while I still had breath in my lungs. "Sorry, I have no idea. He was just some guy..."

A soft laugh sounded from outside, and I glanced over my shoulder. Of course he'd heard that. I turned around and smiled at Marie. Luckily, she was too distracted to see the falseness behind the gesture. That, or she didn't care.

"Actually," I said, leaning closer. "I think he's gay."

"Really?" Marie gasped, her cheeks flushed. "Are you sure?"

I nodded, grinning when I heard a few mumbled curses from outside the open window. "Positive. He kept talking about Cory and asking if he was single."

Marie sighed. "It's true. All the good ones are gay or taken."

"Sadly so," I said, keeping my voice solemn, even though I wanted to cackle with glee. I pointed at a cute guy across the room, who was watching us. "But *he* looks single and straight."

Marie licked her lips. "Wish me luck."

"You don't need it," I said, smiling. "But good luck."

Marie took off, a swing in her step that hadn't been there a second before, and crossed the room to the guy. Within seconds of Marie leaving my side, Cory arrived. He threw an arm around me, throwing us both off balance. I didn't know how many drinks he'd had so far, but it had to be a lot.

Too many for him to be trustworthy.

Maybe he needed some fresh air to sober up. I fanned my cheeks again. "I'm hot. Can we go for a walk?"

Cory straightened and let out a hiccup. "Sure. Let's go."

He stumbled across the room, looking way too close to passing out, and I followed him. As soon as we stepped out into the night air, I took a deep breath. All of the colognes and booze had mixed into an unpleasant odor inside, and the fresh ocean breeze was a welcome change. I looked out toward the ocean and wrapped my arms around myself, reminded of another night just like this one.

The night I met Finn…

God, I missed him.

I gritted my teeth and turned to Cory, forcing a smile. I wasn't going to think about Finn anymore tonight. I refused. "It's been fun tonight."

"Yeah, I'm glad you came."

He wrapped his arms around me. It felt nice to be held by him. Secure, even. But I didn't itch to jump his bones. Didn't want to climb into his bed and lick him from head to toe. Maybe I was doing something wrong. Or maybe there was something wrong with me. Either way, I was done for the night. I wanted to go home.

I looked up at him, intending to tell him goodbye. I opened my mouth…and he was on me. His lips met mine, and it felt…nice. There might have been the slightest stirrings of desire, but it was so quiet a tiny breeze would have put out the fires. Cory groaned and crushed me against his chest, his tongue sliding in between my lips. I tried to feel something…*anything*…but it didn't work. There was nothing there, just like the other time he'd kissed me. Yeah, I was broken.

Why was it that only Finn could make me want him?

Just as I was about to pull back and make my excuses to go home, something crashed behind us. Cory jerked back from me and looked around. I, of course, knew who was out there. How could I have forgotten about Finn following me, for even a second? He'd seen us and probably thought I was moving on. I wasn't.

Probably never would be.

"Who's out there?" Cory asked, stalking toward the noise. "Show yourself."

I grabbed Cory's elbow, trying to bring him back. I didn't want them to see each other. "Don't worry about it. It was no one."

"Someone's watching you," Cory said, his jaw squared. "And I bet I know who it is."

"No!" I cried, trying to pull him back toward me. "There's no one out there. Let's go."

"I can *see* him." Cory pointed at where he supposedly saw Finn. "Come out here, surfer boy."

Finn stepped out of the shadows, his eyes hard and mouth pressed tight. His gaze skimmed over me, then slid back to Cory. "Don't call me that, Cody."

"I knew it was you. Why are you following her around?" He pushed Finn's shoulders and Finn stumbled backward. "Are you some kind of sicko who can't take no for an answer?"

Finn curled his hands into fists and stepped forward, his eyes narrow slits. "Push me again, and I'll be the sicko who breaks your fucking face."

Cory pushed him. Finn snarled and hauled back his fist, ready to do some damage. Cory, the fool, didn't even back off. He was either too drunk to see the immediate danger he was in, or he seriously underestimated Finn's strength. This wasn't going to end well.

I couldn't sit by and let Cory get hurt because I'd kissed him in front of Finn. Couldn't let *either* of them get hurt. I threw myself in front of Cory, arms akimbo. "Finn, *no*! Don't hurt him. I'm fine."

Finn's fist remained raised and something in his jaw ticked. "Get out of the way, Carrie."

Cory shoved me aside roughly, and I fumbled to regain my balance. "Yeah, let the freak stalker take his punch. I'll slam his white trash ass in jail so fast, he won't have time to say *lawyer up*."

"Stop being such a jerk, Cory. He's not a stalker," I said, tugging Cory back. My anonymity would have to come to an end. If I didn't tell Cory who Finn really was, he'd never shut up about this. Never back off. "He's my bod—"

"Ex-boyfriend," Finn interjected. "And I can't stop following her because I want her back."

I blinked at him. "We don't have to do this, Finn. Just tell him—"

"Good luck?" Finn slammed me with a look that clearly told me to play along. He didn't want me telling Cory who I really was. Why not? "I can't. I can't let another man have you."

Cory laughed. "Well, too late. She's already mine."

The hell I was. We would have a talk about Cory claiming me like that, but not now. Not in front of Finn. I shot a cautious look Finn's way. He still looked like he was ready to kill Cory, but at least he'd lowered his fist. "Let's go, Cory."

"Not until he tells me that he'll stop following you around all the time." Cory pulled free of my hold and stumbled back into the reach of Finn. "Did she tell you she wants to be with me instead? Are you mad she's mine instead of yours?"

Finn's fingers flexed. "Keep talking. Give me a reason to take a swing."

"It was only a matter of time until she came to her senses, you know." Cory smirked. "You might be fun for a while, but that's all you'll ever be to her—a fling."

I stiffened. I didn't like this side of Cory. Not one little bit. "Cory, stop it. You're being nasty. It's gross."

"Oh, *excuse* me. Should I bow at your feet?" Finn snorted. "Yeah. Keep dreaming, asshole."

"Go back to whatever trailer park you crawled out of, and leave us alone."

"*Cory*. Stop it!" I snapped. Finn's face revealed nothing, but I could feel how Cory's words affected him as if we were attached to one another. As if when Finn hurt, so did I. "Stop being this way. I don't like it."

"You'd best listen to her." Finn's nostrils flared and he advanced on Cory. "I suggest you leave before I forget that Carrie asked me not to kick your pasty white ass, *Cody*."

Cory took a swing at Finn, connecting with his eye. Finn could've avoided it easily, I'd seen him do so. But he let Cory hit him. Why? Finn rubbed the spot where Cory had hit him, but not before I saw the blood and the bruise already forming. And then he grinned. *Grinned*.

"Game on," Finn said as he stalked toward Cory.

Cory paled, but stood his ground. He held up his fists. "Bring it."

That's it. I was leaving now, before I killed them both. Other girls might like being fought over, but I wasn't one of them. "Finn, *no*."

Finn stopped midstride, his entire body humming with anger and something else I couldn't quite figure out. He took a step toward me and stopped. He tugged on the back of his head, torturing a poor curl. The look in his eyes haunted me. I'd hurt him. I could see it. Feel it.

"Leave. Now."

Cory smirked and walked right up to Finn. He leaned in and whispered something. Finn's face turned red, and then the next thing I knew, Cory was on the ground. He clutched his stomach, moaning and rolling around on the stone walkway. "You hit me. You actually *hit* me."

Finn dropped to his knees and hauled Cory up by the shirt, his face inches away from Cory's. "You ever say anything like that again, I'll fucking kill you. You hear me?"

Cory pressed his hand to his stomach. "I'm going to report you to the police."

Finn grinned, his eyes glinting maliciously. "Go ahead. Tell them I said hi." He dropped Cory back to the ground. "Now get the fuck out of here before I change my mind and kick your ass."

Cory stumbled to his feet and ran off, not even looking at me. His next stop would probably be reporting Finn to the police, and there would be repercussions from tonight. I closed my eyes and counted to three. "He's going to call the cops, and you're going to get arrested."

"Fuck him," Finn said, his voice tight.

I turned around to face Finn, but he had his back to me and his hands braced against a tree. "Did you *hear* me?"

His breath came fast and shallow. "I don't give a flying fuck what the hell he does."

"Well, I do." I grabbed Finn's shoulder and yanked. "What the hell is wrong with you?"

He spun on me, his entire body trembling with rage. "What's wrong with me? Do you actually have to ask me that?"

"Yeah, I do!" I grabbed his arms and shook him. "You aren't allowed to fly off the handle like that. You aren't allowed to draw attention to yourself. You *know* that. What will my father say about this? What about your dad?"

He flung me off him. "I don't give a damn anymore. Not about you. Not about anything."

I stumbled back from the force of his words. It would've been kinder if he had hit me. "You know what? Go to hell."

"Too late. I'm already there."

"You have no idea what hell is. Hell is falling for someone for the first time and finding out that everything he ever told you was a lie. That everything you wanted to believe in was all a ruse to get close to you."

He swallowed hard and closed his eyes. His hands fell at his sides, limp. "I didn't lie to you about us. I've already told you that a million times, didn't I?"

I shoved his shoulders, choking on the huge lump in my throat. Tears filled my eyes, but I blinked them back. I didn't have time for tears right now. "You're not allowed to be hurt in this situation. *You* were the one who did this. *You* were the one who went and ruined everything."

"You think I don't regret it? Huh?" He ran his hands down his face and let out a strangled growl. "You think I don't wish I could make it all go away, if only for one more night in your arms?"

I wanted that too. Only I wanted more than a night. I wanted to go back to what we'd been to each other. No lies. No secrets. "Well, we can't have that, can we?"

He dropped his hands to his side. "And I can't sit here watching you fall in love with someone else. Especially him."

"I'm not falling in *love* with him," I said, my voice coming out thick. No, I was in love with Finn and had been since the second he walked into my life. There wasn't room for anyone else in my heart.

"I quit."

"You can't quit," I cried. "You promised me that you'd—"

"I promised to keep you safe. To watch over you." He slashed his arm through the air. "I didn't promise to watch you suck face with an asshole like him."

I swallowed. "I don't even like him like that."

"I wish you the best of luck with life, but I can't do this anymore. I care about you too much to stay at the side, watching you move on. I just…can't."

And with that, he turned on his heel and disappeared.

I wrapped my arms around myself and blinked back tears. He was leaving, and I'd never see him again. I should be happy. Thrilled. Instead, I wanted to chase after him and beg him to stay.

CHAPTER TWENTY-FIVE

Finn

The next morning, my temper had cooled quite a bit, even if my feelings for Carrie hadn't. One thing I knew I had to do? I had to tell her I loved her before I left. I had to give it one last shot. If she told me she didn't give a damn about my feelings, then I'd leave. At least I would know I gave it all I had. I wouldn't spend my life wondering what would have happened if I'd gotten the balls to tell her I loved her.

I hadn't been lying when I told her yesterday she deserved better than me. She did. But no one else would love her as much as I could. No one else could make her feel as good, either. My phone rang and I glanced down. When I saw it was the senator, I sighed and picked it up. "Good morning, sir."

"What's this I hear about you punching Cory Pinkerton? What happened?"

I rubbed my temples. "Who told you?"

"The police called the campus, and the campus called me." The senator sighed. "I'll get it taken care of, but you better have a damned good reason for punching someone who could very well be a huge contributor to my campaign in the future."

I swallowed the curses wanting to escape. "Yeah. Because your *campaign* is the most important thing here."

"Are you insulting me, son?" His tone dropped, and I clenched the phone. "I can just as easily let the cops get their hands on your sorry ass. I'm sure your father would be displeased."

Minus a huge pension, no doubt.

"No, *sir*." I cleared my throat. "No disrespect."

"Good." I could practically hear the smug grin the senator wore. "Now tell me what happened."

I filled him in, but in my version of the story, Carrie had already left and my cover hadn't been blown. "So, I told him I was a jealous ex, punched him, and told him never to come near her again."

"I'll kill the little brat," the senator said. "How dare he act that way toward my girl?"

I clenched my jaw. "I felt the same way, sir."

"Good work, son. Keep in the shadows, and don't be seen."

This was the time to tell him I quit. Tell him I couldn't stay here anymore, but I hung up on him without another word and tossed my phone across the bed. I'd had to make up a story, so now I had to fill Carrie in on the tale I'd told. Time to track her down and fill her in. And while I was at it, I'd tell her I was in love with her too.

I'd leave after she laughed in my face.

Carrie

I lifted my hand to knock on Finn's door, but it swung open before I could. There he stood, looking breathtakingly gorgeous as always. I had spent an hour out on the water, enjoying the solitude of the ocean. Everyone out there seemed to be trying to escape something. I wanted to escape it all. My life. Cory. My father.

And most of all…Finn. He was leaving me.

I didn't even know how I felt about him anymore. I knew when Finn was around, my heart begged for me to forgive him. To give him another chance. But my head screamed just as loudly, and it called my heart a fool. How could I trust him after everything he'd done? After everything we'd been through?

I couldn't. That's how.

"Carrie? What are you doing here?"

I licked my lips and focused on him. I wasn't sure what I was going to say yet. I probably should have thought that through. "I'm checking in to see if you heard from my dad yet."

"He called. He was informed that Cory pressed charges against me."

I closed my eyes. I'd been up all night worrying about that. "I *told* you he would do that. We'll fix this. I'm sure if I speak to him, tell him who I really am, he'll—"

"No."

I stiffened. "Why not?"

"Because you're not blowing your cover for me."

"What if I want to?"

"I don't care." He lifted a brow. "Besides, your father's taking care of it. I had to fabricate a story so that he wouldn't know I was outed to you, but he bought it."

Wait, if he lied and didn't tell him about me knowing his identity, did that mean he was staying? *Please God, yes.* "What did you tell him?"

Finn quickly relayed the fabricated story, and I nodded. "That was quick thinking."

"No, it wasn't. I was up all night, waiting." He shrugged. "I couldn't sleep, anyway."

I looked up at him. "Me either."

Our gazes latched, and he turned a little bit red. "Look, Carrie, I—"

"Are you still leaving?" I asked at the same time.

He broke off. "Do you want me to?"

"I don't want you to," I said slowly, not dropping my gaze. "I want you to stay, but I get it if you can't."

"Can you ever forgive me? For lying?"

"I do forgive you." I took a deep breath. All night long, I'd been asking myself this very question. Asking myself if I could ever understand his motivation. It wasn't until I answered just now that I realized I already had. "I forgive you for it all. I understand why you did what you did."

His eyes lit up. "Do you think you can ever... Can we ever...?"

I wished I could say yes, but he'd hit me where I was weakest. All my life, Dad had been paying people to get close to me. And the first man I fell in love with was one of them. It hurt too much. Brought back too many memories—none of them good.

He made a choking sound. "You don't have to answer. I can see it in your eyes."

"I'm so sorry," my voice a mere whisper. It's all I could manage past my aching throat.

He swallowed hard. "I love you, will always love you. I'm sorry I killed us before we even had a chance."

And with that bombshell, he shut the door in my face.

CHAPTER TWENTY-SIX

Finn

Well, there you had it. I'd told her I loved her. Had asked for another chance. She'd said no. Chapter over. End of our story. I'd always known she was smart, and she'd proved it even more by rejecting me. She deserved more than I could give her. Security. Diamonds. A fucking mansion.

With another man, she could get all those things and more.

I slammed my fist into the wall, trembling from the force of the frustration and anger and pain storming through me. What had I been thinking, falling for her? What made me think I could find a way to make her forgive me, when I had so clearly fucked up? She didn't love me. She never would.

A knock sounded on the door, and I yanked it open. Carrie still stood there. "How dare you?"

I closed my fist around the knob, ignoring the way my heart leapt at the sight of her. "How dare I what?"

She shoved my shoulders, and I backed up. "You don't tell someone you love them and then just *leave*. What the hell is wrong with you?"

I rubbed where her hand had impacted with my shoulder and raised a brow. "You might as well sit if you want me to list everything. It could take all day."

"*Shut up*, you idiot. God, you make me so...so..." She made a frustrated sound and covered her face. "Mad."

I dropped my hand and held my breath. "Carrie?"

"Did you mean it?" She lifted her head, her eyes shooting a challenge at me I would gladly accept. Any day. Any time. Anywhere. "Do you really love me? Or are you just trying to trick me into thinking you do?"

I frowned at her. I wouldn't dignify that with a response. "What do you think?"

"*Finn.*" She advanced on me. "I need to know. I need to hear it."

I growled. With one quick step, I had her in my arms and I was kissing her. Kissing her so she would shut the hell up and stop shooting questions at me. Kissing her because if I didn't, I might die. When she stopped squirming in my arms, and instead clung to me, I broke off the kiss.

Cupping her cheeks, I met her eyes and said, "I want to be your man. To show you how happy I can make you. I promise you, with all my heart and soul, that I'm not lying about this. I'm not making anything up. Not anymore."

"Finn…"

"I'm falling in love with you, Ginger." I kissed her nose. "Hell, who am I kidding? I'm already there. I'm not exactly used to this feeling. If you want me to leave, then I'll go. You can fall for someone who is much more appropriate for you. If you want me to stay, I'll spend the rest of my life making you happy, or I'll die trying. Just say the word."

"My father's going to kill you," she said, tears falling out of her eyes. "Because I love you too."

My heart stuttered to a stop, then sped back up to light speed. Beam me up, fucking Scotty. She loved me. "You do?"

"I do." She kissed me gently, then shoved me back again. "But if you ever even *think* about lying to me again, I'll cut off your balls and shove them so far up your butt you won't even know they're missing. Got it?"

I laughed. "Got it."

My phone buzzed in my pocket, and she raised a brow. "Who is that?"

"Your father, no doubt." I twisted around to yank it out, holding it down so she could see. No more secrets. *Got the problem taken care of. Where is she now?* "Hm. I can't lie, so…" I picked her up and carried her to my bed, falling down on top of her. Then I texted, *She's still in bed.*

Carrie laughed when I showed her what I wrote. "Tell him I'm with three different men, but not to worry. They're all Ivy League."

I growled and nibbled at her throat. "No way. You're all mine."

"No arguments here. Not anymore." She clung to my shoulders and arched her throat to give me better access. "But he doesn't know it, and he can't."

I lifted my head. "Why don't you want to tell him? Is it because you don't want anyone to know about me? About us?"

"What? No. *No!*" She smoothed my hair off my face. "I don't want your father to lose his pension. He's always been kind to me, and I need to return the favor. After this year is over, and after your father is done, we'll tell my father together. Until then, we'll wait."

The fact that she cared enough about Dad's well-being to lie to her own father only made me fall for her even more. "Are you sure?"

"Positive as a proton."

I laughed and kissed her. My phone buzzed again, and I held it up so she could read. *You'll be returning home with her for winter break. Your father has requested you visit, so I arranged it all.*

Yes, sir.

I chucked the phone aside and settled in between her legs. "Looks like we'll be spending Christmas together, Ginger."

"Good." She trailed her fingers down my spine, then over my ass. "I can't go too long without this."

"You're going to have to if you want us to be a secret." I lowered my body, nibbling at her shoulder now. "Because when I make you come, you scream, babe."

"I do *not*," she said haughtily. "I never scream."

"Oh yeah?"

I ran my hand down her stomach, tracing the waistband of her shorts. "I just might have to prove you wrong…"

I closed my mouth over hers, and she slipped her tongue inside my mouth. I groaned in satisfaction, savoring her taste. Her smell. The way she moved underneath of me, undulating her body and asking for more. More that I'd readily give her. Anything she wanted. The moon. The stars. It would be hers.

She gripped my ass, yanking me against her. "God, I need you."

"Not nearly as much as I need you."

I kissed her gently before I took off her sweatshirt. I made quick work of her bra, and then closed my fingers around her bare breasts.

When I kneaded them and bit down on her shoulder, she cried out and dug her nails into my back. I hissed, half in pain and half in pleasure, and captured her mouth once more.

I rolled her nipples between my thumbs and fingers, tugging with just enough pressure to make her squirm. When she trembled and moaned into my mouth, I lowered my hands to her waist and yanked her shorts off. Once she was blessedly naked, I made quick work of my own shorts, then grabbed a condom and tossed it on the bed. I laid down on the bed and rolled her on top until she straddled my hips.

The sight of her perfect breasts hanging above me was almost too much to take in. I lifted my head and urged her down, closing my mouth around her nipple while gripping her hips with my hands. She let out a surprised cry and speared me with her nails, leaving little half-moon marks on my pecs.

She shoved my shoulders back and took a shaky breath. "That's enough of that. I want to explore this new position."

Her long hair cascaded around her breasts and her back, making her look wanton. Sexy. "You look so hot right now."

She looked down at me with smoky eyes and crawled down my body. When she nibbled on my abs, I flinched and buried my hands in her hair. Without hesitation, she closed her lips around me, sucking me in deep. I groaned and closed my eyes, letting her mouth move over me. Torture me. When she rolled her tongue over the head, I bit my tongue to keep from crying out. From begging her to stop...or to never stop.

I didn't know which need would win.

Reaching down, I picked her up and set her aside. After grabbing the foil and putting on a condom, I lowered her to my cock, spreading her legs wide. "I need you *now*."

She gripped my shaft and lowered herself onto me, inch by torturous inch. My balls tightened, and I practically came right there. I'd never been one to get carried away by passion, but with my Carrie...I didn't have a choice. She touched me, and I was gone.

I reached up and cupped her face, bringing her down for a slow, passionate kiss. She whimpered into my mouth and moved faster on me, trying to find a rhythm that would give her what she needed. What I needed too.

I ended the kiss. "Let me try something I think you'll enjoy." I tucked her legs behind her body, lifted her up, and then rocked my hips into hers. She shrieked, her nails digging into my skin. "You like that?"

"Again," she rasped, her perfect lips parted. "Do it again."

I lifted her up a little bit, then lowered her body as I lifted my own, and she cried out. I grinned. "See? Told you you were too loud."

"Just shut up and do it again," she said, ending on a plea.

I did it again. And again. By the time I reached the third thrust, we were both too lost to talk anymore, let alone think. When her tight muscles clenched down on my cock, warning me of her impending orgasm, my own pleasure grew to a pinnacle. With one last thrust, we both exploded and sank into the mattress, her sweaty body resting against my equally damp one.

I ran my fingers over her back and smoothed her hair over her face. She cuddled in closer, letting out a contented sigh. "Yeah, I can't live without that."

I chuckled. "I don't think I can either. We'll find a way to keep you quiet."

"Me?" She reared back and glowered at me, but the sparkle in her eye ruined the effect she was going for. "I think we need to worry about you, not me."

I hugged her close. "I have no idea what you're talking about."

She climbed off me and headed for the bathroom. "I'm going to go in here for a minute, and then you're going to cook for me."

"Is that all you want me for?" I rolled onto my stomach and grinned. "Food and sex?"

Her head poked out of the bathroom. "And booze."

"Brat," I called out.

She shut the door in my face and I laughed. When I stood up, I stretched my arms high over my head and made my way to the trash can to get rid of the condom. I couldn't believe she'd forgiven me. Given me a chance to prove to her how much I could be trusted. Life couldn't get any better than this.

After I stepped into my shorts, I heard my phone buzz. Padding across the room, I bent down and picked it up. I'd apparently missed a call earlier, and had a voicemail notification. When I recognized the number, I sank onto the bed and swallowed hard. This couldn't be good news. I just knew it. Could *feel* it in my gut.

I hit the *play message* button, then listened to the brief but life-changing message. When it ended, I let my hand fall to my side. Fuck. This wasn't going to be good, and it was going to make Carrie cry. I didn't want to make her cry ever again.

But I couldn't hide the truth from her. Not again.

The door opened and she came out wearing my favorite red shirt. The same one she'd worn twice already. I tossed my phone aside and plastered on a smile. "Damn, babe, you look better in that than I do."

"You think?" She posed in the doorway, bending one perfect leg and shooting me a *come get me* smile. "I might just keep it. It smells like you."

I stood up and swept her into my arms, hugging her as tightly as I could. "If you want it, it's yours. Anything you want."

"Well, then." She lifted her face and smiled up at me, her eyes shining with tears. Happy tears. "All I want is you."

I swallowed hard. "You got me."

"I did," she whispered, rising up on tiptoes and kissing me. "And now you need to *feed* me."

She skipped toward the kitchen, and I followed her with a smile. After dinner, I would fill her in. Give her the news. But we could be blissfully happy for a few hours, right? Because right now, I was too busy being fucking happy that I'd gotten the girl of my dreams. The girl I loved, and who also loved me.

Imagine that.

ACKNOWLEDGEMENTS

First and foremost, I'd like to thank my family. I crammed in the time to write this book for Carrie and Finn, but in turn, my family got to see me hunched over my desk as I did so. Thank you for your love and understanding. Without your support, I'd never have gotten this done.

To my agent, Louise Fury, and her wonderful pit crew, thank you so much for your advice and editing help! And all your guidance and advice and the support. Oh my God, the support! You are all like magical unicorns in the publishing world. You're the bee's knees, and I heart you all.

To my wonderful publicist with InkSlinger PR, Jessica Estrep, thank you for all the unwavering support and dedication you gave to this book and to me. I'm so, so happy I signed with InkSlinger PR, and even happier I got you!

To Heidi McLaughlin and Caisey Quinn, thank you for listening to me panic, whine, bitch, and moan as I learned the ropes of this crazy new adult world. And thanks for all the tips, pointers, and help, too. You two are the best friends a girl could ask for! Lots of hugs and kisses!

To my beta readers, thank you! You all gave me invaluable advice and support, and you helped shape *Out of Line* into what it is today. I'll be sure to send book two your way once I, you know, write it.

To Casey Harris-Parks, Jessica Estep, Louise Fury, and all of her pit crew—thank you for the hours and hours and hours spent deliberating over the perfect title for Finn and Carrie. I couldn't have done it without you! Seriously!

And to all of the readers out there, keep on reading.

Jen McLaughlin

Edited by: Coat of Polish Edits
Copy edited by: Hollie Westring at hollietheeditor.com
Cover Designed by: Sarah Hansen at © OkayCreations.net
Interior Design and Formatting by: E.M. Tippetts Book Designs

This one is for Tessa, Jill, and Trent. You guys kept me sane during my writing spree, and you're the best friends a girl could ask for.

Desperate to keep him...

I've finally gotten everything I ever wanted: love, freedom, happiness, and, most importantly, Finn. Our love is everything I expected it to be and more. We've finally found each other, but the world seems determined to tear us apart. We thought my father was the only obstacle between us, but now it's the military. With Finn's departure looming, we're squeezing in every moment together before we run out of time.

Trying to make every moment count...

Being Carrie's bodyguard was one thing. Being her boyfriend is another. Every day she's mine is a day the sun shines in my life. Yet our time together is running out. Her father will never think a tattooed Marine will be good enough, so I'll do with whatever it takes to be worthy of her love. But the road will take me away from the girl who makes me feel alive—the girl I can't live without.

Time only gets us so far...

Never letting go…

He closed his arms around me and carried me to his bed. He was so hard and solid and it drove me insane every time he moved his tongue over mine like that. His teeth scraped my lower lip, and I whimpered into his mouth. His fingers moved over my butt, slipping between my legs and rubbing against the spot where I needed him most.

As he lowered me to the mattress, he started to climb on top of me, but I broke the kiss and shoved at his shoulders. "No," I said, locking gazes with him. "It's my turn. Just stand there."

He stilled, instantly giving me what I wanted. "Your turn for what?"

"Control," I said, my cheeks heating. "I want to undress you."

He fisted his hands at his hips, watching me from beneath his lowered lids. When he looked at me like that—like I was his dessert or something—it made everything inside of me quiver and beg for his touch so much it hurt. I licked my lips and crawled to the edge of the bed on all fours. He twitched and took a step toward me; as if he couldn't hold himself back anymore, but then he stopped.

He stood there because I'd asked him to.

I ran my hands over his chest, then up over his shoulders. Just touching him made me feel like the luckiest girl in the world, and I wanted to do everything to him. Everything in the romance books I read at night, and then *more*. Even though my mother had never figured it out, I used to sneak them out of her library after she was finished with them. I'd started it in sixth grade. Now I bought them with my own money.

And I had a lot of ideas stored away in my mind that I wanted to try out on Finn.

CHAPTER ONE

Finn

I pulled Carrie tighter to my chest, closing my eyes, even though I was fully awake and alert. I just needed a second to hold her. To breathe her in. I wanted to ignore life for a second longer, because today was the day I had to tell Carrie I have bad news, and I was not looking forward to it. But hell, I didn't even necessarily know what the message was about yet. Maybe I was jumping to conclusions.

Maybe I was full of shit. Or...maybe it was bad news.

The sun came through the curtains, and I opened my eyes again, sighing. When I had woken up earlier, my first conscious thought had been: *Please don't let this all be a dream again. Please don't make me wake up alone.*

But then I'd breathed in her familiar scent that instantly calmed my racing heart, and I had relaxed again. It hadn't been a dream. Thank fucking God. The real world was just as happy as my dreams—which made sense since she starred in both anyway. The woman I loved had forgiven me for secretly working for her father and all was right in the world. Her bright blue eyes were shut tight, her long red hair lay splayed all across her white pillow, and her soft lips seemed to be begging to be kissed.

Her ginger eyelashes were swept low, shadowing her pale cheeks. If someone would have told me last week that Carrie would be back in my bed, in my arms, and in love with me, I would have laughed and asked them what the fuck they were smoking.

Yet here she was. *This* was real.

And she was late for class.

"Ginger...?"

I kissed her lips, savoring the unique flavor that was my Carrie. I made sure not to press too close to her, though, and give her the wrong idea. Or maybe it was myself I was trying to remind. But either way, there wasn't any time for a quick morning fuck.

I pulled back, and her lids fluttered open, showing me those baby blues I loved so much. "Hey," she said, her voice soft with sleep.

"It's time to wake up."

She smiled up at me, stretching like a cat. "Why are you all the way over there?"

I trailed my finger down the little strip of skin on her stomach, right above her green panties. Would I ever get sick of seeing little pieces of her skin bared for me and only me? "Because you're—"

Without warning, she snaked her arms around my neck, hauling me closer until I lay on top of her. So much for keeping my distance. Her hands played with the back of my hair. I loved it when she did that, and I had a feeling she knew it. She could ask me to walk along hot coals for her, and as long as she was playing with my hair like that, I'd do it happily.

Without hesitation, she kissed me, her tongue slipping inside my mouth and entwining with mine. Damn it, I loved it when she took the initiative, but I had to stop this before it went too far. I pulled back and unwound her arms from my neck. Then I scooted out of her reach. "You're late for class."

She sat upright, blinking rapidly. "I am?"

"Yep." I rolled out of bed, and away from the woman who held my heart in her hands. "You get in the shower, and I'll make you breakfast to go."

"Thank you," she called over her shoulder, bolting toward the bathroom in her tank top and satin underwear. I had to pause to appreciate the back view, but then I hightailed it into the kitchen to make her an egg sandwich.

I passed my phone as I went, snatching it up, and quickly called her a cab before setting it down on the counter. As I made her breakfast, I eyed the fucking thing as if it was going to jump up and bite me in the ass. Sometimes, I felt like it could. It had been the root of all bad things that happened to me lately.

First it had shown Carrie I was a liar. Then the call last night…

Nothing was definite yet. Nothing at all. But when you got a mysterious phone call from your commanding officer on a Sunday night…well, you could put two and two together pretty easily. In this fucked-up world, someone was always a finger push away from starting a war with *someone*. And who were the first ones sent in?

Marines. Always the Marines.

But some small, stupid part of me couldn't help but hope the call was nothing more than a red herring. God had a twisted sense of humor like that, didn't He? It seemed like something He would do. Give me the sun and the moon, and then pretend like he was going to snatch away the sun. Then, at the last second, he'd laugh and be all, "*Ha! I got you, didn't I?*"

I shook my head at myself. Was I seriously having a fake fucking conversation with God in my head? I was losing it. Losing my mind. I needed to look at this rationally.

Maybe the military thought there would be another attack in Egypt or something and were readying troops just in case. There were a hell of a lot of *just in case* situations in the military. It didn't have to *mean* something.

The possible threat could fail to come to fruition. Then I'd get to stay with Carrie.

It's not that I was scared to go fight for my country. I wasn't. But I *was* scared of how Carrie would handle the news of me going. That's not to say I didn't think she was strong enough to handle it, because she was. She just worried about me.

I flipped the egg and popped some bread into the toaster. As I waited, I eyed my phone and replayed the message in my head. Screw this. I needed to hear it again. I picked it up and hit *play*.

"*Sergeant Coram, this is C.O. Gunnerson. Report for duty at Pendleton Saturday morning at oh-eight-hundred, and be advised there will be news regarding a possible deployment for you in the near future.*"

The commanding officer's gravelly voice rang in my head, making me want to throw the phone across the room. But, instead, I slammed it down on the countertop, my heart thumping loudly. Yeah. That didn't sound good at all.

I shouldn't be surprised. This was a pattern in my life. The second things started to look up for me, shit always blew up in my face. Like the time I'd gotten the job of my dreams, only to learn it would require me to travel out of the country for ten months of the year. Or the time I'd gotten my Harley, and then an asshole in a pickup truck smashed it into pieces.

This certainly wasn't the first time I'd gone through this type of thing, and it wouldn't be the last.

The toast popped and I set it down on the Saran Wrap. After putting the rest of her sandwich together, I poured her a to-go mug of coffee and waited at the door. She came charging out of the bathroom with jeans and my t-shirt on; her hair in a sloppy ponytail. Hot damn, I didn't want to let her walk out the door.

But I knew I had to.

She grabbed her bag, slung it over her shoulder, and came my way. "You giving me a ride?"

I raised a brow. "Can you eat and drink coffee on a bike?"

"No."

"Then no." I kissed her quickly, not wanting to hold her up even more, and handed her the coffee. Her fingers brushed against mine, and I wanted to capture them and hold them close to my chest. Right above my heart. "I called you a cab, and it's out there waiting for you."

She grinned at me, her warm eyes shining up at me. "Thanks, love."

"*Love?*" I scratched my head. "That's new."

She shrugged and took the sandwich from me. "I'm trying it on for size. You have so many nicknames for me, it's only fair I think of one for you."

"Hm." I patted her on the ass, the universal signal to get going. "Well, *Ginger*, I'll pick you up after class. Five, right?"

"Yes." Her cheeks flushed, and her gaze dipped to my mouth. "I have to study afterward with a friend, so make it six?"

"Which friend?"

"A new one you don't know." She kissed me. "A girl. She's majoring in biology, too, with the end goal of occupational therapy. Just like me."

"Ah. I suppose I'll share then." I slapped her ass gently. "Off you go."

Her eyes darkened. "Do I *have* to go?"

"You know you do. If your grades fail, then I do, too."

She huffed. "I *had* to go and fall for the guy whose job it is to make sure I don't fail, didn't I?"

"Don't look so sad. If you hurry up and get to class—*and* behave yourself all day—maybe I'll help you study again."

She perked up at that. "Deal."

I pulled her in for one last kiss. "I love you, Ginger."

"I love you, too."

I watched her climb down the stairs and make her way toward the yellow taxi. She took a sip of her coffee and slid into the cab, her eyes on me as she pulled away. Once she was out of sight, I sighed and went back inside. As I made myself a sandwich and brewed another cup of coffee, I picked up my phone and unlocked it.

Two texts already.

Ever since I got sent here to guard her—babysit her, more like—I'd been on a daily text routine with her fucking father. He was like a needy teenager in some ways. If I didn't immediately text him first thing in the morning, I got at least three texts before I could finish my coffee. The funny thing was she didn't even need watching.

Well, maybe she did a little bit.

Only because she'd gone and fallen in love with me, despite my initial lies about my real identity and the fact I was her father's lackey sent to spy on her. But no one was going to take her from me—not even her dad. I needed her too badly.

She reported to class on time.

Barely thirty seconds passed before the phone buzzed again. *Good. Check on her after and make sure you actually text me back.*

I snorted. *Will do, sir.*

After I sent the text, I spun the phone in my hand, debating my next move. Maybe I should call Dad and see what he thought was up. He'd been in the military long enough to get how things ran. I could practically hear his voice now. He'd say something along the lines of, "*Griffin, you know what this is as well as I do. You're going to war, son.*"

Maybe I would check in with one of my squad members. See if they knew something I didn't. After flipping my egg in the nick of time, I dialed my buddy Hernandez.

"Hello?" Hernandez said, his voice rough.

"Hey. It's Coram."

Hernandez set something down. Maybe his coffee mug? "What's up, man?"

"Did you get a call last night?"

"From who?"

I leaned against the counter. "Our C.O.?"

"Um, no." Hernandez cleared his throat. "Should I have? What's going on?"

"Shit, I don't know. I thought…" I rubbed my forehead, but it did nothing to take away the ache between my eyes. "Fuck me."

"No thanks," Hernandez said. "You're not my type."

I snorted. "The hell I'm not."

"Yeah…no. I prefer blondes. But why would he call you and not me?"

I shook my head. "I got a call from him that I have to show up this weekend. But if I'm the only one, what the fuck does that mean?"

"I don't know." I heard a door shut. "I hung out with Smith last night, and he didn't mention it either. So I don't know, man."

So two people hadn't gotten the call, but I had? What the fuck did that mean? It didn't make any sense. "All right. Thanks, man."

"Do you think they—?" A muffled knock sounded through the phone. "Shit. I gotta go, Coram. I'll call you later."

"Yeah. Sure."

I hung up the phone and set it down, my head hurting even more now. So I wasn't being deployed with my unit, but I might be deploying soon?

None of this made any sense, damn it.

CHAPTER TWO

Carrie

Later that day, I shoved all my school crap into my brown messenger bag. I'd just finished my study session with my partner from chemistry, and still had a crapload of homework to do, but that was hardly a surprise. Going to school to become an occupational therapist was not an easy thing.

With it came tons of homework and labs and studying. I'd known it was what I wanted to do since I'd entered high school, and I hadn't wavered from it at all. I loved helping people, so it seemed like a good fit for me to pick a career where I was, well, helping people. Hands down.

But now I was finding that juggling a love life and school and lying to Dad about it was a *bit* hard to keep up with. Not that I was complaining or anything. It was a lot to handle sometimes. Tonight before I left, I needed to drop off a few articles of clothing in the main room so people could take what they wanted, then I also had to grab a change of clothes for me.

I had a feeling I would be spending the night at Finn's house again, and that was A-okay with me, thank you very much. Heck, if I had it my way, I'd never leave his side again except for school. Even that was a challenge, to be honest.

I knew I had to focus on studies, and so I did. There wasn't a question of me slacking in that area. I had goals and dreams, and they didn't include flunking out of college. But it was better when Finn was with me. I even slept better with him beside me. I *needed* him there, being all hot, smart-assy, annoying, and irresistible all at once.

You know. Being Finn.

When I'd found out he was my father's spy *after* falling in love with him, I never would've thought we could move on from that. Never thought *I* could move on from that. But when it came to a life without Finn, well, I didn't want to live that life.

I'd tried it. It sucked. I wasn't going back.

I heard someone come up behind me in the library and I gazed over my shoulder. One of the last people I wanted to talk to right now stood there, looking ashamed of himself.

Good. He should be.

"Hey, Carrie."

He scratched his head, barely managing to muss up his blond hair, and gave me a sheepish smile. His gold Rolex—which almost made me laugh, since Finn called him Golden Boy—glinted in the light, so at contrast with Finn's G-Shock watch he sometimes wore that it made me wonder what the hell I'd ever thought Cory could give me out of life. He was my politician father about thirty years ago.

I had no idea why there'd even been a hint of interest in my mind for this man when Finn was within a five hundred-mile radius of me. Cory was everything my father would want for me, and everything I did *not*.

I tensed. "Hi."

"Uh…" Cory cleared his throat. "Can we talk about the other night? I saw you over here studying earlier, but didn't want to interrupt."

I was trying to forget all about that ugly scene outside of the frat party where he said those awful things to Finn about him being nothing more than trailer park trash. *Really* freaking hard. It was kind of difficult to be the bigger person when I wanted to punch him for being so darn condescending to the man I loved.

No one insulted Finn and got away with it. Call me overprotective, and maybe I was more like Dad than I cared to admit, but I wanted to claw out Cory's eyes.

I blew my hair out of my face and shoved my last book into my bag. It barely fit. "I don't really think there's anything to say."

"Look," Cory said quietly, his eyes lowered, "I'm sorry that I—"

"How's your stomach, by the way?"

Cory flushed and shifted on his feet. "It's fine. I don't even really remember what happened that night. I was pretty drunk."

"Yeah, I kind of noticed." I headed down the stairs to the classroom's exit, and he walked with me. "You said some pretty nasty things, you know."

He stopped walking. "To you?"

"To Finn." I looked at him out of the corner of my eye.

He totally relaxed when I told him it wasn't me he hurt. The jerk.

Cory rubbed the back of his neck. For his part, he did at least look slightly ashamed of what he'd done. "I really don't recall. I just remember waking up with a sore stomach and a copy of the police report I apparently filed. I feel horrible about the whole thing. You have to believe me."

"I'm sure you do," I said, gripping the shoulder strap of my bag even tighter. My anger faded away a little bit, but not all the way. "He'll be outside waiting for me, so you can apologize to him if you want."

He flushed and stumbled on a step. "Are you two…you know, back together?"

"Yeah, we are." I pressed my lips together, feeling as if I needed to explain myself or something. "I know you thought we were—"

He laughed uneasily, but his red cheeks gave away his discomfiture on the topic. "I didn't think anything. Really. It's fine. I hope you're happy with him. That's all that matters."

"No speeches about how it'll fail this time?"

He lifted a shoulder and averted his eyes. "I think I said enough on this topic already, don't you?"

"I guess you did, yeah."

He opened the door for me and motioned me through. Today he seemed different. I lifted my head, squinting through the bright sun for any signs of Finn. And then I saw him.

He leaned against a huge palm tree, his bike parked behind him. He wore a pair of ripped blue jeans and a green T-shirt with a stick figure missing his back on the front. The other figure held it in his hand and smiled. It was funny and stupid and so *Finn*.

His tattoos flexed on his muscular arms, making me want to trace each one with my tongue, and I took a big step toward him.

Would that urge, that *need* for him, ever go away?

God, I hoped not.

I knew the exact moment he noticed me. His eyes warmed, and he ran his left hand over his short brown curls. His mouth tipped into a bright smile…that is, until his gaze skidded to the side and he noticed who was with me.

Then he looked less sunny and more dangerous. Go figure.

He tugged on his curls and he pushed off the tree, stalking toward me. As he crossed the grass, Cory stiffened beside me. "Is he going to hit me again?" he whispered.

"No, he wouldn't do that." I hesitated, watching the storm gather in Finn's blue eyes, making them look almost gray. "I wouldn't say anything cocky, though, if I were you."

"God, no," Cory said, straightening to his full height. "I'm not an idiot."

That might be debatable, but I kept my mouth shut. He'd said he was sorry.

Finn reached us in record time, and he held his hand out for my bag. I gave it to him without a fight. As he slipped it over his own shoulder, he shot Cory a foul look.

"What the hell is Cody doing here?" Finn snapped, his entire body throwing off anger in heat waves.

I didn't bother to correct him about Cory's name. He knew darn well he'd said it wrong. I walked over to his side and rested a hand on his chest. "Finn, let him talk."

"Why should I?" His heart thumped erratically beneath my hand, and he looked down at me, the anger softening slightly. "I've got nothing to say to him."

"Because he has something to say to you." I moved to Finn's side, entwining his fingers with mine. Finn held on, his grip firm. "Cory, go ahead."

"I'm…" Cory looked at me, pale. I nodded, giving him the encouragement he seemed to need. "I'm s-sorry I was a jerk the other night. Whatever I said…I didn't mean it."

"Oh, but I think you did." Finn snorted. "Maybe, for the first time in your entire life, you were completely honest with me."

Cory flushed. "Seeing as how I don't even remember what I said, I can't agree or disagree."

"Let me enlighten you. You said that—"

I nudged Finn with my elbow a little harder than necessary. I could tell he was itching for a fight and would gladly give it to Cory if given the slightest provocation. "*Finn.*"

"Fine." He sighed and smiled at Cory, but it came across as more predatory than friendly. "You're forgiven. I won't punch you, and you can go back to silently hating me and waiting for Carrie and me to fall apart. Deal?"

Cory choked on a laugh and took a step back from us. "Uh, yeah. Sure. Whatever you say, man."

Finn narrowed his eyes at Cory. I tugged on his hand, trying to distract him, and started talking way too fast. "Well, now that that's over and everyone is friends again…" Finn still didn't look away from Cory, and Cory was growing paler by the second. I tugged harder. "Hello? Earth to Finn."

Finn finally looked down at me, his hot eyes searing into mine. He seemed to shake off whatever he'd been thinking. "Yeah. I'm here."

"Good." I smiled at him, my heart skipping a beat when he placed his hand on the small of my back. His hard chest pressed against mine, making me want to press closer and rub up against him like a stripper doing a lap dance. "You ready?"

"Hell yeah," Finn said, leading me toward his bike. He glanced over his shoulder, his brow furrowed, and his eyes on where Cory probably still stood. "That took a lot more self-control than I thought I had, I'll have you know."

"Why?"

"I don't like him."

"I know, but he's harmless enough."

"Yeah." Finn snorted. "As harmless as a sniper."

I looked back at Cory. He wore a lavender shirt, was going to school to become a doctor, and had manicured nails. He turned and walked away, his stride slow and laid-back, just like he was. Call me crazy, but that didn't exactly scream *dangerous thug* to me. "I just don't see what you see."

"It's simple, really. He likes you. I don't like him,'" Finn said, grabbing my helmet off the bike. "Need I say more?"

He stuck my helmet under the crook of his elbow and smoothed my hair from my face. With his hands on either side of my head, he leaned down and pressed his mouth to mine, stealing my breath away with a simple kiss. My stomach twisted in knots, and my heart thudded in my ears.

When he pulled back, he ran his thumb over my lower lip and gave me a small smile. The way my body reacted to the simple touch, he might as well have stripped naked in the street. His blue eyes skimmed over my body, making me tense with anticipation. "Were you a good girl today?"

"Of course I was," I answered instantly. "When am I *not*?"

"If you got down on your knees with my cock in your mouth," he said, his gaze fastened on my mouth. "You'd be pretty damned bad then."

"*Finn.*"

My cheeks heated and so did other parts of my body. Namely, in between my legs. I'd be lucky if I made it home before jumping his bones. And man, I wanted to do what he described now that he'd put the image in my head.

I wanted to kneel at his feet and taste him with my tongue, sucking him in deeper and deeper until he came in my—

"Hello?" He waved his hand in front of my face, his lips curved into a smile. "Did I break you?"

I licked my lips and he watched me hungrily, his gaze flashing as he read my expression. "Nope, not broken. I want to go home and do exactly what you just said, so hurry the heck up, will you?"

His eyes widened. "Fuck yeah." He slid the helmet over my head, slammed his own on, and climbed onto the bike. "Climb on."

Oh, I wanted to. And I would…as soon as I got rid of some clothes. It was the perfect time to do it, because most of my dorm mates were at dinner. "Hold on. I need two minutes."

I grabbed the bundle of shirts I was donating, ran inside my building, and threw the clothes in the normal spot. Mom sent me way too many clothes, so I shared. No biggie. I darted back outside without being seen.

As I got on the bike behind him, I let my hands dip lower to his erection. Man, he was hard and ready and *mine*. He revved the bike and hissed when I closed my hand over him through his jeans. "Fuck, Ginger, keep that up and we won't even make it home."

"Then drive fast," I said, resting my head on his shoulder. "Now."

The tires squealed as we pulled away from the curb, and I laughed.

When we got home, I planned on doing all the things I'd been dying to do since this morning. If I had it my way, we wouldn't even say a freaking word once we cleared his door.

I needed him too badly.

I closed my eyes, enjoying the air whipping around us as he buzzed through the crowded streets, darting in between stopped cars as if we were invincible. And lately I'd been feeling pretty darn invincible. I felt like I could handle anything life threw at me from now on.

I had a freedom I'd never had before. My lifelong goals were all laid out and in motion, including acing classes and having a great GPA. I was making more and more friends every day. And to top it off, I had a hot, surfing, tattooed, bike-riding Marine for a boyfriend.

Even better? He loved me as much as I loved him.

We *were* invincible.

As long as we had each other.

CHAPTER THREE

Finn

As soon as I turned off the bike, she was standing and removing her helmet. After I took it from her, she held her hand out to me. The image of her there, the sun setting behind her and silhouetting her perfectness, was so fucking beautiful that I wanted to take a picture of it and carry it with me wherever I went.

I was never one for taking pictures, but she had changed a lot of things about me. Now I *talked* and *forgave* instead of kicking ass and asking questions later. Now I was a fucking softie, and I didn't even mind.

If I had a camera in my pocket, I'd have snapped it right then and there. But no one carried around cameras anymore. Not with cell phones.

No shit, Sherlock. Use the fucking phone.

"Don't move a muscle. Don't even twitch a finger." I hung the helmets on my bike and took out my phone, grinning at her. "Hey. I saw you blink."

She shifted on her feet. "Blinking is kind of essential. Are you taking a picture of me?"

"Yep." I grinned. "Isn't that what boyfriends do?" I opened the camera app. "Take pictures and set it as their backgrounds or some shit like that?"

She laughed and I snapped the picture. She still was silhouetted perfectly, but she was smiling. Fucking perfect. Her hand dropped. "Let me see it."

"Nope. It's all mine." I shoved the phone into my pocket and grabbed her hand, hauling her up against me. She rested her palm over my heart and I smiled down at her, so fucking happy it hurt. "Just like you are."

She opened her mouth to talk, but I didn't let her. Instead, I trapped her mouth under mine, swallowing the words. My mind returned to the odd phone call I'd gotten earlier. I'd called three more members of my unit, and none of them had gotten a call. Just me. I didn't know what to expect or what it meant, but I needed to tell her about it.

Where were they sending me? And why? How long would I be gone? I had all these unanswered questions in my head, and it was driving me fucking insane. If they sent me away, I couldn't be Carrie's bodyguard. And if I wasn't *here*, I couldn't be with Carrie.

If I didn't have Carrie to kiss every single morning…then who the hell was I? I wasn't sure I wanted to know, but I had a feeling I was going to find out.

Her arms wrapped around my neck, dragging me closer, and I deepened the kiss before swinging her into my arms. As I walked up the pathway and up the stairs, I refused to break contact. I needed her as desperately as I had before I'd ever had her.

Maybe even more, if that was possible.

I unlocked my door and kicked it open, then shut it with my hip. Even though I wanted to carry her straight to my bed, I didn't. I needed to tell her about the strange call I'd gotten first. No more secrets. No more waiting.

She tried to kiss me again, but I stepped back and unwound her arms from my neck. "Hold on. We need to talk."

"Why?" She bit down on her lower lip. "What's wrong?"

"Nothing too serious." I cupped her cheek, running my thumb across her lower lip. I loved doing that. Loved seeing her smile, and the faint freckles that danced along her cheekbones when she did. Loved seeing her light up when she helped another person. Loved seeing her on a surfboard. Fuck, I loved *her*. "I got a phone call from my commanding officer. I have to report to base this weekend."

She blinked at me. "But it's the wrong weekend, isn't it?"

"It is." I hesitated and tugged on my hair. I'd have to cut it again. "I don't know what he wants with me, but he mentioned a possible deployment."

She lowered her eyes. "You mean war?"

"I'm not sure yet." I cleared my throat and met her eyes. "The thing is, I called a bunch of guys from my unit, and none of them have to go in. It's just me."

She shook her head. "But what does that mean?"

"I have no fucking clue," I said, reaching up and playing with her hair. I loved the way it felt against my fingers. "It could mean ten million things. I really have no way of knowing until I go and hear the news. But there's definitely *something* going on."

She nodded, her eyes never leaving mine. "Is this a bad thing or a good thing?"

"I really can't say," I said, shrugging. "I can speculate and freak you out with all the what ifs, but until I go and hear the news? It's pointless. I just didn't want to *not* tell you."

"Thank you for being honest right away," she said, after letting out a sigh.

"I won't keep anything from you. Not anymore." I leaned down and kissed her gently, knowing she probably needed a minute to absorb all this. "We're in this together."

She rose up on tiptoe and kissed me, not replying. She curled her hands into my shirt, a desperation in her kiss that hadn't been there before. She was freaking out, and I needed to make it better. I broke off the kiss again, taking a deep breath of air.

"Ginger, it'll be okay."

She nodded, her mouth pressed tight and her eyes narrow. "I know. Just kiss me. I need you to kiss me *now*."

Well, when she put it that way, who was I to say no?

So I kissed her.

Carrie

Okay, I was trying really, really freaking hard not to start panicking.

I mean, he'd said he wasn't going to war, or at least his unit wasn't, so that sounded promising. But still, he'd thrown out the word *deployment*. I might not know much about the military, but even I knew that meant he'd be leaving me.

And if he was leaving me, I wasn't happy.

When he closed his mouth over mine, I shut off my mind and stopped thinking. He'd already told me all he could tell me about the call, so focusing on it wasn't the healthiest choice. We had to wait until this weekend to hear anything more. Until then we were just sitting ducks.

And if I was going to be forced to wait, then I'd do it my way.

He picked me up and carried me to his bed. He was so hard and solid and it drove me insane every time he moved his tongue over mine like that. His teeth scraped my lower lip, and I whimpered into his mouth. His fingers moved over my butt, slipping between my legs and rubbing against the spot where I needed him most.

As he lowered me to the mattress, he started to climb on top of me, but I broke the kiss and shoved at his shoulders. "No," I said, locking gazes with him. "It's my turn. Just stand there."

He stilled, instantly giving me what I wanted. "Your turn for what?"

"Control," I said, my cheeks heating. "I want to undress you. And then I want to wrap my lips around your…your…"

When I drifted off, uncertain what to call his penis, he chuckled. "Cock. It's a *cock*, Carrie. Say it."

My cheeks heated. I knew what it was called. It just sounded so dirty and wrong. "Around your cock," I said in a rush, my cheeks getting even hotter.

"Okay." He fisted his hands at his hips, watching me from beneath his lowered lids. When he looked at me like that—like I was his dessert or something—it made everything inside me quiver and beg for his touch so much it hurt. I licked my lips and crawled to the edge of the bed on all fours. He twitched and took a step toward me; as if he couldn't hold himself back anymore, but then he stopped.

He stood there because I'd asked him to.

I ran my hands over his chest, then up over his shoulders. Just touching him made me feel like the luckiest girl in the world, and I wanted to do everything to him. Everything in the romance books I read at night, and then *more*. Even though my mother had never figured it out, I used to sneak them out of her library after she was finished with them. I'd started it in sixth grade. Now I bought them with my own money.

And I had a lot of ideas stored away in my mind that I wanted to try out on Finn.

I climbed off the bed and rose on tiptoes, kissing him. His tongue rubbed against mine, making my stomach clench. When I slid my hands down over his pecs and abs and then up under his shirt, he groaned into my mouth. My nails scraped his skin, and I pulled back long enough to pull his shirt over his head.

I stood back and looked at him, his gaze burning into mine as I did so. His dark ink swirled up his arms and over his biceps before it crept over his shoulders and chest. I never got sick of looking at his tattoos. I loved deciphering them and admiring how they intertwined with perfection.

He looked the part of the stereotypical bad boy...when he was anything but.

He was a contradiction at its hottest. I ran my tongue over the black tattoo that swirled over his left pec, grinning when he hissed and gripped my hips. After I nipped at the skin, I pulled back enough to say, "New rule, love. You aren't allowed to wear shirts around me anymore."

"Ever?"

"*Ever.*"

He lifted a shoulder. "It might take some explaining when we go back to D.C., but I bet I can make it work."

"I bet you could, too."

I stepped closer, my leg between his, and tipped my head back to look up at him. His blue eyes shined down at me, and his light brown curls stuck up a bit, probably because I'd run my fingers through them a few times.

His hands still gripped my hips, and they flexed on me. "Ginger..." he said, his tone strained and raspy. The way he sounded, all turned on and needy, washed over me and landed somewhere in my stomach, twisting and turning into a knot. "I'm going to—"

"I know," I said, smiling up at him. "Believe me, I know."

I dropped to my knees and undid the button of his pants. As I unzipped his jeans, he clenched his jaw and closed his eyes, letting me work as slowly as I wanted. It might be torture for him, but I knew he'd let me do whatever the hell I wanted, even if it killed him.

When I pulled down his jeans and let them fall to his feet, he kicked out of them without opening his eyes. Leaning in, I cupped his erection through his boxers, closing my hand around him and squeezing. He hissed and moved his hips back, my hand tight on him. Then he arched into me.

The look of pleasure on his face almost did me in. Touching wasn't enough. He seemed to agree. Reaching down, he yanked off his boxers, and as soon as he was out of my way, I flicked my tongue over the head of his erection.

"Jesus, Carrie." His hands burrowed into my hair and held me in place. "Give me *more*."

I groaned and took him into my mouth, swirling my tongue in circles around him. My God, he felt good there—almost as good as he felt when he was inside me. The skin was so smooth and hard at the same time… and so freaking *intoxicating*. I'd never get enough of him. I took more of him in my mouth, and he looked down at me—his jaw ticking and his body tightly wound.

His blue eyes burned with heated need, and he urged me even closer, his jaw flexing as he arched into my mouth. I closed my eyes and let out a soft moan. The urgent need to be taken by him was growing even stronger. Especially when I tasted the salty tang of something I could only assume was his semen. And I wanted more.

"*Enough*," he said, his voice harsh.

He groaned and lifted me to my feet, crashing his mouth into mine before I could even protest that I hadn't finished. Within seconds, all thoughts of protesting faded away behind the need to be touched. My nails raked over his shoulders, trying to get him even closer to me, and he deepened the kiss until I was flat on my back on the bed. He moved between my thighs, where I needed him so freaking much, and rolled his hips against me.

I might not have control anymore, but I didn't care.

I just needed him.

I wrapped my legs around his waist, but my stupid clothes were in the way. I pulled back and undid my pants, my hands trembling too badly to be fast.

"Hurry up," he growled, ripping them down my legs and tossing them onto the floor. He continued removing my clothing with jerky movements, his hands steady and sure. He stopped when I was in my red bra and lacy red thong. "These can stay."

Without warning, he flipped me onto my stomach and lowered

himself on top of me. It took me a second to adjust to the new position, but then I was ready and willing to move on to the next step. Him—inside of me.

But instead of moving forward to give me what I wanted, he nibbled on my earlobe, biting down just enough to sting. I moaned, the sound escaping from somewhere deep within me. The way he felt, cradling me from behind, drove me insane with want.

"Finn, now." I moved underneath of him restlessly, my whole body humming with desire and electric need. "*Please.*"

He groaned, his hands flexing on my hips, and bit down on my shoulder before licking away the pain. "Fuck, Ginger. I need you so bad."

"Then take me," I breathed, my fingers digging into the mattress and clinging to the comforter. I had a feeling I'd be hanging on for dear life soon. "Right here. Like this."

He moaned. "Not quite yet. You're not ready."

He kissed a path over my shoulder blade, then nibbled on the spot right over my bra clasp. I let out a ragged moan I barely recognized as my own and arched my back. He needed to touch me more. Kiss me more. *Do* more, before I exploded.

He undid my bra and I impatiently threw it to the side, and he cupped my breasts from behind. I cried out when he rolled my nipples in between his fingers, squeezing with the perfect amount of pressure, and my stomach hollowed out.

He rolled his hips against me again, mimicking making love, and I clenched my teeth. He was driving me insane with desire and he wasn't even really *trying*, damn it. I needed…needed…*him*. Now.

He pushed off me and positioned me with my legs spread more widely, but I was still on all fours. I felt extremely exposed in this position, but it was Finn. And with Finn, I could do anything. I studied him from my weird position, watching as desire darkened his gaze. Watched his erection grow even harder and his breathing become even more erratic.

I watched hungrily as he rolled a condom on. He watched me as if I was his reward for good behavior—and I really hoped he never stopped looking at me like that.

He crossed the room, his eyes on my spread thighs. "You might want to hold on tight, Ginger."

I fisted my hands tighter into the comforter when he positioned himself behind me. He slid the small scrap of my lace thong to the side and ran his tongue up my slit. I cried out and dug my knees into the mattress. The shock of pleasure his tongue brought me hit me hard and fast. "Oh my God, Finn."

"You have no idea how fucking beautiful you look right now," he said, his voice so low I barely heard him. I wanted to press my thighs together to ease the empty ache I was feeling without him inside of me, but I couldn't. Not with him in between them. "I bet you want me to taste you again. Don't you?"

"*Yes.*"

He didn't tease me. Didn't waste any time. He flicked his tongue over my clit, then sucked me in between his lips, rolling his tongue perfect circles. When he scraped his teeth against me gently, I cried out and pushed back, demanding more. He gripped my hips with his hands, kneeling behind me and going down on me from behind.

The erotic image this presented made me twitch with pleasure, building higher and higher until I couldn't stand it for another second. Everything inside of me burst into fragments, shattering into even smaller pieces until I wasn't even sure if I existed anymore. I cried out and froze, seeing and hearing nothing. Only *feeling.*

He pressed his tongue against my clit, prolonging the orgasm even more, and cupped my butt. "Fuck, Carrie," he groaned.

Then he drove inside me—hard and fast. Having him inside me felt so fabulous I wondered for a second if I was dreaming. But then he thrust back into me, and I snapped back into reality. And Finn in real life was *so* much better than a fantasy.

I dropped my head to the mattress when he withdrew almost all the way, closing my eyes tight and holding my breath in anticipation. When he was almost all the way out, he thrust back inside of me, then repeated the motion until I was whimpering and moaning his name.

He picked up the tempo, and tears stung my eyes. The amount of pleasure he was bringing down on me was actually making me cry. Pleasure so strong I couldn't even freaking handle it without whimpering into the mattress as he barreled into me again and again without restraint. He withdrew, flipped me over on to my back, and drove inside me again. When he changed his angle, going even deeper, I screamed.

Actually *screamed.*

My toes curled and I clenched down on him, my walls squeezing. He groaned and pumped faster, his face lost in the rapture of the moment. When he thrust inside me again, he went spiraling over the edge and collapsed over me, keeping his weight on his elbows.

Once we regained control of our breathing, he rolled to the side and dragged me with him. I clung to him and rested my head on his chest, right over the spot where there wasn't a tattoo. It was on the tip of my tongue to ask him if he had plans for that spot, but I realized I couldn't form a coherent word.

So I smiled instead.

"That was a nice way to forget about the stress, huh?" he asked, his lips twitching. He played with a piece of my hair, gently tugging on it. It made me shiver. "And here I was going to suggest surfing as a good method of forgetting about shit."

I took a deep breath, hoping when I opened my mouth that something besides an unintelligible grunt came out. "We can do that in the morning. I have a late class," I said, my heart finally settling back into a normal rhythm. And, lo and behold, I could talk. "But as far as this particular method of distraction goes? I plan on doing it again and again and again until this weekend…"

"Uh-huh. I see, I see." He nodded and pursed his lips seriously, as if we were discussing world politics. "But then what? We just stop?"

"No, then we find out what's next." I leaned up and kissed him softly. "And we deal with it."

But I really wanted to know what *it* was.

Sooner rather than later.

CHAPTER FOUR

Finn

"Let's go do something fun," I said, my hand on her lower back. She'd just finished studying, and we'd been sitting in silence ever since. I needed to make her stop thinking about what we'd be going through. "What's something you've always wanted to do but never did?"

"Skydive?"

I flinched. "I can't pull that together on short notice."

"Bungee jumping?"

I laughed uneasily. "Do you have a fucking death wish? Jesus."

She rolled her eyes. "Nope. I just like the rush."

"Yeah, well, tone it down a notch. How about roller-skating? Or ice-skating? Or what about—"

"Rock climbing." She sat up straight, her eyes lighting up. "I've always wanted to rock climb."

"Seriously?"

"Seriously." She nodded enthusiastically. I hadn't seen her this excited since the time I told her I'd teach her how to surf. "Do you know how?"

"I used to do it as a kid. Back when my dad still worked here."

"Were you good?"

I tugged on my hair. "My mom had tons of videos of me doing it. I found them the last time I went through the boxes in our attic. I guess I was okay."

"Your mom recorded you?" She smiled and squeezed my hand. "That's so cute."

I nodded. "She was that kind of mom. She came to everything with that damn camera in her hand."

Without even realizing it, I grinned, remembering how much it used to embarrass me. Now, I'd give anything to have her on the sidelines, watching me through a lens and cheering me on. She'd died of cancer when I was sixteen. I hadn't been the same since.

Carrie squeezed my hand again, then dropped a kiss on my jaw. "Let's go do it. Your mom would like to see you back up on a wall, I bet."

She probably would. She'd always said she loved seeing me out there, climbing higher and higher as if I already owned the world. I used to think I did back then. I stood up and helped her stand. "All right. But it's been years, so I'm probably not going to be the best teacher."

"I don't care." She laughed and headed for the door, her step already lighter. She picked up her helmet and grinned at me, her blue eyes dancing with excitement. "It'll be fun. Just you and me and the memory of your mom. Maybe I'll even take a video, love."

I swallowed hard and picked up my phone. I shot a quick text to her dad, then shoved it into my pocket. He'd been a little quiet lately. Must be busy working.

But still. Weird.

"Yeah. Fun." I grabbed my motorcycle keys and my helmet. "So, we'll need to make sure the place supplies the helmets, elbow guards, and knee pads."

"Or we could just climb." She opened the door. "I'll hardly be going that high. I think I'll be all right without all the padding."

I considered this, but shook my head. "I have a feeling they require safety equipment."

"Finn." She sighed. "Don't be my dad. You know I have enough of that in my life. I've already surfed and rode a bike. What's a little harmless rock climbing?"

She had a point, but it was my job to keep her safe. I sighed and followed her down the stairs. "Be that as it may, you will still need protection. They won't let you climb up without it. You might want to be free and wild, but they'll disagree."

"If they do, I'll listen to them." She pulled her helmet down over her head. "Just not you."

"Wow." I frowned at her. "I love you, too," I muttered.

She snorted. "Stop pouting. I'll probably fall off as soon as I get off the ground, which is why they make you wear a harness thingy," she said, motioning for me to get on the bike. "I wouldn't worry about me going too high up."

"Not helping my confidence here." I revved the bike. "Climb on, Ginger."

"Later, maybe," she replied, climbing onto the bike and holding tight. She yelled over the engine of my Harley. "But first, we rock climb!"

I laughed, loving her enthusiasm. She always dived in to new things with wide-open arms, never showing a hint of fear. Hell, she'd even done that with me. Just kind of opened up and accepted me for what I was. That never ceased to amaze me.

The whole ride to the closest rock climbing gym—a quick Google search had showed me the one I used to go to still existed—she held on to me, leaning when I leaned, resting while I rested. She had the bike thing down more perfectly than some drivers did. Maybe some day I'd teach her how to drive this thing. I bet she'd like that.

I parked and we went inside. It took all of five minutes for us to pay, then we were strapped into the harnesses and standing in front of a wall that looked a lot higher than I remembered.

"Okay, you put one foot on and kind of push up like this." I did what I described and climbed up a little unsteadily, almost catching myself off guard. Hell, it had been a long time for me. "But make sure to hold on tight with your hands while spreading them—but not too far. You don't want to throw off the balance."

She watched me, her brow furrowed, then did as I said. She set one foot up high, tested her weight, but then righted herself. She lifted her other foot, her brow furrowed with concentration. "Like this?"

"Yep." I climbed up a little higher again. "Do it again."

She did it, much more steadily this time. "It's almost rope climbing, only you're stepping instead of wrapping yourself around something."

"Except the wall," I said dryly.

"Well, duh," she said, rolling her eyes. "Obviously."

I stretched my arms and took another step higher. "Attitude, Ginger. Attitude."

"Now you're just showing off." She followed me, going a lot faster this time. I wanted to grab her and steady her when she wobbled, but I clenched my fists and let her do it for herself. She needed this. "Look, that was pretty good, huh?"

"Yeah, it was." I grinned at her. "Watch this."

I climbed double the length that I'd been doing, stretching my muscles as far as they could go without falling off the damn wall. She laughed, her eyes shining. "I can do that, too."

I side-eyed her. "You think?"

"Dude." She pursed her lips and looked to the top of the wall. "What is the worst that can happen? I fall and the harness catches me? Somehow I think I'll survive."

I shook my head. "Fine. It's your ass, not mine."

Technically, it was mine, too. I was supposed to be protecting her, not taking her rock climbing, but whatever. The girl needed to live, for fuck's sake.

She'd spent her whole life being watched by men like me not letting her step out of line for even a second. Now she was able to do so. I might be watching her, but I'd be damned if I suffocated her like her father.

We spent the next half hour climbing higher and higher, then we practiced climbing down. She slipped and fell more times than I could count—fine, it was seven—before we finally called it quits. I let her be the one to decide when she'd had enough.

She stood at the bottom of the wall after her last fall, snapping pictures and a few videos with her phone. Her laugh rang loud and clear as I descended to join her. She was so fucking bright and happy. She really was the sun to me.

The only thing that brought true brightness to my world.

I pushed back off the wall, landing nimbly on my feet, and she clapped, her phone held in her hand. "I got the perfect shot of that." She walked over and held out her phone. "And now I have a wallpaper for my phone, too. Nice, huh?"

It was of me in midair, about to land. It was a pretty cool shot. "Good one."

"Thanks. But I'm hungry now," she said, tucking her phone away. "You ready for some burgers or something?"

"McDonald's or Islands?" I asked, unclicking my harness and

grabbing her hand. "You can pick tonight."

After we cleaned up and squared off with the workers, we walked toward my bike, her under my arm. "I think I'm gonna have to go Islands."

I grinned. "Did I convert you?"

"Maybe." She pointed a finger at me and glared, but the effect was ruined by how damn happy she looked. "But I'll forever be a McDonald's girl, too."

I shrugged. "Whatever you say, Ginger. Whatever you say."

CHAPTER FIVE

Finn

The next morning I woke up to Carrie climbing on top of me, kissing me until I forgot what the hell color the sky was. Her hands moved all over me, slowly waking me up, and by the time we were finished with each other, I was exhausted and naked and sweaty. I looked over at her and grinned at the smug smile on her face.

"More distraction, I see." I tapped her nose. "You look awfully proud of yourself."

"That's probably because I'm feeling pretty darn proud of myself."

She rolled over on her side, folded her hands under her cheek, and smiled at me. Something in her eyes pulled at me. Told me that beneath the smile and laughter was fear. Lots of fear.

But how could she manage to look so sad while still looking so damn happy?

"Get over here," I said.

When I opened my arms, she rolled into them and closed her arms around me. I held her for a few minutes, enjoying the closeness, not needing to talk. It was nice having a person with you where you didn't feel the need to blabber on and on just to fill the silence. As I was beginning to wonder if she fell asleep, she sighed and squirmed.

I played with her hair. I was beginning to think I had a hair fetish when it came to her. I couldn't stop myself from doing it. "Hey, you want to go out on a date tonight? Are you all caught up on your homework and shit?"

She rested her chin on me. "A date? Like, dresses and suits and a fancy restaurant?"

I hadn't been thinking of wearing a suit, no. I'd been thinking burgers or something along those lines. But I guess that's what a girl like Carrie expected when the word *date* came up. She'd grown up in the lap of luxury after all. If she wanted to wear a dress and go to some French restaurant I couldn't even pronounce, then so be it. I could certainly afford it.

I smiled at her. "Yeah. We can go to that French place on Pico. The one with the swans."

She brightened up, her smile wide. "Oh my God, yes! I've been wanting to go there for a while."

"Great," I said, smiling, even though I didn't feel like smiling.

"But I have to admit, I'm surprised to hear you suggest it. You're more of a burger-and-shake kind of guy," she said, her voice cheerful.

"And you're not?"

Her mouth twitched. "I'm not a guy."

"And thank fucking God for that." I tapped her nose with my finger. "But you know what I mean."

"I like them both," she said, lifting a shoulder in a tiny shrug. "A little bit of variety never hurt anyone."

Having her get all excited about a date in an expensive restaurant made me feel anxious and wound up. Shaking off the weird feeling creeping up my spine, I asked, "Do you still want to go surfing?"

"I do." She rested her chin on my chest. "It looks cloudy out, so there might be some awesome waves."

I tucked her red hair behind her ear and forced a smile. "All right. Want to eat before or after?"

"After." She got out of bed and looked over her shoulder at me. "But make sure you get some coffee in your system. I don't want to deal with cranky Finn."

I laughed and rolled out of bed. "*Cranky* Finn?"

"Mmhm." She reached into her bag and pulled out her red bikini. "He's miserable without coffee in him. A real jerk."

I came up behind her and nuzzled her neck. The feel of her skin on mine almost made me say the hell with surfing...but if she wanted to surf—then she'd get it. "Don't worry. I'll go make some now." As I headed bare-assed naked into the kitchen, I called out, "I'm surprised you remembered your suit."

"I thought we might end up going." She peeked over her shoulder at me as she stepped into the bottoms. "But we'll need to get my board from my dorm."

"You can leave it here if you want," I said, slipping a K-cup into the Keurig. "I don't mind."

"Really?" She stood up straight, wearing nothing but her tiny red bikini bottoms. Fuck, if she would let me, I'd snap a picture and make *that* my wallpaper. "Okay, sure."

"You look surprised," I said, raising a brow at her. "Why?"

She picked up the bikini top and turned almost as red as it was. "I always thought guys were weird with girls leaving their stuff at their places. They get all paranoid she's trying to stake a claim or something."

"Maybe some guys are, but I'm not one of those guys." I pulled two mugs out of the cabinet and headed back into the bedroom portion of my apartment. The light blue comforter was halfway off the bed, thanks to our morning sex. I straightened it, then pulled it up over our pillows. "Besides, the guys who don't want their girls' stuff at their places are the ones with something to hide. I don't have any more secrets."

She nibbled on her lower lip as she did up her bikini top, tying it in front of her breasts before sliding it up over her neck. "I know that. But you had a pretty big secret before that."

"You mean the fact that I was your father's secret bodyguard sent to watch over you?" I snorted. "That's nothing. What you really should know about me is this: I snore when I'm drunk."

She smacked me playfully. "Don't make me hurt you…and in that case? Maybe I'll need to leave some earplugs here."

"You can leave them right next to the bed." I hauled her into my arms, liking the idea of her leaving her shit here more and more. "You can leave some shirts and stuff, too, if you want. In case you ever need a quick change. Maybe a few of those books with abs on it that you like to read when you're not busy reading for school."

She blinked up at me. "Okay."

"Why are you looking at me like that *again*?" I flexed my fingers on her hips, not sure what the confused stare she wore meant. Did she not like the idea of leaving stuff here? Maybe I was moving too fast for her. Shit if I knew. "It's just clothes, Ginger. It's not a big deal. You have tons of them—just leave a few here instead of leaving them in a box that says 'free: take one' on the front."

She laughed and pushed out of my arms. "I *know*. Now shut up."

"Yes, ma'am." I tied my swim trunks and headed back toward the bathroom to brush my teeth. "Let me text your dad real quick. I've probably got like twenty texts from him already."

She rolled her eyes. "Remind me to tell you about Italy."

"Oh, that sounds…" I picked up my phone and swiped my finger across it. There wasn't a single message from him. Not a single one. That *never* happened. "What the fuck?"

She came up behind me and rested her hands on my shoulders, peeking around me to check my phone. "What? What's wrong?"

"He didn't text me." I opened his messages, scanning the time of the last text I'd gotten. "Shit. He hasn't texted me since yesterday."

"Is that different than usual?"

"Fuck yeah, it is." I swiped my finger up, showing her how many times he usually texted me. "He texts me like ten times a day, Ginger. But I've got nothing. *Nothing.*"

She kissed my shoulder. "It's probably nothing to worry about. He's just busy, I bet. He called me yesterday at lunch and sounded fine. He wanted to let me know he might be a little bit quiet because of his schedule."

I relaxed a little bit, but it didn't feel right. Something was off, and I'd learned long ago to listen to my gut. If it said something was wrong, something was fucking wrong. "Yeah. Sure."

She let go of me. "Now go get ready. I want to get out in the ocean."

I headed for the bathroom, my phone still in my hand. As I brushed my teeth, I jotted off a quick text to Senator Wallington. *Carrie's okay. All is well.*

Within a minute I had a reply. *Thank you.*

That was it. A thank you. There was nothing wrong with the text, per se. But it wasn't right, damn it. I shook off the feeling that was bugging the fuck out of me, and focused on the date I'd promised Carrie. She had enough to stress about, what with that weird phone call I'd gotten that neither of us could make any sense out of, so I didn't need to go obsessing about the tone of a text message like some pansy-assed little girl.

I leaned against the door, my eyes on my reflection. The nagging sensation that something was wrong wouldn't let go. On top of that, I figured out what was bugging me from when we'd talked about our date.

I stared at myself, all tattoos, dog tags, muscles, swim trunks and five-o-clock shadow—it hit me. The problem with her wanting a fancy date with flowers and dresses and jewelry and valet parking was *I* wasn't fancy.

I could put on an expensive suit and pretend.

I could afford to be that guy, money-wise.

But underneath the suit and the charming smile, I was the tatted-up Marine that had no place dating the daughter of a prospective President of the United States of America. She was supposed to be with a trust fund baby. One who had money and wealth and recognition.

Me? I *so* wasn't that guy.

I never would be.

CHAPTER SIX

Carrie

The waves were strong, but not so much that I had to worry about being taken under. Thank God. I'd already been there once before, right after I found out Finn was working for my father, and I had no desire to be there again.

I looked over at him, and he was watching me, his warm blue eyes shining. His light brown hair looked almost blond in the sunlight, and his wetsuit clung to his muscles like a second skin. And I knew under that suit was a perfect body with an even more perfect heart underneath of it. He smiled at me, but I could tell it was strained.

He was upset about Dad not texting him, and I was, too. Even though I played it off like it was no big deal, it did sound bad. I called him while Finn was in the bathroom, and he hadn't answered. That freaked me out.

Almost as much as the call Finn had gotten from his commanding officer.

And it was killing me to act like it wasn't killing me.

"Hey, back at my place you told me to remind you about a story," he said, his tone light and teasing. It didn't fool me, though. He was stressed—and so was I. "What happened in Italy?"

My cheeks heated, and I looked over my shoulder. Why had I told him I'd tell him about that? Ugh. "Well, for me to explain, I have to tell another story first. You might already know it. Did you hear about what happened in Nevada when I was ten?"

Finn's brow creased. "No. My dad wasn't there yet. I was still in California. My mom was still alive…" He trailed off, his eyes focused on a past I couldn't see. "At that point in my life, I was a carefree surfer boy who thought he was invincible. My dad worked on a high-security detail for the governor, and my mom was healthy as a horse."

I nodded, wanting to probe more about what his life had been like before his mother died, but knowing now was not the time. He wanted his story, so I would give it to him. "There's a reason my dad is as crazy as he is. Back then, he wasn't so insistent we have security on us twenty-four/seven. I had freedom and there were actually times when I was on my own. We were free."

"You didn't have someone on you constantly?"

I shook my head. "Nope. In fact, Mom and I got bored while Dad was campaigning, so we decided to go shopping at the local mall to pass some time. We didn't bring anyone with us."

"I think I see where this is going," he said dryly. "You got lost and he panicked?"

I shook my head. "Nope. We got abducted."

"W-What?" he said, sitting up straight. "Are you fucking kidding me?"

"I wish." I sighed and looked over my shoulder. I hated talking about it. It had been a nightmare. "The guy was a complete idiot, so they found us pretty quickly, but my dad got really shaken up about it. We all did. And ever since then, he's been different. Controlling."

He sighed. "I almost get it now. If something happened to you on my watch, I'd probably go insane, too."

"Even though we were the ones who were abducted, I think he's the one who had the major post-traumatic stress issues. Mom and me?" I shrugged and stared out at the ocean before turning to Finn. "We moved on, but with the security that Dad insists follow us *everywhere*. And it's stayed that way ever since."

Finn nodded, his hands tight on his board. "So that's why he makes me follow you around out here."

"Yeah." I watched a fairly large wave form in the distance, rolling slowly toward us. I loved the way the waves did that—started small but slowly built up height before crashing to the sand. I could sit here all day and watch Mother Nature do her worst. "And in Italy, I escaped the watchmen."

Finn flinched. "Please tell me you weren't kidnapped."

"I wasn't." I smiled at him. "But I didn't answer my dad's texts and he freaked the hell out. I mean, catastrophic panic."

Finn tapped his fingers on his board, playing a tune I didn't recognize. "I would've been away then. I missed the show."

"You're lucky. I hear it was quite ugly." I sighed and tore my eyes from the water, looking back at my other favorite sight—otherwise known as Finn.

"Where did you go? In Italy?"

"I wanted to flirt with that guy I told you about when we first met. The Italian guy I mentioned. Remember him?"

His brows slammed down. "I do. But do I want to hear anything else?"

He was glowering at me now, but at least he looked more alive than he had for a while. Ever since he asked me on a date he'd been acting weird. Brooding, almost. I could tell something was bothering him, but I had no idea what it was or if it was even related to our date later tonight.

"Oh, don't look at me like that. I never even got close to him. My dad's guards found me and *took care* of it," I said, lifting my hands and doing air quotes. "But for those thirty minutes when no one knew where I was? Dad texted me every single second, I kid you not. I'd ignored him because I knew he was being his normal spaztastic self, and I told him as much. But after that, he promised to only text me twenty million times if it was an emergency."

Finn pressed his lips together. "So you're telling me this to make sure I don't panic like him, or what?"

"Pretty much." I reached out and caught his hand, squeezing it tight. "It'll be okay. You'll see."

"I know." He lifted my hand and kissed my fingers, making my stomach clench. "With you at my side, how could it not be?"

My heart melted at that sentence. Combined with the way he looked at me—his eyes soft and his lips even softer—I wasn't sure I had the muscle power to surf right now.

"You catch the first wave," I said, my voice practically a whisper. I cleared my throat and tipped my head toward the approaching wave. "It looks pretty big."

He nodded once. "And you'll wait till I come back to catch another one."

"Yeah, yeah." I waved a hand at him impatiently. "I remember the rules, master of the sea."

He looked over his shoulder, more than likely calculating the time it would take for his ride to arrive. He had a few seconds at most. He shot me a look and started paddling forward, his back muscles bunching and rolling flawlessly. "You can give me all the attitude you want, but I almost lost you once—I won't do it again."

"I know," I called out, splashing water at him. The drops barely reached him. "Now go before you're too late."

He grinned and flawlessly caught the wave, riding it to shore like the pro he was. He sliced in and out, doing moves I didn't even know the names of, never once tipping off balance. He was mesmerizing and beautiful to watch out here.

Well, *anywhere*. But especially on the water.

I watched him with awe, quite certain I'd never get to that level of skill, but I was okay with that. I just liked coming out here, hanging out in the water and enjoying the time with Finn. For the most part, we were left alone. There were a few surfers out this morning, but it was much emptier than on a weekend.

A blond man prepared to catch the next wave a few hundred feet over, and past him a woman with black hair bobbed in the water. It was a perfect, peaceful morning.

But I felt anything but peaceful.

Finn swam back to my side and I forced a bright smile. If it was the last thing I did, I would hide my anxiety from him. He didn't need my baggage sinking him down to the bottom of the Pacific. "That was a good one."

He climbed back on his black board and shook his hair like a wet dog, spraying me. "It was. Next one's yours, though."

"As long as it's little enough to pass your test," I added, unable to resist teasing him. Truth be told, I liked how protective he was. He loved me and he didn't want to lose me. I totally got that. "Right?"

"Right." He looked over his shoulder and trailed his fingers through the water absentmindedly. "Here comes a good one."

I paddled forward, watching the wave swell closer. "See ya on the flip side."

"Remember, if you go under, wait it out," he called, his voice tight.

I nodded as I paddled faster, ignoring the fear surging through me as the wave grew and grew. Apparently, that near drowning affected me more than I thought. I refused to let it conquer my enjoyment of the sport. Heck, people got limbs chewed off by sharks and went back out there. What was an almost drowning in comparison?

I struggled to my feet, wobbling a bit at first, but as I straightened my legs and stood, I gained my footing—and my confidence. As I rode the wave, holding my arms out for balance, I laughed from the sheer joy of the rush. I didn't attempt any fancy moves or anything—it took all my concentration just to stay upright.

But my head pounded and my heart raced, making me lightheaded. God, I'd become such an adrenaline junky since meeting Finn. I wanted to do all the things, and I wanted to do them now—with him at my side. Once my ride was over, I stood up and squeezed the excess moisture out of my hair.

I made my way back to Finn, a smile on my face the whole time. I'd missed this. Missed surfing, even though it had only been a week or two since we last came out. Maybe this weekend when Finn was gone, I would—

I stopped walking, a tingling sensation creeping up my spine. I had the weirdest feeling that someone was *watching* me, but when I looked over my shoulder, the beach was empty. The only people out and about were surfers, and none of them were paying any attention to me. I shook off the creepy sensation, forcing myself to keep walking.

It was all the uncertainty messing with my head, I'd bet. All the what ifs and Finn's own suspicions about my father's silence were screwing with me. Maybe reliving the time I'd been kidnapped contributed to my imagining someone watching me. That hadn't exactly been a walk in the park or a happy memory to retell.

All of this stressful crap was obviously combining in one tight ball in my head, making me think the shadows were chasing me. Making me think I was being watched, when the only one watching me was my bodyguard *slash* boyfriend.

I had enough to stress about. I needed to stop imagining new things.

The whole way back to Finn, I thought about what life would be like after this year was up.

I was terrified about what Dad would do when he found out Finn and I had fallen in love. He could totally flip out, or he could—unlikely, as it might be—accept it for what it was. Maybe he would be angry, but he'd get over it with time. Or maybe we would never be welcome in his house again.

He *could* be quite stubborn when he wanted to be. It's admittedly where I'd gotten my stubborn streak from. And I wouldn't put it past him to make it a point to show me how many different ways I'd disappointed him through lectures and maybe even a little bit of a disowning shame. But he wouldn't actually cut the ties with me all because I dared to fall in love.

At least I hoped he wouldn't.

It was a risk I was willing to take for Finn.

CHAPTER SEVEN

Finn

Later that night, I waited in the living room as Carrie finished getting ready in my bathroom for our date. Even though we were only going out to dinner, I was nervous for some stupid ass reason I couldn't quite put my finger on. It was our first real date, yeah, but I didn't think that's what was bothering me. I just felt...

I don't know. Different somehow.

As if I was pretending to be something I wasn't. *Again.*

I tugged on my collar. Jesus, I swore the thing was single-handedly attempting to choke the life out of me. I was also starting to think it might win. My palms were sweaty, and I was so hot I didn't think I was going to make it through the night in this damned contraption. Maybe I'd had more Cali Surfer Boy left over in my blood than I'd thought.

Or maybe I was going soft.

I flopped down on the couch, setting my legs on the coffee table. This dress-up date was probably a bad idea. I wasn't a fancy guy, even if she was a fancy girl.

I was just *me*.

Why did I feel like I needed to be this guy for her all of a sudden? Maybe it was because I was more than likely leaving, and I was having a panic attack of sorts, trying to be everything she could ever possibly want me to be. Or maybe part of me just now realized that no matter what she said or thought, she came from a world where tuxes and champagne were more common than beer and movie nights...and if we were going to be together, I had to be in that world, too.

If I had any chance in hell in getting her father to accept me, I had to change. I had to be respectful and honorable and dress like *this*.

Go on dates like *this*. Be like *this*. And I fucking hated it.

Thinking about all the ways Carrie and I could go wrong made me realize her father still hadn't texted me even once. My heart clenched and I picked up my phone, scanning through our messages. The last text he'd sent on his own had been the morning Carrie had woken up late for school.

I tightened my jaw and typed: *Carrie is home and taking it easy tonight.*

A whole minute passed with no reply. What. The. Fuck?

If he wasn't answering my texts, I didn't know what the hell to think. First the odd call from my commanding officer, and now I was being ignored by a man who had previously needed me to hold his hand all this time. These were *not* good things. I knew it—even if I had no clue what the hell was going on in my life lately.

The bathroom door opened, and I stood up, tugging on my suit jacket as I turned to face her. I was about to ask her if she'd heard from her father, but then I turned around, and she stole the words right off the tip of my tongue. She took my breath away with her beauty, and it would never cease to amaze me how much of an effect she had on me.

I'd told her to wear a dress because we were going out somewhere nice, and she'd pulled out all the stops. She wore a dark purple dress that I suspected might melt if I touched it, it looked that soft. It clung to her body perfectly, highlighting everything that made her...well, her.

She topped it off with her long, red hair cascading down her back, just enough makeup to bring out her gorgeous blue eyes I loved so much, and a pair of black heels that would be over my shoulders by the end of the night if I had anything to say about it.

I didn't know whether to drool, throw her on the bed and hide her from the world, or take her out for all to see. The old me would've hidden her. Kept her to myself selfishly. But the new me? The *me* I was trying to be for her?

Not so much.

"You look beautiful," I managed to say through my tight throat and the even tighter tie. "Really fucking beautiful."

She dipped her gaze over me, her eyes lighting up in that way that told me she liked what she saw. "Dude. You look *hot* all dressed up. Like, really hot. I never thought I'd prefer you in something besides a pair of board shorts and a bare chest, but *hel-lo.*"

I grinned, but my heart dropped to the pit of my stomach. I'd been right. This is what she wanted from me, even if she didn't know it yet. "If you like it, then you'll get it anytime you want."

"I'll take both versions of you, please," she said, grinning. She ran her hands over my shoulders, smoothing my jacket. "I never thought I'd see you in one of these. It's blowing my mind."

I forced a smile. "I wear them for work all the time, Ginger."

"I know." Her hands fell back to her sides and her smile faded. "Is something wrong? You seem…upset or something. Different."

That's because I feel different right now. I shook my head and continued smiling, wanting nothing more than a shot of some hard liquor right now. "No. Nothing's wrong. You ready to go?"

"Sure." She started to grab her helmet, but I tugged her away. "Fancy people don't ride motorcycles. They take limos."

Her eyes went wide. "Limos? Seriously?"

I tried to read the expression in her eyes, but I couldn't tell if she was pleased by my surprise. I knew she was trying to get away from the life of glamour and glitz, but I needed to prove to her, and maybe myself, that I could do this. That I could thrive in her world, even if I wasn't so sure I could.

I opened the door for her. "That's what you ride back home, right?"

"If we're going to some sort of event?" She walked past me, her grip on her purse firm. "Sure. All the time."

I closed the door behind us and locked it. "We're going to an event. A date. Kind of our first date, I guess."

"You didn't have to…" She trailed off and stopped walking halfway down the stairs. "Oh my God. Is that…?"

When she didn't finish, I cleared my throat. "The same type of car you use back home? Yes."

"Wow," she said, her voice strung tight.

She wasn't happy with my surprise. It only seemed to solidify my belief that I didn't belong in her world. I tugged on my hair and eyed her. "We can cancel this whole thing if you want. Take the bike and go to Islands or something."

She pressed her lips together. "It's fine. I'm fine. Come on."

Deep in the back of my mind, I wondered if she was trying to picture me sitting in a fancy restaurant and not meshing the Finn she knew with the Finn I needed to be. Maybe that's why she looked as if I was torturing her instead of taking her out.

I urged her along, using my hand pressed against her lower back to propel her along. The sooner we got this date over with and I made her happy, the better. Then we could come back home, shed our clothes, and maybe share a cold drink over some good old-fashioned American television. Maybe some football, if I could find a game.

Man. I couldn't wait for that.

The driver opened the back for us, and I helped her inside. After following her, I settled into my seat and reached for the stocked bar. I poured myself a hefty dose of whiskey. Thank God they had the good stuff in here.

I took a long draught and reclined in the seat. When I looked at Carrie, she was watching me with narrowed eyes. I froze with the glass pressed to my lips. "What?"

"Why are we even doing this? You look miserable."

That's because I am. But it wasn't her fault. It was my own. I'd done this to myself, and I would damn well suffer through it with a grin on my face. "I'm taking the woman I love out on a date. How could I be miserable?"

She eyed me. "I don't know, but something's off. What is it? Is it the suit?"

How could she read me so fucking well? "No. I'm fine, Ginger."

"Yeah. Okay."

I gritted my teeth. "Drop it. Kick back and enjoy the date, okay? Stop worrying about everything so damn much and relax."

Her eyes flashed at me. I'd gone and pissed her off now. "No, I'm not going to *relax*. Something's wrong and you're not telling me what it is," she insisted, her eyes flashing with determination. "Just tell me why you're being all pissy and we can fix it."

"Jesus, Carrie. We can't fix everything with a conversation," I snapped.

She blinked at me, her cheeks flushed with color. "You're being a jerk," she said, her voice soft. "I don't like it."

Immediately, shame rushed through me fast and hard and relentless. I was yelling at her when I was supposed to be showing her a good time. Being a good fucking boyfriend. I dragged a hand through my hair and forced a smile. "I'm sorry. That was mean. I'm just…tired and stressed out. Maybe I should have had another cup of coffee tonight."

"I don't believe you," she said, her voice small and hurt. "You're not being yourself right now, and it has nothing to do with coffee."

Something snapped inside me, and I replied without thinking. "You're damned right I'm not, because right now I'm realizing that this is the *me* I'm going to have to be from now on. I guess I hadn't really thought about it much, but now it's the only thing I can think about." I finished the last of the whiskey and grabbed the bottle for some more. I could feel her watching me the whole time. "I used to attend these damn balls and galas, but I stood in the shadows, where no one saw me. Now when I go? I'll be judged…and more than likely found lacking."

"Welcome to my world."

I slapped my hand on my knee. "I didn't know it would be mine, too. I didn't know…" I fought for the right words, but nothing came. "I didn't know, okay?"

She looked confused. Her nose wrinkled up and she looked at me as if she didn't even recognize me. "I didn't ask you to dress up for me or to stand in the spotlight. You don't even have to go with me when I go to those things. And I wouldn't make you do anything you didn't want to do, so don't act like I would."

That might be true for now. But what if we got married? Had kids? The likelihood of me being off in the background was slim to none. People would want to know all about me—all about us. I couldn't let her down.

"But don't you see?" I splayed my arms. "I'll do it for *you*, damn it. To make you happy."

"This isn't you. It's not us." She motioned at me, then the limo. "We don't dress like this, and we don't scream at each other in a limo. And it's not making me freaking happy."

"But you *want* it to be us." I took a long drink, welcoming the burning sensation, and pointed my glass at her. "You do. Admit it."

"What?" She paled, but her curled hands twitched in her lap as if she was considering hitting me. I deserved it. "Why would you say that? I've never—"

"I asked you on a date, and you got all excited about fancy dresses and limos and all that shit. You know where I wanted to go? Islands. Burgers and shakes. And as you so aptly pointed out—I like them. I'm that kind of guy."

"And I *like* that guy. Actually, I love him," she said, her eyes narrow on me. "But I'll be honest. This guy?" She gestured toward me and the bar. "I don't like him very much."

I sat up straight and finished my drink, then set it down a little too hard. Maybe I'd had too much too fast. "Yeah, well, it's the guy you're going to be stuck with, so get used to it. I'd have been just as happy eating at a burger joint."

"So we should've gone there," she snapped. I knew she was angry with me now. Knew I'd gone and ruined everything. Hurt her. But I couldn't seem to stop myself from lashing out at her. "You don't have to take me out to an expensive restaurant to make me happy. *God.* You should know that by now."

"Should I? I don't think so." I grabbed her hands, trying to entwine my fingers with hers, but she didn't uncurl her fists. "The girl I know surfs and goes to soup kitchens and isn't afraid to get dirty. The girl I know loves McDonald's and Islands and doesn't care about tuxes and dresses."

She snatched her hands back. "Yeah, and that's still *me*. Fancy dresses don't change what's underneath."

"That's exactly what I'm saying." I sighed and shut my eyes for a second, trying to find the right words to make her understand what I was thinking. When I opened them, she looked at me as if I'd killed her puppy in front of her and then served him up for dinner. "Look, I've been thinking, and—"

"Oh my God." She scooted into the corner of the limo, her lower lip quivering. "Are you...are you breaking up with me? Already?"

My mind whirled at that. "What? *No.*"

She took a shaky breath. "You scared the heck out of me. Never start a fight and then say, '*I've been thinking*' ever again." She smacked my arm hard, then did it again even harder. "Got it, *love*? And also? Don't take me on dates you're going to hate. That's not my idea of a fun time, for future reference."

"Fine. But tell me one thing, *Ginger*," I said, emphasizing the nickname in the same sarcastic way she'd done to me. "Why can't you admit you fucking wanted this date and stop acting like you don't? Why can't you admit you want suits and jewelry and limos? Why can't you admit who you are?"

She threw her hands up. "Okay, maybe I did want it for *one* night. Jeez, is that so bad? Does that warrant you yelling at me and acting like an alcoholic because you're forced to go out with me?"

"Are you fucking kidding me?" I looked out the window, trying to regain the calm I'd lost the second we'd started arguing. I'd been trying to tell her I had to change and would—but that it wasn't easy for me. And now we were in each other's faces screaming about shit that didn't matter. "I had two drinks. Two. Drinks."

"In three seconds," she snapped. "Why can't *you* admit *that*?"

I snorted. "When you're old enough to drink, you can lecture me about my drinking habits. Until then? Not so much. You're barely more than a baby as it is. You can grow the fuck up before you judge me."

She stiffened. "Excuse me?"

I swallowed hard, realizing I was being a complete ass. I was a failure and I was only making it worse with every word I said. How had we gotten here, and how the hell did we get out of this train wreck of a night? "Shit. This is getting out of hand. Maybe we should stop talking now."

"Yeah. Maybe we should. And maybe this whole date thing was a horrible idea," she agreed, her voice shaking. She jammed her finger into the button for the intercom, speaking to the driver directly and ignoring me. "Change of plans. Take me to the dorms at the University of—"

I zoned out as she gave her instructions, my head making a hollow ocean sound. How many chances would I get before she said the hell with me and moved on? I swallowed the bile rising in my throat and tried to fix the fucking mess I'd made by opening my mouth in the first place. "Carrie, look. I'm sorry. I shouldn't—"

She shot me the death glare from hell. "Don't. I don't want to hear it. I'd storm off right now if you wouldn't follow me because you *have* to because it's your *job*. This is a fight, and we'll get through it. But right now? This date? We're done. We're *so* freaking done."

My heart lurched and I scrambled to grab her hands. She jerked out of my reach and gave me a look that froze me in my tracks. She'd never looked at me with such…disappointment. Not even when she'd found out who I really was.

I swallowed past the crippling guilt trying to kill me. "Please, don't go. We can go back home and talk. There's nothing we can't work through without—"

The limo stopped and she shot me a dark look. "Conversations don't fix *every*thing," she threw back in my face.

She opened the door and got out, and I scooted after her. "I didn't mean that. I didn't mean any of this. I was just trying to explain how I feel."

"Well, you suck at explaining feelings." She stopped walking and scowled at me. "Tonight you're not my boyfriend. You're my bodyguard. So watch me go inside so you know I made it home safe—and then leave me alone. It's your *job*, right?"

I bit my tongue from lashing out at her. I didn't want to keep fighting, damn it. I wanted to *fix* this. "Are you always going to throw that in my face every time we fight?"

Shit. I hadn't bitten hard enough.

"Yeah. Maybe. Or, at least, I will until I *grow up*."

She stormed off, and I watched her go, knowing I was a fucking idiot for taking what should have been a great night and turning it into an awful memory.

As if we didn't have enough of those already.

CHAPTER EIGHT

I stomped my way upstairs and made it to my room in record time. I hadn't slept in this room since the night before Finn and I got back together, and I really didn't want to be here now. I don't know what had happened out there, but it had escalated really, *really* fast. Like, supersonic speed fast.

I unlocked the door and shut it behind me, breathing heavily. I squeezed my eyes shut, refusing to cry. Refusing to let this get to me. We had enough crap going on right now, and then we had to go and ruin what should have been a date night with anger and shouting. What was wrong with us that we couldn't gain some sort of equilibrium where there wasn't something *wrong* all the time?

I smacked the door behind me with my open palm so hard it made my hand sting and ache. "Goddamn it all to hell."

"Uh, Carrie?" Marie asked, her voice quiet. "You okay over there?"

I opened my eyes and quickly located her. She sat at the table with her books open. She had her long platinum blonde hair in a sloppy bun, and black glasses perched on her perfect nose that only brought out her bright eyes even more. The irony of Marie home studying while I was out with a guy struck home as it well should.

That's probably what I should have been doing instead of fighting with Finn.

"Not really," I managed to say before I broke down and burst into tears. I quickly covered my face, trying to hide myself from her and the world. I didn't do this. Didn't cry in front of people. What had happened to me lately? "Oh my God. I'm so sorry."

"Shh," Marie said. I heard a shuffling sound and then her arms were around me. "Don't apologize. Just cry if you need to."

I took a gulping breath and sobbed into her shoulder, holding on to her as if she was the only thing keeping me afloat in the middle of the ocean. This whole situation was ridiculous, because we weren't even close, really, and yet I was crying all over her. By the time I finished, she was soaked and I was embarrassed more than words could say.

I pulled back and she hugged me tighter, not letting me go. "Give it another second. You might not be done yet."

I swiped my hands under my eyes and laughed nervously, feeling like a complete idiot. "I'm good."

"Okay." Marie let go of me and backed up a few steps, her lips pursed as she studied me through her glasses. "Now tell me what happened."

"I…well…" I broke off, not sure where to start or what to say. Or how much of it to say. "I got in a fight with my boyfriend."

"Boyfriend?" Her eyes narrowed. "Who is he?"

"No one you know. He doesn't go here." I waved a hand. "It's not important. He might be leaving soon, and we tried to have a romantic night, but we got in a fight."

"Where's he going?"

I swallowed hard. Call me crazy, but I wasn't ready to trust her with all my juicy secrets. We barely talked aside from the pleasantries most roommates shared such as *I'll be out late tonight* or *I'm bringing a guy home.*

I met her eyes. "His work might be sending him away."

"Oh, that sucks." She nodded. "I dated a guy once who was a drummer in a band. It was right when we moved out here for school. He was never around, and when he was, all he wanted was sex. We never even talked, really. It took me a little while to realize I was nothing but a convenience for him when he was in town. He probably had one of me in every city his band played."

Marie pressed her lips together, looking angry at the memory. I reached out and squeezed her hand reassuringly. "He sounds like a real jerk."

"He was." Marie gave me a small smile. "Is that how your guy is?"

"No. He's…he's great," I said, my voice breaking. "That's why I have no idea what the heck happened tonight. One second he was fine, and the next he was yelling and being nasty. I've never seen him like that."

Marie nodded. "Do you think he's stressed out about maybe leaving? Stress can cause men to act like weirdos. One time my dad was acting like a jerk, and we had no idea why. Turned out, he had learned he had cancer and was processing it all. And one of the ways he did it was by ranting at the whole world."

I swallowed hard. It hadn't occurred to me until now, but Finn and Marie had both lost a parent at the same age. "God, that's awful. I'm so sorry."

"Yeah, it sucks," she said softly, her eyes sad despite her words. "But thanks."

I hugged her, feeling like an idiot. All this time I'd been judging her as vapid and empty, and here she was making me feel better. Sharing life stories with me. I hadn't treated her fairly, but I made a vow to stop doing it. "I'm sorry I've been so quiet with you. I…I'm not used to this kind of life. I'm not good at this."

Marie grinned. "You mean like how you didn't want to bathe the first week because people might see you in the communal shower?"

I facepalmed myself. "You noticed?"

"It was pretty hard to miss. You were hand bathing for a while."

"Yeah. It was pretty pathetic."

"Pretty much," she teased, her eyes sparkling again. "But anyway, about your man…do you think that's what this was about? Him taking out his stress on you?"

I straightened my back. "Now that you mention it, that's probably what this was. He's nervous and he lashed out at me. That's what he was trying to talk to me about. I'm such an idiot."

"It's not your fault. Guys are weird," Marie said, patting my back. "How are we supposed to understand how their brains work?"

"I have to go find him." I grabbed the knob, but froze with my hand on it. "Hey, thank you. I'm sorry I cried all over you. I owe you a shirt."

Marie grinned. "It's okay. It was kind of nice to be the one comforting someone else for once. I'm usually the one who's a mess." Marie met my eyes. "Besides, I picked one up from the lobby earlier. Thanks for the donation."

I froze. "You know?"

"Well, I did see it laying out on the bed earlier, and then it was in that mysterious donation box." She shrugged. "It wasn't hard to figure out. But don't worry. Your secret is safe with me."

"Thank you." I hesitated. "You can have first pick if you want."

She laughed. "I might agree to that."

"Okay." I still didn't leave. Instead, I looked at her again, trying to see past the smile and glasses. Maybe it was time to try being friends with a girl for once. I hadn't really wanted to try again, after all the girls I grew up with turned out to be major bitches. But maybe it was time to grow up a bit, like Finn said. "Hey, want to go get coffee sometime? Maybe talk some more?"

Her cheeks flushed and she wrapped her arms around herself. "I'd like that. Now go get him…whoever he is."

Maybe I'd tell her tomorrow, but tonight I had to go get my man.

I closed the door behind me and rushed down the stairs, passing a surprised-looking Cory without so much as a word. As I dialed the local cab company, I decided to see what I could do about getting a car ASAP. Calling a cab every other day was ridiculous.

"Yes, hello. I'd like a cab to get me at—" I broke off as soon as I saw him. Finn hadn't left. He sat on the bench outside my dorm room, his face in his hands. "Never mind."

I hung up on the cab company and slowly walked over to him. He looked so vulnerable.

He'd taken off his jacket and tossed it on the ground, and his tie hung loosely off his neck. My heart broke at the sight of him. When I stopped directly in front of him, I fisted my dress in my hands and tried to figure out what to say that wouldn't lead to another fight.

"You ready to talk without the fighting?"

His head snapped up and his bright blue eyes pinned me in place. He swallowed hard, his Adam's apple bobbing. "I'm sorry. So fucking sorry."

"I know." I sat down beside him and sighed. "I am, too."

He gave a harsh laugh. "You didn't do anything to be sorry for. I'm the one who took a simple conversation and turned it into this."

"I'm the one who got angry and didn't let you talk." I took a deep breath and rested my hand on his knee. "You're nervous, aren't you? That's what you wanted to talk about? What you were trying to say?"

He shook his head, his expression ironic. "Nervous? I'm fucking terrified. I'm scared because your father isn't texting me, and I have to go talk to my C.O. I'm terrified because the one time that I try to do something nice for you, I fucked it up."

"It's okay. I get it."

"It's *not* fucking okay. That's not all I'm scared about." He dragged his hands down his face and looked at me, his eyes raw and open. "I'm scared your father is going to shove me out of your life when he finds out about us. That he's going to make you see I'm not good enough for you or your world. But most of all? I'm scared you'll realize it all on your own without him there to tell you."

I recoiled. That's not what I'd expected him to be scared of, for God's sake. He was supposed to be afraid of leaving and war and guns. Not something that would never, *ever* happen. "That's ridiculous."

"No, it's not. It's the fucking truth." He lifted his head. "How many presidents' daughters have you seen married to bikers, standing up there on the stage during the primaries, with their ink hanging out for all of America to see?"

All my life, I'd lived according to my father's plans. I'd missed my own graduation because we had to go out of town campaigning for the senatorial primaries. I'd given up everything for my father's agenda, but I *wouldn't* be giving up my Finn.

I pressed my lips together. "None. Now ask me how much I care about that?"

"You might not care now, but you will eventually." He gestured toward the moon, his entire body seeming tense and angry. And a little bit...defeated, maybe? "It's only a matter of time, but I have a plan. I'm going to—"

"Shut. Up."

He turned to me, his jaw squared off in that way he always did when he was determined to win a fight, but there would be no victory this time. "I know I said some mean things in our time together, but the truth is...you *are* younger than me. You don't know how cruel the world is. The first thing your father is going to say when he finds out about us—once he's done pounding me into the dirt, that is—is that I'm not good enough for you. And he'll be right. But I'm going to fix it."

"How many times do we have to go over this?" I asked through my teeth. "There's nothing to *fix*. We're not broken in the first place."

"I know you love me and you know I love you, too." He reached out and grabbed my hand, squeezing it tight. "But I can see how this is going to end, Ginger. I'll stay until you send me away, but it'll happen at one point *if* I don't take the necessary steps to avoid it."

I blinked away tears. "It sounds to me like you're just making excuses so you can walk away with a clear conscience."

He made a tortured sound and shook his head. "Hell no. Never."

"If you want to walk away…" I said, my voice breaking so badly I couldn't even finish the sentence. The mere thought of Finn leaving me was enough to break me.

He swiped away tears off my cheeks I hadn't even realized escaped, hugged me tight against his chest, and buried his face in my neck. "I don't want to lose you. I just say all this shit and ruin perfect nights because of my stupid fears, but I'm not scared anymore. I know what to do to make us work."

I curled my hands into his shirt. "We *already* work."

"Now, yeah. But once you graduate, it'll be different. We'll have to be different."

I wanted to fight him on this, but I knew no matter what I said, he wouldn't believe me. He was convinced I was my father's puppet who would break up with him if Daddy told me to. I'd have to prove him wrong. "What are you planning to do?"

"I'm going to change."

I narrowed my eyes, trying to make sense of his words. "I don't want you to change. Even if he doesn't like you, I won't care."

He rubbed my head almost absentmindedly. "It's the one conflict in our life I can see coming—and avoid. He's going to fire me. Hell, he could even sue me. It was in the contract that I couldn't touch you."

"He put that in there?" I asked, gripping my dress tight.

"Yeah."

I shook my head. My father was freaking ridiculous. "If he does, then we'll handle it together. Right?" I bit down on my lower lip. "Maybe you could do something else."

He pushed me away and squeezed my arms with a smile on his face.

266

"Exactly. Like I said. *Change.*"

I hesitated, my heart picking up speed. This kind of *change* I could probably work with. "What are you going to do?"

"I can maybe change my MOS."

I blinked. "What's an MOS?"

"It stands for Military Occupational Specialty, but it's basically my position. My career in the Marines."

I nodded. "What would you change it to?"

"I'm not sure. Maybe I could go into active duty with the Marines. I bet that will look good on Election Day. Having a Marine up on the stage with him in Dress Blues. He can't complain about that, can he?" he asked me, his eyes on mine.

"No. Of course not." And just like that, down came my bubble. "But what about going back to school? Becoming a chef or a surf instructor? I don't know. *Something.*" I shrugged. "Growing up, was there something you wanted to be?"

He blinked at me, a weird look on his face. "Um, I wanted to work on computers as a kid. You know, build them."

I perked up at that. Computers were safe. "Well, you could go to school for that."

"I could." He straightened up, blinking rapidly. "I don't even have to re-up when my time is up, if I don't want to. Or, I can become a commissioned officer and get a job in that field *through* the Marines." He snapped his fingers. "Ooh, yeah. That'll look really good on your father's campaign. An *officer* at his side."

"I don't care about his fucking campaign!" I shouted, my hands curled into tight balls. God, Dad had gotten to Finn, too. Without even trying. His reach was that freaking far. "I care about you. About *us.*"

"But this *is* for us." He stood up and paced, his steps hurried and uneven. He stepped on his jacket and didn't even care. "We won't have to worry about what happens after he kills me—as long as he doesn't *actually* kill me, that is." He swung me into his arms and hugged me tight. "This obstacle between us? It's gone. I can be that guy."

The obstacle that didn't exist? Yeah. It was gone.

"I don't think you need to be any guy but you. I love you the way you are—tattoos and all."

He grinned down at me. "And I love you for that."

OUT OF TIME

He kissed me hard, right in front of my dorm in the moonlight. I clung to him, gripping his dress shirt in my fists and pulling him closer. By the time he pulled back, I forgot all about what we were saying.

All I knew was Finn was smiling at me, and he looked happy.

I wasn't about to ruin it.

CHAPTER NINE

Finn

Wednesday night I waited on my bike outside Carrie's dorm. She had to study late with some friends from chemistry, so I told her I'd pick her up at eight. After our fight last night, I wasn't sure what to expect from her when she came outside. Would she still be mad at me, or had she really forgiven me for being an ass?

All I knew was I needed to get through the rest of the week, find out what my C.O. wanted from me, and then move on with my new life plan. I was more determined than ever to get through this year alive, get out of the Marines, and go back to college. Until Carrie, I hadn't wanted to do that. I had been perfectly content being a Marine.

But now? I wanted more. I wanted to be more.

For her *and* for me.

My phone buzzed, and I looked down at it with my heart racing. Had her father finally texted me on his own? I glanced down at it, but it was from Carrie. *Be down in two minutes.*

Okay. I shoved the phone into my pocket.

A few minutes later, she came out of her dorm, her usual bag over her shoulder and a gorgeous smile on her face, and she looked so damn happy. So much like my Carrie that she took my fucking breath away. I had no idea what I'd done to deserve her in my life, but I'd do it again and again if it meant I got to keep her forever.

I shook my thoughts and straightened my back, waiting for her to make her way over to me. When she was within reaching distance, I snatched her up and kissed her before she could say a word. I slipped my hand into her back pocket before carefully removing it.

Then, and only then, I let myself get lost in our kiss. I needed the affirmation that she was here and mine and happy, as pathetic as that might be. I pressed my mouth to hers, urging her to open to me. And when she did, I slipped my tongue between her lips and kissed her hungrily. As if I would never get enough of her sweet taste.

And I didn't think I ever would.

When I broke the kiss, she rested her hands on my shoulders and blinked up at me. "Wow. I should be late more often."

"That had nothing to do with you being late."

"Then what was it?"

"I wanted to kiss you, so I did." I shrugged, trying to play it off as if I wasn't going completely crazy right now. Because I abso-fuck-ing-lutely was. "Why were you late, anyway?"

"I was chatting with Marie." She glanced up at me. "We've been talking, and we have a lot more in common than I thought. We're getting coffee later this week."

I'd told her she should try talking to Marie some more. My Ginger wasn't the most open when it came to making friends—with reason. But Marie seemed a pretty safe bet. "That sounds fun."

"Yeah." She bit down on her lip. "I think she's homesick, and sometimes I get that way too, even with my crazy parents. She doesn't seem to have many people here, besides me. I'm lucky I have you."

She had a knack for finding the loneliest sucker and making her feel welcome with nothing more than a smile. It was one of the things I loved most about her. "She can have me too if you want."

She slapped my arm. "Haha, really funny."

"What? I was just trying to be supportive." I threw my arm around her. "But you know I'm kidding. I only have room for one college student in my life."

"I might take her to the soup kitchen with me this weekend while you're gone." She stole a quick peek at me. "If you don't mind, of course."

"Of course not," I said through the nervousness trying to strangle me. "But you have to leave with her, and not walk down any dark alleys."

"I'll leave before it's dark, I promise." She grabbed her helmet and tugged it on. When she was finished, I held out my hand for her bag. She handed it over and I slid it over my head, watching her the whole time.

I slipped my own helmet over my head and revved the engine, disgusted with myself. "You ready, Ginger?"

She glided on behind me and wrapped her body around mine. I'd never get sick of this feeling with her. This utter shiny happiness at her arms wrapped around me, her head on my shoulder. It never got old and I hoped it never would.

"Ready," she called out.

When we pulled up to my apartment building, I stopped the bike and took a deep breath. I'd made a move that she may or may not appreciate, and I was about to find out.

"I'm exhausted." She took off her helmet and started up the pathway toward the stairs. After yawning loudly, she added, "I need to do some more homework, then we're going to bed early. I didn't sleep well after you left last night."

I hadn't asked her to come home with me, and she hadn't suggested it. It still stung that after our first fight as a couple, we'd spent the night apart. "Yeah, me either."

"Next time, no matter the fight, we sleep together. Deal?"

"It's a promise," I said, leaning down to kiss her.

When she broke off the kiss, we walked hand in hand to the door. Halfway there, she looked over her shoulder, her brow furrowed. "Did you hear that?"

"Hear what?" I immediately stopped walking and pushed her behind me. I scanned the shadows for any sign of movement. "What did it sound like?"

"A footstep." She bit down on her lip. "Is someone watching us?"

I closed my eyes and listened. There wasn't a sound, not even a breath or a footstep. She was getting as paranoid as I was, because as far as I could tell, no one was there.

"I don't think anyone is there," I said, reaching behind me to squeeze her hand. "Maybe it was a raccoon or something."

"Yeah. Probably." She laughed uneasily. "I'm imagining things."

"Hey, better safe than sorry," I said, smiling at her. "If you ever think you see or hear something, definitely let me know. You might notice something I don't."

"I will." We reached the door and she waited for me to open it. When I didn't, she shot me a look. "Uh, are you going to open the door?"

My heart skipped a beat or two, and my palms grew sweaty. Was this a good idea? It was too late to go back now. I'd already made the steps toward this, and I wasn't one to back down. "*You* open it."

She looked at my empty hands first, then up at my face, her brow crinkled. "Okay? Give me your key."

I crossed my arms. "Why don't you use your own?"

"Maybe because I don't have one?"

"Check your back pocket," I said, my voice low. I really hoped she didn't freak out or throw the key back at me or tell me I was moving too fucking fast. When she just stared at me, her cheeks flushed, I tapped my foot. "Well? Go on. Check."

She slid her hand into the wrong pocket, then moved on to the right one. Hopefully it hadn't slipped out on the ride, or all this show was for nothing. When she pulled her hand out, the little gold key in her fingers, I held my breath and waited to see her reaction.

Slowly, her wide eyes rose from the key until her gaze collided with mine. "You gave me a key? To your place?"

"I did." I tugged on my hair and shifted on my feet. "If you don't want it, it's cool. I just thought it would be nice for you to be able to come over here whenever you wanted, even if I'm not here. You could come here and study, or sleep, or eat, or whatever you wanted even if I'm…"

…not here.

Yeah, I already said that.

I stopped talking and stared at my feet, because I was babbling like a fucking idiot. I didn't like acting like an idiot, although I'd been doing it way too much lately. Apparently, love and idiocy went hand in hand.

"Finn?"

I lifted my head and dropped my hand. "Yeah?"

"This is so…wow," she said softly. "Thank you."

I nodded, not sure what else to say. I wanted her in my home all the time, so I gave her a key. It was simple. "Go ahead and see if it works."

It did. I already tested it.

But at least it gave her something to do besides stare at me looking all happy and yet somehow sad. It's like she knew why I was really doing this. Even if I was gone, it would be like she was with me whenever she came here, and that meant something.

She slid the key into the lock and turned it, giving me a shaky smile when it opened. "It works."

"Good," I said, my voice gruff. "Go in, then."

She went inside and flipped on the light, stopping a few steps in. She stood in the middle of the living room area, her eyes on my closet. Not a big shocker there. After all, it became clear, quite quickly, that I'd cleared some space in my closet for her—complete with pink fucking hangers waiting for her shit.

Yeah. *Pink*.

"Did you…is that…?"

"For you?" I leaned against the door and crossed my ankles, trying to go for casual and unconcerned. "Yeah. Last time I checked, I didn't use pink. I know it doesn't go with your hair, but…" I shrugged, even though she wasn't looking at me. She was still staring at the closet. "I figured that would make the clothes stand out more, since you never wear it. Ya know?"

She walked up to the closet and ran her hands over the pink hangers, then touched my cammies before letting her hand drop to her side. "Are you sure?"

"Yeah, I'm sure." I crossed the room and came up behind her, resting my hands on her shoulders. I leaned down and kissed the top of her ginger head, breathing in the scent of the shampoo that I'd bought for her. "But are you?" I asked softly. "It's not like you're moving in or anything. It's just an open-door policy."

She nodded. "You know I'm not going anywhere, right?"

"I know you think that, and I know you want to believe it. And so do I." I wrapped my arms around her and hugged her close, more so to hide my face from her than anything. And I *really* didn't want to fight again. "But I've seen a lot more of the world than you have. Shit happens and life is hard. If I leave—"

She smacked me. "I'm not going to move on or forget you."

I flinched. "I know." Or, at least I knew she didn't *plan* on it. But plans changed, and so did people. Especially when they were separated. "That's not what I'm saying."

She tensed in my arms. "But you are. You're worried if you go on deployment I'll move on to another guy, aren't you? You don't trust me."

Oh, fuck. This was going to be another fight if I didn't fix it and fix it now. "Ginger..."

"No way. You're not getting off that easily."

My hands flexed on her, but she moved out of my arms. I missed her already. The softness in her blue eyes gave way to her icy look, and she put her hands on her hips. Oh yeah. I'd pissed her off. Damn it. "I trust you, Ginger."

"Don't *Ginger* me, mister." She poked a finger in my chest and I held my hands up in surrender. "Do you have such little faith in me that you think I would freaking leave you when you're off defending our country? *Really*?"

"You're not the one I don't have faith in," I said, squaring my jaw. "I'm worried I'll do something to fuck this up."

"How could *you* mess this up?"

Well, for starters I could *die*. But I didn't say that. She would only worry even more. I scrambled for some bullshit reason to give her, but came up a round short. So I shrugged and said nothing. She pushed me hard, back toward the bed, and I stumbled a little bit before I could catch my balance.

Was it somehow perverted that I liked her beating me up? Because I did.

She shoved me again. The back of my knees hit the bed, and I fell onto it, not even bothering to fight it. When I hit the mattress, she climbed on top of me and held my hands down. "I'm going to tell you this once and once only: I will not leave you. And if you leave, I will always be here waiting for you when you get back. Whether it's in a few days, a week, or a freaking year. I'll be *here*. I'll be *yours*."

Something inside of me gave way and broke. Maybe it was my doubt. Maybe it was something else. All I knew is what caused it. Her. "Fuck, I love you. So damn much it scares the shit out of me. I've never been scared of anything before. Guns. Surfing. War. But now I have the biggest fear of all—losing you."

"Finn..." she whispered, her voice breaking.

I slipped my hand behind her head and urged her down, kissing her the second her lips touched mine. Her fingers flexed on mine, and she moaned softly, straining to get closer to me. I slanted my head, deepening the kiss even more, and she wrapped her arms around me.

Man, I needed this in my life. Needed her lips on mine, her arms around me tight, her grip on my heart secure and complete. Without it, I'd be alive, and I'd be here, but I wouldn't be *me*. I wouldn't be *living*.

My hands moved down her back slowly until I cupped her ass, urging her even closer to my cock. She pressed down, a soft moan escaping her. She adjusted herself slightly so she straddled me, her legs tucked behind her, and she moved against me in a sensuous, perfect circular motion.

I lifted my hands higher, burying them in her hair and yanking her down harder. She whimpered into my mouth and curled her fingers into my pecs, moving her hips faster. She tugged on my shirt impatiently. I broke the kiss off long enough for her to yank it over my head, and then I rolled her beneath me.

Her legs closed around my waist, urging me closer, and my gut tightened. If she didn't stop making those little sounds, I'd be inside of her before she even came for me once. Slowly, I ran my hands over her breasts, lightly teasing her nipples. She arched into my hand, begging me for more without words, and I gave her what she wanted. Hell, I'd always give her what she wanted.

I was that much of a sap.

I cupped her, rolling my palms over her. The shirt had to go and so did the bra, so I stopped kissing her long enough to get her naked and grab a condom. As I stripped off her pants, I kissed a path down her thigh, over her knee, and nipped at her ankle. She cried out and pressed into the mattress, her breath coming in tiny bursts.

As I removed all my clothing, I watched her. I rolled the condom over my cock, never dropping my eyes from her. Her cheeks were flushed and her eyes were closed, and she trailed her hand lightly over her own stomach, a small moan escaping at the touch.

Holy fucking hell, she looked like a naughty angel brought to Earth. My angel…and I was never letting her go. Her father could kiss my ass. I was the man for her, and we both knew it. And wasn't that all that mattered? I'd spent all this time stressing about her father's reaction, when I should have been focusing on her.

I wouldn't make the mistake again.

I crawled up her body, leaving kisses and nips as I went, stopping only once I was at her hip. I rolled my tongue over her hipbone, my heart quickening when she cried out and scraped her nails across my shoulders. I loved the way she looked when she was turned on. All rosy cheeks and soft lips. All *mine*.

I flicked my tongue over her clit, my finger thrusting inside of her at the same time. She screamed and arched her hips; her breath coming out harsh and uneven. "God, *Finn*. Don't stop."

Oh, I wasn't planning on it. Not until she was a quivering mess.

I rolled my tongue over her, pressing a little harder, and moved my fingers in and out, building up the speed with each motion. When she tightened her legs on my head, a cry escaping her lips that sounded more like a breath than a word, I positioned myself between her legs. She scrambled to hold on to me, and I lifted her hips, driving inside of her with one smooth thrust.

"*Finn*," she cried, her nails raking down my back.

"Come for me again," I demanded in her ear, biting down on her shoulder and thrusting harder. "Let go for me."

She dug her nails into my back and held her breath, her pussy clenching down around my cock so hard that she almost pushed me out. When she came, her walls squeezing me until I couldn't fucking stand it anymore, I was right there with her, my hands gripping her as tight as I could as I soared into the sky.

When I came back down, she was running her fingers up and down my spine, kissing my shoulder over and over again. I knew, right then and there, that she'd meant every word she said. She'd be here waiting for me no matter what happened.

And it felt fucking amazing to finally, *truly* believe in that kind of love.

CHAPTER TEN

I looked up at Finn, trying to let my love shine out onto him, or light him up or something. It sounded stupid, in theory, but how many times have you looked at a couple and *known* they were completely in love just from the way they looked at one another?

If ever a girl looked at a guy that way, it had to be Finn and me.

I cupped his face like he always did to me, running my finger over his mouth. I could see why he liked doing it. It was sweet and made me feel closer to him. I repeated the gesture, rubbing the lip I had been kissing. "You okay?"

Because I couldn't live in a world where Finn wasn't okay.

"More than okay." He kissed me, light and teasing, then pulled back again. "But you have to study. I distracted you."

"I know." I smiled up at him. "But I guess I have some unpacking to do first, huh?"

"Lots."

He pushed off me, and I got dressed, watching him as he lounged back on the bed naked and completely okay with that. And so was I.

I could stare at him all night long, admiring the way the colors swirled over his hard muscles the whole time. His tattoos were perfect to me, but he seemed to think there was something wrong with them.

The fact that he thought he wasn't good enough for me and my father

277

made my throat tighten. Would I ever be able to convince him I loved him exactly how he was, not as a version of what he could be? That I didn't want him to change at all?

Once I had on one of his green Hollister shirts and a pair of panties, I headed for the closet. His uniforms stared back at me, and I swear the things were alive. Like they were watching me. I was trying to act all confident about this whole possible deployment mess, but the truth was…I was scared, too.

He lifted on his elbows and watched me from the bed, his steamy eyes on me the whole time. I wanted nothing more in this world than to climb on top of him again and curl up in his arms. There was nothing in this world that his arms around me couldn't fix.

I picked up my bag and took out one of my shirts, hanging it up on the hanger. It meant a lot to me, him offering me this space in his life and his key. It was almost as if, when he was gone, I'd get to be here with him—even without him.

It didn't make much sense, yet it totally did.

And I liked the idea of sleeping in his bed when he wasn't here. Smelling him on his sheets. But how long would the scent of Finn linger if he left? A day? A month? I had no freaking clue, but I did know one thing: I needed to spend as much time as possible with him.

I put a shirt on the hanger and gathered by thoughts. My phone rang from beside Finn on the bed. He glanced down at it and his mouth tightened. He picked it up and held it out to me. "It's your father. He still isn't texting me like he used to, so be careful what you say. Try to get intel from him."

I nodded, crossed the room, and sat at his hip. After taking my phone out of his hand, I said, "Hey, Dad."

"Hello," Dad said, his voice clear and crisp. "Where are you?"

"You're up late." I checked the time, ignoring his question. It was almost midnight back home. Finn toyed with my hair, sending little shivers down my spine. "Shouldn't you be sleeping by now? And why have you been so quiet this week?"

"I told you I'd be busy," he said. "My turn for a question. Shouldn't *you* be in *your* room?"

I tensed, and so did Finn. He must've heard Dad's voice through the speaker. He dropped my hair and rolled off the bed. After grabbing his own phone, he swiped his finger across the screen. I raised my brows at him and he shook his head with a frown. He hadn't gotten any texts from my father asking where I was.

What was Dad up to, and what did it mean for us?

"Uh…" I forced myself to pay attention to Dad. "What makes you think I'm not in my room? Did you put a webcam up in it or something? I'm pretty sure I forbade cameras in my bedroom once I hit puberty."

He snorted. "Don't play coy with me, missy. I'm here, at your dorm, with your mother—and you're not here. Where are you?"

"Wait, *what*?" I leapt to my feet, my pulse racing and my knees trembling. "Why are you here in San Diego?"

Finn cursed under his breath and dialed someone. He grabbed his pants off the floor and stepped into them without boxers, his movements jerky and fast. I picked up my own pants, holding the phone to my ear with my shoulder.

Dad sighed. "We wanted to surprise you with a visit. We barely hear from you anymore, and your mother was worried. But all I really care about right now is where the hell—"

"*Hugh*." There was a commotion, something that sounded like a fight, and then Mom's voice came through. "Don't mind him. We know you're an adult now and you're out with friends. We missed you, dear. Where are you? We could come there to meet you and your friends."

"*No*." I shot Finn a desperate look, and he stepped into his motorcycle boots without a word. "I'll come to you. Just give me, like…?" I shot Finn a look and he held up his hand. "…five minutes, and I'll be there."

Mom sighed. "All right. I'll hold off your father. But hurry up, dear. I need a Carrie hug."

My heart wrenched with a bit of homesickness, despite the stress of the situation. That's what Mom called it when I hugged her as tight as I could. When I was a kid, every night she would pick me up and I would cling to her, all arms and legs and giggles, giving her the biggest good night hug I could.

When she let go and I stayed in place without her support, I would giggle harder—until I lost my grip and fell to the bed. Now I was too big to hang off her, but we still called our hugs *Carrie hugs*. "I'll hurry, I promise."

"Give me the phone, Margie."

"No."

"Give me the—" Another commotion. "And you'll be telling me who you were with," Dad called out. "Missy."

I could just picture him, pushing in to Mom to get another word in. Finn furiously typed something on his phone. Probably texting my dad in an attempt to cover both our asses before it was too late. Before Finn came under suspicion.

"Oh, leave her alone," Mom said. "See you soon."

"Bye," I said, hanging up. I looked at Finn. "What the heck are they doing here?"

"I don't have a fucking clue. I didn't know they were coming," Finn said, grabbing his keys and heading for the door with large, hurried steps. "Why didn't he tell me he was coming? This isn't good. This isn't good at all."

I followed him to the door, swallowing hard. Half my clothes were hung up in his closet and the other half were on his bed. I grabbed my empty bag. "I'll clean these up and then—"

Finn waved a hand and made an impatient sound. "Leave them. There's no time for that. We have to leave, and we have to leave yesterday."

I hesitated. "It'll be a little rough for a while, I get that, but why are you so upset?"

"Because I'm wondering why the fuck he didn't tell me he was coming, why the hell he hasn't texted me during the past two days, and why, even now, there's no text from him." His phone chimed, and he closed his eyes, his jaw ticking. "There it is."

He took his phone out of his pocket and opened the door for me. He scanned it and typed, while I tried to hold on to my patience. "What does it say?"

"He wants to know where you are." More typing. "I'm telling him you went out to eat with a new friend. Give me the name of someone you talk to in class. Someone new?"

I scrambled for the first name that came to mind. My lab partner I'd studied with the other day popped into my head. "Susan Williams."

"Good. He won't be able to locate her that quickly, so she's a good cover story. Your dad didn't tell me he's here in California, though." More typing, then he lifted his head. "Keep walking, Ginger. I can text and walk."

I clenched my fists. "I don't like this."

He didn't look up, just kept typing. "Don't like what?"

"You're acting different," I said, my voice cracking. "Again."

He'd barely looked at me at all since the phone call, and now he was acting cold. Distant. It freaked me out. Was he regretting the fact that he had me in his house when his boss came to visit? Kicking himself for being with me?

I didn't know, but I knew *something* was off.

He looked at me, his eyes as closed off as his voice. "Of course I am. I'm trying to cover our tracks. Your daddy's out there, thinking God knows what, doing God knows what, and I need to get you there without him knowing where the fuck you were. This is me in work mode, Ginger."

"He won't find out. You'll be fine."

"No, I won't be fine." He pressed his lips together, his nostrils flaring. "Because on *top* of that, the whole time he's here I have to stay the hell away from you when I don't even want to be away from you for a fucking minute. So, yeah, I'm a little bit distracted and cranky, to say the least."

He hauled me up against him and kissed me hard, not giving me a chance to reply. What would I have said anyway? What he said pretty much summed up my feelings, so instead, I clung to him, knowing we shouldn't be kissing like this in public, but unable to help myself.

I curled my hands into his shirt, twisting the fabric in my hands. I could feel the tears threatening to escape me, trying to run down my cheeks. But I wouldn't cry. It wasn't like this was goodbye or anything. It was a temporary setback—nothing and no one would make me walk away. Not even Dad.

He ended the kiss way too fast, resting his head on mine. "Let's get you back to your dad. Remember, if you see me watching you—don't even *look* at me. Act like you've never seen me before. Act like I'm no one and nothing. Don't save my name in your phone, and no incriminating texts."

"I can't even tell you I love you?" I asked, my throat swelling with the tears that were trying to escape.

"Not in those words. Text me...*the sun is finally shining*."

"The sun is finally shining?"

"Yeah. It's the first thing I thought of when I met you—that the sun was brighter and shiny and good."

My heart melted. How the heck was I supposed to walk away after that? "I don't want to go."

"I know." He kissed me one last time. "But you have to."

I stopped at the bike, but he tugged me past it. "Wait, where are you taking me?"

"You're taking a cab. I quietly called one while you were on the phone. We can't risk being seen together," he said matter-of-factly. When I opened my mouth to tell him no, he shook his head. "I know. It sucks, but it's how it has to be for now."

I blinked back tears. "Will you stay here?"

"No, I'm getting rid of your helmet and watching from the shadows, like I'm supposed to. And when your dad confronts me and asks where I was, I can tell him that I was watching you the whole time." He slapped my ass. "Now off you go, Ginger."

I walked to the cab, each step I took away from him becoming harder and harder. By the time I slipped into the seat, I was ready to turn around and bolt toward him. It was like something inside me thought this might be the last time I saw him. I didn't know what caused my racing heart and my fear, but it was tangible and undeniable.

And I somehow *knew* as the cab pulled away from the curb and Finn got rid of my helmet and climbed onto his bike…

Something was going to go terribly wrong.

CHAPTER ELEVEN

Finn

After I stashed Carrie's helmet inside my apartment in record speed, I hopped on my bike and followed the cab back to the dorms. I knew Carrie's parents were rich and a flight out didn't exactly break the bank or anything, but why had they come out all of a sudden? Had they just missed her, or was it something more?

Something like suspicion?

Maybe the senator had caught on to some weird vibe coming from across the fucking country and just instinctively known something was going on with his baby girl. But he couldn't. It's not like he was a psychic or some shit like that. He couldn't possibly know that I'd gotten a little bit *too* close in guarding his precious cargo.

…Could he?

Oh, fuck me. What if he'd sent over some extra security and I didn't even know about it? What if, right now even, he had a man watching *me*?

If he did, I was so screwed.

Carrie had thought she heard someone earlier. I had brushed it off, but maybe I'd been wrong. Maybe someone had been there, watching us and reporting back to her father from the shadows?

Son of a bitch…

I revved my engine, gripping the handlebars so tight it hurt, cursing myself ten times over for not considering this angle earlier. The cab pulled over and Carrie climbed out, her eyes seeking me out immediately. I parked my bike and tilted my head, telling her silently to look away and act like I didn't exist. Something told me she'd fail miserably. She wasn't a good liar, my Carrie, and it's one of the things I loved most about her— her honesty.

But it just might be our downfall.

She walked up to her parents, her steps quickening as she grew closer. After one last look over her shoulder at me, she ran into her mom's open arms. Her mom hugged her tight, burying her face in her hair and inhaling deeply. As if she missed Carrie's scent and needed to get as much of it as she could while she could.

Fuck, I got that. I got that all too well.

Next, her dad—the man I've never even seen crack a smile—grinned and hauled her into his arms, spinning her in a wide circle and saying something I couldn't make out. Carrie laughed in reply, the sound breaking through the night, and I closed my eyes.

Ah, that sound…

It had the power to save me from anything.

I watched from the shadows, my heart as heavy as a bowling ball in my chest. They looked so happy and normal right now. I had a hard time placing the man who was paranoid enough to send me to watch his daughter in secrecy with the man who stood here now, laughing and bussing Carrie's nose with a huge smile on his face.

And watching her in the arms of her parents just made our whole situation *real*. Would they ever welcome me into their family with open arms like that? All smiles and kisses and hugs? Doubtful. But I'd do my damned best to make it happen.

I'd make him accept me if it was the last thing I did, damn it.

The next morning, after an hour of watching Carrie bond with her parents and a mostly sleepless night, I woke up hung over and yet way too sober. I'd spent all night plotting and trying to come up with every possible scenario that could occur with her father's visit. I also tried to figure out why he was here.

And I failed.

I checked my text messages. One was from the senator. *I'm in town.*

It was a test. He knew I knew, but wanted to see what I said. *I saw you last night while I stood post. Welcome to California, sir.*

Thank you. Consider yourself off duty until I leave. I'll be in contact ASAP.

I clenched the phone. In other words? Stay away. *Looking forward to it, sir.*

I also had a text from Carrie. It was ridiculous how happy that made me. *The sun is finally shining today, Susan.*

I grinned. She'd saved me in her phone under a woman's name. How smart and devious. I liked it. *Indeed it is. You ready for chemistry class?*

I flopped back on my bed, resting my phone on my bare stomach as I waited for a reply. I didn't have to wait long. My phone vibrated, and I picked it up. *I prefer anatomy.*

Ha! Of course she did. That was our code for exploring each other's bodies, after all. I grinned. *Oh, me too. Believe me.*

As I waited for her to reply, I checked the time and realized she might not reply at all. She'd be walking into class right now, so she'd be silent for a while. Maybe I'd go to the beach. Ride a wave or two and try to figure out what was going on with my boss. Between the unusually quiet days leading up to this visit and the visit itself, I *knew* he knew something.

The question was *what*?

A knock sounded on the door, and I rolled out of bed wearing nothing but a pair of boxers. If someone wanted to knock on my door at this ungodly hour in the morning, then I reserved the right to open it half naked.

But when I opened the door, I wished I'd put some clothes on.

Senator Wallington, Carrie's father in the flesh, stood on my porch staring at me with what I could only describe as speculation in his eyes. Fucking sneaky bastard. I stepped in the doorway, not letting him inside. "Sir? I didn't realize you were texting me from my porch."

"I figured as much." He looked over my shoulder, so I closed the door even more. "Yet…here I am."

He craned his neck to try and see past me, but I didn't budge. Boss or not, he didn't get to drop in at my place unexpected like this. And Carrie's clothes were all over my room right now since I hadn't cleaned them up.

If he came in, he'd know. And I'd be done for.

"Is there something I can do for you, sir?"

"Yes." He crossed his arms over his flawless gray suit. Behind him, security stood in their black suits and shades, watching us both *Men in Black* style. Did I look that constipated when I stood behind the senator, not moving or talking? "You can let me inside, for starters."

I motioned down my body, my other hand gripping the door as tightly as I could. "It's a mess and I'm not dressed. I wasn't prepared for company."

"I don't care if it's a mess, and it's nothing I haven't seen before," he said simply, his voice perfectly calm. His eyes moved over my tattoos, seeming to fall upon each and every one. Then he snapped his attention to my face again. "Let me inside, Coram."

I knew he wouldn't walk away, and since he was my boss, I couldn't exactly refuse him entry. Fuck, I wanted to. Standing here talking to Carrie's dad while half naked with the scratches down my back that she'd made were perfectly visible was *not* my idea of a good start to my day.

I tugged on my hair and sighed. "You'll need to at least give me a second to pick up a little bit. Give me that much."

"You hiding something, Griffin Coram?"

I winced, hating the fact that I was being forced to lie again. I'd hoped my lying days were over when Carrie figured out who I was, yet here I was—lying through my teeth to her father—my boss. "No, sir. The only thing I'm hiding is a mess that I'd rather you not see."

He sighed impatiently. "Go on, then. Clean up and throw some clothes on. We'll go out to eat once you're clean enough."

I nodded and closed the door in his face, taking a second to brace myself for the upcoming confrontation. If he was taking me out to eat, then it couldn't be a bad thing that he was here, could it? Fuck if I knew.

I pushed off the door and made quick work of throwing on a pair of shorts and a T-shirt. Next, I tossed all of Carrie's clothes into a box, along with the pink hangers, and shoved it under my bed. After I made my bed, I stepped back and did a once-over of my place.

It looked Carrie-free again, unfortunately.

I smoothed my hands over my hair, took a calming breath, and opened the door. Senator Wallington still stood there, looking as poised as ever. I motioned him in. "If you'd like to come in now, you can."

The senator walked in, his gaze scanning the interior. His eyes seemed to touch upon anything and everything he could without digging through my drawers. I couldn't help but shift on my feet uneasily. Knowing my luck, I'd probably missed something. Maybe I'd left out a shirt or a hair tie.

He turned to me with his brows up. "This big enough for you? I can get you a bigger place if you prefer."

And just like that? The stress faded away. If he was talking about getting me a bigger apartment, I wasn't getting fired. It pretty much ruled out the possibility of there being another security guy out here with us. If he knew I was in love with his daughter, I would be at the business end of a fist right now.

Everything *had* to be okay. And my father would still get his retirement pension, and all was okay in the world. Minus the fact that I was a big fat fucking liar.

I forced a smile. "I'm fine here, sir. It's close to campus, and that makes my job easier."

"Good." He slid his phone into his pocket, his eyes on my bed. Could he tell that only a few hours earlier, his daughter had been with me in that bed he studied so closely? "Why do you have two surfboards in here?"

My breath slammed out of me. I eyed Carrie's blue surfboard and thanked God she didn't pick a girly one. "Why not? I like variety."

He gave me a hard look and sighed. "Let's go."

"After you, sir," I said quietly. I followed him outside, my palms sweating the whole time. I scanned the faces of the guards following the senator, then slid my shades onto my nose. "Cortez. Morris. Nice to see you again."

"You look different out of a suit, Coram," Morris said, his voice flat. "Like a surfer boy."

I *was* a surfer boy, but I kept my mouth shut on that matter.

"You look different *in* one while standing in California." I shrugged. "I need to blend in, so surfer boy I am."

"Makes sense," Cortez said.

"Yeah. How many of you are there out here?"

"Just us, to the best of my knowledge," Cortez said, his eyes on the senator, who walked in front of us. "But with the senator?" Cortez caught my gaze, not dropping it. "You never know."

Well, shit. That sounded an awful lot like a warning. "I'll remember that."

"You should," Cortez said, motioning me forward into the town car.

I nodded to both of them, then slid into the back of the car, settling into the far side of the seat to make room for all four of us. I kept replaying Cortez's words in my head, dissecting them and trying to make sense out of the whole thing.

My mind raced and my heart raced even faster. Was Cortez trying to warn me about something? Maybe he was trying to tell me that the senator had sent another man out here. If so, it would mean Carrie and I wouldn't even be able to be together. Could I handle that?

I'd been waiting to come clean for my father, but if I couldn't even see the woman I loved, would it be so cut and dry? Suddenly, I wasn't so sure about that.

When the senator sat beside me and closed the door, I blinked at him. "Where's the rest of your team, sir?"

"They'll watch Carrie today. After all, I have *you* with me."

"I don't even have my weapon, sir." I tapped my fingers on my knee. "It doesn't go with the clothes."

He waved a hand. "It's fine. I doubt we'll be attacked at breakfast."

"All right." I cocked a brow and buckled up, not sure how to take the senator's behavior. "She'll see them in those suits."

"I know." He shrugged and looked out the window, gripping the side of the door so tight his knuckles showed. His entire body screamed of impatience and anger and something a hell of a lot like *knowledge*. "She knows they're here now, so she won't question it."

Okay, he had a point, but she wouldn't like them being there. I fidgeted with my seatbelt, but forced myself to stop. It made me look guilty—which I was. Damn it, I hated this shit. Maybe I should come clean. Spit it out. Get it over with.

He wouldn't really cut off my father without a penny, would he? I didn't know, and I couldn't take that chance. If it were just me, I would open my mouth right now and tell him I loved his precious daughter. I'd accept the consequences of my actions. But with Dad months away from retirement, I couldn't take that chance.

I forced myself to nod. "That's true," I said, my voice stiff sounding even to my ears. "Do you have other guys besides me out here, sir?"

He looked at me, his eyes so like Carrie's it gave me the creeps. Even though they were the same shade, they were completely unreadable to me. He also had a way of staring me down that made me want to confess all my sins. Hard. Cold. *Calculated.*

He clenched his jaw. "Have you seen anyone else following Carrie lately?"

"Just thought I saw a few shadows moving." I shrugged. "Could've been my imagination."

"Keep an eye on it. As of now, you're the only one out here."

Thank fucking God. "I will, sir."

He tapped his fingers on the door. "If you need backup…"

"I don't. I'm fine." I adjusted my seatbelt again. "If that changes, I'll let you know."

"Are you juggling the Marines and my daughter with ease?"

Was it just me, or was that question rife with innuendo? "Yes, sir. I have to report for duty this weekend, but I'm sure she'll be fine without me watching her. She's proved to have a remarkably good head on her shoulders. You must be very proud of her."

The senator smoothed his jacket, a look of pride taking over his face. Not a smile, but the closest thing I've ever seen from him that wasn't directed toward his family. "Indeed, I am."

"As well you should be, sir."

He looked out the window. "Your father says hello."

I swallowed hard. Part of me had hoped he would have come here, too. I missed him. "I look forward to seeing him once I return home for the holidays."

"He was going to come along, but something got in the way." The senator turned away, his jaw hard but his eyes somehow softer. "Something unavoidable."

"Oh?" I loosened my seatbelt, my heart quickening at the odd reply. I hadn't heard from my father a whole lot lately, and it hadn't even registered on my radar with all the other shit I had going on, but now it was glaringly clear. "And what would that be? Is everything okay with him, sir?"

He looked back my way, and the momentary flash of emotion had dissipated. The relentless politician I was accustomed to had returned. "I think that's something you need to talk to him about."

That didn't sound fucking good at all. What unavoidable thing could my father have had come up? "I'll call him after breakfast, sir."

"Good." Senator Wallington looked out the window again, giving me a reprieve from the nonstop scrutiny. I'd never seen the man so damned restless before. "I have to say, I had my suspicions in coming out here. Suspicions that led me to come out here directly."

And just like that, my heart stopped beating, then painfully accelerated. "Sir?"

"I knew Carrie was hiding something. I came here because I knew she wasn't being completely honest with me, and now I know what she's hiding."

My chest squeezed tight. "What would that be, sir?"

"Don't you know already?" He leaned closer, eyeing me like a predator with its prey. "I think you do. I think you know exactly what I want to know, and you're going to tell me every detail without leaving a single thing out."

"I don't know what you want to hear from me, sir," I forced myself to say. My voice sounded pretty damn calm. I leaned back against the seat, even though I wanted to bolt and warn Carrie. My heart pounded in my ears, echoing like a drum solo in an empty room. "I've been doing my job. Watching your daughter. Keeping her out of trouble."

He leaned forward and gripped my shoulder far too hard to be comforting. "Well, tell me everything you know."

This was it. This was the fucking beginning of the end. Even knowing this, I forced myself to calmly ask, "About *what*, sir?"

He narrowed his eyes at me, for once not looking cold. No, he looked fucking pissed off. "Why don't *you* tell me?"

CHAPTER TWELVE

Carrie

Mom tilted her head, fingering the sleeve of the soft teal sweater in front of her. "I don't know, honey. Which one do you think you'll get the most use out of?"

"I like this one," I said, my mind not really on the sweater. It was on Finn and the chemistry homework I'd never finished, and the lab I had to do tomorrow morning. "It's a lighter shade."

Mom nodded. "And feel how soft it is."

I sighed, reaching out and touching the soft sweater, trying my best to look as into the whole shopping experience as she was. I'd never been able to last as long as she could, and today was no exception. We'd been shopping for three hours, and I was *done*. D-O-N-E, *done*. I didn't care which one she bought thirty minutes ago, and I didn't care now either.

It was a shirt. A shirt Finn would undoubtedly rip off me at some point.

"It'll go better with your hair." She held the sweater up to me, and I held my arms out as she studied my complexion. "Yes, this'll do. Now, for some pants..."

I followed her, barely biting back a groan. Truth be told, I wasn't much of a shopper, but she was, and it made her happy. I smiled and acted as if I cared what color socks I wore with my sweaters because it made *her* smile. As she combed through a rack of black jeans, I peeked over my shoulder for the ten-millionth time.

Finn still wasn't out there. Just a pair of suits.

Where was he? Was I just not seeing him? For a while after our big fight, he'd done a good job at staying hidden from me. Maybe he was incognito or something.

"Oh, look at the pockets on these." Mom pulled out a pair of black jeans with zippers on a bunch of pockets from the back of the rack. "They look like something a biker chick would wear, don't you think?"

They did. I could easily picture myself sitting on Finn's bike, wearing those pants and wrapping my arms around his waist. I bet he'd like them, too. For the first time this whole shopping trip, my heart picked up speed. "Yeah, and I like them. Are they my size?"

She looked at me with a raised brow. "Of course they are. I wouldn't have pulled them out if they weren't."

"I'll take them." I smiled at her, my eyes still on the pants. "Thanks, Mom."

"You're welcome, dear." She pursed her lips and looked at me, her eyes narrowed. I stiffened. Last time she looked at me like that, I'd been forced to get a haircut because it was fresh and fun. I'd hated it. "Shall we get you some biker boots to go with it?"

I tensed. She sounded *suspicious*. As if she knew I was riding a bike now. She couldn't possibly know that. I forced myself to relax and smile. "Um, sure. Why not? They're fashionable now. Maybe with some laces that go all the way up?"

She tapped a finger on her lip. "Your tastes have changed."

"I've grown up." I looked over my shoulder, searching the crowd outside for Finn. Still no sign of him. I turned back to Mom. "Is that so bad?"

She smiled and headed for the register. "Of course not. As a matter of fact, I think I like the changes. You look happier."

That's because I was. I had Finn. "I am, Mom. Really, *really* happy."

"Good. And I'm glad you're free of all the stresses from our life out here." Mom stood in line, tapping her foot as she waited. "Last week, we hosted three senators and a governor for dinner. Everything was rolling along smoothly, but then, wouldn't you know it? Christy got the flu and couldn't make the dinner. We had to scramble for a replacement chef at the last second, and Dad was on a rampage."

I flinched. I was all too familiar with the stresses that came with being a Wallington. "Who did you find?"

"The Stapletons loaned us theirs. He was delightful." Mom looked over her shoulder, her eyes lighting up. "Hey, you remember them, right? They have a son who's a couple of years older than you. His name's Riley."

I scanned my memory. I vaguely remembered a guy a few years older than me at Dad's last gala, but to be honest, most of those events passed in a blur. "Blond hair, green eyes, and tall?"

"Mmhm." She smiled even bigger. "You remember him."

"Yeah, sure." I shrugged. "He seemed nice enough."

"Well, he wants to go sailing with you over the summer break." Mom stepped forward in the line a little bit more. "They visited the night of the disaster, and we got to talking about you. You'll never believe it, but he goes to school upstate, near San Francisco."

I tensed. Why hadn't I realized where this was going? "Mom…"

"Oh relax, dear." She patted my arm. "It's a sailing expedition, not a betrothal."

I choked on a laugh. "I know, but I'm not looking for a boyfriend right now." *Because I already have one.* "Besides, why would he be thinking about taking me out? He doesn't even really *know* me."

"Your father and his are in the same political party, as you know, so it's an advantageous move for both families." She sighed and hugged the clothes tighter to her chest. "You do know at one point, you'll have to come home and play the game. Be the daughter your father needs you to be. Right?"

I stiffened and swallowed hard. In other words, I was expected to come home and marry a Stapleton like a good little girl. Yeah. That wasn't going to happen. I didn't need a *Stapleton*. I had a *Coram*. This was exactly what Finn had been worried about. And I'd laughed it off, as if it didn't matter and would never come into play.

I'd been wrong. It did matter. Finn was smart to plan ahead.

"Mom, I'm not marrying someone to further Dad's career," I said, my voice low. "I love you, and I love him, but *no*."

"You're not going to marry a man for your father. That's not what I meant." She shrugged. "But you'll marry someone who will be a benefit to the family, I'm sure. Someone who is worthy of standing beside a Wallington. You should take more pride in who you are."

"I have plenty of pride." I crossed my arms. "But you have too much. We're no different than anyone else."

"I didn't say we were. You're putting words in my mouth." Mom sighed. "It's hard to see the big picture when you're so young." She reached out and squeezed my arm, her eyes kind, even though her words made me want to scream. "You have time. There's no rush for you to accept this all right here."

I clenched my teeth. I wouldn't be accepting it ever. "*Mom.*"

"It's about more than what we want out of life. There's your father's career, the presidential campaign, the opportunities…you're just too young to see that." Mom dropped her arm. "Looks like it's my turn to pay."

Mom stepped forward and chatted up the store employee, acting for all the world as if she hadn't just dropped a bombshell on me and walked away. I fidgeted and looked over my shoulder. Dad was out there talking to the suits, but still no Finn.

Not able to stand it another second, I pulled out my phone and texted him. *Everything okay, Susan?*

My phone buzzed and my heart sped up. *Yeah, I'm fine. What are you up to?*

I peeked at Mom, making sure she wasn't watching me. Luckily, she was too busy chatting. *Shopping with my mom.*

Oh boy. Sounds…fun? Okay. I can't lie. Not really. You know I'm not much of a shopper.

I held back a smile. *Yeah, I know.*

Are you going to buy something pretty?

I grinned. *Like…?*

I don't know. A skirt for church? Maybe we could share it.

I snorted, then glanced up cautiously. Mom was almost finished. *Uh-oh. We're done paying. I have to go.*

Okay. Hey, the sun is finally shining.

I looked out the window and smiled. *It really is.*

I shoved my phone back in my pocket just in time for Mom to stop yakking to the cashier. She looked at me, taking in my flushed cheeks more than likely. She arched a dainty brow. "What were you doing, dear?" she asked.

I scrambled for something to say and blurted out the first thing that came to mind. "Looking at used cars."

"Cars?" Mom blinked at me. "Do you want one?"

I nodded frantically, wiping my sweaty palms on my thighs. "Yeah, someday. Something inexpensive to get around in, you know? I spend a lot in cab fare."

"Okay." She shrugged. "Tell your father. He'll buy you one."

"I will." *Not.* If I told him, he'd buy me some expensive, top-of-the-line car. I wanted something old and rusty. Nothing fancy. I cleared my throat, ready to change the subject. "By the way, how's your friend Mary? The one who went for surgery on Monday when we talked?"

"Oh, I think she's better."

I nodded, letting her walk in front of me and following her closely. "How do you know? Did you go see her again?"

"No. She's back on our *Words With Friends* game as of an hour ago." Mom looked back at me and shrugged. "She can't play if she's not feeling better, so she must be fine."

I choked on a laugh. "Uh…yeah. I guess so."

I followed her out the door, my attention focused on Dad. I looked for any signs of anger or frustration or knowledge, but he just smiled at me and hugged Mom. When he hugged me, kissing the top of my head like he always did, I wanted to shake him and ask him where Finn was. I couldn't.

I had to play the game.

"Where have you been?" I asked him.

I looked up at him like I used to do when I was a little girl, with my chin resting on his chest. It took me back to a time when I'd thought he could do no wrong. I'd thought he was perfect back then. Invincible. How naïve I'd been. He was a good man. He really was. But he had flaws like the rest of us.

"You weren't done until three and I knew your mother wanted to go shopping with you like old times." He eyed the bags in my hands and Mom's. "Looks like you were both successful."

"Of course we were," Mom said, fluffing her light red hair. "But where'd you run off to all day, Hugh?"

"Oh, you know, taking care of some business." Dad averted his eyes and let go of me, pressing his lips together. His dark brown hair was immaculately in place, and he was clean-shaven. If he smiled, he'd flash those famous dimples that made all the women in America swoon. He could probably win the campaign with those two assets alone. "I'm starving. You two ready to eat something?"

I nodded. "Sure."

"Absolutely," Mom said.

He grinned, his dimples popping out. "All right. Off we go, the fearsome threesome."

I didn't follow him as he walked, and it took him all of two seconds to notice. When he turned to me with a curious expression, I gave him a level look. A few months ago, I wouldn't have had the courage to stand up to him like this, but I'd changed. Finn had shown me how life was supposed to be, and it wasn't *this*. "Lose the suits. I'm not ruining my cover because you're scared we'll be attacked at the restaurant."

If Finn still followed us, Dad wouldn't even hesitate to send the men packing. He would shrug and tell them to go eat. "You know I can't do that."

"Sure you can. Normal people do it all the time."

"We're not normal," he stressed, looking pointedly at Mom. "A little help here, Margie?"

"But—"

"*I* am normal when I'm here." I caught his gaze, biting down on my lip so hard it hurt. He wasn't sending them away. This wasn't good. Wasn't good at all. "Back home I follow all your rules, even though it kills me to be so freaking sheltered. Out here, you need to follow mine. You promised I could be normal here."

His tough façade cracked. "Carrie…"

"Please?" I curled my hands into fists, not dropping my gaze. "Daddy?"

Yep. I pulled out the big guns. Worked every time.

"Hugh…" Mom grabbed his elbow, holding on tight. "They can take our bags home, dear. It'll be fine. Plus, it'll be nice with just the three of us."

Dad released a breath and motioned them over. "You can take our bags and head back to the hotel. We'll be there after dinner."

The security man nodded, took our bags, and motioned for his buddy to follow him. He wore the same black suit they always wore, and I tried to picture Finn standing beside them perfectly immobile and serious.

The image of the Finn I knew didn't mesh well with the security guard Finn, but I knew that's what he was. What he did. "Thanks, Dad."

"You're welcome," he said, his voice gruff.

Mom grinned, looking back and forth between us. "So, where are we going?" Mom asked, linking her arm with Dad's.

I forced myself to pay attention. "There's a great burger place called Islands. We could—"

"Burgers?" Mom snorted. "I don't think so, Carrie."

Dad looked down at her. "I hear there's a great five-star sushi place in town. Let's go there. Sound good, Carrie?"

No. I hated sushi, and he knew it. Or at least…he should. Then again, maybe I'd never bothered to mention it to him. But there would be something besides sushi at the restaurant, so I could work with it. "Sure. That sounds great."

"What time are your classes tomorrow?" Dad asked.

I had to think about it for a second. "Nine to four."

"Any plans afterward?" Mom asked, her eyes on mine.

"Nope."

Dad stiffened. "Do we have to do this right here, Margie?"

I looked at both of them, unable to follow whatever the heck was going on right now. I slid into the town car and waited for them both to be seated before answering. "I'd assumed I would be hanging out with you two, since you're only here until Saturday night."

"No hot date?" Mom asked, a smile on her face.

She wasn't making any sense. One second she's asking me to come home and marry a Stapleton, and the next she's asking me if I have a hot date planned. I blinked at her. "Uh…no? Why?"

"Well…" Mom smiled even wider, but Dad grew even tenser, if possible. "Your father thinks you're dating someone and hiding it. And I *hope* you are. Well, the dating part. Not the hiding, because I want to hear all about him. We all need to have some fun in college before settling down."

Ah. So that's why she was acting all happy to hear about the possibility of me dating someone. She viewed it as a fling or sowing wild oats or something equally untrue. I gripped my knees so tight it hurt, focusing on Dad instead of her. "Why would you think I'm seeing someone?"

"I have my reasons." He looked over at me, pinning me against the door without even touching me. "Are you?"

My heart beat so loudly in my ears I couldn't hear anything but my own panicked thoughts. "N-No...?"

Oh my God, did he know? *Could* he know? Had Finn told him?

He tilted his head. "Is that a question or an answer?"

"An answer," I said, straightening my spine. If I was going to save Finn's job and keep his father employed through his last few months, then I needed to do better at lying. I tried to ignore my racing pulse. "Of course it's an answer. What kind of question is that, anyway?"

"The question of a concerned father."

"Well, my *concerned father* needs to realize I'm not a little girl anymore, and he needs to relax." When he opened his mouth to argue, I shot him a look that probably could have set coals on fire. "And this goes for you, too, Mom. I'll date who I want, when I want, and I won't answer to either one of you for it."

Mom gasped, covering her mouth. "Carrie, don't yell at us."

I closed my eyes for a second. I hadn't even raised my voice in the slightest. "I'm not yelling. I'm simply letting you two know that *if* and *when* I'm dating a man, I'll bring him to meet you when I'm good and ready. Not a second before. You flying out here to check on me and try to catch me in a lie isn't going to hurry me up any. You don't like that? Then stop trying to dig into something that isn't your business. Last time I checked, I was a legal adult. I expect to be treated as such."

Mom's eyes went wider, and Dad turned red...then even redder. I never stood up to them like this, so I got the shock they were experiencing—but dude, it felt good. Really, *really* good. "You listen to me, young lady, you'll—"

Mom squeezed his arm, but didn't look away from me. "Dear? I think this discussion is better ended right here and now. I know that look in her eye all too well. Let it go."

"But I—" He broke off and pointed at me. "And she—"

Mom patted his arm. "I know, Hugh. It's called growing up. Kids do that."

"They don't talk to their parents like that," he huffed. "If I'd done that to my father, I wouldn't have been able to sit straight for a week."

The car stopped in front of the restaurant, but none of us moved. "I love you both very much," I said softly, "but *some* things have to be done in my time, on my terms. That's all I'm asking."

Dad pressed his lips together, looking as if he wanted nothing more than to shout, but he nodded. "Fine. If you choose the wrong man, I will do everything in my power to send him packing."

I had no doubt that Finn was probably the "wrong guy" in Dad's eyes, but nothing would send Finn running. I was confident in his love for me, and in our love for each other. "You can try."

He narrowed his eyes on me. "Are you at least going to tell me who he is?"

"There is no 'he' at all," I stated, opening the door. "Now let's go eat."

I heard my mother whisper something to my father, and he answered back in hushed tones. When they climbed out of the car, he looked even more pissed off, but he was quiet. I couldn't shake the sinking suspicion that Dad knew more than he was letting on—that he was playing us both against one another until one of us broke and gave away our secrets. It wouldn't be me.

I was determined to keep my silence, my freedom, and my Finn...

No matter what I had to do.

CHAPTER THIRTEEN

Finn

Friday night I tossed all my shit into the green field bag on my bed, my mind at least a million miles from this damn drill weekend. It had been two days since I last saw Carrie, and I was like a man detoxing from heroin. I had the shakes and I needed her *now*. If I could hold her for one minute, and inhale her sweet scent, it would be enough to get me through the weekend. Just a small fix.

I hugged her sweater she'd left here, holding it to my nose to inhale deeply. It wasn't enough. I needed more. I needed *her*. But I couldn't have her until her parents left. It was fucking ridiculous that I was so impatient considering the fact that it would only be a few days apart. It shouldn't be so damn hard to be without her.

But it really fucking was.

Even worse? Her father suspected I was hiding something.

I *was*, but I couldn't say it yet. Not until my father retired. And the really shitty part about this plan? My silence would only make him hate me in the end.

I couldn't betray my own father. Not even for my own chance at happiness.

Knowing I'd possibly lost the one chance I had to come clean with the man didn't exactly sit well, but it was my *dad*. What was I supposed to do? Throw him under the tires to save myself? Over my dead body.

Still, it sucked ass.

My phone rang, and I crossed the room to pick it up off my bed. Once I saw the number, I relaxed a bit. I'd called my father the other day, after the cryptic lunch with Senator Wallington, but he hadn't called me back. Dad *always* called me back right away. "Hey, Dad. It's about time you returned my call."

"Hello, son. I heard that you—" he cleared his throat and continued, "that you were getting company out there."

"Yeah. I kind of expected you to come." I reclined on my bed, Carrie's sweater still in my hands. I absentmindedly ran my fingers over the bandage covering my chest. I'd gotten new ink today. "And don't avoid the question. Why didn't you call me back?"

I played with her sweater as I waited for Dad to answer. He sounded sluggish tonight. He made a weird moaning sound. "I wasn't invited to come along, and I was busy."

I cocked a brow. "Doing what? Guarding the dog? The rest of them are here."

Dad laughed. "You know how much they love this stupid thing. He asked me to stay behind and take care of her."

That was a lie. Dad *never* lied to me.

"You were invited. The senator told me," I replied, sitting up straight. "He said you were going to come out, but something came up. Then I call, and it takes you two days to get back to me? Tell me the truth— what's up, Dad?"

"Oh. Okay, then." Dad sighed, sounding old and tired even through the phone. "I'm sick. I have a pretty nasty flu. It's knocked me down pretty hard."

Well, that explained the weak tone of his voice, at least, and the non-visit. I rolled to my feet and went back to packing, balancing the phone on my shoulder and tossing Carrie's sweater on my pillow. "Oh, that sucks. Are you on the upswing yet?"

He laughed lightly. "I'm trying."

"Do you want me to let you go to bed? You know rest is the best thing for a flu, right?" I ran a hand over my short hair. I'd gotten it cut earlier this morning. "That and the chicken noodle soup Mom used to make, of course."

"I am. And I do." He coughed lightly, then laughed. "It's not as bad as it sounds. I feel fine most of the time. It just gets worse at night."

He didn't sound fucking fine to me. My heart picked up speed. The sound of his weak voice brought back bad memories of Mom lying in bed, slowly wasting away till nothing was there but death. "Are you s-sure? I could come home and check on you—"

"*No,*" he said, his voice perfectly strong that time. "I'm fine. You focus on your job and stop worrying about me and my stupid virus."

Which reminded me about the call I'd gotten—and the possible deployment. I couldn't tell him that shit when he was sick. It could be nothing. And if it *was* something, then I'd tell him about it after this weekend. I didn't want him losing sleep when he needed the rest. "If you're sure…"

"I am." He cleared his throat again, sounding like he choked back a cough at the same time. "I'm going to go now. I love you."

I swallowed hard. He sounded like shit. "I love you, Dad."

I hung up the phone and started to set it down, but my phone vibrated in my hand. A text from Carrie. *You home?*

I sighed and tried to brush off the phone call with my father. He was sick, but he'd get better and be back to his happy self soon enough. *Yeah. Packing for cheerleading camp. You?*

I grinned as soon as I hit send. She'd get a kick about where I said I'd be going, and I couldn't wait to see what her reply was. But it didn't come.

A few minutes passed, making me grow twitchy and forget all about my dad's cold. Lately, the texts had been shorter and fewer, making me wonder if she was already pulling away from me. Then I remembered she was with her parents, and I kicked myself in the nuts for being such a neurotic fucking mess all the time.

My phone buzzed and I looked down at it with a hunger that was laughable. Who the hell got so excited to get a fucking text? *I'm home.*

I pictured her lying in her dorm bed, all alone in a pair of skimpy shorts and a tank top. Was her hair down or in a ponytail? My heart squeezed tight. I shouldn't miss her this much, damn it. It had only been a few days of no contact. We'd gone longer before, but that had been before we became a couple.

I guess that made a difference in my tolerance. I shook my head and focused on my phone. *Going to bed now?*

Barely a second passed. *Maybe...*

It's either a yes or a no. What's the hesitance?

Hold on.

The key sounded in the door, and I lurched to my feet. The only other person with a key was Carrie. And if Carrie was here...I didn't know whether to kiss her or yell at her for being so damn reckless. With her parents in town, the last place she should be is with me.

Her father had said no one was watching us, but that didn't mean he wasn't lying. The man was more slippery than an eel in salt water. I didn't trust him one bit. She walked in, closing the door behind her quickly, her eyes locking with mine. All that mattered was she was here.

A fist of emotion knocked the breath right out of me, making it hard to breathe. I took a stumbling step toward her, then another. Yeah. I wasn't going to yell at her. I was going to kiss her and hold her and thank God she came to see me because I'd missed her way too much. My fingers itched with the need to touch her, to have her.

All I could manage to say, amidst all the feelings she brought to life with her reappearance, was one word. "*Carrie.*"

"Before you say anything, I know I'm not supposed to be here." She leaned against the door and breathed heavily, her eyes on mine. Her gaze dipped lower, lingering on the bandage on my chest, but then she tore her eyes away. "But I have a car now. Dad bought it for me. I told Mom I wanted one and the next day it was there. It's ridiculous how easy it was, but it got me here, and that's all that matters."

I blinked at her. She had a car now? I hadn't even known she *wanted* one.

She continued on, obviously not needing a reply from me. "I parked at the store down the street. Then I went inside, left through the back, and walked here. I won't stay long, so no one will guess where I am. Don't yell at me."

I opened and closed my fists. "Why would I yell at you when I could kiss you instead?"

"Then do it already," she said, her eyes flashing at me.

I let out a broken sound I didn't even recognize and closed the distance between us. I didn't stop until I had her pinned against the door, my body glued to hers. I ran my hands all over her, starting at her shoulder, then dipping down her side and brushing against her breast.

Her breath hitched in her throat, and I yanked her against my body, knowing I should be sending her away but unable to.

Because I was fucking lost.

"You're really here," I breathed. "It's not another dream."

"I'm really here." She tilted her face up, her nails digging into my chest. "Are you going to kiss me or not?"

I groaned and closed my mouth over hers, slipping my tongue inside her lips as if I were a starving man and she was my last supper. And if she was? Well, at least I'd die a happy man. She let out a whimper and clung to me harder, her tiny nails piercing my skin. I couldn't give a damn.

She could draw blood from me as often as she wanted, as long as she was *here*.

Our kiss seemed to break something inside of me. I growled as I lifted her against the door, my hands on her waist. As I undid the button, she trembled and grabbed her shirt, breaking off the kiss long enough to rip it over her head before fusing her mouth to mine once more.

I tugged her shorts over hips, letting them hit the floor, then slid my hand between her legs, expecting to feel the smooth satin of her underwear. Instead, I touched bare skin, and I shuddered with the need that punched through me. It would drive me fucking insane from now on—wondering whether she had anything on under her fucking pants.

I let go of her and crossed the room in record speed, grabbing a condom out of my drawer and tearing it open impatiently. After I had the protection aspect of what we were about to do under control, I stepped between her legs and lifted her higher against the door. I wanted to take it slow and be all seductive and romantic and shit, but she was driving me insane with the little noises she was making and the way her hips rose toward me, begging for more. And I was a desperate man.

I broke off the kiss, my breathing harsh and my cock positioned at her pussy. "This isn't going to be sweet or soft. Are you okay with that?"

"Yes." She buried her hands in what was left of my hair and wrapped her legs around my waist. "Just hurry *up*, damn it."

I groaned and kissed her again, plunging inside of her in one smooth thrust. When I was buried inside her all the way, I tightened my grip on her and pressed her against the door even harder to make sure she had good support. Then…I fucking lost all control. I pulled out of her and thrust back inside—hard and fast and rough. And I didn't stop.

She clung to me, crying out my name. For a second I thought I hurt her, and started to pull back, but she dug her heels into my ass and held me in place, her hips moving restlessly against me. "Don't…stop."

I growled and plunged inside of her again, even harder. I wanted to tell her how much she meant to me, and how much I needed her in my life, but all I could do was move inside of her, making her moan and scream out my name and draw my blood.

Her nails raked down my chest to my abs, leaving a stinging sensation behind them, and I drove deeper inside of her. Her hands faltered over my bandage, but she closed her eyes and lost herself in the rhythm. When she started trembling, her thighs quivering around me, I positioned myself so that I brushed against her clit with each thrust and bit down on her neck. Within seconds, her pussy clenched around me and she tensed, her whole body going tight and hard.

I pounded into her once, twice, and one more time, my entire body shutting down from the force of the orgasm rocking through me. I collapsed against her, still supporting her weight with one arm, and dropped my head against the door by her shoulder. She breathed as unevenly as I did, and she held me close, her arms tight around me.

I didn't want to ever move. I wanted to stay like this, buried inside of her against my fucking apartment door. Because once I moved, I knew she would have to leave, and I'd be alone again, with nothing but my thoughts to keep me company.

She lifted her head from my shoulder, looking up at me with her bright blue eyes. "I think we needed that. These past few days have been rough."

"I know. I never thought I'd be one of those guys who needed his girl with him to be happy, but…" I shrugged and smiled at her. "I am now, and I don't mind. What did you do to me, Ginger?"

"I don't know, but you did it to me, too." She blew her hair out of her face and eyed me. "What's up with the bandage? You okay?"

I sighed and lifted her off the door, setting her down on her feet gently. She clung to me for a second, then seemed to gain her footing. Bending down, I picked up her shorts and handed them to her. "Yeah. I'm fine. Where's your dad right now?"

She gave me a lopsided grin. "Probably still recovering from me yelling at him. I kind of told him to mind his own business from now on." She stepped into the shorts and buttoned them, then took her shirt out of my hand and smiled her thanks. "Went all independent woman on him and everything."

"Man, I would've paid to see that." I snorted, picturing the look on her dad's face while Carrie told him off. "I bet he didn't know what to say."

"Oh, he definitely didn't." She pulled the shirt over her head and leaned against the door, right where I'd fucked her. I would never be able to look at a door again without getting a hard-on. "It was pretty funny. I should have taken a picture of his face for you."

I pulled on my shorts and sat down on the edge of my bed, not bothering with a shirt, and held my arms out for her. "Come here, Ginger. I can't stand not having you in my arms for another second."

She crossed the room and sat in my lap, curling up against my chest in a little ball. She rested her hand over my chest, right above my new tat. "Now *answer* me. What's with the bandage?"

"I got new ink."

She perked up at that. "Cool. Show me?"

I grinned and hugged her closer. "I will in a minute. Right now I just want to hold you before I send you back to your dad."

"Do you think he knows about us?"

I sighed, carefully choosing my words. "I think he knows you're seeing someone, but he doesn't know who."

She placed her hand over my heart. "Did he ask you if I'm seeing anyone?"

I nodded and rested my cheek on top of her head. She didn't smell like my shampoo. For some reason, that made me sad. "He did. I told him I'd seen you with a few guys, but they all seemed to be just friends. I said you were focusing on your studies for the most part."

"A *few* guys?" She slapped my arm hard. "You made me sound like a slut?"

I laughed. "I said they were friends."

"But you made—"

"Oh, shut it already." I tossed her onto the bed and climbed on top of her, laughing and kissing her into silence. When she was clinging to me and squirming beneath me, I pulled back and looked down at her. Everything from her flushed cheeks to her swollen lips screamed for me to keep her here, under me, but I knew I couldn't. So I did the first thing that came to mind.

I tickled her.

For a second, I wondered if she wasn't ticklish. She just stared up at me with narrowed eyes, but then her eyes went wide, a whoosh of air left her lungs, and she broke into laughter, squirming and begging me to stop. I joined her, laughing my ass off and tickling harder.

Only once tears were streaming down her face and she was begging for mercy did I stop, and she still laughed, clinging to me. We both struggled to catch our breath, and I rolled onto the side, holding her close. "You're extremely ticklish, Ginger."

She took a shaky breath, finally seeming to have herself under control. "I had no idea. I've never been tickled."

"Seriously?" I asked her incredulously. Well, I guess I shouldn't be too surprised. The senator didn't exactly seem the tickling type, but I'd thought her mother might have been... I guess not. My own mother had been. "I'm going to tickle you all the time now."

"God, no." She laughed lightly but pressed her lips together, her eyes on my bag. "Are you going to show me your tattoo before I have to go?"

I hesitated. It was the most telling piece I'd gotten since I got Mom's birthdate on my shoulder. "Yeah. Soon."

She ran her fingers over my head lightly. "You cut your hair, huh?"

I kissed her gently. "Yep. I have to report for duty in the morning."

"I know," she said, her eyes still on the bag. She sighed and looked away, her gaze on my pillow. "Are you bringing my shirt with you?"

I arched my neck, spotting the purple sweater I'd been hugging earlier. My cheeks heated, and I debated whether to admit why it was there. Would she think it was pathetic or sweet? If I told another guy, he'd call me names *I* didn't even say out loud.

But this was Carrie.

"Well, you see..." I cleared my throat. Something told me I was turning in my man-card by admitting this, but fuck it. I didn't need it. "I missed you. So I may or may not have been sniffing your sweater right before you came."

Tears filled her eyes and she wrapped her arms around my neck. "That's way too cute."

"Are you sure?" I kissed her, keeping it light and sweet. "It might just be creepy."

"I'm positive as a proton that it's cute and not even the slightest bit creepy."

I chuckled. "I missed hearing that phrase...." I trailed off and kissed her neck, desperately breathing in her scent so I could carry it with me all weekend. "Did you want to see my ink now?"

"Uh, *yeah*," she said, craning her neck and trying to peek. "I've only been begging for the past five minutes. What is it?"

I peeled it back enough for her to see. "It's our tattoo."

I watched her as she read it, her mouth silently moving along as she read the words. It was in a script-type scrawl: *the sun is finally shining*. It was over my heart, which was fitting since she owned it.

"It's perfect." She looked up at me, tears in her eyes. "I want one, too. When you get back, you'll take me. Got it?"

"You want ink?"

"I do. I want that one." She ran her fingers over it gently, making sure not to hurt me. It was still raised and red and covered in the antibacterial goo, but I didn't tell her not to touch it. I didn't give a damn. "That same exact one."

"Then you'll have it." I kissed her gently. After grabbing her hand, I helped her to her feet and hugged her tight, my heart hammering away at the idea of her walking away from me. "But now you have to go. Don't miss me too much while I'm gone."

"I'm not making any promises." She buried her face in my chest. "Hey, where are the rest of my clothes?"

"Under the bed. You can hang them back up once your parents are gone."

"I will." She hugged me tighter, obviously as reluctant as me to let go. "Do I *have* to go?"

I wanted to say no. I wanted to tell her she could stay, her father be damned. But I knew it wasn't the right thing to do, even if it felt like it right now. "You do."

"But the sun is finally shining," she said, her voice muffled because she had her face pressed against my bare chest.

My heart fisted painfully, making it hard to breathe. "It really fucking is." My fingers flexed on her, but I forced myself to let go. "I'll follow you from a distance, okay?"

"Okay." She bit her lip. "But it's only a two-minute walk to my car. I'll be fine."

"The day I let you walk around at night by yourself is the day I'll be dead in a coffin." Which reminded me… "Are you going to the soup kitchen with Marie?"

She nodded. "Yeah, I think so. I have tons of McDonald's gift cards sitting in my room."

"That's fine, but leave before dark—no matter what." I shooed her out the door. "Now get that perfect ass walking out that door so I can follow you."

She gave me one last longing look, then opened the door and left without another word. I silently slid out of my apartment about ten seconds later and followed her. She didn't acknowledge my existence, but she knew I was there.

When she got in her car—which turned out to be a used 2003 Mercedes SL500—and drove off, she craned her neck to watch me until I worried she'd crash into a telephone pole. I had to tackle the desire to chase after her car and drag her back to my apartment where she fucking belonged.

I leaned against the wall in the alleyway and closed my eyes. I couldn't believe how much a man could change in the blink of an eye. Before her, I didn't want a relationship or love. I wanted to focus on work and life before settling down, *if* I ever did. Now, all I could think about was love and marriage and babies and all the shit that came when you signed your heart away to another person. And yet, amidst all of the dreams, hopes, and desires, I knew that this time tomorrow…

I would find out whether our love would withstand what the world was going to throw our way.

Carrie

I crept up the stairs to my dorm, my heart racing as I hid in the shadows. I was fairly certain Dad's guards hadn't caught on to my ruse, but with them, you never knew. They were all sneaky bastards that made a living off following you around. And they were *good* at it, too. After all, Dad only hired the best.

I slipped into my dorm room, closing the door behind me quietly. As I leaned against it, I pulled out my phone and shot off a quick text to Finn to let him know I got home all right. He replied immediately, wishing me a good night, and I closed my eyes, holding my phone to my chest.

Going to see him had been a risky move.

But he was leaving tomorrow morning, and I'd missed him, and it had to happen. I was terrified that once he showed up tomorrow, he wouldn't be coming back. Scared that something or someone wouldn't let him. He couldn't leave me.

I pushed off the door and crossed the room quietly. I peeked in the direction of Marie's bed, but it was empty. Guess I didn't have to be so quiet. I flopped back on the bed and looked up at the dark ceiling. I should probably shower or something, but I didn't want to move.

I kept replaying the short visit with Finn over and over in my head, like a baby's lullaby. He'd actually gotten a tattoo for us. That was huge for him. We didn't talk much about his tattoos, but I knew each one had a special meaning behind it. He didn't mindlessly ink himself.

And he'd put me there. *Me.*

I'd have to decide where to get mine. I hadn't been kidding about that. I wanted one just like his. Maybe on my wrist? Oh, God. Dad would flip. I might be braver and a little bit more rebellious now, but not so much so that I'd go that far. It would have to be in a hidden spot. One Dad wouldn't have to look at. Maybe my hip?

I didn't know. All I knew was I needed one.

Just like I needed Finn to come back home to me, as soon as possible. I closed my eyes and for the first time in years…I prayed.

CHAPTER FOURTEEN

Finn

I shifted in the fake leather chair, tapping my foot in a rhythm that even I didn't recognize. All I knew was the longer I sat here, staring at the receptionist as she typed on her computer, the more impatient I got. If the receptionist sighed and clicked her mouse one more time, I might throw the damn thing out the window.

I'd gotten here at oh-eight-hundred sharp, but when I arrived on base, no one had known what the hell I was doing there. It wasn't a drill weekend—which I already knew—and no one else had been called in for duty. After a few phone calls, they'd sent me to this office, and I'd been counting fucking sheep in my head ever since.

Oh, and it wasn't *my* commanding officer who wanted to see me. It was Captain Richards who wanted me, aka *the* commanding officer of the whole fucking company. For the life of me, I couldn't figure out what he might want. I checked my watch, frowning when I saw it was already noon. How long were they going to leave me here doing shit?

The receptionist sighed and clicked again, and I narrowed my eyes at her. She wore pearls and a gray dress, and those glasses that women seemed to wear when they wanted to look smart. Her red lips were pursed, and she tapped her manicured nails on the mahogany desk.

The inactivity was getting to me. I didn't do sitting well, and I'd been sitting all damn morning. I was *this close* to lying on the floor to do a round of push-ups when the office door opened.

Captain Richards stepped out, and I stood at attention, saluting him and waiting for him to speak to me first, staring straight ahead at nothing.

"Sergeant, thank you for coming on your off weekend," he said.

I didn't move a muscle. "Good afternoon, sir."

Captain Richards studied my posture before stepping to the side. "At ease, sergeant. You may come in."

"Thank you, sir." I relaxed fractionally and nodded to him as I headed his way. "And I'm more than happy to be at your service."

Even if I had no clue what that *service* was.

He followed me in and shut the door behind us, making his way to his desk. "Well, you're probably wondering what you're here for." Captain Richards sat down behind his desk, motioning for me to sit in the wood chair in front of it. "And why I wanted to see you."

I perched on the edge of the chair, keeping my back straight. "I will admit to a certain level of curiosity, sir."

"Tell me, sergeant." Captain Richards rested his elbows on his desk and steepled his fingers. "Do you like being a Marine?"

"Of course, sir."

"Excellent." He tapped his fingers together, really slowly. "Where do you see yourself in ten years?"

Well, if that wasn't a loaded question I'd never heard one.

A few months ago, before Carrie, I would have had an easy answer. I'd be a Marine, and I'd still be guarding Senator Wallington. But now? It wasn't so clear-cut. In ten years, I'd hopefully still be with Carrie. Maybe we'd be married? Shit, I didn't know.

And more importantly? Why the hell did he care?

I cleared my throat. "I would imagine I'll be working in security, sir. Maybe something to do with computers. I've been thinking about getting my degree."

"What is your MOS now?"

"I'm a mortar man, sir."

"A grunt." He arched a brow. "So you want to go from infantry to a commissioned officer? Is that correct?"

"It's quite possibly my goal, yes, sir." I shifted in my chair, clutching my knees. "I've recently re-evaluated my life, sir, and am in the midst of trying to figure it out."

"Ah." His jaw squared off. "What caused this re-evaluation, if I might ask?"

My heartbeat thumped in my ears, louder than drums. "Sir? Why do you ask, if you don't mind my asking?"

His eyes narrowed on me. He was pulling rank on me. I knew it before he even opened his mouth. "Answer my questions, and maybe I'll answer yours."

"Sir, yes, sir." I cleared my throat, hating the fact that I had to sit here like a puppet while this man interrogated me, but it came with the dog tags. Obedience. Discipline. Respect. "I met a girl, sir."

"Might I ask this girl's name?" The captain reclined in his seat and crossed his ankle over his knee. "I do believe I'm acquainted with her father."

I must've blacked out for a second. God knows I felt as if he punched me in the fucking chest. He *knew* Senator Wallington? Well, there you go. Now I knew why I was here. Her father knew and sent me into a situation where I couldn't possibly lie.

God damn it.

I tried to remain calm on the outside, even if I was flipping the fuck out on the inside. "You know the Wallingtons, sir?"

"I do. Carrie is a sweet girl." He looked out the window for a second, then turned those piercing brown eyes back on me. "I've known her since she was in diapers."

I nodded, but didn't say anything.

"You're probably curious how I know."

I shifted on the seat. "Yes, sir."

"Her father asked me to track you. To make sure you were doing your job." Captain Richards eyed me. "Do you feel you're doing a good job, sergeant?"

"I feel she wouldn't be safer with anyone else watching her, sir." I met his eyes, refusing to flinch or back down. "I would guard her with my life."

"Would you do that even if you didn't love her?"

"Yes, sir." I tapped my fingers on my knees, but made myself stop. "It's my job. I take that responsibility very seriously."

"So if you were to guard another young woman, one whom you didn't love, you would still guard her to the best of your abilities?"

I blinked at him. "Yes, sir. I would."

"I heard about what you did when Carrie was almost robbed. Those were some impressive moves."

My cheeks heated up. "I was simply doing my job, sir."

"My man came home right afterward to tell me how impressed he was." Captain Richards raised his brow. "Keep in mind, he's a black belt in karate, among other things."

I bit down on my tongue, trying to figure out where the hell he was going with this. "I'm flattered, sir."

"Does her father know you love her?"

I swallowed hard. "No, sir."

"Why not?"

"We're waiting, sir." I gripped my knees even tighter. "My father is about to retire, and Carrie and I decided to hold off until after the fact."

"Ah." He nodded, his lips pursed in thought. "You're afraid he will withhold funds from your father?"

"Yes, sir," I admitted, sweat dripping down the back of my neck and rolling under the collar of my cammies. I wanted to yank at the collar, but I sat perfectly still. "That was our fear."

"*Our* fear?" He eyed me. "Carrie is in on this?"

Should I deny it? I didn't want her to catch any flak for my lies. But this was a captain in the Marines. I couldn't fucking *lie*. It's not the way the military worked. "Sir, I'd rather not say."

He considered me. "You're protecting her?"

"Sir." I didn't say anything else, but I didn't need to. My point was clear. I wouldn't be saying another word against the woman I loved.

He chuckled under his breath. "You know, I think he would approve if he saw you protecting her from me of all people."

I inclined my head. "Is this why I'm here, sir? Are you going to tell him about us before my father retires?"

"What?" He shook his head. "No. He doesn't know about you. But *I* do."

I wanted to ask him how or why, but it wasn't my place. This wasn't the civilian life where I was entitled to answers. Here, I got them if and when I deserved to hear them. "You're a smart man, captain."

"Indeed. You know what else I know?"

I'd *love* to fucking know. "Sir?"

"I believe you love her, and would do anything to protect her." He leaned forward again. The man was more fidgety than a fucking teenager.

"Somewhere along the way, you fell for her, and she fell for you. Am I right?"

I tensed. It was none of his business. "Sir."

"You don't have to treat me as an enemy, son." He stood up and walked over to the window. "I have a proposition for you."

"I'd love to hear it, sir."

I wanted to get up and pace as I waited, but I sat on the chair like a fucking invalid. And worse? I felt like one. This man knew all of my secrets, and he didn't hesitate to air them in front of me like dirty laundry.

"Did you know how hard it is to get out of the infantry? Lots try, but it takes a hell of a long time and a lot of letters of recommendation."

"I did know it wouldn't be an easy move, yes."

I bit down on my tongue to keep from asking what his point was. If I couldn't make the move, then I'd get out. Go civilian. I'd thought it through. I had a plan.

I wasn't an idiot.

"I can help you make the move you need. One signature from me, and you're moving up the ranks." He leaned against the wall and crossed his arms. "It would be a simple matter."

I stiffened. I think I had an idea where this was going. "Sir..."

"Your unit is up for deployment soon," he said, cocking his head. "You will go overseas, away from Carrie, if you don't accept my help."

"I'm flattered and honored for the offer, sir," I said through my teeth. "However, with all due respect, I'd like to hear the cost of this favor before I accept."

Because everything came with a price.

And if he said what I thought he was going to say, it would take all my self-control not to punch him in the mouth, fucking C.O. or not.

He nodded. "You're a smart boy. I like that about you."

"Thank you, sir," I said stiffly.

"The cost isn't much." He uncrossed his arms. "Stop seeing Carrie."

I stood up, rage making me see red. I'd known—*known*—this is what he would say, but it didn't stop me from wanting to punch him in the fucking face. "No, thank you, sir."

I only made it one step to the door before he spoke again. "Don't you dare leave my office without leave, sergeant. You will hear me out. Sit *down*, boy."

I clenched my fists and turned back, sitting even though I didn't want to. "With all due respect, sir, I will not accept those terms. I will stop seeing Carrie if she asks me to. Other than that, I am not open to discussion."

"Not even to advance your own life?"

I clenched my fists so tight if hurt. "Not even to *save* my own life, sir."

"Good." He sat back down, his lips pressed tight. "Now that that's out of the way, let's move on to the real proposition."

I blinked at him. "Sir?"

"I wanted to make sure you really love her before I offered you this opportunity." He picked up his coffee mug, which said World's Best Daddy on it, and took a sip. "You obviously do, so I feel comfortable in offering you the chance of a lifetime."

"You're saying you were *testing* me?"

"Indeed. And you passed." He set the mug down. "Now we can talk business."

I stood up again. "Sir, what do you want from me?"

"I want you to *sit down*."

For a second, I considered walking out. Not sitting. But the years of military discipline wouldn't fucking let me. So I sat. "*Sir*."

"I'll tell you everything. It involves doing something similar to what you're doing now, but with a huge reward."

"And what would that be, sir?"

He pursed his lips. "You'll find out. But first?" He picked up a pen and shoved a piece of paper at me. "Sign on the dotted line."

I eyed the paper. "I don't sign anything without reading it first, sir."

"Then by all means, read it." He leaned back in his chair and crossed his fingers over his stomach. "I'll wait."

I picked up the paper, scanning it quickly. By the time I was finished, I looked up at him, my eyes wide. This was a mission. A huge mission I didn't think I should be reading about, hence the top-secret security clearance application I could see sitting on the desk. "Sir, is this what I think it is?"

"It is. And I can give you all the knowledge you need to pull it off if you sign."

I picked up the pen, hesitated, and signed on the line.

CHAPTER FIFTEEN

Carrie

Saturday evening I shoveled more food onto a man's plate. I usually came to the soup kitchen on Sundays, but I was trying to keep myself as busy as possible. This time I'd dragged Marie with me. Speaking of which...

I met her eyes from across the room. She made a face at me and I nodded discreetly. It was time to go. There were only a few people here and it was getting dark. It had been a heck of a day. I'd said goodbye to my parents and then studied English with Cory for a few hours.

I felt exhausted yet wide awake at the same time. It was time to get out of here, maybe grab a bite to eat, and try to get some sleep. I had no idea what to expect when Finn returned. Or what to hope for, besides him not leaving.

As Finn would say...*this fucking wait was fucking killing me.*

I took off the hairnet and smiled at the woman who ran the place, earning a wave in return, set down some McDonald's cards, and made my way to Marie. "You ready to go?"

She nodded and headed for the door. "I don't know how you do this all the time. It's depressing."

Deja vu. "It's not depressing. They're hungry and need food." I shrugged. "It's simple."

She rolled her eyes. "Well, now I'm hungry and need food, so feed me. Where are we going?"

I always went to Islands with Finn after the soup kitchen. It was weird not having him here with me. I missed him, and it had only been a few hours. What would it be like when he was gone? No, *if* he was gone?

"How about some Mexican?" I unlocked my car. "I could go for a quesadilla."

"Sure." She slid into the seat and pulled the mirror down, fluffing her hair. "If we go to that place on Pico, we could dance, too."

"Dance? Yeah. I don't think so."

Marie rolled her eyes and buckled up. "You need to lighten up, Carrie. There's nothing wrong with dancing."

"You haven't seen me dance," I pointed out. "You'd disagree if you saw me in action."

She laughed. "That bad?"

"*That* bad."

"Okay, no dancing then." She looked at me, her eyes shining with excitement. "Hey, we're going skateboarding next weekend. How about if instead of feeding homeless people, you come with us? It'll be fun."

"That does sound fun." I buckled up and pulled out of the parking lot. "Count me in."

After we ate, I was on the way home alone. Marie had run into some guy she'd been flirting with lately and had chosen to stay with him. It was a relief, almost. It felt good to stop acting normal when I didn't feel normal.

I felt stressed, exhausted, and way behind on life. And so freaking *tired*. Plus, I couldn't stop thinking about what Finn was going to find out this weekend.

The whole way home, I went over every possible scenario that could come up. He could be going to war. Or maybe he was getting a promotion. Then again, he could be in trouble. Or he could be getting re-stationed across the country. The possibilities were endless, and I was driving myself crazy trying to figure out which one was the most statistically realistic one while also trying to figure out what my reaction would be.

If he had to move, would I move? Could I even do that?

I parked my car at the curb, not even realizing until I got out that

I had gone to Finn's apartment. I'd been on autopilot…but since I was here, I could use my key to get inside and take advantage of the shower. This morning I'd woken up too late, and the line for the showers had been horrendously long. I hadn't had a good, hot shower in days, and I couldn't wait to feel the hot water running down my body.

I slipped the key into the lock, turning it and pushing inside without lifting my head from my phone. I had two missed calls. One from Marie and the other from *Finn.* My heart picked up speed as I kicked the door shut behind me, swiping my finger over the screen so I could listen to the voicemail.

But the voicemail wasn't from Finn. It was from Marie. Mexican music played in the background. *"Hey, it's me. I just wanted to let you know I won't be home tonight. Enjoy the empty room."*

I dropped back against the door, the disappointment at missing Finn's call so heavy that I couldn't stand it. I hugged the phone to my chest, tears filling my eyes. Why hadn't he left me a message? Even a simple *I love you* would have been better than nothing. "Damn it."

"What's with the cursing?" Finn asked, his voice loud and clear.

For a second, I thought I'd called him and somehow put the phone on speaker, but he switched on the light, and he was standing there in his uniform.

"Finn?" I stepped closer but then froze, my heart racing and seeming to painfully climb up from my chest until it felt as if it rested in my throat instead of my chest. I knew that wasn't possible, of course, but I'd swear to it. "How are you home early?"

"They only needed me for a few hours," he said, his tone neutral. "So I came home and called you right away. I saw you pull up, so I hung up."

I knew his being home meant something to us. Something good or bad. But suddenly it didn't matter anymore, because he was *here.* And that's all that mattered, wasn't it?

I took a step toward him, then another. By the time my foot hit the floor a third time, I was running. I'm talking hair-flying-behind-you, full-on sprint. Finn took a few steps toward me and opened his arms. I flung myself at him full force, holding on to him as if he alone could keep me on the ground.

He hugged me close, his arms wrapping around me so securely I couldn't even move, and he kissed my temple. I pulled back, meeting his eyes, and forced a smile. "I'm so happy you're home early."

He smiled back at me. Even though he hadn't opened his mouth, I just *knew* he was going to say something I wouldn't like. I could feel his heart thumping, beating against my own almost in tandem. "Carrie, I—"

"*No*. Not yet."

And I kissed him with all the emotions I had bottled up inside me all this time. I didn't want to hear what he had to say. Didn't want my worst fears to become so utterly, horrifically, devastatingly *alive*. When I had been a little girl, I'd been terrified of monsters that hid under my bed. Now, as an adult, I knew the real terror lie in words and actions. In life or death. Not in scary, hairy, huge beasts.

I kissed him with a desperation I hadn't felt before, knowing if I stopped he'd tell me the words I didn't want to hear. All those silly fears I'd had over the years seemed so freaking pathetic in the face of what I was feeling in Finn's arms.

He moaned into my mouth and stumbled back, his hands supporting me. I knew I was attacking the poor man, but I couldn't stop. Not now. Not ever. When he broke off the kiss, his breathing heavy and his grip on me unbreakable, I dared a glance up at him.

"Ginger," he said. "We need to talk."

I forced a smile for him, my hands gripping his shoulders so hard it probably hurt him, but he didn't so much as flinch. "I know," I said, my voice breaking on the last word. When he shot me a concerned look and opened his mouth to talk, I pressed my fingers against his mouth. "No. Don't say it. Not yet. I need a drink first."

He kissed my fingers and nodded, his bright blue eyes latched on me. "Have I ever denied you something you wanted?"

I wanted to demand he not leave me. He'd promised to give me everything I wanted, hadn't he? But that wouldn't be fair. Even *I* knew he didn't have a say in whether he left or stayed. It was all up to men like my father. To the men in the government who sat behind their desks, moving men like Finn across the world like chess pieces.

I noticed the outline of his dog tags, so I gently grasped the chain and pulled them out from under his shirt. I scanned the words that denoted his name, social security number, blood type, and religion. I now knew he was O positive. What a weird way to find out. I didn't even know what the heck type of blood I had, but I knew his.

Oh, and he was Catholic. He'd never mentioned this before. But we hadn't talked about God much, besides when he'd told me surfing was his version of church. We hadn't gotten to that part of our lives yet, I guess.

Knowing that this was how they kept track of who was who felt so cold and impersonal. But then again, that's how life was, wasn't it?

"Carrie…"

"I *know*. I need a drink first."

He gave me a look, one that said he didn't like this not-talking thing I was doing any more than he liked giving me alcohol, but I stubbornly ignored it. I went into the kitchen, grabbing him a beer and me a wine cooler. After I opened them, I went back to his side and handed him his beer.

He took it and sat down on the couch, his eyes never leaving mine. Then he held it out to me. "To us?"

"To us," I echoed, tapping my bottle with his. I brought it to my lips and drank it, not even taking a breath between swallows. Finn threw me a concerned look and pried it out of my fingers before I could drain it. "Hey."

Finn cupped my chin and turned my head, forcing my face toward his. "Carrie. Look at me."

"I can't. I just…can't." I closed my eyes tight, scrunching them shut. "I don't want to do this."

"Ginger…" He pulled me into his lap. "I need you to *look* at me."

I rested in between his legs, but facing him, a leg on either side of his hips. I squeezed my eyes shut even tighter, like a kid terrified to open her eyes and see the monster looming over her bed late at night. I couldn't handle this. I wasn't strong enough.

Wait. Yes, I was. I had to be strong for him. He needed me to be strong.

I took a deep, shaky breath and opened my eyes, my chest moving far too rapidly and my heart echoing in my head so loudly it freaking hurt. I knew that I wasn't going to like what he had to say, and I knew I was going to lose it. Completely lose it.

I rested a hand behind his neck, directly between his shoulder blades, and the other on his shoulder. I nodded, knowing he was waiting. Waiting for me to be ready.

It's not that I couldn't handle it. I could. I'd just needed some time.

And I loved him even more for totally getting this about me. I nodded once. "Go ahead. Tell me everything."

CHAPTER SIXTEEN

Finn

I looked at Carrie, her blue eyes on me and so breathtakingly beautiful, and I clammed up. I had so much I wanted to tell her, but I wasn't allowed to. I could only give her a fraction of the details, and then in a few days, I wouldn't be able to tell her anything. I knew she wouldn't like that any more than I did.

Our relationship had been built on secrets and lies, and now I had to go right back to not telling her stuff. To keeping secrets. I didn't like it, but my eye was on the end goal. And it would be worth it once we got there. *If* we got there.

I closed my hands around the back of her waist, holding on tight in case she tried to bolt. I needed to hold her. "I saw an old friend of yours today. Captain Richards. Does the name ring a bell?"

"Yeah, he went to the same college as my dad. They've been close ever since. I think he's coming for our Christmas dinner we always do." She shook her head, watching me closely. "What did he want with you?"

"He had an offer to make." I hesitated. "There's something I have to tell you first, and please try to understand this isn't up to me."

She stilled. "What?"

I rubbed her back in big, wide circles. "I can't tell you all the details of what I got asked to do. It's got a high-security clearance—one I just obtained today—and I am legally not allowed to tell you everything I know."

She blinked at me. "I won't tell anyone."

"It doesn't matter. I'm not allowed to tell."

She nibbled on her lower lip. "Do you not trust me to keep a secret? I mean, I know I'm not the best liar in the world, but I could do it."

I cupped her cheeks. "Ginger, it's not that. I fucking trust you with my life. But it's my job, and I *can't* tell you. It has nothing to do with trust, okay?"

"Fine. Yeah." She nodded jerkily. It wasn't fine with her. I could see it. "I get it, but what *can* you tell me?"

"Captain Richards asked me to take on a special case. It will involve me leaving in two days."

"What? Why? *No.*" She gasped. "Where are you going?"

"Away." I flinched. "Out of the country."

Her eyes flashed. "Where?"

"I can't say," I said, closing my eyes. "That's part of the deal, Ginger."

She pushed off my lap and paced. "Seriously? I can't even know where or why? That's ridiculous."

"I can kind of tell you why." I stood up and grabbed her, stopping her in her tracks. "I'll be doing something similar to what I'm doing here. Protecting someone."

She looked up at me, her red hair falling behind her shoulders. "A girl?"

"Yeah." I let go of her and tugged on my hair. "I can't say who."

"Shocker," she said dryly as she covered her face. "I'm sorry, that was bitchy. But I don't get why you can't tell me."

I pulled her hands down from her face, squeezing them slightly. "Wasn't there ever anything your father was working on that he couldn't tell you about? A bill or a law?"

"Well, yeah." She blinked at me. "Lots."

"Did he tell your mom?"

She shook her head. "No."

"See? It's like that."

She sat down on the couch, but she didn't make a sound. She just sat there, her eyes staring straight ahead. I sat beside her and held her hand, letting her process it all, and tried to keep quiet for her. I needed her to be okay with this.

After what felt like fucking hours, she looked at me again. She looked so resolute and strong. "Tell me everything you *can* tell me," she said, her voice surprisingly steady.

"He knows about us." I rubbed her lower back gently. "He confronted me, and tried to bribe me to walk away from you. When that—"

She held up a hand. "He did *what*?"

"He offered me a prestigious promotion. Everything I wanted, if only I walked away from you," I explained, keeping my voice level.

"What did you say?" she asked, her eyes narrow.

"No, of course." My hand tightened on hers. "What do you *think* I said?"

"I don't even know," she said, her voice soft. "How did he find out about us?"

"You know how you thought someone was following us?"

"Let me guess. It was his guy?"

"Yep." I smiled at her and tucked her hair behind her ear. "Your father asked him to send a guy to watch *me*. To make sure I was doing my job and not lounging about my apartment all day. He started watching when we were in our fight." I cleared my throat and looked away. I didn't like to think about that time of my life. "So at first, he didn't see anything but me following you. But then…"

"We made up."

I nodded. "And he saw a hell of a lot, and reported back to Captain Richards."

"Oh God." She paled. "Did he tell Dad?"

I shook my head and grabbed my beer. "Nope. Because he has a plan for me, and it involves me leaving on Tuesday morning."

"Which is the part you can't tell me."

I took a long sip. "Right. Maybe afterward, but not now."

"How long will you be gone? Will he tell Dad after? What does he want from you? When will—?"

I chuckled and pressed a finger to her mouth. "I don't know. And no, he's letting us handle the when and how of telling your dad, but after this it'll be easier."

"Why?" she asked through my fingers.

I got all excited thinking about what I was going to get for just a few weeks of work. "He's giving me the opportunity to change my MOS and become an officer, no military hoopla or shit to deal with. Just a quick transfer. I can go to college, fully paid for by Uncle Sam, and enter any field I want after this mission is complete. I can *do* anything. *Be* anything."

She bit down on her lip, her blue eyes examining my face. "Are you sure this isn't a way to split us up?"

"I'm sure." I leaned back against the couch. "After this, your father will have no reason to object because I'm going to be a commissioned officer."

She forced a smile. "That's great, and I'm happy for you. I really am, but what will this mean to us?"

"I can go to college, here even. We can be together, and even better? He promised to make sure my father gets his bonus, no matter what."

Her fingers tightened on mine. "So no more lying?"

"I still want you to wait until I'm back to tell your father." I drank another sip of my beer, and she picked up her wine cooler with a shaking hand. "I don't want you to do it alone. Once I'm home, we can come clean. Tell him we're in love. No more lies."

Her eyes lit up for the first time since I'd told her my news. She licked her lips, not dropping my gaze. "How long will you be gone?"

"It's looking like I'll be home after Christmas. It's in the early stages, but I think it'll be January at the latest."

"That's…" She swallowed hard. "More than a month away."

"Yeah, but it'll pass fast, I'm sure." I grabbed her hands, holding them to my lips and kissing them. "And when it's over, we'll be free. We can be together, no guilt or deception. Just us, going to college together like normal people."

She smiled at me, but the tears in her eyes kind of ruined it. "That's great, Finn."

"You don't look happy." I kissed her hand again. "This is good. I know it sucks I won't be home for Christmas, but it's worth it. I'm doing this for us, Ginger."

"I know." She pulled free and placed her hands on both my cheeks. "And I love you *so* freaking much for it. For making this happen. I'm just scared. I can't…I can't lose you, Finn. I just can't."

Her voice broke off, and she pressed her lips together, tears streaming down her cheeks. My heart clenched in my chest. I'd been expecting anger about having to keep my whereabouts a secret. Maybe a fight. I hadn't been expecting *tears*.

Logistically, this move made sense. It would solve all our issues, and give me a huge pay raise and life change. A fucking gigantic one. I'd only be gone for almost two months, and then I'd be back, and we'd be free. It was a simple decision.

This was a good move.

"I don't get why you're crying. I'll be fine, babe. It's not as dangerous as war, I promise you that," I said, kissing her tears away. They were salty and warm on my tongue, and I couldn't fucking keep up with them. "Please don't cry."

"I'm s-sorry." She took a shaky breath and closed her eyes. "I'll stop. I'm being stupid."

I hugged her close, breathing in her scent. Her hair was hard against my cheek, and it smelled a little funky, but I didn't care. I just wanted her to smile again. "Carrie, if you're not okay with this…"

"I'm fine. We're fine." She smiled at me, even through the tears, and rested her hand over my heart. "I love you, and you made a good move. I just needed a second."

I swallowed hard, the emotions inside of me warring with one another. I let go of her and lowered my head, not wanting her to see the emotions that were probably quite clear in my eyes. If I didn't do this, then I'd only be deploying next year, which was a hell of a lot worse than what I'd be doing overseas now.

But that didn't make it any easier on her.

Her fingers flexed on my shoulder. "You will *not* die. Tell me you won't. *Promise* me."

My heart wrenched. "I can't make a promise I can't keep, Ginger. I couldn't even make it if I stayed here and never left my apartment. Shit happens. You know that, but this is a hell of a lot safer than getting shot at in the desert. I can tell you that much."

"Then I guess I'll have to take it." She picked up her wine cooler and took a long sip. "I'd rather you stay with me, but I accept you can't."

I pulled her onto my lap and buried my face in her neck, hugging her against my chest as best I could. I swallowed hard, my chest and throat tight. "I promise to be diligent and to keep myself as safe as possible. I promise not to be an idiot. I promise not to be a martyr. But most importantly, I promise to fall asleep every night with you on my mind, and wake up smiling because I'm lucky enough to have you in my life."

She kissed me. She tasted like tears and watermelon wine cooler. "I'm the lucky one, not you."

Ha. Not true. I gripped her hips tight. "So we're okay?"

"Yep." She took a deep breath. "I'll be here when you get back, and then we can move on. Be happy and normal. Right?"

I chuckled. "As normal as I can possibly be, sure."

"Which is not at all," she said, smiling at me and nudging me with her elbow. "Will you be able to call me? Or text?"

I nodded. "Yeah. Email, if nothing else, but you'll be going home soon, so we'll have to be careful. I don't want you to have to tell your father without me. I want to be by your side, holding your hand when he finds out."

"I'll wait for you," she said, meeting my eyes. "Don't you worry about that."

I knew she meant more than the words sounded at face value, and I loved her even more for it. "And I'll be thinking of you the whole time."

She gave me a shaky smile. "You only have two days to get ready to leave?"

"Yeah." I flopped back against the couch, and she curled up against my side. "I guess I should call your dad."

"He's still on the plane. They'll land soon."

I nodded. "I'm going to be busy getting ready to leave, but I want to make sure we make time for us before I go. Monday night, it's just you and me. Got it?"

She patted my chest. I wished I could see her face, but she had it buried in my chest. "You tell me when, and I'll be here. You know that."

"Maybe," I said, grinning and kissing the top of her head.

I could feel her smile against my chest. "Your favorite word, if I remember correctly."

"Nope." I hugged her closer, so at peace with my decision and the future that I felt like I was floating on a cloud. "I have a new favorite word now."

"Oh?" She rested her hands on my chest and looked up at me, all wide-eyed and softness. "And what might that be?"

"*Ginger.*"

She smiled up at me and pressed her lips to mine. As I slanted my chin and took control, deepening the kiss, I knew it would all be okay. I'd get through this assignment in one piece, and then she would be happy because I'd be here with her.

Her father would accept me, since I was now going to be a commissioned officer, and I'd also have the backing of one of his oldest friends. I'd been promised that, too. This assignment wasn't without danger, but I'd told the truth when I said it wasn't as dangerous as war.

At least this was short term, and I more than likely wouldn't get shot at...

More than once or twice.

But it didn't matter, because we had each other. We had love. And we had commitment. On top of that, I had the belief in my heart that we could survive this. Actually come out of the other side still happily together, as strong and steady as we were now. And if I managed to avoid getting killed over there?

Then *maybe*—just maybe...

We'd even get our happily ever after.

CHAPTER SEVENTEEN

Carrie

Monday afternoon, I closed my eyes for a second and took a deep breath. Right now, Finn was packing the last of his belongings, and I was going a little bit crazy. I know he thought this was for the best, and it very well might be true. But until he was home safe, and in my arms, I was not going to be okay with this. In fact, I was a mess.

A hot freaking *mess*.

Marie kicked me under the table. "Dude, are you sleeping over there or what?"

"Huh? No." I straightened and cleared my throat, then smiled at her. "Sorry. It's been a long couple of days on top of the late night."

And it had. Dad was scampering to find someone to watch over me while Finn was gone, and Finn had been a whirlwind of activity since the night he told me he would be leaving. He'd had to get a whole bunch of shots, and then the packing and the phone calls…

He was doing this for us. Trying to make our life easier. But right now, all I knew was my boyfriend was leaving to go somewhere dangerous, and I wasn't even allowed to know *where*.

My phone buzzed and I picked it up eagerly. It wasn't Finn messaging me. It was Dad. *Where are you?*

I'm having coffee with my roommate.

A few seconds passed. *Call me when you're home.*

I didn't answer, and Marie sighed again. "You're ignoring me for your man, aren't you? And when will you tell me his name?"

"I wish. It's my dad." I showed her my screen. "And I can't tell you. It's too risky. The less you know, the better."

"Ah." Marie read the messages and rolled her eyes. "It's all so secret and *hush hush*. You'd think you were dating Channing Tatum or something."

I laughed. "Channing has nothing on him."

"I wouldn't know," Marie said, frowning at me. "But since you refuse to tell me more, I'll politely change the subject. Are you going home for the holidays?"

"I am." I looked out the window, my eyes on the people walking by. They all wore sweaters and hats, but it was only in the low sixties. I missed the snow. The cold, brisk air. Even with all this mess with Finn going on, I was excited to go back. "Are you?"

"Yep. I leave the Friday after this one."

"Saturday for me." I swallowed hard and turned back to Marie. "Where are you from again?"

"Three hours from here," she said, smiling. "So it's not that long of a trip. You're from back East, right?"

"Yeah." I swallowed a sip of coffee. "D.C., to be exact."

"Ah." She laughed. "So you probably laugh at me when I put on a sweater out here, huh?"

"Laugh? Not exactly." I smiled. "But it's not cold to me, no."

Marie looked out the window, a far-off look in her eyes. "I've never really been in snow. We drove to Bear Mountain a few times, but it doesn't feel like winter when it only takes ten minutes down a mountain to get back into the spring, you know?"

"Yeah, I totally get it. I miss the snow." I stared down at my coffee. I was supposed to be going home *with* Finn, not alone. "I miss home, too."

"Me too." Marie cleared her throat and reached out to grab my arm. "Speaking of missing things, whatever happened with your man, anyway? I didn't get a chance to ask how things turned out after your parents came to visit."

She flopped back in her chair, her Starbucks coffee in between her hands. She wore light gray fingerless mittens that were super cute, a matching sweater, and a pair of curve-hugging dark blue skinny jeans. Her blonde hair was soft and clean, and she wore her glasses again. She looked flawless.

I looked down at my own baggy T-shirt and jeans and tried not to compare us. She looked perfectly put together while I looked…well, like a hot mess.

If we weren't friends, I might hate her.

"Well…" I took a sip of my drink and swallowed. "Remember that job I told you about? The one that might take him away?"

"Yeah."

I set down my skinny white chocolate mocha. "He's leaving tomorrow."

"Ouch." Marie flinched. "How long will he be gone?"

"Until after Christmas." I licked my lips and looked out the window, half expecting to see Finn out there watching me. "I don't really know, because he can't tell me. His work is kind of…secret."

"Oh." Her eyes went wide. "*Oh.* Wow. Like, a secret agent or something?"

"Yeah." I forced a smile. "Kind of."

"Does he wear a black suit and look all hot in it?" Marie leaned in. "Oh, and does he drive a Ferrari and wear sunglasses at night like a movie star?"

I laughed. "No, not all that. He wears suits sometimes, but he has a Harley. Not a Ferrari."

"Oh, that's even hotter." She tapped her fingers on the table and bit down on her lip. "Does he surf and have tattoos, too?"

I blinked at her. "Yeah. But…how'd you know it was him?"

"I saw you two together at the beach the other day." She narrowed her eyes on me. "You told me he was gay."

"Yeah…about that?" I leaned in and motioned her closer, as if I was about to impart a big secret. "I'm really a dude. That's why I didn't want to shower in front of everyone."

Marie burst into laughter. "Yeah. Sure. And I'm Kim Kardashian."

"Hey, it's possible." I leaned back and smiled at her. This was fun. I was glad I stopped keeping her at arm's length. Turned out, Marie was a pretty great girl. "You never know what I have under these jeans."

"I saw you changing, and I've seen your tits." Marie snorted. "You're a girl, and he's straighter than an arrow."

"Guilty." I offered her an apologetic smile. "Sorry I lied. We were kind of sort of involved at that point, but in a fight."

She waved her hand dismissively. "It's fine. If I had that man in my hand, I'd lie to anyone who asked about him, too."

"Thanks for understanding." I reached out and squeezed her gloved hand. "I'm glad we did this. I needed the distraction, and it's been great."

"You need distractions because Double-oh-Seven is leaving?"

I laughed. "Double-oh-Seven?"

"Yeah." Marie shrugged, a small smile tipping one corner of her mouth up. "It seems fitting, since I don't know his name."

"I like it."

"Good. Now answer my question."

"Yes, I need distractions." I sighed. "I mean, it's tough to accept all this. I don't know where he's going, or how long he'll be gone. I don't even know how much danger he'll be in…" I broke off, not continuing on. What more was there to say? I think I pretty much covered it all with that sentence. "So, yeah. I'm a bit of a mess."

"It explains the dark bags you have going under your eyes." Marie pointed at my face and moved her finger in a circle. "And the pale face, too."

"Is it that bad?"

"That depends." She pursed her lips. "Will you be seeing him again before he leaves?"

"He's packing now, but we're meeting at his place tonight. I'm supposed to dress up and be ready to be wined and dined."

"In that case? Yeah, it's that bad." Marie stood up. "We need to get going. If I'm going to make you look human and fuck-able, I'll need all the time in the world."

A surprised laugh escaped me as she tugged me to my feet. "Geez, don't sugarcoat it or anything."

"Honey, we don't have time for that." She looked me up and down. "We've got to get to work if we're going to make you look drop-dead gorgeous for your last night together. Are you in, or are you out?"

I followed her, clutching my coffee to my chest. "I'm so in."

After all…I *did* want to look perfect for him.

Finn

I shoved my T-shirt into the suitcase on my bed, then headed into the kitchen. I had lasagna in the oven, and a bottle of champagne on ice waiting on the table. I didn't like supplying her with booze, but this was a special circumstance. It called for a romantic dinner by candlelight…

Oh, shit. I forgot to light the candles.

I grabbed the lighter out of the junk drawer and lit the wicks, making sure not to get too close since I wasn't wearing a shirt, then stood back to admire my handiwork. The table was set, the food was cooking, and the champagne was ready to go. I had an artificial tree set up in the corner, and a few boxes of ornaments and lights ready to go. We'd decorate it together later.

All I needed was the girl, and she should be here any minute now.

My phone rang, and I crossed the room to see who it was. Her father. Fucking fabulous. I swiped my finger across the screen. "Hello, sir."

"Coram," he said, his voice tight. "I spoke to Captain Richards, and he assures me he set a man on Carrie for while you're away. He says you know this man? This Hernandez?"

"I do, sir." I sat down on the couch. I still had to get dressed in the suit I'd planned to wear for Carrie, but obviously her father needed a bit of handholding right now. I played with the strings of my board shorts. "He's a great guy. Excellent at his job."

Papers shuffled. "And you know him how?"

"We're in the same unit," I said, dragging a hand down my face. "And he's in security, too. He's basically the California version of me, sir."

Only he won't fall in love with your daughter.

"And he'll take good care of her?"

"Yes, sir. I wouldn't trust him if he wouldn't." I yawned and tried to hide the sound behind my hand. I was fucking exhausted, but I could sleep on the plane tomorrow. I'd be spending half a day up in the air, without much else to do. "He's good."

"All right." He sighed. "I guess she'll be coming home in a little while, anyway, so it's not too long without you there. And you'll be back in January?"

"I believe so, sir."

"You know…" Senator Wallington paused and cleared his throat. "Arnold told me a little about your mission. Stay safe, son."

I blinked. Was that actual concern for my welfare I heard? That couldn't be possible. Could it? I nodded. "Yes, sir. I will."

"Good. Happy Thanksgiving and Merry Christmas. Keep me posted on, well, you know, your status." Papers shuffled again. "Also, call your father soon. He misses you."

I'd talked to him this morning. He'd sounded much better. Even though I had wanted to, I hadn't told him about Carrie. I'd gotten close, but I decided to wait until we told her father. He didn't need to be burdened with my secrets.

"Yes, sir," I agreed. "I will."

The phone clicked off, and I sat there blinking at it. That had to be the strangest conversation I'd ever had with him. I stood up, fully intent to go get dressed, but my phone buzzed again.

Jesus, what was with the calls tonight? I picked up my iPhone and glared down at it. I sighed and answered. "What's up, Hernandez?"

"I won't keep you long, but I have a few questions," he said, his deep voice coming through the line with perfect clarity. "Can I run them by you real quick?"

"Sure." I walked to the closet. "But make it quick. Carrie will be here soon."

"Right. So she knows I'll be staying at your place while you're away, right?"

"I'll tell her tonight," I answered distractedly. I'd left one suit unpacked, and I couldn't find it. Ah, there it was, behind my jacket. I pulled it out. "What else?"

"She surfs, but she's not supposed to surf without you?"

"Correct." I flinched. "Though I didn't tell her that part yet."

"Okay. Please do. I don't want to do it."

"I will," I said, yanking the tie off the hanger. "What else do you need to know?"

We spent five minutes going over her schedule, then Hernandez sighed. "Okay. I think I got it."

"It's easy. She goes to school. She studies. She shops." I snorted. "It'll be the easiest job you've ever had."

Hernandez sighed. "Why does she need someone, anyway?"

"Got me." I sat down on the edge of my bed. "She got kidnapped as a kid, so I guess he's more paranoid than normal. Honestly? She's fine alone, but don't let that fool you into thinking you can relax. He will want constant updates—and if you let something happen to her? You'll answer to me."

Hernandez laughed. "Down, boy. I'm on it."

"Good." I paused. "Thanks, by the way. I appreciate it, man. I can't go over there without knowing she's okay, ya know?"

"I do." Hernandez sighed. "Or, I guess I do. I mean, I'm not in love and never have been, but I heard it can be rough on the mind."

I snorted again. "That's putting it lightly."

"I'll take good care of her, bro. I promise." I heard him shut a door or a cabinet. "You go focus on the job, and keep yourself safe."

I hesitated. "If I don't come back…"

"None of that," Hernandez said. "You'll come back."

"But *if* I don't," I said, my heart squeezing tight. "Tell her I love her, and take care of her until she moves on. Okay?"

Silence. "All right, man. I will."

I nodded, my throat aching in a weird way. "Thanks."

"Go woo your girl now. All's well here."

I nodded. "Later."

"Later."

I hung up and stared down at my phone. I hadn't really thought about the whole danger involved when I'd agreed to this plan, but hell, *life* was dangerous. Just because I was going into a hostile environment didn't mean I was going to die.

A bus could hit me tomorrow outside my apartment, for fuck's sake.

Why start worrying about what might happen over there when anything could happen here? It was pointless. Life was life.

You lived, and if you were lucky? You loved and got loved in return. And then, no matter how safe you lived your life, when it was all over, you died.

Staying in California wouldn't change that.

CHAPTER EIGHTEEN

Carrie

I smoothed my short red dress over my thighs and blotted my lips together. Marie had spent more than an hour on my hair, and even more time debating the best makeup, shoes, and dress to wear. I *knew* I looked good, even if I felt like a wreck. I wouldn't let my fear over the future ruin what tonight could be. What it *would* be.

It was our last night together, and I was going to make the most of it.

I slid the key into the lock, took a deep breath, and walked inside. The lights were dim, and candles were on the table. The whole apartment smelled like Christmas dinner, and soft carols played in the background. A bare tree stood in place at the window, and Finn was nowhere to be seen.

A suit was laid out across the bed, next to his phone. I smiled and walked up to it, running my hands over the soft fabric. I knew how much he hated dressing up, so knowing he was doing it showed me how special he was trying to make tonight. He didn't have to dress up to make me happy, but he didn't get that yet.

That's all right. I'd have all the time in the world to show him that... once he came back. And he *would* come back. There was no alternative in my mind.

The bathroom door opened, and he came out with nothing but a towel on. He saw me standing there and froze mid-step, his gaze sliding up and down my body. "Holy shit, babe. You look gorgeous."

"Thank you." I walked up to him and ran my hands over his damp chest. "So do you. Screw the suit, just lose the towel and we'll be good to go."

He grinned and leaned down, kissing me gently before he stepped out of my arms. "Not happening. We're having the date I should have given you the other night."

I pouted. "But—"

"No *buts*." He dropped the towel, and my jaw dropped as I watched the back view. Hot damn, the boy was fine. I mean, I already knew that, obviously. But still. The way his butt curved from his lower back to his hard upper thighs? *Wow*. "We're doing this my way. It's Christmas Eve."

I blinked at him. "No, it's not. It's not even Thanksgiving yet."

He stepped into his boxers and shot me a disappointed look. "Look at the calendar on the wall."

"Okay…" I walked over to the Santa calendar and looked. He'd left the month open to December, and he had crossed off all the days up until Christmas Eve. My heart twisted and tears filled my eyes, but I blinked them away before turning back to him with a smile. "You're right. Silly me."

He grinned and stepped in to his pants. "It's okay. I'll forgive you this one time. But as soon as I'm all dressed, the festivities begin. We have a tree to decorate, presents to open…" He walked over to me and wrapped me in his arms, smiling down at me the whole time. "And, of course, some good old-fashioned holiday sex to partake in, too."

I rested my hands over his heart, which sped up as soon as I touched him. "Of course. I wouldn't miss that for the world."

"Let me get dressed." He leaned down and kissed me. "Then we'll check on dinner." He kissed my nose this time. "And after that we'll get started."

"Okay," I said, my voice cracking. This was all so sweet and perfect and so *Finn*. And I was going to miss him so freaking much. I swallowed hard as he turned away, sinking down onto the couch. He'd put out a bunch of tiny Santa figurines on the coffee table, and cinnamon potpourri, too. "You even got Christmas potpourri."

He looked over his shoulder at me. "Huh?"

"This stuff," I said, pointing at the bowl.

"Oh, is that what it's called?" He shrugged into his shirt. "It reminded me of what my home used to smell like when my mom was alive." He looked off toward the tree, his brow furrowed. "At Christmastime, she used to put out Santa figures, angels, and bowls of that smelly stuff all over the house. Even in my bedroom."

"She sounds like she was wonderful," I said, standing up and crossing the room to place my hand on his arm. "I bet I would have loved her very much."

"And, man, she would have loved you." He met my eyes, the far-off look he'd had earlier disappearing. But the sadness lingered, despite the smile he gave me. "When I was planning on how to make it feel like Christmas for you, the only thing I could think of was what she would have done. I copied it."

"I love it." I reached up on tiptoe. "It's perfect."

He curled his hands around my waist. "No, *you're* perfect."

He was wrong. He was the one who said and did all the right things. I was fumbling along, trying to act as if I wasn't a complete mess. I was probably failing miserably.

"What did she do for a living?"

"She was a teacher. Third grade." He buttoned his shirt, his hands steady. "She said that was the best age to teach because they were old enough to take care of themselves, but they hadn't reached the cocky, know-it-all stage yet."

I laughed. "That sounds about right."

"Do you want kids someday?" he asked, his voice deep as he buttoned his shirt. "Little Carries running around the house causing trouble?"

I snorted. "I think it's the little Finns that will be causing trouble. Not the Carries. And yeah, I'd like two or three kids in, like, ten years maybe. You?"

His fingers froze on the second to last button. It wasn't until he looked at me, all heated eyes and *kiss me now* lips, that I realized why. I'd mentioned having kids *with him* instead of the fictional kids with my fictional husband. But when I pictured that life, I saw him at my side. I knew it. He knew it. Why pussyfoot around?

"I want two or three, too," he said, his voice raw and his eyes on mine. "And ten years is perfect."

I let out the breath I'd been holding and smiled at him. "It's a plan."

"It's taking all my control not to pick you up right now, throw you onto that bed, and practice making babies with you without actually making any." He finished up the last button. "But I have a plan on how tonight is going to go, you see. And I'm trying my best to follow it. So if you could stop looking so damn irresistible and stop saying all these things that make me want to kiss you, I'd appreciate it."

He curled his hand behind my neck and hauled me against his chest, and the breath *whoosh*ed out of my lungs right before he melded his mouth to mine, stealing all conscious thought. I closed my fists over his white dress shirt, wrinkling the material, but I didn't think he'd mind. Right now all that mattered was this. *Us.*

His mouth worked over mine and he pressed his hands to my lower back, his tongue gliding over mine perfectly. I moaned into his mouth and pushed him back against the wall. He went without a fight, but when I tried to start unbuttoning his shirt, he broke off the kiss and grabbed my hands. "Uh-uh. That's not supposed to happen yet."

I let out a small protest. At least, I think that's what came out. Maybe I just cursed. I didn't know, all I knew was I needed to feel his skin against mine. "We can go out of order, can't we?"

"Nope."

"*Finn.*" I slid my hands under his shirt, skimming over his hard abs, following along the top of his trousers, then dipped lower, barely brushing against his erection. "Are you so sure about that?"

His head dropped back against the wall and he swallowed so hard I could see his Adam's apple give way. "Nope…"

I stuck my leg in between his, liking the extra height these heels gave me. It let me brush my knee against the undersides of his balls, and when I did that, he groaned and flexed his fingers on my hips. He curled them around my sides and cupped my butt, yanking me even closer.

Then he kissed me again, and I was lost.

He backed me toward the bed, his lips never breaking free of mine. As he kissed me, his mouth moving over mine with a hunger he seemed to have lost control of, his hands roamed under my dress, skimming the top of the thigh-highs Marie had insisted I wear tonight so "nothing would get in the way."

She'd been right. That was an excellent move.

We fell back on the bed and I closed my legs around his waist, whimpering when he pressed against my core, rolling his hips ever so slowly. I tried not to focus on the fact that this would be the last time I'd get to have him like this for more than a month, but it was hard to do that when it's all I could think about.

This whole scene was romantic and *perfect*.

But it was still a bittersweet goodbye, no matter how sweet it might be.

He slid his fingers in between my legs, tracing the line of the panties I wore before slipping underneath them. He ran his finger over me, breaking off the kiss. "That day you came over without wearing any of these? That was fucking hot. From now on, I'll spend half my life trying to figure out if you're wearing anything underneath your clothes, and the other half finding out."

I scraped my nails down his back. "I'll keep changing it up then, so you'll never know."

"Jesus, Ginger." He nibbled on the side of my neck, then swirled his tongue over my pulse. "Are you trying to kill me?"

I shook my head. "Never that."

First, I undid the top button of his shirt with trembling hands, then the next and the next. The whole time I undid his shirt, he kissed me. My neck. My shoulder. My jaw. Anywhere and everywhere that he could reach without moving, he did. I had my legs around his waist, holding him in place, so he only had so much to work with…but *man*, did he make it work.

"Ginger," he murmured in my ear, rolling his tongue over my earlobe. "This strapless dress you're wearing is perfect, and you look un-fucking-believably gorgeous in it, but it's gotta fucking go."

He tore free of my death grip and stood, urging me onto my stomach before I could so much as say *get back here*. He bit down on my shoulder and I groaned, gripping the comforter. His fingers found my zipper and he slid it down, slow and agonizing. He kept dropping kisses over my skin as he bared it, and it was driving me insane with want.

By the time he reached the bottom, I was quivering. He nipped the skin right over my butt, his teeth sinking in just enough to sting. "*Finn*."

"Yeah, babe?" he asked, dropping to his knees behind me and shimmying the dress down to my feet. "You need something?"

"You." I pressed my thighs together. "I need you."

He skimmed his hands up the outside of my thighs, then kissed the same spot he'd bitten, only on the other side of my butt. He ran his fingers down the backs of my thighs…and back up again. "Soon, my love. But not yet."

I shivered and buried my face in the mattress. How dare he ask me if I was trying to kill him? *He* was the one who was going to freaking kill *me*. He glided his fingers down my legs again, but this time he came up the insides. And when he reached the top, oh God, he finally gave me what I wanted.

He slipped his fingers between my legs, rubbing his thumb against my clit in slow circles. I whimpered and pressed back against him, wanting more. He flicked his tongue over the back of my thigh, quickening his strokes. I was so freaking close to what I wanted, but he stopped and stood up, leaving me high and dry.

"*Finn.*"

He undid his pants, let them hit the floor, and yanked his shirt over his head. "Don't move a muscle. I'm not done with you yet. But first…" He opened the drawer by his bed and pulled out a condom. "We need one of these since we're just practicing."

I grinned and wiggled my butt. "Hurry up or I'll get started without you."

"Fuck yeah. Do it."

My cheeks heated up. That had so been an empty threat. I hadn't actually been planning on *doing* it. I couldn't take it back now.

I rolled over and shot him a look that I hoped was more *seductress* than *deer in headlights*, and scooted back on the bed. When I was reclined against the pillows with nothing but my undergarments and a pair of heels on, I trailed my hand down my shoulder.

I felt stupid and ridiculous until I looked up at him and saw the way he stood there, his fists clenched and his gaze locked on my hand as it moved. Then I felt powerful. So freaking *powerful*. I bit down on my lip and moved my hand lower, tracing the curve of my breasts while he watched.

He ripped the condom open and pulled it out, his gaze latched on my hand as he did so. "Take off everything but the heels and the…" he said, his voice gruff. He gestured to my thigh-highs, "…the tights or whatever the fuck they're called."

I sat up and undid my bra, letting it fall to the side. Then I reclined back and closed my hands over my breasts, letting out a small moan. He took a step toward me, his blue eyes dark and his lips parted. "Jesus."

"Nope. Stay there," I said, not taking my hands off myself. This new strength I'd found was exhilarating, and if I was going to do this for him? I was going to do it right, thank you very much. His tattoo-covered muscles flexed when he stopped in his tracks. "No touching yet."

He curled his empty hand into a fist at his side. "You're touching."

"Only me." I rolled my hands over my nipples, licking my lips at the thrill that shot right to my core. Seeing him watching me do this was so freaking hot. "You'll get your turn."

He stepped closer and gripped his erection. "If you get to touch, so do I."

I looked down at his hand moving over his shaft and my stomach hollowed out. His abs clenched as his hand worked over himself and I moaned, sliding my hand even lower over my stomach. When I closed my fingers over my mound, he jerked his cock harder. Funny how I still blushed when I thought about that word.

I bit down on my lip and moved my fingers over myself, feeling the pressure building up even more so as I watched him touch himself.

He took a step closer. "Take off the panties, or I'll take them off for you. But if you make yourself come, with me watching, I'll blow your fucking mind right after. So I suggest you lose them."

I took them off in record time and pressed my fingers against my clit. I was so freaking ready it wouldn't take much to send me over the edge. I knew it. So I rubbed them in a circle, increasing the pressure when a jolt of pleasure hit me hard. "Oh *God*."

"Fuck," he muttered, climbing onto the bed. He grabbed my ankle and nibbled on it, then kissed higher on my calf. "Keep going, Ginger. Show me how good you feel."

I whimpered and moved my fingers faster. Harder. "Finn…"

"I'm here," he said, his voice raw.

He slid his hands up my body and under my butt. Having him so close to where I was touching myself must have sent me over the edge, because I tossed my head back and forth and my entire body clenched. I increased the pressure, the pleasure and painful need ravaging me until I exploded, squeezing my eyes shut tight at the sheer intensity of it all.

I didn't even have time to crash and burn before he was in between my legs, his mouth fastening to mine and his erection pressing against my throbbing clit. All it took was one bump from him, and I came again—miraculously and explosively.

He deepened the kiss, his teeth digging into my lower lip, and then thrust inside me with one quick stroke. I closed my legs around him, digging my high heels into his bare ass, and clung to him for dear life. He moved fast and hard and heavenly. I wrapped my arms around him and dug my nails in, lifting my hips to take more of him.

The pressure was building up again, driving me higher and higher until I wasn't sure I'd ever be able to come back down. But then he swirled his tongue over mine and changed his angle, brushing against my clit, and I did crash down.

But first, oh my God, I soared. I freaking flew.

He thrust into me one last time, deep, before he tensed over me, breaking off the kiss long enough to utter, "*Carrie.*"

He made my name sound like a miracle or some amazing thing only he could have, and I didn't know what to say in reply. So I wrapped my arms around him and clung tight, squeezing my eyes shut. "I love you."

"I love you, too," he whispered, his face buried against my neck. He kissed me gently, right under my ear. "I'm going to miss you so damn much."

I swallowed hard. "I'll miss you, too."

It was almost funny. I'd been so high moments ago, but now I was back on the ground, and I didn't want to let go of him.

I didn't want to let go because I knew once I did…

He would leave me.

CHAPTER NINETEEN

Finn

I finished my lasagna pretty quickly and studied her from across the candlelit table. She was still eating, so she wasn't watching me like I was watching her. As a matter of fact, she hadn't looked up in a while. I knew why. She was sad I was leaving, and I wished I could take it back, almost. Wished I hadn't agreed to leave. But if I hadn't, then next year it would have been war.

I'd only have been delaying the inevitable. At least this way it was on my terms.

And once it was over, well, then I'd have Carrie. And I'd never leave her side again, if I had any say. I picked up my champagne and finished it with one swallow. I had to be up bright and early at five a.m. tomorrow, but I could indulge a *little*. No matter how I looked at it, or how many ways I tried to spin it into some bright shiny angle that would make me feel better, I was leaving the woman I loved behind. And I didn't fucking like it.

"You're awfully quiet over there, Ginger."

Her head snapped up and she swallowed her last bite. Picking up the cloth napkin with the Christmas tree on the corner I'd bought just for this dinner, she swiped it over her mouth and picked up her glass of champagne. After taking a hearty sip, she cleared her throat and smiled at me.

It was a strained smile. She was trying to hide how upset she was that I was leaving. "I was busy enjoying the dinner you made. It was delicious."

"Thank you. It's all part of the plan." I stood up and grabbed the bottle. I stopped at her side and wiggled it in the air. "You ready for a refill yet, slowpoke?"

"Usually you yell at me for drinking too much." She downed the rest of her drink and extended her arm, so I filled her glass and then mine. "Now you want me to drink more? Make up your mind."

In the background, Perry Como crooned on about a white Christmas. The flickering candlelight played with the shadows across her face. I smiled down at her and held out my free hand. "Well, tonight it's Christmas Eve, so the rules don't apply."

She slipped her hand into mine and I helped her stand. Once she was on her feet, I led her over to the bare tree. "Look up."

She did, her long, graceful neck arching as she did so. "Ah." She chuckled and tightened her hand on mine. "Mistletoe. That means we have to—"

I kissed her, not giving her a chance to say another word. When I pulled back, I rested my forehead on hers and clenched my glass tighter. "Kiss."

This moment right now? Fucking perfect.

"Mmhm." She smiled up at me, finally looking not so sad. "Are we going to dress this naked tree or what?"

"Of course." I dropped her hand and cleared my throat. "Do you want colored lights or white? I bought both because I wasn't sure."

"Mom only let us use white. She said it was more elegant, and that the future President of the United States deserved elegant," she said, her eyes latched on the tree. I reached for the white lights, figuring she'd want to make it like home. "So colored, please."

I froze, the white lights in my hand. "You don't want it the same?"

"Nope." She set her glass down and spun on me, her eyes shining. "We're not them. Why should we have the same things? I want cheeseburgers and beer, not caviar and three-hundred-year-old scotch. I want lasagna and mistletoe kisses, not press photos and chaste handholding. I want this. Us. And nothing you do or try to transform will change that. You make me happy. This makes me happy, and I love you so much for being *you.*"

The breath slammed out of my chest and I swear I might have staggered back, her honesty hit me that hard. She really liked me just like I was, and that fucking amazed me. "Then you'll have this every year. Anything you want, it's yours."

"I want you and only you." She curled her hands around my neck. "So come back home safely, or I might shrivel up and die."

My gut twisted and curled until I thought I might hurl all over her pretty dress she'd worn for me. The words were lovely and sweet, and I knew she intended them as such, but the thought of me dying and her being ruined by it made me sick. Fucking *sick*.

I'd never had someone depend on me like this. Need me like this. Not even my father. He'd be upset, but he would move on. She needed me, and *damn it*, I needed her.

I rested my cheek on the top of her head, which was a hell of a lot closer with those *fuck me* shoes on, and closed my eyes. "Sweetheart, I promise you that I'm not planning on going anywhere."

"Good." She rubbed her nose against my chest. "That's all I need to know."

I tightened my arms around her again. "Now let's get this tree decorated so I can give you my present."

"I don't have one for you." She nibbled on her lower lip. "I didn't know we were doing Christmas early."

"You don't have to give me anything." I kissed the top of her head and reluctantly let go of her. "You're all the present I need."

"I could tell you the same thing," she said, cocking her brow in a perfect imitation of me. "But you got me something anyway, didn't you?"

"That's different."

"How so?"

I opened the box of colored lights. "Because I want to spoil you rotten."

"So do I." She bent over and pulled out a white angel. "This is cute."

"You can't do that yet. It's last."

She turned to me, the angel perched between her fingers. "Says who?"

"Me." I pulled out the lights. "And, like, every single Christmas movie *ever* made."

She waved the angel under my nose. "Remember? No movies as a kid?"

"Poor, depraved child," I said, grinning at her. "Don't worry. I have the best Christmas movie in store for tonight."

"What's that?"

"*National Lampoon's Christmas Vacation.*"

She laughed. "It sounds interesting."

"Ginger, you have no idea." I handed her the end to the string of lights. "Hold that."

"I've never done this before." She frowned at the green corded lights in her hand. "Be warned."

I shook my head and squatted at the bottom of the tree. She was close enough that I had an interesting view up her skirt. I'd feel like a pervert staring up at her, but hell, she was mine and I was hers. I was allowed to look. "Just wrap it around like this." I wrapped it around the base of the tree. "And make sure you don't wrap yourself in it."

She rolled her eyes. "I'm not that bad."

"If you say so." I stood and wrapped the light around her legs. "Oops. Would you look at that?"

She burst into laughter and stepped free, her heel getting tangled in the little spot between the cords. "You're such a dork."

"You mean I'm adorkable, right?"

"Oh yeah. So much so." She snorted. "Help me out some more, will ya?"

We spent the next few minutes joking around and putting the lights on the branches. As I reached high, using the last of the lights, she stood back and wrapped her arms around herself. She looked happy enough, but she looked pretty damned sad, too. I bent over and picked up the plug. "You ready to see our handiwork?"

"Yes," she said, nodding at me with a smile. "Do it."

I plugged them in and crawled out from underneath of the tree. I stood up, brushing my hands off, and cringed. There was a whole spot in the front of the middle that had no lights. *None.* "Holy shit, we suck."

She turned her head to the side, squinting. "If you look really, *really* closely, you can see the extra lights we put in the back shining though the tree."

"Hm." I squinted and turned my head. She was right. I snapped my fingers. "I've got it." I crossed the room and slowly turned the tree. "Tell me when it looks best."

She tapped her chin and watched with all the scrutiny she would if someone had told her there would be a quiz later. Must be that attention to detail that would help her become an occupational therapist.

She brightened. "Right there. That looks good."

I stopped turning it and went back to her side. She was right. It looked perfect now. "Well, the window will get a bad view, but it looks good to me."

"Totally." She nodded decisively and headed for the couch. "Do you want the red balls or the green ones?"

"Green. Duh."

She laughed. "Sor-*ry*."

I slapped her on the ass, playful and silly. "The red ones are for my Ginger."

"And green are because…?"

"I like green." I shrugged. "I didn't really care what I had, only you."

"Is green your favorite color?"

"It used to be. Now it's the color of your eyes." I should have kicked myself in the nuts for that sappy sentiment. It sounded corny, but it was true. "They don't have a lot of blue ones, though. Mostly gold, silver, red, and green."

She swallowed hard and smiled. "Right. Christmas colors."

I hung an ornament, and watched her out of the corner of my eye. "My buddy Hernandez will be watching you while I'm gone."

She stopped with a ball half on the tree. "I hadn't even thought of that option. My dad's okay with it?"

"Yeah, he is." I guided her hand to the tree, urging her to hang the ball. "He'll be staying here so he can watch you close enough. I gave him a copy of the key earlier today."

She nodded and pulled out another ornament. "So no more free showers here, huh?"

"Nope. You'll have to slum it with the rest of the freshmen."

"Hey, that'll be you soon, too." She peeked at me out of the corner of her eye. "You'll be a grade under me."

"Fuck, you're right." I moved to the other side of the tree so we didn't get another bare spot. "You'll be robbing the cradle."

She snorted. "Oh yeah. Let me tell you."

Talking about the future made me feel a little better about what was coming tomorrow. We'd get through this and everything would be fine. We just had to keep the faith. I couldn't wait to enter this new life with Carrie at my side.

And I couldn't wait to be the man I knew I could be with her by my side.

If Captain Richards asked me where I wanted to be in ten years, I'd have an answer for him. I'd want to be right here, decorating a sloppy tree with Carrie. Maybe with a baby in my arms. That's where I wanted to be.

And I would be, damn it.

When we were finished, I guided her to the couch. After I had her seated and refilled with champagne—though I left mine empty since it was after midnight—I pulled out the long, skinny red box from the coffee table. It was next to my Glock, which Carrie was looking at with pursed lips.

"Are you bringing that with you?" she asked, swiping her hands across her dress.

"I am." I pushed it aside. I'd been cleaning it earlier, and left it out to dry. "It's kinda necessary in my job."

"You don't wear it here."

"It's not a hostile envir—" I broke off, realizing I was about to blurt out shit I wasn't supposed to. And she, of course, knew what I'd been about to say. "I mean, it's different."

She paled and bit down on her lip. "Right."

"Carrie…" I leaned forward and smoothed her hair back from her forehead. "Enough sad talk. Let's focus on this, because it's after midnight. That means it's Christmas Day."

She curled her hands into fists. "Merry Christmas."

"Merry Christmas." I pressed my lips to hers, savoring the kiss. Soon enough, we'd be falling asleep, and I'd be leaving. "Santa brought you a present."

She took the box from me, her gaze locked with mine. "I still wish I had something for you."

"You can give it to me after I come back. Now open it."

She nodded and ripped open the present. She ran her hands over the velvet case, her head lowered so I couldn't make out the expression on her face. When she flipped open the lid, she gasped and touched the pendant of the necklace I'd picked out for her.

It was yellow gold, and it had a sun hanging off the delicate chain. I shifted my weight, wondering if she'd get the significance behind the gift.

She looked up at me, tears in her eyes. "The sun's finally shining," she said softly. The tears that had filled her eyes just seconds before spilled over, and she threw herself at me. "I l-love it. Thank you."

I hugged her close, blinking because my eyes were stinging for some strange reason. "The sun will continue to shine because I have you. And you have me. Nothing will change that, okay?"

She nodded against my shoulder, her shoulders trembling as she cried. I held her close, making shushing sounds and saying words I didn't even pay attention to. Hell, I'd have promised her the moon and the stars if it would make her smile again.

Anything for her.

By the time she pulled back, her mascara was all over her cheeks and she was a wreck, but she'd never looked more perfect to me. I swiped my thumbs across her face, but I only smeared her makeup even worse.

"Want me to help you put it on?" I asked, my voice coming out strained.

She nodded and handed me the box. After I took out the necklace, she lifted her hair so I could clasp it on. After it was securely fastened, I kissed the back of her neck and she shivered. "Thank you," she said.

I nodded. "You ready for bed, or do you want to watch the movie?"

"Bed. I want to hold you until I have to let go."

My heart twisted. "Deal."

I led her to the bed and pulled back the covers, once we were naked, we made love. I held her in my arms until she fell asleep. The last thought on my mind, before I gave in to the overwhelming exhaustion that had been hitting me ever since I found out I was leaving, was that something that was this good couldn't possibly end badly.

We deserved our happily ever after, damn it.

OUT OF TIME

Carrie

I didn't want to fall asleep. Didn't want to close my eyes. I lay there for a long time, my eyes on the cheery Christmas tree and my ears tuned in to Finn's even breathing. His arms were around me, and I had my ankle looped over his. It was heaven. How could I fall asleep when I didn't know how long it would be until I felt this way again?

My eyes drifted shut, but I forced them open again. I didn't want to miss a single moment of tonight. Wanted to cherish it. Hold it close to my heart in the upcoming weeks. My lids drifted shut again. I tried to lift them, but it didn't work. Maybe I would spend one minute resting them. I wanted to stay awake so badly. Wanted to hold him. Love him. Hug him. I wanted...

Him.

CHAPTER TWENTY

Finn

I brushed her hair off her cheek, my chest so tight I couldn't even fucking breathe. I'd already gotten dressed in my cammies, finished packing my last-minute stuff, and cleaned up dinner from last night so Hernandez wouldn't come home to a pigsty later this afternoon. She hadn't stirred through all the noise I'd made, proving how heavy of a sleeper she really was, but now I had to wake her.

All that was left was saying goodbye.

The hardest fucking part.

It was four forty-five in the morning, which meant my ride would be here in less than fifteen. It also meant I had to walk away from the one thing in this world that made my world brighter. I'd known it wasn't going to be easy, but I hadn't realized exactly how hard it would be.

The sun necklace I'd given her rested directly on the pale skin over her pulse, and all I could think was this was it. This was the beginning of a time when she wouldn't be with me, and I'd be off doing God knows what, while she was here without me.

There were so many things wrong with those sentences.

I leaned down and rested my forehead on her temple, my mind flashing back to the first time she'd slept over my house. I'd been dying to touch her, but unable to, and she'd been feeling the same way. I'd felt so desolate that I'd never get to have her, and now I had her, but I was walking away.

I breathed in her scent and kissed her on the tiny freckle under her eye, high on her cheekbone. "Ginger, I have to go."

"Hmm," she mumbled, rolling her head toward me but not opening her eyes.

She wasn't awake.

Part of me wanted to leave her sleeping peacefully. She was going to cry when we said goodbye, and all I wanted was to make her happy. So why should I wake her up to let her cry? But leaving without that goodbye didn't feel right either.

"Carrie," I whispered, kissing her lips gently. "I have to go."

"Go?" Her eyes fluttered open and she smiled at me for a fraction of a second before it faded away. That must have been when she remembered where I was going. "Oh. Oh God. Okay."

Her arms snaked around my neck and she held on so tightly what I could barely talk, let alone breathe, but I didn't protest. Why would I?

I needed her love more than I needed to breathe.

I hugged her close, burying my face in her neck. Walking away might be one of the hardest things I've ever done, but it would be worth it in the end. And if I kept telling myself that, then it would be true…ish.

I kissed the side of her neck, wanting to apologize for leaving even though I was doing what I had to do, and it would be okay. We'd be okay. "It'll be all right."

She nodded frantically, but didn't release her death grip on me. "I know. I just need a second."

I kissed the side of her neck again, since that's all I could reach with her stranglehold on me. "This isn't a goodbye. It's a see you later."

She made a small sound. "That's true. It's only, like, a month."

Actually, it was two. But I didn't feel the need to point that out. "Right." I pulled back to look at her, and she let me. I smiled down at her, trying to show her how calm I was about this whole situation so she'd feel at ease. "It'll pass by fast with Thanksgiving and Christmas…then before you know it, I'll be back here bossing you around, annoying you, and making you roll your eyes."

She let out a small laugh and her dimple popped out. Fuck, I loved that dimple. "You don't annoy me…too much."

"There you go sugarcoating things for me."

She kissed my jaw. "I don't sugarcoat. I tell it like it is."

"Oh, do you really now?" I turned my head and kissed her, keeping it sweet and gentle since my ride would be calling any minute to let me know he was here.

She smiled up at me. "I know this is going to work out in the end, and so do you. We'll skip the rest of the tears. Deal?"

I nodded slowly, smiling even though it fucking hurt. "Deal."

My phone buzzed on the nightstand, and I picked it up. "That's my ride. I've gotta leave now."

"Okay." She took a deep breath and kissed me. "I'll walk you out."

I pushed off the bed and slid my phone into my pocket. "If you want to."

"I do," she said, sitting up and sliding her legs over the side of the bed. She wore a pair of short shorts and one of my tank tops. She slid her feet into flip-flops, yawned, and reached out for my hand. She clung to me tightly, and I had a feeling I did the same thing to her. "Let's do this."

We walked to the door in silence, her hand entwined with mine. As I opened the door, I had to let go so I could wheel out my luggage. She picked up my laptop bag and slung it over her shoulder, and I let her because I could tell she wanted to help.

And if that's what it took to make her feel better, then so be it.

Carrie

I wanted to punch myself in the face right now. Anything to keep the tears at bay. I'd lectured myself so many times last night *not* to cry when he left, but it was getting harder and harder with each step we took toward him leaving. He didn't need to see me panicking and blubbering as he walked away.

He needed to see me standing there—strong and steady and *sure*. When he left, I could break down, but not a second before.

I straightened my shoulders and thought of anything I could think of besides the fact that my heart was being ripped out of my chest. My upcoming flight home. The lasagna last night. The way he'd held me all night long as if he didn't want to let go…

No. I shouldn't think of that.

Bad idea.

I followed him out the door, staring straight ahead and not meeting him in the eye. If I looked at him and he looked sad, I'd lose it. A black government-looking vehicle sat by the curb, right behind my car, its hazard lights flashing. That must be the car that would take him away to…wherever he was going.

I wasn't allowed to know. Stupid, stupid rules.

As we climbed down the stairs, each step felt heavier. Longer. Because each step we took would take us to that car that would spirit Finn away. I hated that freaking car with a passion. It represented everything I couldn't deal with right now.

We reached the bottom of the stairs and Finn set his suitcase on its wheels, then reached for my hand. I clung to it, knowing it was the last time I'd be able to do so until next year. He was my person. My rock.

What was I going to do without him here?

"You hanging in there, Ginger?" he asked, watching me with a furrowed brow. "If you want to go back up, it might be easier. Saying goodbye is never easy."

"It's not goodbye," I reminded him, smiling through the pain. "It's see ya later."

"Right," he said, his voice coming out rough. Oh God, if he cracked, I'd freaking lose it. Like, the nuclear warfare level of losing it. "I knew that."

We stopped at the side of the car and the trunk popped open. Finn wheeled his suitcase to the back and put it inside, then held his hand out for his laptop bag. I handed it off to him, our fingers brushing. He set the bag inside and shut the trunk with a *clunk*.

The sun was just starting to lighten the sky with tiny little tendrils of grayish-pink, and the birds around us were silent—still sleeping in their nests. It was just us and the guy in the car. And we…

We were out of time.

I held my arms open, and he closed me in his embrace, hugging me so tight he might have cracked a rib. I didn't care. He could take the freaking thing with him as long as he came home safe and sound. I cupped his cheeks and kissed him hard, squeezing my eyes shut so I didn't cry.

Not yet. Not now…

He pulled back and looked down at me, his bright blue eyes grave. Gone was the dancing blue eyes I loved so much. He looked sad, scared, and alone.

"Hey, none of that," I said, using his own words back on him. "I'll be here waiting for you when you get back, and it'll be over before we know it." I looked down at my hands on him, willing them to let go. To let him go. But my fists tightened on his shirt even as I told myself I had to do it. "Stay safe and write to me as much as possible, okay? And Skype if you can."

"I promise," he whispered, kissing me one last time. "See ya later, Ginger."

I forced a smile and let go. As he walked away, I wrapped my arms around myself and smiled at him so big that my cheeks were about to fall off. When he got to the car and opened the door, he looked back at me one more time.

I widened my smile even more and called out, "Hey, look. The sun's about to shine."

"Yeah." He looked up at the sky and let out a small laugh. "Yeah, it is."

With one last look at me, he got in the car and shut the door. The guy driving waited all of two-point-two seconds before he pulled away from the curb. A few seconds later, the car turned around the corner…and my Finn was gone.

As if in a trance, I turned around and walked back up the steps to his apartment. I'd go home later this morning, but right now I needed to be here. With him. Even if he wasn't here, it still smelled like him and his stuff was here and I needed to be, too.

I walked inside, shut the door behind me, and walked to his bed, my eyes barely blinking. As I passed the closet, I bent over and picked up one of his dirty shirts from the floor. Finn never left dirty shirts laying around, so it was like a bonus find. I held it to my face, breathed in deeply, and fell back into the bed.

I rolled onto my side, but on his side of the bed because I swore I could feel him there, his shirt pressed to my face. He was gone. Actually, truly gone. What was I going to do without him here, teasing me and loving me?

And now that he was gone, I could finally break down and feel the things that had been trying to kill me since he told me he was leaving.

Fear. Anger. Resentment. Fear. Love. Sadness. Fear.

It all crashed down on me, hard and fast, and I burst into tears. The pain and numbness—yeah, I knew that didn't make any sense—spread from my heart on out, slowly taking over my legs and arms. Even my fingers and my toes. I couldn't feel *anything* except the absence of Finn, and the fear he wouldn't come home.

I clung to Finn's shirt as if it alone had the power to make me feel better. It didn't. The only thing that would make me feel better was Finn, and he was gone. Just…gone.

What was I supposed to do with that?

CHAPTER TWENTY-ONE

Carrie

A few days later, someone knocked on my dorm door, and I put my history book aside, climbed out of bed, and answered it. Marie wasn't here, and I was catching up on some studying I'd been severely behind on lately. I had been missing Finn and crying myself to sleep.

It was the weekend, and I'd been dragging myself around with less than an hour of sleep per night for almost a week. Tonight I might break down and take a Nyquil or something that would knock me flat on my back. This no-sleep stuff was for the birds.

But first, I had to open the door.

I yawned, covering my mouth, and swung the door open. As soon as I could see who stood in the hallway, I cringed inwardly. It was Cory. He smiled at me and smoothed his light blue polo. "Hey, Carrie."

"Oh." I forced a smile. "Hey."

"We haven't talked in a while, so I thought I'd stop by." He paused. "Can I come in?"

I hesitated. Cory was harmless and all, but it felt wrong to invite him in when Finn wasn't here. "I don't know. I'm kind of a mess right now."

"You look fine to me." He looked me up and down, taking in my gray sweatpants and pink T-shirt. "What's wrong? You look upset."

That's because I *was* upset. Finn was gone. "It's been a rough couple of days." I stepped out of the way and let him in. "You can stay if you want, but I'm just studying. Nothing too exciting."

"Want to study and eat?" He looked at my open book, then at my bed. "You look like you could use a good meal. Or we could go do something fun for a change."

I stood in front of my bed. Should I sit down on it, or would that be weird? "I already ate. And I told you, I have to study."

"When's the last time you did something besides hang out with your boyfriend or study?" Cory asked. "I never see you around anymore. You don't go to parties or mixers. Don't hang out with any of us. It's like you don't exist."

I smoothed my hair self-consciously. Marie had been telling me I needed to go out and socialize, too, but I hadn't been in the mood. Was that so bad? What if Finn called when I was out? Or if he emailed me and…

Oh my God. I'd become one of those girls without even realizing it. I'd turned into a shell of the person I'd been. "I've been busy," I said a bit defensively.

"I know. We all have been, but we're about to all go home for the holidays. Wouldn't you like to have some fun first?"

I pictured Finn's face. He wouldn't like me going out with Cory. But he was here, and he had a point. I'd been a bit of a hermit. "I have a boyfriend."

"I know." He rubbed his stomach in a distracted manner. "I remember him quite well, actually. I'm not going to hit on you or anything. We'll just go out and eat."

"I don't know…"

"We can do something fun, you know." He grabbed my hand and pulled me to my feet. "Marie is going skateboarding with some guy she met the other week, at a place down the road. Want to meet up with her? That way it's not just the two of us."

Crap. Skateboarding. I'd forgotten that's what she was doing tonight. No wonder she kept trying to get me to come. I'd already said I would. It would be safer, too, since Marie was there. Going out alone with Cory felt wrong. "You know what? Let's do it. Let me get changed."

He grinned and sat down on Marie's bed. "I'll wait here."

"Okay." I dug through my clothes and pulled out jeans and a green shirt. "How long of a walk is it? Or should we drive?"

"Driving would be quicker."

"Give me five."

I left the room and headed into the communal bathroom, shutting a stall door behind me. Pulling out my phone, I texted Marie and confirmed she was skateboarding. Next I texted Hernandez—even though his name was Joseph, I could never remember to call him that.

Finn called him Hernandez, so I did. *Going skateboarding.*

He wrote back right away. *What is this, high school? And with who?*

Marie and some other friends. Cory too.

Coram hates him.

I rolled my eyes. *Yeah. I know. But it's fine.*

All right. I'm outside.

I set down my phone, got dressed, and fixed my appearance a little. I was out in less than five minutes. As I breezed back into my room, I called out, "Ready?"

"Yeah." Cory stood up. "And Carrie?"

I picked up my keys. "Yeah?"

"I know who you really are." He shoved his hands in his pockets. "Just wanted to put that out there."

I blinked at him. "What are you saying?"

"Carrie Wallington. Daughter of Senator Wallington, who is pro—"

I held up a hand, my heart thumping in my ears so loudly I could barely think. This wasn't good at all. If he knew, he held the power in our relationship. He could do anything he wanted, and I wouldn't be able to stop him. I swallowed hard. "When did you figure it out?"

"When they came to visit. I saw you out at the sushi place with them. I realized who he was, and I put two and two together." He shrugged. "Plus, you had security following you while they were here."

I closed my eyes. Dad and his stupid insecurities ruining everything. Now I had a potential blackmail situation on my hands. "Did you tell anyone?"

"No, of course not," he said, looking at me as if I'd hurt his feelings. "I wouldn't do that. You didn't tell me, or anyone else that I know of, so why would I do it for you?"

I studied him. He looked as if he actually meant it…for now. Would that hold true over the next four years? Maybe even more, if we went to the same grad school. I'd have to tread carefully from now on.

I gave him a small smile, trying to hide my suspicion behind a calm façade. If he knew I was freaking out, he would know how much power he held over me. "Thank you. I don't want people knowing about it."

"I figured." He took his hands out of his pockets and opened the door for me. "Don't worry. Your secret is safe with me."

I looked over my shoulder at him, trying to look as if I believed him one hundred percent when I *so* didn't. "All right. Let's go skateboarding."

Finn

I leaned back against the cracked wall, my computer on my lap. It was the first night in a while we were actually in a hotel instead of a fucking tent or some other shithole. This building was hardly the Ritz or anything, but it had walls and a roof and minimal bugs. I'd take it.

Plus, it had Wi-Fi. Fuck, I'd missed Wi-Fi.

I logged into my email, immediately opening Carrie's latest one. It was from last night at about midnight her time. I waited for the words to load, tapping my finger on my knee the whole time.

Hey Susan,

I hope you're doing well. Guess what? I went out last night, despite my melancholy mood. You would've been proud of me. I went skateboarding—yes, skateboarding—with Marie, Cory, and a bunch of friends. I didn't even fall off...a lot.

Can you believe that?

When you get home, we should go. You'd like it.

Well, it's after midnight and I'm sore and tired. Wear sunglasses today. I hear the sun is shining really bright.

Carrie

I closed my eyes and grinned, picturing her skateboarding with a big smile on her face. Not even the fact that she'd gone with Golden Boy could ruin my happiness for her. She was out living, even without me, and that made me happy.

I didn't think anything would make me happy in this shithole I was stuck in.

I pulled her picture out from underneath my pillow. The one I'd taken outside of my apartment a few days before I'd left. I ran my finger over the smooth surface and swallowed hard. Sometimes I wished I hadn't taken this offer. I could have been the one skateboarding with her. I could be holding her in my arms right now.

Shaking my head, I set her picture down and typed a quick reply. I only had two hours of down time, and I needed to catch some fucking *zzz*'s.

Carrie,

Skateboarding, huh? That sounds fun…for a thirteen-year-old. ;)

I'm doing well here. Sunning every day. You won't even recognize me when I get home. That's how dark I'm getting in all this bright sunshine.

Get some sleep.

Susan

The door opened and I looked up. It was my roommate for the night, my superior, Eric Dotter. He rubbed his eyes and flung himself on to the bed next to mine. "Jesus, I've never been so fucking tired in my life."

I hit send and looked down at the twenty other emails I had—some from Dad, some from Hernandez—and sighed. I couldn't leave it open and disturb Dotter. "I hear ya, sir." I closed the lid to my laptop and set it aside. "I could sleep three days straight and not even roll over."

"I could do five." Dotter yawned, long and drawn out. "Nope. Make it six."

I settled back against the pillows, my hand going out to the spot Carrie was supposed to be. The bed felt foreign and empty. This wasn't where I was supposed to be, damn it. "Yeah, me too."

"We're going even deeper into the desert tomorrow than we did yesterday." Dotter heaved a long sigh. "Can you believe her? She's got a death wish."

"Yeah, and she's going to drag us all down with her." I tucked Carrie's picture under my pillow. "We've got almost two hours left. I'll catch you on the flip side of our night."

Dotter chuckled. "Good night."

"Night," I replied.

I laid there, looking up at the dark ceiling for a few minutes, willing my brain to shut down. It finally did, as Dotter's soft snores filled the room. But that's not what I heard as I drifted off. No, I heard Carrie's soft laughter as she climbed the rock wall on that day that felt like a year ago.

And I fell asleep with a smile on my face, despite the hell I was in.

CHAPTER TWENTY-TWO

Carrie

I leaned back against the car seat, my eyes focused out the window. Hernandez was driving me to the airport so I wouldn't have to leave my car there, and all I could do was sit there listlessly.

It had been close to two weeks now. Two weeks with no Finn.

I was absolutely miserable.

I kept going out of my way to live my life like normal. To not be one of those girls who was miserable because her boyfriend was gone. But my boyfriend wasn't away on a vacation or visiting home. He was away getting shot at or attacked.

I had nightmares about it every night, and I barely slept.

I'd tried to fill my days with activities. I'd studied. I'd even rock climbed and dragged Marie there with me. We'd skateboarded again a few times for fun, drank more coffee than was healthy, and even gone out dancing a few times.

Yeah. Me. Dancing.

Finn would never believe it, even though I told him every day what I did.

He always wrote back with encouragement and enthusiasm about my activities, but I felt almost guilty telling him the things I was up to.

While he worked, I danced and drank coffee. How was that fair?

Hernandez cleared his throat. "I heard from Coram last night."

"Oh yeah?" I sat up straight. "What did he say?"

"He thanked me for watching you and threatened my life if I failed in my job of protecting you." He shot me a grin. "You know, the usual."

I rolled my eyes. "He wouldn't actually kill you. He likes you too much."

"Um, I think he likes you more." He chuckled. "I don't kiss him or fu—" He broke off, his cheeks going red. "Well, you know."

"You can say dirty words in front of me," I said, my tone dry. He reminded me of how Finn was before we connected—all cautious and reserved. Ah, who was I kidding? He had never been cautious around me. "I won't tell my dad."

"I'm more worried about you telling Coram. I don't want him getting the wrong idea. You know?"

Like what? That we were flirting?

I looked over at him, eyeing him critically. I hadn't really paid him much attention, to be honest. He'd just been the guy who followed me around. The guy who wasn't Finn. I mean, he was nice and all, but we hadn't talked much.

He was cute. Really, *really* cute.

He had the same lightly tanned skin and dark hair that most men of Spanish descent had and dark brown eyes. There were tons of muscles and a few tattoos, just like Finn. He was a stunner.

If Marie ever saw him, she'd be all over him like white on rice. She loved exotic men, and he definitely fit the bill. Which got me thinking... "Are you single?"

He shot me a narrow eyed look. "Yeah."

"I have a friend. Her name's Marie. Blonde. Pretty." I tapped my fingers on the door. "Maybe when Finn gets back we can double-date or something."

"Uh..." Hernandez ran a hand over his short hair. "Yeah, maybe. We'll see."

I pulled out my phone. The home screen was Finn and me on "Christmas" night. I'd have to fix that before I touched down in D.C. I pulled up the picture of Marie at Starbucks the other day and held it out. "Here she is."

He stopped at the stoplight and looked, disinterest on his face until he focused on the phone. He leaned closer and grinned. "Okay. We'll do it once Coram's back."

"Deal." I laughed and shoved the phone in my purse. "Tell me, how did you two meet?"

He pulled forward and merged into the left lane. "At drill. When he moved out here, he told me how he was babysitting some spoiled little brat for a year." He shot me an apologetic smile. "Oops. Sorry."

"I know what he thought of me at first," I said, shaking my head. "It's not exactly news to me."

"I know. But then I asked for the whole story and all he would tell me is you were a politician's daughter and you'd never known a day of freedom in your life. We got closer over the weekend, and made plans to hang out the next weekend."

I nodded. "And then?"

"We met up for drinks and he said, 'Dude. I was wrong. She's not spoiled and I like her a lot. I'm fucked.'" Hernandez laughed. "I remember the look of panic on his face. He looked like he was in hell and about to fall off a ledge into the fiery pits."

I pursed my lips. "How long after he met me was this?"

"I think a week?"

"So we'd already kissed." I smiled. "Yeah, he was 'fucked,' all right."

"He told me about it. Told me he'd never met anyone like you but he couldn't have you." Hernandez pulled into the airport. "He also told me about your dad blackmailing him, basically, about his dad's pension. Did you know they've been friends for years? His dad and your dad? He begged Coram's dad to come work for him in D.C."

I blinked at Hernandez. "I didn't know that, no. If he's friends with Larry, why would he threaten to take away his bonus?"

"I think it's just that. A threat."

"You don't think he'd do it?"

"I don't know much about your dad. Just what I've gotten from his texts. But it seems to me that if a man begs a buddy to come out and work with him…" Hernandez turned the car off and gripped the door handle. "Then the last thing he'll do is take his friend's money. Right?"

I nodded. "You'd think so."

"I think your dad struck where he thought it would hurt Coram most. To make sure he would keep his hands to himself." Hernandez opened the door. "So he got Coram to agree to those terms."

I opened my door and got out, meeting Hernandez at the back of the car. "Yeah. Maybe."

"He's been very nice to me. Checks in a lot, but I already knew what to expect." He pulled out my luggage and set it on the pavement. "You have everything? Passport, ID, tickets?"

I patted my purse. "A politician's daughter never travels without that stuff. I got that drummed in to my head at a young age. Oh, and hey?"

He looked at me. "Yeah?"

"Thanks for taking me to Finn's guy for my tattoo. I can't wait to show Finn when he gets home." I pressed a hand to my hip. "It's his present."

He smiled. "Anytime. It gave me some ideas for my next one." He motioned me forward, my luggage behind him. "You walk, I'll pull."

We passed a military vet with a sign asking for a ride to San Diego. I reached into my purse and handed him some money and a gift card to McDonald's. "Good luck, sir. I hope you get home."

"Thank you, miss," the man said, squeezing my hand and smiling up at me.

Hernandez stood behind me, hovering close enough to grab me and protect me if necessary. "If you don't mind, I can give him a ride there after I leave," he murmured in my ear. "But it's your car."

I nodded. "This man will give you a ride, if you'd like. He'll be out in a few minutes."

"Bless you." The man shook Hernandez's hand. "Bless you."

Hernandez inclined his head. "I'm always willing to help out a fellow member of the military, sir."

After the arrangements were made for the man to remain where he was and wait for Hernandez to come back, we went into the airport. He shook his head. "Coram wasn't kidding about you wanting to save the world and everyone in it, was he?"

I flushed. "I wouldn't say that. I just like to help."

"You're going to school to be a therapist, right?"

"Yeah." I smiled and swiped my card down the slot for the baggage claim and ticket printout. "It's a good fit for me."

"I believe that." He set the baggage on the scale and watched as I checked in and paid. Once I was finished, he held out his right hand. "Well, have a nice trip. I'll be here waiting for you, if Coram's not stateside yet."

"Thanks, Hernandez." I shook his hand and laughed at myself. "I have to stop calling you that. Your name is Joe, right?"

"Yeah. Well, Joseph." He dropped my hand. "But Coram calls me Hernandez, so it makes sense for you to do the same."

"Well, goodbye, *Joseph*." I waved. "See you later. Don't forget about our double date."

"I won't." He pointed at me and backed toward the door. "Now get through that gate so I can give that guy a ride home. He's been waiting long enough."

I laughed and left, a smile on my face. He turned and walked out the door, his steps sure and powerful. He looked pretty darn good leaving, too. Even *I* had to admit it.

Marie was going to *love* him.

The next morning, I rolled over slowly, knowing when I opened my eyes that I'd be alone. Utterly, horribly *alone* in my parents' house. I closed my eyes, trying to hold on to how wonderful that last night with Finn had felt. I wanted to remember the way I'd felt after we made love—close and naked. And so freaking *happy*.

I did it every morning.

Then every morning, reality came crashing back down on me. It sucked.

I reached up and fingered the sun pendant I hadn't taken off since "Christmas morning" when Finn had given it to me. I still had no idea when he'd be home. I missed him so much it actually *hurt*. It was like I had this big, gaping hole inside of me that oozed pus and blood until I felt I couldn't go on anymore. I just wanted to hurry up through Thanksgiving and Christmas and get to the part when Finn came home.

My parents knew something was up with me. They kept bugging me and asking me why I was so silent, and I kept blowing it off. I wanted to tell them it was because I was missing a piece of me, but I couldn't.

I'd promised Finn I would wait for him, so I was. It still stunk.

Last night, I'd hung out with Finn's dad for a little while. He didn't know about Finn and me, but we used to hang out when I was younger, so he didn't question why I wanted to play chess with him last night.

He was trying to hide it from me, but I could see he was sick. I had a horrible feeling it was his heart or something like that. His skin was a pasty gray that couldn't possibly be healthy. Most of his duties had been delegated to younger men in the squad. Dad kept talking to him in low voices, and on top of that? He looked worried.

My dad. *Worried.*

If that wasn't bad, I didn't know what was. It made me want to demand he tell Finn, but I didn't have that right. Not yet. He might be fighting as hard as he could, but Finn deserved to know. I'd almost emailed him about it last night, but then I deleted it.

It didn't seem like something I should tell him over an email. We'd promised no lies or secrets, but I didn't even know for sure if his dad was sick.

I sat up and shoved the blankets down to my feet. I'd get an answer out of him soon, one way or the other. Tomorrow was the Annual Wallington Holiday Dinner, which was like Thanksgiving and Christmas rolled in to one. All of the house staff and security guards ate with the family at this party.

Dad and Mom always bestowed bonuses and gifts upon everyone, and the booze flowed freely. It was my favorite dinner of the year. As soon as my feet hit the floor, I had my phone in my hand. My heart skipped a beat when I saw I had an email from Finn. I opened it with excitement, eager for my dose of Finn.

Hey, Ginger.

It's hot here, and it makes me think of the cold ocean water in Cali. It's been a long day, and all I want to do is sleep, but I have to pull an all-nighter.

Remind me to show you my latest cheerleading move when I'm home. Camp's been fun because the sun is always shining.

See you soon,

Susan

I closed my eyes and fell back against the bed, my phone clutched to my chest. Every time I heard from Finn I relaxed for a few hours, because I knew he was alive and well. Then, a few hours later, I'd start worrying again.

But right now, directly after contact, was the highlight of my day. He was okay and so was I.

I smiled and typed a quick reply to him telling him I was sleeping well—even though I wasn't—and I told him it was sunny here, too. After I hit send, I nibbled my lower lip and looked outside. It was cloudy and gray and the snow was coming down so heavily you couldn't even see the driveway.

Sunny, indeed.

Last night, I'd asked Dad about his relationship with Larry—poked and prodded a little. Turned out Joseph—as I was now calling him in my head—was right. He and Larry *were* close friends. This only confirmed my suspicions.

Dad wouldn't screw over his friend. He might be a politician and controlling in a creepy way, but he wasn't that kind of guy. Dad wouldn't take away his friend's bonus. As soon as Finn came home, I'd tell him. It would remove one more worry from over his head.

I'd also found out some more about the commanding officer that sent Finn overseas—who was actually coming to dinner tomorrow night. He always did.

But Dad had been talking about visiting Arnold when he'd come to see me, and then he'd told me that Arnold was in charge of getting high-detailed security for important politicians and politicians' families.

Is that what Finn was doing over there…wherever over *there* was? Guarding a politician? That didn't sound too dangerous. I mean, it's what he did for me.

I liked the idea of him following some rich snob around Europe. It was safer than the nightmares that plagued me every night. A knock sounded at the door and I lifted my head to call out, "Come in."

"It's me," Mom said, peeking her head inside before opening the door all the way. Her faded red hair was pulled back impeccably in a tight bun, and her light green eyes sought me out. "Are you dressed?"

Her reactions never failed to make me smile. Did she really think I'd tell her to come in if I was naked on the bed? "Yeah, Mom. I'm dressed."

She came in and closed the door behind her. Tinkerbell, Mom's little terrier, whined from the hallway. "Tomorrow night's the Wallington Annual Holiday Dinner."

I almost rolled my eyes at how she used the *official* name for it, but held back.

"I know." I slipped my phone under my pillow in case Finn wrote back. I mean, he used the name Susan—he'd even created a *SusanCheers@ gmail.com* account to stay in character—but I still didn't like to risk it. I sat up and hugged my knees, resting my chin on them. "Dad reminded me last night."

"I got you a new dress for it." She reached out and smoothed her hand down my head in the way she always did when I was upset. I was trying to act all happy and cheery, but it was hard when a piece of me was gone. "We're going to have some extra guests, too."

"Okay..." I rolled my head her way. "Who?"

"Arnold and his family, the Christensons," Mom turned her head and stared out the window, "and the Stapletons."

Why did that name sound familiar?

"Sounds nice." I wiggled my toes and sighed. "Do you need help setting anything up?"

She laughed, seeming to be relieved about something. "No, we hired temporary help so the normal help could relax before the big event."

Ha. Only in *my* life would that sentence make total sense.

Finn would've laughed at that, too. My heart panged, and the happiness I'd found moments before simply faded. "Mom, can I ask you something?"

"Sure." She crossed her legs and perched on the edge of my bed. "What is on your mind? Are you finally ready to talk?"

She wore a flawless pair of black dress pants and a light pink satin top. She looked every inch the lady. As a kid, I'd always wondered if I would turn out like her. If I would end up being soft spoken yet strong. Kind yet stern. Always the lady.

I didn't think I would anymore. It wasn't *me*.

"If I loved someone who wasn't from our normal crowd, would you approve?" I met her eyes, curling my hands over my calves. "If he made me happy, would you accept him?"

She pressed her lips together. "I don't know, dear. It would depend on the boy, I guess." She turned to me, bending and sticking her foot underneath of her thigh. "Why? Are you seeing someone you don't think we'd approve of?"

"No, not exactly." I shook my head. "I like a guy who isn't from our world. He's not a Christenson or a Wallington."

Mom nodded slowly. "Would he make your father's campaign look bad?"

"I don't think so, no." Finn's words echoed in my head. He'd said he wouldn't fit in on the stage with us, with his tattoos and his motorcycle, but I didn't care about that. "He's not a criminal or anything."

Mom sighed and rested her hand on my back. "Life is hard, and sometimes the heart doesn't make much sense. Sometimes it knows best, and other times it's wrong. You have to pay attention and decide when it's right and when it's off. If you're questioning our acceptance of this boy, chances are this time it's off and you know it."

"*Mom.*" I stood up and spun on her. "That's not true. It's not wrong."

"Are you sure about that?" She stood as well, remaining perfectly poised. "If you weren't uncertain, you wouldn't even have to ask. You'd just introduce us to this boy, and you'd be certain we would like him. Let's count the ways this doesn't add up."

"It's not that. I—"

"Hm. Let's see." She counted off on her fingers as she said, "Instead of telling us you have a boyfriend, you hide him and pretend he's not real. Then you ask me if I'd like him even if he wasn't one of *us*, whatever that means. Then you tell me the heart is right, even though it's not."

She had a point, but I wasn't hiding him because of what she said. I was hiding him because of his job, and because he wasn't *here*.

But I couldn't tell her that, could I?

"It's right and you'll see it." I put my hands on my hips. "When I'm ready to tell you about it, that is."

"I'll look forward to that time." Her chin lifted. "Until then, I'll assume we won't like your boy, because you won't tell us who he is." Mom sighed and walked to my side, not even narrowing her eyes or acting the slightest bit angry. "If he makes you happy, we'll like him."

I nodded. "Then get ready to knit us matching sweaters for Christmas."

"Good." She inclined her head toward my closet. "The dress I bought you is in your closet. I had Frances put it in there this morning."

"Thanks," I said stiffly.

She started to walk away, but then stopped again. "You know, I'm not a snob. You seem to think I am. I've just been around a lot longer than you have. I've seen a lot more than you, and I know how the world works."

"Maybe I want to change the world," I said, lifting my chin.

"Maybe you will."

And with that, she opened the door and left with Tinkerbell trailing behind her, like always.

CHAPTER TWENTY-THREE

Finn

I hated this fucking place. All I'd done for the past three weeks was eat sand, get shot at, almost get blown up twice, and miss Carrie. I walked around like some lovesick fucker who didn't know how to live without a woman at his side.

And even worse? I was *absolutely* that fucking guy. And this assignment sucked donkey balls.

I'd been given three hours of down time, and I had every intention of using it to sleep and dream of her—even if it *was* seven o'clock at night. When you only got a handful of hours to sleep on any given day, you took them when you got them.

I closed my eyes and tried to pretend I was with her. We were laying side by side, our hands touching and her ankle thrown over my calf like she always did in her sleep. Or maybe we were about to get ready for the big Wallington Annual Holiday Dinner.

I think that was today or tomorrow...

I'd kind of lost track of time lately. All the days blended into one long, drawn out nightmare. It would have been the perfect night to tell everyone we loved each other. We would all be together, with the normal social hierarchy gone.

We could have stood up, entwined hands, and announced our love for each other. I would look her father in the eye and assure him that I would never hurt Carrie...

Knock, knock, knock.

"Come in," I called out, sitting up straight and rubbing my eyes. Had I dozed off for a second there? It felt like it. "I'm up."

Dotter popped his blond head in through the crack of the door. "We're getting word of a disturbance up north about a mile. We have to go check it out."

I was on my feet within seconds, shrugging into my bulletproof vest. "Yes, sir."

He closed the door and I stomped into my boots, then grabbed my helmet off my bare bunk. I was halfway to the door before I realized I didn't have the most important item with me. I crossed the room and snatched Carrie's photo from under my pillow, tucking it securely inside my vest—next to my dog tags and over my heart.

As I walked out the door and nodded at my superior, he came to my side. "I heard a rumor we might be going home soon."

I stopped walking. "She's done exploring the rough and tough Middle East already?"

He snorted and opened the door. "I guess so. When she heard there was another disturbance she said maybe she would return home for the holidays. We might be stateside for Christmas."

I grinned. "That's the best news I've gotten all month."

"I hear ya, Coram." He slid into the Humvee and started the engine. I climbed up beside him, cocking my rifle and looking out the window. "Do you have a girl waiting for you back home?"

"Yeah." I closed my eyes for only a fraction of a second, picturing Carrie's sweet smile. I opened them when we pulled forward and onto the makeshift road. "You?"

"A wife and two kids." He drummed his thumbs on the wheel. "If I could be home for Christmas for once, I'd be quite happy."

"I'm sure they would be, too, sir." I scanned the shadows for any movement, but all was quiet on the western front. Okay, maybe that was a bad analogy to make when I was in this fucking place. "God willing, she'll realize she did enough pilgrimage and we'll be all set to go home for the holidays."

"From your lips to God's ears," Dotter said.

"I'm not seeing anything." I looked over my shoulder. "What was supposedly seen here?"

"We had a report of a suspicious blue vehicle, lurking by the entrance of the compound. And someone heard some loud booms." He shrugged. "Out here, that's not exactly the weirdest thing in the world."

"Damn straight." I kept looking. Nothing. "I think we can head back, sir."

"I think you're right, but, first, let's go west a little more."

I nodded and turned back out the window, watching for any signs of life. But in my head, I offered up a silent prayer that God had been listening earlier. That we were going home early, and that this nightmare would be over.

But most of all? I prayed we walked away from this fucking mess alive.

Carrie

The night of the party, I stood in front of the mirror and smoothed the maroon satin over the tulle that made it poof out underneath. Mom had picked the dress, and it *so* wasn't my style, but I wore it anyway. She'd gone through the trouble of finding it, so the least I could do was wear it once before I donated it to charity.

I looked at the necklace she'd bought for me to wear with it, but I didn't pick it up. If I wore that, I'd have to take off Finn's necklace, and that wasn't something I was willing to do. Not even for Mom.

I picked up the necklace she bought and shoved it inside the drawer by my bed. Then I went back to the mirror and studied my reflection. I looked tired and miserable. There were humongous bags under my eyes, and my cheeks looked hollowed out a little, too, no matter how much blush I applied.

But besides that, I guess I looked okay.

The dress was pretty. My hair was swept into a pretty updo that Marie had coached me through, and I had soft pink lip gloss on my lips. I picked up my phone and snapped a picture, then sent it off in an email to Finn.

He would like this dress. It looked easy enough to remove.

I waited to see if I got a reply, but none came. That wasn't a huge surprise. Communication from him was sparse at best, but I ached to get something from him. Anything. It was the only way I had of keeping track of him.

Of knowing he wasn't lying dead somewhere. I shook my head, trying to ditch that train of thought before it ruined my halfway decent mood. My phone buzzed and I picked it up, my heart racing. It wasn't Finn. It was Marie. *How's it going?*

I sent the picture I'd sent to Finn to Marie. *Good. Do I look okay?*

A few seconds, then: *Geez, girl. Have you slept AT ALL?*

Yeah. I tapped the phone on my chin. *Okay, not much. I miss Double-oh-Seven.*

As soon as I sent the message, I deleted it. She wrote back. *Ah. Well, it's almost over. Then we can have some girl time. For now, go to that party (I'm assuming you're going to a party) and have some fun.*

I smiled. *I'll try. Thanks for the pep talk.*

And SLEEP.

I tossed my phone on my bed and headed for my door. The guests would be arriving soon, and I had to be there to greet them, or Mom would have a heart attack. I walked down the carpeted stairs, my hand gripping the white bannister at the end in case my heels decided to slip on the marble foyer.

Dad turned to me and smiled wide, his blue eyes lighting up. He smoothed his graying hair and held his hands out to me. "Ah, it's my princess. Don't you look beautiful?"

"Thanks, Dad." I walked over to him, and he grabbed my fingers, squeezing them tight. "You look wonderful, too, of course."

He hugged me and kissed my forehead. His familiar cologne washed over me, and I hugged him, closing my eyes as I rested against his chest. "Thanks, princess."

"*Hugh.*" I heard heels come up behind me, and Mom said, "Watch the dress, you'll wrinkle it."

I looked up at Dad, rolled my eyes—which made him laugh—and turned to Mom. She headed toward us, Tinkerbell at her heels. Even the dog had dressed up for the occasion. She wore a red satin bow around her neck. "Well, you both look pretty. Very festive."

Mom wore a deep crimson dress that flowed to the floor in elegant swirls, and diamonds in her ears that would probably make the Queen of England jealous. She did a little twirl, her heels clacking as she did so, and leaned forward to kiss my cheek.

"So do you, dear," Mom said, smoothing her dress, even though it was flawless. Tinkerbell shot between her legs, tongue hanging out in excitement. "The first guests should be arriving soon. The house staff and guards are already drinking champagne in the dining room."

"Should I go in there with them so they're not alone?"

Mom shook her head. "No. You should wait here and greet our guests."

"Did you tell her that the Stapleton boy is coming tonight, Margie?" Dad nudged me with his elbow. "That's an *excellent* family if I do say so myself. Their son, Riley, is going to school in San Francisco."

Now I knew why I recognized that freaking name. That's the guy mom had been trying to marry me off to. No wonder she'd been so nervous when she mentioned their name yesterday. This was a setup. A date of sorts.

I turned to Mom and smiled, even though it probably looked more feral than kind. Her cheeks were flushed. "Oh, how *lovely*. I can't wait."

Dad patted my arm. "You'll like him. He has the same beliefs as us."

Then I probably wouldn't get along with him. But I didn't say that. "I can't wait," I said, smiling so wide it hurt my cheeks.

Laughter came from the dining room, and more joined in. The house staff and guards sounded like they were having a blast. I wanted to go in there with them and sneak a drink, but I forced myself to stand still. To play the part of dutiful daughter.

Soon enough they would see it was all an act. I loved them, and I was their daughter, but I wouldn't be their pawn. Not anymore. I pasted a smile on when the doorbell rang. Time to play the part.

"They're here," Mom said, clapping her hands excitedly.

"I'll open it, you two stand there." Dad headed for the door, his steps wide and sure. "Ready, girls?"

"Ready," Mom said.

They were acting like this was some huge thing, but we were standing here in dresses and heels like idiots. Even Tinkerbell stood at attention, for the love of God. This is why I'd never be like my mother. I felt like an idiot—and rightly so. I mean, why were we so freaking special that we were lined up like royalty on an episode of *Downton Abbey*?

It was *stupid*.

"Happy holidays," Dad boomed, clapping some gray-haired man on the shoulder. "Arnold, how good to see you."

I stiffened at the familiar name. He was the man responsible for sending Finn away. Even if he was helping, right now I didn't like him. His eyes clashed with mine over Dad's head. "It's a lovely night out for a party."

Dad nodded and laughed. "Indeed it is. Though it's not as nice as that California weather, is it?"

Arnold shook his head, his eyes still on mine. "Not quite. Right, Carrie?"

"Uh, right." I lifted my chin, raising my voice to be heard over Tinkerbell's incessant barking. "Nice seeing you again, captain."

He came to my side and dropped a kiss on my head. "I trust you'll be wanting to speak with me tonight?" he asked quietly.

"You'd be right," I gritted out. "After dinner."

"I'll meet you in the drawing room," he agreed, squeezing my hand before moving on to my mother. "Darling, you look fabulous."

I smiled and greeted his wife and two young children, then took a steadying breath. I had a lot of questions for him, but they would have to wait for now.

The doorbell rang again, and Dad opened it. Tinkerbell barked even louder. "Ah, hello, hello. Happy holidays," Dad boomed. "Come in. It's great seeing you again, Chris."

Chris. That didn't tell me which one this was. But then I saw the guy with him—young, tall, blond, and *really* hot—and I knew right away. It was the Stapletons.

My intended family...if my family had their way.

Dad beamed at me. "Ah, Riley. Carrie is home, so you won't be drowning in old people talk tonight."

"Sir, I must be old myself, because I've never been bored." He placed a hand on Dad's arm and met my eyes, his smile widening. He had dimples. Freaking dimples. "But I must confess, I'm excited to get to know you better, Carrie. I've heard so much about you."

I pasted on my generic smile and extended my hand, shaking his. His hand was rough and huge on mine, and he seemed friendly enough. If I had met him on this level before I'd met Finn, maybe he would have stood a chance with me. Unfortunately for him, he wasn't Finn. "I hope it was all good."

He laughed, deep and rumbly. Tinkerbell hopped up on hind legs, whining at his feet. Riley squatted down and pet her, grinning. "Indeed."

"Good." I bent over and whispered. "Then they were lying."

His smile slipped for a second, but he laughed and straightened to his full height again. Tinkerbell slinked back to Mom's side. "I think we're going to get along nicely, you and I." He held out his arm. "Shall we go get a drink?"

I made a face. "I'm not old enough."

"I won't tell," he whispered. "Come on, cutie."

I raised a brow. "*Cutie*?"

"Too soon?" He sighed. "I thought since we were getting along so well, we were there. Nicknames and all that."

"Uh…" I eyed him, torn between genuinely liking him, and not wanting to lead him on. He might be handsome and he might be a catch, but he wasn't mine to catch. My hook was already taken…or whatever fishing metaphor fit in this situation. I wasn't exactly the fishing type. I leaned in and dropped my voice. "Look, I have a boyfriend. My parents don't know about it, so they didn't tell you, but I do. Have a boyfriend. Who I love."

He held a hand to his heart, his other arm still extended to me. "You wound me. What part of my drink invitation said 'I'm looking to get into your pants'? I must've missed it, because I'd swear I simply asked you to keep me company in a dining room—not my bedroom."

I laughed, then covered my mouth. Mom looked over and smiled, obviously thinking her plan was working. "So you're *not* trying to get into my pants?"

"No, of course not." He skimmed his gaze over me. "Not yet, anyway. I mean, I just met you. Give a guy a little credit, will ya?"

I rolled my eyes. "Yeah, because not knowing a girl has stopped guys before."

"I'm not just any guy. I'm one of a kind. A Stapleton through and through." He put a hand on his chest, and for a second I thought he was serious, but he broke out in a grin and dropped his hand. "Was I cocky and serious enough? Did I pull it off?"

"Yeah, you almost had me." I laughed. "You're something else."

"I get that a lot."

I blinked up at him, fluttering my lashes a little. "From girls you flirt with?"

"I'm not flirting. I'm chatting, darling," he said, drawing out the syllable to sound snobby. "And while I'm sure you're quite lovely under that dress, I have a secret, too." He offered his arm again. "If you want to hear it, you have to follow me."

This time, I curled my hand into his elbow and let him. "Spill it, Stapleton."

He looked at me out of the corner of his eye. "Oh, you're bossy. I like that in a woman."

I sighed, but inside I felt alive. It had been so long since I'd gotten to relax and be myself. It felt *good*. "It comes part and parcel with being a Wallington."

"Ah, yes. I think I saw that in the informational packet your dad gave me about your blood lineage." As we crossed the foyer, he added, "Did you know my parents want me to marry you and make little trust fund babies? They made it quite clear."

I stopped walking and looked at him, my jaw dropping. "Uh, okay. That was a sweet proposal and all, but no thank you."

"Sweetie, that wasn't a proposal." He shuddered. "I am not my parents, and I have a feeling you aren't yours either. I'm betting you don't like being told what to do. Am I right?"

I bit down on my lip and nodded. "They told me the same thing— that I should marry you for the greater good."

"I'm shocked." He snorted and opened the door to the dining room. "Or not. But at least they're open and honest with us, right? They seem to forget this isn't the Victorian times, and we're not—"

"And we're not children who will do as they're told," I finished for him, smiling. I liked this guy. There was something about him that made me relax. "You're right, I think we'll get along great."

He nodded and picked up a glass of pink stuff, handing one to me. "Drink it before they come in."

"On it." I tipped it back and took a big gulp. It was fizzy and slightly sweet. And delicious. After I swallowed, I lifted my glass and pointed it at him. "You don't act like them."

"Neither do you." He took a thoughtful sip. "I think it's why we like each other. I mean, really, why am I in a tux for dinner with friends? How pretentious can we be?"

I giggled and took another sip. This stuff was even better than the wine coolers Finn always got me. I'd have to figure out what it was so we could keep it stashed at his place. "We hired help to replace the help. For *one* day. Like, what?" I held out my arm. "The house will fall apart in twenty-four hours?"

He rolled his eyes. "My parents are the same. When I'm done with college, I'm going to get a normal-sized house, a normal job, and marry a normal girl."

"They'll just die," I said fluttering my lashes. "Can you imagine the reaction?"

His gaze dropped to my mouth and heated, but then he looked away. "They'd have a heart attack, I'm sure."

I tried to ignore the look he'd given me. So what if he'd stared at my mouth for a fraction of a second? It didn't have to mean anything. And honestly, I didn't want to stop being silly with him. Ever since I came home, I'd been pretending to be something I wasn't. I wasn't the girl who left here all those months ago. *I* was different.

Finn had changed me, and I had no desire to go back to being that girl.

He took another sip of his drink, then grabbed both of us another one, stepping even closer to me. "Let's go sit over there. They'll think we're off flirting and maybe getting a head start on those trust fund babies, and we can drink. Maybe spend some time getting to know one another since we'll be married soon…"

"You *are* flirting with me," I said, narrowing my eyes on him. "The question is: why bother?"

"Dude, I'm respectful of the fact you have a man back in Cali," he said, his eyes drifting down my body. "But I'm not dead. I see a pretty girl? I flirt. Don't look too much into it. Although…wait. Scratch that. I *did* ask you to marry me."

I laughed and led him into the sitting room. "You're horrible."

"If our parents knew we were wandering off together, they'd be cackling with glee. I can picture them now, standing on the sidelines and rooting us on." He lowered his voice. "No, son, you have to move slower. Make it last. It's not a rush to the finish line, boy. Conserve your energy for round two. Stapletons *always* have a round two."

I choked on my drink and gasped for air. "Oh my God."

"Too much?" he asked as he sighed and leaned against the wall.

"Nope. It's just enough," I said, grinning. "You remind me of…well, my boyfriend."

He narrowed his eyes. "If you're going to ask me to stand in for him in a dark bedroom, I'll have to say…*yes*. Absolutely yes."

I rolled my eyes. "Yeah. Totally something he would say."

"He sounds like a smart guy." He finished his drink and sat down on the couch. "Come. Sit. Tell me about this paragon of a man."

"Well…" I took a sip and sat down next to him, setting my full glass down on the table next to his empty one. "He's a Marine. And he surfs. And rides a bike. And he's the sweetest guy ever. He treats me so…so great."

I broke off and played with the sun necklace. There weren't enough words to encompass all that was Finn.

"Mm." He tapped his fingers on the side of the couch. "Sounds like Mommy and Daddy will *love* him."

I snorted. "You have no idea, but I don't care."

"The heart never does," he said softly.

His words reminded me of Mom's, and all that "the heart is right or wrong" crap. I considered him. He looked awfully melancholy. "What about you? You have a girl back in San Francisco?"

"I did." He lifted a shoulder and offered me a twisted smile. "But we broke up when I found her in bed with her professor."

"Ouch." I patted his back. "Sorry."

"Eh, it's okay." He leaned his elbows on his knees. "It's not like she was *the one* or anything."

I pursed my lips. "Do you believe in that?" I asked.

"I do." He turned to me. "Don't you?"

"I do. I mean, I found him." I picked up my drink. "So I know it's real."

"I'm kind of jealous." He nodded. "Enough about me. Drink that and we'll go back in. It's time to act the part of the spoiled rich kids."

I finished my half-empty one and picked up the full glass, resting my chin in my hand. "You're so different from them."

"You are, too." He watched me, his green eyes sparkling with life and kindness. "I wonder why?"

"I…" I paused and tapped my finger on my lips. "I don't have a freaking clue."

He laughed. "Me either. Maybe it's the generation we've been born into."

"Yeah, maybe." I thought of Cory, who was the epitome of what my parents had to have been at my age. "Then again, maybe we're just freaks."

"Maybe," he agreed, laughing. "But the best kind."

I chugged the rest of my drink and stood up, smoothing my dress over my thighs. "You ready to go into the ranks again?"

"Yep." He rose to his feet and offered his arms. "Shall we?"

Such an old-fashioned phrase. I dropped into a curtsy, grinning up at him before taking his arm. "We *shall*."

I locked arms with him and we headed for the double doors that would lead us into the room where everyone—waitstaff, cook, house staff, and bodyguards—would be mingling with senators and governors. All dressed alike, all eating and drinking the same stuff.

We pushed through the doors and walked into mayhem.

CHAPTER TWENTY-FOUR

Carrie

Everyone was mingling and chatting, and the noise was incessant. Mr. Richards's kids were running around pretending to shoot at each other, and the conversation was deafening. I cringed and tightened my grip on Riley's arm. Suddenly, the empty sitting room seemed a heck of a lot better place to be. At least I could hear myself think.

Riley scanned the room. "Holy crap, this is insane."

"Yeah." I sighed and patted his arm. "Welcome to the Wallington Holiday Dinner."

"It's…different," he said, grinning.

"Ah, there you are," Mom said, smiling at me and then smiling even wider at Riley. "We were wondering where you two got off to."

Riley nudged me and I bit down on my tongue to keep myself from laughing.

"Oh, you know, Mrs. Wallington." He bowed at the waist. "Just talking and getting to know one another. Your daughter is fascinating."

"Perfect." Mom clapped her hands. "Come, come. There are refreshments of the spirited kind for you, Riley, and some sparkling cider and soda for those of you who aren't twenty-one."

I rolled my eyes. "Otherwise known as *me*."

"Yes, dear," Mom said, patting my arm. "Well, I'll leave you two young ones to yourselves as I mingle. Ta-ta."

I cringed and waved. "Bye."

"She's too cute," Riley said, smiling after her. "My mom is nothing like her. She's a bear disguised as a sheep."

I looked at his small, blonde mom. She looked sweet and rich, like the rest of the women in the room. She talked to her tall, gray-haired husband, while a few feet away Larry and Christy talked between themselves.

"If you say so. She looks harmless enough." I smiled at him and untangled myself from his arm. "If you'll excuse me, I'm going to go talk to some of the staff."

He bowed. "Have fun."

I nodded and made my way over to Finn's dad. He saw me coming and turned to me with a smile so much like Finn's that it hurt to see. "Carrie, doll. You look gorgeous tonight."

I smiled and hugged him. "You do, too. Very dashing."

"Thank you." He patted his thinning belly, sweat covering his forehead in a thin sheen. He looked exhausted. "I love these dinners."

"So do I." I pointed to an empty row of chairs. "Come, sit with me."

He smiled and followed me. "You're worried about me."

"You look tired is all," I protested. "Are you feeling well?"

"As well as a man my age can feel, yes." He sat down and stretched his legs in front of him, then turned his shiny blue Finn eyes on me. "Getting old is no fun, doll."

"I'm sure," I said, sitting down beside him. "Besides that...are you well?"

He looked at me, his brow furrowed. "I'm fine. I'm just worried about my son."

"O-Oh." I reached out and grabbed his hand, squeezing tight. "He's fine, I'm sure. He knows how to take care of himself, and I'm sure he wouldn't want you to worry about him."

God knows I'm doing enough of the worrying myself.

He froze and raised a brow, his eyes locked on mine. "Do you know him?"

"What?" I froze up, realizing what I'd done. I might as well have admitted to his father that I knew Finn and that we were dating. "I...I... no. I just meant that—"

"Carrie, dear?" Mom came up behind me and rested her hand on my shoulder. "It's time to sit down, so you'll have to follow me."

I swallowed hard, gave Finn's father one last look, then stood. "Of course."

As she led me away, I looked at Finn's dad again. He was watching me, his brow furrowed, and I know my heated cheeks were a dead tell, so I turned forward again. Mom led me to a seat that was next to Riley—of course—and next to one of the downstairs maids.

"You're here." She motioned Riley over. "And Riley, you're here."

I sat down, my heart thudding in my ears the whole time, and watched Larry as he sat across the table from me, but down a few chairs. Next to him was Mr. Richards, and they spoke to each other in low tones. I wanted to go sit next to them and eavesdrop, but I'd probably make a bigger mess out of it than I already had.

I stared down at my empty plate instead. I had a sinking suspicion that something bad was about to happen. It didn't make any sense, but I did. Maybe it was just paranoia about what I'd said to Larry. Maybe it was the drinks I'd had.

But something felt off.

"Hello, again." Riley sat next to me and waved his hand in front of my face. "Hello? Earth to Carrie? Are you in there?"

"Huh?" I looked up at him, blinking. "Oh. Yeah, sorry."

"You okay?"

"Yes." I nodded and picked up my water. "Got distracted for a minute."

He leaned closer, his hot breath washing over my ear. "Well, I am starving. Do you know what we're having?"

"Um..." I took a deep breath and scooted away. The light flirtation we'd been sharing felt a little too close now. Especially with my parents watching and scheming, and Larry across the table. "I think it's turkey and ham."

He nodded. "Excellent. I love them both."

"I hate turkey." I lifted my chin and stared at the table. "I prefer lasagna."

"That's good, too," he agreed. "I love lasagna."

"Is there any food you don't love?" I asked drolly.

"Um, nope."

I laughed and shook my head. "You're something else."

"I've been told that once or twice. By you even."

"By other women, too?"

"Of course," he said, grinning. "They all love me as much as I love food."

Such a cocky statement, but coming from him…it wasn't cocky at all. I had no doubt it was true. He was kind, hot, and smart. What wasn't to like? "I love food more than you."

"That's because you haven't kissed me," he said, shrugging. "That tips the scales in my favor."

I snorted. "Yeah. Sure."

"Care to find out?" he asked, raising his brow.

"I'll pass." I frowned at him. "But thanks for the offer."

"Suit yourself," he said. "Why isn't your boyfriend here, anyway? If I were your man, I wouldn't be sending you home alone at Christmas."

I took a second to choose my words carefully. "He's not—"

A phone rang, and everyone looked up. Then another phone joined in. I zeroed in on both the owners. Larry and Mr. Richards. Larry stood and fished out his phone, smiling at the table. "Sorry, I kept my phone on me in case my son called." He looked down at the screen and frowned. "Excuse me for a second?"

"Yes, of course," Dad said, nodding once.

Mr. Richards also answered, walking in the opposite direction of Larry. The two of them getting a phone call at the same time? That couldn't be a coincidence, could it?

My gaze darted between Mr. Richards and Larry, my heart racing and my palms going sweaty while my mouth dried out. Larry lifted the phone to his ear as he walked toward the double doors. If that was Finn, I wanted to know. No, I *had* to know.

I started to stand up, but Riley put a hand on my thigh. "*Dude*," I snapped, shoving it off. "Keep your hands to yourself."

"Whatever you're thinking about doing right now? Don't. Your dad is watching you and he looks *pissed.*" Riley leaned in and smiled, completely at odds with his warning. "Something tells me you'd like to know about that call."

I took a deep breath and forced myself to sit back down. "H-How do you know?"

"I could see the tension in you when those men answered their phones," Riley said, picking up his glass of water. "And then the answering anger in your father. Who are they to you?"

"One's a bodyguard and the other is a family friend," I answered dismissively, stealing a quick glance at Dad. He was totally watching me, so I forced myself to look at Riley instead of Larry. "That's all."

Riley shook his head slightly. "If you say so."

A masculine cry sounded, and a phone hit the marble floor, clattering once or twice before landing. It was like a slow-motion nightmare. You know, the ones where a murderer is chasing you and you're running as fast as you can, only you're moving in slow motion? Yeah, that. Only ten times worse.

Dad was the first one on his feet, followed by me. Larry leaned against the wall, a hand to his mouth and his face even paler than before. I shoved my chair back and took off running in my heels, knowing I needed to get to Larry's side. Knowing I needed to help him, but also knowing he'd gotten bad news.

Bad news about Finn.

I bolted around the edge of the table. Mr. Richards grabbed my elbow even though he was still on the phone. "Carrie, wait. He'll know what's going on if he sees your face."

"*I don't care.*" I shook free, stumbling backward when he let go. "I'm going."

I took off again. Vaguely, I heard people shouting, and talking loudly, and Mom shouting my name, but I didn't even register any of it. All that mattered was getting to Larry. My throat ached with tears that were already threatening because I knew, I just *knew*, this was bad.

Dad got there first, and I wanted to shove him out of the way. "What is it, Larry?" he asked, throwing an arm around his shoulders. "What's wrong?"

"It's Griffin. He's been…oh my, God." Larry fell to his knees and scrambled for his phone with shaking hands, crawling forward on all fours. "I have to go. I have to go now."

"I'll take you," Dad said, squatting beside him and handing him the phone. "Larry, come on. Where are we going?"

I finally reached their side, but I'd already heard all I needed to know. I pressed a hand to my speeding heart, wondering how it could be beating when it had been ripped out of my chest just seconds before.

"W-What happened to him?" I asked, my voice barely more than a whisper. "Larry?"

"Larry's fine," Dad said quietly, standing up and smiling calmly at the people gathering behind me. "It's his son who's not all right. Stay here and control the madness with your—"

"*No.*" I grabbed the lapels of Dad's tux and shook him, then shouted, "What happened to Finn?"

Dad paled and gripped my hands. "Carrie…how…why…?" He turned red in the face. "*I knew it.*"

Larry stood up and started walking for the door. I didn't have time to waste trying to get answers out of Dad. I shoved off his chest and raced after Larry, grabbing his arm. The panicked rush of adrenaline was taking over my body, numbing the pain I knew would hit me any second. Right now I needed to *know*.

"Larry, tell me." I gripped him tighter. "Is he…is he…?"

I gulped in a deep breath and a sob escaped, so I covered my mouth. I couldn't even say the word. Not in the same train of thought as Finn. It wasn't right.

Larry paled and gripped my hands with his own trembling hand. "I don't know how bad it is. I think they said something about him being in surgery, but I dr-dropped the ph-phone."

I didn't know whether to shake him for doing something so incredibly stupid or hug him because he was obviously breaking. "Okay. Okay… we'll go there right away and find out. Where is he? Who called you?"

"He's in Germany. I don't know anything else," he rasped. "That's all I know," he repeated, his eyes focused on a spot on the wall. He looked like he was in shock, so I rubbed his back. "My boy. I don't even know…"

I nodded, trying to remain calm for Larry's sake, but inside I was freaking the heck out. This couldn't be happening. Not to my Finn. It had to be a nightmare. That was the only explanation. But I didn't wake up, and the pain wracking through my chest was all too real. I was awake. "Let's go find out more. Just let me grab my passport."

"No way, missy." Dad grabbed my upper arm. "You're staying here with your mother. I can handle this."

"*No.*"

"She can come," Larry said, his voice cracking. "It's fine."

My father stiffened and rose to his full height. "Carrie Louise Wallington, you *will* listen to me and you'll—"

"No, *you* will listen to me." I yanked free and glowered at him and everyone else who had huddled around to watch the show. Riley looked at me with sad eyes, and Mom was wringing her hands. "I am going because his son is Finn, and I *love* him."

Mom gasped and covered her mouth, her cheeks fusing with color. "*Carrie*. You don't even know him."

"Don't I, Dad?" I put my hands on my hips and stared him down. "Tell her why I know Finn, won't you?"

"Hugh? What's the meaning of this?" Mom asked.

"Oh for the love of God…" Dad said, covering his eyes.

"Carrie, go get your things," Mr. Richards said, laying a hand on Dad's shoulder. "I got this."

Dad yanked on his tie and threw his arms up in the air. "We don't have time for this melodramatic scene. Larry and I have to go. *She* is staying."

"*I* am going," I shouted. Tears were streaming down my face, and I didn't even care I had a whole freaking audience in front of me. "Do you even *hear* me? I love him, and *I* am going."

Larry grabbed my hand. "She's coming, and you can too, if you want. But we're going *now*."

Dad sputtered, his fists clenching and unclenching, then headed for the door without a word. I didn't have time to worry about him. I needed *Finn*.

He was okay. He *had* to be okay. Because if he wasn't okay…

I'd never be okay again.

CHAPTER TWENTY-FIVE

Carrie

The town car sped down I-95, leading us to the airport. Dad had secured a private jet for the flight, and apparently he was going to Germany with us. He was going, despite his stony silence and glowers. All I cared about was getting to Finn.

"H-Hello?" Larry said, his voice soft. "Yes, this is him." Silence, then he sagged against the back of the seat and ran a hand down his face. "Can you tell me anything at all?" Larry nodded. "But how?" A moment of silence. "I...I see. Yes. We'll be landing at six your time." More silence. "Okay. Thank you."

He hung up and I reached out, grabbing his knee. "Tell me everything."

"There was an ambush. IEDs and guns..." He drew in a deep breath and covered his face with his hands. "He's in surgery, but I already knew that. They won't tell me anything else. They claim not to know." He dropped his hands from his face. "I think he's alive. I'd know it if he wasn't, wouldn't I?"

I didn't answer. I couldn't. I was too busy trying not to break down. We clung to each other's hands, not speaking. The whole ride to the airport felt like a nightmare. And the long plane ride turned out to be even worse.

I spent the whole flight praying and praying that Finn would be all right. But even more so, I prayed that this was all a dream. I was so sure I'd wake up in Finn's arms. He would laugh at me for being such a paranoid wreck, and I would snuggle in. I looked out the window and saw the clouds beneath us, and the pain hit me all over again.

It wouldn't leave me alone.

Dad swiped his finger across his phone. What was he doing, anyway? He couldn't be messaging anyone or doing something important since we were flying. I swear to God, if he was playing Candy Crush when I was dying inside, I'd kill him. He hadn't said a word to me this whole flight, but I didn't care.

I didn't have time for my daddy issues. Not when Finn…

God, he couldn't be dead. It wasn't possible. I had to believe, like Larry, that I would *know* if he was gone. I covered my mouth with my free hand, fighting back another sob trying to escape me. Wouldn't I know it, deep inside?

I had to believe I would, because the alternative wasn't acceptable. He'd left the country for me, for us, and now he could…he might be… *dead*.

And this was all my fault. If he died, that was on me.

After all, if he hadn't met me, and wanted to change for my father, he wouldn't have been offered that assignment. And he wouldn't have taken it. This had all been for us, and now he'd paid the ultimate price. While I…while I what? Dined and chatted with Riley, pretending I was single in front of my parents?

And why? All because he didn't fit in my world?

I was done. So freaking *done*.

I turned on my father, who was still staring at his phone. "He did this for you, you know," I said, a sob breaking up the last word. "He said you wouldn't accept him as he was, so he was trying to *fix* himself. Trying to make himself *better*. Are you happy now, Dad?"

Dad sat up straighter, the color draining from his face, but he didn't answer me. I knew what I was doing. I knew I was transferring my anger at myself onto my father, but I didn't freaking care. "Carrie…"

Larry squeezed my hand. "This isn't your father's fault, doll."

"Yes, it is," I said, sinking back against the plane seat. "It's his fault, and it's *mine*, too. Finn didn't think he was good enough for us. Didn't think my world would accept him. Well, I don't want a part in a world that doesn't accept a man like Finn. Not anymore. I'm done with it all.

Done."

Dad finally broke his silence. "Carrie, don't be unreasonable. It's not like I knew about this. Griffin couldn't have known my reaction. He did this to better himself, not to better himself for me."

I laughed hysterically, then covered my mouth. "Don't you get it? He can't *better* himself because he's already perfect. He's the nicest guy I've ever met, but when you look at him, you won't see that. You'll see the tattoos and the motorcycle. Let's not pretend otherwise, especially not in front of Larry."

We all fell silent, and I closed my eyes. Tears rolled down my cheeks, but I didn't bother to wipe them away. What was the point? Nothing mattered until the freaking plane landed in Germany and we got to Finn. Until I got to see him. Nothing mattered until I knew whether he was still here with me.

The rest of the flight passed by with agonizing slowness, but I didn't break my silence the whole time. None of us did. We just sat there. Waiting. Hoping. Praying.

When we landed and got in the waiting town car, my mind was numb. And when the car pulled up in front of the hospital, after a series of ID checks and verifications, I was the first one out of it. I offered Larry my hand. He took it as he came out, holding on to it for support as we made our way in through the revolving glass doors.

Dad walked beside us, his tie loose, and his security behind us. I glowered at him. "You brought them here?"

"Yes, Carrie, I brought them here," he said, his voice tired. "They go where I go. And, as you obviously know, where you go, too."

I turned my head, not wanting to do this right now. Not able to do it. "Do we know where to go, Larry?"

"They said the third floor." He pointed at the elevator. "So I'm guessing we start there."

We walked to it in silence, holding hands still. By the time the elevator arrived, and we rode it to the third floor, I wasn't sure my legs would work anymore. But somehow, when the doors opened, I walked out. And then I took the steps that led us to the receptionist, who wore a scrub top with cartoon turkeys on it.

"Can I help you?" she asked, pushing her glasses up her nose.

Larry stepped forward and rested his hand on the desk. It looked casual enough, but I knew he rested on it for support. "Y-Yes, we're here for Sergeant Griffin Coram. We don't know if he's…"

When he didn't finish, instead covering his mouth and closing his eyes, I stepped forward and I squeezed his hand tighter. "If he's still alive, he means."

God, even saying that hurt.

The nurse's brown eyes flashed with pity, and she looked at her computer. "Go have a seat, and someone will be with you."

"Can you tell us anything?" Larry asked, his face pale. "Anything at all?"

She hesitated. "It's not my place to do so, sir. There's protocol and rules…"

"P-Please?" I added, catching her gaze. "Even something tiny."

She sighed. "He's here. That's really all I know. I don't know where or how he's doing. I don't even know if he's…living. I just see his name in the system—and that's all I can tell you."

Tears fell down my cheeks and I nodded, biting down on my lower lip. "Th-Thank you," I managed to say before I led Larry to his seat.

Dad followed, his fists tight at his sides. "That's bull. They can't tell you anything?"

"It's the way the military works," Larry said, collapsing in the plastic chair. "It's always been this way."

"Someone ought to fix that," Dad grumbled.

Larry and I both gave Dad a pointed stare, and then we all fell silent again. We sat there for what had to have been two hours before we saw anyone. A nurse in pink scrubs came up to us—her eyes empty and her face carefully neutral. "Sir? I can take you to your son now. The rest of your party will have to wait out here."

I stood up, almost falling over in my haste. "Can't I come, too?" I asked, my voice cracking. "Please?"

"Family only, ma'am," the nurse said, her eyes showing me she didn't want to refuse me. "I'm sorry."

I bit back a sob and covered my mouth. I didn't want to stay out here. I wanted to be with him. With Finn. "Okay. I'll wait here."

"You'll let her go back," Dad said, his voice clear and strong. "I'm Senator Wallington from the United States Senate, and that boy back there is one of mine. I'll gladly follow your rules and wait, but you'll let *her* go back."

I looked at him in surprise, tears still blinding my vision. "D-Dad?"

"Sir…I can't."

Larry rested a hand on her arm. "He'd want her back there. Whether he's alive or not…he'd want her there." He paused. "Please."

She hesitated, still gazing at my father, who stared her down until she finally nodded. "All right. She can come, but not for too long."

Not for too long? Did that mean he was alive? I was trying to dissect everything she said and it was driving me insane. When would they tell us something?

I looked at Dad, but he didn't look at me. Instead, he headed for the elevator without a word. Larry tugged me into the back room, and then we were entering a room with beeping noises and a lot of bright lights and…*oh my God*.

He was there. *Finn* was there, but he didn't look like Finn at all.

His head had white gauze wrapped all around it, and he had scratches all over his face, a black eye, and a bloody lip. It looked as if they'd shaved all his hair off, too. All I saw was skin, scars and stitches. There were stitches over his forehead that ran long and deep, extending underneath the bandage around his head. And he looked so pale. Almost as if…

As if he wasn't *alive*.

But the machine was beeping steadily. He had a heartbeat. He was alive.

I kept echoing that in my head.

I took a step closer, my own heart squeezing so tight that it hurt to move, let alone breathe. His eyes were closed, but his lips moved restlessly, as if he was having a bad dream or talking in his sleep. They were all scabbed up and dried out, and he looked as if he hadn't had a drink in days. His left arm was in a cast from the elbow down, and then a sling, too, as if it needed all the support it could get. His legs were covered with a blanket, but I didn't think he had any casts on underneath.

"Oh my God," I said, taking another step closer. "*Finn*."

Larry cried out and rushed to Finn's side, and I watched as if I was out of my body. Unable to move or talk or do anything besides stare. I wanted to feel relieved that he was alive, but how could I feel anything resembling relief when he was in a bed—bloody and bruised and *hurt*?

The arm that wasn't in a sling rested at his side, but he had his hand fisted tight. As I watched, he loosened the fist, then tightened it again. He was holding something. I leaned closer, squinting. It took me maybe three seconds to recognize it. It was tattered, but I'd know it anywhere. It was the picture he'd taken of me outside his apartment. I hadn't even known he printed it out.

My gaze flew to his face, but his eyes were still closed. "I'm here, love," I whispered, even though he probably couldn't hear me. I stood there, not sure where to touch him…if at all. It didn't look safe to touch him anywhere. "I'm with you."

"Is he going to be okay?" Larry asked, his eyes on Finn. "Will he recover?"

"He's been confused and in pain," the doctor said. He walked to Finn's side and checked his vitals. "We've been keeping him dosed with morphine, and he's been pretty out of it because of that, so it's hard to tell what kind of effects the explosion might have had on his brain. We did an MRI, but we're still waiting on the results from that. With crude IEDs, you never know."

Larry covered his mouth. "What got broken?"

"He was lucky," the doctor said. "It was just his arm. Lots of bruises and stitches all over his body. There will be scarring on his face and his arm. And he got a concussion, as I said. We won't know the long-term effects until he wakes up. When his arm broke, the fibula came through the skin, so it was touch and go for a while. He lost too much blood before they could get him here, so he's weak. But he really lucked out."

I walked toward Finn slowly, my eyes on his cast. *That was lucky? How could that be considered lucky?*

"The rest of his unit died," the doctor said, watching me closely. "That's how he's lucky."

I hadn't even realized I'd said that out loud. I reached Finn's side, the one without the broken arm, and I slowly closed my fingers over his hand. I made sure not to crumble the picture, even if it was almost unrecognizable already. Even though he didn't so much as blink or wiggle his fingers, I swear…

I swear he *knew* I was there, and that was enough for me.

CHAPTER TWENTY-SIX

Finn

I kept seeing it over and over and fucking over again. The bright flashes as the IED went off. The deafening boom where I heard nothing at all, followed by me wishing I *still* heard nothing at all. The screams. The blood. The dead men...

Then there was my superior's leg getting blown clear off his fucking body, and then blood spurting everywhere, even in my face and burning my eyes. I swear I could still smell it. Taste it. I'd never forget that hellish night.

I'd tried my best to slow down the bleeding, even as it stopped squirting and just started to trickle slowly, I didn't let go. Even as his face went lax and cold, losing all traces of life. Everyone around us went into panic mode, shooting at anything that moved. I didn't let go until they dragged me away kicking and screaming.

And the pain...

God, it wouldn't fucking leave me alone.

I'd been fully conscious when my arm snapped in half and I flew from the Humvee, and I'd been so sure this was it. That I was a fucking goner. And in a weird, twisted way, I kind of wished I *had* died. At least then, I wouldn't be living through an endless replay of the attack in my mind.

I was fairly certain they had me doped up on some strong pain meds, so I didn't feel the pain. But yet…I did. Maybe I was dying. Or maybe I was already dead.

All I knew was that I was in *hell*.

I felt someone poking at my head, and a masculine voice talking about brain damage and possible long-term repercussions. I wanted to shove him off me and tell him to leave me the fuck alone so I could die in peace. I wanted to shout at the world, demanding they shut the fuck up. But then…

Ah, then I heard *her*.

I felt her soft hand touch mine, immediately calming me, and I tried to open my eyes. Tried to see if I was really dead, or if I was alive with Carrie at my side. If Carrie was here, I was alive. It felt unfair, almost. I knew no one else had made it out alive. Only me. I should have died. I really *should* have fucking died.

"Finn? Can you hear me?" Carrie's voice asked, the hand on mine tightening. "I love you. I love you so much. You've got to wake up for me. Open those blue eyes."

Either I was alive, or I was right and I was burning in hell, because I swear that was actually Carrie. I tried to open my mouth to ask her if she was real, but only a squeak came out. A small, pathetic sound.

"Oh my God, he's waking up," Carrie called out, holding on to me with both hands. Her grip on me hurt. That's how fucked up I was, but I didn't care. "Doctor Sloane, he's waking up."

I felt a man's hands probing me, then heard, "Be prepared for the worst. He might not remember things. Might not remember you two at all."

The fuck I didn't remember her. She was my Carrie. I managed to make my fingers move, and she cried out. "Larry, he's moving."

My father was here? But where *was* here?

"Son, I'm here with you." What I assumed to be Dad's hand fell on my arm, gentle and yet rough at the same time. He sounded fucking exhausted, and he sniffed loudly. "We're both here."

I managed to crack my eyelids open, but the bright lights shining down on me hurt, sending shards of pain through my brain. I slammed them shut again, then opened them more slowly. I blinked against the bright light and managed to turn my head *just* enough to see who stood by me.

Jesus Christ, I hadn't died. Carrie was here with my father.

She wore a short purple-ish dress, a pair of ripped tights, and her hair was falling all around her face. Her makeup was smeared across her cheekbones, and she had the hugest bags under her eyes I'd ever seen … but she was my very own angel.

"C-Carrie?" I managed to croak.

She burst into tears and nodded, smiling at me. Fuck, she looked perfect. "Yes, it's me," she said. "I'm here."

Dad gripped my arm and kissed the left side of my forehead. "You scared us, son."

I'd scared them? How had they even known about it? I had so many questions to ask, but I didn't want to. Not now. All that mattered was they were here. And I was alive.

Fucking *alive*. I wasn't sure how I felt about that yet.

Carrie kissed my hand, her hot tears hitting my skin. She blinked at me, a soft smile still on her lips. I knew she was putting on a show for me, trying to be brave and all that shit. And I loved her so much for it.

"I know you feel horrible right now, but I've never been happier to see those blue eyes," she said, kissing my hand again.

"You…" I took a deep breath. It hurt to fucking talk, but I had to say something to let them know *I* was still here, under all the scrapes and bandages. "Look like hell."

She blinked at me, then a surprised laugh escaped her. Dad chuckled, too, and I eased my head back on the pillow, closing my eyes. That's what I'd needed. Right there. I needed them to take a break from crying or worrying about me.

And it's what they needed, too, even if they didn't know it.

"I'm sure we do," she said, her voice still light.

"It's been a rough night, son," Dad said. "Not anything like yours…"

"I'm feeling pretty good right now," I said, trying to make light of the fact that I felt like I was dying slowly. "I'm h-h..."

My voice broke and I swallowed hard. I kept picturing the life leaving Dotter's eyes as I clung to his bloody stump of a leg. Jesus Christ. I'd never forget it.

The doctor cleared his throat. "I think we should let him rest now. I'm going to get him another dose of morphine. You'll have to say your goodbyes till tomorrow."

I tightened my fingers on Carrie. I'd just found her again. I didn't want her to leave, but the nurse pushed a button on my IV station, and the world spun in front of me, taking away my vision and even my concentration. "C-Carrie?"

"I'm still here," she whispered.

"Tell me something before they dope me up again," I whispered, urging her closer. "Before I'm g-gone."

I felt her move closer to me. "Yeah?"

"Is the sun shining?"

Her tears hit my arm, rolling off onto my hospital bed. "It is. And it won't stop. I'm right here with you. I'm not going *any*where."

I nodded and drifted off, the nightmare starting all over again. I could still smell the flesh burning, and I could hear the cries of the dying men all around me, but I knew I wasn't there anymore. I was home. And Carrie was here, too.

I'd be all right.

What might have been minutes or hours later, I opened my eyes again, blinking into the empty hospital room. I heard someone move closer and slowly turned my head, hoping to see Carrie. Instead, I saw her father. Senator Wallington.

For a second I thought I was hallucinating, so I blinked again. He was still standing there, watching me with those intense blue eyes. I tried to speak, but nothing came out. I was too damn high to make a fucking sound.

When he saw my eyes on him, he took a step closer and rested his hand on my bedrail. "I know you probably won't remember this, but you're a hero, son."

I blinked. Yeah, I was totally fucking high right now.

He sighed. "I know you love my girl, Griffin. And I know she loves you, too." He looked down at me. "I get why you fell for her. Who wouldn't? It doesn't mean I'm *happy* about it, though. Or that I'll accept it."

I wanted to reply so fucking bad, but nothing came out.

I swallowed and tried to open my mouth to talk, but the drugs were still dragging me down. All that came out was a moan sounding like, "*Sir?*"

He flinched and reached out, pushing a button on my IV that

controlled my morphine drip. "Get well, son. For both of our sakes."

Within seconds, the screams of the dying men took over my head again…

And I fell back into my own version of hell.

ACKNOWLEDGEMENTS

I have to first and foremost thank my family. My husband, Greg, for being so supportive every time I have to hunker down and get to work. And for my kids: Kaitlyn, Hunter, Gabriel, and Ameline...you're the best things I ever did. Thanks for being you.

I also have to send my love to my parents, sisters, nephews and brother-in-law. Thanks for being my cheerleaders and also for pimping out my books occasionally. I know you always have my back, and that's an amazing feeling.

And my amazing agent, Louise Fury from The Bent Agency. You've been my nonstop supporter, backbone, guide, and are just all-around awesome to be with. I don't know what I'd do without you there, helping me make the right choice. You're a rock star! Much love to you and your hubby, too.

To Team Fury, and everyone at The Bent Agency, I have to say it: I love you all. You're a great team to be on, and I thank my lucky stars I get to be a part of the group every day!

And thanks are also due to my fabulous publicist at InkSlinger PR, Jessica Estep. You're the best, and I couldn't possibly handle all these blog tours and blitzes without you. And thank you so much for all your excitement and confidence in this book, and in me.

I couldn't leave out my best buddies: Trent, Jill, and Tessa. You three are my rock, and I love how close we've gotten lately. NYC crew forever, man!

To my wonderful, fabulous, amazing critique partner, Caisey Quinn.

You never let me down, and you're always here for me, no matter what. I love you, girl!

Thanks to Casey, as well, for your expertise in all things Finn. You're the best.

To my editor, Kristin; my copy editor, Hollie Westring; my formatter, Emily Tippet; and my cover artist, Sarah Hansen: thank you so much for giving me the best quality service out there! I love you all.

A huge, huge thanks goes out to all the Carrie and Finn fans out there. Thank you for joining me for the second part of their journey. I hope to see you for the final portion of the journey next year!

And to all my writer friends…you know who you are. There are *way* too many to name in this small section, and I don't want to leave you out. You know I love you. You know how much you mean to me. And thank you for being you!

THANK YOU!

sometimes love isn't enough...

OUT OF MIND

Jen McLaughlin

Edited by: Kristin at Coat of Polish Edits
Copy edited by: Hollie Westring
Cover Designed by: Sarah Hansen at © OkayCreations.net
Interior Design and Formatting by: E.M. Tippetts Book Designs

Reaching for sunlight...

Finn survived the ambush and came home to me, but in his head, the battle is still raging. He's falling apart and I'm trying my best to pick up the pieces of him, to find the *us* we used to be. I love him as much as I ever did, but love isn't enough to fix this. I thought telling my father about our relationship would be the hardest thing we'd ever have to face. I was wrong.

Lost in shadows...

All I wanted was to be worthy of Carrie. One mission, just one, and I'd be able to give her the future she deserved. Then everything went wrong, leaving me tainted and broken. Carrie wants me to be who I was, but all that's left is what they made of me. I'm no good for her. No good for anyone like this. I have to figure out how to move forward. Alone.

Sometimes love isn't enough...

This one goes out to all the men like Finn who fight, come home, and struggle to fit in with everyday life. Especially my friend Tim, who we all still miss dearly.

CHAPTER ONE

Finn

"Don't let me die...Please don't let me die..."

Explosions boomed in my ears, shooting me upright into a sitting position in bed, gasping for air and crying out into the empty bedroom. Gunshots still echoed in my head, along with the gurgling of Dotter's blood as it poured out of his body until there was nothing left. I looked down at my hands, half expecting to find them bloody. They weren't. But metaphorically? That was a whole other fucking story.

Trembling, I rose to my feet, my broken arm casted and hanging uselessly in a sling. My body was coated in a light sheen of sweat, and even my sheets were dampened and dark. Blinking at the sunlight that crept through the closed curtains, I tried to remind myself where I was. I wasn't fighting for my life. Wasn't watching people die. I was safe.

As safe as I was going to be, anyway.

Pushing the curtains back, I squinted outside. After spending a couple of weeks in a hospital in Germany, followed by another couple of weeks in a hospital in D.C., it was nice to be in a home. But instead of the sandy beaches and hot weather of California, I saw a foot of snow reflecting the sun, blinding me. And we were supposed to get even more tomorrow night. Fucking ridiculous. I studied the position of the sun in the winter sky. Damn, what time was it now? Last thing I remembered, I took a few pills and zonked out. It had been...morning? Maybe? Now, judging from the sunlight streaming through clouds, it was mid-afternoon.

I'd missed a whole day.

Sure. I could act shocked about this, but that happened more often than not lately. I slept away the day, high on painkillers and drunk from whiskey. When I woke up, I swore I wouldn't touch another drink. I'd last an hour or two.

Then I'd do it all over again.

I ran my hand over my shaved head, wincing at how rough it felt. I'd been back in the good old USA for a couple of days now. I still felt like I was trapped in the fucking desert. Instead, I was in the winter wonderland from hell. Carrie's parents' house.

A knock sounded on the door, and I dropped the curtain. I glanced down at myself. I had on a muscle tank and a pair of black basketball shorts. Decent enough, I supposed. "Come in."

The door cracked, and the red hair I'd recognize anywhere appeared before the face I needed so damn much did. "You're up?"

"Yeah." I tugged on my tank and crossed the room. "You can come in."

Carrie entered, shutting the door behind her. She hesitated, looking torn. Her blue eyes were sober and crystal clear, while I was a fucking drunken wreck. I'd been snapping at her lately. Pushing her away. I hated myself for it, yet I couldn't seem to fucking stop.

"Did you sleep good? I thought I heard you cry out."

I fingered the puckered wound on my head. It was still sensitive to the touch and ugly as fuck. Not as ugly as the rest of my scars. Inside *and* out. "I had another nightmare. Same old thing."

She approached me slowly. "Anything I can do to help?"

"Yeah." I met her eyes. "You can come hug me."

She gave me a smile. "Anytime."

Within seconds, she was in my arms. Well, my arm. I glowered down at my broken arm, knowing it was as marked up as my head. You just couldn't see it right now. I closed my arm around her, burying my face in her neck. "Fuck. I missed you."

She tilted her face up to mine. "I missed you, too."

"You should start sneaking in here to see me at night." I dropped a kiss on her forehead. "Then I can at least hold you for a little bit before I fall asleep."

She did sneak into my room every single night, but we never acknowledged her visits. It was our unspoken agreement. Without fail, I would have a nightmare every night. Also without fail, she would come in and comfort me until I fell back asleep. Then, in the morning, we pretended it never happened. I could tell she wanted to talk about it, but she kept silent.

She just gave, without asking for anything in return.

She was too good for me.

"I'll try tonight," she agreed, stretching up on tiptoes to press her mouth to mine.

I tensed and pulled away. I couldn't...she couldn't really want me right now. Not when I looked and felt like this. She stepped back, the disappointment in her eyes way too fucking clear. "I'm going out to refill your prescription. Want to come with me?"

I'd love to, but I couldn't. I wasn't ready for the world to see me yet. "Nah. I'll stay here."

"O-Okay." She watched me, her brow furrowed. "Did you see the sun is shining?"

My heart wrenched. We used to say that, back when I'd been overseas. It had been our code for "I love you." Back when we'd been a secret. Back before her father found out about us. Before he'd threatened me if I ever hurt his baby girl.

I didn't want to hurt her, and yet I was.

I needed to start acting *happy* better. I pasted a big grin on my face. I felt like a fucking clown. "I did. It's so bright."

She nodded, perking up a bit. "Are you sure you don't want to go out with me? It could be fun. Maybe we could go out to dinner? Have a little date."

I started to waver. A date sounded fucking fabulous. It had been so long since I felt normal. Since I felt human. We hadn't had any alone time together, unless you counted stolen moments like this one, and it had been way too long since we acted like a couple at all. I was a fucking mess, and I knew it.

Could I pretend not to be, for her? I could try. "Well..."

I looked over at the nightstand. The mirror over the top of it showed us in perfect profile. She watched me with a hopeful look in her eyes. All red curls, gorgeous skin, and bright blue eyes. She was flawless. And then there was me…Beauty and the Beast.

The wound on my head ran a thin line across my skull, extending down past my eyebrow. My shaven head was patchy at best, due to some lovely hospital clippers that had been used on me. I was told my hair would grow back in eventually, but I was supposed to go out with her like this? I could picture the looks now.

The disgust. The pity.

No. I wasn't ready.

"We could go Christmas shopping, too," she said, her voice excited. "It's only six days away, and I know you didn't get anything for your dad. I still need to shop for mine, too." She grabbed my hand, squeezing it. "We could have fun, like old times."

"I'm sorry, but I can't," I said. "My head…" *is fine.* "Hurts."

"Oh." The smile slipped, but she forced it back into place. She was better at acting happy than I was. "Okay."

"Can you open my pills for me?" I sat down on the edge of the bed. "Maybe get me a drink, too?"

"It's a little early for another pill. You need to wait another hour. And you know you're not supposed to mix booze and painkillers." She looked at me, pressed her lips together, and set my unopened pills on the table. "But I'll grab you some water if you're thirsty."

"Not what I meant, but thanks."

She nodded, grabbed a water bottle, opened it, and handed it over. "You're almost out of pills already. You took too many. I think there should be more."

"I dropped one," I said, averting my eyes. "It rolled away, and I couldn't find it."

"What way did it go?" she asked, dropping to all fours. "I'll find it."

"I don't know. It was dark."

She looked up at me, not saying anything. She didn't believe me. Good. I wouldn't believe me either. I watched her, daring her to argue. To stop treating me as if I might break. She shook her head slightly, stood up, and brushed her hands on her perfect thighs. "Okay, I won't look then."

I frowned and glanced away. "Hey. Have fun shopping."

"Yeah. Thanks." She kissed my bald head, hovering awkwardly. "I love you."

I cringed. She trailed her fingers over my naked scalp. She used to love my hair. Now I didn't have any. "I love you, too."

Once she left, I grabbed the bottle of meds off my nightstand. Another hour, my ass. I'd find a way to open this bottle even if it killed me. After a brief struggle, I managed to pop the lid off on my own. After a while of sitting there in silence, the pill hit me, making the world spin around me. Everything faded away but the blissful silence.

It was the only time I felt like myself anymore.

CHAPTER TWO

Carrie

It had been four months and twenty-three days since I met Finn. He'd told me he was a surfer who didn't have any aspirations above being a Marine, but he'd really been my father's spy. It had been two and a half months since he told me he loved me. I'd told him I loved him, too, and we'd sworn never to lie to each other again. And it had been a month and two days since he got injured, and I thought my world would end. Three days since we came home, and he shut me out of his life. I didn't know how to get back in.

The days kept swirling around my head, over and over again. I guess in a way, I was trying to reassure myself of something. I mean, he was home. And he was getting better. He was trying, anyway. He'd get better. But my world still felt like it was ending. It still wasn't right.

Finn wasn't really Finn anymore.

So instead of going inside my parents' house, I sat in Dad's car for a while, staring up the driveway at the way-too-large-for-normal-humans house I'd grown up in. Part of me wished we'd gone straight to California, instead of back to D.C. like Dad wanted. But Finn's dad was here, and it was winter break, so here we were. Dad let Finn stay at the house, despite his frequent disapproving frowns and his long, lingering looks. But Finn was alive. And he was with me. That's all that mattered, right?

I sighed and slid out of Dad's car, waving at the security dude who got out of his car. He'd wanted to ride with me, but I'd wanted to be alone, so he'd followed me to the store, where I'd wandered around aimlessly. "Finn: Part Two" I liked to call him in my head. Dad had placed a detail on me again, and even though I hated it, I let it slide.

At least he was letting Finn stay at the house.

His room might be on the complete opposite side of the house from my room, sure, but it was something. And it was only temporary. Christmas was coming up, and then we would go home right before New Year's. After that, we'd be fine. And if I kept saying that, maybe it would be true. Finn tried to act normal. He held me close and told me he loved me.

But he wasn't *Finn*.

I opened the front door and blinked. Every single light was on downstairs, and laughter came from the living room. Christmas music played in the formal sitting room, and I could hear my mother on the phone, talking quietly. I was pretty sure I heard my name, so I decided not to go in there. Instead, I'd follow the laughter because I recognized it. It made my whole body tingle and go warm. It was Finn.

Laughing. Actually *laughing*.

I crept into the room, my breath held. My dad, the same man who told me he didn't want Finn and me together, was sitting next to Finn, laughing his butt off at something Finn had apparently just told him. Finn lounged back against the cushions, his casted arm resting against his chest with the help of a sling. He was laughing, too, those blue eyes shining.

So. He'd been drinking again. It's the only time he laughed anymore. He held a mostly empty glass of whiskey in his good hand, and the wound crossing his forehead and creeping into his shaved scalp gave him a ragged appearance. Kinda piratical. All he needed was a hoop earring and some buckskin pants. It was hot. His black tattoos stood out against his paler-than-normal skin, and his dimples were shining full force. He looked happy—normal, even. I knew better.

It was the alcohol talking.

Finn's dad, Larry, was also there, but he wasn't laughing. He was watching Finn with the same concern I felt. The same undying certainty that all was not quite perfect under that flawless smile and never-give-up attitude he kept showing to the world.

"Did that actually happen?" Larry asked, smiling when Finn looked at him. Playing the part, just like me. Was that how I looked? Scared when Finn wasn't looking, and perfectly content when he was? I had a feeling I did. "Or are you making that up?"

I came more into the room, forcing a smile. "What did I miss?"

Dad stood up and held his arms open, a grin still on his lips. "Griffin here was just telling me a story about his buddy from overseas. He was apparently scared of spiders."

"Really?" I hugged Dad. Crossing the room, I bent down, kissed Larry's forehead, and squeezed his hand. Last, but not least, I turned to Finn. "What kind of big, scary fighter is scared of spiders?"

Finn's smile slipped for a fraction of a second. He lifted his glass to his lips, drained it, and smiled up at me as if he didn't spend half the night pacing in his room instead of sleeping. As if he didn't wake up screaming every night.

As if I didn't know all about it.

"That's what we said to him," he said lightly. "But he was. We found that out one night, for sure."

I sat down beside Finn, resting my hand on his knee. He had one leg bent over the other, so it was the perfect snuggling position. He wrapped his good arm around me, his gaze shifting to my dad before he hugged me close. When he held me like this, I almost believed the façade he showed the world. Almost believed we were okay.

"Did you put one on his pillow to mess with him?" Dad asked.

He was being polite, but now that I was here, next to Finn, I could hear the tension in his voice. He didn't approve, but he knew forbidding it wouldn't work, so he was being quiet…for now. I couldn't help but wonder how long that silence would last.

"I did," Finn admitted, a side of his mouth quirking up into a lopsided grin. "When he came into the room, I laid there as if I didn't have a clue what the hell was going on."

Larry shook his head. "I'm sure he was pissed when he saw the beast on his bed."

"He screamed like a little girl." Finn's hand flexed on my shoulder. He gave a long, hard look at the empty glass on the table before turning back to his dad. "That was the second to last day we were there. He didn't sleep the whole night."

Which meant the next day, the guy Finn was talking about had been killed. And Finn had watched it happen. My heart twisted, and I looked up at him. He stared off into the distance, his brow furrowed. He looked lost. I wished I could find him.

Dad cleared his throat. "And that was that."

"Yes, that was that," Finn rasped. He seemed to shake himself, and then he was back on earth again. "He was scared to surf, too. I told him I'd teach him sometime."

"You're an excellent teacher," I said.

"Wait." Dad sat up straighter. "How would you know how good of a surfing teacher he may or may not be?"

I froze. "Uh…"

Finn closed his eyes and sighed. "I taught her."

"You did *what*?" He rose to his feet, his face turning an alarming shade of red. "Griffin Coram, I'll have your skin for—"

"Dad." I glowered at him. "In the scheme of things, do you really think it's that big of a deal? I'm obviously okay."

"*Obviously* okay?" Dad sputtered. "I…he…you…" He cut off. "Argh."

Finn cleared his throat and made as if to rise. "I think that's my cue to grab another whiskey."

"I'll get it." Dad looked at me. "I need the fresh air."

Once my dad left, Finn looked at me and smiled, his blue eyes softening as they usually did when he looked at me. I ran my hand over his head, smiling back at him in return. I used to play with his hair. I missed that. "Oops," I said. "My bad."

"He was bound to find out eventually. Might as well be now," Finn said, reaching out to tug a strand of my hair. "Where'd you go earlier?"

"I picked up your medicine." I reached into my purse and put his bottle of pain pills on the coffee table. I'd be keeping a close watch on how many disappeared. "Remember? I told you before I left."

"I must've forgotten." He ran a hand down his face. "Sorry."

He'd been forgetting a lot of things lately. I wasn't sure if it was from the pills, the booze, or the injury. Maybe a combination of all three. Either way, it kind of freaked me out. "It's okay. Maybe I was wrong and I forgot to tell you."

"Maybe." He shrugged. "Either way, I'm glad you're back now."

Larry stood up. He looked a little bit pale and unsteady. I started to rise, but he shook his head. Finn looked over at him, and Larry gave him a smile. "I'm going to crash early tonight, son. I'm exhausted."

Finn studied him. "You feeling all right, Dad?"

"Yeah, of course. I'm fine," Larry said, shaking his head and chuckling. "Don't you worry about me. You worry about you."

Finn narrowed his eyes. "You look pale. Are you getting sick again?"

"No, not again." Larry headed for the door without looking back. "Good night."

When Finn started to stand, I tugged him back down. "Let him go. He's tired. You can talk to him in the morning."

Finn tensed. "Something's wrong, and he's not telling me. Do you know what it is?"

I was pretty sure Finn's father wasn't doing well. I *thought* it might be something to do with his heart, but I'd never gotten it confirmed. "I don't. I have my suspicions, like you," I said, squeezing his hand. "We'll talk to him together in the morning, okay? Not now."

He nodded and let out a sigh. "You're right. But don't let me forget to talk to him tomorrow. Promise you'll remind me."

I swallowed hard. "I promise." I rested my hand against his cheek, trying to enjoy the moment. "How's the head feeling tonight?"

He met my eyes, relaxing under my touch. "It hurts," he admitted. "A lot."

"Have you had any more pills since I left?"

He shook his head but didn't meet my eyes. "Nope."

"Okay." I hesitated before grabbing his pills. For what had to be the millionth time, I said, "But you've been drinking. You're not supposed to mix—"

"They just say that shit to scare you. I'm fine." His hand shook as he took the bottle from me. He seemed to remember he couldn't open it with one hand, so he held it back out. "Can you help me?"

"Of course." I opened the bottle and poured out a pill, wishing I hadn't asked him how his head felt. I'd had to beg to get a refill for him, since it was a full day too early. "You're not supposed to mix them, and you know it."

"I don't give a damn, and *you* know it." He took a deep breath. With a small grimace, he popped the medicine into his mouth. After he swallowed, he gave me a long, hard look. "I'm fine, Carrie. Don't worry."

I froze, the lid half on. "I didn't say you weren't."

"I watch you all the time. You always look worried, unless you see me watching. Then you laugh and smile." He cupped my cheek and ran his thumb over my lip. "I'm okay. You don't need to worry about me. I'll get through this."

I wished that was true. "I'm not worried about that."

"I know," he said, his tone playful despite the shadows I could see in his eyes. The ones that chased him every night no matter how fast he ran. "I've got you. What more could I possibly need?"

I leaned in and brushed my mouth across his. He tasted like alcohol. "Nothing," I whispered against his lips.

His good hand flexed on my thigh. "Careful. Your dad's coming back any second now."

"He knows about us. Why worry about a kiss?"

"He knows, but he doesn't like it." He leaned back against the couch. "And he definitely doesn't want to see us kissing in his living room." He closed his eyes and pressed his lips together tightly. When he opened his eyes, all signs of tension dissipated. "We won't be here much longer, and then we can go back to normal. We'll be back in California, and I'll be back to annoying you twenty-four-seven."

I smiled, knowing that was what he wanted from me. He loved to make me happy, after all. "I know. I can't wait."

"And, hey, at least I'm home for Christmas. We didn't think I would be." His mouth twisted, and he fingered my sun necklace. "We even celebrated early and everything."

I thought back on the night Finn had created Christmas for me. We'd decorated a tree, shared a romantic dinner, and spent the night in each other's arms. It had been the last time we made love, and the last time I'd seen him *really* smile.

"I know. It was lovely." I kissed him one more time, keeping it short. "Maybe the actual Christmas will be even better. I'll get to show you the present I got for you."

He ran his free hand over his shaved head, touching the shiny, puckered wound. It started at the corner of his eye and then extended to the back of his skull. I knew he was self-conscious about it, but he shouldn't have been. He was gorgeous as always. "I don't think it will top our other one. I can't even use my fucking arm, and we won't be alone.

There won't be any hot holiday sex to finish off the night."

"Oh, I think you could do plenty of damage with just the one arm," I teased, running my hand over his chest. I placed my palm right over the spot where he'd gotten our tattoo. "And if not, well, you can still hold me. That's all I need to be happy. Your arms around me, and us together. Fighting the world as a team."

"You and me against the world, right?" Meeting my eyes hesitantly, he looked down at where my hand rested. His were blazing with heat, desire, and love. He leaned in and rested his forehead against mine, taking a shaky breath. "I love you so fucking much, Carrie."

My heart melted and I blinked back tears. This was the first time he was acting like my Finn, and it was breaking my heart. "I know. I love you, too."

"I don't know what I did to deserve you." His fingers moved to the back of my head, cradling me and holding me closer. "I hope I don't fuck it up."

"You won't." I pulled back and smiled at him, trying to show him there was nothing—*nothing*—he could do to send me running. "We've been over this before. I'm not going anywhere."

He drew in a ragged breath. "I didn't deserve you when I was whole, and I definitely don't deserve you now, looking like Frankenstein's monster."

"*Finn.*" I ran my hand over his head, scowling at him. "Don't you ever say that again. You're perfect. We're perfect." I lightly kissed the spot where his injury started. "And a few scrapes isn't going to ruin that. You're as hot as ever."

He let out a small sound and caught my mouth with his. It was the first time *he* kissed *me* since he came home. Every other time, I'd been the one initiating it, and he'd been pushing me away. He always had a good reason for doing so, but it didn't change the fact that it was true. He was pushing me away, and I couldn't do anything to stop him.

Footsteps approached, and my dad came into the living room. Finn let go of me as if I were diseased and stood shakily. Dad handed him a drink and looked at me. He scanned my face, his brows lowered. Finn took the drink and inclined his head. "Thank you, sir. If you don't mind, I'll take this up to my room. I just took a pill, and I'll be tired soon."

I stood up. "I'll come and—"

"No. I'm fine." Finn offered me a smile, but the real smile I'd gotten earlier was gone. In its place was the one I'd gotten all too used to. "Spend time with your dad. I'll see you in the morning when the sun's shining nice and bright. Maybe we can go out to breakfast."

I watched him go. He snatched up an entire bottle of whiskey off the side table as he passed it, and walked out into the hallway. He was going to drink himself to sleep again. He'd still wake up screaming, though. I knew it and so did he. Or maybe he didn't. Maybe he'd forgotten about his night terrors.

I hadn't.

I took a step after him, planning on ripping it out of his hands, but Dad grabbed my arm. "Let him go. He needs some time alone," Dad said, reaching out and squeezing my hand. "I don't like you two together, and you know that, but I'm telling you this much for your own sake. He needs time and space to accept what happened to him over there, and you need to give it to him. Let him drink. Let him sleep. He'll come out of it."

"But I don't think he needs space." I swallowed hard. "I think he needs me."

Dad flinched. "I think he needs you, too, but not right now. He's not ready yet."

"Why are you telling me this?"

"Because you're my daughter, and I love you." Dad stood. "And because I won't be the one to break you two up. Unfortunately, I think he'll be able to do that just fine without my help."

I stiffened. "We're *not* breaking up."

Dad rested his hand on my shoulder. "Even you have to see the changes already. If you want to make this thing between you work, give him space. He needs it. And pray that he comes out of this resembling the guy he once was."

"How do I know you're not telling me what's worse for him so we break up?"

He hesitated before heading for the doorway. "You don't. You'll have to just trust that I know what's best for you—and him."

He left, and I was alone for all of two seconds before my mom came in. "Did the men abandon you?" Mom asked, her phone still in her hand. She sat beside me, grabbing the remote and switching on the television.

"Did I hear you went shopping without me?"

I forced a smile. "Just to CVS. Nothing too exciting."

"Oh. Well, *Downton Abbey* is on. You know how much I love that show." And it was on the only pre-approved channel in this house: PBS. Educational and political all at once. "Want to watch with me?"

I sighed and settled into the corner of the couch, pulling a throw blanket over my lap. "Sure. Put it on."

As Mom started the show, I glanced over my shoulder. I wanted nothing more than to chase after Finn, take away the whiskey, and hold him until he was better. But something told me Dad was right this time. I probably couldn't fix him with a hug. And maybe it was time to accept one thing about this whole mess.

He needed more help than I could give him.

CHAPTER THREE

Finn

Bombs exploded all around me, punctuated only by the screams of the dying men. I could smell the blood. Taste the fear. Feel the pain. I was sent back there again, living through the attack while everyone else died. But at the same time, I also *knew* I wasn't there anymore. I was in bed, alive and safe—unlike the rest of my squad. It was almost like an alternate universe where I wasn't sure what was real and what wasn't.

Which haunted me now: Nightmare or reality?

I sat upright, my eyes scanning my surroundings. Lightly painted walls and expensive furniture surrounded me instead of blood and bombs. Another nightmare. I'd been stuck in the same hell I was in every night, and no matter how much I drank, nothing made it go away. Nothing saved me. I was starting to think nothing could.

I must have been tossing and turning in my sleep, because my broken arm throbbed like a bitch. My sheets had tangled themselves around my bare feet like a noose, but even so I was still covered with sweat. My door opened and closed. I turned toward it, breathing heavily. It would be Carrie. It was always Carrie. She always calmed me down. Always took care of me.

I loved her for it, but I hated the need for it at the same time.

"Are you all right?" Carrie sank on the bed beside me, her hands reaching for my one good one. "You were having the dream again, weren't you?"

I flopped back down, hating that she was seeing me like this. Scarred. Weak. Broken. Scared. Maybe I should start gagging myself when I went to bed. Or just give up sleeping altogether. "I'm fine," I said, my voice a lot harder than I'd wanted it to be. "Just fucking relax."

She stiffened. If this had been before I'd been fucked up, she would have snapped back at me. Given me as good as I gave her. But she was walking on eggshells around me. Pampering me. I just wanted her to fight with me and be my stubborn Carrie. I wanted that easy camaraderie back so bad that it hurt more than my arm and my head combined.

She nodded, nibbling on her lower lip. "I'm sorry. I—"

"*Don't.*" I rolled out of the bed. "Don't apologize to me again."

"Excuse me?"

"You keep apologizing when I'm the one being a prick. Stop it."

She shook her head. "You're not being a 'prick.'"

"Yeah. I am."

She stood up, too, and curled her hands at her sides. "I know you're stressed and not sleeping well. It's okay to be a little cranky after what you experienced."

"A little bit *cranky*?" I locked the door. "That's the understatement of the damn century."

She ignored me. Just lifted that stubborn chin of hers higher. "I know this is hard for you to deal with, so I'm not going to fight with you, no matter how hard you try to piss me off."

"You never do anymore, Carrie." I crossed the room slowly, never taking my eyes off her. "You're too scared to."

She bit down on her lip. I watched her, studying the curve of that lip. I loved that little pink mouth of hers. And suddenly, I wanted to taste it. No, *needed* to taste it. Wanted to feel normal for one fucking minute of today, before I lost myself in the agony that wouldn't leave me alone. Wanted to go back to how I'd been, instead of what I'd become. "I'm not scared of you, Finn. But tell me, what do you want from me? You want me to fight with you?"

"Sometimes, yes. But not right now—not anymore." I stepped closer. "Right now? I want you. Nothing more. Nothing less."

"*Finn.*" She held her hands out. "You already have me."

"No. I had you." I shook my head. "But I haven't *had* you since I've come back."

Comprehension lit her eyes, and she flushed. "Then you can have me." She closed the distance between us, reaching up to close her palms around the back of my neck. "What are you dreaming about every night? Tell me about it. Talk to me."

Talk? I didn't want to fucking talk. I wanted to *feel*. Forget. Move on. "I c-can't, Carrie." I shook my head, dissipating the bloody images she'd brought to life with her words. "I'll tell you anything you want to know about anything else, but I can't talk about that night. Not to anyone."

"Okay. Okay." She made a soothing sound, as if I were a baby or some shit like that. That needed to end right fucking now. I was a man. A broken man, but a man nonetheless. "You're not ready."

"I never *will* be ready," I managed to say through my suffocating anger. "It's not something I'm willing to relive through conversation. I already see it every night, and that's enough for me."

She shook her head. "But if you talk to someone, it helps."

"Yeah, well, you're not a therapist."

A flash in her eyes answered me before she even opened her mouth. A hint of the real Carrie shined through. About damn time. "No, but I *am* going to school for it."

"Occupational."

She pressed her lips together. "Still—"

"Nope. Not happening."

She narrowed her eyes on me. "You don't have to talk to me if you don't want to, but you need to talk to someone. It will help you recover."

Recover, my ass. Therapists made you talk because it made them money. End of story. It wouldn't help me. Wouldn't fix me. They'd just tell me to pop some pills and call me healed. Bullshit. I would do it my way, in my own time. "I'm already recovering."

She pursed her lips. "I'm not talking about the visible injuries, Finn."

"Yeah, well, they are the only ones that matter, as far as I'm concerned." I hauled her closer. "Can you ever want me again, even with how scarred I am now?"

She shook her head, and for a second my worst nightmare came to life. "Finn, I never stopped wanting you, and I never will." She rested her hands on my chest, and I almost collapsed from the relief surging through me. "So how can I possibly answer if I'd ever want you again?"

I tried to believe that. Tried to be optimistic like I'd been before I went overseas and almost got blown to pieces like the rest of my buddies. But she had the benefit of not seeing inside my head. She didn't know just how far gone I was—so she was still blissfully optimistic. Her world still had rainbows and butterflies and all that shit.

But me? I saw it all, and part of me thought it might be better for her if I walked away. But we'd promised to stay with each other. Promised no more running or lies.

Her eyes lowered, and her stare lingered over my abs before dipping even lower. Good. She could see what I fucking wanted right now—*her*. I wanted to remind her why she was with me, since she probably couldn't see it anymore. Not when she looked at my wounds.

All she saw was what I used to be.

She hesitated. "Finn, I don't know if you're ready yet…"

"Why wouldn't I be ready?" I stepped closer, and she tilted her face up toward mine. Her pupils flared, and she bit down on her lower lip again. "I've been ready since I met you."

Her mouth twitched into a reluctant smile. "You know what I mean. With people recovering from trauma, sex can be a trigger. It can make things worse. I don't want to make you suffer—"

"The only way I'll suffer," I cupped her face with my good hand, my thumb under her jawline, "is if you say no. So don't say no."

Part of me needed to know she still wanted me, scars and all. She might be right, and this might not be good for my head, but fuck it. I needed it. I needed *her*.

Carrie

I knew this wasn't a good idea. But when he looked down at me like that, all blue eyes and soft words, I couldn't stop myself from giving him what he wanted—even if it wasn't what he *needed*. The two didn't always go hand in hand, did they?

Reaching up on tiptoe, I curled my hands around his neck and kissed him, keeping it light and easy. I didn't want to scare him off or be too pushy. I didn't need to worry, I guess. He backed me across the room, his breath coming fast, his hand flexing on my chin. I knew he was frustrated with feeling helpless and broken, and I wished I could help him.

Wished he would let me help him.

I spun him so his back was toward the bed and pushed him gently onto it. Good thing he'd locked the door. As long as we were quiet, no one should know what we were up to. I straddled him, skimmed my hands up under his shirt, and sighed with satisfaction even as it bugged me that he was wearing a shirt. He never used to sleep with a shirt on. Was he hiding his wounds from himself, too? It seemed that way.

I pulled back and studied him. His eyes were shut, and his cheeks flushed. He looked so freaking hot like this. Turned on and ready for me. All mine. "Are you sure you're ready?"

He smoothed my hair off my face. "Of course I'm sure."

"Okay." I reached for the bedside light, but he snatched my hand before I could turn it on. "What? What is it?"

"No lights," he rasped, his fingers tightening on mine. "I like it like this."

"Finn…" I swallowed hard. "You don't need to hide from me."

"I'm not. I don't want your dad to know." He let go of my hand and hauled me closer. "That's all."

I wanted to believe him, but I didn't. He hadn't let me see him yet. Hadn't even taken his shirt off in front of me. But I couldn't push it. Couldn't push him. "Okay."

I kissed him, holding myself back again. I wasn't sure how to be with him when he was being like this. Should I be bold? Or should I let him take the lead? I was out of my league here, and I knew it. He broke off the kiss and cursed under his breath before saying, "If you don't want this from me anymore, then you can leave. I understand."

"I want this." I tried to kiss him again, but he didn't let me. "Finn, what's wrong?"

"You're acting as if you can't stand the thought of kissing me," he rasped, his hand flexing on my hip. "I get it. I'm fucked up now and—"

I slammed my mouth down on his, shutting him up before he insulted himself again. It was killing me to act as if he was going to break at any point, and I was done listening to him put himself down. Freaking *done*. He was gorgeous, injuries and all.

His mouth opened under mine, so I slid my tongue inside, seeking his. As soon as I found it, heat shot through my body, making me tremble.

I deepened the kiss, needing more of him. Needing to kiss him, touch him, love him. It had been too long since I'd gotten to kiss him like this. Feel him like this.

His uninjured hand skimmed up my side before running down my arm. I shivered and ran my hands down his pecs, to the waist of his boxers. He arched his hips a little bit, pressing his erection against my core. God, that felt good. *So* good. For the first time since he'd come home, I wasn't thinking of him as Finn, injured Marine.

He was my Finn, and I needed him as badly as he needed me.

"Fuck," he moaned, arching into me again. "Lose the clothes."

"Yours first." I slid down his body, pressing my open mouth against his neck.

He gripped my hair tight, holding me in place. "Help me get these off."

I closed my hands over his boxers and nipped at his abs through the shirt. He hissed and tightened his grip on my hair. I wished I could see him right now. See him watching me with those blazing blue eyes I loved so much. But for now, quiet and rushed would have to do. I lowered his boxers over his hips, and he helped me get them off by lifting his hips slightly. I tossed them off the bed and climbed between his legs. "Condom?"

"Drawer," he said, his voice strangled. "Left side, top."

I didn't bother to ask him when and how they'd gotten there. I climbed over him and retrieved one, but didn't put it on him yet. I lifted his shirt and licked his abs, grinning when he groaned. I loved driving him insane. Loved making him squirm with need. Loved *him* so much it hurt. I skimmed my hands up his thighs while flicking my tongue over the head of his cock. My cheeks heated as I did so, knowing I was totally disobeying pretty much every rule my parents had laid down when they allowed Finn to stay here to recover…

And not even caring a little bit about it.

He gripped my hair, begging for more without making a sound. I closed my mouth around him, swirling my tongue over the smooth skin of his erection. He squirmed, moving restlessly against the white sheets. "*Carrie.*"

I sucked him in deeper, taking as much of him into my mouth as I could, and yet still wanting more. I'd never get sick of this. Never get sick of him. I cupped his balls, squeezing gently as I increased the suction, going up and down with perfect timing.

He let out a ragged moan, but bit it back abruptly. It brought me back to a time when he'd teased me about being too loud in bed. He'd proceeded to prove his point by making me scream his name repeatedly, and I'd done so quite happily. It had been back when we'd thought we were going to D.C. together. Before he deployed.

My heart squeezed tight at the memory. Of his laughter ringing in my ears on that day. He'd been so light. So free. I didn't think he'd ever be that way again.

"*Carrie*. I need you so damn much." He threaded his hand in my hair and tugged me up his body. "Kiss me. Love me."

My heart twisted at the need in his voice. I couldn't help it. "Always."

I kissed him, making sure to not press my weight on his broken arm, while putting all the emotions I couldn't put into words into that kiss. He didn't want to talk about anything, and that was fine for now. But he needed to know I was *here*. Needed to know I wasn't leaving. His lips hesitated under mine, almost as if he was receiving my message loud and clear, and then he groaned and held me against his body as tight as he could with a casted arm between us.

Then he let go and picked up the condom, ripping it open with his teeth before holding it out to me. "Put this on me."

I took it and rolled it down his cock with trembling hands. Once the condom was firmly in place, I tried to kiss him again, but he pressed his fingers against my mouth. "Get naked first. Then I'll make you come so many times you'll lose count. It's been too long."

He was always alpha in bed—and out of it—but this was different. And it was hot. I slid off the bed and quickly stripped out of my pajama pants and tank top. Next, I shimmied out of my underwear. I stood there for a second, knowing I was silhouetted in the moonlight for him. And he seemed to appreciate the view, judging from the way his voice rasped when he said, "Get back here now."

I climbed onto the bed, my heart racing as I crawled between his legs and kissed him again, my bare butt in the air. It felt decadent to be so casual about what we were doing—and where we were doing it. He curled his hand around the back of my head and hauled me closer, kissing me passionately. My stomach twisted into a tight coil, demanding more.

Demanding what I knew he could give me. It had been so long. *Too* long. And I needed more. I let out a moan of my own when he dipped his hand between my thighs, finding my clit easily. He rubbed two fingers against me in a circular motion, applying the perfect pressure to send me over the edge.

He broke off the kiss and bit down on my shoulder, drawing a ragged gasp from my lips. "*Finn.*"

"You like that?" he asked, his voice rough and low. "You want more?"

"God, yes." I dug my nails into his sides, making sure that I didn't bump against his injury as I squirmed. "*More.*"

He rubbed my clit rougher, making me bite back a scream. God, I was so close. I could feel the pressure building higher and higher, and soon I would break. He knew it, too. I could tell by the way he was playing with me. Torturing me.

It was oh-so-delicious and incredibly frustrating.

I didn't know whether to beg for mercy, or kick his butt for doing this to me.

"Did you touch yourself while I was gone?" He increased the pressure. "Did you rub your fingers against yourself and pretend it was me? Did you come with my name on your lips?"

I groaned and moved my hips restlessly. I was almost there. Almost to heaven. Part of his words didn't even register with me. I was that far gone. "I…I can't talk like that."

"Answer me." He thrust a finger inside me, and I whimpered and buried my face in his neck. I had to be quiet. Had to make sure no one knew what we were doing. "Did you fuck yourself when I was gone?"

Of course I had, but it had never felt like this. Only he made me feel this good. But I couldn't tell *him* that. "J-Just keep touching me. Don't…" I moved against his fingers, straining to get even closer. "You…dare… stop."

And then he did. He stopped touching me. Just hovered there, almost brushing against me, but remaining still. Yeah. I was going to beg for mercy. Then, after I was done, I'd kill him. "Tell. Me."

"*Finn.*" I grabbed his hand and pressed it back where I wanted it. No, where I *needed* it. He couldn't stop now. Not when I was so close. "Please."

"Tell me the truth, and then I will."

"Y-Yes. I did it, okay?" I moaned when he rubbed me again, but too lightly. Not enough. Not nearly enough. I knew I was being too loud, but even knowing it didn't make me stop. "Finn, please."

"You touched yourself and imagined it was me?" He nibbled on my neck and thrust a finger inside me again. Thank freaking God. "Was it my lips or my fingers when you did it?"

I whimpered, low and desperate. "Your lips. Always your lips."

His fingers stilled. "Then I can't disappoint you now." His hand was gone, and I wanted to shout, scream, and cry. He slapped the side of my ass. "Climb on top."

"I am on…" Comprehension lit up within me, as well as desire. So much desire. "You don't mean for me to…"

"I do." He tugged my leg. "Hurry the fuck up. I need to taste you. To make you come on my mouth."

I trembled just from the words. And the image…oh my God, the image that gave me. I wanted it *now*. I positioned myself so I straddled him, a knee on either side of his head—and clear of his injured arm—and then lowered myself to his face. It was so dirty and raw and right. So freaking right.

God, yes.

His tongue touched my clit, and I closed my hands over the top of the headboard so tight it hurt my palms, and dropped my head against the light blue wall. God, this must look so hot. Him under me, with me basically sitting on his face. We'd never done it this way. It was different and amazing. And oh my God…

His good hand cupped my butt, his fingers digging in enough to hurt just enough, and his mouth moved over my clit with the perfect amount of pressure. I stopped thinking, stopped picturing this, and just lost myself in his touch. The tightness in my belly grew harsher, focusing on his mouth moving over me.

His tongue, his teeth, his hands…

Everything within me gathered real close before exploding in fragments of pleasure and need. I collapsed with my forehead against the wall, and he kept his tongue pressed against my sensitive clit as I came back down from the high he'd given me. By the time I could gather my thoughts, he moved his tongue, which was featherlight and almost nonexistent on me.

I came again, explosive and hard. Much harder than the first time.

I tore free of his grip when he tried to keep going down on me, and he let me. I slid down his body, kissing him hard. He tasted more like me than him, but I didn't care. I needed him. Needed this. I positioned his cock at my entry and lowered myself on him, swallowing his groan with my mouth.

His hand gripped my hip while his broken arm rested on his chest, and he urged me to move faster. I didn't have any complaints about that. I pumped my hips fast and hard, my breathing growing more and more fevered with each thrust. His fingers dug into my thigh, and a tortured groan came from him as he tensed beneath me.

I closed my eyes and moved even faster. I was *so* close to coming again. I could feel it. Taste it. Sense it. I pressed my mouth to his and lost myself in the pleasure, the kiss, and him. The orgasm took me by surprise, even though I'd known I was close. But it felt different this time. More whole. As if it was more intense than ever before, and maybe it was.

He froze beneath me, his back curved and his fingers tight on me, and then he collapsed onto the mattress, his breathing unsteady and hard. I melted against his chest, my head on his good shoulder and my hand curled under his neck. "Wow."

His hand flexed on me. "Yeah," he rasped.

Something in his voice told me he wasn't all right. I lifted my head and checked his broken arm. I hadn't been lying on it or anything. I tried to search the darkness to see his face, but I could only make out vague shapes. I couldn't see him. "Are you all right? I didn't hurt you, did I?"

He laughed, but it wasn't his laugh. It was strained. "I'm fine. I'm just tired, that's all."

"Oh." I scooted off him. "You'd tell me if you weren't all right, right? We promised, no more lies."

"Honestly? I don't think you'd want to know whether I was lying right now." He stood up, removed the condom, and came back to the bed. "You don't need to know everything that's in my head. I just need time to adjust."

That's exactly what my father had said. That he needed time.

"Okay. Then I'll give it to you. Just know I'm here to talk, or whatever."

After a second of hesitation, he lay back down and wrapped his arm around me before kissing my forehead. "I know you are. If I need to talk, I'll let you know."

"That's all I can ask for, minus one thing."

He stiffened. "What?"

"Don't lie to me again." I propped myself on my elbows. "Whatever happens, whatever you go through, just don't lie to me. I can handle a lot, but not that."

He nodded slowly, his shadowed face intent on mine. "Okay. No lies. But don't ask me things I'm not ready for. The stuff that happened over there…"

His voice cracked, but he cleared his throat to hide it. It broke my heart that he was so vulnerable, yet unwilling to show it. "I won't push," I promised. "Not yet."

"I can't talk about it." His jaw flexed. "I won't."

"Okay." I scooted up and kissed him. "Want me to stay until you fall asleep?"

He hesitated. "Would it make me less of a man if I said yes? If I admitted I needed you more than I need medicine? You're the reason I keep going. You're why I'm still here, instead of in that fucking nightmare I can't escape."

My heart… Yep. It totally melted.

"Nope, not at all." I sat up and pulled the covers over us before settling back down on the pillow. It was weird, in a way, how you went from sitting on a guy's face to snuggling under the covers and holding each other for support. "It would make you the man I love more than anything."

His fingers flexed on my hip, and he nodded. "Are you too tired?"

I was freaking exhausted. I'd been sitting up with him almost every night. But if he knew that, he'd send me away. His sleep was more important than mine, so I lied. Ironic, considering I'd just lectured him about not lying to *me*.

This was different. He needed me here.

"Nope. Wide-awake. I had coffee earlier." That much was true.

He smiled. I didn't see it, but I could feel it. "I wish I could manage without sleep like you. I used to be able to…before…"

He broke off. He wasn't going to finish that thought.

I rested my hand over his heart. "You'll get there again."

"I know." He yawned, loud and long. "It'll happen soon."

I smiled and ignored the tears in my eyes. "Get some rest. I'm here with you, and I'm not going anywhere."

"And neither am I," he whispered sleepily.

CHAPTER FOUR

Finn

The next afternoon, I stood at the window, watching the snow fall to the snow-covered lawn, and let myself breathe it in. I'd dozed off on the sofa for a little while after eating my lunch, and I'd woken up sweating and screaming. Not knowing exactly where I was or even if I'd live. Like fucking usual.

Good thing no one had been here to see or hear it. It was bad enough *I* knew about my weakness—I didn't need Senator Wallington knowing too. He'd already warned me he wouldn't stand by and watch me hurt his daughter when he'd visited me in the hospital in Germany. His words may have been cryptic, but they were crystal clear.

I know you love my girl, Griffin. And I know she loves you, too. I get why you fell for her. Who wouldn't? It doesn't mean I'm happy about it, though. Or that I'll accept it. Get well, son. For both of our sakes.

That last part? Yeah, it meant "get better, or get the hell out of her life." I knew it. He knew it. And I wasn't getting better. Not yet. Maybe not ever. My good hand tightened on the coffee mug I held. I wanted something stronger. Something to take the pain away. But I resisted, for Carrie.

I'd gone through hell and back to keep her at my side.

I wouldn't…no, I *couldn't* lose her.

A car pulled up, and I narrowed my eyes. It wasn't Carrie or her parents. They were out getting a Christmas tree. They'd waited till the last minute since Carrie hadn't been home to go with them until a few days ago. I'd stayed behind because walking around in the freezing cold with an aching arm while the senator frowned at me wasn't the best thing for me. Carrie had tried to stay behind but I'd insisted she go.

She needed to spend time with them before we went home. Needed to feel normal as badly as I did. I knew it, so I made her leave by telling her I wanted to nap.

I had. Then I'd had a nightmare. Go fucking figure.

The red Porsche parked at the front, but I couldn't see who got out of it. I made my way over to the front door just in time for the butler to open it. "They're not at home, Mr. Stapleton."

"I know. Carrie texted me and told me, but I thought I'd stop by and wait." He laughed. "She told me she wouldn't be much longer because they're freezing outside."

"Ah, well, come in. You can wait in the family living room, if you'd like."

I stood in the shadows, waiting to see who the fuck this was. Carrie had been texting him, but I didn't know a single thing about him. "Thank you, George."

He knew the butler's name?

"Can I get you a cocktail?" George asked.

Another laugh. "I'd love a whiskey, if you don't mind."

I stepped closer. There was a shuffling sound, and then a tall blond guy stepped through the door. He was handsome, had bright green eyes, and was wearing an impeccable blue sweater and a pair of khakis. He looked...fucking perfect, damn it.

He was everything I wasn't right now. Who the hell *was* he?

He pulled off his scarf and kept talking to George, but I didn't hear a word. I was too busy trying not to be jealous of a guy I didn't even know. He laughed and turned my way...and the smile faded. He looked me up and down, concern clear in his eyes. I *knew* I looked like hell. I *knew* I was a wreck. But seeing him looking at me as if he felt sorry for me?

Fuck no. Not happening.

"Hi," he said, hesitating. He crossed the room and held out his hand, offering me his non-dominant hand since he knew I couldn't use my broken arm. How thoughtful of him. "I'm Riley. You must be Griffin, right?"

Son of a bitch, he was nice, too.

I knew right away, within seconds of eye contact, that while this guy was rich, he was *not* another Cory. This guy was kind and seemed to be a guy that even I could like, under different circumstances. In fact, even I had to admit he was the perfect guy for Carrie…

If it wasn't for *me* being in the way.

"It's Finn," I managed to say without my voice cracking. I set my mostly empty coffee mug down on the side table and shook his hand, not dropping his stare. He was sizing me up, and I had a feeling he'd find me lacking. So I stared right the fuck back. I wasn't one to back down, even when I was clearly the one who lost this battle. My mind was not whole, and neither was my body. "And you are…?"

"Riley Stapleton." He was a little shorter than me, but not by much, and he was strong. His grip didn't relax on mine at all, even though I didn't let go of him as quickly as I should have. "I'm a friend of Carrie's, and our dads are political affiliates."

I nodded and released him. He watched me with bright green eyes. His flawless skin and impeccably styled hair made me run a hand over my own roughly shaved head, ending up on my long, jagged cut. "I've never heard of you."

He smiled easily. "It's not too surprising. I didn't really become friends with Carrie till the holiday party. And after that, she left and stayed with you. We've only been talking via text and phone." He nodded toward my arm, his eyes warm and compassionate. "I hear you're doing better?"

"Oh yeah. Much." I looked him up and down, trying to dislike him on principle, but failing. He genuinely seemed to care. Un-fucking-believable. "So you were there when the call came in about me?"

"I was."

I flinched. "How bad was it?"

"It was pretty bad," Riley admitted, laughing lightly before motioning me into the living room. "Please. Let's sit. I don't want to tire you. Carrie would be angry with me."

Tire me? What was I, a fucking baby? "I'm fine."

"Still. Let's sit."

Damn it, I should have been the one to invite him to sit, since I kinda sorta lived here. I should have been polite and mannerly, and invited him inside. Instead, I'd questioned him in the foyer like a dickhead. I led him into the opulent room, hovering by the couch awkwardly while Riley seated himself. I sat beside him, letting my broken arm rest against my chest, and gripped my knee with my hand.

George came in with two glasses of whiskey and set them in front of us. He left the bottle behind and I knew it was because of me. One drink wouldn't hurt, would it? I eyed it, knowing I wanted it way too badly and unable to stop myself from picking it up. I drained it in one gulp, turning to Riley with more confidence. I wasn't used to this feeling. It fucking sucked.

I felt inferior and incompetent in the face of such perfection.

"So." I looked at him again. He'd been watching me drink. When I met his eyes, he quickly looked away and picked up his own whiskey. "You're a friend of Carrie's, huh?"

"I am." Riley's hand tightened on his crystal glass. "You don't need to worry about me, man. I'm not after her or anything."

I blinked at him. "I never said you were."

"I just wanted to make that clear. I mean, she's a great girl, and you're a lucky guy." Riley looked down at his drink and shrugged. "But anyone with eyes can see she loves you, and I've never come between a guy and a girl before. I won't be starting now."

"You don't get why she loves me though, right?" I poured more whiskey with a trembling hand. "You don't understand why we work."

Riley let out an uneasy laugh. "I get it perfectly fine." Riley reclined against the couch and watched me. I half expected to see criticism in his eyes. Or judgment. There wasn't, damn it. "You seem like a good guy. Why would I question that?"

"I'm not one of you." I motioned down his body. "I'm different."

"Different is good sometimes." Riley took a small sip. I forced myself not to gulp down the contents of my whole glass. "I'm not like her father any more than she is. Don't assume I am just because I run in the same circles."

I set the bottle down and raised the glass to my lips. As I drank, I thought on his words. He was right. I was judging him, and that wasn't fair of me. "I'm sorry."

Riley started. "Excuse me?"

"You're right. I shouldn't make assumptions." I lifted my glass to him and tried to brush my prejudice and insecurities aside. "If you're a friend of Carrie's, you're a friend of mine."

He seemed surprised at my about-face. "Uh, good." He shifted his weight. "How's the arm doing?"

I looked down at the sling. "Still broken."

"That's unfortunate," Riley said dryly, amusement in his eyes. "Maybe tomorrow it won't be?"

"Maybe." I smiled. I couldn't help it. "What do you do when you're not here?"

Riley took another sip. "I'm still in college. Upstate California, but I'll be finished with my bachelor's degree soon. Then next year I'll be moving to Southern California for my master's and doctorate."

So he'd be by Carrie and me soon. Fucking fabulous. "Let me guess, somewhere really close to the University of California in San Diego?"

"Yeah." Riley flushed and looked out the window, so I took the opportunity to study him. I tried to picture him as this villain who was out to steal my girl, but I couldn't. I really wanted to, but it wasn't there. "That's the plan anyway."

I nodded even though he wasn't looking at me. "I plan on starting at Carrie's school soon, too."

Riley turned back to me. "Oh yeah? What major?"

"Uh…" I racked my memory for what I'd decided to do, but the word wouldn't come. I knew it, but my fucking mind wouldn't work. Another side effect of being almost blown to pieces, I guess. I couldn't remember a damn thing. "I'm still deciding. Things got a little confused when I came home like this."

Riley nodded. "I can see why. I wish you all the best of luck, man."

"What are you going for?"

"Law, of course." Riley twisted his lips. "My father wouldn't have it any other way."

I was about to ask him what he would do if it weren't for his father, but the front door opened. "Is that Riley's car I see out front?" Senator Wallington asked. "Where are you, boy?"

George cleared his throat. "He's in the living room, sir."

"They're back," Riley said unnecessarily. My brain might be scattered, but it wasn't completely useless. Riley rose to his feet and smoothed his shirt. "You need a refill?"

I looked down at my glass. I hadn't even noticed I'd finished it again. How many had I had? My head was spinning a little bit already. Shit. "No, thank you. I'm fine."

My voice slurred on *fine*. Riley was polite enough to pretend he didn't notice. "All right."

"Riley? Sorry to keep you waiting. We had to search for the perfect tree and—" Senator Wallington stopped in the doorway, his eyes going from me to Riley. I didn't have to be sober to know who he preferred. "Oh. I see Griffin was keeping you company." He eyed the whiskey on the table, and then pointedly looked at my empty glass. "Hopefully you two got along all right."

I flinched. Riley laughed and dragged his hand through his perfect hair. I missed my fucking hair. "How could we not? He was wonderful. Welcomed me into the home with open arms."

"Indeed." Senator Wallington eyed me dubiously. He wasn't flat-out rude, never that. But I knew he didn't like me with Carrie. He tolerated me. Nothing more. "I'm glad to hear it."

I looked past him. "Where's Carrie?"

"She's coming." The senator gave me a tight-lipped smile. "She stopped to talk to your father."

Right. My father. I should have been spending time with him instead of drinking in the living room. I had questions to ask him. "Oh."

Senator Wallington turned to Riley. "Come and see the tree. It's humongous."

"Sure thing." After a quick nod, Riley turned to me. "You coming, Finn?"

I shook my head. I didn't need to go out there with a man who hated my guts to stare at a tree that would be inside the house soon enough. Especially when my head was spinning like a fucking carousel. I'd rather wait for Carrie to come inside. "Nah. Go on without me."

Senator Wallington eyed me suspiciously, but grinned at Riley. "Come on, then."

Riley went outside with him, not looking back again. Unable to resist, I stood at the window and watched him and the senator as they stood next to the car with the tree on the roof. It was fucking *huge*. Would probably fill up my entire apartment.

But in this house? It would be just right.

As I watched, the senator threw his arm around Riley's shoulders and said something that made Riley laugh. He'd never accept me like that. Broken or not, he never would have been so friendly to me. It was time I accepted it. I was second choice.

Hell, probably his last choice.

Riley gestured to the tree while saying something that had the senator grinning. Carrie and her mother came up. While her mother beelined for Riley and the senator, Carrie started for the door. Her father called her over, and she turned to him and walked to the car.

As she talked, she turned to Riley, smiled, and smacked his arm while also laughing at something he said. She didn't hit me anymore. Was probably too scared to hurt me or some shit like that. As a matter of fact, she didn't smile with me anymore. Not like that. I hadn't seen her smile like that for way too long. Not even with me.

But without me?

She looked happy. A hell of a lot happier than she'd been.

I grabbed the bottle of whiskey off the table and stalked out of the living room, out into the foyer, and headed for the servant's entrance into the kitchen. I needed to clear my head. Maybe some fresh air would help me think clearly, since I couldn't seem to do that anymore. Hell, if I was smart, I'd see the one thing that was staring me right in the fucking face, even if I was too selfish to admit it.

She was better off without me.

And she was better off *with* Riley.

CHAPTER FIVE

Carrie

I took my teal cashmere cowl off and peeked into the living room. Empty. Riley came up behind me and helped me remove my coat, and I smiled at him in thanks as I strained to see if Finn was lurking somewhere. He was nowhere to be found, even though he'd been with Riley only minutes before.

Part of me wondered how that had gone. Finn had a tendency not to like guys who were my friends, so it made me think maybe Finn tried to scare Riley off. Or maybe he'd been as taken in by him at the first meeting as I'd been. Something about Riley screamed for you to like him instantly. Outside, he'd been cracking jokes to me about how much my father kept pushing him toward me, despite my very real boyfriend inside the house.

On top of that, he'd told me he'd met—and loved—Finn.

That made me like him even more. He obviously had good taste. "Where were you two hanging out?" I asked him.

"In the living room." Riley hung my coat on the coat stand and motioned me forward. "I'm sure he's still there. Let's go find him."

We walked into the living room, but it was clear he wasn't there anymore. An empty glass sat on the table, but nothing else. "He's not here." I picked it up and sniffed it. Whiskey. So, he'd been drinking. "But he obviously was at one point."

"Yeah. With me." Riley watched me closely. Too closely. "That's my glass, though. Not his."

Hope surged through me. "Oh. He wasn't drinking?"

"He was. He must have cleaned up after himself when he left." Riley shrugged. "He must've put the bottle away, too."

I swallowed hard. He'd probably taken it with him to finish it off. But Riley didn't need to know that. I'd hoped that after last night, he might not feel the need to drink himself into oblivion. I'd hoped... It didn't matter what I'd hoped.

It hadn't happened.

I gave Riley my back while I composed myself. Once I was ready, I turned to him with a bright smile. "I can get you a refill, if you'd like."

"Yes, please." He hesitated, reached for my hand, but dropped it by his side without me having to reject him. Good, because I didn't want to. "Are you okay, Carrie?"

"I'm great," I said, forcing a cheerful note to my voice. "I mean, it's hard to see him like this." I motioned toward the empty glass. "But he's working his way through it. We're working our way through it."

"I didn't ask how *he* was." He stepped closer, watching me from under his lashes. "I asked how you are."

I swallowed past the lump in my throat. "I told you. I'm fine."

"Carrie..." He looked over my shoulder and smiled brightly, changing his tone of voice. "Ah, there you are. We were about to send out a search party for you."

Finn stood in the doorway, watching Riley and me with narrowed eyes. When I smiled at him, he smiled back, but I could see the look in his eyes didn't match. Not at all. If anything, he looked sad. He set down his empty glass, and put the bottle on the table. It was almost empty. "I went looking for my dad, but I couldn't find him."

Riley picked up his cup and headed across the room, talking about having another drink. I trailed behind him, my eyes on Finn. He seemed as if he was being friendly enough. He hadn't called him Miley or anything else that was close to his name, but not quite right. "I was just talking to him when I came home. He went out to the store."

"Oh." He ran his hand over his head. He used to tug on his curls when he was nervous. Is that what he was trying to do? "I would have gone with him if I'd known. He shouldn't be going out alone."

But he hadn't wanted to go shopping with me? I wasn't sure what that meant. "Sorry, I didn't think you'd want to."

He smiled at me. "It's fine. Now I get to spend time with you… and Riley." He popped the lid off the whiskey and poured Riley a good amount. "Can't let you drink alone, now can I?"

Riley grinned. "Course not. Short Stuff over here isn't old enough, so I've only got you."

"Yeah, she's not quite old enough yet," Finn murmured as he poured himself another glass. He watched me as he poured, almost as if he was daring me to say something. To start a fight with him. And, man, I wanted to. "We've had a few discussions about that, though, haven't we, Carrie?"

I curled my hands into balls and bit down on my tongue. Glancing at his glass pointedly, I said, "We have. Too much alcohol is never a good thing."

He laughed. "She thinks I drink too much when I'm stressed out." He turned to Riley and held his glass out for a toast. "Lately, that's been all the time, hasn't it?"

"Finn…" I started, but he threw his arm over my shoulder and hugged me close. I stole a quick look at Riley. He was watching Finn with concern in his gaze. My cheeks heated. "You doing okay?"

"Fabulous now that you're back." He kissed my forehead, his lips lingering. Despite my uneasiness about his current state of mind, my heart flared to life as the gesture. It was so much like something the old Finn would do. "I missed you."

"Did you nap?"

He fingers tightened on his glass. "Yep."

I wanted to ask him if he'd had the nightmare again, but I wouldn't in front of Riley. "Great. So I see you met Riley?"

"I did." Finn led me to the couch, making sure I sat between him and the arm of the couch. Riley sat on Finn's other side. "We were talking about the night you two became friends."

I stole a quick glance at Riley. "Oh yeah?"

"Yep." Riley sipped his drink, looking slightly uncomfortable if his furrowed brow was any indication. "How long are you two staying here?"

"We go back on the thirtieth."

"Is that what we decided?" Finn blinked. "I thought we were leaving on the twenty-seventh."

I shook my head and rested my hand on his thigh. "No, because you have an MRI that morning." I softened my voice. "Remember? I put it on a Post-it."

"No. I don't remember." Finn took a long drink, his leg going hard under my hand. I could practically feel the frustration rolling off him. "How long are you in town, Riley?"

"Through the afternoon of the first. Then it's the red-eye flight back to California that night."

I nodded. "We were going to stay through then, too, but I thought it would be best if we got Finn back to Cali so we could start setting up his physical therapy appointments, and all the other stuff that goes with his injuries." I lifted a hand before letting it fall to my lap. "There's a lot to organize before classes start."

Finn cursed under his breath and stood. "You make me sound like I'm an old man who can't take care of myself. I'm injured, not useless. I can organize it all."

"I know. I didn't mean—"

"I know you didn't mean anything by it, Carrie. It's just that I'm realizing I'm not your boyfriend anymore. I'm a fucking burden." He gripped his head and gave me his back. "You know what? Forget I said that. I think I'm going to excuse myself before I say something else I'll regret."

I lurched to my feet. "Don't go. I'm sorry."

"I told you to stop fucking apologizing to me," he snapped.

"But—"

My dad came up behind Finn. "Is every—?"

Finn whirled on my dad, fist raised, his breathing coming fast. He looked a second away from clocking my dad in the jaw. Dad jumped back, his eyes wide and his hands up in surrender. I ran to Finn's side, and Riley bolted around the couch to Dad. "Finn."

"Shit." Finn covered his face with his good hand. "I'm sorry. You snuck up on me." He shook his head, but didn't drop his hand. "I'm sorry. I'm sorry."

"Shh. It's okay, Finn." I locked eyes with Dad. "It's okay. He's all right."

Dad broke gazes with me, his face pale but otherwise seeming unaffected. "Yes. I'm fine, Griffin."

Finn turned to me and finally showed his face. He looked ravaged. Terrified. *Broken.* It's the first time he'd dropped the act around me, and it hurt so freaking much. I opened my arms, and he dove into them, bending down and hugging me with his good one. "Fuck, Carrie. I'm sorry. I love you. I'm *sorry.*"

"Shh." I hugged him as tight as I could, meeting Riley's gaze over Finn's shoulder. "I'm here with you."

They needed to go. Needed to let Finn recover without an audience. He seemed to get my message. "Mr. Wallington?" Riley said a bit haltingly. "Let's go check on your tree and see if the household staff needs any help. It's a fine tree, if I may say so myself."

Dad looked less than willing, but good manners won out. "Sure thing. Let's go." He started for the door but froze. "Carrie, if you need help, I'll be right out there."

I nodded but didn't answer. I was too busy holding Finn and trying to calm him down. Once we were alone, I kissed the top of his head. "I'm here, and you're okay."

"I'm not okay. I'm *not.*" He clung to me so tightly I could barely breathe. His face was pressed into my chest, but I could still feel him shivering in my arms. "Shit, I can't do this to you anymore. I can't be this guy."

My heart stuttered. "You didn't do anything to me, Finn. I'm fine." I ran my hands over his bald head, skipping over his puckered wound. I didn't know if they still hurt. "You're fine. We'll get through this."

He shook his head but didn't release me. "You don't deserve this."

"Hey. Stop that." I pulled back and forced him to look at me. Cupping his cheeks, I narrowed my eyes on him. "*You* don't deserve this. You went there because you were trying to make life better for us. For me. If anything, this is all my fault. If we hadn't met, and you hadn't loved me, you never would have taken this job." My voice cracked. "Anything you're going through right now, it's on *me.* Not you."

He shook his head frantically. "This isn't your fault. It's mine. I lived. They died." He stared off into the distance. "They all died in front of me. I saw it happen. They all just *died.* Why did I live? Why me?"

I swallowed back a sob. He looked so lost. "Because I need you."

"I need you too." He seemed to snap back into reality. He turned to me and his face softened a fraction. "So damn much, but it's not fair.

459

None of this is fair."

Was it not fair that he needed me, or was he saying it wasn't fair he was still alive? I wasn't sure, and I wasn't sure I really wanted to find out. "I know it's not."

"I can't do this to you," he repeated. "I won't do it. I won't ruin you. I won't take you down with me."

His words filled me with fear. It was as if he was telling me he was leaving. We'd promised to love each other forever. He couldn't leave. I gripped him even tighter. "Stop talking like that. You're scaring me."

"You should be fucking scared of me." He laughed harshly. "*Look* at me."

"I *am* looking at you." I leaned in and kissed him gently, even though my fingers ached to slap him until he stopped talking nonsense. "I'm always looking at you. You're gorgeous, brave, kind, and loving. You're Finn, and I love you just the way you are. Forever, no matter what."

He drew in a ragged breath. "Yeah, but I think you see the old me. Not the 'me' I am now. The *me* I'll always be from now on. The guys died. Every. Single. One."

"But you lived." I shook him a little. "You're here, with me. There's a reason for that, don't you think?"

"I know, but I'm not here," he whispered. "Not really. You'd be better off if I just—"

"Don't you even think about finishing that thought," I hissed. "I'm telling you right now, I won't accept it."

He averted his eyes. "But it's true. You're just too stubborn to admit it."

I pushed him a little bit, anger taking over and making me forget I might hurt him. What had he been about to say? Was he going to say I would be better off if he'd just leave me…or if he'd died? Either way, he was wrong. *So* freaking wrong. "I will kick your ass so fucking hard you won't be able to sit straight for a week. Do you *hear* me?"

That seemed to bring him back to life. His lips even twitched as he turned back to me. "Is that so? A whole week?"

"Yeah. That's so." I curled my hands into fists so hard my nails dug into my palms. "I can't live without you. I can't do anything if you leave me. Don't think it. Don't dream it. Don't even *say* it. I'll never forgive you if you do. Not in a million years. Got it?"

His Adam's apple bobbed as he swallowed. "I hate doing this to you. Hate being fucking broken. This isn't who you fell in love with."

"We're all broken in different ways. You feel shattered now, but it'll get better." I ran my fingers over his jawline. It was so strong. So resilient. Just like him. He didn't realize how strong he still was. "Love is about staying with each other, in sickness and in health. I'm not leaving because you've been injured. And you can't push me away. I won't *let* you do that to us."

His resolve cracked. I could see it, as if it was a physical thing. "Carrie…"

"No. Don't *Carrie* me."

I kissed him, trying to convey the depth of my devotion and love in that simple kiss. He clung to me, making a broken sound in the back of his throat. His hand trembled as he cupped the back of my head, deepening the kiss.

Something crashed behind us and he jumped to his feet, shoving me behind him. Riley stood at the door, his eyes locked on us. "It's just me," he said softly. "I'm going to head out now. The snow is getting pretty heavy."

Finn relaxed marginally. "I'm sorry about earlier. I…well, I'm…"

"Dude." Riley held up a hand. "No explanations needed. Seriously."

Finn gave him a long look and nodded. "Thanks, man."

"Are you sure you can make it home okay?" I glanced out the window. The snow was coming down really heavily now. I felt bad that he'd come all this way to visit us and I'd basically said hi and that was it. "You just got here."

"I'll be fine." Riley smiled. "I might be in California now, but I'm still used to the D.C. winters. I'm not that much of a surfer boy."

No, I only had one surfer boy in my life.

Finn gave him a small smile. "It was nice meeting you. Hopefully the next time we see each other, I'm a little more put together."

"I think you're exactly the way a man should be after going through what you went through." Riley offered his hand. "Take it easy."

Finn shook it. "You too."

"I will." Riley turned to me and hesitated. "Carrie? Want to walk me out?"

I looked at Finn. "I should probably—"

"You should walk him out." Finn let go of me and stepped back, running his hand over his head. "Don't worry. I'll be right here when you get back."

I didn't want to leave him, but I couldn't refuse. That would be rude. "All right."

Riley started for the door, and I fell in to step with him. As we turned the corner, I peeked over my shoulder. Finn stood exactly where I'd left him. All alone.

"He's having a hard time," Riley said under his breath. "Be patient. I had a buddy come back from Iraq like this. He was drinking. Having panic attacks. It lasted for a long time. If he'd had someone who loved him the way you love Finn, then maybe…" Riley shook himself. "Keep being loving and kind, like you're doing. Don't let your dad tell you Finn needs space. He doesn't. He needs you."

I blinked back tears. "Finn thinks I'm better off without him, though. He told me so."

"Right now, he thinks it's true. Men like him push away their loved ones. They think they're failures and not good enough to be loved." Riley opened the front door and grabbed his coat. I followed him outside, hugging myself. "He will keep pushing you away. Just keep pulling him closer."

I nodded and swallowed hard. "I'm trying."

When we reached the front of his car, Riley brushed a finger across my cheek. It came back wet. I hadn't even realized I'd been crying. "Keep trying. And if you need to vent, give me a call. I'm an excellent listener."

I nodded and forced a smile. "Thank you. You're a good friend."

"I know," he teased. "You'd be a fool to not take me up on that offer. I'm a catch."

"Yeah, you are." I laughed. "I should hook you up with someone from my dorm."

"I don't know about that. I'm not ready for love yet."

"You still love your ex?"

He hesitated and avoided my eyes. "Yeah. Something like that."

"Well, when you're ready."

"It's a plan." He opened his car door and started to get in. "Bye, Carrie."

"Wait." I stepped closer. "How long did it take your friend to get better?"

"He didn't. He shot himself in the head a month and two days after he came back home. I found him that way." Riley met my eyes. "Take care of him, Carrie. And watch him closely."

I nodded and walked backward as I watched Riley get into the car, eager to get back to Finn. God, just the thought of him doing something like that…

I couldn't even think it.

CHAPTER SIX

Finn

Ring, ring, ring.

No matter how many times I called, the result hadn't changed. Dad's voicemail picked up, announcing joyfully that he couldn't come to the phone right now. I sighed and hung up without leaving a message. I'd already left him one. The snow kept coming down heavier and heavier, and it would only get worse after sunset.

Hell, even Riley was leaving.

I walked to the window and peeked through it, watching them like a voyeur. Riley had pulled his car up when they'd been carrying the tree inside, so I could see them perfectly from where I stood. When Riley reached out and touched her face, I wanted to scream at him to back the fuck off my girl, but I didn't. I just watched.

They looked good together.

Pushing away from the window, I straightened my spine and grabbed my pills off the table, staring down at the small orange bottle. It was time for another dose, judging from the pain ripping through me.

"You need help with that?" Carrie's mom asked hesitantly.

I jumped, my heart racing. Would I ever stop panicking when someone walked up behind me? Or would I forever be the scared, pansy-ass, shell of a man I'd once been? "Yeah. I can't open it, ma'am."

She approached slowly, as if uncertain of her welcome. "I'll open it for you."

"Thank you," I said, holding it out to her. "I appreciate that."

Senator Wallington followed her into the room, his blue eyes locked on mine. As his wife opened my pain meds, he grabbed an unopened bottle of Aquafina off the bar. My half-eaten turkey sandwich was still there, too. "You'll need this opened, too, I presume?"

I licked my parched lips. I'd rather have a stiff drink, but the water would look better in front of them. God knew I already looked bad enough. "Yes, please, sir."

He twisted the lid off and handed it to me. "You doing all right? Mixing alcohol and pills is generally discouraged."

"I'm fine." In a half an hour or so, I'd be feeling even better. I set the water down. Next, I took the pill from Carrie's mom and popped it in my mouth, watching him the whole time. "Sorry about earlier."

"It's all right." He sat down and crossed an ankle over a knee. "What time is your father expected back? It's getting nasty out there."

"I'm not sure. I called him a few times, but he's not answering." I shifted on my feet, blinking when the room spun. Weird. I didn't remember it doing that before. "I might have to go out and look for him. Maybe Carrie knows where he went."

"Where who went?" Carrie asked, her voice tight. "Sit down, Finn. You look dizzy."

I wasn't dizzy. I was fucking high. But I sat down anyway. She came to my side and curled her hand with mine, holding on tight. She seemed freaked out by something. "My dad. It's getting bad out there, and he isn't answering his phone."

"We can go look for him if you want," she said quickly. "He went to Target."

I nodded. "Let's go. I'm worried he'll—"

"You're not going anywhere," Senator Wallington said, his eyes on Carrie. For a second, I'd thought he was talking to me. "We'll send out security in an all-terrain vehicle. You're not going out in this mess in your Volvo."

"I'll go," I said.

"No, you won't. If you go, *she'll* go." Senator Wallington arched a brow at me. "Do you really want her out in this?"

I looked out the window, squinting. It looked blurry. "I guess not…"

"That's what I thought." Senator Wallington smoothed his suit jacket. "I'll send Cortez and another man."

"Hugh, are you sure we should make them go out in this?" Carrie's mom asked, her voice worried. "It's getting pretty dark out there, and the roads are bound to be treacherous."

"All the more reason that we need to find Larry," Carrie said, her voice insistent. "I can do it. I'll be—"

"*No*," Senator Wallington snarled. "Absolutely not."

"Hugh. We need to—"

"Someone needs to go," Carrie insisted.

"Enough of this!" I shouted, heading for the door. I stumbled on my second step. "*You* can argue about who should go. *I'm* going before it's too late to get out of here."

Carrie rushed after me. "You can't drive. You're…you're…" She paused, and I could see her arguing with herself how best to get me to listen. She should just say it. *You're drunk. Say it, Carrie, say it.* "Your arm is in a sling, so you won't be able to control the vehicle if it slips."

She didn't say it.

"I don't care, Carrie. He's my dad." I yanked the door open. "I'm not losing him, too."

"Not losing who?" Dad asked, blinking at me. He looked past me, no doubt seeing Carrie, Senator Wallington, and Mrs. Wallington all hovering in the doorway. "What did I miss?"

"You," I snapped, curling my hand around the knob so tight it hurt. "What did you need that was so important you had to drive in the snow?"

"My medicine," Dad said calmly. He held up a prescription bag and shook it under my nose. "I knew the weather was going to get worse, so I figured it was now or never. I chose now."

"I don't know what medicine was worth risking your life over." I snatched the bag and struggled to pull out the orange pill bottle. I scanned the pill name before looking at Dad with a hollow pain in my chest. I recognized the name of the meds, damn it. "Why are you taking this? What aren't you telling me?"

"My heart is acting up." Dad took his medication back and dropped it into the bag. "It's not a huge surprise. Your grandfather had issues, too."

"Yeah. I remember." I swallowed hard. It was all coming together now. "And he died of a heart attack. Did you have a heart attack? Is that why you didn't come to California when the senator did?"

Dad flushed. "Yes."

Anger rushed through me, red-hot and burning everything in its path. It collided with the ice-cold fear also coursing through my veins, creating a monstrous storm within me. "And you didn't tell me because…?"

"Can I at least come inside before you ask me a million questions?" He huddled into his coat, his bright red cheeks looking chafed. "I'm freezing."

I hadn't even realized I still stood in the doorway with the door wide open, blocking his entry. I backed out of it and looked over my shoulder. Carrie's parents were gone, but Carrie still stood there. She looked unsure of her welcome. I met her eyes. "Did you know about this?"

"I didn't *know*, but I suspected." She wrapped her arms around herself. "I didn't tell you because I didn't have confirmation. We were going to talk to him today, remember?"

I nodded once. "Yeah. I remember. You didn't remind me, though, like you promised you would."

"I'm sorry. I—"

"Can we talk in my room, son?" Dad came inside and closed the door, looking at me with disappointment clear in his blue eyes. "I'm exhausted."

"Of course." I forgot all about being pissed he didn't tell me about his illness. He looked even paler than he'd been, and I couldn't shake the feeling that he was acting as if he was feeling much better than he actually was. You know, like *me*. "Let's go. Did you eat dinner?"

"Of course I did." Dad rolled his eyes and shuffled toward the stairs. He looked weaker than ever. Same gray hair. Same blue eyes. But so much fucking older. "I have a bad heart, not a bad stomach."

I forced a laugh. "That's true. You were never one to skip a meal."

"And I never will," he said, laughing along with me.

As soon as he turned around, the smile on my face disappeared. I stopped at Carrie's side and leaned down until my mouth was a whisper away from her ear. "We'll talk later."

She caught my hand. "Take it easy on him. He's worried about you."

"And *I'm* worried about him." I watched him climb the stairs, one slow step at a time. The pain pills finally kicked in, giving Dad a weird shimmery haze around him. Almost like an aura—or what I guessed an aura looked like. Fuck if I actually knew. "I just want to know all the details. Then I'll let him sleep."

"Okay." She rose up on tiptoe and kissed me. "I'll see you soon."

"I'll be waiting."

"The sun is finally shining," she said softly.

I tensed. "Yeah, it is," I managed to say through my swollen throat.

Not because it made me happy, but because it made *her* happy. Those words used to mean so much to me when she said that, but now it brought back memories of men dying. Of Dotter's blood squirting all over my face and in my mouth. It meant something completely different to her—and it sucked that was the case now.

Fuck, I wished…

I wished we could go back.

We made it into his room, and I switched the light on. I hadn't been in his room since we got here. I'd been so absorbed in what I'd been dealing with that I totally missed all the signs. That's the kind of man I'd become. A whole shitload of orange pill bottles sat by his bed. I walked up to them and ran my fingers over the lineup. "You should have told me."

"What good would it have done? When it's our time to die, it's our time. There's nothing you or anyone can do to stop it."

I threw the covers back off his bed. "Lay down."

"I will." He scratched his head. His half-bald head. When had that happened? He's always seemed so strong. Ageless. Now, as I thought it over, I realized he was over fifty. Too young to die, but old enough to be way too fucking close to it. "There's nothing you can do to stop time from moving on. Nothing you can do to change the past."

I let out a harsh laugh. "Yeah. No kidding. I learned that up close and personal. One might even say I had a front row seat."

"I know, and I'm sorry you did." He ran his hands over his hair. "I wish I could change that. Wish I could take it all away."

"Yeah, well, you can't change what already happened."

I opened his dresser and pulled out a pair of pajamas. They were blue and had stripes on them. They'd been his present from me last year for Christmas. That seemed as if it was a lifetime ago, not only one year. It had been before I met Carrie. Before I learned what love really was.

Before I'd watched my whole unit die and then lived to tell about it.

A hell of a lot could happen in a year.

"No, but we can change how it affects us." Dad pulled his sweater over his head, and I handed him the pajama top. "You're pushing her away."

"I know. I can't help it." I picked up the pants and held them out as Dad shrugged into his shirt. "I keep saying I'll stop. Keep waking up with the best intentions. But then I fuck up and I still push her away."

"You have to stop hurting her. Have you talked to her about it?"

I hesitated. "We haven't really talked much at all."

"Because you're pushing her away."

"Yes." I crumpled his pants in my hand. "Sometimes I think she would be better off without me."

He shook his head. "She wouldn't be. She'd live. She'd laugh. She'd smile. But she wouldn't be better."

Dad's hands were shaking too badly for him to button the shirt himself, so I tossed his pants to the side and went to help him button his shirt…right until I realized I could barely manage to button my own damn shirt. So I just stood there, helplessly watching my father struggle to dress himself.

How the fuck had I missed this? How could I be so self-centered?

"You're not self-centered. You're recovering. There's a difference." Dad frowned at me. Those pain pills must've messed with my head. I hadn't even meant to talk out loud. "But the kind of love that you two have doesn't come around often. To waste it on pride and self-pity would be a crime."

I swallowed hard. Damn it, he was right. I was being an idiot, but I already knew that. I just couldn't *stop*. Too bad they didn't make a pill for that. "I hate that she's stuck with this. Stuck with me."

"She's not stuck with you; she chose you." Dad caught my hand and squeezed it tight. "You can't lose her, too. Don't let that happen, because I guarantee you'll regret it if you do."

I met his eyes. "Are you saying I'm losing you?"

"I'm saying I'm old and sick." Dad lifted a shoulder. "It's not rocket science, son. Everyone dies. I'm not sad that my turn is coming. You shouldn't be either."

"I can't lose you, Dad."

"I'll try my best to stay, but it's not up to me." Dad pointed up toward the ceiling. "It's up to Him."

At first I thought he meant Senator Wallington, whose bedroom suite was upstairs on the third floor, but then I realized he meant God. The same God I wasn't even sure I believed in anymore. Why would the "merciful" God kill all my squad members, but let me live? Why would He take my mother away?

And why was He trying to take my father, too?

Later that night, I sat in my dark bedroom, staring out the window. The moon was full, and it made me think of the last time I'd seen it that way. I'd been with Carrie on my bike. We'd whipped through the streets of San Diego, and she'd clung to me the whole time. We'd been so wild and free and in love.

My dad kept insisting I stop pushing her away, but maybe I should be pushing her away even harder. Maybe I should break it off with her. Set her free. Wouldn't that be better than this? I eyed my pill bottle. It hadn't been long enough for me to take another one yet, but the urge was there. I tried to ignore it.

The door opened, and I lurched to my feet unsteadily. She slid inside the door, shut it, and then stood somewhere close to it. I couldn't see her because it was too dark. "Finn? Are you in here?"

For a second, and only a second, I debated not answering. She would go away, and I could drink myself into oblivion, and top it off with another pain pill or two. But then I remembered I loved her, and she loved me, even if I was an ass. "I'm here."

I heard her come closer. "Can I turn on the light?"

"I prefer the dark. It soothes me."

"Okay." Her weight dipped down on the bed beside me. "How's your dad?"

"He's dying." My voice cracked on the last word. I couldn't fucking help it. I needed him here. God didn't need him. *I* did. "It's not fair."

Her arms wrapped around me from behind, entwining in front of my heart, and I clung to her joined hands with my good hand. It felt good. Right. Human. "I'm so sorry. But he's still here. He could live another twenty years and surprise us all."

"Yeah. Maybe. He is stubborn like that." I laughed. It felt foreign in my throat. "Must be where I got it from."

She was silent for a second, almost as if she couldn't believe I made a half-assed joke, and then she laughed. It washed over me, soothing my soul. "Yeah. Must be."

"That was the wrong answer," I teased. My fingers twitched on hers. "You were supposed to say I'm not stubborn at all."

"I would, but we promised not to lie to each other." She kissed my shoulder. "So the truth it is, love."

Love. She hadn't called me that since Germany.

I closed my eyes, pretending I hadn't just found out my dad was sick. On top of that, I pretended I wasn't fucked up. Pretended we were in California, not D.C. Then I opened my eyes and woke the fuck up. "I appreciate that about you. You always tell me the truth."

She shifted behind me. "I try to, anyway."

"Do you still love me, Carrie?" I tightened my hand on hers when she tried to pull away. "And before you answer that, let me be clear. I'm not talking about the man I was before I left. I'm talking about the man I am now. *Me.* Do you love *me*?"

"Of course I do." She wiggled free. I let her this time. "This will pass, Finn. I know you're upset because it's been a battle every second of every day, but it'll get better."

"It might not." I stared out the window. "I might be like the moon now. It will come and go in phases, but I don't think the pain, the sheer helplessness and anger I feel at the world right now, will ever fully go away."

"Why are you angry?" she asked, her voice whisper light.

"Because He took everyone else, but He let me live." I shook my head and forced a laugh. "No matter how many times I look at it, and no matter how many different ways, that will never make sense to me."

Her hand found mine and held on tight. "Do you wish you'd died?"

"I don't think you want honesty on that question," I said, my throat tight. "Not tonight, anyway. Ask me another time."

She made a weird sound, but stayed silent on the issue. "I'm glad you lived. It might make me selfish and horrible, but I'm glad."

"You don't think it would be easier on everyone if I'd just died?"

I asked, my voice oddly distant in my own head. "I think He made a mistake. I think I was supposed to die, too. That's why I feel the way I do. That's why I can't let myself be happy. I'm supposed to be dead, like them. Hell, I feel like I'm dying already."

She cried out. "Don't say that. It's not true."

"I have to be fucking honest, right?" I rubbed my head, my gaze on my casted arm. "This is me right now. This is the real me. No pretending I'm okay. No lies."

She crawled into my lap and cradled my face. "I know, but I'm here. And I'm not letting you waste away. I refuse to let you wither away into nothing because you feel like you should be dead. If you were supposed to be dead, you'd be dead. You're here, and you're mine."

"I'm a drunk and I can't even relax or sleep." I bit down on my tongue hard. "Why do you want me to stay?"

"Why would I want you to leave?" She kissed me, perfect and sweet and so very *her*. She pulled back, but I could still taste her on my lips. "I love you, and I'm not leaving you. I'm here to stay, and so are you."

I dropped my forehead to hers. I *wanted* to believe it. Hell, deep down I *did* believe it. Once upon a time, I'd been sure we would get our happy ending. I'd known, deep down to my soul, that we were meant to be together forever. That I was the best man for her, because no one would make her happier than I could, because our love was just that fucking strong. I'd been certain of it.

I couldn't say the same thing anymore.

CHAPTER SEVEN

Carrie

There was a shift in him tonight. I could feel it. Sense it. He was still trying to convince me he wasn't good enough for me, just like when we'd first gotten together, but now it was more of a hindsight type of thing. He wasn't pushing me away, but he was being painfully honest with me.

Maybe he was actually starting to heal.

It was way too early for recovery. I knew that. I'd done my research. Even now, I had an open book on PTSD and all its lasting effects on my nightstand. It was part of my bedtime routine. I also had countless books on being the support system for someone with PTSD, and how best to handle certain types of episodes. That's what he'd had today.

An *episode*.

He worried that he might not go back to normal. I wasn't sure he would either, but I knew one thing: he might never get back to normal, but he would get better. And if he didn't ever return to normal, well, then, he would have to achieve a new standard of normal. We'd have to adjust our expectations.

His hand skimmed down my sides and settled on the curve of my hip. "Ginger…"

God, I'd missed him calling me that. He used to do it all the time. Now, it was always Carrie. *Carrie* this and *Carrie* that. Never Ginger. "Yeah?"

"I'm going to stop telling you to leave me." He caught my hand. "I'm going to stop pushing you away, but know this: I still think you could do better. This isn't a heroic action of mine; it's a selfish one. I don't want to lose you, because I need you. But you *should* walk away from me."

My heart twisted painfully. The fact that he believed this, with all his heart, broke mine. "You're wrong. You're the most unselfish man I've ever met." I wiggled my hand free. "And I think you're blind to yourself."

"I think it's the other way around," he said sheepishly. He ran a hand over his head, probably looking for those curls again. With a grimace, he dropped his hand to his lap. "I'm going to try to get better for you."

"Don't do it for me." I undid the last button of his shirt. "Do it for you."

"No." He ran his hand up over my body, tipping my head back. "For *us*."

I swallowed hard and unclasped his sling, my knuckles scraping against the hard cast. Desire unfurled in my belly at the way he watched me. I couldn't see it, but I could feel it. "Let's get you out of this shirt."

"Only if you get out of yours, too," he said, his tone light.

Hope, small and distant, flared in me. I'd been right. He was different tonight. Maybe his talk with his father had helped. Whatever it was, I was happy for the change. "That could be arranged."

I took the sling off and laid it on the side. He flinched. "I think it's time for another pill."

"Has it been four hours yet?"

He hesitated. "Yeah, a little over, I think."

I gently slid his shirt off his shoulders. His hard muscles taunted me. I wished I could run my tongue over each one, but he wasn't ready for that. "And when was your last drink?"

"With Riley."

"Okay. I'm going to turn the light on so I don't spill them."

Silence. "All right. But stay on my lap."

"Gladly. It's my favorite place to be."

He chuckled lightly. "The feeling is mutual."

I stretched my arm and turned on the light by his bed. It was very dim. Perfect for what I needed. I grabbed the bottle and undid the cap. When I turned back to Finn, he was watching me with a soft look in his eye. One that I hadn't seen in a long time. I swallowed and poured one big pill into my palm. "Do you need a drink to wash it down?"

"I *need* you." He took it and tossed it into his mouth. "But, yeah, I could go for some water. My bottle is next to the lamp."

I closed the meds and set them back where they'd been. Picking up the water, I undid that cap, too. "We need to get you a glass in here."

"I'm fine."

He tipped his head back and chugged the water. As he did so, I let my gaze skim over his body. He had injuries, sure, but he looked beautiful to me. Even more so than before, if anything. His ink still stretched over his muscles, and his muscles were still ridiculously hard and huge.

The heart under those muscles was still the same, too.

My stomach tightened and I forced my gaze away. I didn't want him feeling pressured to do anything with me. Heck, last night had been pushing it. Although, it had seemed to maybe help a little bit... But the books said it didn't.

"You can turn out the light now," he said. I looked back at him, and he looked so vulnerable it hurt. "I know it's not a pretty picture."

"Finn, you look delicious." I skimmed my fingers over his shoulders. "When I look at you, it takes all my control not to attack you. You don't see what I see." I touched the cut on his shoulder. "I see bravery. Love. A good man."

I lowered my hand over the tattoo he'd gotten for us. It said: *the sun is finally shining.* Our code word for *I love you.* Guess we didn't need a code anymore, though.

Everyone knew about us.

"I'm only good because of you," he whispered. "You're the only good part about me."

"That's a lie." I placed my hand over his heart. "Your goodness is in here. It was there long before you met me. It was there when we met, and it's what made me want to kiss you that first time. It's what makes me want to kiss you now."

He made a small sound and squeezed my thigh. "Then fucking kiss me already, Ginger."

There he went using that nickname again.

He kissed me, his hand skimming up my body, and over my breasts, before settling on my lower back. He pulled me closer as his lips crashed over mine, stealing away all my thoughts. All my doubts. All he left behind was this. *Us.*

His tongue slipped between my lips, and I whimpered into his mouth. He swallowed my cries and his own moan melded with mine. I pressed down against his erection, my entire body begging for more, and I knew I was lost.

I always had been when it came to Finn.

Finn

I could feel her hesitation. Her doubt. She was worried she might break me even worse than I already was, but it didn't matter. I needed her more than I needed my sanity.

I needed her to need me.

And I knew the exact second she stopped fighting me internally. She melted against me and gripped my good shoulder, her nails digging in. I deepened the kiss and cupped a breast, toying with her nipple with the perfect amount of pressure. When I tugged hard, she cried out into my mouth, grinding down against my cock.

When she pushed down, I arched up, stealing her breath in the process. Good. I still had it in me. I might only have one good arm, but I'd still make her come so hard she wouldn't be able to look at me without blushing for a week, damn it.

Her nails dug into my shoulder, her other hand dipping past my broken arm and between us to massage my cock. "Finn. God."

"Undo my pants," I commanded, my own voice a little bit broken. "Then take yours off, too, but hurry up. I need you."

A desperate need to be buried inside of her consumed me. While she took her pants off, her hands trembled over every button and zipper. It consumed her, too. I could see it. Even though the light was on and I was looking like I now looked, she still wanted me.

This was what love was.

She dropped to her knees between my thighs and undid my button. I gritted my teeth and helped her remove my jeans. Next went my boxers, and then she grabbed a condom out of the drawer by my bed. Instead of putting it on me, she lowered her mouth to my cock and licked it.

Holy fucking shit.

"Carrie, not tonight. I need…I need…" I grabbed the condom and ripped the foil open with the help of my teeth. "I need to fuck you. Hard. Hot. Now."

"*Yes.*"

Her cheeks flushed, she rolled the condom on my cock. She straddled my hips, her pussy right where I needed her, and lowered herself onto me with a soft sigh. With my good hand, I gripped her ass and drove into her fully. She let out a strangled scream, biting down hard on her lip. I paused. "Are you okay?"

"No." She shook her head, still biting her lower lip, and smacked my uninjured arm. "You stopped. Don't. Stop."

Game fucking on. I moved beneath her, and she rode me hard. I could tell she was close, and I was close, too. So fucking close. "Touch yourself. I can't do it, so you have to do it for me. You have to be my hands. Play with yourself like I do."

She skimmed her hands over her belly. There was no hesitation. My Ginger was getting bolder. I loved it. "Where do you want to touch?"

I used my good hand to roll her nipple between my fingers. I wasn't gentle or sweet at all, and she loved it. "Massage your clit while I fuck you."

She let out a moan, lowering her hand inch by torturous inch. When she started moving her fingers in a circle, masturbating in front of me, my stomach tightened and twisted. I almost came right there. I needed her that bad. "Oh my God. *Yes.*"

I squeezed her breast and pumped my hips up hard. She moved over me faster. Her fingers picked up speed, too, and then she was arching her back and tensing. Her pussy squeezed down on me, and I let myself go. I didn't close my eyes this time. I just watched her as she came; her lids squeezed shut and her pink lips parted.

She was fucking gorgeous.

I came so hard it almost hurt, and I clung to her as well as I could with one hand. She collapsed against my good shoulder and I let myself fall back against the mattress. I rubbed her back gently, trying to catch my breath. She seemed perfectly content to stay there on me, snuggled up as if we hadn't just fucked each other rather than sweet lovemaking.

We'd both needed it.

She traced an invisible pattern on my shoulder. Or maybe she traced my tattoo. I couldn't tell. "When I sleep next to you, do you have the nightmares?"

"No." My hand stilled on her back. "But you usually only come in after I've already had at least one."

"Want me to stay the whole night?"

Fuck yeah, I did. "Your dad won't like it."

"If he isn't happy with it, we can go get a hotel room." She lifted up on her elbows, resting on my chest. It was then that I realized she hadn't even taken off her shirt. I'd have to make sure she got naked for me next time. "Your peace of mind is more important to me than my father's rules."

The painkillers kicked in, thank fucking God, making my mind all fuzzy and loose again. "Then stay. I miss sleeping with you in my arms. Maybe you'll chase away the nightmares."

She nodded against my chest. "Get on your pillow. You look like you're about to pass out."

I scooted up backward to my spot, rolling halfway over on my side. I didn't even bother to remove the condom. She rolled me onto my side more fully, removing it for me. Even though I wanted to protest, I couldn't say a word. My eyes closed, and I started drifting off into my drugged la-la land.

Maybe with her here at my side, I'd actually sleep. Maybe she was my pretty little dreamcatcher, fighting to keep the demons at bay.

She turned off the light, pulled on some clothes, from the sound of it, and then slid into bed beside me. As she tucked me in, my last conscious thought was how very like my father I was right now. I'd tried to help him undress for bed so he could rest, and now Carrie was doing it for me. He and I were kinda the same.

We were both slowly dying from the inside out.

CHAPTER EIGHT

Carrie

I got ripped from my sleep when Finn's door flew open, banging against the wall. Finn cursed and sprung up as well as he could, picked up a knife I hadn't even known he had from beneath the bed, and faced the door, breathing heavily. I scooted back against the headboard and blinked against the hallway light. Finn was completely naked, holding a knife, and mumbling under his breath.

He looked…terrifying.

"Who's there?" he snarled, positioning himself between me and the *threat* at the door. "Speak now before I kill you."

"It's me." A man cleared his throat. And, God, I recognized that voice. "Senator Wallington. Sorry to barge in unannounced, Griffin, but you have to—"

"*Stop.*" Finn looked over his shoulder at me, his face highlighted by the moonlight. I could see that the look in his eyes was somewhere between anger, fear, and desperation all mashed into one. He still held on to the knife. "Can you please give me a second to get dressed? I'm… I'm not decent."

I couldn't see my father, but I could picture him taking in Finn's nakedness. And he'd realize *why* Finn might be naked in three, two, one…

"Who is in there with you?" Dad asked calmly. I heard him come closer. "You're not alone." It wasn't a question.

"Stop right there." Finn stepped forward, blocking the light switch. "You're not turning that light on, sir."

"The hell I'm not," Dad growled under his breath. "If you're messing around behind my daughter's back, I assure you that my wrath is worse than what you experienced over there. You will never sleep again without picturing *my*—"

Finn let out a strangled sound. "I'm not cheating on Carrie, sir."

"Then who...?" He broke off. "Carrie. That had *better* not be you behind him."

I closed my eyes in embarrassment. This was hell. Right here. Right now. I opened my mouth to talk, but Finn beat me to it.

"Which is it you prefer, sir? For me to be cheating on her, or for her to be here instead of someone else?" Finn asked, his voice strained. He set down the knife on the nightstand. "What makes you think someone is here at all? Maybe I just sleep naked."

"I can see it all over you," Dad said, his voice tinged with disgust. "*Who* is back there?"

A light shone, and I cringed away from it. Damn those flashlight apps on the iPhone. Finn tried to jump in front of me, but it was too late. He'd seen me in Finn's bed. *Gr-eeeeat.* "Hi, Dad," I said softly, waving a hand. "Fancy seeing you here."

Dad shut off the light, completely ignoring me. "I was quite clear about my rules, Griffin."

"Yes, sir." I saw Finn's shoulders droop. "I'm sorry."

"I came to him, Dad. Not the other way around." I tugged the covers higher, even though I had a shirt on. I felt exposed. "Stop yelling at him and yell at me."

"Or better yet, tell me why you're in my room at—" Finn picked up and lit up his phone, "—one in the morning."

"I...you..." Dad trailed off, making a frustrated sound. "It's your father. Get dressed and come quickly."

"My dad? But what—oh God." Finn tossed his phone to the side, and I lunged out of the bed. "Oh God."

Before he could turn the light on, I already had his plaid pajama pants out of the drawer and was holding them out for him. The room flooded with light, and I thanked God I'd gotten dressed before I'd fallen asleep because my dad was standing right there watching us with disapproval clear in his eyes.

"Is he okay?" I asked, helping Finn into his pants. He was trembling. "Is Larry…is he…?"

"Dead," Finn said, his voice hollow. He met my eyes, looking broken and terrified. "She's asking if he's dead."

My dad's face finally cracked. "No, but he had another heart attack. The ambulance is on its way, but with the snow this heavy, it might take a while."

"Shit," Finn said, his voice broken. He closed his eyes, his jaw flexing. "Please, no. Not him, too. Not my dad."

I swallowed and placed a hand on his biceps. "Shh. Let's go to him and—"

Finn shook me off and pushed past Dad, bolting toward Larry's room. He was only wearing his pajama pants, so I grabbed a sweatshirt out of the drawer and followed him. Dad stepped in my path before I could leave the room. "Carrie."

I glowered at him. "Now isn't the time to lecture me for disobeying you. Finn needs me."

"I know. And I'm angry. Make no mistake." Dad hesitated but grabbed my hand. "It's bad, Carrie. He's dying. He won't make it this time. I can see it."

My heart slammed to a halt and sped up, all within the span of two seconds. My chest heaved, the tears that wanted to escape choking me, but I refused to let them free. "B-But he can't die. Finn…h-he…*no.*"

I slipped past him, running after Finn. If my dad was right, and Larry was dying…God, this would kill Finn. He was already going through so much. Could he possibly recover from this, too? He was still an unstable mess after all he'd been through overseas. If he had to bury his father on top of that, he would never be the same.

He'd never be able to heal.

I stopped in the doorway of Larry's room. Finn knelt at his side, holding Larry's hand with his uninjured one. "Dad, I'm here. You'll be okay. Help's coming."

I hovered in the doorway for a second. Finn kept talking to Larry, but Larry looked…oh God, he looked dead. His skin had an ashen gray color to it, and there were no signs of life left within him. Finn squeezed

Larry's hand and called out to him, but there was no reply.

He was dead. Larry was dead.

I blinked away the tears blurring my vision, not even bothering to try to hold them back. I hugged Finn's sweatshirt to my chest and stepped forward, my grief choking me. He must've heard me. He turned around and his gaze fell on me. He looked scared, but not sad. It confused me until I realized…

Oh my God. He didn't know.

"Is the ambulance here yet?" Finn asked, his voice rushed. "He said my name when I got here, but then he passed out."

I pressed my lips together tight. I couldn't break down. Couldn't cry. "They're not here yet." I went around to the other side of the bed and touched Larry's hand. It was already getting cold and a little bit stiff. So freaking fast. "Finn…"

He shot me a look. "Don't talk to me like that. He'll be fine." Finn dropped his head to the mattress. "He *has* to be fine. We were just talking. Just…" Finn lifted his head and glowered at me. "Stop looking at me as if he's dead. He's not. He's okay. Got it?"

I nodded, not sure what to do or say. "O-Okay."

Finn placed a hand on Larry's forehead. "He's cold. Can you get him some extra blankets?"

"Uh, y-yes. Sure." I left the room and opened the linen closet down the hallway. As I pulled out some comforters, Mom and Dad came around the corner, talking quietly. When they saw me, they stopped in their tracks. "He's still alive, right?"

I closed the door and juggled the blankets. "I don't think so. But Finn…he doesn't know. I think he knows, but he can't know. He can't accept it yet."

Dad rushed past me, his face pale, and Mom hugged me. "Oh dear. This is going to hit all of us hard, but Griffin, well, he's going to have a difficult time."

I released a huge sob, clinging to my mom and letting the comforters hit the floor at our feet. "I'm so scared. He can't handle this right now. It's going to kill him."

"I know." Mom hugged me tight. "He'll need you with him."

I nodded, let go of Mom, wiped my hands across my cheeks, and then picked up the blankets. I felt like shit, and knew it was only going to get worse, but Finn needed me at his side. I had to pull myself together. At some point, he would realize Larry was gone, and he'd need someone at his side when that happened. He'd need me.

"This is going to kill him," I repeated.

Maybe I was in shock or something.

"I know." Mom grabbed my hand and didn't let go. "But he has *you* to help him."

"I don't think I'm going to be enough this time," I said, my voice hollow and distant in my own head. "I'm not enough."

Finn

I clung to Dad's hand, praying with my eyes closed. I didn't fucking pray anymore. God had stopped listening to me a long time ago. He'd taken my mom. Taken my unit. And now He was trying to take my father, too. Well, fuck that.

I wouldn't let Him.

"You can't have him," I whispered, my face pressed to my father's cold hand. Where the hell were those blankets, anyway? "I still need him. He's not done here yet."

A footstep sounded in the doorway, and I didn't bother to lift my head. I couldn't look at her right now, those sad blue eyes of hers shining with pity. I didn't need her pity. Dad wasn't dying tonight. She could save her empathy for someone else.

Anyone else.

"Did you get the blankets?" I asked.

"She's getting them," Senator Wallington said. Oh. It wasn't Carrie behind me this time. "I'm just coming to check in on Larry. To s-see how he's doing."

I struggled to my feet and stood between him and the senator, looking at him defensively. "He's not dead."

"I didn't say he was." He held his hands up. "He's my friend, Griffin. I just want to see him, like you. To make sure he's okay."

I hesitated, letting him pass through. For some reason, I didn't want anyone looking at him too closely. Didn't want them to tell me he was…

I stopped that thought right fucking there.

Carrie's dad sat on the opposite side of the bed and reached for Dad's fingers with his trembling hand. "Larry." He closed his eyes and swallowed hard. "I'm so sorry."

"*No.*" Rage swept through me, strangling me with the strength and depths it struck in me. I snatched Dad's hand back and gave the senator what I hoped was an eat-shit-and-die look. "You don't get to say a word about being sorry for him. He's *fine.*"

He stood up and covered his face. "Look, son, I know—"

"I'm not your son!" I held Dad's hand to my chest. "You don't even like me, and don't approve of me and Carrie at all. Let's not mince words tonight."

He dropped his hands. "I don't *dis*like you, Griffin."

"But you don't like me, either."

He didn't say anything to that.

I squeezed my dad's hand. Was it just me, or was it even colder? "Where is the ambulance? And where's Carrie with the blankets?"

"I'm here," she said from behind me. She came to my side and gently laid blankets over Dad. "You doing okay?"

I swallowed hard at the look of concern in her eyes when she glanced my way. She was looking at me as if she was scared I'd fall apart. I wouldn't. "I just want the ambulance to get here already. Then I'll be fine."

Senator Wallington cleared his throat. "Griffin, your father isn't cold. He's—"

"Dad, don't." Carrie kneeled beside me and rested a hand on my upper back. "Just don't. Let me handle this."

"I don't need to be *handled.*" I looked at Carrie, swallowing hard when I met her eyes. There wasn't pity, but there was sadness. So much fucking sadness. As if she knew he was gone, accepted it, and was worried for *me.* "He's not dead, Ginger. He can't be dead. I…he…*no.*"

The senator stepped forward again. "I know this is hard, Griffin, but—" Sirens sounded outside the window, and he cut himself off. "They're here now."

"About damn time," I said, my voice even. I knew what he was trying to say, but I didn't believe him. I'd know it if my father was dead, damn it. I'd seen dead. *This* wasn't it. "Can you let them in? I don't want to leave him alone in case he wakes up."

"I'll do it," Carrie's mom said. I hadn't even realized she was here.

"You stay with them, Hugh. Just in case."

Just in case *what*?

Senator Wallington nodded. Carrie rested a small hand on my arm. "It's going to be okay, Finn."

I nodded, but didn't say anything. I could sense more than see the long, shared look between Carrie and her dad. I ignored it. "I know."

She laid her hand over mine and I clung to her, needing her strength now more than ever. But I didn't let go of Dad. It seemed like it took ages for the paramedics to come inside, but when they did, I finally released Dad's hand, but not Carrie's, and moved out of their way. They came to the side of the bed and checked his pulse.

Carrie's dad leaned down and whispered something to the man. After he finished, they both looked at me. The paramedic bent over Dad, his fingers doing something I couldn't see. Senator Wallington approached me, his eyes filled with sadness and acceptance. I wasn't accepting a damn thing he told me. "Griffin, I know it's hard, but he's gone. There's nothing we can do to save him now."

"You're wrong." I shook my head, my vision blurring. My heart thudded in my ears, and I backed up, dropping Carrie's hand. I looked at the paramedic, who looked fucking terrified of me. "He's alive, right? *Tell me he's alive.*"

The man looked at Senator Wallington before studying me. "His heart gave out. If it's any consolation, he went fast. There wasn't time to—"

"*No!*" I fell to my dad's bedside and shook him. "Dad. You have to wake up. Wake up right now, and show them you're not gone." I shook him harder. "Wake. *Up.*"

Carrie let out a sob behind me and squeezed my shoulder. "Finn, he—"

"No. Don't." I shrugged her off and shook Dad again. His lips were already turning that bluish, dead-like color that all corpses got. "But he was just here. He was just talking to me...*no.*"

Senator Wallington covered his mouth, his eyes watering.

Carrie nodded. "I know, but he's gone."

"No." I swallowed past my aching throat. I ran my fingers over his cold forehead. He looked like he was sleeping. Not like he was gone forever. "I need you. Dad, *please.*"

Nothing. He'd left me, too.

Everyone kept fucking dying.

I stood up, roared, and punched the wall. My fist sank into it, sending pain flying up my good hand, but it didn't numb the pain in my heart. The absolute, agonizingly real pain that choked me. So I punched the wall again. And again. And again. I lost count after the fourth time. When that stopped feeling satisfying, I started breaking shit.

Anything.

Carrie cried out my name, and tried to rush to my side, but her father held her back. He tossed her to a paramedic, who grabbed her arms and held her back, then stood in front of her protectively. Tears streamed down her face, and she was shouting words, but I didn't hear anything. All I heard was my own heartbeat thundering at breakneck speeds. And these words kept repeating in my head: I lived. He died. They all died.

It wasn't fucking *fair*.

By the time I was focused on the world around me again, I had no idea why the hell everyone was crying, or why Carrie was holding her face and sobbing her heart out. I collapsed against the wall, my breath coming out in ragged gasps. I stared at my feet, because why the fuck not? They were the only things standing still right now.

Everything else was spinning.

Someone came close to me, and I snapped my head up. It was Carrie's dad. He looked scared of me. I was kind of scared of myself, too. "Griffin, you need to calm down. Don't make them sedate you."

I stiffened when he came closer, blinking rapidly. The room was in shambles, vases and glasses were broken, and Carrie was sobbing. The paramedic was still holding her back, and everyone was looking at me like I was crazy. Even Carrie looked scared.

What had I done?

I tore my gaze from Carrie's wet face, looking down at my hand in surprise. It was dripping with blood, all over the pristine white carpet, and the skin was ripped back from the knuckles. It looked as if a storm had gone off in the room, and that storm had been me.

I'd done this.

"C-Carrie?" I looked up at her, swiping my forearm across my cheeks. It came back wet. I'd been crying? I didn't fucking cry. "He's gone?"

She shoved the paramedic off her and stood, her legs barely supporting her. She took an unsteady step toward me, and then another. Her father watched, looking as if he was going to step in the way. She shot him a look, brushed past him, and walked up to me. "Y-Yes, he's gone."

I choked on a sob, and she threw herself at me, hugging me tight. I clung to her with one arm, letting myself cry. I hadn't cried since my mom died, and now here I was again. *Alone.* "I'm alive, and he's dead. They're all dead."

I buried my face in her neck and squeezed my eyes shut. I didn't want to see the senator watching me, looking horrified and sad. Didn't want to watch as the paramedics zipped my father in a black bag and hauled his lifeless body away. And I didn't want to accept the fact that I was the only one who kept living, while everyone else around me died.

Who was next? Carrie? I was a toxic bomb, killing everyone who cared about me.

She hugged me tighter. "It's not your fault. None of this is your fault."

But she was dead wrong. It should have been *me.*

CHAPTER NINE

Carrie

A little while later, I pulled the blankets over Finn's shoulders, kissed his forehead, and turned out the light. He hadn't really said anything after he'd gone insane and started breaking things. He kept just staring off into the distance, talking when spoken to, but in a way that told me he wasn't really there. He might have been holding my hand, but he might as well have been across the country—or the world, for that matter.

He was gone.

Right now, he was buried in grief, and there was nothing I could do to help him. Sure, I could love him and be here for him, but I couldn't bring his dad back. He'd already been struggling with the deaths he'd seen, and now he had one more to add to the pile. The worst one since his mother died.

I was scared he was going to drift away from me. Heck, he'd already started to. Absentmindedly, I touched the tender spot on my cheekbone. When he'd started bashing the wall, I'd tried to stop him. Tried to calm him down. Stupid, really. When a huge guy is going insane and breaking things, you shouldn't jump in the way.

If he knew something he'd broken and/or thrown had hurt me by accident, he'd never forgive himself. That's why he'd never find out. It hadn't been on purpose, after all. He didn't need to know.

I stood up, ready to find my bed. It was already five in the morning, but I could maybe sneak in two hours before the household rose and started preparing for the funeral. I almost cried out when he grasped my hand. He'd finished almost a whole bottle of whiskey and taken two pain pills. For once, I hadn't even harped at him for mixing the two. But I thought he'd been out.

"Carrie?" His voice slurred. "Where are you going?"

I sat back down. "Nowhere. I'm right here."

"Don't leave me," he whispered. "I can't lose you, too."

I squeezed his hand. "I'm not going anywhere, love."

He drifted off to sleep again, and I rested my head on the mattress. Dad came up behind me, his shadow falling over the two of us. "Are you going to bed now?"

I shook my head, but didn't bother to lift it. "He needs me tonight."

"Carrie..." He came closer. "I care about him. I really do, but if he continues in this self-destructive behavior, this has to end. He's dangerous right now. He could hurt you."

I sat up straight and glowered at him. "His dad just died. Think about that before you go judging him. When he flipped out, he wasn't himself." I looked back at him. His brow was wrinkled, but his breathing was even and deep. He appeared to be asleep. I hoped he was. He didn't need to hear this. "He wouldn't...he doesn't *do* this stuff. He's not himself right now."

Dad nodded. "That's exactly what I'm worried about."

"I'm not leaving him. I love him."

"I know, and I know he loves you. I never disputed that." Dad headed for the door. "You can spend the night. I happen to agree with you on one point—he needs you right now. But leave the door open."

He walked out into the hallway, leaving us alone. His words kept ringing in my head. I pressed my fingers to my cheekbone. Dad hadn't seen me get injured, thank God. His reaction would have been just as bad as Finn's if he ever found out about it.

"He's wrong." Finn's eyes opened again. He pulled the covers back with his bandaged hand. "I would never hurt you. I'd sooner kill myself."

I couldn't tear my eyes off his injured hand. The paramedics had taken care of it after they removed Larry's body. They'd also asked us if we wanted to press charges against Finn for the damage done to our home. Dad and I both said no immediately. Mom had agreed with us after a small moment of hesitation.

He had a broken arm and a busted hand. How was he supposed to take care of himself now? Easy. He wouldn't. I would have to be his hands.

"I know," I whispered, climbing in beside him. "Don't listen to him."

His unbroken arm wrapped around me, holding me close. He kissed the top of my head, letting out a shaky sigh after. "I love you, Ginger. You know that, right?"

I blinked back tears and nodded, not answering him.

"I'm sorry I lost it like that. Something just…I don't know. I didn't think I'd lose him, too. Not yet." His voice cracked, and he let out a strangled groan. "I didn't know I'd be so alone. Didn't know I could hurt more than I already was."

I lifted my head and cupped his cheek. "You're not alone, Finn. You have me and my parents."

"I know." He paused, the words slurring together. "But it's just not the same. Nothing's the same anymore. And I'm sorry for that, too."

"Things don't have to be the same to be good," I whispered. I ran my thumb over his lower lip, like he used to do to me. "People change. As long as we change together, we'll be fine."

"I don't think you have any idea how much I need you, Ginger." He rested his bandaged hand on my hip. "I love you so damn much. You have no idea how much."

"I do, because that's how much I love you." I kissed the spot above his heart before resting my hand over it. "Now get some rest. It's almost morning."

He nodded sleepily, and within seconds he was breathing evenly again. Tears fell from my eyes, and I didn't wipe them away. If anything, it would draw notice to them and possibly wake him up, and he didn't need to know how upset I was. I needed to be the stronger one right now.

For him. For us. For me.

These next couple of weeks would suck for all of us, but once we got through them, the healing process could start. Finn would bury his father, and over time he would stop drinking so much. His arm would heal, and then he would stop taking meds. Maybe he would be able to laugh again. Smile again. We could go home to Cali, and he'd be able to surf, ride his bike, and start school. Everything would be fine.

Everything *had* to be fine.

A few hours later, I woke up when someone knocked on the door lightly. I rolled over and squinted toward the noise, trying to remember where I was and why someone was knocking. Then I remembered it all. Oh, boy, did I remember it all.

Mom looked at Finn and the way he was holding me, her lips pressed together. "It's time to wake up. We have to start the funeral arrangements."

"All right," I whispered. "I'll be right there. I think he should sleep a bit more, because—"

"I'm up." Finn's bicep flexed under me. "I'll be down."

Mom nodded, giving me one last look before she left the room. I lifted my head and studied Finn's face. His eyes were bloodshot with dark circles under them, and he looked as if he hadn't slept at all. His blue eyes met mine, and he tried to give me a small smile. "My arm's asleep, I think."

"Oh." I scooted back and sat on the side of the bed, facing him, hugging my knees. "Hey."

"Hey yourself." He lifted his arm and rotated it, flinching. "Ow. What the hell happened to my hand?"

I looked at him, not certain what to say. "You don't remember?"

"I remember losing my shit, but I'm a little sketchy on all the details." He reached out to brush my hair off my face before glaring down at his bandaged fingers. "Oh, fuck. I broke stuff, didn't I? Punched the wall and all that?"

I swallowed hard. "Yeah. It's okay, though."

"In what world is that behavior okay, Carrie?" He sat up and rested his arm on his knees, in almost the same position as me. His slinged arm was the only difference. "Hitting things and throwing fits are never okay. I'm not a child."

"Your dad just died." I flinched when he paled at the words, reaching out to squeeze his foot. "I think we all understand why you lost control like you did. No one holds it against you."

He met my eyes, but glanced away just as quickly. "I do. I hold it against me."

"Finn…"

He got out of bed. "Don't make excuses for my behavior. You deserve better, and you know it." He turned back to me, his bandaged hand at his side. "What if I had hurt you? What if I...?" He broke off, his jaw flexing. "God, what if I lose it and hurt you, Carrie? I'd never forgive myself."

I fought the undeniable urge to press a hand to my cheek, hiding the mark he'd made last night. I knew he hadn't meant to. He'd been out of his mind. Inconsolable.

But I wasn't making excuses for him.

I shook my head. "It will never happen, so you don't need to worry about it. You'd never hurt me like that."

"I promise to try to do better. I know yesterday was—" he sighed, "a fail of epic proportions. Today will suck too, and the next day. But I'll do better."

I gave him a small smile. "You're doing just fine."

"No, I'm not." He sat down on the edge of the bed, glowering down at his bandaged hand. "Can you take the bandage off? I need to have at least one hand."

"Are you sure—?" When he gave me a look that clearly said *take it the fuck off*, I came around the side of the bed and knelt at his feet. "If it hurts too much, I can put it back on. I watched them do it yesterday."

His Adam's apple bobbed. "I can't believe he's gone. Just like that. No matter how much I see death, no matter how many times I lose someone, I will never get over how fucking fast it happens. One second they're there, and the next...just gone."

I undid the silver clasp that held the Ace bandage on before slowly unwrapping it. "I won't pretend to know what you're feeling right now, because I can't possibly understand it until I'm there, but I know it sucks, and anything you need? I'll give it to you."

He met my eyes. "I know. You're too good to me."

"You keep saying that."

He shrugged with one shoulder. "Because it's true, and I promised not to lie to you anymore."

I shook my head and bit down on my lower lip, focusing on the task at hand. From what I could see of his knuckles, things weren't looking promising for him. He thought he'd be able to use his hand, obviously, but it looked mangled, bruised, and thoroughly unusable.

After I finished the task at hand, I settled back on my haunches. He flexed his fingers, paling and flinching. "Fuck, that hurts."

"I know." Automatically, I reached for his pain pills. At some point, the bottle had fallen to the floor and rolled partially under the bed. There were only three left, so I'd have to get more this afternoon. That meant he'd taken more than he was supposed to. There should still be six. "I'll open this and—"

"*No*." He rolled his shoulder, flexing his hand again. "I'm done taking those things. They're fucking with my head. Flush them."

I looked down at the bottle in my hand. "What if the pain gets worse later?"

"It's going to get worse. There's no way it won't." He looked back at me, his eyes solemn and way too somber. "But if they're here, I'll find a reason to take them, and then I'll turn into a raging fuck-head again. I'm done with those, and I'm done with drinking. I'm just done with it all."

I blinked rapidly, trying to fight back the tears of relief I felt. For a while there, I'd been worried he might become addicted to the escape the pills and booze gave him. I worried he might fall apart, and there would be nothing I could do to save him. But he was saving himself. *Thank God*.

"Okay. I'll get rid of them."

"Thank you." He held out his hurt hand, and I latched on to his wrist so he could pull me up to my feet without too much pain. "For everything."

I reached up on tiptoe and kissed him. I'd expected him to be a mess this morning, but if anything, he seemed stronger than before. More determined to be the man he wanted to be. I wasn't sure what to make of it. "You ready?"

"Yeah. My dad wouldn't have wanted me to fall apart. I promised him—" His voice broke, and he stopped talking. He ran his hand over his head, watching me. "I promised him I'd pull myself together and stop being an ass. I'm starting now. It's what he would have wanted."

I rested my hand over his heart. "He was very proud of you. You know that, right?"

"I know he *was* proud of me." He closed his eyes. "But he wasn't proud of the man I'd become since I came back home."

The thin wound that ran down his forehead looked more pronounced this morning. I reached out and traced my hand over it. "I think you're wrong. He knew you were in there, and he knew what you were going through—what you went through to get back here. He didn't judge you at all."

He caught my hand, trapping my fingers against his jagged gash. "He didn't, but I did." He gave me an inscrutable look and released his hold on my hand. I didn't miss the pain that crossed his eyes at the movement. "Let's brush our teeth, then we'll go down. There's a lot to get done today. I have to contact the church, get a coffin, write a eulogy…"

I nodded. "One step at a time, together. Okay? First step? Teeth."

"Okay." He kissed the top of my head. "Let's go."

I followed him out of his room. For a second, just a second, I wanted to grab him, shove him back inside the bedroom, and lock the door. Inside here, he was just my Finn. It was the only place where we felt and acted normal. As soon as we got out there, with my parents and the rest of the world, there was no telling what would happen.

And selfishly…I wanted to keep him *just like this*.

CHAPTER TEN

Finn

"That one." I pointed to the wooden casket at the end of the row, my throat tight and my arm throbbing like hell. Everything hurt, but I refused to ask Carrie to get my prescription refilled. I deserved the pain. Every. Fucking. Second. It fueled me. Made me put one foot in front of the other. Distracted me from the *real* pain that was killing me.

The pain of losing my father.

Carrie tightened her fingers on mine. "It's beautiful. He would have loved it."

"Thanks."

I closed my eyes for a second. It was ridiculous that people spent so much damn time picking out a casket based on what the dead person lying in it would have liked. They wouldn't ever see it—so why the hell did it matter if it was the right color? Or if it had top-of-the-line pillows? They wouldn't feel a fucking thing.

They were blissfully, blessedly unaware of all these proceedings. If Father Thomas was to be believed, Dad was in a much better place now. He was with Mom in heaven, smiling down on me. I'd rather they got their asses back down here with me. That way I wouldn't be the only one left.

Senator Wallington pulled the man aside and spoke to him in a low tone. He'd come along with us, and kept adding things—then insisting to pay since he'd "adjusted" the order. I knew what he was doing. He was taking care of the bills for me, but trying to do so in a way that I wouldn't take offense.

I gritted my teeth and looked down at Carrie, forcing a smile. If it was the last thing I did, I wouldn't let her know how fucked up I was right now. Oh, who was I kidding? She knew. She'd seen me last night. I still couldn't believe I'd let myself break like that, and in the process broken so many things in that damn bedroom. I could have hurt someone— hell, I could have hurt Carrie.

I would fucking walk away before I ever, *ever* let myself hurt her.

End of story.

I looked into her eyes, trying to latch on to the serenity that I usually felt. She looked different today. She'd put on makeup, even blush. Was she trying to look less exhausted for my behalf? If so, she was failing. I knew how tired she was because she'd been taking care of me. Well, no more.

Tonight, I'd make sure she went to bed at a decent time.

"All right. We're all settled." Senator Wallington came over. "I added a few things to the order, so I paid for the coffin myself. I hope you don't mind."

Enough. "Sir, I can't let you keep doing that. I have money, and I can—"

He held a hand up. "You caught me. I promised him I'd take care of the bills when his time came. I won't break that promise, no matter how much you hate it. Besides, last time I checked, you were too injured to work. You'll need to save money, since you don't know how long you'll be unemployed."

I flushed. I hadn't even considered the fact that I couldn't do my job anymore. Or was that not what he meant? Was he suggesting I was fired from being Carrie's bodyguard not because of my injury, but because of our relationship? No one would guard her better than me, damn it.

My own life depended on her survival.

"Dad, he can still guard me." Carrie frowned at him. "An injury won't stop him from babysitting me for you."

"Oh, and how would he stop a kidnapper with a broken arm and a mangled hand?" Her dad cocked his head. "Will he kick them? Shout for help?"

Carrie glared at him. "He'll heal."

"Yeah, but until then, he can't work as a guard." He looked over his shoulder while straightening his tie. "Besides, contracts were broken and lies were told. I'm still not sure what I'm doing about that yet, but now isn't the time or place to discuss this. All I was saying was that I was paying, and I wouldn't take no for an answer. That's it."

I inclined my head, not dropping his stare. "Yes, sir."

I practically spit out that last word. Fuck, I needed a drink. I understood what he wasn't saying: I wasn't getting my job back. I'd lied to him. Fallen for his daughter. Lied some more. And then gone crazy. It wasn't exactly a shocker that I'd lost my job.

"We'll talk later," the senator repeated.

"No need. I understand completely."

Carrie might not realize it, but I'd known all along how this would end when he found out about us. I'd be fired and looking for a new job. It's why I'd left on that assignment in the first place. Why I'd tried to better myself, only to end up broken and damaged.

Carrie shook her head. "This isn't over, Dad."

"This has absolutely nothing to do with you, and like I said—" He motioned security over. Cortez and Morris walked over our way, their expressions solemn. "It's not the time or the place."

After Cortez nodded at me, he turned to Senator Wallington. "What can I do for you, sir?"

"You're going to leave with me," he paused, "and Morris?"

Morris stepped forward. "Yes, sir?"

"You stay with them."

Carrie stiffened. "We don't need a guard."

"It's fine," I said, catching the senator's eyes. He didn't trust me around his daughter anymore. That much was clear. And honestly? I didn't blame him. "I can't protect you, Carrie. He's right."

He was *so* fucking right.

"I don't want anyone watching me besides Finn," Carrie protested. She shot Morris a smile. "No offense, but I've already got my—"

"*No.*" Senator Wallington balled his fists, his face turning an alarming shade of red. "I've put up with a lot from you, Carrie, but this is not up for debate. Morris stays."

I squeezed Carrie's hand. She was about to start a fight, right here in the fucking casket store, for the love of God. "It's fine, Carrie. He's right."

She whirled on me, eyes narrowed. "No, he's not. You wouldn't let anything happen to me."

"I'm not quite myself." I smiled, even though I wanted to fucking scream. "You can't deny that."

She hesitated. "But still…"

"It's just for now. Things will go back to normal after I heal. Isn't that right, sir?"

Senator Wallington met my eyes. "Right."

"See?" I let go of her hand. "Where are you going, sir?"

"I'm going to stop at my office on the way home. I'll be home in time for dinner." He hesitated. "Riley might be stopping by. He heard about your father, and wants to give his condolences."

"Excellent."

"That might not be the best idea," Carrie said, looking at me. "You might need some down time."

"Then he can keep you company." I smiled again. It fucking hurt to smile when everything was breaking inside me. I wasn't worried about her and Riley. I trusted her, and that meant I had to trust him, too. "My head is killing me, so I do need to rest. It'll be good to know you have a friend nearby while I'm sleeping."

She bit her lower lip. "All right, if that's what you want."

I didn't. What I wanted was a fucking drink, but I couldn't have that, could I?

So I nodded. "It's what I want."

The next day was Dad's funeral. It was cold, dark, depressing, and fucking hard to get through. There were tons of people there. People I'd known over the years. People Dad knew. And then friends of the senator. We'd actually had to turn some people away, as we couldn't all fit inside.

It should make me feel happy to know so many people cared about him, but instead I felt empty. I sat in a room surrounded by people who cared about my dad, but there were only two people in this room who actually gave a damn about *me*—and one of them was in the coffin at the front of the room.

People came to say goodbye to my dad, but every once in a while, I heard someone laugh as they caught up on the "good old times." I wasn't fucking laughing. I hadn't laughed since the night before my dad died.

Hell, I didn't know if I'd ever laugh again.

After I delivered my eulogy, which I'd managed to get through without breaking down, I stared at the open casket as Father Thomas droned on and on about redemption, heaven, and hell. I couldn't take my eyes off Dad, knowing it was the last time I'd ever get to see his face again. I think part of me was hoping this was all a dream or some shit like that. Like he'd pop up and be all, "Ha! I tricked you, didn't I?"

But he didn't move. He was really *gone*.

I clung to Carrie's hand, my dry eyes stinging. She sniffed beside me, tears running down her cheeks, and I almost envied her. I couldn't let myself go again. Couldn't release the grief. Look what had happened last time. So I sat there, staring straight ahead, and pretended I was anywhere but here. Surfing. Riding my bike. Laughing with Carrie on my lap.

Some undetermined amount of time later, Carrie shook my knee. "Finn? You ready?"

I blinked, looking around in surprise. The room was empty. Only Carrie and I remained. We sat in the middle of the front row, and everyone else waited outside. I could see them through the window. Waiting for the next step—the gravesite. "N-No. I'll never be ready."

"Take your time." She didn't let go of me. If anything, she held on tighter. "They can wait for you."

"Fuck." I swallowed hard. "I have to say goodbye now, don't I?"

She nodded slowly. All traces of her tears were gone, and she looked at me with clear eyes. "Yes. You have to say goodbye."

I looked over at the casket. After he was in the ground…what then? I just went about my life acting as if I was normal when I wasn't? "This sucks."

"Yeah, it does." She kissed my temple. "Do you want to say goodbye alone?"

I thought about it before nodding. "Wait for me outside?"

"Always." She let go of me and started for the door. She wore a black dress and a black pair of heels. Her long red hair fell down her back freely, and she looked gorgeous. "And Finn?"

I stood up and straightened my black suit jacket. "Yeah?"

"You're not alone. You have me."

My heart clenched tight. She was right, and I knew it, but I still felt alone. I was the only family member left. My grandparents were long gone. And now my parents, too. But I didn't say any of that. "I love you."

She smiled sadly, her red lips parting to show her perfect white teeth. She had a lot of makeup on again today. "I love you, too."

After she left, I turned to my father. The undertaker nodded at me and retreated to the back of the room to give me privacy. He joined the group of pallbearers, talking quietly. They all gave me their backs. I was alone. It was time to accept it.

I walked up to the casket slowly, each step taking longer than the next. By the time I reached the side and knelt beside it, my feet felt as if they weighed a thousand pounds each and my palms were sweating. I reached out and held his hand with my only semi-functioning hand. It didn't feel like his skin, and yet it did. "I'm going to miss you, Dad."

He didn't reply, obviously, but I swore his fingers tightened on mine.

"I'm going to go to school. I'll make you proud. I know I made a big mess of things. I know I screwed everything up." I looked up at the window. Carrie stood there, next to her parents. Riley was with her. I tore my eyes away. "But I did some things right lately. I know what I have to do, and I'm going to do it."

I looked at my dad again. He was pale and lifeless, but he was still *here*. And soon…he wouldn't be. "I wish you hadn't left me. Everyone is dying. Everyone but me. I just don't get it. It's not fair."

I swallowed past my throbbing throat. Visions of Dad teaching me how to drive hit me. "Remember when you used to blare the radio and crank the windows down when you were teaching me how to drive? That way when I mastered driving with the music blaring, nothing would faze me after that." I let out a small laugh. "And you used to sing Tom Petty at the top of your lungs, your face glowing every time I mastered a new skill, and I told you I was going to pretend like I didn't know you if you didn't quiet down." I cleared my throat. "I never would have done that to you. I loved you then for being so silly and free, and I love you even more now. Just thought you should know that."

I dropped my head onto the side of the casket, swallowing hard. "And I keep remembering how you looked the day I went away to boot camp. You looked so proud of me that day—the proudest I've ever seen you look. Your eyes were all bright and shiny with tears, and you smiled throughout the whole damn ceremony." I lifted my head, my eyes stinging. "You haven't looked at me once like that since we got back to D.C. I'm sorry I let you down. So sorry—"

I broke off. Knowing he'd died while being disappointed in me killed me. He might not have told me as much, but I'd seen it in his eyes that last night we had together. Heard it in his voice. He'd wanted me to do better, and I hadn't had the chance to do so. His last memory of me would be me as a pill-popping drunk.

I curled my hurt hand into a fist, grimacing through the pain. I deserved it. "I love you, Dad. And I'll never stop loving you. Never stop missing you. I'm sorry I fucked it all up, but I'll fix it. I promise."

Was it just me, or had someone touched me on the back? I looked, but I was still alone. I gave my dad one last look, stood up, cleared my throat, and nodded at the men in the back of the room. "I'm done. He's all yours."

I walked out the door, my eyes scanning the crowd until I found her. As I walked toward Carrie, I heard whispers of "the heir" dating "the help," and I knew they were talking about Carrie and me. Someone snickered and replied about how it was fun "to date below rank sometimes," but that it "wouldn't last past the grieving."

Fuck them. Fuck them all.

Riley bent down to Carrie, talking to her quietly, and she shook her head. I approached slowly, not wanting to interrupt the two people in this room who everyone would agree was a perfect match. She must have sensed me coming, because she broke off midsentence and rushed to my side.

"You okay?"

No. "Yeah."

She claimed my hand again. It hurt like hell, but I didn't care.

I needed her too badly to let go yet.

CHAPTER ELEVEN

Carrie

I walked into the empty family room, a glass of water in my hand, and sat down on the edge of the couch. The whole day had been nonstop mingling, comforting, crying, and then more crying. Finn had gone upstairs to lie down for a few minutes, and I'd escaped the crush of people still hanging around our house.

I wish I could have lain down, too, but my mom would've had a heart attack if I escaped mid-party. Bad manners and all that jazz. I finished off my water, set it down, and laid back against the couch. Silence. Silence was good. The door opened behind me and I leapt to my feet, forcing a smile to my face. When I saw it was Riley and my dad, I let the smile slide away and sank down on the cushions. "Oh, it's you guys."

"You sound disappointed." Riley sat beside me, amusement in his eyes. "Were you hoping for someone else? Maybe someone with tattoos?"

I shook my head. "He's resting. He just went upstairs."

"That's good," Riley said.

Dad opened the liquor cabinet. "Riley, would you like a—?" He squinted. "Oh, wait. My scotch is missing. Maybe Griffin took it up with him."

"No. He's not drinking anymore." I looked down at my lap. "He stopped after Larry died."

"Uh…" Dad closed the cabinet, a bottle of whiskey and two glasses in his hands. "I thought I saw him drinking last night. Are you sure?"

I swallowed hard. He'd sworn he wasn't drinking anymore, so that didn't sound right. "I'm positive he isn't drinking. He's not even taking pills anymore. I flushed them all."

Dad and Riley exchanged a long glance. "Okay," Dad said.

"I, for one, haven't seen him drinking today," Riley said, offering me a smile. "Maybe you were mistaken after all, Mr. Wallington."

"Yes. Maybe." He poured two glasses of whiskey, putting the bottle back into the cabinet. After handing the glass to Riley, he headed for the door. "I'll leave you two alone. If I don't go back to help with the guests, your mother will kill me."

I looked at Riley and rolled my eyes. It was clear he'd brought Riley in here just for this purpose—to leave us alone together. Once the door closed behind him, Riley shoved his glass at me. "Drink it. You need it more than I do."

"Oh, thank God," I said, downing the nasty beverage in one gulp. I didn't know why anyone would drink this crap willingly. I swiped my forearm across my lips and handed the empty glass back to Riley. "Is this ever going to end?"

"Is what ever going to end?"

I stared out the window. Snow was falling again, and the sun was setting, casting the sky in hues of pink and orange. It looked so peaceful. Too bad it was anything but peaceful in here tonight. "The pain. The nonstop crap being piled on Finn. First he gets injured, and then his father dies. How much can one man take?"

"Finn's strong." Riley got up and made his way over to the cabinet. He refilled his cup, drank it, and poured some more. "He'll recover, and he has you to help him."

"Yeah, but what if I'm not enough?"

Riley gripped the side of the cabinet with both hands, his knuckles going white. Pushing off it, he came back to my side, sat down, and offered me his cup again. "How could you not be?"

I took the drink, swallowing it quickly. I didn't even flinch that time. "Easily. I'm not his father, and I can't give him back his father."

"You don't need to be his dad. You just need to be you." He shrugged before crossing one ankle over his knee. "That's all he needs."

"Yeah…"

I stared off into the distance, watching the snow falling. It would be Christmas in a couple of days—two, I think? I'd lost track of the days. But it didn't matter, I was only thinking of the days because there wasn't really much more to say. I *knew* I wasn't enough. If I were enough, he'd be sitting next to me, instead of Riley. If I were enough, he wouldn't be sitting in his bedroom alone, instead of being with me. Ever since my father basically fired him yesterday, he'd been quiet. We'd slept together again, with the door open, but he'd barely said anything besides "good night" to me. It scared me.

Riley reached out and touched my cheekbone. "What happened there?"

"It's nothing." I flinched away and covered the bruise with my hand. All my crying must have removed the heavy makeup I'd put on to hide it. I couldn't let Finn or my dad see it, so I'd have to reapply. "Nothing at all."

Riley's brows slammed down. "Did someone *hit* you?"

"N-No, of course not." I stood up shakily, walked to the mirror, and studied the mark. I'd need to sneak up to my room for some concealer. "It was an accident. I'll go get my—"

"*Carrie,*" Riley said. He caught my gaze in the mirror. He looked ready to kill someone. "Was it Finn?"

"No. Yes. Kind of." I closed my eyes. I didn't want to look at Riley right now. Not when he looked so freaking angry. "When his dad died, he went a little crazy. Punching things and throwing crap around. Breaking stuff. My dad tried to pull me back, but I moved too fast. Finn kept hitting things, and stuff was going all over the place, and something went flying…and bounced off my cheek. He didn't mean to do it, and he doesn't even know it happened. That's how far gone he was. My dad was there. He saw the whole thing." A white lie. My father had seen it, sure, but he didn't know I'd been hurt. I spun around and gripped the mantel behind me. "You can't say anything to Finn, though. If he knew he hurt me…I don't know what he'd do."

"But he *did* hurt you."

"Not on purpose." I crossed the room and grabbed Riley's hands. "Please don't tell him. Finn can't ever find out about it. It would kill him."

Riley shook his head. "But—"

"I can't ever find out about *what*?" Finn asked from the doorway, his voice low and broken. "What did I miss in the five minutes I was upstairs?"

Riley tensed and dropped my hands, and I stumbled back. I realized, at the last second, what it looked like. It looked as if we'd been caught red-handed in an intimate moment, and we'd been talking about keeping secrets. "It's nothing, Finn."

Finn met my eyes, his gaze neither accusing nor untrusting. "Then tell me what it is if it's no big deal."

"Look, man." Riley cleared his throat. "It's not what you think. I would never—"

"I know. I assure you, I trust Carrie implicitly." Finn looked at Riley, staring him down. "But you should leave us so we can talk in privacy. Now."

It was the first time I'd seen him actually act like my arrogant Finn in way too long, and it sent a shaft of pain to my chest to know it was because he'd overheard me. Why hadn't my father closed the freaking door? "You can go, Riley. We'll be fine."

Riley looked at the spot on my cheek where I knew it was discolored, shifting on his feet uneasily. "Yeah. Sure. I'll go find my parents."

"Close the door on your way out," Finn said. He watched Riley pass, doing the manly head nod they all seemed to do, and then turned his attention back on me. As soon as the door closed behind Riley, Finn crossed the room and stopped directly in front of me. "What's going on, Ginger? What are you hiding from me?"

"I…it's nothing."

"If it's nothing, then you wouldn't be acting like this." He reached out and caught my chin, lifting my face up to his. His gaze latched on to mine. "Tell me the truth. We promised, no more lying."

I crumpled my dress in my hands. "Did you drink last night?"

"What?" He blinked at me. "No. Why?"

"Dad said he saw you drinking."

He shook his head. "I promised not to touch it anymore, and I didn't." He looked at the empty glass on the table. Slowly, he turned back to me. "Were *you* drinking?"

I flinched. "Riley got me a drink…well, two. Two drinks."

"It's okay. Just because I can't handle it right now doesn't mean you have to be scared to have one." He lifted a shoulder. "I still don't like it, but hell, I'm not in charge of you anymore. I got fired."

510

"No, you didn't. Not technically. He just said—"

"He fired me." Finn flexed his jaw. "Plain and simple. I knew it was going to happen, so it's not a surprise."

"You'll be fine once your arm heals. If nothing else, he probably meant you couldn't do it for a while," I said in a rush.

"Carrie." Finn met my eyes again, his own looking a little bit hard. "He didn't fire me because of my injury. He fired me because I fell in love with you. I knew it was going to happen, and I did it anyway."

I flushed. "But—"

"It's *okay*." He pressed his fingers to my mouth. "I made plans for this, remember? I can call Captain Richards and see if the offer for college is still open and—"

"Wait. You want to stay *in*, after what happened to you?"

He frowned at me. "Well, maybe. If I'm not discharged. That's always been the plan. What else am I supposed to do with myself?"

"Go to college. Be normal. *Live*."

"This is me being normal." He stepped back, letting go of me. Then his brow crinkled, and he grabbed me again, turning my face toward the light. He paled, and his fingers faltered on my chin. "Where did this mark come from?"

"It's nothing," I said quickly, my voice quivering. I tried to think fast. "It's a silly bruise that I can't even remember—"

"Don't fucking lie to me," he said, his voice hard. "Did Riley hit you? Is that what you were talking about earlier? Is that what you couldn't tell me?"

"N-No." I closed my eyes and shook my head as best as I could with him holding me like that. By the time I opened my eyes, he looked like he was ready to explode. "Of course not. Please. It's nothing."

"Then who did it?" He ran his fingers over the discoloration, his voice tinged with concern. "I know it wasn't your dad, and the only other person you were with besides him was…was…" His gaze snapped back to mine, comprehension turning the blue stormy and violent. "*Me*. Holy shit."

I shook my head frantically. "Finn, you didn't do this. Not really." I tried to grab his hand, but he jerked away and backed off, his eyes wide. "It wasn't you. When you went crazy that night, something flew back and scraped against me. It was nothing."

He growled, his chest rising and falling rapidly. "It's everything! I fucking *hurt* you."

"It was an accident!" I cried out, holding my hands in front of me and taking another step toward him. He backed away again. "Don't you see? This wasn't you. It was just a freak occurrence—"

"Stop. Making. Excuses." He ran a hand down his face. The empty hollowness I saw in his eyes killed me. "I hurt you, Carrie. The one person I swore I would never hurt. The one person I swore I would never, ever let down. The one person left on this world I need—and I hurt you? How the fuck is that *okay*?"

"Because you didn't mean to do it, damn it," I shouted, stomping my foot. "Why do you insist on always making yourself out to be the bad guy who ruins everything? This was an accident. Simply an accident."

"Fuck that." He stalked to the bar and yanked it open. "Me hurting you is never, ever acceptable. You've been tiptoeing around me, acting like you're scared to set me off—and now I see why. You should have been scared, damn it."

He was right. I'd totally been walking on eggshells around him, and look where it had gotten us. Here. "You know what? You're right. I've been scared about doing anything to set you off or make you upset, but maybe you need that now." I slapped his uninjured arm, and, man, it felt good. "Stop being an asshole. Stop hurting me. And stop acting like *this*."

He flinched, but I knew it was from my words, not my blow. "I can't. I keep hurting you, and it's not fair."

"Then don't do it again," I snarled, wanting to hit him again, but holding myself back. "Simple solution, really. No need for dramatics and heartbreak. You know where you can start? Close that stupid cabinet, and back away from the alcohol. You *promised* me you wouldn't drink anymore. Why don't you follow through on that? It's a good start."

He froze with his hand on the knob. "I hurt you, Carrie. What makes you think I'm worthy of keeping promises? What makes you think you can trust me at all?" Then he looked at me and he looked…different. It reminded me of something, but I couldn't put my finger on it. "What makes you think I give a damn about what promises I've made you if I can hurt you like that? You can't fucking trust me. Not anymore."

I curled my hands into fists. He was ruining everything, all because of a stupid mark he hadn't even meant to put there. God. "Stop this right now, or maybe *I'll* decide *I'm* done with you. Is that what you fucking want?"

He hesitated. Actually hesitated. "And if I do?"

"You don't," I said quickly, not giving up on him. I couldn't. "I know you, Finn. This isn't you." I wrapped my arms around myself. "Stop being like this."

He yanked the cabinet open. "Ah, but you're wrong. This *is* me now, Carrie, and it isn't changing. The problem is, neither are you. Which is why…" He hesitated, his knuckles white on the handle. "Th-This isn't working anymore."

I gasped, unable to believe what he was saying. What he was *doing*.

And then, oh God, then I realized what I was thinking of when he'd reminded me of something earlier. The way he was looking at me right now, all cold calculation and separated, it reminded me of when we'd first met…

Before he loved me.

Finn

She gasped behind me, and the pain she felt right now sliced through me. I'd swear it did. *You have to stop hurting her if you love her.* That's what Dad had said before he died. It was time I did what he'd asked. I'd been selfishly keeping Carrie at my side, treating her like shit the whole time.

It was time to admit that I wasn't getting better anytime soon. I was hurting her constantly, and I couldn't do it anymore. I'd been ignoring it up until now, but seeing that bruise on her face? Well, I couldn't fucking ignore that. I always swore I'd leave her before I'd hurt her. It was time to follow through on that promise.

"Finn, don't do this to me. You didn't even know it happened," she whispered, her voice broken and shaken.

I closed my eyes, pain ripping through me. "Is that supposed to make it better? That I was so fucked up I didn't even realize the person I love more than life itself was hurting?"

"It's not like that," she said, her voice growing stronger with each word. "You were upset. Anyone would have—"

I slammed my hand down on the bar. From the corner of my eye, I saw her jump. Good. Maybe if I scared her more, she'd finally give up on me. I'd already given up on myself. "Anyone would *not* have done what I did. I'm not fucking normal, Carrie. I'm a mess, and all I can think about at any given time of day is drinking, pain pills, or *dying*. That's all I care about anymore."

"You care about me. Don't pretend like you don't. You can say it all you want, but I'll see it for what it is. Another fucking lie." She glared at me. "I can't help you if you refuse to help yourself."

Good. She was mad. When she cursed, I knew she was pissed.

"You're right. You can't, so stop trying to." I set down a glass and filled it with whiskey. I didn't even want the drink, but I had to make a point. Had to show her that right now, I wasn't capable of being saved. She needed to physically see it to believe it. Lifting it up, I toasted her. "That's why I'm letting you go."

She watched me as I downed the whole fucking drink in one swig, her cheeks flushing. Then her gaze snapped back to mine, flashing fire. "You don't get to *decide* what's best for me. You don't get to *let me go*. I get a say, damn it. And fuck you for thinking I don't. I'm not walking away because you think you're too scary for me. You're not. You're just being an asshole."

"I know I am, damn it." I laughed harshly, letting all my frustration and anger out on her. Because even though I knew this was the right thing to do, it was killing me. This conversation hurt more than the IED or the broken arm, or even my father dying. It. Fucking. Hurt. "Jesus, Carrie, do you see me right now? Do you even fucking see me?"

"*Yes!* I've never *stopped* seeing you. Never stopped loving you. I've been here, with you, this whole time!" She stalked across the room and shoved my shoulder. "And what do I get for it? This! You giving up on yourself. On us."

I twisted my lips into a poor imitation of a smile. "Yeah, well, that's me. I'm an asshole. It's how I was before you, and now I'm back to my old ways. Get used to it."

She came closer, her eyes shining with tears and anger. So much anger. She looked like she was going to hit me again, and I wanted her to, because I deserved it so damn much. But she stopped short. "You're upset and not thinking clearly. You need to put away the drink and go to bed. In the morning—"

"I'll feel exactly the same." I met her eyes, squaring my shoulders. It was time to really hurt her, and I didn't want to. But if I could hurt her this one last time, she would be better off. Free of the emotional wreck I was. It was time to help her be happy again, because I never would be. "I can't love you like this, and you can't love me like this." I paused, gathering up the nerve to say, "I don't love you anymore, Carrie."

She gasped and covered her mouth. I immediately wanted to take the words back. "Wh-What? Don't say that if you don't mean it. Don't you dare say it again."

Of course I didn't *mean* it, but I'd say it anyway. I had to, for her. "I. Don't. Love. You. Anymore. We're done."

Tears poured out of her eyes, and she shoved me backward. I stumbled this time, welcoming the pain it sent shooting up my arm. "You're only saying that because you refuse to help yourself. You're giving up. Lying to me again. We swore—"

"I swore a lot of things." I forced a cocky grin. It hurt. "I lied to you, plain and simple. It's what I do. But I'm not lying now. This isn't about giving up. It's about letting go. We're over. The love is gone."

"Finn…" she whispered, broken and hurt. "I don't believe you."

I poured another drink, hating myself for every single drop that went into it. Hating myself because I'd let it get to this. Let it go this far, when I should have never let her fall in love with me in the first place. We were fucking doomed from the start, and I'd known it. I'd just chosen to ignore it. Now, I was even more fucked up than before.

She deserved better, damn it.

"Yeah, well, believe it." I saluted her with the glass. "It's over, Ginger. I've been faking feelings for you this whole week. I'm too tired to fake it anymore just so you don't get hurt. I'm done protecting you."

She lifted her chin stubbornly. "I can't save you if you're giving up."

"I don't want you to fucking save me!" I shouted. "I want you to leave me the hell alone!"

She backed up, her lower lip trembling. "Fuck you, asshole."

"And she finally sees the truth," I drawled, my heart ripping in two. "It's about damn time you accepted it."

Tears poured down those smooth cheeks of hers, and her blue eyes were coated in moisture, making them brighter than usual. It went against every single instinct inside of me not to walk up to her and hug her. To not take it all back. She might not know it now, but I was doing her a favor. I had to remember that, even if it was too late to save her from the pain. I couldn't regret loving her. Knowing her. So, no matter how selfish it might be, I didn't regret the time we had together. I'd never love someone the way I loved her.

She'd always be the one for me. I just couldn't be hers.

"Even so, I'm not giving up on you—but you need to fight, too. You're going to realize this is wrong. You're going to regret this, and I'll forgive you. But you can't say things like that to me and expect me to forgive *that*." She reached for my hand. If she touched me, I'd be a goner. I'd lose my resolve to save her. "I love you, and I'll always love you, but this isn't okay."

"Don't say that," I rasped, backing away from her. I ran my hand over my shaved head, wishing I could tug on my hair. Wishing I wasn't me. "You need to forget this ever happened. Move on. This was all a huge mistake between us. Stop trying to be a rebel, and stop trying to piss off Daddy Dearest all the time. Marry a guy like Riley."

I choked on the words. This wasn't right. She was supposed to marry *me*.

Fuck, I needed to get away from her.

"I'm not marrying anyone but you," she said, her voice completely calm. "When you wake up in the morning, come find me. Say you're sorry, and maybe we can forget this happened. *That's* how much I love you."

Without warning, she lunged across the distance between us, closing it with one giant step. Her arms snaked around my neck and she kissed me. She tasted like tears, whiskey, and Carrie. God, she felt so fucking good. So fucking right. How was I supposed to give this up? Give her up? I'd never get to taste her again, and that hurt, too.

I broke off the kiss, a ragged moan escaping me. Tears burned my vision, but I turned away from her before she could see. "It's over. Just give up already. I don't want to be with you anymore. It's…it's your fault this happened to me. I blame *you*."

She gasped and backed off, covering her mouth. I hated myself right then, for striking where I knew she'd be weakest. I knew, deep down, she blamed herself for this. And I'd used that to hurt her. To make her back the hell off.

I deserved to die right now.

The door opened. Senator Wallington walked in, took one look at me, skimmed over to Carrie, and rushed inside. "What's going on here?"

I poured myself another drink. "Your dreams have come true. I've finally accepted I'll never be good enough for your baby girl, and I broke up with her."

Carrie shook her head but didn't say anything.

She just stared at me, looking broken.

I faced her father, letting all my rage at this situation come to the surface. Letting them see how much of a fuck-up I was, finally. "Since she's having difficulty accepting this, why don't you tell her how wrong I am for her? Did you ever tell her about that time I almost got fired for bringing a girl back here with me? We got caught naked in the—"

Carrie cried out and spun on her heel, giving me her back and hiding her gorgeous face from me. I wanted to demand she turn around so I could see her. After all, I wouldn't be seeing her again. I needed to see her—to memorize everything about her.

"Griffin, you're drinking. You're not thinking this through." The senator cleared his throat. "Maybe you should put that aside and go to bed—"

"Sleep won't change a damn thing. I'm done trying to make myself better for this family. Done trying to be good enough for her, when that will never happen." I chugged the drink before I slammed the glass on the bar. "Be happy. You got what you wanted. You predicted it, even. Warned me in the hospital that I'd become too dark for her. Well, you're right. So I'm leaving."

"Then go," Carrie said, her voice so soft I almost missed it. "You don't love me anymore?"

I looked at her, wanting nothing more than to take it all back, but she was finally accepting it. I couldn't give in to temptation now. "I can't love you anymore, not like this."

Carrie flinched, but didn't say a word. Senator Wallington wrapped an arm around her shoulders. Glaring at me, he said, "Then you need to leave."

I laughed, even though I wanted to shout at the top of my fucking lungs. "I've got nothing left here, so I'll gladly leave."

"You had me," Carrie said, her voice steady despite the tears streaming down her cheeks. She lifted her chin and stared me down. "But that wasn't enough, was it? It was never enough, because this was always my fault. You blame me."

I met her eyes, my heart shattering into pieces. I wanted to deny it. Wanted to tell her how much she meant to me, but I just stared back at her, not saying a word. Carrie stared right back at me, not flinching. She waited for a second, obviously giving me one last chance to take it all back. I wanted to do it so damn badly. But instead I inclined my head, agreeing with her without speaking, because quite frankly? I couldn't even if I tried right now.

The tears I was holding back were choking the life out of me.

She swallowed hard, nodded, and walked out of the room. The last vision I had of her was her leaving the room, her head held high, as she walked away from me.

And she didn't even look back.

CHAPTER TWELVE

Carrie

I dashed up the stairs full speed ahead, slowing down once I rounded the corner. I walked down the hallway toward my room in a daze. I couldn't believe what had just happened, and yet in some ways, I'd known it was coming. The whole flight to Germany, I'd been going over and over in my head how I'd done this to him. Our relationship had ruined him. Had ruined his life. How could he ever love me after that?

Easy. He didn't. He'd told me as much.

I'd ruined our chances at a happy ending. He blamed me for his injuries. So did I. Over the last month, I'd seen him pushing me away constantly, and I'd made excuses for it. I'd seen him deteriorating in front of my eyes every single day, and I'd let him. He hadn't been shutting me out because he was healing. He'd been shutting me out because he didn't want me around. He'd realized he didn't love me anymore.

I couldn't fix that.

I'd been out of my league with him, and he'd been going slowly out of his mind—with no one to help him stay afloat. We'd been a ticking time bomb, and it had only been a matter of time till it all exploded. I covered my mouth and choked on a sob, picking up the pace before someone saw me. My mom opened her door at the same time I ran past it. All it took was one look at me, and she was following me into my room.

She closed the door behind her and opened her arms for me. "What happened?"

I shook my head, my hands fisted together in front of me. "He...he doesn't love me anymore, and it's all my fault."

"What?" Her face fell. "Oh no. I'm so sorry, baby."

"How...why...oh my God, he doesn't *love* me."

And then I burst into tears. I threw myself into her arms, finally letting myself cry. Really, *really* cry. I'd never cried like this before, and I didn't think I ever would again. There would never be another love like Finn's in my life, and I knew it. Knew this was it, the best love of my life. Gone forever.

"Shh." Mom rubbed her hand down my hair, over and over again, soothing me without words. But really, what was there to say? Nothing would ease this aching emptiness inside of me. Nothing ever could. "Shh, baby."

I couldn't believe it. It was over. He was gone.

Our first fight. Our first kiss. The way he'd laughed at the movie we'd watched that first night we spent together. Him on our "Christmas night," so stoic and scared, but determined to better himself for *me*. It was all gone. All a memory.

I shouldn't have let him go overseas. That had been my first mistake. My second had been blindly believing in love. I wouldn't be making that mistake again.

Love obviously didn't conquer all.

By the time I finished sobbing all over Mom, she was soaked and I was exhausted. I pulled away from her and avoided her eyes, feeling like a child all over again. "Thanks, Mom. I'm okay now."

Only I wasn't. Not at all.

"Our first heartbreak is always the toughest." She tucked my hair behind my ear and gave me a small smile. "It'll get better."

I swallowed hard, looking away. I didn't want to talk about it. It hurt too much. "I think I'm going to stay up here for the rest of the night, if you don't mind? I'm not fit company."

"That's fine, dear. People are clearing out now." She stood up. "I'll get you some cookies and milk. That always makes you feel better."

That might have worked for scraped knees and bad dreams, but nothing would fix this. I smiled anyway. "Yeah. That sounds lovely."

"Okay. I'll be right back. Why don't you get more comfortable?"

I nodded, not saying anything. As soon as the door closed behind her, I ripped the stupid black dress off and threw it across the room. Next went my bra, my panties, my tights. *Everything* had to go. Everything that reminded me of this day.

I hated him a little bit right now. I loved him. But, God, I hated him too.

I stood naked in front of the mirror and looked at myself. I looked a little bit crazy right now, with black mascara running down my cheeks and my hair a hectic, frizzy mess. All I wore was the tattoo I'd gotten for Finn—which he'd never gotten to see—and the necklace he gave me.

I closed my fingers around the clasp, ready to take it off...

But I couldn't.

He might not love me anymore, but God, I loved him so much. I ran my fingers over the sun pendant before pulling pajamas out of my closet. I barely had them on when the knock sounded on the door. I sat down on the bed and started twisting my hair into a ponytail. "Come in."

The door cracked open, but instead of my mother, Riley poked his head in. I wanted to tell him to fuck off, channeling Finn one last time, but it wasn't his fault Finn kept saying Riley was better for me. It wasn't his fault Finn didn't love me anymore.

"Hey," I said, my voice coming out hoarse and kind of frog-like. "You leaving?"

He came inside, leaving the door wide open, carrying a tray of cookies and milk. "Yeah, I'm about to head out, but your mom asked me to bring these up real quick." He set them on my nightstand, his green eyes studying me. "You okay?"

I laughed. It sounded foreign to my ears. "Do I *look* okay?"

"It's Finn, isn't it? You got in a fight because of the bruise. Maybe I could talk to him?" Riley shoved his hands into his pockets. "See if he needs a guy's perspective on things? It might help."

I looked down at my lap, wringing my hands into knots. "He doesn't love me anymore, and he blames me for his injuries. For his dad...for all of it..."

Riley's eyes went wide. "What? Bullshit. He loves you."

"No, he doesn't." I bit down hard on my lower lip. "He told me he doesn't love me. We're done. I wanted to be with him the rest of my life, and now it's over. Just like that. Gone. Dead."

"Shit." Riley hesitated for a second. He sat on the bed beside me and pulled me into his arms, but not too close. "I'm sorry. Are you sure he meant it? Maybe he just thinks he isn't good enough for you anymore, and is pushing you away. It's standard PTSD behavior."

I shook my head, blinking back tears. I refused to cry again. Finn had made me cry too much as it was. I knew why he was being this way, and I even understood it. But it didn't mean I had to roll over and accept it without feeling mad, hurt, and betrayed. This sucked. "He looked me in the eye and said it to my face. It's over."

Riley smoothed my frizzy hair back. "I know how you feel right now, but it'll get better. Over time, it'll hurt less."

I fought the urge to throat punch him for that platitude. It wouldn't get better, and it wouldn't fade. It would always hurt, like a festering, open wound that never healed. Did anyone realize how much I needed Finn? This wasn't puppy love, and it wasn't infatuation. It was soul-searching, heartbreaking, undying *love*.

"Yeah, I don't think it will. But thanks anyway, Riley."

I pulled back and looked into his eyes. He gazed at me with so much compassion that for a second, only a second, I wished I could have fallen in love with him instead. He was so nice. So perfect. I could totally see why Finn wanted me to be with Riley.

Too bad he didn't get to pimp me out like a rental doll.

Riley patted my head. "Give it time. You'll go back to school, hang out with friends, and it'll all fade away to a painful memory."

I nodded, not having it in me to argue anymore, and swiped my hands across my damp cheeks. "I'm sorry you had to witness all this drama."

"It's fine. We're friends, and friends help each other out." He pointed at the plate. "They also share their cookies with each other, and those look delicious. So…?"

Despite the blinding pain I was in, I laughed. I actually laughed. "Fine."

Reaching out, I grabbed a cookie for the both of us. We ate in silence. What would Finn do now? Where would he go? Would I ever see him again? Did he really not love me? How could something so strong and real die so fast?

I guess I'd never find out.

Riley took his last bite and dusted off his hands. "Well, I guess I'll get going. Remember, this too shall pass."

Another useless platitude. My fingers twitched with the urge to maim him. "Yeah. Sure." I finished my cookie, my eyes on the door. "I can't believe I'm going back to Cali alone. That he's not going to be there…"

"Hey, I'll see you in California, don't forget. You won't be all alone. I'm not that far away. We could get together over the weekends and drink the pain away."

"Yeah." I nodded without really listening. My mind was on Finn. "That'll be fun."

He walked past me, dropping a brotherly kiss on the top of my head. "Rest up. It'll look better in the morning."

I highly doubted that.

Finn

This was the end. There was no coming back from this.

She could never love me again after what I'd done. What I'd said. I'd had a similar thought before, when she'd found out who I really was in California. Back then, I'd still been naïve enough to think we could be together. That had been before I morphed into a monster who hurt everyone I loved.

It had been before I became…*me*.

"You need to cool it," Senator Wallington snapped. "I'm going to give you the benefit of the doubt and assume this is the alcohol talking, but you're done treating my daughter this way. And I'm cutting you off too."

Senator Wallington snatched the whiskey up and held it against his chest, making sure I didn't get another glass, I could only assume. He didn't need to worry. I didn't want any more. She was gone, so there was no one left to horrify. I didn't need to make her hate me anymore. She already did. "Don't worry. I'll be gone soon."

"Carrie loves you, and you're being an idiot." The senator shook his head. "I don't know what's gotten into you, but you need to snap out of it before it's too late."

I laughed. "*Now* you're championing us?"

"No, I'm championing her. She loves you, and you broke her heart just now." He cocked his head, his gaze scanning over mine. "How's that feel?"

"Like fucking hell," I rasped, curling my hand into a fist. "But she'll realize I did her a favor once she moves on. I hurt her. You see that mark on her face? It's from me. I did that."

Senator Wallington stiffened. "Excuse me?"

"The night my dad died. Something I did hit her." I tightened my fist. "I hurt her."

His eyes narrowed on me. "In that case, maybe you're right. Maybe you need more help than we can give you. Go find—"

"Save your words of wisdom for someone else. I don't need them anymore." I laughed harshly. "And, hey, she can marry Riley now. Have trust fund babies who don't have a daddy with tattoos behind them. That should make you happy."

The senator shifted on his feet. "You know that's not true. If I wasn't okay with you being here, you wouldn't be here, damn it. What would your father say about how you're acting right now?"

"*Don't.*" I took a step toward him, fury raging through me. It felt better than the agony. "You don't get to say that to me. He knew I was messed up, and he told me to stop hurting her. Now I am, because we're done. She'll move on, and I'll…I'll…" *I'd go crawl into a hole somewhere and forget the world existed.* "I'll be fine, too."

The senator scowled at me. "Go to bed. Talk to her in the morning when you're sober. And if you don't want to fix this, get the hell out of my house before dawn. She doesn't need to see you again."

I stormed past him. Every step I took felt harder than the last, because I knew if I was going to follow through on my promise to stop hurting her, I needed to leave before I caved. Senator Wallington was right. I needed to leave tonight.

I went outside, ready to run away right then and there, but I had too much shit upstairs in my room. I'd have to get at least some of it if I wanted to make a clean break. I sank down to the ground and covered my face with my hand, unable to believe that my life had come to this. How had this happened?

How had I lost her too? I had nothing left.

No reason to go on living.

I'd turned into a drugged-out, alcoholic, raging lunatic—and I'd hurt

Carrie in more ways than one. I'd never wished I was dead more than in this moment.

Some unknown amount of time later, I stood up and went back inside. I passed Riley on the stairs, only just managing to hide my surprise at seeing him coming down from the direction of Carrie's room. Irrational, misplaced jealousy hit me in the gut. I nodded at him. "Hey."

"Did you mean it?" Riley asked, his voice hard. "Do you actually not love her anymore?"

I stopped mid-step, my hand tight on the banister. So. Carrie had already told him about the breakup. That hadn't taken long. Again with the jealousy. I wanted to take a swing at him. Kick his ass until he couldn't stand up. I didn't. "I really don't see how it's any of your business. We broke up. That's all that matters."

"Ah, but you see, it's not." Riley crossed his arms. "I had a friend with PTSD once, you know."

I shrugged. "Your point?"

"He killed himself after pushing all of his loved ones away." Riley laid a hand on my shoulder, and I swallowed hard. Shrugging free, I gave him a look that clearly told him to keep his hand to himself. "Don't be him. Don't do anything stupid. If you love her, don't let her go. And don't think you can let her go and then sweep back into her life when you're all better. Someone else will snatch her up, and it'll be too late. She'll have a long line of guys waiting for her to get over you."

I cocked a brow at him, but damn it, he was right. Just the thought of her being with someone else tasted bad in my mouth. "Will you be the first in that line?"

Riley twisted his lips. "If I thought I stood a chance in hell? Yeah. But she loves you, and you're an idiot to throw it all away."

Again. He was right. But so was I. This was the right thing to do. I was sure of it. I kept dragging her down, drowning her slowly. It was time to sink alone. "Then I guess you'll win in the end, because I'm not changing my mind. I'm no good for her like this." I caught his gaze. "But if you manage to get her to fall for you, you damn well better take good care of her, or you'll answer to me."

With that, I climbed the rest of the way up the stairs. When I opened my bedroom door, I stopped in the frame, one foot in and one foot out. She was there. In my room. The first thing I noticed was that she'd changed into pajamas. The second? That she wasn't crying anymore. She didn't look pissed, though. She just looked empty.

She looked up when I came into the room, her ravaged face sending a fist of pain through my chest. The black makeup that had streamed down her cheeks like a child's first finger painting had been washed off at some point. Christ, I couldn't do this anymore. Couldn't keep fucking hurting her. I closed the door behind me and collapsed against it.

"Carrie…"

She stood up unsteadily. "Don't worry, I'll leave you alone in a second. I just wanted to ask you something without my father standing there watching." She met my eyes one last time. "Are you just pushing me away for my own good? Or did you really mean it when you said you didn't love me anymore because of what I'd done to you?"

No. No, no, no, no, no.

I opened my mouth, ready to beg for forgiveness, but then I saw it. The bruise I'd given her. "Y-Yes. I meant it." I swallowed hard. "Too much has changed between us. I went over there to make myself better for you, to save us, but instead it ruined everything. I'm sorry for that. I'm sorry it has to be this way, but I can't love you like I used to, and you shouldn't love me either."

She bit down hard on her lower lip and nodded, still not crying. "I think it's my fault, too. I totally get it if you can't love me because of what I did to you." She bit down again, even harder. "But we promised each other no more lies. If you do this, if you say this, you can't show up later and take it all back."

I shook my head, even though I wanted to hug her. Kiss her. Love her. "I'm not lying."

"Okay." She tilted that stubborn chin of hers up again, looking more like her father than ever before. "If it wasn't for me, for *us*, you would have never been offered that job. You would have never been hurt, and you'd still be the you that you so clearly want to be. I'm sorry for that. So, so sorry."

My heart wrenched. She couldn't take the blame. It wasn't on her shoulders, damn it. She wasn't the broken one here. "It's not your fault. None of this is your fault. It's all me. Forget what I said earlier. I didn't—"

"Don't go backing down now," she snapped. Then she regained that calm she'd been showing me, and looked at me with a cool smile. "One more thing. I love you, and I'll always love you, but I don't want to ever see you again if this is the end. Don't come looking for me. Don't come check on me. It's done."

I counted to three in my head. I wouldn't tell her the truth. I wouldn't fall to my knees and beg her to forgive me. And I definitely wouldn't tell her it had all been an act. That I hadn't really broken any promises to her.

That I loved her with all of my fucking heart and always would.

I closed my eyes. "Carrie…"

"Don't." She headed for the door. "Just d-don't."

She was making this so damn hard, when all I was trying to do was save her. She needed to leave before I snapped. But when she grabbed the knob, finally ready to leave me alone, I laid my hand over hers. Stopped her. Her skin was so soft. So perfect. So *mine*. How was I supposed to live without her by my side? How was any of this right?

"You won't see me again," I promised, meeting her gaze before looking at the bruise again. It kept reminding me I was doing the right thing. "Someday you'll love someone who actually deserves your love, and I'll be happy you found him."

"Yeah. Okay." She looked away first, tears finally escaping her eyes. "Whatever."

I moved away from the door, and for the second time that night…

I watched her walk away.

CHAPTER THIRTEEN

Carrie

Month one

Without opening my eyes, I shut off my blaring alarm. I slowly rolled over and blinked at the window. The sun was shining bright and cheery, completely opposite of the weather in D.C. It had been so weird coming home without…without *him*. I refused to even think his name—it hurt too much. I fingered my necklace, still staring outside at the bright blue sky. Funny that it was so pretty and cheery outside, when my life felt so dark I didn't want to move. I rolled over, pulled the covers over my head, and went back to sleep.

Finn

I chugged back another shot, squinting through the dim bar across all the bodies, shouting, and laughter. A girl with red hair turned my way, smiling coyly when she spotted me watching her. It only made me think of Carrie, which made me want to drink more, damn it. I motioned the bartender over, pointing at my empty shot glass. Where was she right now? Was she happy? Sad? Did she miss me as much as I missed her? I didn't know, but fuck, I wish I did.

CHAPTER FOURTEEN

Carrie

Month two

I sat up in bed, smoothing my messy hair out of my eyes. I was five minutes late to class, so I needed to move fast. Throwing the covers over the side of the bed, my feet hit the bare floor within seconds. After I tossed my scattered homework into my bag, I hobbled over to my closet, eyeing the shirt I'd left curled up in a ball on my pillow. Finn's shirt. It had taken me three weeks to find it mixed in with my stuff; I'd been that much of a mess. Now I slept with it every night. It calmed me, even while it made me cry. I couldn't let it go.

Couldn't let him go.

Finn

I sank onto the bench, a bottle of beer in my hand, glowering at the ocean. I had thought it would bring me peace, being back out here in California. Being near her. But she didn't even know I was here, and I hadn't gone near her. I looked down at my ripped jeans and trailed my hand over my scar. The cast was off my arm now, but it still hurt like a fucking bitch. Everything hurt. I had no meaning to my life. Nothing to live for.

No one who cared.

CHAPTER FIFTEEN

Carrie

Month three

I entered my dorm room, smiling as I shut the door behind me. I'd been out to dinner with Marie and her latest love interest, Sean. For the first time in months, I thought maybe I was starting to feel alive a little bit again. I walked up to the window, staring out into the night. I played with my necklace as I stared at the full moon, wondering where he was right now. If he was okay. If he was happy. I glanced down to where he used to always stand while watching over me…and my heart stopped. I swore, I freaking *swore*, I saw him out there, looking up at me. Pressing my forehead against the glass, I squinted into the darkness, desperately seeking him.

He wasn't there. I'd imagined the whole thing.

Swallowing past the tears that welled up in my throat, I rested a hand against the glass window. "I miss you, Finn."

The door opened behind me. I swiped the tears away and left the window.

Finn

I looked up at her, my heart racing so fucking hard I swore she could hear it. I saw her scanning the shadows, looking for me. Had she seen me, or had I imagined that? I tightened my fist around the bottle of whiskey I always seemed to carry around with me, wanting so badly to step into the light and shout her name at the top of my lungs. To beg her to forgive me. To love me again. Then I saw the empty bottle in my hand…and I hated myself.

"I miss you so much, Ginger," I whispered, dropping the bottle to the grass at my feet. "So fucking much."

I stumbled forward. I shouldn't be alive. Shouldn't be here anymore. Maybe I should go to the beach, take all my pills, and end it. End the suffering, pain, and agony. No. That wasn't painful enough. I deserved worse.

I deserved to fucking suffer.

Slowly, I made my way to the store, my heart in my throat the whole time. As I stood in the camping aisle, staring at the rope that could end my life, I tried to think of how best to do it. Where best to do it. I didn't have a house, and hanging myself from a tree seemed too poetic. I just stood there calmly contemplating the best place to die, and I didn't even care.

I'd hit rock bottom.

CHAPTER SIXTEEN

Carrie

Month four

I blinked up at the blinding light, covering my eyes with my hand. Peeking through my fingers, I just managed to catch sight of the bright blonde hair hanging down over my head. I'd been blissfully sleeping moments before, but now the light was freaking killing me. "God, Marie. What the hell?"

"Get up." She yanked the covers off me, leaving them tangled around my feet. "We're going out."

I pulled the covers back up over my sweats and loose T-shirt. "What? No. I'm not going out. It's…" I looked at the clock. "Uh…eight o'clock at night."

Wow. I'd have sworn it was at least midnight.

"Yeah. Just noticing the pathetic depths to which you've fallen, huh?" She ripped the covers off again. This time I let her. "It's a Friday night in spring, the weather is perfect, and we're going to a party whether or not you like it. Enough moping around over him."

"I'm not moping," I protested, sitting up and rubbing my eyes. "I'm just tired."

"You've been moping ever since you came back from D.C., and you know it. You woke up and he was gone. It was over. It was tragic and sad.

He broke your heart." She put her hands on her hips. "I've allowed you four months to get over it, but enough is enough already. You need to come back to the land of the living. Finn's gone, but you're not."

I swallowed hard at the mention of his name, my fingers automatically closing around the sun pendant. Had it really been four months? It felt like only days ago that I'd woken up to find his room empty. No goodbye. No hugs. Nothing. Just empty, like me.

I nodded. "I know that."

"Then get the hell up." Marie headed for the drawers, rummaging through them and slamming them shut in progression. "Ugh. You need one of my dresses. All of yours aren't right."

"Right for what?" I asked, shoving my hair out of my eyes. "I really don't want to go to a party. I'm tired. And there's—"

"'No other Finns out there.' Yeah. I got that loud and clear the other twenty times you told me." She rolled her eyes and pulled out one of her black dresses. I hated black dresses now. They reminded me of *him*. "How's this?"

"No."

She rolled her eyes and pulled out a dark green one. "This?"

"Marie…" I met her eyes. "Don't make me go. I-I'm not ready."

"You'll never be ready." She sat down beside me and hugged me so tight I couldn't breathe. I didn't mind one little bit. "But all you've done is sleep, hang out with me, study, and study some more. The only person you get dressed nicely for anymore is Riley, and even that's a chore for you. Do you really want your life to be like this forever? To be stuck in mourning like this?" She squeezed my shoulder. "You broke up with him, he didn't *die*."

It felt like he had. I hadn't heard a word from him since he'd packed up and left my parents' house in the middle of the night. Lately, I kept thinking I'd seen him here and there. Outside of my classes. At the gym. At the cafeteria after dinner. But then I'd look again, and he wouldn't be there. His ghost kept haunting me, even though he was still alive.

Hernandez was my guard now, and by unspoken agreement we didn't discuss Finn at all. I didn't ask, and he didn't tell. Heck, I didn't even know if they still talked. It was better that way…or so I kept telling myself.

Maybe Marie was right.

Maybe I needed to stop being so darn sad all the time. It had been four months, and he'd obviously moved on with his life. Maybe I should try to do the same, no matter how dull and boring it might be now. "Where's the party?"

"At Sean's fraternity." Marie's eyes lit up at the mention of Sean. All I knew about the dude was that he was loud when they made out, and he had a hell of a smile that Marie couldn't shut up about. "You in?"

I sighed. "Yeah, I guess so. I'll have to let Hernandez know."

I'd told her who I really was two months ago, when I'd finally stopped moping around long enough to actually form a coherent sentence. We'd gotten even closer since she knew the real me. It was so refreshingly fun to not have to hide my identity from someone like Marie.

"Oh." Marie's smile faded. "Does he *have* to come? He ruins the fun with that frown and serious disposition of his. And those judgey eyes."

"He'll stay back," I said, grabbing my phone. "And he won't stare at you. Why do you hate him so much?"

"He's Finn's friend. That makes him the enemy in my book," Marie said. She stood, the dress still in her hands, looking less than convinced. "I wonder if Riley could come down to meet us? What do you think?"

I pulled up Hernandez's number and jotted off a quick text. *Going to party.* "I doubt it. He'd need more notice than twenty minutes."

"Well, about that…" Marie fidgeted, her gaze skittering away. "I kind of sort of invited him down yesterday. Thought it might be time for you to open your eyes and see the boy's in love with you."

I tightened my grip on the phone. It vibrated, but I didn't look at it. "No, he's not. We're friends. That's it. Why does everyone keep shoving us together like we're suddenly going to fall in love or something?"

Marie snorted. "*You* might want to be friends, but *he* wants more."

"No, he doesn't." My stomach twisted at the thought. "He really doesn't."

"Yeah. Sure he doesn't." Marie pulled out a clean—maybe?—towel and chucked it at me. I caught it reflexively. "He'll be here in ten minutes, so you better go shower and shave."

"I don't have to shave," I said, my voice low.

"Have you seen those legs?"

"Yeah, it's not that bad." I lifted my leg and looked at my calf. Then, well, I flinched. "Okay, you're right. I'll shave." I looked at my phone and opened Hernandez's text. *Address?* I gave it to him before I tossed the phone aside. "'K, off I go."

"Is Sourpuss coming?" Marie asked, applying her eyeshadow.

She acted as if she hated him all the time, but every time we got together with him, Marie came to life. I'd bet my bottom dollar that she got off on their arguing. "Yep. Wear red. He likes it."

She rolled her eyes. "Now *you're* the crazy one."

I laughed and headed for the showers, feeling a little bit lighter for the first time since I'd gotten my heart broken by the guy who'd sworn he would always love me. I tried not to think about it much, but it was hard. Especially when my new guard was his freaking BFF. At first, I'd tried to avoid Hernandez out of principle. Dad kept sending him after me, though, and I'd realized I wasn't punishing Dad or Finn by avoiding the tail. I was punishing Hernandez, because he was getting in trouble for losing me.

So now I played along. I hated it.

I turned on the water, stripped, and stepped under the stream. The hot water woke me up even more, and I shaved and cleaned up as fast as I could manage with the jungle I'd been growing on my legs. As I dried off, I looked down at my tattoo. I wish I could say I regretted it, but I didn't. It represented a short period in my life where I'd been happy—really, truly happy—and even if he didn't love me anymore, he had.

And I'd loved him, too. So freaking much.

My heart wrenched, and I wrapped the towel around myself before making my way back to my room. I passed a few people on the way, but for the most part the halls were empty. When I opened the door, I called out, "You win. I'm no longer a hairy Amazon beast."

A man cleared his throat. "Uh, that's good."

"Riley?" I scanned the room and found him sitting on the edge of Marie's bed, his cheeks red. "You're early."

"You're naked." He raised a brow, looking me up and down casually. "Call it even?"

I clutched the towel tighter to my boobs, swallowing hard. It was longer than most dresses, yet I felt horribly exposed. "Uh, where's Marie?"

"Someone knocked on the door, and she left." His gaze dipped low again before slamming back up to my face. His gaze heated significantly, making me shift on my feet. "I guess I should do the same so you can get dressed. Or are we wearing towels to this party? I could totally rock that."

I laughed. "Yeah, you probably could. But I kinda need to get dressed, so…"

"I don't suppose I could sweet-talk you into letting me stay?" He stood up and crossed his arms. "I make excellent company."

"Bad boy," I said, laughing and pointing at the door. "Out."

He laughed and held his arms up in surrender. "Yes, ma'am."

"I'll call out to you when I'm decent," I said, grinning.

"You already look decent to me."

I cocked my head. "Are you flirting with me?"

"And if I am?" He brushed past me on his way to the hallway, his arm rubbing against my bare one. "Would that be so bad?"

I rolled my eyes and closed the door in his face. I couldn't answer that. Any girl would be lucky to have a guy like Riley flirting with her, but I wasn't *any* girl. I might not be with Finn anymore, but I knew I wasn't ready to fall for someone else.

I wasn't even sure if I could.

I slipped into my panties, bra, and then slid the dress over my head. It was soft, short, and sexy. For a second, I debated taking it off and changing into my usual jeans and loose T-shirt, but then I shook off the urge. I refused to be that girl anymore. Marie was right—enough was enough. It was time to move on…

Even if I still felt like I was dead inside.

"You can come in now," I called out, walking up to the mirror where all our makeup was. "I'm dressed."

As I applied light gray eyeshadow, Riley came back inside and sat down on my bed this time. He whistled through his teeth. "Damn, girl. You look good."

"Yeah, yeah." I leaned closer to apply my eyeliner. His gaze dipped down. *Oh my God, he's totally checking out my ass.* "Hey. Eyes at face level."

He met my eyes in the mirror. "They are at my face level. That just happens to be at your ass. It's a nice one, you know."

"Sorry to bail, I had to lend my curling iron to—" Marie stopped in the doorway, a smirk on her face as she took in me at the mirror and Riley on my bed. "Oh. Am I interrupting something?"

"No," I said.

"Yes," Riley said at the same time. Then he grinned. "I was staring at her...dress."

Marie snorted. "Yeah. Sure you were."

"He's being a typical dude. Staring at anything in a dress." I looked at Marie as I slammed the lid back on my eyeliner. She had on a short red dress that barely skimmed mid-thigh. "Speaking of which..."

She flushed. "Oh, shut up. It's the only one I had."

"Mmhm." I applied mascara, grinning the whole time. She had it bad, she just didn't want to admit it. As if on cue, my phone buzzed. I glanced at it and put the finishing touches on my lashes. My hair was still wet, so I grabbed a hair elastic off the shelf. "He's outside waiting for us."

"How much longer are you going to be?" Marie asked.

"Three minutes tops."

She backed toward the door. "I'll go let him know."

And then she was gone. I rolled my eyes. "She's half in love with him, you know."

"Who?"

"My new bodyguard, Hernandez." I checked out my hair. For once, my updo managed to look decent. I'd done a half-up, half-down twist. "He replaced...Finn."

I flinched. Even saying his name hurt.

"How are you doing with that?" He came up behind me but didn't touch. "Have you heard from him at all?"

"Nope, when we broke up, we broke up. I woke up the next morning, and he was gone. Haven't heard from him since. It's over." *Yeah. Even though I still slept with his shirt, I was so over him.* I smoothed my hair for lack of something better to do. I didn't like talking about it. It hurt too much. "How have you been?"

"Good." He studied me. "But you didn't tell me how you've been."

"I'm fine," I said softly. "Really. I don't like talking about it, or him. That's all. It hurts too much, you know?"

"I know. Hey, I like the darker red." He gave a small nod toward my hair. I'd dyed it a little darker after the breakup, and I had side bangs now. I was still adjusting to the darker red. "It's nice."

"Thanks."

"You're welcome. I like the bangs, too." He stepped closer. "Ready to go?"

I smiled at him gratefully. One of the best things about him was that he knew when not to push. "Yeah, just let me get some shoes."

Once I had a pair of heels on, I walked out into the hallway with Riley. Cory was walking down it at the same time as we left. He looked at Riley, and then stared at me. "Oh. Hey."

I gave him a little smile. We might not be friends anymore, but he *did* know my secret. I hadn't forgotten about that. "Hey, how's it going?"

"Good." Cory held his hand out. "I'm Cory."

"Riley Stapleton." He shook Cory's hand. "Nice to meet you."

Cory nodded and looked back at me. "Where's Finn?"

"We broke up." I swallowed. "We're on our way to a party, so I'll catch you later?"

"I'm going, too." Cory grinned. "So, yeah, you will."

Great. I nodded. "Bye." I headed down the stairs, grimacing. "Remember the guy I told you about who Finn hated?"

"That's him?" Riley asked dryly. "I can see why. I don't like the way he looks at you."

"Now you sound like *him.*"

Riley shrugged and opened the door at the bottom of the steps for me. "Sorry, but it's true. He's sleazy."

I rolled my eyes. "He's harmless as a—"

"Oh, don't be such an ass," Marie snapped. "God, why did I come out here at all?"

"I'm simply pointing out that if you wanted to wear a short dress, you should have put on—" Hernandez cut off, his eyes narrowing on me. "Oh. Hey, Carrie. What's he doing here?"

"Put on a what?" I asked, my eyes wide.

"Nothing," Marie snapped.

"Pair of underwear," Hernandez said at the same time. "That doesn't leave ass cheeks hanging out."

"I...I see." I looked at Marie, whose face was bright red, and she looked as if she wanted to punch Hernandez. I forced myself not to ask how he knew what she had on under her dress. Forcing my attention back to Hernandez, I smiled. "And *he's* here to go to the party with us."

Hernandez frowned. "You come down here an awful lot, considering your school is so far away."

"Yeah. I came down for the weekend to see Carrie." Riley eyed him, his blond hair reflecting the full moon. "Is that a problem?"

"No, of course not. It's just a long way to travel for a little party when you're going to school for law. How long did it take? Five hours?"

Riley laughed uneasily and rubbed his jaw. "Yeah, something like that."

I frowned at the way Hernandez was watching Riley. To quote Marie, he was looking at him with *judgey eyes*. "How do you know where he goes to school, and what his major is? From my dad?"

"No, from—" Hernandez hesitated. "I mean, yeah. Sure. Your dad."

My heart stopped before painfully speeding up. If he hadn't heard about Riley from my dad, that meant he'd spoken to Finn. Was he here, in Cali? I looked over my shoulder, half expecting to see him behind me. He wasn't. "You talked to him."

It wasn't a question.

Hernandez flexed his jaw. "Let's not do this. You ready to go?"

"Y-Yeah, of course." I took a steadying breath. "You're right."

"Carrie?" Riley placed his hand on my lower back. "You still want to go?"

No. "Of course. Let's go have some fun."

Hernandez looked at Riley's hand, stiffening. "After you guys."

I walked by him, Marie on my other side, trying to resist the urge to shrug Riley's hand off. It was an innocent enough touch, and despite what everyone seemed to think…

He wasn't in love with me.

CHAPTER SEVENTEEN

Carrie

The music was so loud I couldn't hear myself think, let alone carry on a freaking conversation. But I guess that was the point of a party like this. You were supposed to let loose, stop thinking, and just drink. Dance. Have fun. Be young and free.

I was trying so hard to do all of those things.

I lifted my cup to my mouth, draining the last of the wine. It tasted okay, but I missed my pink wine coolers that Finn had always kept stocked for me. I paused, the cup still pressed to my lips. That's the first time I'd thought about Finn without wanting to cry in…well, since the breakup.

Maybe that meant something.

"Want to dance?" Riley asked me, leaning down to shout in my ear. "With me, that is?"

My head spun a little bit from the amount of booze I had already. The last thing I should do is dance, yet that's exactly why I would. I'd been living my life doing all the things that I *should* be doing, instead of being crazy every once in a while.

Maybe it was time for a change of pace.

"Sure, let's go. But first…" I took his drink and finished it. When he looked at me with wide eyes, I laughed, tossing my head back and everything. "What?"

"Nothing at all. I like seeing you happy, is all."

He grabbed my hand and led me to the dancing area—which, in all reality, was nothing more than a cleared out living room. Couples danced all around us, half of them caught in the moves, and half of them caught up in each other. Some had stopped with the pretense of dancing, and were just plain old getting it on without caring who saw.

It made my cheeks go all hot, and it made me miss how Finn had made me feel when he touched me like the dude in the corner was touching his girl.

"Who says I haven't been happy?" I called out to Riley. "I'm good. Excellent. Wonderful."

And a horrible liar.

He pulled me in his arms and moved to the music without hesitation. Turned out, he was a pretty amazing dancer. Was there anything this guy *wasn't* good at? His hips swung to the music, mimicking sex, almost, and it was hot. Damn, the boy moved like Bruno Mars. The urge to fan my cheeks hit me strongly. "Since when do you dance like that?"

"Since forever. You just didn't notice before because you weren't looking." I stared at him in surprise, and he grabbed me and pulled me closer. "You going to dance, or stand there moping about Finn?"

I gave him my back, moving my body to the music. He brushed up against me, all hard muscle and hot skin. "Stop talking about him," I called over my shoulder. The tempo picked up, and we matched it effortlessly. Grinning, I moved closer, feeling so freaking alive. "He's not here, but you are."

"About time you noticed."

I looked back at him, ready to make some sarcastic remark, but he was watching me with a weird look in his eye. As soon as he saw me looking, though, it faded away and he grinned. I swallowed hard, realizing he'd been looking at me as if he *wanted* me. How often had he done that, and I missed it? Was I really that blind?

The song ended, and a slow one took its place. We both stood there awkwardly, staring at each other. I might be able to break it down with him, sexy style, but I couldn't be that close to him. I fanned my face with my hand. "I'm going to head outside for some fresh air. Want to get some more drinks and meet me out there?"

He nodded. "Don't wander off far."

544

"I won't. Besides, Hernandez is out there." I shrugged. "I'll be fine."

I walked away without waiting for an answer, needing to get away from him and all the possibilities that look he'd given me represented. It made me nervous and anxious at the same time. My stomach fisted into a knot, making me wonder if I was about to puke up all the wine I'd just drank. That would be a fitting end to this night, wouldn't it?

I stumbled out into the cool night, taking a big gulp of air. I could still hear the music, so I moved away from the doorway, wanting some peace and quiet. Someone stepped out of the shadows and I jumped, my hand to my chest. For a second, a split second, I thought it was going to be Finn.

It's how we met, after all. Outside a party.

But I was wrong. It was Cory. "Where are you going?"

"Nowhere. I needed some fresh air." I dropped my hand back to my side. "You scared me."

He laughed. "Sorry. Where's Riley?"

"Getting us some more drinks." I wrapped my arms around myself, eyeing him. I could tell with only one glance that he was drunk. Last time he'd gotten drunk at a party with me, it hadn't been pretty. "He'll be out any second."

"I'll only take a second." He walked right up to me, his jaw hard. "You're single again, and you're with a guy who looks like me. He's basically me, but not. Is he a senator's kid, too?"

I laughed, unable to stop myself. I'd been caught off guard by the cocky statement. "Um, I'm not with him. And he doesn't look like you at all."

"Yeah, he does. He comes from money, like us." He stumbled a little bit. "Answer my question, Carrie."

I backed up a step, stalling for time. Riley would come out soon, I was sure. "Which one?"

"Is he a senator's kid, too?"

I blinked. Why did he care? "Uh, yeah. He is."

"Of course." He smirked. "You had enough of playing on the wrong side of the tracks, huh? I don't blame you. Finn was a huge mistake."

I frowned at him and backed up. "Someone should really lock up the alcohol so you can't get a hold of it. When you drink, you don't play nice."

"I'm not drunk." He stumbled again, totally ruining the denial. "I'm just telling the truth. Finn was horrible for you. Stay on this side of the tracks," he slurred.

"Finn wasn't from the wrong side of the tracks. He was a good guy." I curled my hands into fists, taking another step back from him. He was pissing me off now, talking badly about Finn. He had no right. No right at all. It was deja vu. "Better than you've ever been."

Cory laughed and followed me, backing me up to the beach. "Doubtful. He's gutter trash."

My heart sped up, and I finally saw what Riley and Finn saw. For the first time ever, Cory creeped me out. "You're scaring me. Stop following me like that."

"Why? Because your big bad ex isn't here to beat me up? You don't have him here guarding you anymore. I could kidnap you now," he whispered, grinning evilly. "You're used to that, I bet. Being stolen away by ruffians. I bet you like it, too. You like it rough, don't you?"

"God. You're such an idiot," I snapped. "Leave me alone."

He grabbed my hand and jerked me closer. His breath reeked of cheap beer and even cheaper vodka. "You know, you *should* be nicer to me. I know things about you that no one else knows. And I've kept all your secrets…for now."

I tried to pull free, but he tightened his grip. "Let *go* of me."

"Fine." He released me and ran his hands down his face. "You treat me like I'm the enemy."

"You were mean to Finn," I said, rubbing my wrist. "And you're being mean right now, too." Where the hell was Hernandez, anyway? Shouldn't he have come out, even though I'd warned him only to show himself if it was life or death?

I scanned the shadows. Nothing.

"Well, he's not here anymore, is he?" He shrugged. "So why hold it against me? I was obviously right about him, or you'd still be with him."

"Just because he's gone doesn't make it okay to talk crap about him," I said, frowning at him. "You really don't get it, do you?"

He stepped closer and ran a finger over my jaw. "I never got what you saw in him, no. You should be with someone like me."

Over my dead body. "Stop it."

"You deserve so much better. Someone like me."

He lowered his face and kissed me before I could even remotely guess what he was going to do. His tongue probed my lips, making me gag. I gasped and shoved him back, swiping my hand over my mouth while trembling. "Don't do that again. We're not together, and we will *never* be together."

"That's why I did it. I had to do it just one more time." He balled his hands at his hips. "Before you're with that Riley guy next."

A scuffling sound came from the shadows. Hushed voices, too. Footsteps approached rapidly before slowing down. "Everything's fine, Hernan—" I broke off. It wasn't Hernandez; it was Riley. "Oh, hey."

"Hey." Riley held two bottles of water in either hand. "Everything okay?"

"Yeah, I was just leaving," Cory muttered. He gave me one last look before walking away. "See ya," he called out over his shoulder.

I let out a sigh of relief and looked at Riley. He was watching me closely. "Did he kiss you? I thought I saw…"

"He did. I told him not to do it again." I sat down on a big boulder and looked up at him. "He's always liked me, I guess. Which is why Finn hated him."

Finn.

"You still love him, don't you?" He perched next to me on the rock. "You're not over him even in the slightest."

I swallowed hard. "I don't know if I'll ever be *over* him, really. What I felt for him isn't something that just goes away with time. It'll always be there."

"Yeah. I get that."

I looked over at him. He looked pensive. "Are you still in love with your ex, too?"

"No." He laughed. "God, no. I don't think I really ever loved her. She was a girlfriend, but that's it. Nothing more."

"Have you ever been in love?"

"Well…" He looked over at me, and his eyes latched on to mine. "I think I could be, easily, but it's not the right time."

I sucked in a shaky breath, my heart wrenching. Darn it, I'd been a blind fool. Everyone was right. He wanted more from me, and I couldn't give it to him. "Riley, I can't—"

He leaned in and placed his fingers over my lips. "Don't. There's nothing to say. I know already."

"But—" I pulled his hand away from my lips, but didn't let go of his fingers. "There is. You're such a good guy. The perfect guy, really. I wish that things could be different. That I could be different. I'm just not ready to try again."

"I know." His fingers flexed on mine. "Do you think, once you are, that maybe we could, I don't know, get a coffee? Go to dinner?"

"You have to understand, the love I had for Finn?" I shook my head, not dropping his gaze. His eyes looked even greener in the moonlight. I didn't even realize that was possible. "I'm not sure it will ever fully go away. That's not fair to you. You deserve more than half a heart from a girl."

He reached out and cupped my cheek. It felt good. "Let me decide what I deserve, okay?"

I'd said something similar to Finn once. He'd pissed me off by deciding what was best for me without asking. Is that how Riley felt now? Frustrated and angry at me for trying to decide what's best for him? I didn't want to do that to him.

"Okay." I forced a smile, still holding his hand. "You really are a great guy, you know. If I'd met you first…"

His gaze dipped to my lips. "But you didn't."

"I didn't."

He set the water down, and framed my face with his other hand. "May I kiss you? Just a little kiss to see if we're compatible, before I try to win your heart?"

"I don't know." Speaking of hearts…mine picked up speed at the thought of kissing Riley. I'd only ever kissed Finn and Cory. There was no comparison there. Maybe with Riley it would be different. "I guess we could try if you want."

He grinned. "You make it sound like a prison sentence."

"Sorry." I laughed, reaching out to grasp his wrists lightly. "It's just—"

He leaned down and kissed me, cutting me off mid-sentence. His soft lips touched mine, applying the perfect amount of pressure. Perfect setting. Perfect weather. Perfect touch. Perfect guy. The gentle way he held me. The way he tilted his head just right to get access to my mouth. Everything about the kiss was *perfect*.

But he wasn't Finn. There were no explosions or fireworks.

It just felt nice.

He pulled back, resting his forehead on mine. "That wasn't so bad, was it?"

"N-No." I tightened my grip on his wrists. I wished I were different. Wished I were healed already so I could try this again with an open mind. "It was great."

"Good." He grinned down at me, looking way too happy. It made me feel guilty. "I can wait for you to be ready now."

"What if I'm never ready?"

He shrugged. "Then you'll never get to kiss me again."

"Ouch." I laughed. "That's harsh."

"I'm just kidding. You can kiss me anytime." He let me go. "You wanna kiss me again now, don't you? Admit it."

I smiled at him. He was so freaking charming that it was hard not to. "Actually, I think I'm going to go back to my room now. I'm tired."

"I'll go with you," he said quickly.

"*No.*" I winced at how harsh that sounded. I just needed to be alone right now. Kissing Riley and kind of liking it was like putting the nail in the proverbial coffin that held my relationship with Finn. I needed time to recover. "You stay and have fun since you drove this whole way down. Don't leave for me."

He studied me. "I want to, but I can tell you want to be alone, so I'll stay. Maybe we can have breakfast in the morning before I head back?"

"Sure, where are you staying?"

"With a buddy here." He quirked a brow. "Why? You offering to let me stay with you? 'Cause I could ditch him and crash with you instead."

"Ha! You could totally—" Something scratched on the concrete behind us, and a crashing sound broke the relative quietness of the night. I whirled around to look. "Hernandez, is that you? Are you okay?"

A shuffling sound, and then Hernandez came stumbling out of the shadows, tripping over his own feet. "Sorry, I, uh, I kicked a potted plant by accident."

I squinted at him. "You kicked a…plant?"

"Yep. That's me." He glowered over his shoulder. "Always being a clumsy asshole."

"Oookay." I stood up and picked up the bottle of water Riley got me. "Well, you're just in time. I'm ready to go back to my room, so you can walk me, and then go home."

He eyed Riley. "Alone, I assume?"

"Yes, of course." My cheeks heated. "If I wasn't going to be alone, I wouldn't ask you to walk with me."

He looked over his shoulder again. "I'm ready when you are."

I smiled at Riley. "Anyway…"

Riley came up to me and kissed my lips gently. "See you in the morning?"

"Sure. Nine?"

"It's a date," he said, grinning. He backed off, not dropping my gaze. "It's supposed to be sunny tomorrow, so maybe we can go to the beach, too."

The sun is finally shining, Ginger. Finn's voice echoed in my head, loud and clear. It was almost as if he'd actually said the words, and it hurt. Would he ever stop haunting me? My smile slipped. "Great. See you then."

I watched him head back into the party, tossing his water bottle from hand to hand. A super-hot girl walked up to him and started flirting, but he looked back at me. Well, crap. He really did like me. I wasn't sure what to do about that. I waved one last time before walking toward my dorm.

Hernandez fell into step beside me. "So…moving on, huh?"

"I don't know." I lifted a shoulder. It felt weird talking to him about this, when he may or may not be in contact with Finn. "Maybe."

"He seems…nice."

As if stuck in a time warp, Finn's words from all those months ago rang in my head: *Nice. That's the word for a puppy, not a man. Nice won't make you scream out in bed.* I straightened my spine and glanced around, half expecting to see him standing somewhere in the shadows, smirking at me. God, I was losing it. "Uh, yeah. He's very nice. There's nothing wrong with being nice."

"I never said there was." He shoved his hands in his pockets and looked over his shoulder again. "Where are you two meeting tomorrow for breakfast?"

"I don't know. He'll probably come up to my room first, and then we'll decide." I looked at him. "Why do you ask?"

"So I can follow you there." He raised a brow at me. "It's kind of my job," he lowered his head and mumbled, "no matter how much I might wish it wasn't."

"Why don't you quit if you hate it?"

"I can't." He looked at me, then glanced away. "I need to watch over you for him. He'd want me to."

"He doesn't love me anymore," I said, my voice soft. "You're off the hook."

He laughed. "No. I'm not."

We walked the rest of the way home in silence. I hesitated at the entrance to my dorm. Hernandez hovered, all of his weight on his left foot, as if perched to leave.

Still, I didn't move. My hand gripped the door tight. "Is he…is he okay?"

"Finn?" Hernandez looked away. "What makes you think I've talked to him recently?"

I tucked my hair behind my ear, my heart racing at the mere thought of hearing how Finn was doing. I was like a starved dog, desperate for any scrap of information I could get about him. "Please. Tell me if he's okay. That's all I want to know. I don't need to know anything else."

Hernandez looked out toward the shadows and shoved his hands in his pockets.

"I get wanting to move on, but don't do it if you're not ready. That's not fair to anyone involved."

"Has Finn moved on?" I asked. Immediately, I regretted the question. I didn't want to know. I held up a hand and scrunched my eyes tight. "You know what? Forget I asked that. Forget it all. Just go home."

I opened the door and walked inside, trying not to look back at him. Trying not to go back and beg him to answer my question. I *needed* to know.

I couldn't know.

CHAPTER EIGHTEEN

Finn

I rocked back on my heels and cursed under my breath, an empty hollowness residing where my heart used to beat. It had felt that way ever since I walked away from Carrie, and I didn't think it would ever go away, not without her in my life. She owned my heart, carrying it with her wherever she went, and she wasn't with me anymore. I missed her more than I missed having a heart. I'd finally learned how to *live* when I'd been with her, and now I wasn't living.

I was just surviving. Barely.

Dr. Montgomery opened the door and smiled at me. She wore her usual business suit, and her brown hair was pulled back in a bun. She was a creature of habit, if nothing else. "Griffin, you can come in now."

"All right."

I walked into the office and sat down on the couch. I drew the line at lying down on it, though. It was hard enough to walk in those doors. But after hitting rock bottom, I realized I needed help. And it *was* helping. I was still here, after all.

I almost hadn't been.

Dr. Montgomery settled in her chair. "So, how was your Friday night? What did you do? When you called for an emergency meeting, I figured something had to be up."

"It was…hard. Bad." I ran a hand over my hair. It was growing out a little bit now. It was as short as it would have been if I had been going to drill weekend. "I almost did something I would have regretted, but I held myself back."

"Did you try to hurt yourself again?" she asked, her forehead creased. "I thought we'd gotten past that point."

"No, that's not it."

"Were you upset over your honorable discharge from the Marines again?" she asked.

"No." I dragged my hand down my face. "And before you ask, no, Captain Richards didn't try to contact me about that job again."

Dr. Montgomery nodded. "Ah. Then it was Carrie. Did you try to go see her?"

"I *saw* her," I admitted, touching the scar on my forehead. "But I made sure I stayed hidden from her. She dyed her hair a different color—it's a darker red now. And she has bangs. She wears more lipstick, too. It's like she's trying to change herself now that I'm not there. She was with a guy we both know, and she looked happy. So fucking happy." I cut off. "Sorry."

"You can curse—God knows I do when I'm not working. This is a safe environment for you." She leaned forward. "So. How did seeing her look so happy and different make *you* feel?"

"Empty. So fucking empty." Rubbing my jaw, I laughed uneasily. "Lonely. Sad. Full of regret and wishes and useless hopes. What else would it make me feel? I love her so much it *hurts*, and she's not mine anymore. She never will be. I broke her heart."

She nodded. "But you let her go. Set her free. Do you now think that was the wrong decision?"

"Fuck if I know. I was so messed up, I wasn't even *me*." I tugged on my hair. "I wasn't good for her. She needed someone stronger than I was. A man who could protect her, be her partner. Not a burden."

Dr. Montgomery steepled her fingers. "But you think you could be that man now? Is that what you're saying?"

"I...I don't know. She looks pretty happy without me."

"Looks can often be deceiving." She leaned back and studied me. I hated when she looked at me like that. She saw way too much. "So can words. After all, you told her you didn't love her, but that was a lie."

"Yeah, well," I swallowed hard. "She didn't seem to be broken up or anything. She looked like she's moved on, and I'm happy for her. I am."

"But…?"

"But I miss her so damn much." I stood up and paced, my heart beating faster even though I swore it wasn't there. "I want to go up to her and beg her to forgive me, but then my head gets in the way. What if she's better off without me in her life? What if Riley makes her happier than I ever did or could? What right do I have to jump back into her life and fuck it all up again?"

She inclined her head, still watching me. "Is she with this Riley guy?"

"Not yet." I looked out the window. "My buddy is her guard. He says this is the first time this happened."

"The first time what happened?"

"They kissed." I looked at her. "I saw it."

She sat forward. "Did it trigger anything?"

"I had another nightmare last night." I looked out the window. "I'm not sure if it's because of that. They never really left. They just got less frequent."

"All right." She studied me, her eyes locked in on something I couldn't see. "What else did it trigger?"

"Nothing, besides the need to get her back." I sighed and headed back toward her. "And they're meeting up for breakfast."

"Ah, so there's something *starting*."

"I guess so." I turned around at the wall and headed back toward the window, my steps agitated. "But if there's nothing there yet, I'm not messing anything up, right? It's not like they're in love or anything."

"The real question is: Are you ready for all that talking to Carrie would entail? The possibilities? The pain?"

I looked at her. "Isn't that where you come in? Tell me. Am I ready?"

"You've been doing well. For all intents and purposes, you're more yourself then you were when you showed up here the first time." She crossed her arms. "Tell me again about that night. The night you turned it all around."

I sat down on the couch and rubbed my temples. "Why?"

"Just trust me this time, Griffin."

I rested my elbows on my knees. I hated when people used my full name. It reminded me of the senator. "I was drunk off my ass and went to Carrie's dorm. It was the lowest point in my life." I looked up at her.

"I was ready to end it all; the pain was just too much. I couldn't take it anymore. Couldn't stand that I was the only one alive, and I was alone. And I missed her so damn much."

She nodded. "And then…?"

"I went to the store to get rope to hang myself," I whispered. "I deserved a rough death. Slow, painful, horrible. The whole way to the store, I was so fucking calm. No panic, no doubts. It's what I wanted to do. But when I held the rope in my hand, deciding the best type…something stopped me. I thought about her, and I couldn't do it. I couldn't do that to her. It would devastate her knowing I'd died alone and miserable."

"Good." She cocked her head. "And then…?"

"I took a deep breath, put down the rope, and walked to my buddy's house, which used to be mine. Pounded on the door till he answered, and I told him I needed help before I hurt myself." I sighed. "You already know this shit. Why are we going over it again?"

"I have a point." She pursed her lips. "And he said…?"

"'No shit, dude. You look like a fucking zombie.'" My lips twitched into a reluctant smile. "Then he hugged me, made me shower, and I slept for a day and a half. I made an appointment to see you, and I've been getting better every day. Really getting better, not just trying to."

"And you haven't thought about ending it all again?"

"No, not even once." I dragged a hand down my face. "Does that mean I'm ready? Is that your point?"

"I don't know. When you saw her with Riley, did you want to hurt yourself?"

"What? No." I shook my head. "I was upset, but I'm done with that portion of my recovery, if you could call it that. I don't even think about it anymore. It won't make the pain go away. Nothing will. I miss my dad. Miss my friends. And I miss her the most, because she's still here, but not with me."

"What do you do instead of thinking about hurting yourself?"

"I accept the pain. Deal with it. Move the fuck on." I tugged on my hair. "Life is full of shit. There's not much to be done for it, and I've accepted it. My PTSD isn't gone, but I'm coping."

"What are your plans for the future?"

I laughed. "I have no idea. I'm out of the Marines, thanks to my injuries, and I'm not in private security anymore."

"Do you want to be in either one?"

"I got offered a job with a private security firm." I shrugged. "I said no."

She nodded. "Why did you do that?"

"It was in Chicago." I paused, knowing what she wanted to hear from me. "She's here, in California. Why would I move there?"

"Ah, so you don't want to leave her, but you don't want to be with her?"

"I never said that," I snapped. "I said I wasn't sure if I would be best for her. That's why I'm here, asking you if I'm ready. If I can try to get her to forgive me yet or not."

She pushed her glasses up on her nose, her green eyes on me. "If she rejected you, would the pain send you spiraling again? Would you want to hurt yourself? Drink a few bottles of beer? Pop a few pills? Buy a rope?"

"No. I don't know. I don't think so." I scrubbed my face with my hands. "I love her. That's all I fucking know. Every day I spend away from her is a day I'm in hell."

"Sometimes loving someone is letting them go," she said softly, her eyes still on me. "I can't tell you whether you're better for her than this Riley guy is. No one can, except for her. Maybe you *should* talk to her. Test it out. Let her decide this time, since you decided for her last time."

My heart twisted at the thought of going up to her. Actually saying hello. Seeing if she hated me. Oh, fuck. What if she looked at me with hatred shining in those pretty blue eyes I loved so much? What then? "She could despise me," I rasped. "What if she can't even look at me without wanting to punch me?"

"Then that's a cross you'll have to bear," she said, taking her glasses off. "The question is, do you want to know for sure, or do you want to spend your whole life wondering what would have happened if only you'd said hello?"

I swallowed. "I don't know. Can't you just tell me what's better? Fix it?"

"I'm sorry, but I can't do that," she said, smiling a sad smile at me. "This one's up to you."

I stood and dragged a hand through my hair. "Fine. I'll think about it."

"I look forward to hearing which option you chose on Tuesday." She also stood up, smoothing her black skirt. "But Griffin?"

"Yeah?"

"Don't jump blindly into either choice. If you do see her, make sure you take things slow. You have to remember: She thinks you don't love her. You broke her heart into pieces, no matter how honorable your intentions might have been. These things take time to heal. Even if she rejects your offer of friendship at first, try to be patient. She might come around." She pointed her pen at me. "And that's all you should offer in the beginning. Friendship. Another chance to get things right. No rushing into anything in a single day."

I nodded. "Thanks, Doc."

"Good luck."

I left the office, paid my copay, and stepped out into the sunlight. Squinting into the brightness, I headed for my bike. It had taken a while for my arm to heal, but now I could act like myself again. I rode my bike. I hung with Hernandez. But…

I didn't have a job. Didn't have a plan. Didn't have Carrie.

I scanned the crowd on Ocean Drive, looking for a redhead out of habit more than anything. I knew she was around her somewhere, eating breakfast with Riley. The desire to find out where she was hit me pretty strong, but I shook it off. If and when I saw her again, it wouldn't be with Riley watching. We would be alone.

Maybe I'd buy her some flowers.

I revved the engine, looking over my shoulder at the spot where Carrie used to sit. There hadn't been another woman in my life since her. Even at rock bottom, I couldn't let myself fall even lower. Carrie owned my heart, and no other woman would do.

It had to be *her*, damn it.

"Hey, how did it go?" Hernandez shouted in my ear from behind me.

Jumping, I looked over my shoulder, shut off the engine, and frowned at him. "Aren't you supposed to be guarding Carrie?"

"I am. She's in that restaurant." He pointed over his shoulder at a restaurant that was about three hundred feet away. "With Riley the Perfect."

I picked up my helmet. "Shit, man. I gotta go before she sees me."

"So you're not allowed to approach her yet?"

"It's not that." I gripped my helmet tight. "I don't know what I'm doing yet, but I'm not making rash decisions this time."

Hernandez grinned. "That sounds like a therapist talking."

"It was her advice." I lifted a shoulder. "It seemed like it made sense, so I'm gonna take it. And while I might say hi to her at some point, it won't be while she's on a date with another guy."

Hernandez nodded. "She almost saw you last night, when she kissed Riley and you knocked over that damn pot with your elbow."

I flinched. "Yeah. I wasn't watching where I was going."

I'd been too busy watching her *kiss* Riley.

"I noticed," Hernandez said dryly.

The restaurant door opened, making a bell jingle. Both Hernandez and I turned slowly. I knew it was going to be her. Just knew it. She walked out, holding Riley's hand and laughing, and a fist punched in my chest. Riley's eyes latched with mine, but Carrie didn't look this way.

I knew the second he realized it was me. He paled and went all tense.

I slammed my helmet over my head and started my engine, watching as Hernandez headed her way without another word to me. She still didn't see me, so I revved the bike and took off. As I passed her, I saw her turn my way with wide eyes, her mouth parted. She spun as I passed, following me with her eyes. I drove faster.

If I didn't get away now, I'd go back.

And I'd beg her to love me again, Riley be damned.

CHAPTER NINETEEN

Carrie

I walked Riley to his car with my mind a million miles away on the motorcyclist that I was ninety-nine percent sure had been Finn. I hadn't seen his face or anything, but there was no doubt in my mind that I'd seen Finn today.

Same type of bike. Same type of build. Same helmet.

"You're thinking about that guy on the bike, aren't you?" Riley asked, his voice level. "I saw him, you know. Before he put the helmet on."

I stopped walking. "Wait. What?"

"I know you're not mentioning it because you don't want to hurt my feelings, but you're dying to know if it was Finn." He met my eyes. He looked so handsome in the sunlight. So tall and perfect. It almost made me sick to my stomach just looking up at him. "I can tell you, if you want."

I sucked in a shaky breath. "I'm sorry. I know you want—"

"Sh." He hugged me close, resting his cheek on the top of my head. It was intimate and yet withdrawn at the same time. "We both know what I want, but it doesn't mean you have to give it to me. If you still have feelings for him…"

"Sometimes, I wish you were Finn. That you'd been sent here to protect me, not him." I rested my hands on his arms. "It would be so much easier."

"Me too." He tilted my face up to his. "Maybe you could move on from the past at some point, though? From his hold over you?"

I swallowed past my aching throat. I wasn't sure how to answer that. "I don't know. He still owns the majority of my feelings; I know that. I don't know what I feel for him anymore, but he fills my head all the time."

"Fair enough." He stared at my mouth, his eyes darkening. "How about one more kiss before I go?"

Before I could answer, his lips were on mine again. He kissed me, and it felt good. I even felt a little bit of desire stirring within me. But it just wasn't Finn.

It wasn't fair.

He deepened the kiss, his tongue touching mine. Even though I wanted to pull away, to end it, I kissed him back. Heck, I even pulled him closer. I owed it to both of us to at least try to feel something here. To try to get over Finn. Something within me came to life, a small flicker of something, but it almost wasn't strong enough to notice.

I curled my hands behind his neck, moaning into his mouth, and he crushed me against his chest. When he groaned and cupped my butt, hauling me closer against his erection, desire hit me pretty hard, but it didn't feel *right*. Panic crept up my throat, choking me. I gasped and lurched back, my hand covering my mouth. "I'm s-sorry. I can't. N-Not yet."

"I'm sorry. I got carried away." He gave me a small smile. "But that was perfect. Just perfect, Carrie."

Yeah. Perfect. "I know. It was…nice." *Nice won't make you scream out in bed, Ginger.* "Unexpected, even."

He grinned. "I'll take it."

"Riley…" My heart wrenched. "Was it him?"

The grin slipped away. I felt like crap for asking, but I had to know. He slid his shades in place. "Yeah. It was Finn. He looked better than the last time we saw him. More whole." He looked away. "Are you going to get back together with him now?"

"No." I shook my head for emphasis. "Absolutely not. He's over me."

Riley hesitated. "I'm killing my own case here, but I have to be honest or I'll never be able to live with myself. The way he looked at you today? He didn't look *over* you. He looked like he wanted you back, Carrie."

A small thrill shot through me, but I stifled it. He'd hurt me. Broke my heart. Even if he was regretting it now, it didn't mean I would fall into his arms and hug him.

My heart was still broken.

"Well, it's a little too late for that now." I crossed my arms and forced a smile. If I were smart, I'd fall for Riley. I'd forget all about the boy who'd broken my heart. If only my darn heart would get the memo. "Thanks for visiting me this weekend. I had fun."

"Should we do it again soon?"

I hesitated. My heart said *no*, but my mind screamed *yes*. "You know I'm still not over him, right? I can't commit to you fully yet."

"But you could in the future? I could definitely work with those odds. I'm a gambling man when the occasion calls for it."

I bit down on my lip. "I want to, but I can't promise anything."

"Especially since he's back."

"That's not why—"

"Carrie. I get it. You loved him, and still do—maybe, kind of, sort of." He cupped my cheek, his thumb resting on my chin. It made me think of how Finn used to do something similar, but he'd run his thumb over my lower lip instead. My stomach clenched tight at the memory. "Those feelings might come back to the front if he comes to see you. And if that does happen, that's okay. I know what I'm up against, but unless you get back together with him? I'm not going anywhere. I'm determined to throw my hat in the ring, or whatever people say nowadays."

Tears filled my eyes, but I laughed. "You're too good for me."

Funny. Finn used to say that to me all the time. I finally understood what he meant now. Hindsight was twenty-twenty, after all.

"Nah. I'm just patient and understanding and…okay, maybe I'm a little too good." He kissed me, smiling against my lips when I laughed again. "I'll call you later this week to see if you want to get together. No pressure or anything, but I'll be expecting a yes. Don't break my heart, Carrie."

I shook my head at his teasing. "Okay."

After watching him drive away, I headed back toward my dorm. Hernandez stepped out from the shadows once I got close to him, a disinterested look in his eyes. "Here."

"Um…thanks." I took what he handed to me. It was a small rose. "You're giving me a rose?"

He rolled his eyes. "No. Read the little paper."

I opened the tiny scrap of paper that someone had wrapped around it. *Keep smiling.* I looked up at Hernandez, feeling more confused than anything. "Who gave you this?"

"No one. I found it on your car, so I took it off to make sure it wasn't a death threat or something."

I blinked down at it. It was yellow. Yellow roses were my favorite. "Maybe it was from Riley?"

He looked away. "Maybe," he mumbled. "So. What's next for today?"

I sniffed the rose and walked toward my car. "I don't know." I stole a glance at him. "Have you seen Marie this morning? Is she back at the dorm?"

"I don't know. Last I saw, she was out with some guy getting coffee." Hernandez tightened his fists. "She was wearing the same clothes she had on last night."

"Oh. That must have been Sean. He seems like a nice enough guy." When Hernandez clenched his jaw, I looked over at him. "You know, if you want her, you should just ask her out before she gets serious with some other guy—maybe even Sean. Right now, they're having fun. There aren't feelings involved or anything."

He gave me an incredulous look. "Why in the hell would I want to do that?"

"Because you seem to like her. And believe it or not? I think she likes you, too." I stopped at my door. "You should ask her out already. We'd planned on doing a double date when Finn came home, if you recall. We can't double-date anymore, but you could take her out without me."

He frowned at me. "Yeah, I don't think so. We would be horrible together."

"If you say so."

"I do." He leaned on the passenger side. "So, you staying in, or going out?"

"Um…" I looked up at the sky. It was a pretty warm day, and there was a good breeze for an early spring morning. I hadn't been surfing since…well, since Finn. Suddenly, it seemed like the best idea ever to get out there again. To do something that I hadn't done in months. To get back to living. "Actually, I'm going to go surfing."

His brows slammed down. "You can't. Finn said you're not allowed to go out without him."

"He did, yes, back when he was my bodyguard and my boyfriend. He isn't either of those things anymore." I raised my brows. "So why should it matter? It's irrelevant."

"Carrie…" He frowned. "You can't go out there alone. Finn had his reasons for not wanting you out there alone, no matter where he is or what he's doing now."

Or who he's doing it with, I added in my head.

"Yeah, well, I don't care what his reasons are. I'm an adult, and he isn't my boss, boyfriend, or father." I crossed my arms, the rose still in my hand. "Last time I checked, he didn't have any say on what I did with myself. Not since he walked away. If I want to surf, I'll freaking surf. You can't stop me."

He dropped his head back and glared up at the sky. "Days like this? I hate my fucking job even more."

"Sorry." I opened the door. "But I'm going anyway."

I climbed up the stairs, feeling free. Feeling light. And for the first time in a while, I was excited about something. I pushed open my door and headed for my bikini and wetsuit. Marie sat on the bed, reading a biology book. "Hey. Whatcha doing?"

"I'm going surfing." I grinned over my shoulder at her and tossed the yellow rose on my pillow. "What are you up to besides doing the walk of shame at a coffee shop?"

She flushed. "Nothing like that happened. I just fell asleep at Sean's place." Then she paused. "Wait. How did you know I got coffee this morning?"

"Besides the cup in your hand? Hernandez saw you." I yanked my shirt over my head. "You might want to look away. I'm about to be naked."

She huffed and turned away. "Why the hell is he watching *me* now? Who does he think he is? He doesn't work for *my* dad."

"I don't think he was watching you." I took my bra off and slipped the bikini in its place. "He just happened to come across you."

"Well, he can just happen to kiss my ass, too." Marie set her coffee down hard. "Is he out there?"

"Yep. He's pissed because I'm surfing."

She stood up. She had on a pair of short shorts and combat boots, paired with a flowing purple tank top. She looked beautiful in her anger. It brought a color to her cheeks that had been missing before. "He's about to be even more pissed after I'm done with him."

She stormed out without another word. I blinked after her.

"Okay, then," I muttered. After I finished changing, I grabbed my board and headed downstairs. I passed Cory, but ignored him. We were *so* done, no matter how much he knew about me. My bullshit meter had filled up and overflowed. I came through the doors just in time to see Marie stomping away from Hernandez. He watched her with a confused look on his face, shaking his head. I almost felt sorry for him.

I walked right by him. "I'm going now."

"I don't like this." He walked beside me, glaring the whole time. "You shouldn't be out there alone."

"I'll be fine. Turns out, I kinda like being alone. There's no one to boss me around, and no one to let down. " I flipped my hair over my shoulder and unlocked the car. "You can watch from the beach if you'd like. Want a ride?"

He sighed. "Sure. Why not?"

The whole time we drove to the beach, my heart raced. I was actually going to do this. Go out there without Finn. It was exhilarating. Scary. Fun. And more importantly, it would prove I didn't need him anymore. I didn't need him to have fun. If I could do this, well, I could move on. I could be free of him.

Maybe, with time, I could even be happy again.

I pulled into my normal spot. There weren't a lot of people out there in the water. It was too late for optimal waves, but I didn't care. I was going to have fun anyway. I hopped out of my car and grabbed my board, closing my eyes and inhaling the fresh beach smell. On the West Coast, it smelled so clean. Crisp, even. The waves crashed on the sand, creating a soothing sound that never ceased to calm my nerves. Today was no exception. I kicked off my flip-flops, eager to get my bare toes in the sand again.

Hernandez shoved his phone in his pocket and scanned the beach. "Where do you surf?"

"Out there." I pointed to my normal spot. It's where Finn had always taken me, and I couldn't imagine going anywhere else. Maybe it was habit; maybe it was sentiment. Maybe I was a glutton for punishment. All I knew was I liked the memories, as painful as they might be at times. "See? There's even a bench over there where you can sit and watch."

He nodded. "Don't kill yourself, or *he'll* kill *me*."

"Don't worry, my dad will never know you let me surf," I called over my shoulder, tossing my flip-flops at him. "Hold these, will ya?"

"Yes, ma'am," he called out sarcastically. "Want me to braid your hair and tell you all my secrets, too?"

I ignored him, grinning as I headed for the surf. As soon as my feet touched the water, I laughed out loud. This was it. This was what I'd needed today. I swam out to the optimal surfing point and climbed on my board. Wringing my hair out, I tilted my face up to the sun, letting it all soak in. Letting the freedom hit me.

I could do this. I could move on. Get over him.

Try again.

"Hey, Ginger." A shadow fell over me, and for a second I thought I was imagining things again. Hearing things. "You know you're not supposed to be out here alone."

I opened my eyes slowly, as if I might find out I'd imagined the whole thing if I dared to peek. It was him. *Finn.* My heart lurched, painfully accelerating so hard it seemed as if it was trying to jump out of my chest and back into his hands where it used to be.

I scanned him, looking for any signs of the haunted man he'd used to be. He still had the scars. Still looked tired as hell. His brown hair had grown in a bit; looking about the same length as it had been last time he'd gone to drill. And his arm was out of the cast. He wasn't wearing dog tags. In fact, he wore nothing but his black wetsuit and a cautious look in his eyes. He looked good. Healthy. Happy.

Holy. Freaking. Crap.

CHAPTER TWENTY

Finn

I watched her, my heart pounding in my ears full speed ahead. I hadn't been planning on saying hello to her. I'd been planning on watching her from far, far away. Hernandez had texted me to let me know she was going out in the water, and I'd rushed so I could get there before her. Waiting. Watching. Guarding.

The usual.

But then I'd seen her, sitting in the sun, looking pretty as hell with her wild red hair blowing in the breeze, and something inside me had broken. Maybe it was something that had been holding me back, restraint even. But now that she was out here, in my territory, there was no holding back.

Her hair was longer, reaching all the way down to the small of her back while wet, and it looked even darker than before since it was damp. Her blue eyes looked bluer than I remembered, too. Fucking gorgeous. That's what she was. She was perfection, while I was not. I was finally starting to be okay with that fact, though. That I wasn't perfect and never would be.

She was just staring at me.

Finally, she seemed to snap out of it. She licked her gorgeous lips, her gaze skimming over me all over again. Did she like what she saw? I'd grown my hair longer for her. It helped camouflage my scar a little. That had to help my appearance somewhat.

She shook her head slightly. When she spoke, her voice came out hoarse. "You…You're *here*."

"I am." I tugged on my hair, watching her. "I've been here for a while, actually. A little over a month now, I guess. Maybe two."

It had been two months, one day, three hours, and twelve minutes, to be exact. She didn't say anything. Just stared at me, not moving besides the lull of the waves that made her board sway. I cleared my throat. "Did you get my flower?"

She blinked at that. "That was from you?"

"Yeah." I rubbed my head. "I left it on your car earlier."

"W-Why?"

I shrugged. "Because I wanted to."

"I…see. Why come back out here?" She met my eyes again. "Instead of staying in D.C.?"

"There's nothing for me in D.C. anymore."

She cocked her head. "And there's something for you here?"

"Yes." *You. I love you. Take me back. Forgive me. Make me whole again.* "The weather's nicer. And there's surfing. Hernandez. My bike…" *You.*

"I see." She stared at me, not moving. "You—" She cleared her throat. "You look good. Better. Are you?"

I couldn't believe she was being so damn polite. "Thanks. Yeah, I am." My heart twisted and turned. "You look beautiful, as always. So fucking beautiful."

"Th-Thank you." She took a deep breath, color slowly coming back to her cheeks. "I don't know what to say to you right now. This feels weird."

I tried to smile at her. It probably came across as a grimace mixed with a grin. It hurt to feel so damn awkward around her. We'd never been like this. "A little bit, yeah. But we've never had to deal with the aftermath of…after saying all that we said."

"And you never snuck away in the middle of the night on me, either," she said slowly, her bright eyes still on me.

"About that?" I looked down at my hands. Should I tell her it was all a lie? That I'd been trying to save her from me? Would she even fucking care? Time to find out. "I fucked up. I never meant—"

"Don't." She glared at me. Now she was pissed. *This* is what I'd expected to see. "Don't go apologizing or backpedaling. And don't you dare try to take it back. You said how you felt, and you left. I shouldn't have even brought it up. You caught me off guard, is all." She let her hand fall back to the board. "I wasn't expecting to see you out here. Actually, I wasn't expecting to see you at all. I told you not to check on me, remember? Said I didn't want to see you again."

Yeah. I remembered. But I couldn't stay away. "I'm sorry. I really am." I twisted my lips. "It's not safe for you to be surfing alone. You know that, Ginger."

She lifted her chin, her blue eyes flaring with anger and maybe a hint of something else. Sadness, maybe. "I'm fine on my own, thank you very much. I've been just fine without you here watching over me, and I'll continue to be fine. I don't need you watching me to make sure I don't drown. I have Hernandez."

I gripped the surfboard. I'd been right. She was fine without me. Didn't need me like I needed her. "Hernandez can't fucking surf."

"Yeah, but he can swim. And even if he couldn't? Even if I drowned out here? That's my problem, not yours." She looked away. "You're not my guard or my boyfriend anymore, so stop acting like you're either one."

I flinched. "I know you're not mine anymore. That's not why I'm here. I was planning on surfing already. You're not the only one who surfs on weekends, if you recall. I'm the one who brought you here in the first place."

She bit down hard on her lip, looking flustered and upset with my reappearance in her life. I shouldn't have said hi, damn it. She fingered her necklace, and I stared at in in disbelief. It was the one I'd given her. She still wore it. "You weren't supposed to come find me. I told you—"

"You're wearing our necklace," I said, my voice sounding way too fucking weak. "You didn't throw it away after I left?"

She dropped it immediately. "No. I didn't throw it away." Her cheeks red, she looked away from me. "I-I forgot all about it, honestly."

Something told me that wasn't true. She was lying to me. She knew she was wearing it, and she wore it because it reminded her of me. I knew it. Happiness rushed through my veins. For the first time in months, I let myself believe I stood a chance with her. Let myself believe I might be able to make her love me again.

God knows I needed her to feel alive.

571

"Ginger. Fuck, I miss you so—"

"*Don't.*" She shook her head, her eyes spitting sharp blades of fire my way. "You don't get to say that to me. Just leave me alone. I'm out here for some peace and quiet, not for a trip down memory lane. We've 'caught up,'" she used her fingers to make quotations marks, "enough. Now go back to leaving me alone, like we agreed upon."

I gripped my board tighter. "I can't leave you."

"You didn't have that issue in D.C." She glowered at me, her eyes still spitting fire. "I haven't forgotten what you said, and I'm sure you haven't forgotten what I said. Goodbye, Finn."

She closed her eyes, obviously intending to ignore me until I left. I sat there quietly, not so much as making a splash, letting my heart break some more. Hell, I was used to it now. After a while, she cracked her eye open and looked at me. I inclined my head and looked her over, trying to act as if there was nothing strange about us being out here alone again. "Yeah, I'm still here."

"I see that," she said, frustration clear in her voice. "What are you trying to do, Finn? What do you want from me? Is there a point to this visit?"

"I wanted to see you again," I said, my voice light. Just being near her, talking to her, felt like fucking heaven. I missed her so damn much. I tugged on my hair. "It's the first time I felt strong enough to come up to you. I didn't want to come back till I was better."

Her gaze flew to mine. "And you're better now?"

"I think so." I swallowed hard. "How have you been, though?"

She turned her head away, hiding her pretty face from mine. "Ask Hernandez how I'm doing if you want to know." She glowered toward where he sat on a bench by the beach. He looked like he was texting someone, or surfing the web instead of the ocean. "I'm sure he could tell you everything you want to know about me."

"I'm not asking him anything. I'm asking you." I hesitated. "I know I'm not supposed to say it, but I've missed you, Ginger. So damn much."

"You really shouldn't call me that anymore," she said, her voice breaking. "It's not right. We're not together, and that was what you called me when—" She broke off, rubbing her hand on her forehead. "It's not right."

"I'm sorry. So fucking sorry." I swallowed hard, my throat aching with the pain I'd caused her. I wanted to wrap her up in my arms and never let go again. To love her like I should have all those months ago. "I never wanted to do this to you. To us."

She looked at me again. The pain in those baby blues hurt. "But you did it anyway."

"I did." I nodded once. "I wish I could take it all away, Carrie. I really do."

"Well, you can't. It's over. When you told me—" She broke off, shaking her head. "You know what? I'm not saying it. Not fighting with you. Our days of fighting are over. We're over. You saw to that."

I gritted my teeth so hard it hurt. "I know. I'll never stop regretting it, and I will never get over it. Over you."

She made a small sound. "Don't go there."

"Why not?" I paddled closer to her. "Are you and Riley an item now?"

She stiffened and held her hand out, wanting me to stay away, I could only assume. "That's not any of your business. *You're* the one who broke up with *me*. That means you don't get to ask about my personal life anymore."

I narrowed my gaze on her. "I might not be your boyfriend anymore, but it doesn't mean I'm fucking blind, deaf, or dumb." I paddled closer, despite her upheld hand. "I saw you kissing him. You looked like you liked it."

She turned to me, her eyes wide. "You were there?"

"Have you ever known Hernandez to knock over a fucking pot?" I asked, raising a brow. I stopped when I was three feet away from her. Close enough to touch, but not so close that I would. "I knocked it over when I backed away, not wanting to watch you 'moving on.' Not wanting to accept that you could be happy with someone besides me when I'm so fucking miserable without you."

"Then you shouldn't have looked," she snapped, her cheeks flushed. "You don't get to come here and swoop in, trying to make me fall into your arms again. It's not going to happen."

I gripped the surfboard. "Tell me about it."

"And how dare you ask me about my love life? Because I'm *so* sure you've been perfectly celibate since you left me," she said, her grip tight on the board. She might be acting as if she was making a point, but I could tell she was dying to know. "You haven't touched a single girl since you left me, right?"

"I haven't wanted another woman at all," I said, dropping my voice low. "I haven't been with anyone else since the first moment you kissed me on my curb. I swear it on my father's grave."

She stared at me, her eyes wide and her lips parted. For a second, just a second, her eyes softened. She didn't look angry. But then she shook her head and glanced away. "It doesn't matter."

Pain sliced through me. It didn't matter to her that I'd been faithful to her? She didn't care anymore. "No, I guess not."

Her back remained ramrod straight. "How long have you been watching me?"

"For a little while. I've been trying to stay away, though. Trying to let you move on." I cleared my throat. "I saw you at the window, when you thought you saw me. It was the night I decided to fix myself."

I didn't mention the wanting-to-kill-myself part. It wasn't necessary.

She frowned at me. "Did you drive away like you did this morning?"

"Ah." I leaned back on my board, relaxing my stance. "You saw me, huh?"

"Of course I saw you," she said, her eyes glaring at me. God, I loved it when she looked at me like that. All fiery and passionate and *hot*. "You were on your bike and you drove right past me. It was kind of hard to miss."

"Riley saw me." I cocked my head. "Did he tell you that he saw me, or did he hide that fact from you?"

She pressed her lips together. "Yeah, he told me it was you. He would never lie to me, unlike you."

Of course he'd told her I was back. Riley was that kind of guy. It made me fucking sick. "He's a good guy. Far better than me. I've never denied that."

"I know he is." She lifted her chin. "I'm *trying* to like him. To care for him as more than friends. You showing up isn't making it any easier on me."

Delight hit me, hard and swift. So she didn't have feelings for him yet. That meant I wasn't too late. I laughed. "If you have to try, it isn't fucking working. There's this thing called *chemistry* between a man and a woman. It's either there, or it isn't. I don't remember us having to *try* to like each other."

"Yeah, and that worked out so well for us, didn't it?" She glowered my way. "Life is just a bucket of sunshine and rainbows now."

"Love isn't always easy," I said, silently begging her to realize that we weren't done yet. I hadn't been thinking clearly. I'd messed up, and I knew it. If she gave me another chance, I'd never let her go again. "I made a mistake back in D.C. One I've regretted since the moment I sobered up enough to realize what I'd done. I shouldn't have left you. *Ever.*"

She closed her eyes. "But you did."

"I know. Believe me, I fucking know it." I reached out and tried to grab her hands, but she lurched back. I let mine fall back to my lap, empty.

Tears slipped down her cheeks. "*You broke my heart.*"

"I broke mine, too." I dragged my hands down my face, releasing a ragged breath. "I was fucked up. More so than I ever let you see. You have no idea how dark I was."

"Which was the problem. You didn't let me in." She swiped her hand across her cheeks with jerky motions. "You didn't trust me, or trust in our love. You just lied and left."

"I know. But if you give—"

She shook her head, her whole body tense. "Don't. Don't ask me that." "*Please.*"

She covered her face, shaking her head. "I can't do this right now. I was getting better. I was finally feeling alive again. And now you're here, telling me you're sorry? What am I supposed to do with that?"

"Forgive me," I said, my voice raw. "Give me another chance."

"To what? Leave me again? Lie some more?" She looked at me, her eyes shining with tears. "You have no idea what that did to me, because you just *walked away.*"

"I know." I held my hands out. "I'm sorry. I can't say I'm sorry enough times, I know, but I am."

"That doesn't mean you get me back." She lifted her chin. "Riley wouldn't hurt me. He wouldn't leave me broken hearted."

"Only because you don't love him," I said, frustration coursing through me. "He can't hurt you if he doesn't have that power over you."

"Which is why he's the better choice," she cried out. "I don't want to be in love anymore. Love isn't worth the pain. Not if it hurts like this. It isn't safe. It's not real. It leaves all too fast, as soon as one person decides they're done." She pressed her hand to her chest, tears streaming down her face. "I can't do this anymore. I don't want to be in pain. I don't want to be in love."

"You don't have to be in pain anymore," I whispered, reaching out for her hand. "I can make it better, and you can make me better, too. I was *always* better with you."

She shook her head and yanked her fingers out of reach at the last second. "No, you weren't. You were miserable. Always trying to change yourself for me and my dad." She looked over her shoulder. I knew what she was doing. She was going to escape. "You think you want me, but you don't. Not really."

"*No.*" I grabbed her knee, my fingers firm on her. "I'm better with you. Don't fucking leave me."

She shoved my hand off with her elbow. "No, you're not. Look what happened to you when you were with me. You were broken and beaten and at the lowest point in your life. I brought you nothing but pain, and you did the same to me."

"My pain wasn't because of you," I argued. "You made me so fucking happy."

"It was because of *me!*" She shouted, tears still running down her cheeks. "You tried to change for me. It's my fault you got injured. It's all my fault, Finn! You left me, and then you got better. Don't you see? We're no good for each other. It's *over.*"

I wanted to push her further. To see if she still had feelings for me, but then she looked at me with tears in her bright eyes. "You're wrong. Don't do this."

She laid down on the board and started forward. "You left me, and you're better off for it. Look in the mirror if you don't believe me."

"I'm only better because of you." I curled my hands into fists, yanking on my hair. "You saved me, even without you at my side, it was you who saved me that night."

She paddled faster and called over her shoulder, "I'm no good for you. Go be happy with someone else. You won't find your happily ever after with me anymore."

She rode the wave away. I could have followed her. Could have forced her to continue this conversation, but I sensed it wouldn't go the way I wanted it to. I'd have to bide my time and wait till she was ready to see me again.

    But I wasn't giving up on us. Not again.

    I wouldn't make that mistake twice.

CHAPTER TWENTY-ONE

Carrie

A few days later, on Friday afternoon, I came out of my last class of the day and found Marie standing outside the exit. She fidgeted while nibbling on her lower lip. As I approached, I noticed she looked upset. I hurried to her side, not sure what was going on. "Hey, what's up?"

She grabbed my hands. "He's there. At our room. Waiting for you again. Just like he has been every single day since he came back. With a pink rose this time."

Finn. Every single day, he'd shown up at my door and asked me to go out to eat with him. Or surfing. Or to the soup kitchen. And he always had a flower with a cute little message on it. *Keep smiling. Don't give up. You make me happy. Forgive me.*

He wasn't giving up. And I was scared one of these times I'd give in.

I smoothed my hair and blotted my recently glossed lips. Pink today. "Seriously?"

"Seriously." Marie eyed me. "But I have a feeling you knew that. Is that a new shirt you're wearing?"

I tugged at it. "No. Yes. Maybe."

"Don't do it. Don't give in," she warned. "He'll hurt you."

The night he came back, I'd told her how Finn had showed back up in my life, after radio silence for months. Once her surprise wore off, she'd

579

been angry at him for bombarding me like that. I'd listened to her rant and rave and call him names, but the whole time, I'd been thinking about him—and I hadn't been calling him names.

I'd been too busy thinking about how he looked better. How he'd filled out a little bit more again, since he'd been so skinny when he came home. I'd been thinking about how his hair was short, but long enough for me to run my fingers through it as he kissed me. But mostly, I'd been thinking about how wonderful he'd looked sitting on that surfboard.

Too bad he'd only gotten better after he left me.

"What should we do?" Marie asked, wringing her hands. "I told him to leave, like usual, but he just stared me down…like usual."

I sighed. "Right now? I'm going to go eat. If he's still there when I get back, I'll deal with him just like all the other times." I paused. "Pink, huh?"

"Yep. Pink." Finn came around the corner, holding out a pink rose. "Oh, and *he's* not there anymore. He's here, and he's starving, too. Let's go eat."

I narrowed my eyes on him, not taking the rose. "You're not coming."

He wiggled the rose. It had a note attached, like usual. I still didn't take it. "Come on, Ginger. You know you want it."

He wore a light blue T-shirt with a motorcycle on it and a pair of ripped jeans. He had on black shades, and he looked freaking hot. Way too hot for me to keep pushing him away. Damn him. His ink swirled up his biceps, and I knew exactly how they intertwined on his chest, right near the tattoo he'd gotten for me.

He'd never seen the one I'd gotten for him.

"No, I don't," I responded, gripping my bag. "I thought I was perfectly clear yesterday, and the day before that, and the day before that, and all the other days that you've showed up at my place with a present, that I'm *not* interested in restarting our relationship."

"Liar."

He stepped into my space, and his cologne washed over me. I closed my eyes, savoring the familiar scent. Smelling him like this made me want to throw myself into his arms and beg him to never leave me again. It made me want to forget.

"I'm the liar?" I snapped, whirling on my heel and ignoring him. I felt so freaking alive right now, with him next to me provoking me all over again.

Marie walked with me, shooting Finn an anxious look. "Hey, thanks for stopping by, but we're going to go eat now."

He grinned at Marie. "Good. I'm starving. Take the flower."

"Dude," Marie looked at him, her eyes wide. "We didn't invite you, and she doesn't want the flower."

"Sure she does," he said, frowning at Marie. "She loves flowers. They make her happy. So do inspirational messages. She used to get one sent to her phone every day."

"I still do," I said, my heart picking up speed. "That's why you give me little notes?"

"Yeah." He held his hand out. "Please take it."

I reached out and took his flower, my hand so tight on the stem that a thorn dug into my palm. "Th-Thanks."

"Don't mention it." He shoved his hands in his pockets, still walking beside me. "I know pink isn't your favorite color to wear, but it reminded me of the hangers I got you. Remember those?"

Of course I remembered them. He'd gotten them for me so I could keep clothes at his place. Ignoring his question, I opened the little note he'd attached to the stem. *I'm sorry.* Swallowing hard, I looked back up at him. "Finn..."

He locked gazes with me. "Wanna go to Islands with me? I have my Harley here. We can take the back roads, like we used to. Enjoy the fresh spring air that God gave us today. It would be a shame to miss out on it."

I stopped walking and curled my fist even tighter on the pink rose. God, yes, I wanted to get on his bike with him. Of course I did. But that's why I couldn't. "No, thank you."

He *tsk*ed me. "Carrie Wallington, I'm ashamed of you. You've lost your fun streak since I left. Your desire for adventure is dead." He took his sunglasses off and walked backward, his gaze locked with mine. "The Carrie I knew wouldn't turn down a ride from me, even if she was pissed. Get on the bike. You know you want to."

I shook my head, but he was right. I really freaking wanted to. "That was before we broke up. I'm not her anymore."

"You'd have gotten on the damn bike before. You changed."

"Says the man who broke up with me because I *hadn't* changed while he had," I said, crossing my arms over my chest. "Be careful what you wish for."

He held his hands out at his sides, pouting at me. Actually. Pouting. He used to give it to me back when we were dating and he wanted to get his way on something. I couldn't resist that look, darn it. Not now. Not then. Not ever. "Ginger, get on the bike. Let's go for a ride for old time's sake."

I wavered. I knew he sensed it, too, because his eyes lit up. "*No.*"

Marie watched us both, looking about as happy as a kid stuck between two quarrelling parents. "This isn't awkward for me at all," she drawled, studying her nails. "Want me to leave?"

"Yes," Finn said.

"No," I said at the same time. "Stay right there."

She craned her neck. "Oh, look. It's Hernandez. I'm going to go fight with him for a little bit."

She took off like her butt was on fire. "*Marie,*" I called out. But it was useless. She wasn't coming back. I turned on Finn, my hands clenched at my sides. "You need to stop doing this."

"I can't." He leaned against the side of the building. "I miss you."

I closed my eyes. "You need to stop saying that."

"Fine. Then make me *not* miss you." I sensed him moving closer, so I snapped my eyes open. He froze. "Go on a ride with me."

"I *can't.*"

"Just one little ride." He reached out and pushed a tendril of hair behind my ear. "I promise to behave myself. Come on. You miss it, don't you?"

"It doesn't matter if I do," I said. "I'm not going anywhere with you."

"If you go with me and hate it," he said, clenching his jaw. "I'll stop coming by your dorm. I'll stop giving you messages and flowers. I'll leave you alone."

I swallowed hard. He'd leave me alone? No more flowers and inspirational notes? The idea was as tempting as it was painful. I was such a mess of emotions right now that I didn't know which way was up and which way was down anymore. "I don't know. There's too much…"
Love. Pain. Desire.

When I didn't finish my sentence, he offered me a small smile. "Well, let's find out. If you still hate me when we're done, and don't want to see me again, I'll back off. Give you some time and space. Stop showing up every day." He held his hand out. "Let's go for a ride and for some lunch. You're done with classes for the day."

I frowned at him, not bothering to admit I didn't hate him. I could never truly hate him. "Someone has an inside source."

"Maybe." He shrugged. "What can I say? You're my favorite subject."

"Then you shouldn't have dropped out." I walked past him. "I'll go with you, but then you'll be leaving me alone. Be prepared. And friends don't hold hands, Coram."

He laughed and followed me, sounding way too happy for someone who was about to be told to hit the road. "Fair enough."

I looked at him again, unable to believe this was the same Finn who had broken up with me. "Why are you acting so normal now?"

He stole a glance at me. His blue eyes shined even brighter in the sunlight, making them seem unrealistically blue. "I told you, I'm better. I go to a therapist now, just like you suggested I should," he said softly. "She's helping me a lot."

I nodded. "I'm glad." I stole another glance at him. "And your arm?"

"Better." He looked down at it, wiggling his fingers. "I only get aches here and there. The headaches are a bitch, though."

I frowned. "You still get them?"

"I'm told I'll always get them." He shrugged. "But I'm not on meds any longer. I just lie down if it gets too rough. And I don't drink."

I stopped by his bike. He had my helmet sitting on it, and I felt a sharp pang of loneliness at the sight. God, I'd missed him. It was true. I watched him closely. He looked so different, and yet exactly the same. "This is weird, isn't it? I should go…"

"No. It's not weird at all. It's just the new normal." He grinned at me and grabbed my helmet off the bike, looking eternally optimistic. "Put this on, get on the bike, and it'll all feel right again."

I took my bag off and handed it to him, just like I used to do. Looking down at the rose in my hand, I tucked it into the bag as an afterthought. He slid it over his shoulder and sat down, lowering his own helmet over his head. I looked back at Marie, who shot me a *Really?!* look. I shrugged and slid the helmet on before settling onto the back of the bike. But once I was there, I didn't know what to do. Should I hold him like I used to, or was it not necessary to get quite so close?

He looked over his shoulder. "What?"

"Nothing," I said quickly. I gripped the side of his shirt loosely, leaving plenty of room between us. His skin burned through the fabric, and his hard muscles taunted me, and I hadn't even touched him. God, he felt so freaking good. And even scarier was the fact that it felt so *right*. As if I'd finally found the missing piece of me I'd lost. "I'm r-ready."

"Only if you're hoping to fall off the back and skin your pretty little ass," he called out. "Hold on tighter, or you'll throw off our balance."

I scooted up more, still not touching my front to his back. To do so would be dangerous to my mental well-being. "Better?"

He shook his head and twirled his finger in a circle. "Scoot closer. I told you I would behave, and I will. Hold me like you used to. Friends do that on bikes, I assure you."

"*Fine*." Rolling my eyes, I glared at his back and slammed my body fully against his. I held back a groan, just barely, but he didn't even bother to try. Hearing him groan made me want to do something else to make him do it again. It reminded me of the sound he always made when I used to…uh, never mind what it reminded me of. "Better?"

"Fuck yeah."

He revved the engine and pulled away from the curb. As soon as the wind hit my face, I grinned bigger than I had in a long time. Being back on his bike, holding on to him, it felt *right*. He swerved in and out of traffic, taking the slow roads to our old restaurant. I hadn't been there since he left for…wherever it was that he went. I still didn't know.

I wonder if he could tell me now?

Man, I had so many questions. Questions I had every intention of asking him once we were at Islands. There was so much I wanted to know. He revved the engine harder, zipping between two cars. I laughed, and if I wasn't mistaken?

So did he. I'd missed that, too. So freaking much.

By the time we pulled into the parking lot, I couldn't hold back my excitement at being back on his bike. Of being with him, if I was being honest. I wasn't. I hopped off the bike and tore my helmet off, laughing. "That was freaking *awesome*."

He laughed, watching me with a warmth in his eyes I hadn't seen in way too freaking long. It stole my breath away. "Yeah, it was."

I smoothed my hair with a shaking hand. "When did you start riding again?"

"Two weeks ago," he said, running his hands over his head. He didn't need to worry about his hair being messy. He looked perfect, as always. "I wasn't ready until then. But my therapist told me I should try again, so I did."

"What does she say about me?"

"She said I should reach out to you, if I was ready." He met my eyes. "So I did."

"And you listened to her." I set my helmet down and twisted my hair into a ponytail. Finn liked it down better, but since we weren't dating anymore? Ponytail it was. I hated wearing my hair down. "That shows a lot about where you are."

"I won't pretend I'm a hundred percent better," he said, motioning me forward. He fell into step beside me as I walked toward the mall where Islands was. "But I'm not a hot mess anymore, either."

He placed his hand at my lower back, just like Riley had last week. But instead of feeling a little awkward, Finn's hand made me all itchy and wound up inside. "Well, there's that. But friends don't hold on to each other. Hands to yourself."

He dropped his hand back to his side. "Damn, you're right…again." He looked at me, giving me a grin. "So what's up with you? Still studying and being a good girl?"

I shivered, a burst of desire sweeping through my veins. Last time he asked me if I'd been a good girl, I'd gone down on my knees in front of him. What a freaking time I'd had. Of course, that had been *after* he told me he might be leaving, and then he had.

I stared at him for so long that he blinked at me.

"Carrie?" he said, looking at me with narrowed eyes. "You okay?"

Quickly, I looked away from him, shaking off the memories. "Y-Yes, of course. My grades are as good as ever. I've had more time to study ever since—"

"Since I was an ass and left?"

"If the shoe fits." I tucked my side bangs behind my ear. "In this case, you might as well be Cinderella."

"I like the new cut and color, by the way."

"You noticed?" I touched my hair self-consciously. "It's not a big change or anything. Just a shade darker."

"I noticed the second I saw you. Favorite subject, remember?"

I shook my head. "Yeah. Sure."

He twisted his lips and opened the door for me. His gaze fell on the spot where he'd bruised me inadvertently. It had faded a long time ago. I wish I could say the same about the rest of the pain he'd inflicted upon me.

I watched him as he walked up to the receptionist, giving her his megawatt smile. She practically melted into a puddle right then and there, and I wanted to gouge her eyes out for it. I guess friends weren't supposed to feel that way. I had a lot to learn about being friends with Finn…if we could even make it work.

I didn't want to hurt him anymore.

CHAPTER TWENTY-TWO

Finn

I watched Carrie close her small hands around the gigantic burger on her plate, her eyes shining with excitement. I knew, right then, that this was the best fucking move I could have ever made. Start out as friends, just like we did before, and eventually? Maybe she would love me again. Fuck, I hoped she loved me again.

Knowing she didn't love me anymore was killing me.

I fingered the envelope in my pocket; uncertain whether or not I should give it to her. Hell, I was uncertain of everything. Twelve times now, I'd reached for her hand, and covered it up by grabbing my drink instead. I was on my fifth fucking lemonade. I didn't even really like lemonade. I'd just ordered it because I'd been too distracted by her to pay attention to the menu. Ten times, I'd gone to entwine my ankle with hers under the table, just like we used to, but quickly jerked my foot back to my side. And six times, I'd almost went in for a kiss, but hidden it by grabbing the dessert card off the table.

Being her friend again was *hard*.

She moaned and closed her eyes, slowly chewing. My cock came to life at the sound, since it's the same one she made whenever I made love to her. Her face was lost in rapturous delight, and, oh my fucking God, I wanted her so badly. Needed her. I cleared my throat and picked up my own burger, unable to look away even though it physically hurt to watch her.

I sank my teeth into the burger, hoping it distracted me from the need that currently attempted to kill me. It did. I chewed, letting out my own groan. Her eyes flew open and she watched me with heated eyes. Oh, fuck. She liked that sound, too.

I didn't know whether that was a good or bad sign right now.

I swallowed past the suffocating need choking me. Trying to play it cool, I lifted the burger. "It's so fucking good."

She nodded slowly, her gaze on my mouth. "Yeah. Yeah, it is."

Need punched me with iron knuckles in the gut.

Before I begged her to forgive me and take me back—and before I could ruin the tenuous peace we had going between us—I shoved the burger in my mouth and took another bite. This time, I groaned even longer, and I even rolled my eyes back in my head a little bit, because why the fuck not? She kept staring at me as if she wanted to close her mouth around *me* instead, and if she was tempted?

I was going to push my luck.

She made a small sound and picked up her lemonade, downing almost the whole glass in one gulp. "It's so freaking hot in here, isn't it?"

"Yeah." I lifted my shirt a little bit, fanning my abs and showing her the goods. It worked. After her gaze dropped, it flew back up to mine. "They need to turn the air on or something."

She frowned at me. "Totally."

I took another bite, once again groaning deep and low. She bit down on her lower lip, watching me with hunger in her eyes. When I chuckled, the hunger faded away, only to be replaced my calculation. She grinned, too. The kind of grin that told me she was up to no good.

Thank God.

Her gaze latched with mine, she took a bite of her burger, letting out the longest, most drawn out moan she'd ever voiced. It was fucking *hot*. "Oh. My. God. Yes." She breathed in tiny little spurts, as if I was going down on her right here and there. "That's *so* good."

Some twenty-year-old brat kid looked over at her, his mouth ajar. It took all my control not to punch the fucker in the face. Those noises were for me. Or, at least, they had been, once upon a time. Another dude looked over, and he looked vaguely familiar to me. He'd been at the beach the other day, when Carrie and I had been surfing.

Coincidence…or not?

I looked back at Carrie, forcing myself to pretend I didn't notice him. "You're playing a dangerous game, Ginger."

She patted at her lips with a napkin, never looking away from me. "I have no idea what you mean. I'm just eating." She leaned in. "Unless you have something to admit to, Coram?"

"Not at all," I said, smiling. I reached out and ran a thumb over her lower lip. "Sorry. You had a little something on your lip."

Her eyes were blazing at me now. "Oh, really?"

"Really," I said as innocently as I could manage. I sucked on my thumb, licking away all traces of her. "Mm. Tastes good. Almost as good as you do."

She gasped, looking over her shoulder as if scared someone might have heard. "You're…you're so…"

"Perfect? Funny? Adorable?"

"*Annoying*," she offered. But the sparkling in her eyes ruined the anger effect she was trying to give off. "Incorrigible. Ridiculous."

I lifted a shoulder, my heart soaring. *Fuck me.* Did I really just think that my heart soared? What the hell was wrong with me? "I can live with those titles, Ginger."

She rolled her eyes. "Of course you can."

"I'm also stubborn. I don't give up easily. Remember that one, too."

She froze with the burger in her mouth. As she took a bite, chewing slowly, I let her absorb that information. I bit down on my burger, studying her as I did so. She looked at me like someone who wanted to be more than friends would, but I didn't point that out. "You know we can't be more than buddies."

I swallowed. "Funny, I heard you said the same thing to Riley the other day when he left."

She stomped her foot. "Oooh, I'm going to *kill* Hernandez."

I laughed. "It's not his fault. I'm irresistible to him, too." I pointed my burger at her. "You should add that to your list of my faults."

She snorted. "Yeah. I'll get right on that. *Not.*"

We ate our burgers in silence, no more competitive sexual groaning going on, but I sensed her watching me the whole time. Every time I looked at her, she quickly turned away. As if she didn't want me to know she watched me. She shouldn't have bothered with the attempted subterfuge. I could feel her eyes burning into me.

After we were finished, I picked up my lemonade. "This was nice."

"Yeah." She leaned back in the booth. "What are you doing with your life? Are you still in the Marines?"

I shook my head, my heart twisting. I still couldn't believe I was out. Honorable discharge and all that, but still. It was so fucking weird. "No. I got honorably discharged, so there wasn't any shame or anything."

She blinked at me. "Oh. So you're actually out?"

"I'm out."

"Are you still in security?" she asked, pursing her lips. Her eyes were narrowed, as if she was figuring something out. "Or do you want to be?"

"No, I'm not still in security. I'm currently jobless." I looked where the guy who'd set my teeth on edge earlier had been. He was gone. I relaxed slightly. "I got offered a job, but I turned it down."

She picked up her lemonade and finished it. "Why?"

"It was in Chicago."

"Ah." She *clunked* the cup down. "No surfing."

I hesitated. Should I be honest? I had nothing to lose anymore. Nothing at all. "No, there's no you."

She froze. "What do you mean?"

"I didn't want to go there because you weren't there." I grabbed her hand, squeezing it between both of mine. I still had scars on my knuckles from the night I'd gone insane in her parents' house. Did they stand out to her as much as they stood out to me? "I wanted to be here with you. I *need* to be near you to live."

She pulled free. "I know what this is all about. Dad hired you again, didn't he? You're guarding me again and don't want to tell me."

I choked on a laugh. "What? Are you fucking crazy? *No*. He didn't contact me, and I haven't talked to him since I left. Why would he? He fired me."

"I don't believe you. You told me you didn't love me anymore. You looked me in the eye and said it." She pressed her lips together. "Now you want to live near me? It makes no sense."

My stomach hollowed out. "I didn't mean it. I was trying to save you. I never stopped loving you, and none of the things that happened to me were your fault."

"Yes, they were."

"No. They. Weren't." I locked gazes with her. "I only said that because I knew you'd believe it. I knew you felt bad, so I used that against you. I'm sorry for that, too, but I never stopped loving you. I lied about that."

"Stop." She reared back, her face pale. "Just stop."

"*I can't.*" I pressed a hand to my heart. "No one will love you like I do, Ginger. I always have. I always will. Even if you hate me for the rest of your long, healthy life, I'll still love you forever. I don't know how to stop. I can't." I reached into my pocket and pulled out a note I'd written her. "Read this later. Please?"

She made a broken sound and slid out of the booth without taking the note. "I can't do this—can't love you like you want me to. I told you, I'm done with love. It *hurts* too much. I made up my mind. You need to stop coming to my dorm. Stop begging me to forgive you. Stop trying to be my friend. Just stop everything."

She bolted for the door. I tossed some cash down on the table and followed her, grabbing the note on my way out, my heart shattering into a thousand pieces even as it sped up. I had a bad feeling that something was about to happen. And when I got that feeling, I was usually right. I followed her out into the dull afternoon sun, scanning the crowd for any signs that something might be amiss.

Nothing stood out to me, except I didn't see Hernandez. That might be nothing, since he knew she was with me, but it might *be* something, too. I shot him a quick text, keeping my phone in my hand as I followed Carrie.

When she saw me behind her, she glowered at me and hurried her steps. She rifled in her purse, pulled her phone out, and put it to her ear. When she stopped walking and stood there, talking rapidly while scanning the crowd, I stopped, too. Talking into her phone, she nodded before heading for the exit. I trailed her, keeping a good distance behind her. Hernandez was missing, so like it or not, I was kind of her guard right now.

She must have spotted me following her, because she whirled on her heel. "Finn. Go. Away. You promised you would after this."

"I will, but not until you're home."

"I will be soon." She gripped her bag tight, not meeting my eyes. "Marie is coming for me."

I crossed my arms and searched the crowd. No sign of the dude who had caught my attention, but another man I didn't know stood to the side, watching Carrie way too fucking closely for my liking. "Fine. But I'm not leaving until she does. I think someone's wa—"

"I thought you weren't my freaking guard anymore," she snapped, eyes flashing. Her red hair blew in the breeze, and she looked picture perfect. I wanted to kiss that frown right off her face, in front of everyone in this outdoor mall. "Yet here you are, guarding me yet again."

I twisted my lips. "Hernandez didn't come, so I have to watch over you. And I saw someone—"

"Actually, you don't." She tossed her hair over her shoulder. "I'm fine alone."

"Jesus, woman, will you let me fucking talk?" Which reminded me why I'd written the note in the first place. So I could get all my words out like Dr. Montgomery suggested. I stepped closer, towering over her short frame. I shook the note in front of her face. "Take this."

"No." She shook her head. "I don't want it. It won't change anything."

I opened it. "Dear Ginger," I started. "I know I was wrong when I left you. I know I broke your heart, but the thing is? I broke mine more. I can't live without you. When I wake up, you're there—but you're not there. When I laugh at something on TV, I look to your spot on my couch to see if you laughed too—but you're not there. When I roll over in bed, I stretch my hand out, looking for your smooth skin—but you're not there."

"Oh my God, stop." She covered her ears, tears streaming down her flushed face. "*Please.*"

Pain sliced through me, but there was no way in hell I would stop now. "Even when I was out of my fucking mind with grief and rage, even when I wanted to fucking die and almost did, you saved me. I was going to end it all the night you saw me outside you room, but when I stood in the store picking out a rope—you were there. You *saved* me. You didn't ruin me. You are all I need in my life to live, and without you, I'm not living. Without you—"

"Wait. Y-You wanted to *die*?" She took a step toward me but stopped herself short. "You almost killed yourself?"

She was close enough for me to touch her now.

I didn't.

"I'm not done yet." I dragged my hands down my face. "Without you, I will never be whole, because half of me will always be gone. You complete me, and without that, I'll—"

She pushed my shoulders hard. "Damn you. You can't *die*."

I lowered my arm, giving up on reading the letter right now. "I know. And I'm not." I fisted my hands. "I'm here, watching you hate me, and I'm not going anywhere. It's my turn to have the broken heart. I can handle that. But it won't make me stop fucking caring, damn it." I lifted my arm. "Without that, I'll keep living, but I'll die alone, because no one else will ever replace you. I. Am. Not. *Leaving*. Not this time." I looked up at her again. "Please forgive me. Please love me again, because I can't stop loving you. I won't. I don't want to be your friend. I want to be your forever. The sun is always shining when I'm with you. Love always, Finn."

She pushed my shoulders ever harder this time, her wet cheeks shining in the dull sunlight. "Fuck you!"

I stood my ground, even though it hurt to see her look at me as if I was the enemy again. I'd done this to myself. I deserved every second of her anger, and more. It was better than her being upset, if nothing else. I crumpled up the paper in my fist. "That's what the letter said."

She growled and smacked my arm. "God, I *hate* you sometimes."

"I love you all the time," I said.

"Stop saying that."

"Or what?" I cocked a brow. "You'll kiss me into submission, like the good old days?"

Her eyes flared, and she stared at my mouth. I could tell she was contemplating it, so I acted without thinking. I hauled her close, spun her against the wall, and kissed her. Our lips met explosively, fireworks going off and all that sappy, sentimental garbage most women said happened when people kissed.

Thing is? Most of them are lying.

But this was real.

Her hands closed on my shoulders, and for a second I thought she was going to push me away. But then she dug her nails into my skin and hauled me closer, whimpering and parting her lips. I slipped my tongue in with a growl, deepening the kiss until I felt her melt against me. When she was all liquid desire, I cupped her ass and lifted her slightly, needing to feel her against me.

Needing her.

She gasped and broke off the kiss, her cheeks bright red. "Oh my God."

"Please." I kissed her again, soft. My heart thundered in my chest, drowning out the sounds of the people all around us. "Don't push me away. I *need* you. Love me again, Ginger."

"Finn…" Her hands hesitated, and she looked up, her blue eyes shining up at me. I held my breath, waiting for her to say *yes*. Hoping she wouldn't send me away, because it just might rip me in half. "I—"

"Carrie?" Riley said, his voice hard. "Are you okay? Marie sent me here to get you."

She bit down on her lip hard, still staring at me. But I could see the difference. The moment had passed, and she was going to reject me. She wasn't looking up at me with warmth. She was scared. Angry. Hurt. But not in love.

It was over.

CHAPTER TWENTY-THREE

Carrie

Oh my God. This was so unfair. I'd been fighting and fighting to move on from Finn when all along…he'd been hiding within me. I thought I could get over him? Well, he'd never left. How could I move on when I was still hopelessly in love with him? The second his lips touched mine, it was like I'd finally come home.

The weight that had been sitting on my shoulders lifted, and I could finally breathe again. It was like I'd been stuck in some deep, endless slumber—and nothing could wake me up but his kiss. Like Snow White or something. That might sound stupid, but it was true. It had always been, and would always be, Finn. There was no escaping it, and if I kept trying, I might drive myself insane in the process.

I could probably love Riley. I could probably be happy.

But he wouldn't make me feel like *this*.

I looked past Finn to Riley, and I could tell he was upset. He deserved better than this. He deserved to feel this way with a girl who felt this way about him. I let go of Finn, and he stepped back, his head lowered. "I need to…I need…Riley. I have to go to him."

Finn nodded, his mouth pressed tight and his eyes achingly hollow. "I know. Go ahead. A deal is a deal."

I didn't know what he meant by that, but I tried to push it aside so I could focus on what needed to be done. As I walked over to Riley, I bent down and picked up the note Finn had written for me as I walked. I could feel Finn's eyes on me. "Riley, I'm—"

"I know. I can see it. There's nothing to say. No explanations or apologies needed. I knew I was the underdog in this match." He shrugged. "I guess I just hoped you had a thing for the underdog. Or that I'd have a sweeping win, Rocky style."

I held his hands, squeezing them. "I'm so sorry. I think I could love you eventually. It would be so much easier. So much…just more everything."

He offered me a small smile. "A wise man once said that the heart wants what the heart wants."

"That wise man was you."

"Was it?" He cocked his head. "I should write that down. It's good advice."

I laughed a little bit. "It is."

"I guess I'm taking my hat back, huh? It's a good thing I look so hot in a hat."

"Yes," I whispered. "I believe love like this, as disastrous as it can be, only happens to a person once in a lifetime. You deserve to find someone who feels that way about you."

Riley cupped my cheek. "If you were mine, I'd never let you go. You deserve a guy who will stand by you, no matter what."

"Thank you." I smiled and dropped back down to my normal height. "Your girl is out there. You'll find her soon. I know it."

He smiled sadly. "We'll see about that."

"Want to say hi to Finn?" I looked over my shoulder. "He really does…like…you." I spun in a circle, searching the crowd. "Wait. Where did he go?"

Riley frowned. "He was just there, watching us."

"Finn?" I called out, rising on tiptoe. I spun in a circle. "Something's wrong. I know it."

Riley scratched his head. "What could possibly be wrong? We're in a crowded mall."

"You don't understand." I grabbed his hand. "I know him, and he wouldn't leave me alone. He'd never leave me unguarded like this."

"Calm down. You're with me. Maybe that's why he left." Riley started leading me to the exit. "Let's get to my car and we'll call him. Maybe he's already on his bike, waiting to follow us back to the college. Okay?"

I looked over my shoulder. "No. I *know* something's wrong."

"Then we'll find him." He squeezed my hand. "Try calling him."

We started for the exit, me fumbling for my phone in my pocket, but someone stepped in our path. He wore a hoodie that covered his face, and he reeked of smoke. I couldn't see his face, but his dirty hand held what looked like an equally filthy blade. "We have your boyfriend, and he's unconscious. You want him to live? You'll both come with us, Ms. Wallington."

My heart stopped. "What did you do with him?"

"It doesn't matter if you don't get walking," the guy said, showing the blade in his hand even more fully to us, "'cause he'll be dead."

Riley stiffened. "We're in a crowded mall. You can't abduct us here."

Another guy came behind us, pressing a knife against my lower back. "Do what he says, princess."

I tried to look over my shoulder. The guy in front of us snarled. "Don't turn around. Don't fight. Just *walk.*"

"No," I said, surprised at how steady my voice sounded.

"Carrie," Riley said, his voice cracking. "Do what they say. He has a knife to your back."

The guy in front of us slashed out at Riley. Riley hissed and jerked back, his hand to his arm. Blood soaked the white shirt, and he glared at the criminal with fury in his eyes. "You *asshole.* I'll kill—"

"Okay, we're going!" I said, my heart racing. "Riley. Look at me."

Riley whirled my way, still looking as if he was ready to fight both these men all on his own. He'd lose. Two to one. "We can take them."

"We have her boyfriend," the guy behind me hissed. "How will you save him, too?"

The guy in front of us smirked. "You'll never find him."

"We're coming." I swallowed hard. "Who put you up to this?"

"A friend of a friend. We were only supposed to scare you, and make this one look like a fool," he said, tipping his head to Riley. "But then we realized you're both worth more money than the other kid offered us. Now, out to the parking lot, real easy like, and no one gets hurt."

Riley's hand tightened on mine. The blood had spread over his forearm, soaking the whole lower half of his sleeve. "Let's go. Do what they say."

I walked with him, my eyes straight ahead the whole time. "Are you okay?"

"I'm fine." Riley's hand tightened on mine. The guy behind me pressed the knife deeper against my back. "Pissed, but fine."

I nodded. I was terrified, so much so that my legs shook. But we'd be okay. These guys would ransom us off, and this nightmare would be over. Finn would be okay, too. Things could go back to normal. Oh, who was I kidding? This was my freaking life. Two kidnapping attempts in one lifetime meant my life would never be normal.

We reached a shady van with dark windows. Of course. This kidnapper didn't have an original bone in his body. For some reason, I wanted to laugh at this whole scenario. Maybe it was paranoia, maybe it was me going crazy.

All I knew was that this seemed extremely funny.

The guy in front of us opened the back door of the blue van and said, "Get in. Quickly."

Before Riley could move, the guy behind us hit the ground twitching. I whirled, my eyes wide as the dude struggled to breathe, his face turning blue. Riley leapt on him, twisting his arms behind his back, forcing the guy onto his knees. Finn leapt around us, attacking the other kidnapper before he could even react. He hit the ground, too, and Finn knelt behind him, choking the dude out and breathing heavily, his eyes narrowed as he searched the rest of the parking lot.

His hard muscles flexed as he gripped the guy tight. I watched as the kidnapper lost all color to his face and finally passed out. Finn hadn't even broken a freaking sweat. "I already took out the driver. Were they with anyone else?"

"I-I don't know," I said quickly, looking around. "I thought they h-had you."

"No, they had Hernandez. I already saved him, though. I saw him get taken. I almost missed it, but when I looked away from you two…I saw Hernandez." He let go of the guy, and his lifeless body slumped to the ground. "Then he was gone, so I followed him."

I let out a sigh of relief. Finn was okay. So were we. It was over. But this whole thing felt fake, as if it were a dream.

Finn stood up and came around us, punching the other guy in the face. He slumped over, too, knocked out cold, and Riley let go of his arms, his face pinched tight in anger. "Thanks, man."

"It's nothing," Finn said, reaching into the van and pulling out some rope. I'd known he was lethal, but seeing him in action again was both frightening and yet…somewhat *hot*. Knowing he could save me from anyone or anything made me all warm and gooey inside. "I was here. Carrie? Are you okay?"

I nodded. "Y-Yes."

He'd never let me down again, and I knew it.

His gaze scanned over me. He opened the van and pulled out rope, tying the kidnappers' feet and hands together effortlessly. It wasn't until he opened the van that I saw another guy in there, also hogtied. He was awake now. "Did they hurt you?"

"N-No. They cut Riley, though." I looked at Riley. I was still holding his hand, but he seemed to need it, so I didn't let go. He looked shaken up. "We're okay. I thought they had *you*."

He snorted. "But they didn't. They'd never have gotten me. I'm surprised they got Hernandez. He must have been distracted by something."

Marie came running up, out of breath. "Is everything okay? I was on the phone with Hernandez, fighting with him over whether he was able to find you, and then he was gone. It sounded like…" Her eyes went wide. "Why are there two unconscious dudes on the ground?"

"We were almost kidnapped, and they knocked out Hernandez." When Marie paled, I quickly added, "We're all fine, though. It was over before it started because of Finn."

Marie looked horrified. "Oh my God. Are you okay?"

"Yes. I am, I swear."

Looking in the van, she nodded distractedly. "Where is he? Where's Hernandez?"

"I left him in Islands after I found him unconscious. He's probably awake by now." Finn looked up from his position on the ground. "You can go check on him, if you'd like."

Marie took off without a backward glance.

"Thank you, Finn," Riley said again, stepping forward. He still didn't drop my hand. "You saved us."

Finn finished tying up the first suspect, stood up, and went to the second. "It's nothing, man." He looked at me before quickly glancing away. "Absolutely nothing."

I let go of Riley when my phone rang. "It's my dad. How does he know already?"

"Hernandez called him, I bet." Finn looked at me and nodded. "Answer it. Tell him what happened. I'm going to stand guard till the cops get here in case there are more of these assholes out here."

I picked up the phone, and instantly my dad started. "Who is this? Give me back my baby girl or I'll—"

"It's me. I'm okay. I'm safe. We're all safe," I said, not bothering with small talk. The world started spinning, as if I'd forgotten to breathe or something. "Finn was here with Riley and me, and he saved us."

Dad was silent for a second. "Who did this to you?"

"I have no idea, but Finn tied up the suspects, so I'm assuming the cops can find out." I took a shaky breath, trying not to break down now that it was all said and done. Funny, I didn't feel scared before, but now? I was literally falling apart. As a matter of fact, I just might faint. Funny. I'd never done that before. "Finn was here, so he took care of it. And we're okay. We're all okay. O-Okay."

Finn tied the man's arms together, his gaze locked on me the whole time. "Riley, hug her or *I* will. She's going in to shock and needs comfort. Comfort her."

Riley hesitated. "Dude, we're not—"

"I don't give a shit," Finn growled. "Just fucking do it already, man."

"Okay," Riley said, pulling me into his arms and kissing my temple. "It's okay. We're here. We're fine."

I just stared straight ahead, not sure what to say or do. It was like I was broken. I held the phone to my ear still, and Dad kept talking, asking a million questions, but I couldn't make a sound.

Finn reached out for my cheek, but then pulled back. After a low curse, he said, "It's okay. You'll be all right." Finn took the phone from my hand. "Sir, she's in shock right now and can't talk, but she's okay. There were three suspects that I took care of. I'm keeping an eye out for others, but there's no sign of any." Sirens sounded in the distance. "The cops are almost here. I called them after I got the first guy, as I searched for Carrie." He was quiet. "Yes, sir. He was with her." Another pause. "No, sir. He's fine. So is she." He blinked. "I'm fine too, sir. So is Hernandez." He nodded. "I'll let her know to expect you." He hung up and put my phone in his pocket. "Your dad is on his way."

I nodded. Or at least I think I did. I tried to say something, anything, but nothing came out. My mouth just opened and closed. Finn stepped forward, his eyes on me, but then he stopped. His fist unfurled, curled again, and he turned away. "She's still freaking out. You need to calm her the fuck down, Riley. Come *on*."

"Shh, you're okay." Riley hugged me closer. Police cars rolled into the parking lot, screeching to a halt by us. I barely noticed them. "What happens now?"

"Police will want statements and all that, but once they're done, you go home and let them do their jobs." Finn tugged on his hair, still watching me. "She's not fucking okay, damn it. Fix it!"

Riley let go of me, making an angry sound. "Maybe *you* should try to fix her. You're the one she loves! She probably just needs you."

"She doesn't—" Finn shook his head and growled. "Fuck it. Come here, Ginger."

He yanked me into his arms. He hugged me so tight I could barely breathe…and yet suddenly, I *could*. I clung to him, releasing a sob. "I-I was…so scared, Finn."

"Shh." He kissed my head, his arms going even tighter around me. "I'm here. I won't let anything happen to you. *Ever.*"

I nodded, burying my face in his chest. "Don't leave me again. Swear it."

"I swear. I'll never leave you again," he whispered brokenly. His heart thundered against my cheek, and I hugged him as hard as I could. He didn't seem to mind. If anything, it made him kiss me even harder the next time. "Even when you're with someone else, I'll take care of you. I love you so damn much."

I shook my head. Didn't he realize what I was saying? I was his, and always would be. "There's no—"

A cop cleared his throat. "We need to speak with her, please?"

Finn tightened his arms around me. "If she's ready."

"I'm r-ready." I let go of Finn reluctantly, but entwined his fingers with mine. "Stay with me?"

He gave me a sad smile. "Always. But what about Riley?"

I looked at Riley. He was talking to an officer and walking toward a paramedic. "He looks okay, right? They'll fix his arm in the ambulance."

Finn nodded, looking confused. "Yeah, but…"

"He'll be brought to the station, too," the officer said, motioning toward his own car. "Let's get her somewhere safe and then they can reunite in the station."

I nodded and took a deep breath. "All right. Let's go."

"Just you, ma'am," the officer said, eyeing Finn. "He can follow in another car."

"He stays with me, or I don't go." I hugged his arm close to mine, gripping his biceps with my free hand. "He's with me."

Finn flexed his jaw. "I go with her if she wants me to."

The officer sighed. "Who are you?"

"Her bodyguard," Finn said, before I could open my mouth to answer. He cocked his head toward the van. "I'm the one who tied them up."

"Oh. Good." He opened the back door. "We need to talk to you, too."

Finn slid into the backseat, not letting go of me. "I'm all yours," he said softly.

I swallowed hard, clinging to him.

Had he been talking to me or the officer?

CHAPTER TWENTY-FOUR

Finn

Hours later, and a million questions later, I finally got released from the interrogation room. I don't know if that's what it actually was, but man, it had felt like it. They'd asked me so many questions, over and over again, that my fucking head hurt more than ever. I rubbed my temples, wanting nothing more than to lie down in a dark room for a whole day.

"Griffin." A door opened beside me and Senator Wallington stepped out, looking as impeccable as always in his gray three-piece suit. "A word?"

Shit. "Yes, of course."

I followed him into the empty room…well, almost empty. Mrs. Wallington stood in the corner, watching me cautiously. "Griffin."

"Mrs. Wallington." I nodded at her and turned back to Senator Wallington. "You two got here way too fast. Or was I really in there that long?"

"We were actually in Arizona for a meeting. We arrived a little more than an hour ago."

"Oh." I dragged my hands down my face. "You're here to ask me to leave Carrie alone, I assume?"

Mrs. Wallington stepped forward. "Griffin—"

"Wait, let me talk first." I lifted my chin. "I was a mess before, and I know it. I wasn't worthy of Carrie like that, but I got better. I've been going to therapy, and I don't take pills or drink."

Senator Wallington shook his head. "But you left her. Walked away and didn't even care."

"I *cared*." I fisted my hands. "I cared way too much."

Mrs. Wallington nodded. "You did. I know that. But what makes you think you're better for her now?"

"Because I'm me again, and I love her more than anything. I love her enough to walk away when I needed to. I'm not walking away again, not if she wants me." I met Senator Wallington's eyes. "She doesn't forgive me yet, but if she ever does, you can be damn sure I will never break her heart again. I'll cherish her till I die. She's…she's my life."

Mrs. Wallington's eyes filled with tears. "I believe you."

"Margie," Senator Wallington hissed. He gave her a long look before turning to me with hard eyes. "Why were you there today?"

"I know I shouldn't have been there, since I don't work for you anymore, but I was—and that's a good thing. I was able to help Hernandez."

"I heard." He crossed his arms and studied me. "You look better. Less…"

"Messed up?"

He nodded. "Yes. That."

Mrs. Wallington gasped. "Don't be rude, Hugh."

"He's right, though," I said, smiling at her. "I am less messed up now."

"Good." He stepped closer, his gaze dipping over me. "I won't pretend you're my choice for her, but if you make her happy, and keep yourself in check, I'm willing to give you a second chance. I might even approve of you, over time."

"Me too," Mrs. Wallington said, resting her hand on my arm. "I know how much you love her, Griffin." She cocked her head. "Finn, I mean."

I blinked, my hands hovering at my sides. What. The. Fuck? "Ma'am…?"

"It's what she calls you, right?" She smiled at me, her eyes tearing up. "If you're going to be with her, we should call you that, too."

Senator Wallington cleared his throat. "I saw what happened to her when you left. I don't want to ever see that again." He held his hand out for mine, waiting. "I'm willing to accept you not because I have to, but because I think in the end…you just might be the best partner for her. You'll die for her. Live for her. Do anything to keep her safe."

I swallowed hard. "Always. But sir, she's with Riley now."

"No, she's not. We tried to urge that along, but it's not going to happen." He frowned at me. "You better love her the right way this time, because I'm determined to see her happy again. No drinking. No drugs. No punching walls."

"I'm better now. Still not the same guy I used to be, and I don't think I ever will be, but I love her with all my heart." I tugged on my hair, eyeing Mrs. Wallington. "I only left her because I wasn't good for her. I—"

He waved his hand. "We all know you were in a dark place, yes, but you seem better now. I hear you go to therapy twice a week, and the nightmares have mostly stopped?"

I stared him down. "Sir, have you been reading my medical records?"

"No." He laughed. "Your roommate, otherwise known as Hernandez, is keeping me informed. He told me when you came back, and I've been watching you ever since. Watching you heal."

"But why?" I asked, more confused than ever. "I don't understand."

"Because I want Carrie to be happy, and you're the one who makes her happy." He laid a hand on my shoulder and squeezed. "Speaking of which, do you want your old job back, Griffin…er, Finn? With our permission to date and love our daughter for the rest of your life, as long as you treat her like you should?"

I swallowed hard. "I have to talk to her first. See if that's what she wants. But I…I want to go to college. I think Richards is still going to pay for me to go, even though I'm not a Marine anymore. He told me he was."

"Then go to the same college as Carrie," Mrs. Wallington said. "That would be perfect."

Senator Wallington motioned in the general direction of the campus. "I'll even pay for your education myself as part of your salary if that's what it takes for you to come back. But if you ever hurt her again, I'll—"

Mrs. Wallington stepped forward. "What he *means*, Finn, is we forgive you. We're willing to move on instead of dwelling on the past." Mrs. Wallington held on to her husband's arm. "Isn't that right, Hugh?"

He flinched. "Yes. That's right."

"Thank you. I…I don't know what to say," I said, my throat feeling way too damn tight.

"She's waiting for you out there," Mrs. Wallington said. "You ready to go back to her?"

I looked at the door. "What about Riley?"

"He's there, too," Senator Wallington said, opening the door. "But I told you, she doesn't love him. I'd *prefer* her to love him, to be honest, but she just doesn't."

"I'll guard her, even if she's with him." I gritted my teeth. "I'll do it anyway, so I might as well get paid for it. I can't trust anyone else. What about Hernandez?"

"He quit already. Said being a Marine was enough danger for any one man," the senator said, straightening his tie. "I never saw him as long-term. I was just waiting."

I cocked a brow. "For?"

"You. I knew you'd be back."

"So did I," Mrs. Wallington said.

I shook my head. This was the weirdest fucking conversation ever. "If she does take me back, I'm not changing for you." I stared him down, running my fingers over my scar. "She likes me the way I am. Or, she did, anyway."

He inclined his head. "Fair enough. As long as you treat her right this time, I can work with that. But if you—"

"*Hugh.*"

Senator Wallington cut off, shooting me one last look before heading for the door. I didn't say anything else. I followed them out into the main area, my heart thundering in my ears. Were they right? Did Carrie want me, even though Riley had come back into the picture at the worst moment? We entered the room, and I saw her immediately. Her hair was down now, and she sat next to Riley.

She looked fucking exhausted.

We walked over to them, me a few steps behind the Wallingtons. Carrie looked up, cried out, and flung herself into my arms. "Are you okay? They had you in there forever."

I hesitated only a second before I closed my arms around her tight. Riley locked gazes with me, nodding once. Saying he was okay with this type of contact with his girlfriend, I suppose. "I'm okay. I just have a headache."

She let go of me, framed my face with her hands, and nodded. "Let's get you home."

"You mean to Hernandez's place?"

"He's not there. He said he was leaving the job and the apartment—since the apartment belongs to Carrie's guard," Senator Wallington said, heading for the door. "We'll take you there."

I had no idea what was going on, but I didn't want to ask Carrie in front of them.

My questions would have to wait.

We all piled in to the limo, mostly silent. Finally, Carrie spoke. "Apparently, they came after us because of Cory."

"Cory?" I snapped, my head lifting instantly. "What did he do?'

"He hired them to scare us, and make Riley look like a fool since he couldn't protect me." She shrugged. "Cory thought that would make me break up with Riley, I guess. Or maybe he thought it would scare Riley off. I don't know."

I curled my hands into fists. I'd kill the fucker. "They did more than scare you both."

"Yeah, they broke the plan. They decided to ransom us off for money and leave us somewhere to be found afterward," Riley said, looking down at his bandaged arm. "They were looking for money for their next fix, and thought they found it in us."

"*Cory,*" I snarled, rage choking me. "I always knew that guy was trouble."

She nodded. "You were right. I should have believed you. He'll be facing charges now."

I snorted. "He should face me. I'll make him sorry he ever thought of endangering you."

"Agreed," Senator Wallington said. "For once."

We all fell silent until the limo stopped in front of my old place. I nodded my head at Riley and the Wallingtons. Finally, I locked eyes with Carrie. "Thanks for the ride."

"You bet," Carrie said, her hands clutched in her lap.

I nodded and got out of the car, heading up the walkway. Swallowing hard, I dug my key out of my pocket. It had been way too fucking hard to walk away from Carrie again. You'd think I would be used to it by now.

"Hey, wait up!" Carrie called out.

I stopped, my heart lurching. Slowly, I turned. The limo left, but Carrie stayed. I didn't know what to think of that. "Yeah?"

"Did you mean it?"

I gripped my keys tight. "Did I mean what?"

"That you still loved me, and never stopped?"

"Of course," I said. "I love you, and nothing will ever—"

She flung herself in my arms, kissing me into silence. I dropped the keys to the ground, picking her up and hugging her against my chest. By the time the kiss ended, we were both out of breath. She pulled back, her cheeks flushed and her blue eyes shining. "Can I come up with you?"

"Yes." I nodded, feeling completely flustered. "Of course."

She bent down, picked up the keys, and headed for the door without breaking stride. "Did you know Hernandez never slept in your bed?"

I rubbed my jaw and followed her, using all my strength and resolve to not grab her and pick up where that kiss had ended. What did it mean? Did it mean she loved me, too? That she forgave me? Fuck, I hoped so. "I did. He was on the couch when I came back. He said it didn't feel right taking over my place when he had his own a few miles away. So I've been sleeping in my bed, and he's been on the couch."

"He never got rid of his place?"

"Nah. He owns it." I glanced her way. "He's had it ever since his grandfather died. He just stayed here for the job."

She shook her head. "He never wanted this job."

"No." I took the keys out of her hand and unlocked the door. "He did it for me."

"I know." She walked inside. She took it all in, her face a mixture of hope and nostalgia. "Now we talk."

I closed the door and tossed the keys on the table. "Okay."

"Do…" She sat down on the bed, bouncing to test it out. She looked back toward the pillow, frowning when she saw the purple rose on the pillow. Reaching out, she picked it up and looked at me. "What's this?"

"I was going to give it to you, but then decided the note was too much." I shifted on my feet. "Too soon, because you hadn't forgiven me yet."

She looked down at it, her fingers lightly caressing the petals. "Can I read it?"

"Yeah, I guess so." I crossed the room and grabbed six more. I'd struggled to pick the right message today. "Here's the rest."

She looked up at me, her eyes filling with tears. "Were these all too personal, too?"

I nodded. "Yes."

She took a deep breath and unrolled the paper. "*Love me.*"

"Yeah." I tossed the red one on the bed. I hadn't even realized that people dyed roses all these crazy colors until recently. I thought they only came in red or pink. "This one says: *The sun is shining. Love me.*" The pale green one. "*I can't live without you. Love me.*" Pink next. "*You look beautiful. Love me.*" Another pink one. "*I'll never make you cry again. Love me.*" Last, the yellow one. I tossed that in her lap. "*I want to marry you. Love me.*"

She looked up at me, tears falling down her cheeks, and picked up the yellow one, holding it to her chest. "God, Finn."

"I'm going to be honest with you here." I paced her way, nibbling on my thumbnail. "I'll never be the same guy you fell in love with. I still get headaches, I have scars, and I occasionally have those nightmares, too. I don't drink to hide the pain anymore, and I don't abuse pain pills anymore, either. I was in a dark, dark hole the last time we were together, but I'm better now."

She stood up, still holding the yellow rose. "Finn—"

"Wait. Before you say anything, I know you could do better. I know Riley is better. But damn it, you love me. You even said it. It might be scary and hard, but I want to spend the rest of my life with you. Making you laugh. Making you cry. Making love to you. I want to be yours…and I need you to be mine. Please. I'm begging you—and I don't fucking beg. You know that."

Tears shined in her eyes. "Are you done yet?"

"I…no." I tugged on my hair, looking at the half-dozen roses scattered across my bed. "I love you, and no one will ever love you like I do. I know I fucked up, and I'll spend my whole life making it up to you, if you'll let me. Please, just let me love you. *Love me.*"

"Yes. Yes, yes, and yes." She launched herself into my arms, hugging me tight and crying. "I love you, too. I do. I love you so much."

"Y-You do?" I looked down at her, my mind spinning and my heart racing. "You still love me?"

"Yes, I love you, you idiot." She cupped my cheeks. "I've laughed with you. I've been blissfully happy with you. I've cried with you. I've cried for you. I've been scared for you. I've hurt for you and from you. I've even been broken hearted over you." She looked up at me, tears rolling down her cheeks. "But I never want to be *without* you again."

"Then you won't be. I swear it."

She lifted her face. "Good. Now kiss me before I die."

CHAPTER TWENTY-FIVE

Carrie

The second his mouth closed over mine, I lost myself. I gave myself over to him willingly, knowing this was the right choice. No second-guessing or wondering. This was Finn, and I was me. We belonged together like this. It was the way we were supposed to be. His tongue touched mine, and he growled, pressing me back on the bed. I wrapped my arms around his neck, holding him close. There was no way I'd ever let go of him again. Not even if he pushed me away. Not even if he tried to make me not love him anymore.

Love like this wasn't meant to die.

He pressed his hard length against me, and I spread my legs so he could rest within them. We both moaned when he fell into place, but we didn't stop kissing. I don't think I could have even if someone forced me to. He slid his hand under my butt, lifting me against his erection. I rolled my hips, desire twisting and turning in my belly.

He broke off the kiss with a gasp, dropping his forehead on mine. "I can't believe we're back here again. I didn't think you'd ever forgive me."

"I love you." I sat up and watched him as he pulled his shirt over his head. "Love is forgiveness, compromise, and dedication. I think we have that all covered. Now get *naked*."

"Fuck yeah." He tossed his shirt over his shoulder, his steamy blue eyes latching on to mine. "Your turn."

I shook my head. "You need to be naked first, because once I get my hands on you? I'm not stopping."

He undid his fly and dropped his shorts, kicking out of them easily. After he shimmied out of his boxer briefs, he stood there naked for the first time since his accident. Staring at me, waiting, letting *me* look my fill. He had scars all over his arm, and the scar on his head was still there, obviously. His muscles were as toned as ever, and he looked tanner than he used to be. He looked nervous, as if I might not like what I saw.

He didn't need to worry. He was *Finn*.

"You're perfect," I said, slowly standing. I trailed my fingers over the red, jagged scars on his arm and shoulder. "Every mark on your body, whether it's ink or a scar, tells a story. I want to know it all. I want to be there for it all from now on."

He relaxed, his eyes lighting up again. "You will be. I swear it."

"I know. I do too. Without you, I go out of my mind."

He laughed. "Yeah. Me too."

"I have a surprise for you." I undid my shorts, letting them fall to the floor. I stared at his tattoo. The one he'd gotten for me. *The sun is finally shining.* On his other shoulder, he'd gotten a new tattoo. It said *Ginger*. Even when we were apart, he'd gotten my name on his shoulder. I blinked back tears. God, I loved him. "I hope you like it, because I have a feeling it doesn't mean the same thing to you as it once did. But it means a lot to me."

He cocked his head. "I'm trying to concentrate, but you're getting naked. I'm finding it increasingly hard to listen."

"It's part of the surprise." I kicked out of my underwear and then grabbed my shirt hem. "I got something for you for Christmas, but I didn't have a chance to show you."

He nodded, his gaze on my stomach area...or maybe lower. "Show me," he rasped. "Hurry, please."

I took a breath and lifted my shirt over my head, letting it hit the floor behind me. The bra came off next, but Finn wasn't watching my movements anymore. He'd spotted my gift since I was officially wearing nothing but his necklace and his tattoo. As he stood there, staring at me, I waited. Letting *him* look *his* fill this time. "D-Do you like it?"

He closed the distance between us. Reaching out, he traced his fingers over the ink with a featherlight touch. "You got our tattoo? When?"

"When you were overseas." I rested my hands on his arms. "I know you don't like saying it anymore, probably because it reminds you of what you went through over there, but I—"

"I fucking love it." He pushed me back on the bed, lowering himself down my body to kiss the ink. "And I fucking love you, too. So damn much."

His hand skimmed lower and dipped down between my legs. I almost fell apart right then and there, because it had been so freaking long since I'd been touched like that. I let my legs fall open and moaned. "Oh my God."

"Jesus, I missed this. Missed you." And then he thrust a finger inside me. I cried out, arching my hips, my eyes rolling back in my head. It felt that good. "You're so hot when you're flushed with need, Ginger."

"P-Please," I begged, moving my hips higher. "More."

He chuckled, the sound low and so sexy it drove me even more insane. My pulse raced, and I moved my hips again, groaning when he thrust inside at the same time. "I am so incredibly moved and touched that you did that for me," he said, withdrawing and then thrusting two fingers inside. "But before I get all sappy and sentimental and shit, I'm going to make you scream my name so fucking loud it hurts."

"God, yes," I breathed. "*Finn.*"

He slid down my body till he knelt on the floor next to the bed. Without a second's warning, he closed his hands on the sides of my hips and his mouth was on my clit. As his tongue moved over me in slow, sensuous circles, I slowly drifted away to a place where nothing mattered but us. Nothing but this.

He cupped my butt, lifting me higher against his hot mouth, and increased the pressure. His fingers dug into my skin, making me cry out from the mixture of pleasure and pressure, and he scraped his teeth against me. It had been so long since I'd had him, so long since I'd felt anything even remotely close to this, that it didn't take much to send me soaring over the edge.

And, man, did I freaking fly. "Finn," I cried out, my entire body bursting with pleasure. "Oh my God. Oh my God."

He let me hit the mattress again, growling as he climbed on top of me and claimed my mouth with a tortured kiss. After he rolled a condom on, he lifted my hips and thrust into me in one hard drive, not stopping once he was all the way inside of me. He pulled out and slammed into me again, making my entire body convulse from pleasure. I screamed into his mouth, unable to hold back the frantic noises escaping me, and closed my legs around his waist.

Freaking *heaven*.

He broke off the kiss and rested his forehead on mine, breathing heavily. His muscled arms flexed on either side of my head, and he rolled his hips gently. "Shit, Ginger. Are you okay? Was I too rough on—?"

"No." I dug my heels into his butt, smacking his arm in frustration. "Don't stop. Keep going. *Harder*."

He growled and moved within me. Slow at first, but quickly picking up speed and friction. I dragged my nails down his back, moaning and whimpering and God only knows what else I did. My body was focused on him and what he was doing to me. Nothing else registered at all. I was so lost in him that I didn't even know or care what I said or shouted or even cried.

As long as he kept pumping his hips like that and kissing me, that's all that mattered. He bit down on my neck, letting out a grueling moan. "I'm so fucking close. I need you to come again, Ginger."

He reached between us, squeezed my nipple between his finger and thumb with the perfect amount of force, and thrust harder. "Yes," I cried out. "Oh my God, yes."

He thrust into me so hard the bed moved across the floor with a loud screech. His hard biceps were so strained his veins were pronounced, and he closed his eyes, his face lost in pleasure. It was so freaking hot, watching him like this. Knowing I was the only one who got to see him like this. I clung to him even tighter. "Fuck, Carrie."

"Let go. I have you," I said, kissing him. "I'm all yours, love."

He let out a broken sound and moved inside of me without abandon. I dug my nails into his shoulders as the bed moved across the floor, the tightness in my stomach coiling so hard that I knew I was close to exploding again. He pinched my nipple, rough and hard, his tongue moving against mine, and I came.

"*Carrie*." He growled and pumped into me once more, harder than ever before, and his body went rock hard as he orgasmed. He collapsed on top of me, his breathing harsh. "Holy shit."

"Yeah." I grinned. "It's been way too long."

He lifted up onto his elbows and smiled down at me, sweeping the hair off my face with his hand. "I feel a hell of a lot less tense now, that's for fucking sure."

"You and me both." I flexed my legs around him, not wanting to let go…like…ever. "You know I wasn't with anyone else while you were gone, right?"

He kissed my nose. "I'd hoped so, but if you moved on when I was gone, it would be fine. I don't have a right to—"

"I didn't." My cheeks heated. "You're the only one who makes me feel this way, and you're the only one who ever will."

He kissed me tenderly before pushing off me. "We need a shower. I want to wash the filth of those assholes Cody hired off us."

I laughed. "You mean Cory?"

"Nope. Cody." He lifted me into his arms. "He doesn't deserve a real name."

I rested my head on his shoulder as he walked into the bathroom. I flicked the light on with my toes. He set me down on my feet, kissed the tip of my nose, and turned on the water. "Still like it scalding hot?"

"Yep." I pulled out two towels and rummaged under the sink for supplies. Two bottles caught my attention. "You still have my shampoo?"

He dropped something into the trash and turned a little bit red. "Yeah. I liked to sniff it when I missed you, which was every night before bedtime. Sometimes in the morning, too." He rolled his eyes. "And there goes my man card yet again."

"You never lost it, and never will. Not with me." I hugged the bottles close to my naked body. "Besides, I slept with your shirt, so I'm not one to talk."

"You did?"

"I did," I admitted. "Do. Whatever."

He laughed and swept me into his arms. He carried me into the shower, depositing me directly into the stream of water. "Are you okay? I mean, after the scare and all…"

"I'm fine." I reached up and cupped his face. "I'm not here because I'm in shock or anything."

"I know." He kissed me. "And I'm not here because your father asked me to be your guard again."

"I know. You're—wait. What?" I peeked up at him as he massaged my scalp under the water. "Did he ask you?"

"Yeah, he did. I want to make sure it's okay with you." His fingers stilled. "He's also giving me a second chance to prove myself. Your mother is, too. I'm not sure what to think about that."

"I'm not too surprised. They want me to be happy, and you make me happy." I rose on tiptoe and kissed him. "Do you want to accept the job?"

"I think I will. Since I'll be guarding you for the rest of my life, I might as well get paid for it and keep some annoying dude from following us around all the time." He poured out the shampoo and rubbed it into my hair. "He offered to pay for my college, but Captain Richards has already informed me that he'll still pay even though I'm a civilian now. I don't know if I can accept that, though."

"Accept it." I frowned at him. "Are you insane? Of course you accept it. He's offering to help you, and you earned it."

"But why? Because I lived and no one else did?"

"Because you were injured, and that was part of the deal—you going to college on his dime. Trust me, he can afford it." I rested my hands over his heart. "And if you won't accept help from Captain Richards, then accept it from my father. He owes it to you after all the crap he's given you."

He stepped back and tugged on his hair. "I don't know. I'll think about it."

I gazed at him, admiring the view. His ink was stark against his flawless skin. His broad shoulders tapered down over his hard pecs, and then narrowed to his impossibly taut abs. His cock—yes, I still blushed at that word—jutted out from his light brown curls, and he looked beautiful.

Delicious, even.

I'd never seen a more welcome sight than him, standing naked and wet in the shower with me. And I never would again. After he finished rinsing my hair, I grabbed his hand before he could snatch up the conditioner. "So…ready for round two?"

His eyes darkened. "Are *you*?"

"Heck yeah." I nodded for good measure, running my fingers down his chest, over his abs, and closing my hand over his cock. "And three…"

"And four…" He dropped his head back against the white tile. I skimmed my fingers over the head of his erection before jerking him in my fist. "Fuck, that feels good, Ginger."

I sank to my knees. "I know what will feel even better."

"Yes." He threaded his fingers in my hair, his Adam's apple bobbing as he swallowed hard. "Do it. *Now.*"

I sucked him into my mouth hard, rolling my tongue over him just like he liked. He tightened his fists in my hair, urging me closer. His body flexed and moved, and he gently pumped his hips into my mouth as I sucked on him. I tasted his semen before he tried to pull away, but I dug my hands into his butt and refused to let go.

I wanted to do this. To taste him.

"Ginger, I'm going to come," he growled, pulling my hair. "Let me make you come, too."

I shook my head and sucked harder, moaning. He growled and moved his hips, seeming to give in. He rested his shoulders against the wall and pulled me closer, instead of pushing me away. When I scraped my teeth over the tip of him, he cried out and came. It was such a heady feeling, knowing I'd done this to him. Made him feel this good.

I swallowed, finally letting go of him after one last kiss to the tip of his cock. He collapsed against the wall, breathing unevenly, his hand still fisted in my hair. "You've been a bad girl," he said, his tone broken.

He tugged me up by my hair, and I stood. Once I was on my feet, he spun me around and entered me from behind. I slammed my hands against the wall, and my forehead smacked against it, too. "*Finn.*"

He reached around the front of me, pressing his fingers against my clit. "My turn to make you scream, Ginger."

As he moved inside of me harder and faster, his hands seemed to be everywhere. He skimmed over my breasts, pinching my nipples, and then dipped down. As soon as he touched me there again, I tensed. He thrust hard. I threw my head back and screamed, my nails scratching uselessly over the tiled wall as I came. "*Yes.* Oh my God."

He moved inside me once, twice, three times, his grip on my hips so tight it almost hurt—but in a good way. He dropped his forehead against the shower wall, cradling me in his arms from behind. "Holy shit, you're going to kill me."

"Never." I slid off him and spun around, wrapping my arms around his neck. "I love you too much."

Grinning, he trailed his fingers over my tattoo. "I love you, too. The sun is always shining around you, Ginger."

My heart warmed. "Indeed it is."

And I had a feeling it would never stop.

CHAPTER TWENTY-SIX

Finn

Four months later

I climbed off my bike and hung my helmet on the bars, taking a calming breath and smoothing my hair as I did so. The crisp early September morning air smelled fresh, sending awareness through my veins. Waking me up. It felt renewing, almost. Since this was the start of a new chapter of my life, it felt fitting. These past few months with Carrie had been pure heaven. We fought. We kissed. We made up. We loved.

I never thought I could be so damn happy.

My phone buzzed, and I pulled it out of my pocket. Senator Wallington. *Good luck, Finn. Let me know how it goes. Give Carrie my love, too. We miss you two already.*

I smiled. We'd spent the summer with them, getting to know each other better. I could almost say that they actually liked me now. They got to see the "me" I was without the pain and grief. It had been good for us. *Thank you, sir.*

I still couldn't believe how much he'd changed. But then again, we'd all changed. I sure as hell had, and so had Carrie. It stood to reason that he would have, too.

My phone buzzed again. *Talk to you later.*

"Who was that?" Carrie asked, smoothing her hair and coming up beside me.

"Your dad." I slipped my phone into my pocket and offered her my arm. "He was wishing me luck."

"Oh, that's nice. I bet he—" She checked her phone and frowned. "Hey. I got nothing."

I shrugged. "What can I say? I'm the favorite child now."

"Only because you can talk with him in his study for hours about politics without getting bored." She pouted, stealing a peek at me. "I had to escape. He can't blame me. Even Riley left after an hour."

I laughed. "That's 'cause he's not as cool as me."

"I know it." She wrapped her hand around my bicep. "But after we spent all summer living with them, I think my father really does love you more than me in some ways—and I love that fact, just for the record."

"That's not true." I grinned. "Okay. Maybe it's a little bit true."

She smacked my abs with her free hand. "*Ha-ha*, really funny, fresh meat."

"Hey, you promised not to call me that."

She laughed. "No, I promised not to call you that in bed. I didn't say anything about not doing it here. And I never promised not to laugh at you if you get lost on campus."

"Brat," I said, kissing her temple. I slid my bag higher on my shoulder and handed her hers. "Somehow I think I'll be fine, though, with or without your help."

"You think?" She smiled at me. "Are you ready for this?"

"Of course I am." I rolled my eyes. "I've been on this campus since last year. What difference is taking a few classes going to make?"

"Tell me that when you're buried in homework later this week."

I readjusted so I could put my arm over her shoulder. "As long as you help me study? I won't give a damn."

"You know I will." She wrapped her arm around my waist and hesitated. "You know...I was thinking."

"Sounds dangerous," I quipped.

She smacked my arm. "Stop it."

"Fine. I'll behave." I grinned and yanked my bag up higher on my shoulder. "What's up?"

"We're going to be studying so much, and at the same school, so I thought," she peeked up at me, "maybe I could move in with you? I mean, I practically live there now, but we could make it official."

I stopped walking, my heart thundering in my ears. "R-Really? You want to?"

"I do." She smiled up at me. "If you do."

"Fuck yes." I picked her up and swung her in a circle. "Yes! Are you sure?"

"I'm as positive as a proton," she said, grinning.

"Me too."

She laughed, and the melody washed over me, washing away any nerves I had—that I'd deny I had if anyone asked. I had her with me. What could ever possibly go wrong? She loved me, and I loved her.

Life was fucking good.

I kissed her, my mouth melding to hers perfectly. Which made sense, since she was made for me. I pulled back and grinned so big my cheeks fucking hurt. "If we weren't on our way to class, I'd celebrate this with you my favorite way—naked and wet."

Desire flared in her eyes. "Meet you out here at twelve for a nooner at home?"

"Yes." I kissed her one last time. "I love you."

"I love you, too."

I looked to the left and sighed. "I have to go this way to my economics class."

"And I go this way to trigonometry." She backed away from me, our fingers still entwined. "Then tonight, we'll tell my dad together? About us living together?"

I groaned, not letting go. "Do we have to? He liked me, but will he like this?"

"I don't know." She grinned. "But we'll find out the best way possible."

"Together."

"Always," she said, looking at me with so much love it almost hurt. "Now get your butt to class, freshman."

"Yes, ma'am." I let go of her reluctantly. "Look in your bag first, though."

She reached in and pulled out a yellow rose. Grinning, she read the message. "*I'll miss you. Love me.*" I'd ended the note the same way as I had the day we'd gotten back together. It was easily one of the best days of my life. She looked up at me, her blue eyes shining in the sun. "I'll miss you, too. And I do."

I blew her a kiss. "Stay in class and don't wander off, since I won't be watching you."

She laughed and called out over her shoulder, "You worry about me too much. Good luck!"

"I'll never worry enough when it comes to you," I said under my breath, watching her walk away. She took my heart with her, but I knew it would be safe in her hands.

Always.

EPILOGUE

Finn

Seven years later

I watched Carrie from across the room, my arms tightening on the precious bundle in my arms as I juggled the phone with my free hand. She stretched her arms up, trying to get the last ornament on the perfect branch toward the top of the tree, her lips pursed in determination. The pink rose I'd given her earlier lay on the table behind her, the message still attached to the stem.

"Are you still there?"

"Yeah, sorry." I forced myself to focus on the conversation I was having with Carrie's father. "We'll be there first thing in the morning for Christmas breakfast."

"Coffee starts at eight," her dad said. I heard paper crinkling, which probably meant he was wrapping his presents at the last minute like usual. "Did Carrie tell you to make the fruit salad? She told me she would remember."

I laughed. "Yeah. It's all ready to go. We'll see you tomorrow, sir. Tell Margie I said merry Christmas."

My father-in-law sighed. "If I ever finish wrapping these godforsaken presents, I will. I should really just hire someone to do it."

But he wouldn't, because he liked doing it. "Well, good luck. I have to hang up now, because your daughter needs help with the tree."

"Don't let her knock it over like she did last year," Senator Wallington said. "She might hurt—"

I rolled my eyes. "I won't, sir."

"All right. Merry Christmas Eve."

"Same to you." I hung up and tossed my phone on the sofa, turning back toward Carrie just in time to hear her curse under her breath. "I heard that, Mrs. Coram."

She shot me a frustrated look, her blue eyes blazing at me. "I'm going to get this last one on if it kills me, I swear it."

"I *can* help you, you know." I crossed the room slowly, trying not to upset my balance. "I am a bit taller than you."

"Nope. I get the red ones, not you." She looked at me, her gaze dropping low and then slipping back up. "It's our Christmas Eve tradition."

I grinned. "Yeah, it is. Then when we're done, we drink and have hot, sweaty—"

"Sh," she hissed, her cheeks going red. "She'll hear you."

"I think we're safe," I whispered, stopping directly in front of her. The colored lights on our tree twinkled merrily, and all that was left was the ornament in Carrie's hand and the angel—which came last, of course. "She doesn't really speak English."

"Still. It's the principle." She peeked at me, a sly grin on her face. "We don't want to have to foot that therapy bill, trust me. We cost way too much."

I rolled my eyes. "Believe me, I know that."

Carrie had changed her major the second year of college. After seeing how much Dr. Montgomery had helped me, she decided she wanted to do that for other people like me. Wanted to help soldiers and others who suffered from PTSD. She worked on base now, and she always looked so damn happy.

I liked to think I had something to do with that.

And I liked that we worked in the same building, so we got to have lunch together every single fucking day. It was heaven, and I never failed to thank God for giving me my Ginger. She was my life. My partner. My world. My everything.

Sometimes it all seemed too good to be true.

She was a therapist, and I was a computer engineer, just like we'd both wanted. We still lived in Cali, thank fucking God. D.C. was way too cold, even if her parents still lived there half the year. They spent a lot of time out here, too.

Everything in our life was perfect. Scarily, unrealistically *perfect*.

Carrie waved her hand in front of my face, laughing when I jumped slightly. "Hello? Earth to Finn?"

I caught her hand and kissed it, right above her wedding ring. I must've zoned out. I still did that sometimes. Got lost in thought. "Sorry, Ginger. I was lost in time."

"What were you thinking about?" she asked, a soft smile on those perfect lips of hers.

"You." I leaned forward and kissed her, loving the way she tasted, even after all these years. "Always you."

She closed her hands on my shoulders before pulling back and looking down for a quick second. "You two ready for the angel?"

I looked down at the baby in my arms, smiling with so much fucking happiness I swear my heart would burst. Our red-haired daughter, Susan Marie Coram, fluttered her lashes open and looked up at me with the same blue eyes as her mother. She was only three months old, but already I knew she would own my heart as fully as her mother did.

"We've been ready for years," I said, making my voice higher as I held Susan's hand. She cooed and closed her tiny little fingers around mine. "She's so f-f—" I cut myself off. I was trying to cut back on the cursing. "—uh, fetchingly perfect."

Carrie laughed, picked up the angel, and came over to us, her eyes on me the whole time. "How could she not be? She came from us." She trailed her fingers over the scar on my forehead, smiling. Then she laid the angel on Susan's belly. "You're up, princess."

I walked up to the tree, lifting Susan above my head. With my help—*aka* I did it myself—we put the angel on top of the tree. Backing up far enough to really see it, I eyed the tree skeptically. We'd gotten better over the years, because it actually looked evenly spread out. Perry Como crowed in the background, and lasagna cooked in the oven.

It was tradition.

No sooner did I nod in satisfaction than the timer dinged. I looked down at Susan. She was fast asleep. Good, it was time for me to have some one-on-one time with her mama. I smiled at Carrie, my heart so full it had to be close to bursting. "You get the lasagna out, and I'll lay down Susan."

"Okay." She walked by me, heading toward the kitchen, her hips swinging with each step she took. She wore a red dress and a pair of red heels. Fucking hot. "Hurry up."

"Oh, I will."

After watching her go, I climbed the stairs to Susan's nursery. I laid her down to rest and snuck into the master bedroom to grab my present for Carrie out of my underwear drawer. I'd gotten her another sun pendant, but this one was white gold with a diamond in the middle of the pendant. She'd love it.

I stopped two steps into the room. Lying in the middle of the bed was my wife, and she didn't have anything on except a pair of red heels and a seductive smile. "Merry Christmas to me," I said, shutting the door behind me.

She opened her arms. "Come here, love."

I crossed the room, climbed onto the king bed, and lowered myself on top of her. She moaned and closed her arms around my neck, arching her back seductively. Trailing my fingers down her side, toward her hip, I kissed her. Her tongue tangled with mine, fighting for control before she gave it to me.

I moaned and deepened the kiss, wedging myself between her legs. Breaking the kiss off, I whispered, "I love you, Ginger."

She smiled up at me, tracing her fingers over my faded scar. "I love you, too."

Unable to resist her when she looked so fucking hot, I kissed her again. I never could resist her, and never would be able to for as long as I lived...because she loved me—and *needed* me—just as much as I needed her.

Imagine that.

Stay tuned for more Finn and Carrie. A new chapter of their lives is coming late 2014/early 2015...and you'll want to be there to see what happens.

NOTE FROM THE AUTHOR

Dear Reader,

Some of you might have recognized this already, but the epilogue in this book is almost exactly pulled out of Finn's thoughts in *Out of Time*. When he and Carrie are decorating their first Christmas tree, he thinks to himself:

If Captain Richards asked me where I wanted to be in ten years, I'd have an answer for him. I'd want to be right here, decorating a sloppy tree with Carrie. Maybe with a baby in my arms. That's where I wanted to be. And I would be, damn it.

Well, Finn got what he wanted, and I hope you all did, as well. I've had tons of fun writing Carrie and Finn's story, and I hope to see you again soon. Even though Finn and Carrie got their happily ever after... Marie, Hernandez, and Riley didn't.

At least...not yet.

If someone asked me where I saw myself in the next ten years, I'd have an answer too—just like Finn. I'll be right here, writing stories for you. Thank you for letting me do that for you. I feel so very blessed.

Till next time? The sun is finally shining.

Love,
Me

First

BONUS SCENE

Finn

This scene takes place a few weeks after the end of OUT OF TIME, but a couple of weeks before the beginning of OUT OF MIND.

I woke up slowly, blinking away the sunlight streaming through the hospital windows. I must have dozed off for a little while. By some miracle of miracles, I hadn't had a nightmare. I usually did. Sighing, I reached out and pushed the morphine button on the machine next to me. My head and arm hurt like a fucking bitch.

The door opened, and I tensed. My last visitor had been Senator Wallington. He'd reminded me exactly how beneath his daughter I was, then left. Ya know, the usual. But this time? It was a most welcome visitor. Carrie's red head peeked inside the hospital room.

"I'm awake," I said, smiling and adjusting myself against the pillows. "Come in."

She grinned at me and slipped through the crack of the door. "I came by earlier, but you were sleeping, so I went to the gift shop. Here. It's for you."

"Thank you." I took the yellow rose she held out for me, not quite sure what I was supposed to do with a flower. I was a dude. We were supposed to be the one's giving out the flowers—not the other way around. "I didn't realize they made yellow roses."

"They make them in every color imaginable," she said, sitting down on the side of the bed gently. "You're probably wondering why I got you a flower, right?"

I chuckled and stared down at the gentle bud. "Uh, yeah, kind of."

"From what I've seen, roses are the toughest flowers out there. One year, my mother's gardener planted the garden way too early. A frost came through, and it killed all the flowers outside." She leaned in and touched the soft petal. "All of them except the roses. They were the only flowers that thrived, despite the cold and the frost. They had the biggest batch ever that year. And they were gorgeous."

I swallowed hard. "Oh yeah?"

"Yeah." She cupped my cheek. Her soft touch was so soothing and perfect that I closed my eyes and savored it. "And those roses remind me of you—of us. You are so strong, and I know it'll be tough, but you'll get through this, and you'll be stronger because of it. I know it."

My heart clenched. "We'll get through this." I squeezed her hand with my one good one. "Together, we can do anything."

"Together," she echoed, her eyes filled with tears that didn't spill out. "I love you."

"I love you, too, Ginger."

I kissed her, my lips fleeting over hers. My grip tightened on her hand, and she strained to get closer. I drew in a ragged breath, my body responding to her closeness. Her tongue flicked over mine, making my stomach get tight and other things go hard. What I wouldn't give to be out of this hospital room, and back in California with her in my apartment so I could take care of this need for her that was trying to kill me.

But we wouldn't have privacy until I got out of this one in D.C., though, so we had a while to go. With that knowledge ringing in my head, I pulled away. "I can't wait to go home."

She sighed. "Me too. It'll be here soon. We just have to get back to my parents house, then get through Christmas. Then things will go back to normal."

Normal? Nothing about me was normal anymore. I was a fucking mess. But I smiled for her even though I knew it was a crock of shit. "Yeah. Normal."

Her smile faltered, as if she saw through my façade, but she didn't say anything. Her phone dinged. She didn't pick it up. "We're going to be okay," she said again.

"Yeah, we will." I hoped to hell we would, anyway. "Are you going to see who messaged you?"

"It's just my daily inspirational message of the day." She lifted a shoulder. "You know how I love those little messages."

I ran my thumb over her lip. "I love that you love those little messages. It's a-dork-able."

She flushed. "Shut up."

"Gladly." I leaned in, the morphine making me feel high and kinda out of it. "Or you could shut me up."

"Gladly," she echoed, completely oblivious to the fact that I was a fucking wreck.

She kissed me, and I tried to stop thinking. Stop feeling.

To just stop it all.

Second

BONUS SCENE

Finn

I looked around our small apartment, my heart racing faster than a fucking racecar at Daytona. I was actually going to do this. Actually going to ask her the question I'd been wanting to ask her since I fell in love with her. I was going to make her my wife...if she decided I was a lucky enough bastard to have that honor.

I still couldn't believe she'd chosen me, after three years of being together.

She really fucking loved me, and God knows I loved her, too. So damn much it hurt. I'd lived life without her, and I'd lived life with her. I never wanted to do the former again, and I wouldn't have to. Not if she said yes.

Stepping back, I studied my handiwork critically. Roses of every color imaginable were in the center of the table in the crystal vase I'd given her two years ago for our anniversary. I'd made lasagna, and had a bottle of sparkling champagne on the table, too.

For her, I'd stick to sparkling cider.

I smoothed my hand over the bulge in the breast pocket of my suit—the suit I'd donned for her—and eyed the clock. She'd be home in five minutes.

For the rest of my waiting time, I ran around the apartment like a fucking lunatic, making sure everything was perfectly in place, and before I knew it, the key clicked in the lock. I froze with a piece of fallen potpourri in my hand. The door opened, and in came my own personal ray of sunshine.

Carrie.

She tossed her books on the counter, her head lowered over something she read in her hand. She hadn't even looked up yet. Hadn't seen the scene I set.

With a small grumble, she chucked the piece of paper on top of the books. "Ugh, you wouldn't believe the crapshoot of a day I've—" She turned, and her voice faded. She stared at the table with wide eyes. "Had."

"Hopefully, it's about to get better," I said, dropping the piece of potpourri in the crystal bowl. Another gift from me. "Go in the bedroom and put on the dress I laid out on the bed."

She glanced toward the big bed that she could see from the door. We hadn't moved yet because we fit nicely here. It was home, and we liked it. "What's going on?"

"Just do it," I said, lowering my brows. "Or I'll be forced to spank you."

She bit down on her lower lip, and her bright blue eyes sparkled. Finally. "That's not exactly a threat…"

"Fine." I crossed my arms. "Then I won't spank you."

"Well, in that case, I'll go get dressed right away." As she walked past me, she trailed her fingers over my arm. "You're all dressed up. Did I forget an anniversary?"

"Not really." But there was one, in a way. It was three years after I'd decided to get better. Three years after I'd decided to live instead of die. "Just get dressed. I'm going to check on dinner."

She pursed her lips. "O…kay."

"Good girl." I swatted her ass as she passed. She shot me a playful grin over her shoulder and hustled. "Hurry up."

While she dressed, I went into the kitchen and pulled dinner out of the oven. I listened to the sounds of her stripping naked, my eyes on her the whole time. Her long red hair cascaded down her bare, porcelain back, and she looked so fucking perfect it hurt. She was so fucking perfect it hurt.

I still had no clue what I had done to deserve her, but I hoped I never fucked it up like I had all those years ago. When I'd been in my dark abyss. I massaged my shoulder absentmindedly. We could be happy. I could be happy.

This was going to work.

She came up behind me, closing her arms around my chest from behind. Her floral perfume washed over me, and I closed my eyes, inhaling her sweet scent like an addict. "You look so serious over here. What's wrong?"

"Nothing's wrong at all." I closed my hand over both of hers. "I'm just thinking about how happy you make me."

I felt her smile against my back. "You make me happy, too."

Closing my eyes, I took a deep breath. She was going to say yes. Of course she was. We loved each other. I just had to open my big fat mouth and ask her. I opened my mouth, but only a squeak came out. Like a little fucking mouse.

Perfect.

"Are you ready to eat?" she asked, her voice a little bit hesitant.

"Yeah. Go head over to the table." After she started that way, I looked down at the counter. "Get it together, Coram."

Sighing, I rolled my shoulders and followed her. She sat down in her usual spot, her eyes on the roses. "Those are pretty."

"You have a job to do after we eat."

She smirked. "Do I, now?"

"Yep." I laughed when her gaze dipped low over my body. "Slow down there, Ms. Wallington. I don't need any help studying tonight."

"Studying." Our code word for making love. Laughing, she picked up her fork and knife. "I'm going to eat this fast so we can move on to the fun stuff. Whatever you want to call it."

We ate in silence—me mostly freaking the fuck out, and her probably picking up on my weird vibe. She kept stealing glances at me, her brow wrinkled, but she didn't say anything. When she finished eating, she set her fork down and turned to me. "What's wrong? The last time you acted this strange, you were getting sent overseas."

"What?" I blinked at her, then set down my utensils. "No. It's nothing like that."

"Then what is it?" She clung to her dress. "Just spit it out."

"Pick up the red rose."

"The rose?" She shot me a weird look. "What?"

I took a deep breath, steadying my fucking nerves as best as I could. "Pick up the red rose."

Letting out a sigh, she tugged it out of the vase. When she saw the little scrolled note attached to it, she froze, her pink lips parted. "Finn…"

"Read it out loud."

"Okay." With trembling hands, she unrolled the note. After licking her lips, she said, "You saved my life with your love."

When she glanced at me, I smiled at the tears in her eyes. Leaning in, I pressed my lips to hers. She was so soft. So sweet. So mine. "Next, the yellow one."

"Finn, what is this?" Her lip trembled, and she bit down on it. "Are you…?"

"Don't ask questions." I tugged the yellow rose out. "Just follow my instructions. Read it out loud."

Blinking rapidly, she unrolled the paper. A small sound escaped her. "You are my sunshine, and I never want to live without you."

I nodded. "Pink now."

Without arguing, she reached out and snatched it up. "I wanted to know if you loved me as much as I love you." She looked at me, tears rolling down her cheeks. "I love you more."

"Not possible," I argued. Gently, I swiped my thumbs over her cheeks, smoothing the tears away. "Purple."

She took a shaky breath. Then she grabbed the rose, and slowly unfurled the paper. "So I have to ask you a question. Look at me."

Gradually, she turned to me with wide eyes. When she looked where I had been sitting, all she found was an empty seat. Then she looked lower, finding me on bended knee at her feet. She covered her mouth, the purple rose still in her hand. "Finn."

"You've made me the happiest man on the planet by loving me, but I'm going to be greedy. I'm going to ask for more." I took a deep breath, and popped open the black velvet case. "Carrie, will you do me the honor of becoming my wife?"

"Yes! Yes, yes, yes!" She launched herself into my arms, making us both tumble onto the floor, with her on top of me. "Yes."

She kissed me, and we both laughed. I curled my hands around her thighs, the ring forgotten on the floor beside us. Tilting my head, I deepened the kiss, taking control. This was it. This was life at its finest.

She said yes. She loved me.

And she was going to be my wife.

We'd got our happily ever after.

Original Ending

This was the original ending to Out of Time, before I decided to change it from a novella to a full length novel. Once I made the book longer, a bunch of stuff changed, including the way/place/time that Finn told Carrie he would be leaving. As did the reasons why. Enjoy! --Jen

Carrie

A. Freaking. Mess.

That's what I was right now. What I'd been ever since Finn told me he might be leaving. Even more so now that I knew the time for the truth grew rapidly closer. It was Sunday evening at five-forty five and I was a hysterical wreck. And I'd been that way all weekend long, especially once my parents were gone.

In a way, I'd been grateful they were here like they'd been. It had been a welcome distraction. But then they went home yesterday, and I was all alone. Last night and today had passed the slowest any day had ever been. I'd gone to the soup kitchen with Darren. Handed out tons of gift cards. Done my homework. Worked on my thesis. Washed my new car. Done research. Cleaned the apartment, which had been an adventure all in itself. Gotten ahead in class, even.

And I'd still had hours and hours to sit around twiddling my thumbs, slowly going insane as I waited for six o'clock to come around. In a matter of minutes, Finn would be here on this beach with me. And knowing he was going to tell me whether or not he was going to freaking war…yeah.

Manic. That pretty accurately described my state of mind.

Despite the "unhappy" circumstances behind this picnic, I'd tried to set a romantic scene, complete with a red and white checkered blanket, a wicker basket, and a pilfered bottle of wine from Finn's cabinet. There was also a bunch of grapes and strawberries, and a couple of sandwiches for us both.

I'd spent the night at his place last night, putting my clothes away and just being there. I slept in his bed, hugging his pillow, and had laid awake almost all night long. I tugged my navy blue and white sweater down and fidgeted with the hem of my jean shorts. I'd left my hair down for Finn, since he liked it that way, but now I was wishing I'd taken the time to do something with it. If I'd done my hair, it would have taken me even longer to get here, and I wouldn't be sitting here fidgeting and wondering and stressing.

As Finn would say…this fucking wait was fucking killing me.

But no matter what he said, no matter what happened, I was standing by him. I wouldn't leave him, and I wouldn't move on and forget about him. Hopefully he didn't really think I would. Long ago—at least, it seemed long ago—he'd told me if he went to war I would forget all about him. God, if he really thought that…

I'd have to do my best to show him he was wrong.

The hair on the back of my neck stood up and I got that tingling sensation that warned me I was being watched. I remembered having the same type of feeling the first night I met Finn, when he'd been guarding me and watching from the shadows.

Who would have known that he would have come to mean so much to me in so little time? That I'd need him so badly I couldn't imagine a life without him in it. Who would have known the man who was sent to watch me would want me, too?

I rolled clumsily to my bare feet, my heart racing and seeming to painfully climb up from my chest until it felt as if it rested in my throat instead of my chest. I knew that wasn't possible, of course, but I'd swear to it anyway. He walked toward me steadily, his light blue jeans folded up at the ankle to keep them clean. He wore a grey hoodie and a pair of sunglasses. I couldn't read his freaking eyes. Had no clue what to expect.

But suddenly it didn't matter anymore, because he was here.

And that's all that really mattered, wasn't it?

I took a step toward him, then another. By the time my foot hit the sand a third time, I was running. I'm talking, hair flying behind you, full on sprint. Finn picked up the pace, too, his long steps growing even faster. By the time we met, I was out of breath and fighting back the tears threatening to escape.

Even though he hadn't opened his mouth, I just knew what he was going to say.

He caught me in his arms, spinning me in a giant circle and hugging me to his chest. I could feel his heart thumping, beating against my own almost in tandem. He opened his mouth to talk, but I kissed him before he could. I didn't want to hear it. Didn't want my worst fears to become so utterly, horrifically, devastatingly alive.

When I was a little girl, I'd been terrified of monsters that hid under my bed. Now, as an adult, I knew the real terror lie in words and actions and in life or death. Not in scary, hairy, huge beasts.

I kissed him with a desperation I hadn't felt before, knowing if I stopped he'd tell me the words I didn't want to hear. Knowing if I stopped, I'd utterly lose it. There was a good handful of people on the beach, and they were probably all watching us with wide eyes, but I didn't even care. All those silly fears I'd had over the years seemed so freaking pathetic in the face of this.

Of Finn.

He moaned into my mouth and stumbled back, his hands supporting me. I knew I was attacking the poor man, but I couldn't stop. Not now. Not ever. From a distance, I heard the waves crashing on the sand and a few voices carrying off from the distance, but I shut it all out. All I wanted to focus on was Finn.

When he broke the kiss off, his breathing heavy and his grip on me unbreakable, I dared a glance up at him. Even with his shades on, I could see the tension in the way he smiled. And the way his shoulders were tight and hard. "Hey, Ginger," he said lightly.

I forced a smile for him, my hands gripping his shoulders so hard it probably hurt him, but he didn't so much as flinch. "Hey, yourself."

"I like this kind of greeting." He swung me into his arms, cradling me against his chest. "But now I'm not going to put you down."

"I don't want you to," I said, my voice breaking on the last word.

When he shot me a concerned look and opened his mouth to talk, I pressed my fingers against his mouth. "No. Don't say it. Not yet."

He kissed my fingers and nodded, but he looked away from me. Probably trying to hide his own tortured feelings from me, to protect me, but it didn't work. I could feel his pain as if it was my own—and he could probably feel mine. "Okay. What's for dinner?"

"Wine. Lots of wine."

He laughed, but it sounded forced. Of course it did. "Let me get this straight. You want me to publicly provide a minor with wine? Seriously?"

"Seriously." He set me down on my feet next to the picnic blanket, and I buried my toes in the cool sand. Funny how that used to feel like such a thrill to me. How naïve I'd been. "I want this to be the perfect date. And once it's over…then we talk. Deal?"

"Have I ever denied you something you wanted?" He sat down and patted the spot directly next to him. "If that's what you want, you'll get it."

I wanted to demand he not leave me. Wanted to demand he not go to war.

He'd promised to give me everything I wanted, hadn't he?

But that wouldn't be fair. Even I knew he didn't have a say in whether he left or stayed. It was all up to men like my father. To the men in the government who sat behind desks and demanded that men like Finn go overseas to fight for oil and other crap they tried to put a pretty face on.

"I want you, here with me." I grabbed a grape and pressed it to his lips. "And I have that now."

He took the grape out of my fingers, licking them as he sucked it in. Something in my stomach tightened, despite the emotional turmoil I was in, and I leaned closer, watching his mouth hungrily as he chewed. It wasn't until I looked away that I noticed he still wore his dog tags. I gently grasped the chain and pulled them out from under his shirt.

I scanned the words that denoted his name, social security number, blood type, and religion. Guess I now knew he was O positive. Weird way to find out, though. I didn't even what the heck type of blood I had, but I knew his. And knowing that this was how they kept track of who was who felt so cold and impersonal.

But then again…that's how life was, wasn't it?

"Carrie…"

"I know." I dropped the cool metal back against his chest and grabbed the bottle of wine with trembling hands. "Can you open this for me?"

He gave me a look, one that said he didn't like this not-talking thing I was doing any more than he liked giving me alcohol, but I stubbornly ignored it. Once he took the wine, I reached into the basket and took out two glasses, two sandwiches, and the strawberries I'd bought at the local market. They were bright red and juicy and perfect. The best I'd seen all year.

It's weird how I noticed this crap now, of all times.

I knew why. Denial and stress and avoidance and some more denial thrown in for good measure. But I embraced it anyway. It was easier than accepting the truth.

"Here you go." He held a glass of white, sparkling wine out for me. It looked stupid in a red Solo cup, but I'd opted to grab something we could easily dispose of instead of bringing breakable glass. After he poured himself some wine, he ripped his sunglasses off and tossed them aside. Meeting my eyes, he held his out and said, "To us?"

"To us," I echoed, tapping his cup with mine before bringing it to my mouth and drinking deeply. Finn threw me a concerned look, then pried it out of my fingers before I could drain it. "Hey, I was drinking that."

"I can see that." He set the cup aside and grabbed my hands, squeezing them in between his. "It's going to be okay. You know that, right?"

I shook my head, my eyes blurring with the tears that I was trying really, really hard to hold back. "Eat your sandwich and stop talking. Or talk about something else. Anything else."

"This is ridiculous, Ginger." When I shot him a look, he squared his jaw and looked out over the ocean. I could read the tension in his shoulders as easily as an open book. The fact that he stayed silent for me only made me love him even more, if that was possible. "What kind of sandwich is it?"

"Turkey and cheese. I got it from your favorite deli on Pico." I scooted closer and grabbed his, opening it up and handing it to him. "It's just the way you like it. I remembered what you…"

I faded off, not finishing my sentence. I couldn't talk past my throbbing throat, anyway. I was a word away from breaking down right now.

"Thanks." He took the sandwich and smiled at me, but it was fake.

Fake, fake, fake. "I saw you were at my place last night."

"I was. Today too." I opened my own sandwich, swallowing hard. I didn't think I'd be able to eat a freaking bite with this huge, aching lump currently choking me. "How'd you know?"

"The clothes were back in the closet, and my pillow was on your side of the bed, and you cleaned. Or at least, I think that's what you were trying to do."

Your side of the bed. I hadn't even realized I had one of those. Funny, how you just kind of fall into a pattern, and don't even know it. "I tried, but that Swiffer thing is weird. I couldn't get it to squirt the right amount."

"The batteries might be dead. I'll check it later." He chuckled. "And my pillow? What did you do to that?"

I lifted a shoulder. "I might have hugged it all night long."

"I've never been so fucking jealous of an inanimate object as I was that pillow." He took a bite of his sandwich, chewed and swallowed. His gaze fell on my sandwich. "You aren't eating."

I looked down at my sandwich. "Yeah, I am."

"Eat, or I won't." He pushed the hand holding my sandwich up toward my face, his mouth tight. "I can't be worrying about you eating, Ginger. Come on."

When he was gone. That's what he meant.

As if that was the biggest thing he had to worry about? Me eating?

I choked down a hysterical laugh and the lifted the sandwich to my mouth. I took a big bite and chewed, but it might as well have been newspaper for all I cared. It was tasteless and horrible. I barely managed to swallow it down. "I'm eating. See?"

"I see," he said slowly, his brow up. "You okay, Ginger?"

No, I wasn't freaking okay. "Yeah, why?"

His brows slammed down. "Gee, I fucking wonder."

"Wonder away, then, babe."

I forced a smile, knowing it was killing him to see me be so…down. I needed to snap out of it for him. When he was gone, I could be as miserable as I wanted. But not now. I took another bite, my eyes on him the whole time. He relaxed a little bit and ate his sandwich, never dropping his gaze from me.

"So we're keeping that nickname, then?"

I lifted a shoulder. "I can't think of a better one."

"You could call me sugar daddy," he said, wiggling his brows. "I give you anything you want, after all."

I rolled my eyes. "No."

"Sweetheart?"

"Gross. My mom calls me that."

He flinched. "Yeah, that's a no. Umm…" He took another bite, his gaze on the ocean. When he swallowed, he said, "Surfer boy."

"Cory called you that."

"You mean Cody." He hesitated. "Where is he lately, anyway?"

I blinked at him. "Why would I care?"

"I don't know." Finn shrugged. "Just curious."

I took another bite, then set the rest of my sandwich down. I'd eaten half. If I tried to shove anything else down, I might vomit all over him and totally ruin the romantic thing we were both trying so hard to hang on to. Reaching around him, I grabbed my cup and drained it, sighing when the bubbly drink went right to my head.

Thank freaking God for small favors.

He finished his sandwich, refilled my glass, then his. "You ready to talk yet?"

"How was your weekend?" I took a long sip. "Did you get any sleep?"

"Yeah, I did." He pressed a hand over his forehead and made an impatient sound. "You know that this isn't going to make it any easier, right?"

"I have no idea what you're talking about."

I scanned the beach. There was only one other couple here with us now, and the sunset was descending rapidly. Soon, the beach would be dark. And we'd be alone on a dark, crazy beach in this dark, crazy world. I took another long sip, desperate to have a buzz going on before we had this discussion.

Finn cupped my chin and turned my head, forcing me to look at him. "Carrie. Look at me."

"I can't. I just…can't." I closed my eyes tight, scrunching them shut. "I don't want to do this."

"Ginger…" I felt his hand take my cup away, and he pulled me into his lap. "I need you to look at me."

I rested in between his legs, but facing him, a leg on either side of his hips. I squeezed my eyes shut even tighter, like a kid terrified to open her eyes and see the monster looming over her bed late at night. I couldn't handle it. Couldn't handle this. I wasn't strong enough, darn it.

Wait. Yes, I was. I had to be strong for him. He needed me to be strong.

I took a deep, shaky breath and opened my eyes, my chest moving far too rapidly and my heart echoing in my head so loudly it freaking hurt. I knew what he was going to say, and I knew I was going to lose it. Completely lose it. I rested a hand behind his neck, directly between his shoulder blades, and the other on his shoulder. I nodded, knowing he was waiting. Waiting for me to be ready.

It's not that I couldn't handle it. I could. I'd just needed some time.

And I loved him even more for totally getting this about me.

I nodded once. "Go ahead. Say it."

Finn

This whole fucking weekend had been hell. My C.O. had waited until the last possible second to tell us what was going on, and even then it'd been with reluctance after countless questions. After they poked us with needles for hours, and had given us God knows how many vaccinations, they made us spend all fucking night filling out paperwork. I hadn't slept at all, but I didn't want Carrie to know that.

She was already worried enough.

There was no reason she needed to know about how I hadn't slept since Friday night, and probably wouldn't be sleeping much at all in the next year. This whole picnic thing was all both bittersweet and ridiculous. The not talking about what we were both so obviously thinking about was even more so.

It was time to just man up and open my fucking mouth. She was ready now.

I closed my hands around the back of her waist, holding on tight in case she tried to bolt or something. Fuck if I knew. I just knew I needed to hold onto her. "I'm going on deployment."

She squeezed her eyes shut again, tears streaming down her cheeks, but she didn't make a sound. She just sat there, her eyes tightly shut like a little kid who was too scared to open her eyes, and didn't move. I held her, letting her process it all, and tried not to freak out myself. Not because I was scared to go over. I mean…I was a little bit.

But mostly because I wanted her to be okay.

After what felt like fucking hours, she opened her eyes. She looked so resolute and strong, even with wet cheeks and makeup running down her face, that she took my breath away. "Where are they sending you?" she asked, her voice surprisingly steady.

"I'm not entirely sure yet. I'm not even sure that I can say, once I do know." I rubbed her lower back gently, still not letting go of her. If I had it my way, I'd never let go of her again until I had to walk on that fucking ship. "I think we're going out on the Cleveland, but I could be wrong."

She licked her lips, not dropping my gaze. She was so strong. So fucking strong. "How soon?"

"It's looking like it'll be after Christmas sometime. It's still in the early stages, but I know we'll be doing workups sooner." I hesitated, not sure how much information I should give her. "We'll be going to a combat zone, but I don't know if I will be able to tell you anything else."

She made a small sound, but clamped her lips together. "I…see."

"Carrie…"

"I'm fine. We're fine." She cupped my cheek with one hand, the other one still pressing against the spot in between my shoulder blades. "I love you."

I swallowed hard, the emotions inside of me warring with one another. I let go of her and lowered my head, not wanting her to see the tears that welled in my eyes. I wasn't fucking crying, damn it. I was just moved by her emotions.

But on top of that, I knew it wasn't fair of me to put her through all this shit. When I'd given her the "I don't date because of my job" excuse, it hadn't been one hundred percent truth. I hadn't even been referring to my job as a Marine.

But now…now maybe I was getting that a little bit better.

Maybe it wasn't fair of me to do this to her.

"I'm sorry, Ginger." I closed my eyes and breathed her in. "I know you didn't sign on for this when we fell in love. I'm sure you weren't thinking of how this would be, or how you would feel if I went away."

"I tried not to think about it, but I freaking knew it was possible." Her fingers flexed on my shoulder. "I'm not as weak as you think I am. I— "

"Weak? Are you shitting me?" I laughed, the words flowing without a stop valve. "I think you're the strongest fucking person I know, but I'm terrified to ruin that in you. Scared to ruin you."

Her eyes flashed at me. "And how the heck are you going to ruin me?"

I should just break it off. Walk away and set her free. But beneath all my brave words and actions, I was a selfish man who didn't want her to leave me. Who didn't want to let her go, even if I knew I should. But I had to be honest with her. "I might die. And if I did, then you'll—"

She made a broken sound, tears filling her eyes again, and smacked me. "You will not die. Tell me you won't. Promise me."

My heart wrenched. "I can't make a promise I can't keep, Ginger. You know that."

"That's why I need you to promise me." She shook her head, the tears streaming down her face, clinging to my arms so hard it hurt almost as much as my heart did at the sight of her tear filled eyes. "If you say it, I know you'll be okay. I know you'll stay safe for me."

I wanted to give it to her. Wanted to make her feel better. But what if I went and died? I didn't want the last promise I made her to be a lie. Fuck no. I ducked my head lower, hiding my eyes from her. She was fucking killing me here. "Damn it, I wish I could. But I can't."

Her lower lip trembled, but she bit down on it so hard I feared she would draw blood. "Please."

I buried my face in her neck, hugging her against my chest as best I could. I swallowed hard, my chest and throat tight. "I promise to be diligent and to keep myself as safe as possible. I promise not to be an idiot. I promise not to be a martyr. But most importantly, I promise to fall asleep every night with you on my mind, and wake up smiling because I'm lucky enough to have you in my life."

And just like that, I broke her. "Finn…"

She let out a shattered sob, her whole body trembling in my arms. She felt so fucking frail and small just now, even though I knew underneath the fragile façade she was stronger than anyone I'd ever met. My heart shattered and I blinked rapidly, my own vision blurring. I couldn't handle her tears, damn it. "Shit, don't cry. Not for me."

"I c-can't stop," she wailed, holding me even closer. "I'm s-sorry."

She was sorry? Seriously. This was all my fault. Not hers. My chest grew even tauter. I wanted to say something, anything, to make her feel better. Anything to make the moment less terrifying for her. Less painful. "I love you, and nothing is going to stop me from coming back here to you. Nothing."

She drew back and looked up at me. Her eyes were red and the tip of her nose was even redder. It was fucking adorable, even if my heart broke to see her so upset. "I love you too. Just…just do your best. That's all I can ask."

I forced a smile. What if I came home crippled or broken or shot? Or what if I came home so fucked up I wasn't even the man I used to be? The man she fell in love with. Would she still love me then? Would anyone? "I will."

She took a shaky breath and swiped her hands across her face, trying to get rid of the tears. All it did was smear her makeup worse. "Will you still be able to come home with me for the holidays?"

"I think so." I twisted my lips into what I hoped was a smile. "As long as I'm not floating in the middle of the ocean for it."

She tried to smile but failed as horribly as I probably did. "And what will my dad do? Does he know about this?"

"He knows it's possible I'm going, but I didn't talk to him yet. I'm sure I've got a million texts from him by now." I dropped my forehead to hers. "This is all just logistical bullshit, really. It'll all be the same except…I'll be gone."

"And Dad will send someone else in your place." Her lower lip quivered. "Maybe we should tell him I know, and then I'll tell him to knock it the heck off."

I cocked a brow even though she couldn't see me. "Do you think it would work?"

"No," she admitted. "It didn't work last time. He sent you."

"No falling in love with the next one," I said, keeping my voice light. "I'll have to come back and kick his ass."

She chuckled, but it sounded forced. Of course it fucking did. "I promise that won't happen."

"And when I'm over there…" I broke off, not sure how to word this in a way that wouldn't piss her off, but then decided I couldn't think of a single way. "Just let me know if something changes, you know?"

She stiffened. "Like?"

"Like if you meet someone who isn't in the fucking desert." I tightened my grip on her when she started to pull away. "Hey, I'm just saying—"

She squirmed. "Yeah, well, just say it one more time and I'll punch you so hard in the balls you won't be able to talk in anything but a soprano for a month."

I pulled back and looked her in the eye for the first time since she started crying. I finally had myself under control. "It's just that I love you enough to be able to let you go, if that's best for you."

"Being without you will never be best for me." She pressed her lips together. "No matter what, it's me and you together—even if we're apart. Promise?"

"I promise." I kissed the tip of her still red nose. "It's us against the world."

She gave me a small smile. "Right. And together, how could we possibly lose?"

Her grip on me tightened, and she kissed me. She tasted like wine and tears, and I pressed even closer to her, needing more. Needing so much fucking more.

The night had fallen, and the dark shadows surrounded us, but all I smelled and heard and felt was her. I knew if a threat came close-by, I'd be on my feet in two-point-two seconds, fists swinging. But right now, we were alone on a dark beach. Our beach.

When I'd seen her, in tiny shorts and a striped sweater looking for all the world like she was standing at gunpoint instead of waiting for her boyfriend to come, my heart had stopped. Literally stopped. I would never get used to the way she made me feel.

How much better she made me.

ABOUT THE AUTHOR

Jen McLaughlin is the New York Times and USA Today bestselling author of sexy New Adult books. Under her pen name Diane Alberts, she is a multi-published, bestselling author of Contemporary Romance with Entangled Publishing. Her first release as Jen McLaughlin, Out of Line, released September 6 2013, and hit the New York Times, USA Today and Wall Street Journal lists. She was mentioned in Forbes alongside E. L. James as one of the breakout independent authors to dominate the bestselling lists. She is represented by Louise Fury at The Bent Agency.

Though she lives in the mountains, she really wishes she was surrounded by a hot, sunny beach with crystal-clear water. Though she lives in the mountains, she really wishes she was surrounded by a hot, sunny beach with crystal-clear water. She lives in Northeast Pennsylvania with her four kids, a husband, a schnauzer mutt, and a cat. Her goal is to write so many well-crafted romance books that even a non-romance reader will know her name.

This paperback interior was designed and formatted by

www.emtippettsbookdesigns.com

Artisan interiors for discerning authors and publishers.